ALSO BY BARBARA WOOD

The Dreaming

Green City in the Sun

Soul Flame

Domina

Childsong

Yesterday's Child

The Magdalene Scrolls

Hounds and Jackals

Night Trains
(with Gareth Wootton)

The Watchgods

Curse This House

Vital Signs

Virgins of Paradise

Barbara Wood

VIRGINS OF PARADISE

RANDOM HOUSE

NEW YORK

Library of Congress Cataloging-in-Publication Data
Wood, Barbara.
Virgins of paradise / Barbara Wood. — 1st ed.
p.   cm.
ISBN 0-679-41579-3 : $22.00
I. Title.
PS3573.05877V48   1993   813'.54—dc20   92-37356

Manufactured in the United States of America
98765432
First Edition

Book design by J. K. Lambert

For Ahmed Abbas Ragab, with love and gratitude.

ACKNOWLEDGMENTS

This book could not have been possible without the help of some special people. I would like to thank my friends in Cairo, in particular the Ragab family—Ahmed, Abdel Wahab, Sana'a, and Fatima. Dr. Khadija Youssef, for enlightening me on Arab feminism and the rights of modern Egyptian women. Samira Aziz, for providing such a wonderful look into the life of Nile villages. Homeyra Akhavani, for sharing her experiences as a Muslim woman adjusting to American life. And most especially, "Sah-ra"—Carolee Kent of Riverside, California—star dancer at the Meridien Hotel in Cairo, for giving so generously of her time, for her marvelous depiction of a dancer's life in Egypt, and for giving me permission to use her description of the zeffa wedding procession. I am also grateful to Anne Draper of Riverside, and my sisters in Middle Eastern Dance, for their support and contributions. Artemis of Pacific Grove, California, and the staff of Sisterhood Bookstore in Westwood are also to be applauded for their efforts and success in filling my nearly impossible requests for hard-to-find research material. Finally, I could not have written this book without the support and encouragement of my husband, George.

Transcribing Arabic into the English alphabet poses a challenge, as there are only three vowel sounds in Arabic. Pronunciation of a word can vary from region to region, even from one person to another, and the same word might appear in a variety of spellings in various English translations. I have chosen a conventional form that is comfortable for the English speaker. All names and foreign words are pronounced as they are written.

The word *fellah* (Egyptian peasant) is pronounced fell-AH, with the accent on the second syllable.

There was a Door to which I found no Key:
There was a Veil past which I could not see;
    Some little talk awhile on ME and THEE
There seemed—and then no more of THEE and ME.

—*The Rubáiyát* of Omár Kháyyám

Women shall with justice have rights
similar to those exercised against them,
although men have a status above women.
Allah is mighty and wise.

—The Koran. II:228

Virgins of Paradise

On an impulse, Jasmine said to the taxi driver, "Could we please drive by Virgins of Paradise Street first?"

"Yes, miss," the Arab driver said, looking at his passenger in the rearview mirror, his eyes lingering for a moment on her golden hair.

Jasmine was surprised at herself. During the drive from Cairo International Airport, and earlier, during the long nonstop flight from Los Angeles, she had promised herself that she would not go anywhere near Virgins of Paradise Street. That she would go straight to the Nile Hilton, find out why she had been summoned back to Egypt, take care of whatever business needed taking care of, and then get on the first return flight to California. Appalled by her impulsiveness, she wanted to tell the driver to go straight to the hotel after all, that she had changed her mind. But she couldn't. She might be afraid to go to Virgins of Paradise Street, but she was more afraid not to.

"Very nice street, miss, very beautiful," he said as he pounded his horn and fought the congested traffic in the center of the ancient city. Jasmine saw the curiosity on his face, a look that told her tourists rarely visited Virgins of Paradise Street. She sat in the belching little car that was decorated with colorful tassels, paper flowers, and, on the velvet-upholstered dashboard, a Koran, the holy book of the Muslims, anxiously digging her fingers into her blue jeans. She preferred jeans to anything else, wearing them even at the pediatric clinic and when she made hospital rounds—"Very undoctorly, Dr. Van Kerk," the chief of surgery had once said teasingly.

As the taxi inched its way around Liberation Square, Jasmine watched the pedestrians crowding the sidewalks. She saw few blue jeans among the young men in outmoded bell-bottoms and tight nylon shirts. There were stylish women in bouffant hairdos and modern skirts and blouses, and men in traditional galabeyas; there were also young women in long dresses and head veils—the "Islamic dress" of the new fundamentalism—and peasant women sashaying down the street with their buttocks slung in tight black cloaks, a garment that revealed the very charms it was intended to conceal.

Jasmine tried to see in the crowd the child she once was, a little girl with pale skin and blond hair, skipping along with her duskier companions, carefree, unaware of the turbulent future that was racing toward her. Jasmine leaned close to the window; was that girl somehow still here? And if she saw her, would she stop the taxi, and say, "Come with me. We will go far away from here, far away from the danger and betrayal that awaits you."

The taxi coughed and lurched past the pedestrians. Then, all of a sudden, she was on a street so stunning in its familiarity that, for a moment, she couldn't breathe.

The driver slowed the car as Jasmine gazed out at trees and garden walls long forgotten. It was as if she had left Egypt only yesterday. And her fear grew.

She could, of course, have thrown away the letter that had arrived at her Los Angeles office a few days ago, with its cryptic message: "Dr. Jasmine Van Kerk, could you please come to Cairo at once, it is urgent. There is a matter about your inheritance which must be discussed." The letter was from a lawyer in Cairo. She remembered him from when she was a child growing up on Virgins of Paradise Street. The man had been the family's lawyer; apparently he still was.

"You should go," her best friend, Rachel, also a doctor, had said. "You'll never be able to get on with your life until you come to terms with your family. Maybe this is a good sign, a chance to lay your demons to rest."

Jasmine had telephoned the lawyer for details. "I am sorry, Dr. Van Kerk," he had said, "but it is very complicated. You must come here."

"Stop, please," she said to the driver, and the cab came to a halt beneath a canopy of ancient cottonwood trees that grew from behind an impressive stone wall. Glimpsed behind the wall was an enormous house surrounded by a peaceful garden, a rare sight in this congested, over-populated city. As she stared at the three-story, rose-colored mansion with ornate balconies and wooden lattice screens over the windows, Jasmine was suddenly overcome. She thought: This is the place where I was born. Here I drew my first breath, shed my first tear, laughed my first laugh.

And here I was banished from the family, cursed, and sentenced to death.

She regarded the house, a stone-and-mortar monument to Egypt's glamorous and decadent past. Those shuttered windows might open and familiar faces appear, faces she had once loved and cherished, or hated and feared—faces belonging to generations of Rasheeds, a power-ful and aristocratic family. They had been rich beyond imagining, inti-mate friends of kings and pashas, beautiful and blessed; but, under the glamour, burdened by secrets of insanity, adultery, murder. Questions crowded her mind: Does the family still live here?

And then she was recalling words from long ago, Amira saying, "A woman might have more than one husband in her lifetime, she can have many brothers and many sons, but she can only ever have one father."

"Driver," Jasmine said abruptly, turning away from the memory of her father, and their last terrible day together, "take me to the Hilton, please."

As the taxi pulled out onto a busy street, Jasmine realized that she was crying. At the airport, when she had stepped down from the plane, she had braced herself for the shock of being back, but she had so prepared herself, so wrapped herself in defences, that no shock had come, there had been no emotions, no feelings; she might have been in any airport in the world. But now, having driven through the city of her childhood, and having seen the house on Virgins of Paradise Street again, she felt the barriers begin to crumble.

Cairo—after all these years! Despite her tears, Jasmine could see changes that astounded her. Many of the aristocratic old houses had been sold to big businesses. Neon signs were affixed to elegant old façades; there were high-rises going up, new construction, the constant noise of jackhammers and pile drivers. It looked as if a war had demolished whole city blocks and surrounded them with chain-link fences. Even so, this was still her beloved Cairo. Brazen, gaudy, audacious, this was a city that had withstood ten centuries of invasions, foreign occupations, wars, plagues, and eccentric rulers.

Her taxi lurched and braked around Tahrir Square, now like the center ring in a circus, chopped up for the construction of a new subway. Jasmine saw how the Cairenes, used to adjusting to new ways, went about their business unperturbed, in veils or business suits or as they sat outside coffeehouses. When Jasmine finally saw the Nile Hilton, no longer seeming as fabulously modern as she had once thought it, she recalled her own wedding there, and wondered if the bronze bust of Gamal Nasser still dominated the lobby. And there, next to the American Express office, was the ice-cream seller she and Camelia and Tahia and Zachariah had gone to as youngsters, a tiny shop where you could get any flavor you wanted as long as it was vanilla. And there were the jasmine sellers, so loaded with garlands that you couldn't see the men underneath, and fellaheen women crouched on the sidewalks roasting husks of corn, the annual sign that summer had arrived.

Jasmine leaned back from the window. She had long ago vowed never to return to Cairo, and she intended to honor that vow. Her body was here, to see Mr. Abdel Rahman the lawyer and to take care of the matter of her inheritance, but her heart and soul were safely back in California.

When the cab pulled up in front of the hotel and the doorman rushed to open her door, saying, "Welcome in Cairo," she saw how he looked at her, admiring her blond hair the way the taxi driver and the customs agents and baggage handlers back at the airport had done. She reminded herself to buy a scarf to cover her head, the way she had remembered to pull on a cardigan before leaving the plane, to cover her bare arms in this Muslim country.

A bellboy came out and looked for her luggage, but Jasmine had only one small case; she wasn't going to be staying long. Only overnight, if she could manage it. And she certainly wouldn't be going back to Virgins of Paradise Street again.

As she entered the lobby, she heard loud music and people cheering. A wedding procession appeared, led by dancers and musicians, with friends and relatives following the bridal couple, showering them with coins for good luck. Jasmine paused to watch the young bride sweep by in a white wedding gown, two little girls carrying her long train. And it brought back sweet memories of the night her own wedding procession had passed through this very lobby, when the hotel had been new, and she had been so happy. She reached into her purse and brought out some dimes and quarters, and tossed them at the couple, murmuring, "Good luck. *Mabruk.*"

At the registration desk Jasmine was greeted warmly with the familiar "Welcome in Cairo."

"Are there any messages for me?" she asked the good-looking young clerk, who offered her the flattering, dark-eyed smile she remembered Egyptian men being so expert at.

He checked behind the desk, and said, "I am sorry, Dr. Van Kerk, there are no messages."

She had told the lawyer the date of her arrival and that she had a reservation at the Nile Hilton, and had expected him to meet her at the airport; when he hadn't shown up there, she'd felt sure she'd find him at the hotel. A bellboy accompanied her to her room, "Nile side," as she had requested, and when she tipped him a pound note, she saw by his smile that it was too much.

Jasmine was tired and hungry—she had been sleepless on the plane, and had eaten little—but she went first to the telephone beside the bed, to call Los Angeles and tell everyone she had arrived safely. As her hand touched the phone, she heard a knock at her door.

When she opened it, she drew back in shock.

A woman stood there, her clothes the traditional robes of one who had made the pilgrimage to Mecca—a long white dress, with a white veil over her head and covering the lower half of her face. She carried a leather bag in one hand, and walked with the aid of a cane. When Jasmine saw the dark eyes regarding her above the veil, she was rocked by conflicting emotions. Amira!

She remembered the last time she had seen this woman, and felt again the anger, the sadness.

In Arabic, Amira said, "Peace to you and the compassion of God."

And Jasmine was suddenly remembering the scent of sandalwood and lilac, the music of the ancient fountain in the garden of the house on Virgins of Paradise Street, the heavenly taste of sugared apricots on hot afternoons. Happy memories, which she had suppressed along with the painful ones.

"And to you," she said, as if she were addressing an apparition.

"Peace and the compassion of God and His blessings. Please, come in."

As Amira entered the room, her white veils giving off the fragrance of almonds, Jasmine marveled at how easily the years suddenly caught up with her. She was amazed at how smoothly and readily the Arabic returned to her tongue. And how good it felt to speak it again. Amira waited until Jasmine invited her to sit down; when she took a chair, she settled into it with the grace of a woman used to granting audiences, although Jasmine noticed her movements were somewhat stiff. After all, Amira was in her eighties.

Jasmine sat on the edge of the bed, filling her eyes with this remarkable vision. So, Amira had finally made the pilgrimage to Mecca.

"I am well, praise God," the older woman said as she lowered her veil, revealing snow-white hair.

"How did you know I was here?"

"It was I who sent for you, Yasmina."

"How did you find me?"

"I wrote to Itzak Misrahi in California, and he knew your address. You look well," Amira said with a slight tremor in her voice. "And you are a doctor now? That is good. It is a big responsibility." She held out her arms. "Won't you embrace me?"

But Jasmine was afraid. This woman had been the midwife at her birth; those almond-scented hands had been the first human touch she had known. Yet when Jasmine looked into the dark, leaf-shaped eyes that seemed to spark with the same fire she had once seen in the heart of a black opal, she could not go into this woman's arms. This woman with the strong features of the desert Bedouin, with arrogance in the tilt of her chin—characteristics all Rasheed women, including Jasmine Van Kerk, possessed. Because Jasmine's real name was Yasmina, and this woman was her grandmother.

"We must not be enemies, Yasmina," Amira said. "You are the granddaughter of my heart, and I love you."

"Forgive me, Grandmother, but I am remembering the last time I saw you."

"Yes. It was a sad day for us all. Yasmina, my darling child, something happened to me when I was a little girl, and it made me cry and cry until I thought I was going to empty myself, like water pouring from a bottle, and that then I would die. I didn't die, but I was left with the memory of that deep anguish, and I vowed that I was never going to let one of my own children know such pain. But even though Ibrahim was my son, he was your father, and I could not intervene. Under the law, a man can do as he wishes with his children, he is the master of his own family. But I grieved for you, Yasmina. And now you have come back."

"Please tell me, Grandmother, why did you have Mr. Abdel Rahman ask me to return? Is my father dead?"

"No, Yasmina, your father is still alive. But it is for your father's sake that I wanted you to come home. He is very ill, Yasmina; he is dying. He needs you."

"So he asked you to send for me?"

Amira shook her head. "Your father does not know that you are here. I was afraid that if I told him I had written to you, and then you still did not come, it would destroy him."

Jasmine fought back tears. "What is he dying of? What is his illness?"

"It is an illness not of the flesh, Yasmina, but of the spirit. His soul is dying. He has lost his will to live."

"How can *I* save him?"

"It is because of you that he is dying. The day you left Egypt, so did your father's faith leave him. He was convinced that God had forsaken him, and now, on his deathbed, he still believes it. Listen to me, Yasmina. You cannot let your father die without faith, for then God will indeed abandon him, and my son will not dwell in paradise."

"It is his own fault . . ." Jasmine said, her voice breaking.

"Oh, Yasmina, do you think you know everything? Do you think you know why your father did what he did? Do you know all the stories of our family? By the Prophet, peace upon Him, you do not know the secrets that make up our family, that make up you. But the time has come for you to learn those secrets." Amira lifted the leather bag onto her lap and took out a handsome wooden box inlaid with ivory, its lid inscribed in Arabic: *God, the Compassionate.* "You remember the Misrahi family, who lived next door to us on Virgins of Paradise Street? They left Egypt because they were Jews. Maryam Misrahi was my dearest friend. We kept each other's secrets. I am going to tell you our secrets now, because you are the granddaughter of my heart, and because I want there to be a healing between you and your father. I will even tell you Maryam's great secret; she is dead now, and it will not matter. And then I will reveal to you my own very terrible secret, one that not even your father knows. But not until you have heard everything there is to hear."

Jasmine stared at the wooden box, spellbound. The drapes, which she had drawn over the sliding glass door to her balcony, fluttered in the morning breeze, and with it came the sounds of traffic on the Corniche below. And a strange thought entered Jasmine's head; she suddenly recalled that there had been a time when that Corniche road along the river had not existed, nor had this hotel; British military barracks had once stood here. And as she watched her grandmother open the box, revealing mementos from generations of a proud family, it struck Jasmine that she and Amira were about to embark upon a journey back into time.

"I am going to tell you all the secrets now, Yasmina," Amira said softly. "And you will tell me yours." The wise, onyx eyes gazed at Jasmine. "You have secrets, too," Amira said. "Yes, you have secrets." She sighed. "We will exchange them, and when God hears our story, I pray that in His compassion He will allow you to see the wisdom of what you must do. The first secret, Yasmina, belongs to the year before you were born, when the war in Europe had just ended, and the world was celebrating peace. It happened on a warm night that was full of hope and promise. It was the night that marked the beginning of our family's downfall . . ."

Part I

1945

CHAPTER 1

L ook there, princess, up in the sky! Do you see the winged horse galloping across heaven?"

The little girl searched the night sky, but saw only the great ocean of stars. She shook her head and received a warm hug. As she continued to gaze, seeking the flying horse among the stars, she heard a rumble in the distance like thunder. Suddenly someone was screaming, and the woman who held her cried "God help us!" In the next instant, fierce black shapes descended out of the darkness, gigantic horses with riders dressed in black. Thinking that they had come down from the sky, the child tried to see their great feathered wings. And then they were running, women and children, trying to hide in the tents, while swords flashed in the light of the campfire, and cries rose up to the cold, impersonal stars.

The child clung to the woman, as they huddled behind a large traveling trunk. "Be quiet, princess," the woman said. "Don't make a sound."

Fear. Terror. The child was roughly torn from the protective arms. She screamed.

Amira awoke. The room was dark, but she saw that the spring moon had spread a silver mantle over her bed. As she sat up and turned on the lamp, flooding the room in comforting light, she pressed her hand to her chest as if to calm her racing heart, and thought: The dreams have begun again. And because they had, Amira had not wakened rested, for the dreams that visited her sleep were troubling—memories, perhaps, although she wasn't sure if they were of real events or of imagined ones. But whenever they returned, she knew they would dog her through the daylight hours, and she would be compelled to live the past during the present—if they were indeed memories from the past—as if two lifetimes were unfolding simultaneously, one belonging to the frightened little girl, the other to the woman who was trying to make order and sense of an unpredictable world.

It was because a baby was about to be born, Amira told herself, as she sat up and tried to determine how long she had slept. It was strangely quiet. With each birth in the big house on Virgins of Paradise Street, the visions came back to haunt her sleep. Calming herself, she went into the elegant marble bathroom that she had once shared with her husband, Ali Rasheed, now five years in his grave, and, without turning on the light, ran cold water from a gold faucet. She paused to regard herself in the mirror and saw how the moonlight bleached her face. Although Amira did not consider herself beautiful, others did, and commented upon it. "Promise me you will marry again," Ali had said on his deathbed, just before World War II broke out. "You are still young, Amira, and so full of life. Marry Skouras, you are in love with him."

Amira splashed water on her face. Andreas Skouras! How had Ali known that she was in love with him? She thought she had kept her feelings so carefully hidden that not even her best friend could have guessed how her heart leapt every time the attractive Skouras came to the house. *Marry Skouras.* Could it be so simple? But how did the king's minister of culture feel toward her?

Straightening her hair and clothes—she had lain down for a short nap in anticipation of her daughter-in-law's coming night of labor—Amira crossed the bedroom to the door. The moonlight was illuminating a photograph on the nightstand, and the mustachioed, hawk-nosed man in the silver frame seemed to be beckoning to her.

She held Ali's picture in her hands, drawing comfort from it, as she always did when troubled. "What do the dreams mean, husband of my heart?" she whispered. The enormous house, normally alive with the noise and sounds of the generations who lived within its walls, was silent.

The only signs of life, she knew, would be coming from the suite below, where her daughter-in-law lay laboring to bring her first child into the world. "Tell me," she whispered to the photograph, to Ali Rasheed, rich and powerful, the last of a vanished generation, "Why do the dreams always come back when a baby is about to be born? Are they omens, or is it my own fear that creates them? Oh, my husband, what happened to me in my childhood that makes me experience such terror each time new life is brought into the family?" Amira sometimes dreamed about a little girl, a child crying deep, desperate sobs. But she didn't know who the child was. "Is she me?" she asked the photograph. "Only you knew the secret of my past, husband of my heart. Perhaps you knew even more, but never told me. You were a man and I was but a child when you brought me to this house. What secrets did we leave behind when you took me out of the harem on Tree of Pearls Street? And why can I remember nothing of my life before I was eight years old?"

There was no answer, only the rustling of cottonwood branches in the garden outside, as a spring breeze swept over sleeping Cairo. She replaced the photograph. Whatever answers Ali might have possessed had gone with him to his tomb. Amira Rasheed was left with unanswered questions about who her family was, where she came from, what her real name was—a secret that not even her family knew; when her children were little, and they would ask about her side of the family, she would say evasively, "My life began the day I married your father, and his family became my family." For she had no childhood memories of her own to share with her children.

But there were the dreams . . .

"Mistress?" came a voice from the doorway.

Amira turned to the servant who stood there, an elderly woman who had been with the Rasheeds since before Amira was born. "Is it time?" she said.

"The lady is very near, mistress."

Placing her dreams and thoughts of Andreas Skouras behind her, Amira hurried down the silent hallway, her slippers whispering along rich carpets, her reflection captured in crystal mirrors and gleaming gold candelabra, the air filled with the scent of polish and lemon oil.

Amira found her daughter-in-law attended by the aunts and female cousins who lived in the house, comforting her, whispering reassurances, and praying. Old Qettah, the astrologer, was there, too, in a dark corner of the room, poring over her charts and instruments as she prepared to record the exact moment of the baby's birth.

Amira went to the bedside to see how far the girl's labor had progressed; she still could not shake off the effects of her recent dream. It had seemed more than a dream, more as if she had actually only just moments before been sitting in a desert encampment gazing at the stars, and then had been brutally taken away from someone who had been trying to hide her. Who was the woman in her recurrent dream? Did those loving arms belong to her mother? Amira had no memories of a mother, only dreams of that strange, star-filled night. She sometimes felt she had not been born of a woman, but had sprung straight from those brittle, distant stars.

But if my dream is indeed the fragment of a memory, she thought, reaching for a cold cloth to place on her daughter-in-law's forehead, then what happened after I was taken away? Was the woman killed? Did I witness her death? Is that why it is only in dreams that I can remember the past?

"How is it, daughter of my heart?" she asked the young wife struggling to bring forth her baby; the poor girl had been in labor since early in the day. Amira prepared an herbal tea made from an ancient recipe that the Prophet Moses's mother had supposedly drunk to ease her own labor, and as Amira coaxed her daughter-in-law to drink, she studied the distended abdomen beneath the satin cover, and was suddenly alarmed: something was not right.

"Mother—" the young woman whispered, pushing away the tea, her feverish eyes shining like black pearls. "Where is Ibrahim? Where is my husband?"

"Ibrahim is with the king, and cannot come. Now drink the tea, it possesses the power of God's blessing."

Another contraction came on, and the girl bit her lip, trying not to cry out, because for a woman to show weakness during childbirth was to dishonor her family. "I want Ibrahim," she whispered.

The other women in the room wore silk veils over their heads, their bodies were scented with costly perfumes and clothed in expensive dresses because they lived in the house of a wealthy man. Twenty-three women and children resided in the women's wing of the Rasheed mansion, ranging in age from one month to eighty-six years. They were all related, all Rasheeds, being the sisters and daughters and granddaughters of the first wives of Ali Rasheed, founder of the clan; they were also the widows of his sons and nephews and cousins. The only males in these apartments were boys under the age of ten, after which, according to Islamic custom, they would leave their mothers and move into the men's wing on the other side of the house. Amira reigned over this women's wing, once known as the harem, where the spirit of Ali Rasheed still ruled. The large portrait that hung over the bed showed him surrounded by his wives, concubines, and many children, his women veiled, his hands adorned with heavy gold rings—Ali Rasheed Pasha, sitting on a chair like a throne, a heavyset, powerful man, wearing robes and a fez like a potentate from the previous century, his name still invoked five years after his death. Amira had been his last wife; she had been thirteen when they married, and he, fifty-three.

Her daughter-in-law's mouth opened in a silent scream. Amira changed the damp pillow for a dry one, and blotted the girl's forehead.

"*Bismillah!* In God's name!" whispered one of the young women who was assisting at the bedside, her face as white as the almond blossoms arranged around the room. "What is wrong with her?"

Amira drew down the satin bedspread and was startled to discover that the baby had inexplicably turned and was no longer in the normal birthing position, but lying transversely. It reminded her of another night, nearly thirty years ago, when she had just been brought to this house as a bride. There had been a woman in labor, one of her new husband's older wives, and that baby, too, had lain sideways.

Both mother and baby, Amira recalled, had died.

To hide her alarm, she said soothing words to her daughter-in-law and beckoned to one of the women, a cousin, who was burning incense to keep jinns and other evil spirits away from the childbed. Amira murmured to her that they were going to have to manipulate the baby back into a normal, head-down position. The delivery was near; if the child became wedged in the birth canal, both mother and baby could be lost.

Like other women in the household, the cousin was greatly experienced in all the problems of a difficult childbirth, but as she gazed down at the distorted abdomen, she froze: which end was the baby's head, and which the feet?

Amira reached for an amulet she had placed earlier among the birthing tools, an object of tremendous power because it had been "starred"—placed on the roof for seven nights in order to absorb the stars' light and power—and clasped it between her hands to draw out its magic. A voice on the radio, tuned to the nightly reading of the Koran, chanted, "It is written that nothing will befall us except what God has ordained. He is our Guardian. In God let the faithful put their trust."

After gentle manipulation, Amira managed to turn the baby into the proper position, but as soon as she removed her hands, she saw the abdomen slowly change shape as the baby turned again to lie sideways across the birth canal.

"Pray for us!" one of the women murmured.

Seeing the look of fear on the other women's faces, Amira said calmly, "God is our guide. We must hold the baby in the correct position until it is born."

"But is this the head? What if we are sending the child down feet first!"

Amira tried to hold the baby in the proper position for birth, but with each contraction, it stubbornly swung back into a transverse lie. Finally she knew what had to be done. "Prepare the hashish," she said.

As a new, pungent aroma filled the room, joining the perfume of apricot blossoms and the smoky frankincense, Amira recited a passage from the Koran while she scrubbed her hands and arms, drying them on a clean towel. She was drawing upon knowledge learned from her mother-in-law, Ali Rasheed's mother, who had been a healer and who had passed her secret arts to her son's young wife. But some of Amira's learning went even farther back than that, back to the harem on Tree of Pearls Street.

She watched while her daughter-in-law drew on the hashish pipe until her eyes glazed over. Then, gently guiding the baby from above with one hand, Amira proceeded to reach up for the infant with the other.

"Give her more of the pipe," she said quietly, trying to visualize the position of the infant.

The girl tried to draw in the smoke from the hashish, but the pain became unbearable; she turned her head away and, unable to stop herself, screamed.

Amira finally turned to one of the women and said, calmly and quietly, "Telephone the palace. Tell them Ibrahim is to come home at once."

——

"Bravo!" cried King Farouk. And because he had just won a "cheval," his winnings were paid seventeen to one, and his entourage gathered around the roulette table burst into cheers.

But one man who applauded the king's victory, Ibrahim Rasheed, and who said, "Take a chance, Your Majesty. Luck is with you tonight!" had no heart for the entertainment. When the king wasn't looking, he stole a quick glance at his watch. It was getting late, and he was anxious to telephone home and see how his wife was faring. But Ibrahim was not free to leave the table; he was part of the royal entourage and duty bound, as the king's personal physician, to stay at Farouk's side.

Ibrahim had been drinking champagne all evening, something he rarely did but had turned to tonight to calm his anxiety. His young wife was pregnant with his first child, and he couldn't recall, in all his twenty-eight years, having ever been so nervous.

But rather than lift his spirits, as he had hoped, the champagne was having the opposite effect. With each glass, with each cheer from the crowd around the roulette table, the more morose he grew, wondering what he was doing wasting time at amusements he didn't find amusing. He looked around at the king's companions and saw a regiment of young men who all looked exactly like himself. We are like identical worker bees, he thought, as he accepted another glass from a passing waiter. Everyone knew that Farouk chose his attendants with a particular eye for attractiveness and polish—olive-skinned young men like Ibrahim Rasheed, who had handsome brown eyes and black hair, all in their late twenties or early thirties, rich and idle, wearing tuxedos ordered from Savile Row in London, and speaking an affected English that they had learned while attending school in England, as had most sons of Cairo's aristocracy. And yet on their heads, Ibrahim noticed with uncharacteristic cynicism, they wore the red fez, the jealously guarded symbol of those who belonged to the Egyptian upper class, and some were worn tilted so far forward on their foreheads that they almost rested on their owners' eyebrows. Arabs trying not to be Arabs, Ibrahim thought bitterly, Egyptians trying to pass for English gentlemen, and speaking not a word of their native tongue, because Arabic was good only for giving orders to servants. Although Ibrahim's was an enviable position, at times it secretly depressed him, for even though he was the king's personal physician, it was not an achievement he could point to with pride. The post had been secured for him by his powerful father.

Being Farouk's personal physician had, in fact, many drawbacks, one of them being having to spend evenings such as this, wasting time beneath bright lights and listening to an orchestra play rumbas while women in seductive gowns danced with men in tuxedos. As the king's doctor, Ibrahim was required to be with the royal personage at all times, or at least on call; he had a telephone in his bedroom at the house on Virgins of Paradise Street that was linked directly to the palace. He had held the elite post for five years and in that time he had come to know Farouk better than anyone else, including Queen Farida. Despite rumors—only one of which was true—that Farouk had a very small penis and a very large pornography collection, Ibrahim knew that, at twenty-five, Farouk was at heart a child. He adored ice cream, practical jokes, and "Uncle Scrooge" comic books, which he imported regularly from America. His other passions included Katharine Hepburn movies and gambling. And virgins, such as the milky-skinned seventeen-year-old who hung onto the royal arm tonight.

The crowd around the roulette table grew, everyone wanting to bask in the royal spotlight—Egyptian bankers, Turkish businessmen, British officers in starched uniforms, and various members of Europe's displaced nobility who had escaped Hitler's army. After having braced itself for Rommel's march into Cairo, the city was now in a frenzy of celebration; there was no room in this noisy nightclub for ill feelings, not even toward the English, who were expected to take their occupying forces out of Egypt now that the war was over.

When the king called out, *"Voisins!"* and arranged his chips on numbers twenty-six and thirty-two, Ibrahim chanced another quick look at his watch. His wife should be going into labor at any time, and he wanted to be on hand to comfort her. But there was another, more shameful reason for his anxiety, shameful at least as Ibrahim saw it. He needed to know if he had fulfilled his obligation to his father by producing a son. "You owe it to me and to your ancestors," Ali Rasheed had said the night he died. "You are my only son, the responsibility lies with you." A man who did not father sons, Ali had said, wasn't really a man. Daughters did not count, as the old saying implied: "What is under a veil brings sorrow." Ibrahim recalled how desperate even Farouk had been that Queen Farida give him a son: he had even secretly asked Ibrahim for advice on fertility potions and aphrodisiacs. Ibrahim would never forget hearing the gun salute the day Farouk's child was born; all of Cairo had listened with held breath. They had been acutely disappointed when the salvo had stopped at forty-one guns rather than the one hundred and one that would have meant a boy.

But more than anything, Ibrahim wanted to be with his wife, the girl-woman he called his little butterfly. The king scored another win, the crowd cheered, and Ibrahim gazed into his champagne glass, recalling the day he had first seen her. It had been at a garden party at one of the royal palaces, and she had been among the lovely young women attending the queen. He had been struck by her frailness and beauty, but the exact moment he had fallen in love with her had been when a butterfly had landed on her nose and she had screamed. As the others clustered around her, Ibrahim had made his way through with smelling salts, and when he had broached the protective feminine circle and found her at its center, he had believed she was crying, but when he realized she was laughing, he had thought: someday this little butterfly will be mine.

Ibrahim sneaked another look at his watch and was trying to figure a way of removing himself from the king's presence when a waiter came up bearing a gold tray. "Pardon me, Dr. Rasheed," the man said, "this message just came for you from the palace."

Ibrahim scanned the brief note. A few private words with the king, and he was hurrying out of the club, barely remembering to get his coat from the hatcheck girl, and hastily draping his silk scarf around his neck. When he got behind the wheel of his Mercedes, he suddenly wished he had not drunk so much champagne.

=

Pulling into the driveway on Virgins of Paradise Street, Ibrahim turned off the engine and scanned the façade of the three-story, nineteenth-century mansion. He listened for a puzzled moment and then, recognizing the strange sound that was coming from within, ran through the garden, up the big stairway, across a large hall and into the women's side of the house, where he found the women wailing loud enough for the whole street to hear.

He stopped when he saw the empty bassinet at the foot of the fourposter bed, with a blue bead suspended over it to ward off the evil eye. His sister ran to him and threw her arms around him, crying, "She is gone! Our sister is gone!" Gently removing himself, Ibrahim slowly approached the bed, where his mother sat with a newborn baby in her arms. He saw tears in her dark eyes.

"What happened?" he asked, wishing his head were clear, cursing the champagne.

"God has released your wife from her ordeal," Amira said, drawing the birthing blanket away from the baby's face. "But He has granted you this beautiful child. Oh, Ibrahim, son of my heart—"

"She was in labor?" he said, wishing his mind wasn't so muddled.

"Since shortly after you left for the palace this morning."

"And she died?"

"Just moments ago," Amira said. "I telephoned the palace, but I was too late."

Finally he brought himself to look at the bed. His young wife's eyes were closed, her ivory face looking peaceful, as if she merely slept. The satin cover reached her chin, hiding the evidence of the life-and-death struggle she had lost. Ibrahim fell to his knees, buried his face in the satin, and said softly, "In the name of God the compassionate, the merciful. There is no god but God, and Mohammed is His messenger."

Amira placed a hand on her son's head and said, "It was God's will. She has gone to paradise now." She spoke in Arabic, the language of the Rasheed house.

"How will I bear it, Mother?" he whispered. "She left me and I didn't even know she had gone." He raised a tearstained face. "I should have been here. I might have saved her."

"Only God can save, may He be exalted. Take consolation in this, my son: your wife was a pious woman, and the Koran promises us that the truly pious, when they die, will be granted the supreme reward of beholding the face of God. Come, see your daughter. Her birth-star is Vega, in the eighth lunar house—a good sign, the astrologer assures me."

"A daughter?" he whispered. "Am I then doubly cursed by God?"

"God does not curse you," Amira said, touching Ibrahim's face and remembering how they had grown together—she a girl of thirteen, he a baby in her womb. "Did not God, the Glorious and Almighty, create your wife? Has He not the right to call her to Him when He wishes?

God does nothing that is not wise, my son. Proclaim the oneness of God."

His voice was tight as he bowed his head and said, "I declare that God is one. *Aminti billah.* My trust is in God." He rose, looked around in confusion, and then, with one final anguished glance toward the bed, hurried from the room. Minutes later he was in his car, speeding toward the Nile, then over a bridge spanning the river, and finally along dirt lanes bordering fields of sugarcane. He was barely aware of the huge spring moon that seemed to mock him, or the hot wind that blasted his car with sand; he drove blindly, in rage and grief.

Suddenly, Ibrahim lost control and the vehicle went into a spin, crashing into the sugarcane. He staggered out, the effects of champagne and shock making his head spin. He stumbled a few yards, oblivious of his surroundings or the village a short distance away, and stood for a moment looking up at the night sky. Finally, with a bitter sob, he raised a fist toward heaven. In a loud voice, he cursed God, again, and yet again.

CHAPTER 2

Dawn came, thin and pale, and as Ibrahim opened his eyes, he saw the sun shrouded in mists like a veiled woman. He lay still, trying to think, to remember where he was; his body ached, his head was throbbing, and he was consumed with a terrible thirst. When he tried to move, he discovered that he was sitting in his car, which was tilted at an angle in a forest of tall green sugarcane.

What had happened? How did he come to be here? And where, exactly, was *here?*

And then it came back to him: the summons from the casino, the drive home, finding his wife dead, then the desperate flight through the night, the car going out of control—

Ibrahim groaned.

God, he thought. I cursed God.

He pushed the door open and tumbled onto the damp earth. He couldn't remember anything after that angry curse, yet he realized he must have climbed into the front seat and fallen asleep.

And now he felt sick, and so thirsty he thought he could drink the Nile.

As he leaned against the car and vomited, he saw to his dismay that he was still in his tuxedo, the white silk scarf around his neck, as if he had just stepped out of the casino for a breath of air. He couldn't remember having felt this wretched ever before in his life. He had dishonored his dead wife, his mother, his father.

As the morning mist began to burn off, Ibrahim sensed the vast blue sky open above him, and he felt his father, the powerful Ali Rasheed, looking down from heaven, thick eyebrows meeting in disapproval. Ibrahim knew that his father had occasionally drunk alcohol, but Ali would never have been so weak as to vomit afterward. For nearly all of his twenty-eight years, Ibrahim had tried to please his father, to meet his high expectations. "You will study in England," Ali had said to his son, and Ibrahim had gone to Oxford. "You will become a physician," the father had commanded, and the son had complied. "You will accept a post on the king's staff," Ali, now the minister of health, had instructed, and Ibrahim had joined Farouk's circle. Finally, "You will continue the tradition of honor in our family, and you will give me many grandsons." But all his efforts to gain his father's approval seemed to have been dashed in this one humiliating moment.

Ibrahim sank to the rich earth and tried with all his heart to ask God's forgiveness for his weakness—for running out on his mother, Amira, for not praying over his wife's body, for driving to this desolate place, and for cursing the Almighty. But Ibrahim could not find the humility within him. When he tried to pray, his father's implacable face kept coming to his mind, confusing him. Did all sons, he wondered, see their father's face when they tried to picture God?

As he looked around in the direction of the Nile—he desperately needed water—he heard his father's voice come thundering through the tall sugarcane: "A daughter! You can't even accomplish what the simplest peasant can do!" Ibrahim wanted to cry to heaven: Did I not try to produce a son? Was I not ecstatic when my precious little butterfly told me she was pregnant? And hadn't my first thought been: Here at last is something that my father hasn't given to me but which I have created on my own?

Holding onto the fender, he vomited again and again. As he straightened up and gasped for air, his mind cleared, and in a single, stunning revelation he saw the root of his anguish. And what he saw shocked him utterly: *It is not her death that drives me to madness, but the fact that I have failed to prove myself to him!*

Ibrahim wished he could weep, but, like the prayer for forgiveness, the tears refused to come.

As he steadied himself against the car, assessing how deeply into the mud it was mired, how he was going to get it out, if there was a village or a well nearby, he suddenly saw a figure standing a few feet away, watching him. He would have sworn that she had not been there a moment before; dark herself, she seemed to have arisen from the dark earth, barefooted, in a long dirty dress, an earthenware jug balanced on her head.

He stared at her, seeing that she was a fellaha, a peasant girl, no older than twelve or thirteen, watching him with large eyes that were more filled with innocent curiosity than fear or wariness. And then his eyes fixed on the tall pitcher she carried.

"God's peace and compassion upon you," he said in a dry voice, barely hearing himself over the pounding in his head. "Will you offer water to a stranger in need?"

To his surprise, she stepped toward him, lifted the jug from her head, and tilted it. As his hands shot out to catch the fresh river water, he recalled the few times he had visited his vast cotton farms in the Nile delta, and how shy the peasants were who worked for him, how the girls would run when they saw the master coming.

God, but the water tasted of heaven! He cupped his hands and drank deeply, then splashed the water over his head, his face, and into his mouth again. "I have drunk the most expensive wine in the world," he said as he ran wet hands through his hair, "and it could not compare with this sweet water. Truly, child, you have saved my life."

When he saw the bewildered look on her face, he realized he had spoken in English. He felt himself smile, a strange sensation against the backdrop of his grief. "My friends tell me that I am lucky," he said, continuing in English as he washed his hands again and splashed the cool water over his face. "Because I have no brothers, I received my father's entire legacy, which makes me a very rich man. Oh, I had brothers once, my father had several wives before he married Amira, my mother. Those wives gave him three sons and four daughters. But an influenza epidemic before I was born carried away two sons and a daughter. My youngest brother died in the war, one of my sisters died of cancer, and my two remaining older sisters live now in my house on Virgins of Paradise Street, because they never married. And so I am my father's only son. It is a big responsibility."

Ibrahim looked up at the sky, wondering if he could see the face of Ali Rasheed in the endless blue, and as he inhaled the fresh morning air, he felt his heart constrict like a fist in his chest and tears rise in his chest. She was dead. His little butterfly was dead. He held his hands out and the girl poured more water into them; he scrubbed at his gritty eyes and ran his wet fingers through his hair again.

He took a moment to look at the fellaha, thinking she might even be pretty under all the grime, but he knew that the hard life of a Nile peasant would make her old before she was thirty. "So I have a baby daughter now," he went on, pressing down his rising grief. "My father would see this as a failure. He considered daughters to be an insult to a man's virility. He ignored my sisters when we were growing up. One of them lives at home now, she's a young widow with two little children. I don't think he ever embraced her all the time she was growing up. But I think daughters are nice. Little girls are sometimes like their mothers—" His voice broke.

"You don't know what I'm saying," he said softly to the girl. "Even if I were to speak in Arabic, you wouldn't understand. Your life is simple and already laid out before you. You will marry a man chosen by your parents, you will have children, you will grow old and perhaps live long enough to be venerated in your village." Ibrahim put his hands to his face and began to weep.

The girl waited patiently, the empty water jug cradled in her arm. Ibrahim finally composed himself. Perhaps, with the girl's help, he could get the car out of the mud. He spoke to her in Arabic, explaining how she must push on the hood when he gave the signal.

When the car was once again up on the dry dirt track, the motor purring softly, inviting him to go home, Ibrahim smiled sadly at the girl and said, "God will reward you for your kindness. And I would like to give you something." But as he went through his pockets, he found he had no money with him. And then he saw how she eyed the white silk scarf that was still draped over his shoulders, so he removed it and handed it to her.

"God grant you a long life," he said with tears in his eyes, "a kind husband, and many children."

After the car disappeared down the track, thirteen-year-old Sahra spun around and raced off toward the village, forgetting that her water jug was empty, thinking only of her prize—a length of fabric as white and pure as the breast feathers of a goose, and so soft that it felt like water in her fingers. She couldn't wait to find Abdu and tell him about her encounter with the stranger, show him the scarf. Then she would tell her mother, and then the entire village. But first Abdu, because of the wondrous thing about the stranger—hadn't he resembled her beloved Abdu?

As Sahra made her way down the narrow lanes, where cookfires filled the early-morning air with pungent smoke, she thought how lucky she was. Most girls never knew what sort of a husband they were going to marry; the bride and groom were strangers on their wedding day. And a lot of girls went on to lead unhappy lives, which they proudly bore in silence, because a complaining wife was a disgrace to her family. But Sahra knew *she* would not be unhappy when she married Abdu. Abdu, who laughed so well, and made up poems, and gave her the strangest feeling deep down inside whenever he looked at her with those eyes as green as the Nile. She had known him since childhood—he was four years older—but it had only been after the last harvest that Sahra had started seeing him in a different light, and Abdu had started paying her a different kind of attention. The whole village assumed Sahra and Abdu were going to marry. They were first cousins, after all.

She looked around for him as she entered the tiny village square, where farmers were spreading out produce for sale; he sometimes helped to bring in the crops. A group of women came over, laughing and gossiping; the loose black caftans they wore over their dresses showed they were married, and Sahra was surprised to see her sister among them. As she watched her inspect a crop of onions, she realized that, in strange ways, her sister had changed. Only yesterday she had been a girl like Sahra, but this morning she was a woman. Her sister had gotten married the night before; Sahra recalled how she had watched her sister undergo the virginity test. "The most important moment in a girl's life," Sahra's mother had called it.

So important, that it had been accompanied by a big celebration, which the entire village had attended. But what was it about losing virginity? Sahra wondered, as she marveled at the change in her sister. When the women had arranged the bride on the bed last night, drawing up her dress and exposing her legs, Sahra remembered a night when the women had done a similar thing to her. She had been only six, asleep on her mat in the corner, when, without warning, two aunts had taken her out of bed and lifted her galabeya as her mother held her from behind. Before Sahra had been able to utter a sound, the local midwife had appeared, a razor in her hand. One swift movement, and Sahra had felt a searing pain shoot up through her body. Later, lying on her mat with her legs bound together, forbidden to move or even to urinate, Sahra had learned that she had just undergone her circumcision, a cutting that happened to all girls. It had been done to her mother, to her mother's mother, to women all the way back to Eve. Sahra's mother had gently explained that an impure part of her body had been cut away in order to cool her sexual passion and make her faithful to her husband, and that without such an operation no girl could hope to find a man who would marry her.

But, last night, the midwife had not been present for her sister's test of virginity and honor, nor had there been a razor. The young bride's new husband had performed his duty with a white handkerchief wrapped around his finger, while the assembled family and wedding guests watched. The bride had cried out, and the young groom had jumped up, displaying the bloodied handkerchief. Everyone had burst into cheers and the women began the ear-splitting *zaghareet,* trilling their tongues in their mouths, a sound of joy and celebration. The bride was a virgin; family honor was safe.

And now, this morning, Sahra's sister had been miraculously transformed into a woman.

Sahra hurried on to the coffeehouse, glancing inside hoping to see Abdu, who often helped Sheikh Hamid set up the tables. The older men of the village were already there, puffing on water pipes and contemplating glasses of dark tea. As she searched for the young man, she heard Sheikh Hamid's croaking voice talking about the war, and how the rich in Cairo were celebrating the end of it. But the lot of the peasant hadn't changed, the old sheikh complained, *they* had nothing to celebrate. His voice lowered as he brought up a dangerous topic—the Muslim Brotherhood, a secret group of over a million men dedicated to overthrowing the lordly pasha class, who numbered, Sheikh Hamid declared, a mere five hundred.

"We are the richest country in the Middle East," said Hamid who, being able to read and write and owning the village's only radio, was looked upon with great respect, and regarded as the village's main source of news. "But how is the wealth distributed? The pashas number less than one half of one percent of all landowners, and yet they own a third of all land!"

Sahra didn't like Sheikh Hamid. Not only was he very old, he was very dirty. Despite being a learned man, and thus earning the respectful title of *sheikh,* his galabeya was filthy, his long white beard was tangled and stained with coffee and tobacco, and he had disgusting habits. He had been married four times, being left each time a widower because, the village women whispered, he literally worked his wives to death. Sahra didn't like the way he had started gazing at her breasts whenever she was sent to his shop.

Suddenly remembering the scarf the rich man had given her, she hid it in a fold of her dress. Surely he had been a pasha, a lord, one of the very men Sheikh Hamid spoke against.

Finally she saw Abdu, and when she heard his odd, distinctive laugh and saw the width of his shoulders beneath his striped galabeya, she wondered what was it going to be like on their wedding night. Will he hurt me? she thought, recalling how her sister had cried out when her husband had performed the virginity test. Sahra knew the test must be done, otherwise how did a family prove its honor, which lay in a daughter's chastity? She thought of the poor girl from the next village, who had been found dead in a field. She had been raped by a local boy, her family dishonored. Her father and uncles had killed her, as was their right because, as the saying went, "Only blood washes away dishonor."

Sahra signaled to Abdu and then hurried away before the men saw her. She went to the stable behind the small house she shared with her parents, and slipped inside the little four-walled, roofed shelter made of bamboo, palm fronds, and cornstalks plastered with mud. On very hot days, the family's buffalo would lie here, her jaws constantly moving as she chewed her cud, and Sahra would sit with her. It was her favorite place, and she came here now to relive the meeting with the stranger, to bring the silk scarf out and draw its softness through her fingers.

As she settled down on the straw, noticing that the sun was climbing high, bringing a fresh new day to the village, she knew she should go to the river and refill her jug, but she wanted to be alone, for just a moment, with her wonderful memory. The rich man had said God would bless her! She prayed that Abdu had seen her outside the coffee-house and had followed her, she so badly wanted to tell him of her adventure. Since he had started working in the fields with his father, and Sahra had been more and more restricted to the house, their childhoods seemed over; no longer permitted to play with each other, but forced to join the separate gatherings of men and women, they had had few moments together. As children they had roamed freely, playing at the river's edge or riding a donkey, Sahra with her little arms around Abdu. But adulthood had brought such freedom to an end. The onset of Sahra's monthly cycle had meant long dresses, a scarf to hide her hair, and modest demeanor at all times. No more running or yelling, no allowing so much as a glimpse of her ankles. After years of freedom such sudden restriction was almost unbearable, especially when she and Abdu attended family reunions and were kept apart.

Why did parents seem so afraid for their daughters? Sahra wondered. Why did her mother watch her so closely all the time now, and make her account for every minute of her whereabouts? Why was she no longer allowed to go to the bakery or to the fish-seller on her own? Why had her father started glowering at her as they sat eating bread and beans, watching her with a ferocity that sometimes frightened her? What harm was there in talking to Abdu, or sitting by the river as they had when they were children?

Did it have something to do with the strange new feelings she was experiencing lately? A kind of all-over hunger that made her so restless? She would be washing clothes in the canal, or scrubbing the pots, or spreading dung patties on the roof to dry, and she would forget what she was doing and start daydreaming about Abdu. Usually she received a harsh rebuke from her mother, but there were times when her mother wouldn't get angry, just sigh and shake her head.

Finally, Abdu did come to the stable, and Sahra jumped up, her first impulse being to throw her arms around him. But she held back shyly, just as he did. Boys and girls were not allowed to touch; it wasn't even proper for them to speak together, except at private family gatherings. Modesty had replaced playfulness; obedience, freedom. But the yearning was still there, no matter what the rules said. Sahra stood in the morning sunlight that filtered through gaps in the wall, listening to the drone of flies, the occasional grunt from the buffalo. She gazed into Abdu's green eyes and thought: It was only yesterday that he chased me and pulled my braids. Now, her braids were hidden beneath a scarf, and Abdu was as polite as a stranger.

"I have composed a new poem," he said. "Would you like to hear it?" Since he was illiterate, like everyone else in the village, Abdu could not write down his poetry. Each piece that he composed he committed to memory, and over the years he had made dozens, to which he now added his latest:

> "My soul thirsts to drink from thy cup,
> My heart yearns to taste thy clover.
> Away from thy nurturing bosom I perish and die,
> Like the gazelle lost in the desert."

Thinking that the poem was about her, Sahra was so overcome she couldn't speak, not even to say, "Oh Abdu, you are so beautiful, you look like a rich man!" But when they went down to the Nile to fill her water jug, she told him about the stranger at the canal, and showed him the white-as-clouds scarf he had given her.

Curiously, Abdu expressed little interest. He had much on his mind, although he could share none of it with Sahra, because he knew she wouldn't understand. He had hoped his poem would help her to see what was in his heart, his deep love for Egypt, but by the look on her face he realized that she had mistaken its meaning. Abdu had been in the grip of a strange uneasiness ever since a man had come to the village to speak about the Muslim Brotherhood. He and his friends had listened to the stranger's passionate speech about the need to bring Egypt back to Islam and God's pure ways, and the youths had felt their souls become inflamed. They had sat and talked late into the night, asking themselves how they could continue to work the rich men's land like donkeys, how they could kneel meekly beneath the heel of the British overlords. "Just because we are fellaheen, are we not also men? Do we not have souls? Were we not fashioned in God's image?" Suddenly they had seen a vision that went beyond the village and their small stretch of river; Abdu knew he had been created for a greater purpose.

But he kept his new thoughts to himself, and finally he walked Sahra back to her parents' house, where he paused in the sunlit lane and spoke to her silently with his eyes. Overwhelmed with love for her, he felt again the war waging within his breast: whether to marry her, live and grow old with her, or to heed the call of the Muslim Brotherhood to serve God and Egypt. But Sahra was so lovely in the sunlight, her face so perfectly round, her little pointed chin so charming, that he had to fight the urge to kiss it, her body ripening so quickly that already her galabeya hugged promising hips.

"Allah ma'aki," he murmured. "May God be with you." And he left her there, in the golden sunlight.

Sahra hurried inside, eager to tell her mother about the stranger. She had already decided to make a gift of the scarf to her mother, who had never owned anything so lovely in her life, even though Sahra had caught her looking longingly at the pretty fabrics that were sometimes on sale in the market. She was afraid for a moment she was going to get a scolding for coming so late from the river with the water, so she was ready with an excuse about searching for a stray goat. But, to her surprise, her mother received her excitedly.

"I have wonderful news!" she said. "God be thanked, you are to be married within the month! And your match will outshine even your sister's, which everyone declared has been the best match in the village in years!"

Sahra drew in a breath and clasped her hands. Her mother had spoken to Abdu's parents! They had finally agreed to the match!

"Praise God, it is Sheikh Hamid who has asked for you," her mother said. "You lucky, lucky girl."

The beautiful silk scarf slipped from Sahra's fingers.

CHAPTER 3

W hat is troubling you, Amira?" Maryam asked, as she watched
her friend snip rosemary leaves and put them in her basket.
Amira straightened up and slipped the veil off her head, exposing
glossy black hair to the sun. Although she was in her garden harvesting
herbs, she was dressed to receive visitors, her expensive silk blouse and
skirt entirely black, out of respect for her husband, Ali, and also for her
recently deceased daughter-in-law. But, as always, she wore the latest
style, made from patterns her dressmakers imported from Paris and
London. Amira had also spent time and care on her face—her eyebrows
were shaved off and painted in, Egyptian fashion, her eyes outlined with
kohl, her lipstick a dusky red. A black veil was draped around her
shoulders; if a male visitor should call, she would cover the lower half of
her face and wrap her right hand in a corner of the veil before shaking
his hand.

"I am worried about my son," she said finally, adding some blossoms
to her basket. "He has been acting strangely since the funeral."

"Ibrahim is grieving for his wife," Maryam said. "She was so young,
so lovely. And he was in love with her. It has only been two weeks since
she died, he needs time."

"I hope you are right."

They were in Amira's private garden, which had been planted long
ago by Ali Rasheed's mother, who had patterned it after King Suleiman's
garden in the Bible, filling it with camphor, spikenard and saffron,
calamus and cinnamon, myrrh and aloes. Amira had added imported
plants with healing properties: cassia, fennel, comfrey and chamomile,
from which she made her own medicinal decoctions, syrups, elixirs, and
salves.

It was the time of the siesta, when all the shops and businesses in
Cairo closed for the afternoon, the time when Amira received visitors,
and also when Maryam Misrahi, who lived in the big house next door,
usually came to call. Taller than Amira, Maryam did not hide her rich red
hair beneath a veil, and her bright-yellow sundress caught the attention
of a curious hummingbird.

"Ibrahim will heal," she said, adding, "by God's grace." This she said
in Hebrew, because Maryam, whose last name, Misrahi, meant "Egyp-

tian" in Arabic, was Jewish. "But there is something else troubling you, Amira. I have known you too long not to know when you are not at peace."

Amira waved a bee from her face. "I would not burden you with it, Maryam."

"Since when have we not shared everything, every joy and celebration, and even tragedy? We helped bring each other's children into the world, Amira, we are sisters."

Amira picked up her basket, filled with pungent herbs and fragrant blossoms, and looked toward the gate in the garden wall; it stood open, for guests. Amira never left her house—she had not set foot beyond the wall since Ali brought her here as a bride—and anyone wishing to see her had to come here, to the house on Virgins of Paradise Street. And often, there were many. Long ago, feeling sorry for the young wife whose old-fashioned husband kept her sequestered, Maryam had introduced her own friends to Amira; over the years, the friendships had multiplied, as had Amira's reputation as a healer, one who knew the ancient remedies. There was rarely an afternoon in which visitors did not come.

"I can keep no secrets from you!" Amira said with a smile, as she and Maryam walked back along the flagstone path. She smiled to hide her falsehood—Maryam knew all Amira's secrets except one: She did not know about the harem on Tree of Pearls Street. "I have not been sleeping well. My dreams disturb me."

"The dreams about the desert encampment, the men on horses? You have that dream every time a baby is born into this house, Amira."

But Amira shook her head. "No, I am talking about new dreams, Maryam, dreams which I have never had before." She stopped and faced her friend. "I am having dreams about Andreas Skouras, the minister of culture."

Maryam gave her a startled look, then laughed and linked her arm through Amira's as they walked in the shade of the old trees. Ali Rasheed Pasha had years ago planted his garden with lemon, lime, orange, and tangerine trees, as well as the feathery casuarina and shady sycamore, and the native figs, olives, and pomegranates. A Turkish fountain dominated a flower garden filled with wild lilies, poppies, and papyrus; an ornate sundial inscribed with the verse from Omár Kháyyám about time's hasty passage stood in a bright corner; and grapevines graced the walls.

"Mr. Andreas Skouras!" Maryam said with delight. "If I were not married, I would dream of him myself! Why does this bother you, Amira? You have been a widow long enough. Didn't Ali express his wish that you should remarry? You are still young, you can still have more children. Mr. Skouras! What a delightful prospect."

Amira could not put into words why dreams of the attractive minister should distress her. If asked, she would say that she would not expect a man to marry a woman who did not know her real family, who did not know where she was born, her background or lineage. But when Amira searched her heart, she found a darker reason for fearing these new dreams about Mr. Skouras—it was the shadow of guilt that caused her anxiety, guilt over the fact that she had fallen in love with Andreas Skouras while Ali had still been alive.

"And how does he feel about you?"

"Maryam, he doesn't feel anything about me. I am simply the widow of his friend. Since Ali died, may God make paradise his abode, I have seen Mr. Skouras only four times. The last time was two weeks ago, when he came to the funeral for my son's wife, God rest her. Before that, it was for Ibrahim's wedding, and before that, for Nefissa's. And before that, Ali's funeral. Four times in five years, Maryam. Hardly the attentions of a man who has a special regard for me."

"Maybe he is simply respectful of your widowhood and honors your reputation. I saw him here two weeks ago, and it seemed to me he paid particular attention to you, Amira."

"I had just lost my daughter-in-law."

"God rest her. But Skouras's eyes followed you."

Amira felt her heart leap, and simultaneously felt another pang of guilt, of shame. How could she, with her young daughter-in-law so recently laid to rest, and her son so unhappy, their baby left motherless, be thinking of romance? She recalled the day she had first met Skouras, when Ali had brought him to the house. Amira had shaken his hand, her own wrapped in her veil as custom required, but even so she had felt a shock pass through the fabric from his hand to hers. And had his eyes rested a moment too long on her face, or had she imagined it? At that moment she had felt she had dishonored her husband, if only in her heart. And now, as she walked through Ali's magnificent garden with her best friend, she felt as if she were dishonoring her children. She must not think of Skouras. And she must find a way to stop those disturbing dreams.

A flock of startled pigeons suddenly flew up from the roof, then settled busily into the cottonwoods that lined Virgins of Paradise Street. Shading her eyes, Amira looked up and saw someone silhouetted against the sun.

"It is Nefissa," Maryam said, also looking up. "What is your daughter doing on the roof?"

It was not the first time Amira had seen her twenty-year-old daughter up there between the grape arbor and whitewashed dovecote.

"Perhaps," Maryam said with a smile, "the daughter has been placed under the same spell as the mother. Hasn't Nefissa been acting like a girl in love lately? How romantic the Rasheed women are!" she added with a laugh. "Oh, young love, how well I remember it!"

It was possible her daughter had fallen in love, Amira conceded, but with whom? Widowed since her young husband was tragically killed in a racing-car accident, Nefissa had been living in the customary semiseclusion. Who then, Amira wondered, could she have met? What opportunity, in fact, had she had to make the acquaintance of a man? Perhaps he is a friend of the princess, someone Nefissa met at court, Amira decided, comforting herself with the image of a man of nobility, well established, from an old and respected family.

A man like Andreas Skouras . . .

"You know what you need?" Maryam said, as they neared the gazebo where Amira received her visitors. "You need to spend time away from this house. I remember when I first met you, Suleiman and I had only been married for a month and he brought me to his house here on Virgins of Paradise Street. Your Ibrahim was five years old and my Itzak had not yet been born. You invited me to tea, and I was so shocked to learn that you had never set foot outside your garden. Of course, a lot of wives lived like that then, but Amira, my sister, that was over twenty years ago, times are changing! The harem is outmoded, women go about the city on their own now. Come with me and Suleiman, we are going to vacation in Alexandria. The sea air will do you good."

But Amira had been to Alexandria one summer, when Ali Rasheed had taken his family to a villa on the Mediterranean. The move from the heat of Cairo to the cool ocean air of the northern coast had been a big and exciting event, with days of preparation that ended with the women, securely veiled, going directly from the house into the car and, when they arrived, hurrying from the car into the villa before the veils were removed. She had not liked Alexandria. From the balcony of their summer house she had seen, out in the harbor, the British warships and the American ocean liners, which, she suspected, brought dangerous ways to Egypt.

"The house and everyone in it," Maryam said, "will manage perfectly well while you are gone."

Amira smiled and thanked her for the invitation, but it was an old argument. Every year Maryam came up with new reasons why Amira should free herself from the old, restricting tradition, inventing lures and enticements, and each time Amira would say, as she said now, "There are only two occasions in a woman's life when she needs to go outside: when she leaves her father's house to go to her husband's, and when she leaves her husband's house in her coffin."

"Such talk! Coffins!" Maryam exclaimed. "You are still a young woman, Amira, and there is a wonderful world beyond this wall. Your husband is no longer here to keep you a prisoner in your house, you are a free woman."

But it was not Ali Rasheed who had made his wife a prisoner; Amira recalled the day he had said to her, "Amira, my wife, we live in changing times, and I am a progressive man. Women all over Egypt are discarding the veil, and they are leaving their homes. You have my permission to go about the city whenever you wish, and without your veil, so long as you are chaperoned."

Amira had thanked him, but had declined to be emancipated. Ali had been bewildered, as Maryam was now, wondering why a woman like Amira Rasheed, still young, in the prime of her health and vigor, should choose the severe restrictions that liberal Egyptian women had been fighting for years to abolish.

Amira knew that the root of her reluctance lay buried in the blank years of her childhood, a vague, haunting fear to which she could not put a name. Somewhere, she knew, among those lost memories of the time before her eighth birthday, lay the cause of her desire to remain cloistered. And until she recovered those memories and was able to get over her fears, she was content to stay within the safe walls of Virgins of Paradise Street.

"You have a visitor," Maryam said, as someone came through the gate.

—

From her place on the roof, where bees hummed among the grapevines and doves cooed under the eaves, Nefissa looked out over Cairo's golden domes and minarets at the sunlight sparkling on the Nile, and thought: this time, when he comes, I will go down and speak to him. I will!

From the roof of the Rasheed mansion, one could see the entire city, from the river to the Citadel, and, on clear moonlit nights glimpse the Pyramids, a ghostly collection of triangles in the far-off desert. But this afternoon, while the city dozed through the siesta, Nefissa focused her attention on the street beyond the high wall that surrounded her house and gardens. Each time a carriage rolled by, the horses' hooves clip-clopping on the pavement, she would lean over the parapet and wonder, Is this he, riding by? If a military vehicle turned onto Virgins of Paradise Street, her heart would skip a beat. She never knew when he would come, or if it would be on foot or by car. When she saw her mother and Maryam Misrahi in the garden below, she quickly stepped back, hoping they hadn't seen her. They would certainly not approve of what she was doing!

Nefissa had been widowed several months ago, just before her second baby was born. According to custom, she was required to lead a quiet and chaste life. But how could she, when she was only just twenty, and her husband had been a man she barely knew, a playboy who had loved nightclubs and the fast crowd, and who had been killed in a car accident? Nefissa knew that she had married a stranger, had lived with a stranger for three years, born him two children, and now was expected to spend a year mourning him.

But she couldn't. Not now. She wanted to fall in love, and she was sure she was doing so.

The first time Nefissa had seen the stranger had been over a month ago. She had been idly watching the street through a small opening in the mashrabiya, the latticework screen that covered her window, when she had noticed a British officer walk by on the sidewalk below, and stop beneath a street lamp to light a cigarette. He had happened to look up; their eyes had met. It had seemed to be by accident, but when he lifted his eyes a second time, Nefissa knew it was not. She had sat frozen, holding her veil to her face so that only her eyes showed. And he had lingered beneath the lamppost longer than was necessary, an intrigued look on his face.

Since then, she had watched for him; he had come at different times, unexpectedly, to stand beneath the lamppost, light his cigarette, and watch her for a few forbidden moments through the smoke. Before he walked on, Nefissa was rewarded with a glimpse of his handsome face— he was blond and fair-skinned and more beautiful than any man she had ever seen.

Where did he live? Where did he walk to when he passed her house; where did he walk from? What was his job in the British army? What was his name, and what were his thoughts when he looked up at Nefissa's window, seeing eyes framed by a veil?

If he came today he wasn't going to see her at the window, she thought with a thrill. Today he was going to have a surprise.

As she watched for him, a daring plan evolving in her mind, she wondered what his thoughts were. Was he as amazed as she that the war in Europe was over at last? Had he and his fellow soldiers expected the fighting to go on for another twenty years, as all of Cairo had? Nefissa could hardly believe that there would be no more blackouts, no more bombing raids, no more hurrying out of bed in the middle of the night to huddle in the air-raid shelter Ibrahim had built within the walls of the estate, it being unthinkable that the women of his family should go to a public one. Did those enchanting English eyes hide the fear that, now the war was over, anti-British sentiment was going to gain momentum in Cairo, and that Egyptians would call for the withdrawal of the English who had occupied Egypt for so long?

She didn't want to think of wars or politics. She didn't want to imagine her beautiful officer being driven out of Egypt. She wanted to know who he was, to talk to him, even . . . to make love with him. But she had to be careful. If her secret flirtation were to be found out, the punishment could be severe. Hadn't Nefissa's older sister, Fatima, been banished from the family for some terrible never-to-be-spoken-of sin?

But she wasn't going to worry about consequences, she cared only about taking chances. Today she was not going to sit at the window with a veil over her face; today she was going to make a bold move.

As she watched the street, Nefissa hugged herself joyfully. She had finally learned something about her officer.

The previous afternoon she had gone shopping with King Farouk's sister, who was her friend, and after they had visited Cairo's fashionable shops, along with the princess's usual entourage and bodyguards, they had gone to Groppi's for tea. The entire shop had been cleared of customers so that the royal group could enjoy privacy, and while they sat over tea and pastries, Nefissa happened to glance out toward the street and see two British officers walk by, wearing the same uniform as "her" officer. A casual enquiry among her companions—"What sort of officers are they?"—had told her his rank. It wasn't much, she still didn't know his name, but it was more than she had known yesterday.

He was a lieutenant. He was Lieutenant So-and-So, and his men would address him as "Sir."

She continued to watch the street, looking out over the tops of the tamarind and casuarina trees that grew in the garden below, praying that he would come. It was such a beautiful day, surely he would go for a walk! The neighboring mansions, hidden behind their own high walls and stands of flowering trees, were washed in warm sunshine; the perfume of orange blossoms was carried on the Nile breeze; and only the songs of birds, the tinkling of fountains, disturbed the silence. Yearning for romance, Nefissa thought how appropriate it was that the street where she lived should possess a legend deeply rooted in sexual passion.

According to the story, centuries ago a sect of holy men had come out of Arabia. They had roamed the deserts and countryside completely naked, and wherever they went, women flocked to them, because it was believed that having sexual intercourse with them, or even just touching them, cured wives of barrenness, and assured virgins of finding virile husbands. In the fifteenth century one of these holy men had visited a palm grove on the outskirts of Cairo, where he was said to have blessed a hundred women in just three days, after which he died. Witnesses at the scene declared that Allah's dark-eyed virgins, whom the Koran promises to male Believers as their heavenly reward, came down from the sky and lifted the holy man bodily up to paradise. Thus the palm grove became known as "the place of the virgins of paradise." Four hundred years later, when the British, who, in their role of "protectors," were occupying Egypt, built their mansions in a newly created district in Cairo called Garden City, they retained this bit of local history by naming one small, crescent-shaped street Virgins of Paradise Street. And it was here that Ali Rasheed Pasha had built his rose-colored mansion, surrounding it with a lush garden and a high wall to protect his women, covering the windows with mashrabiya screens so that his wives and sisters could look out without being seen. He filled the house with lavish furniture and precious objects, and over the front door he placed a sign carved in polished wood that read, O YOU WHO ENTER THIS HOUSE, GIVE PRAISE TO THE CHOSEN PROPHET. When Ali Rasheed Pasha died on the eve of World War II, he left behind a widow, Amira, who had been his youngest wife; a son, Dr. Ibrahim; the daughters of his previous wives; and assorted other female relatives and their children. And Nefissa, his last child, who now dreamed of love.

She saw a visitor come through the garden gate below. Friends frequently visited her mother during siesta, and strangers also, women who had heard of Amira's knowledge of medicines and who came seeking advice or amulets or remedies. Nefissa found their requests fascinating—often they came for love potions or aphrodisiacs; contraceptives or medicines for menstrual problems; aids in fertility for the barren woman or impotent husband.

Nefissa sometimes joined her mother and her guests, as did the other Rasheed women and young girls and children who lived at Virgins of Paradise Street. But today Nefissa wasn't going to take part. If her lieutenant came, she was going to go down to the garden. And she had in mind a daring surprise for him.

—

Amira and Maryam sat in the gazebo, an exquisite work of wrought iron crafted to resemble an elaborate birdcage, covered with filigree and lacy ironwork, its top shaped like the dome of the Mohammed Ali mosque, freshly painted white each spring so that it shimmered in the sun. But the gazebo possessed one flaw: the design around the entrance was asymmetrical. The imperfection was intentional; Muslim artists always included a flaw in their work, believing that only God could create something perfect.

A servant approached the gazebo and said, "A visitor has come to see you, mistress."

A woman Amira had never seen before appeared; she was well dressed, with leather shoes matching her handbag, her hat a European import with a net covering her eyes—clearly a woman of substance.

"May your day be prosperous, Sayyida," the woman said, using the respectful form of address that meant "Lady." "I am Mrs. Safeya Rageb."

Although a woman's status was usually determined by the expensiveness of her clothes, the refined way she spoke Arabic, the number of servants in her household, and her husband's status, even more important was the way she was addressed, as Amira's visitor had been quick to establish. "Mrs." earned the respect of the married woman. But Amira noticed that she had not introduced herself as *Um*, "Mother," followed by a son's name, for the highest respect went to the mother of a son—Um Ibrahim being more highly regarded than Um Nefissa.

"May your day be prosperous and blessed, Mrs. Safeya. Please sit down," Amira said, as she poured tea. She then commented upon the weather, the fine crop of oranges, and offered Mrs. Rageb a cigarette. The woman accepted, observing ritual good manners because for a visitor to get straight to the point of her visit would give offense, and for a hostess to ask why a guest had come would be rude. But Amira had noticed the curious amulet made of blue stone that hung on a thin gold chain around her visitor's neck. As blue was the traditional color for warding off the evil eye, Amira thought: She is frightened.

"Forgive me, Sayyida," Safeya Rageb finally said, barely hiding her nervousness. "I came to your house because I had heard that you are a *sheikha*, that you have wonderful knowledge and wisdom. They say that you can cure every ailment."

"Every ailment," Amira said with a smile, "except the one by which a person is destined to die."

"But I had not known of your recent bereavement."

"Necessity has its own laws. How can I help you?"

Safeya Rageb glanced at Maryam, distress so apparent in her posture and troubled eyes that Amira rose and said, "Maryam, please pardon us. Mrs. Safeya, will you walk with me?"

=

Nefissa made her way along the garden wall, glancing back toward the gazebo to be certain she wasn't seen. There were two gates in the wall:

the pedestrian gate, which was open, and the large double gate across the drive that led to the carriage house in the rear. It was to the latter Nefissa now hurried, pressing close and peering through a crack. She held her breath—what if he didn't come?

But he was there!

He had come, and his eyes were fixed on the upper windows. Nefissa felt her heart race. Now was her chance, before he walked away. Yet she had to make sure no one saw her.

She had thought first she would throw a note to him, telling him her name, asking who he was. But then she had thought, What if he doesn't see it, and a neighbor finds it instead? She had considered something of a personal nature, a glove perhaps, or a scarf. But again, if he wasn't able to pick it up and someone else did, mightn't they recognize it as hers? Nefissa had agonized over this all morning until it had finally come to her. And now—

She froze.

Her mother's voice! Somewhere nearby, and coming closer! Nefissa quickly hid behind a bush. What if he left? What if he thought she had lost interest? Oh, Mother, what are you doing here now? Walk faster, Mother! Walk faster! Go away! She scarcely breathed as she watched Amira stroll by on the stone path, a woman at her side Nefissa had never seen before. They were talking in low tones, and Amira seemed not to have noticed her daughter hiding in the bushes. When they had finally disappeared among the tangerine trees, Nefissa returned to the crack in the gate and looked out. He was still there!

Quickly plucking a scarlet hibiscus flower, she tossed it over the wall and held her breath.

He didn't see it!

A military truck rolled by just then, its great dusty tires nearly crushing the flower. But after it passed, she saw him go into the street and pick up the flower. He searched the garden wall until his eye fell upon the gate, at the very place where she stood. She had never seen him this close: his eyes were the color of pale blue opal, there was a mole on his left jaw—so handsome! And then he did an astonishing thing: with those extraordinary eyes still fixed on hers, he lifted the flower to his lips and kissed it.

Nefissa thought she would faint.

To feel those lips, those arms around her! Surely they were destined to do more than stare at each other over a wall. But how could they meet?

A pang of fear shook her. How would he react when he learned she had been married and had two children? Widows and divorced women were not prized as brides among Egyptian men, sexually experienced women were considered poor wife material because they had known another man's lovemaking and comparisons would surely arise between the new spouse and the old. Were English men like that too? She wondered. Nefissa knew very little about the fair-skinned race that had occupied Egypt for nearly a century, supposedly as "protectors," but really, as some claimed, as imperialists. Did they, too, place a high price on virginity? Would her handsome lieutenant find her less attractive once he knew the truth about her?

No, she thought, please don't let him be like that. For them, it had to be wonderful. And they *were* going to meet, they had to.

"Nefissa?" a voice said.

She spun around. "Auntie Maryam! You startled me!"

"Did I just see you throw something over the wall?" Maryam Misrahi said. "And may I assume there is someone on the other side to catch it?"

As Nefissa blushed, Maryam laughed and put an arm around her. "Ah, to be young again!"

Nefissa felt a tightness in her chest. She wanted to be alone, to watch her lieutenant, to be close to him for another moment, perhaps to hear his voice. But then she heard footsteps on the other side of the wall, fading away.

Maryam smelled faintly of ginger, and her red hair shone like chestnuts in the sunlight. She had helped bring Nefissa into the world and had always felt motherly toward the girl. "Who is he?" she asked with a smile. "Someone I know?"

The young woman was afraid to reply. Everyone knew that Maryam Misrahi hated the British because they had killed her father during the revolt of 1919. He had been among the group of intellectuals and political figures executed for "murdering" Britons. Maryam had been sixteen at the time. "A British officer," Nefissa said at last.

When she saw Maryam frown, Nefissa added quickly, "But he's so handsome, Auntie, so elegant and polished. He must be six feet tall, and his hair is the color of wheat! I know you don't approve, but they can't all be bad, can they? I *must* meet him! But everyone is saying the British will leave Egypt soon. I don't want them to go, because then he will go, too!"

Maryam gave her a wistful smile, recalling a time, twenty-two years ago, when she too had been twenty, and in love. "From what I've heard, my dear, the British aren't going to leave so easily."

"But I hope there won't be violence," Nefissa said unhappily. "I've heard talk. Everyone is saying that if the British don't leave, there will be a fight, perhaps a revolution."

Maryam didn't reply; she had heard the same rumors. "Don't worry," she said, as they headed back toward the gazebo. "I'm sure your officer will be safe."

Nefissa brightened. "I know he and I are going to meet. It's our destiny, Auntie. Have you ever felt that? That you were just meant for someone? Did you feel that way about Uncle Suleiman?"

"Yes," Maryam said quietly. "When Suleiman and I met, we knew at once that we were meant to be together."

"You will keep my secret, won't you, Auntie? You won't tell Mother?"

"I won't tell your mother. We are all the keepers of each other's secrets," Maryam said, thinking of her beloved Suleiman and the secret she had kept from him all these years.

"Mother doesn't have any secrets," Nefissa said. "She's too honest to have anything to hide."

Maryam looked away. Amira's was the biggest secret of all.

"I must find a way to meet him!" Nefissa said, as they neared the gazebo where the Rasheed women had now congregated and were chatting and drinking tea while their children played. "Mother would never allow it, of course. But I'm a grown woman, Auntie. I should be able to decide if I wear a veil or not. Hardly anyone wears the veil any more. Mother is so old-fashioned. Can't she see that times are changing? Egypt is a modern country now!"

"Your mother can see only too well that times are changing, Nefissa. And perhaps that is why she is holding on to the old ways."

"Who is the woman I just saw her with? They looked as if they wanted to talk privately."

"Ah yes," Maryam said with a smile. "More secrets . . ."

=

"No one knows of this, Mrs. Amira," Safeya Rageb was saying. "It is a burden I bear alone." She was referring to the reason for her visit: her daughter, fourteen years old, unmarried, and pregnant. Safeya had heard that Amira Rasheed knew secret potions and remedies.

Suddenly Amira was remembering being a child in the harem, remembering a medicinal tea that was sometimes administered to women who hadn't seemed to her to be sick. But then they were sick for a while after they drank it. She had heard the older concubines call it pennyroyal, and she had learned since that it was an abortifacient.

"Mrs. Safeya," Amira said, offering her guest a seat on a marble bench beneath a shady olive tree, "I know what you have come to ask of me, and although I sympathize with your plight, I cannot give it to you."

The woman started to cry.

Amira signaled to a servant who had been standing at a discreet distance, and a moment later tea was brought, made from chamomile grown in Amira's garden. Encouraging her guest to drink it before continuing with her story, Amira waited until Mrs. Rageb was sufficiently calmed.

"What about the girl's father?" she asked gently. "He does not know?"

"My husband and I come from a village in Upper Egypt, and we were married when I was sixteen and he seventeen. I had our first child, my daughter, a year later. We might still be in that village if my husband hadn't heard about the military academy being opened to the sons of farmers. He studied very hard and was accepted. He now holds the rank of captain. He is a very proud man, Mrs. Amira, he values honor above all else. No, he does not know about our daughter's disgrace. He was transferred to a post in the Sudan three months ago. It was a week after he left that my daughter was raped by a neighbor boy on her way to school."

These are indeed dangerous times, Amira thought, now that girls go out to school, walking unchaperoned in the streets. She had heard talk of introducing a new law that would make it illegal for a girl to get married before she was sixteen. Amira was opposed to it. A mother had only one way to protect her daughter—to make sure that as soon as the girl began her monthly cycle, she was placed in the custody of a husband who would then see to it that she was not promiscuous, and that any children she bore were his. But with people these days imitating Europeans, young girls weren't married until they were eighteen or nineteen, leaving them unprotected for six or seven years, and placing the family's honor at great risk.

But her tone was kind as she said, "The judgments of society are sometimes harsh and it is up to a mother to mitigate them for her family." She thought of Fatima, her own lost daughter, cast out of the family because Amira had not been able to save her. "When will your husband return from the Sudan?"

"His posting is for a year. Mrs. Amira, my husband and I love each other very much, I am lucky in that respect. He asks my advice in many matters, and listens to my counsel. But in this instance, I think he would kill our daughter. Can you help me?"

Amira was thoughtful. "How old are you, Mrs. Rageb?"

"Thirty-one."

"Have you been having relations with your husband?"

"The night before he left."

"Is there somewhere you can send the girl? A relative who can be trusted?"

"My sister, in Assyut."

"This is what you must do. Send your daughter there. Tell your neighbors she has gone to nurse a sick relative. Then wear a pillow under your clothes, increasing its size every month. Tell everyone you are pregnant. When your daughter gives birth, summon her and the child home, remove the pillow and tell everyone the baby is yours."

Safeya was amazed. "Can it be done?"

"By the grace of God," Amira said.

After Mrs. Rageb thanked her and left, Amira started back toward the gazebo, but stopped suddenly when she saw that the path was blocked.

She stared at the man standing in the afternoon sun. Andreas Skouras, the man who had come to her in dreams. She was so surprised to see him that she forgot to cover her hair with her veil, or to wrap her hand in a corner of the silk before offering it to him. Once before she had felt a current shoot through her palm from his; fabric had been between them then, but now she felt the direct, unhampered warmth of his skin. Aside from Ali and Ibrahim and her closest male relatives, Amira had never touched another man, and although it was only their hands that met, the contact communicated an astonishing feeling of intimacy.

"My dear Sayyida," he said, using the respectful formal address. "May God's blessings and bounty visit this house."

An esteemed member of King Farouk's cabinet, Andreas Skouras was not a particularly handsome man, but Amira was enthralled by the way the shadows and dappled sunlight played over his smiling face and silver hair. Of Greek descent, Skouras was only slightly taller than Amira, but his robust physique gave the impression of great power and strength.

"Welcome to my house," Amira said, hardly believing that he was actually standing there. His eyes seemed to look at her, into her, right through her. He made her body sing.

"Sayyida," he said, "I honor the friendship and memory of your husband, may God make paradise his abode. I came today because I wish to present you with a gift, to express my high regard for you."

Amira opened the small box and was taken aback to see a gold antique ring nestled on velvet. She recognized the stone as carnelian, and when she saw that a mulberry bush, a symbol of eternal love and fidelity, had been engraved on it, she was overwhelmed.

"Sayyida," he said. Then, more quietly, "Amira. I am asking you to marry me."

"Marry you! *Allah!* Mr. Skouras, you have taken me by surprise!"

"Forgive me, dear lady, but I have planned this for a long time, and I could think of no other way than to be straightforward. May I be cursed if I have offended you."

Amira tried to find her voice. "I am honored, Mr. Skouras, more than I can say. Indeed, I am speechless."

"I know this is a surprise, dear lady, and that you hardly know me—"

I have made love to you in my dreams, she thought, although you will never know it.

"I ask only that you think about my proposal. I have a large house, where I live alone, now that my daughters are married; my wife has been gone these past eight years, God rest her. I am in good health and am financially well situated. I would see to it that you want for nothing, Amira."

"But how can I leave my children?" she said. "How can I leave this house?"

"My dear Amira, you cannot live in a harem all your life. These are modern times."

She was stunned. Did he know about the harem she had lived in as a child? Had Ali told him about her past? Cautiously, she said, "You know nothing about me, about my life before I met Ali."

"None of that matters, my dear."

But it does, she wanted to say. I do not remember my life before I lived in the harem from which Ali rescued me; my only childhood memories are of that terrible place. She wanted to cry: my mother may well have been one of the harem's tragic residents, a concubine, a woman with no honor! She wanted to tell him that she had once even considered returning to the house on Tree of Pearls Street, to see if the answers to her true identity were still there. But the house, she had been told, had long since been torn down, the women of the harem emancipated and scattered like birds.

"My son is without a wife, Mr. Skouras," she said finally, "and my daughter is husbandless. It is my responsibility to see that they are well situated in life."

"Ibrahim and Nefissa are no longer children, Amira."

"They will always be my children," she said, and suddenly her recurring nightmare—the desert encampment, the riders on horseback, the child being torn from its mother's arms—came vividly back to her. And she thought, Is this why I am afraid to leave my children? Is it because I was taken away from my own mother?

Andreas took a step closer and Amira felt her breath catch in her throat. If he should touch her now, in this garden filled with fruit and flowers, she knew she would succumb. She would say, "Yes, I will marry you." But Skouras only said, "You are a handsome woman, Amira. God forgive me that I speak so freely, but I was attracted to you from the moment I met you. I know that Ali, as he watches us from paradise, will forgive me for saying this. He and I were more than friends, we were brothers."

She felt tears begin, and was ashamed to realize that the tears of sadness were mixed with tears of joy. She thought of everything Ali Rasheed had done for her, bringing her to this house, marrying her, and now she was standing in the garden he had created, wearing the expensive clothes and jewelry he had so generously given her, and she was desiring the embraces and kisses of his best friend! "I owe my husband more than I can tell you. He took me from a life of unhappiness and brought me into a house full of happiness."

"I honor his memory and I honor you, Amira. You are a woman beyond reproach."

She looked away. So he did not know her entire story after all. He did not know that Ali Rasheed was not the first man with whom she had been intimate. And before she could marry Skouras, she would have to confess this. But to do so would be to dishonor her husband. So she said, "My first duty is to my children, Mr. Skouras. But I am honored and flattered that you have asked me."

"Have you at least not a small affection for me, Amira? May I perhaps continue to hope?"

She wanted to say, "It is no small affection, Andreas. It is love I feel for you, and have felt since the day we met." Instead, she said, "Please give me time to think about it." And she handed the ring back to him, adding, "I will accept this when I have accepted your proposal."

She walked with him to the garden gate and watched him get into a long black limousine waiting at the curb. As she stood there, a servant came down the path from the house.

"Mistress," he said, "the master is home and is asking for you."

Amira watched the limousine vanish around the curve in the street, then she thanked the servant and turned away from the gate.

As she entered the house, she felt her fears mount. How close she had come to accepting Andreas Skouras's proposal! How easily she could leave this safe house and go and live with a stranger, simply because she desired him. How frail we women are, how prey to our passions, she thought. But Amira knew she had to rule herself with her mind, not her heart. If she and Andreas were destined to be together, then it would be so, but for now she must think of her children: Nefissa, troubled by the same dangerous romantic longings; Ibrahim, his eyes filled with grief, but also with something more, which Amira could not name but which alarmed her. She thought finally of her other daughter Fatima, born after Ibrahim and before Nefissa, whom Ali had banished from the house.

I will not lose my one remaining daughter, Amira thought, as she mounted the massive staircase that divided the men's wing from the women's. I will find a way to save Nefissa from the passions that have possessed her.

That possess us both.

As Amira entered the dark, handsome rooms that had been her husband's, she thought about the days when she had been young and Ali would summon her. She would wait on him, give him a bath and massage, serve him, make love with him, and then retreat to her own side of the house until he called again. In a few years, Nefissa's three-year-old son Omar was going to move from the women's side and take an apartment here; someday he would be entertaining male guests as Ibrahim now did, as Ali once had. A life separate from women.

As she entered Ibrahim's apartment, Amira was struck by how much her son had changed in only two weeks. He looked alarmingly thin. He addressed her in Arabic: "I have decided to go away for a while, Mother."

She took his hands between hers. "Will going away help?" she asked. "Despair reminds us of joy, my son. Time wears away mountains, don't you think it will wear away your grief?"

"I dream of my wife as if she were still alive."

"Listen, son of my heart. Remember the words of Abū Bakr, when the Prophet Mohammed, peace upon him, died and people disbelieved? Abū Bakr said, 'For those of you who worshiped Mohammed, he is dead. For those of you who worship God, He is alive and will never die.' Keep your faith in God, my son. He is wise and compassionate."

"I must go away," Ibrahim said.

"Where will you go?"

"To the French Riviera. The king has decided to vacation there."

Amira felt as if she had been stabbed. She wanted to reach out to him, her baby, the son of her heart, and take away his pain, persuade him to stay here where he belonged. But instead she said, "How long will you be gone?"

"I don't know. But there is no peace in my soul. And I must find it again."

"Very well then. *Inshallah.* It is God's will. But though the body travels an inch, it seems a mile in the heart. God's peace and love go with you." She kissed him on the forehead—a mother's blessing.

As Amira returned to her own side of the house, she felt her heart become full of misgivings. The dreams . . . A child being torn from protective arms. Was it a memory, or a portent of things to come? Why did she feel such dread over Ibrahim's leaving? Why was she suddenly filled with the irrational fear that she was going to lose her children? Nefissa, restless for love; Ibrahim, going away. She had to protect them, keep the family together. But how? *How?*

She did not return to the garden; the servants would be closing the gate now that it was four o'clock; Amira always ended her afternoon receptions at that hour in order not to miss the afternoon prayer. When she entered her private apartment, she went straight to the bathroom and performed the ritual washing required before prayer. Then she went into her bedroom, where Ibrahim's young wife had died giving birth to the baby, Camelia. She spread out her prayer mat, removed her shoes, and faced east toward Mecca. As she heard the muezzins call to the faithful from Cairo's many minarets, Amira cleared all earthly and material thoughts from her mind, and concentrated on God. Placing her hands on either side of her face, she recited, *"Allahu Akbar.* God is great."

She proceeded to recite the Fatiha, the opening passage of the Koran: "In the name of God, the most Gracious, the most Merciful . . ." And then, in one fluid motion that was the result of years of praying five times a day, Amira bowed, straightened, slipped to her knees and touched her forehead to the floor three times as she said, "God is most great. I extol the perfection of my Lord, the Most High." Finally she stood and closed her prayer with, "There is no god but God, and Mohammed is His messenger."

Amira drew comfort from prayer, and she had raised her family to believe in the power of worship. The women in the Rasheed house were required to go through the ritual five times a day—when the muezzin called: just before dawn, a little past noon, in the afternoon, just after sunset, and in the dark of night. They never prayed exactly at dawn or noon or sunset, because those were the times when pagans had worshiped the sun.

After her prayers Amira felt once again spiritually refreshed and empowered, with fewer doubts, less fear for the future. God will provide, she reassured herself, and as she prepared to go down to the kitchen to give the cook instructions, she suddenly felt God illuminate her heart, and in an instant she saw what she had to do.

Find a new wife for Ibrahim, a husband for Nefissa.

And then perhaps, God willing, she would she consider Mr. Skouras's marriage proposal.

CHAPTER 4

As thirteen-year-old Sahra milked the buffalo, leaning against the great warm body and pressing her face into the coarse hide, she experienced a brief moment of peace. For a spell, at least, she forgot the pain and bruises from the beatings her father had given her; she forgot her misery and the terrible marriage she was being forced into.

Tomorrow she would be wed to Sheikh Hamid.

A muffled sob caught in her throat. "Old buffalo," she cried, "what am I going to do?"

Sahra had seen Abdu only once in the two weeks since she had helped the stranger pull his car out of the canal; when she had told him the news of her betrothal to Hamid, he had been shocked, then angered. "We are cousins! We should marry!"

"You will work in Hamid's shop," her mother had said excitedly. "You will talk to customers and take money and make change. You will be very important, Sahra!" But Sahra had seen the sorrow behind her mother's eyes, and understood that she was trying to play up the only good she could see in her daughter's future. To run a shop was prestigious, and Sahra would have welcomed it, but everyone knew that Hamid didn't have even one servant; as well as working all day at the shop while her husband sat in Hadj Farid's café playing backgammon, Sahra would also have to take care of his house, his cooking, his laundry.

She knew why her father had agreed to the match. He had gone into debt for her sister's wedding feast; Sahra's parents were now among the poorest families in the village. She knew there would be no new dress for her on the Prophet's birthday.

Stepping out of the small stable, she looked at the green fields veiled in the early-morning mist. As the sun broke over the mud rooftops, the water in the canal seemed almost luminous. The village began to stir; smoke from cooking fires and the aromas of hot bread and fried beans started to fill the air; and the muezzin called through the loudspeaker of the mosque: "Prayer is better than sleep."

Sahra watched for Abdu. Since she had told him the bad news, she had not seen him again, either around the village or in his field. Where had he gone? She saw someone walking along the canal, tall and broad-shouldered, his feet stirring the ground fog into misty tendrils. Abdu!

She ran to him, but when she saw that he was wearing his one good galabeya and carrying a bundle, she became alarmed.

He regarded her for a long moment with his Nile-green eyes, then said, "I'm going away, Sahra. I have decided to join the Brotherhood. Since I cannot have you, then I will have no woman, but will dedicate myself to bringing our country back to God and Islam. Marry Sheikh Hamid, Sahra, he is old, he will die soon. And then you will inherit the shop and the radio, and everyone in the village will respect you and call you Sheikha."

Her chin quivered. "Where will you go?"

"To Cairo. There is a man there who will help me. I haven't any money, so I will walk, but I have food with me."

"I will give you the scarf," she said in a tight voice. Because the white silk scarf the stranger had given her would fetch a good price, Sahra wore it hidden beneath her dress, for fear her father would sell it. "You can get money for it."

But Abdu said, "Keep it, Sahra. Wear it at your wedding."

When she started to cry, he drew her into his arms, and the feel of each other's touch, the heat and firm flesh they sensed under their clothes, shocked them both. "Oh Sahra!" he murmured.

"Don't leave me, Abdu! I shall die without you!"

He held her at arm's length and felt her tremble as he said, "Think of our love, Sahra, and be a good wife. Bring honor to us both." And then he set off, toward the north. But when he had gone a few yards along the canal, she cried after him, "My soul goes with you, Abdu. You take my spirit, my breath, my tears. Sheikh Hamid will have nothing but this empty flesh."

Abdu turned. And then he ran to her and she flew into his arms. A pair of startled plovers, nesting in the reeds, darted up, screeching. They both gasped as Sahra's hair suddenly tumbled to her shoulders. Drawing her close, he felt such power surge through him that he knew his entire life had been lived for this moment, that his body had been created to touch Sahra's. His mouth sought hers, his fingers became entangled in her hair. He pressed his face into her neck and smelled Egypt—the fertile Nile, hot bread, musky buffalo, and Sahra's own young, virginal scent.

They sank to the damp ground, the succulent green shoots making a soft bed, the mist swirling gently around them. Abdu spread his body over Sahra's, felt her engulf him with a soft embrace, and as he drew up her dress and touched a firm, naked thigh, he wanted to shout, "Allah! Sahra is my wife, my soul."

=

At sunset, Sahra and her mother went down to the Nile to join the other village women, who were collecting water, pounding clothes with bars of soap, and washing their arms and legs, making certain that no men were around to see. They filled their water jars and gossiped, while children laughed and splashed at the river's edge, darting around the buffalo standing in the water.

"Tomorrow is the big day, Um Hussein!" the women called to Sahra's mother. "Another wedding! We have not eaten for a week in preparation!"

Sahra's friends, girls like herself who had just entered the frightening world of womanhood, giggled and blushed and made sly comments about how well she was going to sleep the next night. "Sheikh Hamid is insatiable," said one of them, not quite sure what "insatiable" meant, simply echoing the women's bawdy comments. "You have your job cut out for you!"

The women laughed, dipped their jars into the dirty river water and swung them up onto their heads. "Keep Hamid hungry, Sahra, and he will come home to you every night!"

"I know how to get *my* husband to come home to me every night," boasted Um Hakim. "He used to come in after midnight, and I got tired of it. So whenever he came in late, I would call out, 'Is that you, Ahmed?'"

"And that cured him?" the others asked.

"It did! My husband's name is Gamal!"

The women laughed as they headed back along the path to the village, the children scampering after them, the older ones leading the tethered buffalo. As the dying sun turned the river orange and red, Sahra and her mother were left alone by the water; finally her mother said, "You're very quiet, daughter of my heart. What's wrong?"

"I don't want to marry Sheikh Hamid."

"Such a foolish thing to say! No girl chooses her husband. The day I married your father was the first day I had ever set eyes on him. He terrified me, but I got used to him. At least you know the sheikh."

"I don't love him."

"Love! What a silly notion, Sahra! A mischievous jinni has placed that idea in your empty head! Obedience and respect are what you must hope for in a marriage."

"Why can't I marry Abdu?"

"Because he is poor—as poor as we are. And Sheikh Hamid is the richest man in the village. You will have shoes, Sahra! And perhaps a gold bracelet! He is paying for the wedding, don't forget. He is a generous man, and he will be good to us when you are his wife. You must think of your family before yourself."

Sahra dropped her water jug and started to cry. "A terrible thing has happened!"

Her mother froze. She took Sahra by the shoulders. "What are you talking about? Sahra, what have you done?"

But she already knew. It was what she had feared ever since her daughter had begun her monthly cycle. She had seen how Sahra and Abdu looked at each other, big-eyed, like two calves; she had lain awake at night, fearful that she might not be able to protect her youngest daughter until she was safely married. And now her worst nightmare had come true.

"Is it Abdu?" she asked quietly. "Have you lain with him? Has he taken your virginity?"

Sahra nodded and her mother closed her eyes and murmured, "*In-shallah*, it is God's will." Drawing her daughter into her arms, she recited from the Koran: "The Lord creates, then measures, then guides. Every small and great thing that we do is already recorded in God's books. It is His will." In a tremulous voice she added, "He sends whom He will astray, and He guides whom He will."

She dried Sahra's tears. "You cannot stay here any more, daughter of my heart. You must go away. Your father and uncles will kill you if they find out what you have done. Sheikh Hamid will find no blood of virginity tomorrow night, and they will know that you have dishonored us. You must save yourself, Sahra. God is compassionate, He will take care of you."

The girl swallowed back her tears and regarded the mother she loved, who had taught her and guided her.

"Wait here," her mother said. "Don't come home with me. I will come back after your father has eaten. I have a bracelet and a ring, your father's wedding gifts to me, and the veil Auntie Alya left to me. You can sell them, Sahra. I'll bring food and my shawl. Don't let anyone see you, don't tell anyone where you are going. You will not be able to come back to the village."

Sahra thought of the rich man's scarf, which she had tied around her waist beneath her dress. She would sell that, too. Then she turned away from her mother and looked at the river; a few miles downstream a bridge led into the city. It was the way Abdu had gone. She would follow.

CHAPTER 5

Nefissa stepped down from her carriage, hastily drew her veil over the lower half of her face, and joined the pedestrians thronging through the ancient Bab Zuweila Gate. Because she was wrapped from head to foot in a black *melaya*—a large rectangle of black silk covering even her hands—she was indistinguishable from the peasants who inhabited this part of Cairo; hurrying past the tentmakers' shops and under the gate that for centuries had been the site of bloody executions, she indeed entered another, older era. In the narrow alleys of old Cairo, away from the fashionable streets, many women wore the melaya over their chic European dresses. Ostensibly meant to conceal the form underneath, the melaya was more often used by younger women for its seductive potential. Draped over the head and shoulders and flowing to the ankles, the lower end was gathered up, pulled tightly around hips and buttocks, and draped over one arm, the result being more form-revealing than concealing. As the material was generally light, it required constant rearranging and adjusting, gestures some women had turned into a skillfully provocative art.

Nefissa didn't pause at the stalls, where everything from vegetables to prayer mats were sold, nor did she glance into dark doorways, where artisans worked at centuries-old crafts; she walked purposefully toward a plain door in an unmarked stone wall. She knocked; the door swung open and she slipped inside.

A female attendant in a long robe accepted a pound note, then led her along a dimly lit corridor whose marble walls were damp, the air filled with a heady mixture of perfume, steam, sweat, and chlorine. Nefissa was taken first to a room in which she removed all her clothes, giving them to another attendant and receiving in return a large, thick towel and a pair of rubber thongs. She then entered an enormous chamber with marble pillars and skylights that admitted a diffuse sunshine, which softly illuminated female bathers and masseuses; attendants walked around with glasses of cold mint tea and bowls of freshly peeled fruit. A large pool with a fountain in the center dominated the room, filled with women wading or floating, laughing and gossiping, or washing their hair, some modestly wrapped in towels, others unabashedly naked. Nefissa recognized a few regulars; other women were here for the ritual bath required after menstruation; still more were taking advantage of the healthful perfumed inhalants and herbal soaks. A wedding party, a common sight in the baths, was also in progress: the bride's female relatives were preparing the bride-to-be, waxing her body to remove all hair.

But Nefissa was here for none of these reasons. Her visit to the baths was for an illicit and forbidden purpose.

This *hammam* was one of hundreds in Cairo; it dated back a thousand years, and had a colorful history. Legend had it that, a hundred years ago, an American journalist, wanting to know what really went on in the women's baths, had disguised himself as a woman and gained entry. When his deception was discovered, the outraged females had seized and castrated him. But he survived, and lived to a comfortable old age, during which he wrote his memoirs, with only a brief mention of the Cairo bath-house incident: "The women were all naked, and when they discovered I was a man, they immediately covered their faces, unconcerned about exposing their other charms."

Nefissa was taken into a room where female attendants were busily at work at massage tables, cracking bones and kneading flesh. Removing her towel and stretching out on her stomach, Nefissa tried to relax and deliver herself into the care of the masseuse's strong fingers. But she was not here for a massage, nor a bath, nor any of the numerous cures the hammam offered. Nefissa was here to meet her English lieutenant, and closing her eyes, she prayed that today was the day he would finally come.

In the months since she had thrown the hibiscus over the wall, she had seen the lieutenant only sporadically. His schedule had grown erratic; she wouldn't see him for two or three weeks at a time, and then suddenly he would appear, walking down Virgins of Paradise Street. But one night, as a yellow autumn moon hung over Cairo, Nefissa happened to look out her window and see him there, at the foot of the street lamp, watching her house. She had expected him to walk on, but he had held something up to the street lamp, then, spotting a beggar girl nearby, had said something to her, pointed to the pedestrian gate in the Rasheeds' garden wall, and handed her the object and some coins. Then he had looked up at Nefissa and tapped his watch, indicating he had to leave. And before he did, he blew her a kiss.

Nefissa had run down and opened the garden gate; there was the beggar girl, holding out an envelope. Nefissa was momentarily stunned; Cairo's wretched poor were rarely seen in this wealthy district, let alone a fellaha barely into womanhood, trying to hide her pregnancy beneath a shawl. Nefissa took the envelope the girl held out, then said, "Wait." She ran back into the house and down to the kitchen where, startling the cook, she took bread, cold lamb, apples, and cheese, and wrapped them all in a clean dishcloth. On the way out she stopped at the downstairs linen cupboard and pulled out a heavy wool blanket. Giving these and some coins to the startled girl, she said, "God be with you," and closed the gate.

Nefissa couldn't wait to open the envelope. She ran down to the gazebo, glittering in the moonlight like a cage of spun silver. The letter was one sentence long: "When can we meet?" That was all. A plain sheet of paper with no names, nothing to incriminate him or get her into trouble if it should fall into the wrong hands, but it filled her with rapture.

Nefissa had gone nearly mad trying to come up with a way to arrange a meeting, for she rarely left the house alone; when she went shopping or to the movies her mother insisted it should be in the company of one of her many cousins and aunts. And then it had come to her. She had heard one of Princess Faiza's ladies-in-waiting remark on the wonderful curative qualities of a certain public bath. It was then that Nefissa's "headaches" had started. She first had to suffer her mother's homemade remedies, but finally she was able to wonder out loud if the baths would help. Her first visits had been with a cousin, but they had found the daily visits boring, and since then Nefissa had managed to come alone.

And that was when she had written a note: "My dear Faiza, I am suffering from headaches and have undertaken a cure at the baths by the Bab Zuweila Gate. I arrive every day shortly after the midday prayer, and spend an hour. I believe you would find the benefits most healthful, and I would certainly welcome your company." She had signed it and addressed the envelope to "Her Royal Highness, Faiza." She had then secretly given it to the beggar girl who was now often glimpsed around their gate, and instructed her to pass it along to the soldier the next time he came. Of what would happen should he decide to follow her and meet her outside the baths, Nefissa had no idea. They certainly could not be seen in the street together; she knew any onlookers would assume the English soldier was accosting a respectable Muslim woman—he wouldn't make it out of the street alive. Any meeting they risked, no matter how carefully planned, would be dangerous. But danger only enhanced the drama of their romance. Nefissa was young and desperately infatuated. But now she was beginning to worry. She had come to the baths nearly every day, and he had not yet appeared. Was he no longer in Egypt? Had he been sent back to England?

And then a new and more fearful thought came to her. What if he had found out the truth about her? Perhaps after he read the note he had made inquiries and been told: "Her name is Nefissa, a friend of Princess Faiza." And had also been told she was a widow with children. That was it! And now he was never coming back!

After being massaged with rose, almond and violet oil—reportedly Cleopatra's own beauty secret—Nefissa concluded her visit with the treatment by which many Egyptian women keep themselves beautiful and desirable. The bath attendant produced a jar of red powder and spread it on Nefissa's forehead; a moment later she carefully tweezed out all Nefissa's eyebrows, which would later be painted in. Then came the *halawa,* lemon juice boiled with sugar until it had a sticky consistency; applied to the skin and then pulled off, it took with it the excess hair the Egyptians considered unsightly, and was a painful but effective depilatory. Nefissa then slipped into a perfumed bath to remove any residual stickiness, emerging as smooth and hairless as marble.

She dressed and emerged into the sunshine, cleansed and refreshed, and as she looked up and down the street before returning to her carriage, she suddenly froze. There he was! He was leaning against a Land Rover parked underneath the Bab Zuweila archway.

Nefissa almost didn't recognize him, because he wasn't in uniform. With a thumping heart she started to walk; for an instant their eyes met, then she hurried on. Once inside her carriage, she asked the driver to walk down the street and buy her a bag of roasted pumpkin seeds, an errand he wouldn't find odd and which she estimated would take him ten minutes. The instant the driver left, her lieutenant was there. He gave her a questioning look through the window, and she moved over to let him get in.

As life ebbed and flowed all around them, the street noisy with people and cars and animals, the two sat in a microcosm that held room for no one but themselves. Nefissa took in every detail of him, this phantom lover from beneath the lamppost, who had visited her bed every night in her dreams. They stared at each other, their fragrances mingling, his aftershave with her roses and violets. She saw a dark fleck floating in one of his light-blue eyes. A thousand questions stood on her lips.

Finally he said, in English and in a voice more compelling than she had even imagined, "I can't believe I am truly here. And that you are here with me. I thought I must have dreamed you."

Her heart pounded as he reached up hesitantly to draw away her veil. When she didn't protest, he pulled it aside. "My God, you are beautiful." His words stunned Nefissa. She felt naked, as if he had completely undressed her, but neither shamed nor embarrassed, just burning with desire. There was so much she wanted to say to him, all the things in her heart. And then she was horrified to hear herself say abruptly: "I was married. I am a widow. I have two children." Best to get it out now, she told herself, let him reject me at once, before things go any further.

But he smiled and said, "I know. I'm told they're as beautiful as their mother."

She couldn't speak, she was so excited.

"I live not far from you," he said, in his cultured British voice. "On the next street over, at the Residence, but I'm headquartered at the Citadel. They've been moving us about quite a lot lately. I was afraid you might forget me."

Nefissa was terrified, dizzy, certain that she must be dreaming. "I thought you might have gone away for good," she said haltingly, amazed at how easily she could speak to him. "That awful business when the students marched on the British barracks. So many killed and wounded! I feared for you, and I prayed for you."

"I'm afraid the situation will only get worse. That's why I didn't wear uniform today. Can we meet somewhere in private? Just to talk," he added quickly, "or for tea or coffee. I can't stop thinking about you. And now that you're actually here, just inches from me—"

"My driver will be back soon."

"Can you arrange for us to meet again? I don't want to get you into trouble, but I must see you."

"Princess Faiza is my friend, she will help us."

"Is it permitted to give you a gift? I've been stationed in Cairo for a while, but I only know a few of your customs. I wouldn't give you anything so intimate as jewelry or perfume. I don't want to offend you. But I was hoping that this would be all right. It belonged to my mother—"

He handed her a handkerchief of fine linen, edged in lace and embroidered with small blue forget-me-nots. Nefissa held it in her hand; it was still warm from his pocket.

"This is very difficult for me," he said quietly. "To be this near to you and yet—I don't know what to say, what I'm allowed to say. The screened window you sometimes sit behind, this veil that covers your face. I want to touch you, to kiss you."

"Yes," she whispered. "Yes. Perhaps the princess will help. Or perhaps I can arrange for somewhere where we can be alone. I'll send a note to you, through the girl who is often at our gate."

They looked at each other for a moment, then he touched her cheek, and said, "Until then, my beautiful Nefissa," and was out of the carriage and disappearing into the crowd before she realized he hadn't told her his name.

———

Maryam Misrahi was telling a story: "Farid took his son to the market one day to buy a sheep. Now, everyone knows that the price of the sheep is determined by how much fat is stored in its tail, and so as Farid was feeling the tails of many sheep, weighing them, squeezing them, his son asked, 'Father, why are you doing that?' Farid replied, 'It is done to decide which sheep to buy.' A few days later, when Farid came home from work, his son ran to him and said, 'Father! Sheikh Gama was here today! I think he wants to buy Mama!' "

The women laughed, and the musicians, hidden behind a screen because they were men, also laughed. Then they struck up another lively song.

The party was being held in the grand salon of Amira's house. Brass lamps cast intricate patterns of light on the beautifully dressed women, who were sitting on low divans and silk cushions as they helped themselves to food set out on tables inlaid with mother-of-pearl. Turkish carpets on the floor and rich tapestries on the walls kept out the cold December night; the room rang with laughter and warmth and music.

Servants brought out platters of fragrantly spiced meatballs, eggs in their shells cooked in a rich lamb stew, great dishes of fresh fruit and the rose-petal jam for which Amira was famous, all accompanied by the sweet, viscous mint tea so beloved of the Egyptians.

The party was being held for no other purpose than to celebrate for celebration's sake, and Amira's guests, over sixty of them, wore their best clothes and jewelry; the scent of winter roses mingled with exotic incense and expensive perfume. Because of the sudden demand in the Far East for cotton, and the need for wheat and corn in a food-rationed Europe, Egypt was experiencing a postwar economic boom, and Amira's guests, whose husbands were enjoying unparalleled prosperity, advertised their wealth in the customary fashion; Amira, too, wore the diamonds and gold her husband Ali had so generous given her.

"Ya Amira!" a woman called from across the room, "Where does your cook buy her chickens?"

Before Amira could reply, Maryam shot back, "Not that crook Abu Ahmed on Kasr El-Aini Street! Everyone knows he stuffs his chickens with corn before he kills them so they will weigh more!"

"Um Ibrahim, listen to me," said a middle-aged woman wearing numerous gold bracelets on each wrist. Her husband owned ten thousand acres of rich delta farmland, and was very rich. "I know this excellent man, very clean, educated, a wealthy widower, very pious. He has expressed great interest in marrying you."

Amira merely laughed; her friends were always trying to play matchmaker. They didn't know about Andreas Skouras, whose handsome countenance now came to her mind. Since the afternoon of his marriage proposal, he had come to the house three more times, had telephoned often, and had sent bouquets of flowers and boxes of imported chocolates. He was a patient man, he had assured her, he would not press her for an answer. But each night, as she continued to dream of his embraces and kisses, Amira felt her resistance wear down.

"And what do you hear from your son?" asked another guest, the wife of the curator of the Egyptian Museum.

At the mention of her son, Amira was reminded of another dream she had had just the night before, in which she had seen herself walking through the men's side of the house, down dark and silent corridors, carrying an oil lamp. When she reached her husband's apartment, which was now occupied by Ibrahim, she had opened a door and seen a room full of evil jinns cavorting among cobwebs and long-neglected furniture. What had the dream meant? Had it been a vision of the future, or only of what the future *might* be?

"My son is still in Monaco," she said to the curator's wife. "But I recently received word from him that he is ready to come home, God be praised."

Amira had thought she would faint with joy when the telephone call came. In the nearly seven months that Ibrahim had been away, she had heard from him rarely. She prayed every night that God would ease his pain and bring him home where he belonged. She had found the perfect bride for him: eighteen years old, quiet and obedient, neat and clean. And a relative, too, the granddaughter of Ali Rasheed's cousin.

However, Amira had so far not been as successful at finding a husband for her daughter. Nefissa was not a virgin: it was going to be more difficult to marry her off. Still, the girl was beautiful—and she was rich, which helped; a man might overlook the drawback of sexual experience, providing a woman brought property into the marriage.

Amira glanced at Nefissa, who was sitting on a divan along the far wall nursing her three-year-old son, while two babies played at her feet: Nefissa's own eight-month-old daughter, small and gentle, and Ibrahim's motherless Camelia, an exotic-looking olive-skinned child, with honey-brown eyes, robust at seven months despite the ordeal of her birth. Amira assessed Nefissa's distracted manner, the restlessness that seemed to emanate from her, and sensed once again that Nefissa was yearning for romance.

When Amira thought of Andreas Skouras again, her own secret

passion, she empathized with her daughter. It was a wonderful feeling to be in love, but she didn't want Nefissa to be hurt. Hadn't love for the wrong man been at the root of her other daughter's, Fatima's, disgrace?

The musicians struck up a popular melody called "Moonbeam, Moonbeam," and one of Amira's guests suddenly got up to dance. She kicked off her shoes and moved to the center of the floor, as everyone began to sing to the music. The lyrics were erotic, like most Egyptian songs, speaking of lingering kisses and forbidden caresses. As little girls and young virgins they had learned to sing such songs, chanting them in gardens and on playground swings, "Kiss me, kiss me, O Beloved. Lie with me until daybreak. Bring warmth to my bed and heat to my breast . . ." The words meant nothing to them at that age.

The dancer sat down after just a few minutes, and another woman got up. She wore high heels and one of the new Dior suits everyone was talking about, and she closed her eyes and flung her arms out, while the women merrily sang of virility. When she made an especially graceful turn, some gave her the zaghareet of approval, and when she sat down, another immediately took the floor. This kind of dancing, known as *beledi*, always formed an integral part of women's gatherings, released pent-up emotions, and expressed secret, forbidden yearnings; because such dancing was a very personal expression, the dancers were not judged or compared to one another. This was not a competition; no one was better than her neighbor, and no matter how poor or unskilled a dancer, she was never criticized; every dancer received only encouragement and praise from her companions.

When Amira impulsively took the floor, taking off her shoes and rising up on her toes, the women shouted. Wearing a tight black skirt and black silk blouse, she moved her hips with astonishing skill, first in a rapid shimmy and then, her hips still vibrating, in a slow figure-of-eight. She beckoned to Maryam Misrahi, who got up, removed her shoes, and joined Amira. The two friends had danced together since they had been young brides, and they perfectly complemented each other's movements; soon the entire party was filling the air with deafening zaghareets.

Amira felt her spirits soar. Beledi dancing—"belly dancing" as the tourists called it—released the soul and produced a giddiness some likened to the euphoria of hashish. She saw the same joy mirrored in Maryam, who had recently celebrated her forty-third birthday, one week after that of her oldest son, who was, Amira knew, the secret Maryam had kept from her husband, Suleiman.

Maryam had been married once before, briefly, when she was eighteen, but her young husband and baby had died in an influenza epidemic that had swept Cairo, and she had been alone and grieving when she had met the handsome Suleiman Misrahi, a wealthy importer, and fallen instantly in love. The Misrahis were one of the oldest Jewish families in Egypt, and when Suleiman brought his young bride to the family house on Virgins of Paradise Street, he had prayed to God for many children.

But a year went by, and then another, and finally a third until Maryam was beside herself with worry. She went to doctors, and was told there was no reason she should not have more children. So she knew the problem lay with Suleiman, but such knowledge, she was certain, would destroy him. She had expressed her anxiety to her friend, Amira Rasheed, who had already given birth to Ibrahim and Fatima, and Amira had said, "God will provide."

But it was an idea that had come to Amira in a dream that had ultimately provided the solution.

She had been visited in her sleep by the face of Moussa, Suleiman's brother, and it had struck her that they so strongly resembled each other that they might be twins. After Amira told her friend about the vision, it had taken Maryam weeks to get up the courage to go to Moussa, but when she finally did, he had listened to her story with surprising compassion. He, too, had thought that Suleiman's learning of his impotence would devastate him. And so they had devised their plan.

Maryam had secretly visited Moussa, sleeping with him until she knew she was pregnant. When the child was born, Suleiman believed it to be his. Two years later, she went back to Moussa, and the daughter of that reunion was again the image of Suleiman. Five children ultimately blessed the house of Suleiman Misrahi on Virgins of Paradise Street, and when Moussa moved to Paris, Maryam told Suleiman that a doctor had advised her to bear no more children. To this day, only she, Amira, and the far-off Moussa knew Maryam's secret.

When Amira returned to the divan, laughing breathlessly, a servant approached, quietly informing her that a visitor was asking to see her—a man.

Amira went out into the hall and was not surprised to see Andreas

Skouras; she had hoped he would visit her soon. He had been so much on her mind lately that she wondered if it was a sign that she was indeed going to marry him.

"Welcome," she said, "and God's peace upon you. Please come in and enjoy my hospitality, such as it is."

"I have come to say good-bye, Sayyida."

"Good-bye!"

"As you know, His Majesty changed his cabinet last month. I am no longer minister of culture. While it might appear that I am the victim of politics, perhaps this is God's blessing in disguise. I have for some time now owned title to several hotels in Europe, left to me by an uncle I barely knew. And now that Europe is being rebuilt, there is promise of a new prosperity. Tourists will come, they will need a place to stay. I am leaving for Rome in the morning, Sayyida, and from there I shall go to Athens, the birthplace of my family. I don't think I shall be coming back to Cairo again soon."

He took her hand, raised it to his lips, and kissed it.

"I don't know what to say, Mr. Skouras. I am saddened by this news, but happy for you also, in your new endeavor, and I pray that God will bless you and give you success. But tell me, please, would you have still made this decision if I had accepted your proposal?"

He smiled. "We were not meant to be, Sayyida. I had held out hope, but falsely, for this house is where you belong, with your family. I wanted you for my own selfish needs, and I have finally come to realize that I have caused you distress rather than joy by asking you to marry me. But I shall carry you in my heart, Amira. I shall never forget you."

"Come inside, please," she said, fearful that she was going to break down and cry. "Enjoy the hospitality of my house before you go."

He looked toward the large, ornately carved doors that stood open to the grand salon, permitting bright lights and music to spill into the hallway. "I fear that if I do, Sayyida, I shall never leave. God's peace and blessings upon you." He clasped her hands again, pressing into them a small box. It was the carnelian ring. "Wear it in friendship, Amira," Skouras said quietly. "So that you will always remember me."

She watched him through tears, and when he had gone, took the ring out of its box, and began to slide it onto her finger. Then she stopped. To wear Andreas's ring, she decided, would mean being untrue to him and to its meaning, for she could never think of him merely as a friend. She would save it, and wear it on the day he returned to her, not as a friend, but as a lover.

As she was about to return to the salon, the little gold box in her pocket, she heard a man's voice calling in the hallway, *"Ya Allah! Ya Allah!"* the traditional warning that a man was about to enter the women's quarters.

When Amira heard the voice, she thought, Ibrahim? Seeing him in the doorway, she let out a cry and ran to him. He pulled her into a tight embrace, tears on his cheeks. "I have missed you, Mother!" he cried. "Oh how I have missed you!"

When they came into the salon, Nefissa ran to her brother, and then aunts and cousins and the children, while the rest of the women chatted excitedly: Dr. Rasheed has returned! What a propitious evening! God is good, God is great!

When Maryam Misrahi came over to embrace him, he took her into his arms, even though it wasn't proper that he should touch a woman to whom he was not related. But Auntie Maryam was like a mother to him; she had taken care of him when his sisters Fatima and Nefissa were being born; he had grown up with her children, had attended the Bar Mitzvahs of her sons, and had taken Sabbath meals at the Misrahi house.

"Mother," he said to Amira with a big smile. "I want you to meet someone." And when he stepped aside, the room fell silent as a young woman came in, tall and slender, with a radiant smile, smartly dressed in a traveling suit with a leather shoulder bag and wide-brimmed hat. But it was her hair that stunned the women, a shoulder-length pageboy that was—*blond!*

"I present you to my family," Ibrahim said to her in English, and to Amira he said in Arabic, "Mother, this is Alice. My wife."

When Alice held out a hand and said in English, "How do you do, Mrs. Rasheed? I've been so looking forward to meeting you," more gasps rippled around the room, as one word was whispered and passed along: British!

Amira regarded the offered hand, then she held out her arms and said in English, "Welcome to our house, my new daughter. God be praised, for He has blessed us with you."

After they embraced, Amira saw what the other women in the room had already seen: the unmistakable swell of pregnancy.

"Alice is twenty, just like you," Ibrahim said excitedly to his sister Nefissa. "I just know you two will be great friends." The sisters-in-law embraced, and then the other women clustered around Ibrahim's wife, fussing over her, touching her hair, exclaiming how beautiful she was. "You didn't give us any warning, Ibrahim!" Nefissa said, as she laughed and linked her arm through Alice's. "We would have prepared a big welcome!"

Amira embraced her son again; they held each other for a moment, then she regarded him through tears of joy and said, "Are you happy, son of my heart?"

When he said, "I have never been happier, Mother," Amira held out her arms and said, "Come, daughter. Welcome to your new home." And she thought: Praise the Eternal One for His blessings upon us, and for bringing my son back to me.

Finally, she thought of Andreas Skouras, and marveled at God's mercy, that, while He had taken away the man she might have married, He had restored her son to her.

CHAPTER 6

Sahra had come to beg from the rich tourists in front of the elegant Continental-Savoy Hotel when her labor pains began. She was think-ing that she had yet to make her quota for the day and that Madame Najiba was going to be furious with her, when the first pain struck—a sharp band circling her waist. Her first thought was that it had been caused by the falafel she had bought from a street vendor, spending money she shouldn't have—Madame Najiba counted every piastre— but she had been ravenously hungry. That had been hours ago, though—would it give her a stomachache now?

When the second pain struck, stronger than the first and radiating down her legs, she realized in alarm that her baby must be coming. But it was too soon!

"When was the child conceived?" Madame Najiba had asked, after

Sahra had joined the gang of beggars. She had been unable to reply, having lost complete track of time as she searched Cairo for Abdu. But she recalled that when she and Abdu had made love, the cotton fields had been filled with yellow flowers and the corn had just been harvested. Madame Najiba had counted on her dirty fingers and said, "It'll be born at the end of February, maybe March, with the khamsin wind. Good. All right, you can stay with us. Listen, you might think being pregnant will get you more alms, but it won't. It's an old trick, people will think it's a melon under your dress. But a girl with a baby brings in good money, especially when it belongs to a skinny little thing like you."

Sahra hadn't minded that Madame Najiba purposely kept her underfed in order to maintain the half-starved look, because at least she had a place to stay, a mat to sleep on, and the company of people she could call friends. Some of the other beggars were far worse off, such as the men who had once been perfectly healthy but who had gone to the "beggar-maker" and had their bodies mutilated and deformed because they could make more money that way. And the girls who allowed men to use their bodies. Even though prostitution was legal, it was a shameful profession. After those first terrifying weeks in the city, when Sahra had thought she was going to die of starvation, the protection of even one as cold-hearted as Madame Najiba was welcome.

When a third pain cut through her body, Sahra dropped back from the crowd and looked for the position of the sun. In the village it had been easy to tell the time of day, but with all these tall buildings and domes and minarets, the sun was not so easily found. But there was the sky, turning red behind the roof of the Turf Club. Evening was coming; her baby was going to be born on this cold January night.

Suddenly excited—it seemed as if she had waited forever for the arrival of Abdu's child—Sahra ducked down a side street to avoid drawing attention to herself, and made her way as quickly as possible in the direction of the Nile. The alley where Madame Najiba and her gang of pickpockets and beggars lived was in the other direction, in the old part of Cairo, but Sahra wouldn't go there just yet. There was something she must do first, and it involved crossing the newest section of the city, where shiny automobiles sped down wide avenues, and women in short dresses and high-heeled shoes walked briskly. A section where grimy fellaheen girls were not welcome.

By the time she was close to the river, the sun had dropped behind the horizon and Egypt's brief twilight stood between night and day. Sahra realized she must hurry. The pains were coming closer together; she would do what she had to do, and then get back to Madame Najiba's. She had to be careful. She was near the barracks of the English soldiers; and just beyond was the big museum, closing for the day. Sahra shivered; the temperature was dropping rapidly. If she were back in the village now, she would be securing the old buffalo in its little stable for the night, and then she would hurry inside her father's mud house, which would be filled with warmth from the oven.

She wondered what had happened after she left. Had Sheikh Hamid been angry over losing his bride? Had her father and uncles gone looking for her, to kill her? Had they beaten her mother to find out the truth? Or had life just gone on and the disappearance of Sahra Bint Tewfik become another village story?

Sahra didn't like to recall those first terrible days in Cairo, when she had been so certain she would find Abdu. She had not expected the city to be so big, so crowded, so full of strangers, who ignored her, or the cars that honked their horns at her—the doormen, who had shouted at her when they found her sleeping on their steps; the street vendors, who had chased her for stealing food; the policeman, who had said he was arresting her, but had kept her in his apartment for three nights before she had managed to escape. And then she had come to that curious bridge lined with cripples and beggars, where Sahra had tried to beg for alms from passersby until a woman with Bedouin tattoos on her chin had run her off, shouting that this was *their* bridge and that if she wanted to work on it, she had to come to some agreement with Madame Najiba.

And so Sahra had gone to work for the formidable Najiba, whose name meant "clever one," turning over to her half of what she brought in each day, which sometimes wasn't even enough to let her buy an onion for her supper. Sahra wasn't good at begging, and once she had almost been thrown out of the gang, but then the beautiful woman in a big pink house to whom she had carried a message had given her a wool blanket, and some food and money, and Najiba had decided that, since the baby was due soon, and it would bring in more money, Sahra could stay.

Somewhere in all those days and weeks, her fourteenth birthday had passed, uncelebrated. The closest she had come to finding Abdu was when she had been standing by the gate of the big pink house where the generous lady lived. A car had pulled up and out had stepped the stranger Sahra had helped by the canal the night after her sister's wedding, the man whose silk scarf she had finally had to turn over to Madam Najiba. Sahra had been stunned again to see how strongly he resembled her beloved Abdu, and so she had gone back to the house when she could, hoping to glimpse the rich man again.

The next contraction was so severe that her knees buckled. She was huddled in a doorway, watching cars and buses swing around the big traffic circle in front of the British military compound. She had to find a way to get to the Nile.

Twilight faded and street lights came on. Skirting the traffic circle and moving through the shadows of big buildings with many glass windows, Sahra finally came to the bridge that began the road out to the Pyramids. It was also the road to her village, but she would never go back there. She hurried down to the riverbank, stopping when the pain became too severe; when her bare feet struck moist earth, she slid the rest of the way down, coming to rest among reeds, litter, and rotting fish. To her left, she could see feluccas moored at a landing and fishermen cooking suppers over braziers in the bows of their boats. To her right, beyond the museum, rich people's houseboats rode the gentle tide, their decks strung with lanterns, while music and laughter poured through open portholes. Across the water was the large island where there were sporting clubs and nightclubs and fancy villas, all starting to light up for the night.

Sahra was not afraid as she struggled down to the water's edge. God would take care of her, and soon she would hold Abdu's baby in her arms, as she had once, briefly, held Abdu. And when she was strong, she would continue her search for him, because she had not even for an hour given up the hope that she would find her beloved again.

In going down to the river to give birth, Sahra was following the custom of fellaheen woman who believed it would help them to eat mud from the bank, because the Nile possessed powerful properties of health and virility and protected the unborn child from the evil eye. But Sahra's pains were so severe that she collapsed and could barely breathe. Too late she realized that she should have gone straight to Najiba's. The baby was starting its push into the world.

She lay on her back and looked up at the sky and wondered when night had fallen. So many stars! Abdu had told her they were the eyes of God's angels. She tried not to cry out and thus bring dishonor to herself. She thought of Hagar in the wilderness, trying to find water for her baby. I will name him Ismail, she thought, if it is a boy.

Sahra concentrated on the lights on the opposite bank, gold and glittering; she could see people dressed in white, like angels, and as the stars spun overhead and she was engulfed in pain, she stared across the water and thought that was what paradise must be like.

—

Paradise! Lady Alice thought as she stepped out onto the terrace of the Club Cage d'Or. Cairo, so brightly lit, and the stars so brilliant, their reflections dancing on the Nile—surely this was paradise! She was so happy that she thought she could dance right out there on the river. Her new life had far surpassed her dreams and expectations. She had heard that Cairo was called "Paris on the Nile," but she had not been prepared for it to look so French! And her new home was like a small palace, on a street of embassies and the handsome residences of foreign diplomats. She could well believe Virgins of Paradise Street was in the fashionable Neuilly district of Paris.

She was glad the war was over. Not that she had really been touched by it—she had lived in the country, on the family's ancestral estate. Her father, the Earl of Pemberton, had offered to take in children from the cities and towns that were being bombed, but it had never come to that, thank goodness. Alice wouldn't have known what to do with them.

She didn't like to think about unhappy things such as war and orphans; she even refused to think of all this talk about the British pulling out of Egypt. An impossible thought. What would happen if they did? Hadn't the British made Egypt the marvelous place that it was? One of the things she had first liked about Ibrahim, when she had met him last year in Monte Carlo, was the fact that he, too, didn't distress himself with unpleasant subjects; when everyone else got involved in heated political or social debates, he didn't participate. But this was only one of the many qualities that endeared her new husband to her. He was also kind and generous, soft-spoken, and certainly modest about himself. She had thought that to be a king's personal physician was terribly exciting, but Ibrahim had confessed that it was easy work, not requiring him to do much real doctoring. In fact, he had confessed that he had only become a doctor because his father had been one; and although he had done fairly well at medical school, and had had an above-average internship, he was pleased he had been spared the bother of setting up a private practice: through his father, he had been introduced into the king's circle, and Farouk had taken an instant liking to him. What Ibrahim enjoyed most about his position was that it required him to do very little, just to take the royal blood pressure twice a day, and occasionally to prescribe medicine for stomach upsets.

Alice didn't mind that Ibrahim truly "didn't go very deep," as he himself laughingly put it. He had gone on to describe himself as even-tempered, with no particular hates or passions, no crusades, no driving ambitions, his proudest boast being that he made a comfortable life for himself and his family. Alice loved him for these things, and for the fact that he understood the need to enjoy life, the need for pleasures and amusements. And he was a good lover, although she had no other men to compare him to, since she had been a virgin when they met.

How she wished her mother were still alive! Lady Frances would approve of Alice's choice of husband, as she herself had had a passion for the exotic, and for all things oriental. Hadn't she boasted about seeing *The Sheik* sixteen times, and *The Son of the Sheik* an impressive twenty-two? But Alice's mother had suffered from a depression of unknown origin—"melancholia," the doctor had written on her death certificate. One winter morning, Lady Frances had put her head into a gas oven, and neither the earl, his daughter, Alice, nor his son, Edward, had spoken of it since.

Hearing laughter inside the nightclub, Alice turned and looked through the glass door. Farouk was at his usual gaming table, with his usual entourage cheering him on. He must have just had a win, Alice thought. She liked Egypt's king, whom she thought of as an overgrown boy, with his funny stories and practical jokes. Poor Queen Farida, unable to give him a son. There were rumors that he might divorce her because of it. A man could do that in Egypt; all he had to do was say, "I divorce thee," three times and it was done.

Alice found this national obsession for boy babies quite peculiar. Of course, all men wanted sons; hadn't her own father, the Earl of Pemberton, been disappointed that his firstborn was a girl? But Egyptians seemed really obsessed with the issue. Alice had discovered that there wasn't even a word in Arabic for "children." If a man was asked how many children he had, the word used was *awlad,* which meant "sons."

Daughters weren't counted, and the poor man who had fathered only girls was often labeled with the humiliating epithet *abu banat,* "father of daughters."

Alice recalled how, back in Monte Carlo, Ibrahim's interest in her had increased when, telling him about her family, she had mentioned her brother and uncles and male cousins, adding with a laugh that the Westfalls' specialty seemed to be producing boys. Of course she knew that wasn't his main interest in her; Ibrahim wouldn't have made love to her, married her, and brought her back to his home just for her boy-producing capabilities. He had told her countless times that he adored her, worshiped her, how beautiful she was, blessing the tree from whose wood her cradle had been carved, lifting her feet and kissing her toes!

If only her father could understand! If only she could make him see that Ibrahim really loved her and that he would be a good husband. She hated the word "wog," and wished her father hadn't said it. The two weeks she and Ibrahim had spent honeymooning in England had been a disaster. The earl had refused to meet her new husband, and had insinuated that he would disinherit his daughter for marrying him. She would lose her title, he warned. She had been Lady Alice Westfall because her father was an earl. But she had said that she didn't care, because having married a pasha, her title was still "lady." But she knew the earl would change his tone when the baby was born. He would want to see his first grandson!

But Alice missed him. There were moments when she felt homesick, especially during her first days at the Rasheed house, when she had discovered she had moved to altogether another world. Just her first meal there, breakfast the morning after they had arrived, had stunned her. So used to the silent, polite meals she had shared with her gentlemanly father and brothers, Alice had been amazed at the noisy affair that breakfast on Virgins of Paradise Street had been. The entire family had sat on the floor, supported by cushions, and helped themselves to trays of food. There was incredible noise and confusion—talking and grabbing and eating as if it were their last meal, each morsel being commented upon, spices and the amount of oil used discussed, with persistent urgings to "taste this, taste that." And the food itself! Fried beans, eggs, hot loaves of flat bread, cheese, pickled lemons and peppers. When Alice had reached for something, Ibrahim's sister Nefissa had quietly murmured, "We eat with the right hand." Alice had said, "But

I'm left-handed," and Nefissa had smiled sympathetically and said, "To eat with the left hand gives offense, because we use that hand for—" and she whispered in Alice's ear.

There was so much to learn, so much intricate etiquette to work out in order to avoid offending. But the Rasheed women were kind and patient; they even seemed to delight in teaching her, and they laughed a lot, Alice noticed, and frequently told jokes. Nefissa was her favorite. The very day after Ibrahim and Alice had arrived at the house, her new sister-in-law had taken her to meet Princess Faiza, and all the sophisticated ladies at court who, although Egyptian, were very European in their manner and dress. That was when Alice had received one of her biggest shocks. After getting all dressed up to go out, Nefissa had wrapped herself entirely in a long black veil, which she called a melaya, until no part of her body was exposed except her eyes. "Amira's rule!" she had said, laughing. "My mother thinks the streets of Cairo are filled with lusts and temptations and men lurking at every turn to rob a girl of her honor. But don't look so horrified, Alice! The rules are different for you, you are not Muslim."

There were other adjustments as well. She missed her morning bacon; there were to be no more pork chops or ham, and as alcohol was also prohibited by Islamic law, there was no wine with dinner, no brandy afterward. And Ibrahim's female relatives spoke Arabic all the time, occasionally remembering to translate for her. But Alice's most difficult adjustment had been with the curious male-female division of the house. Ibrahim could enter any room he liked, whenever he liked, but the women, even his mother, had to ask permission to visit him on the other side of the house.

Finally, there was the issue of religion. Amira had very kindly pointed out to Alice that Cairo had many Christian churches and that she was welcome to attend any she liked. Not having been raised in a very religious atmosphere, Alice had never attended church except on special occasions. When Amira had politely asked her why there were so many different Christian churches, Alice had replied, "We have different shades of belief. Aren't there different Muslim sects?" Amira had said that there were, but even so all Muslims, regardless of sect, attended the same mosque. When she expressed further curiosity about the Christian Bible, wondering why there was more than one version when there was only one Koran, Alice had had to admit that she didn't know.

But she had been accepted into the family; everyone called her either sister or cousin; she was treated as if she had lived there all her life. And when the baby was born, the perfection would be complete.

Ibrahim came out onto the terrace then, saying, "There you are!"

"I had to get some air," she said, thinking how handsome he looked in his tuxedo. "I'm afraid the champagne's gone to my head!"

He laid a fur stole around her shoulders. "It's chilly out. And now I have two of you to take care of." He had brought her a chocolate truffle with a creamy center; he put it between her lips and then kissed her, sharing the truffle.

He drew her close. "Happy, darling?"

"The happiest I have ever been."

"Are you homesick?"

"No. Well, a little. I miss my family."

"I am sorry that you and your father aren't friends. I am sorry that he doesn't approve of me."

"It's not your fault, and I can't live my life just to please him."

"Do you know, Alice, that I have lived all my life to please my father, never being quite successful at it. I have never told anyone this, but I have always felt a little like a failure."

"You are not a failure, darling!"

"If you had known my father, God rest him in peace, you would know what I am talking about. He was very well known, very powerful, very rich. I grew up in his shadow. I don't recall him ever having a kind word for me. He wasn't a bad man, Alice, but he was of another generation, he belonged to the era when it was believed that to show affection to a son would be bad for his character. I sometimes think that my father had expected me to be an adult the day I was born, because I didn't have a childhood, except with my mother. And when I became a man, no matter what I did, I could never please him. That's one of the reasons why," he said, touching her cheek, his eyes glistening, "I want a son. Giving my father a grandson will be the first achievement I can look upon with pride. A son will give me my father's love at last."

Alice kissed him gently, and as they turned away, out of the cold, they did not see a small commotion on the opposite riverbank, Nile fishermen shouting about something they had found.

CHAPTER 7

Y ou are very lucky, my dear," Amira said to her daughter-in-law as they sat on the roof beneath the stars, examining the tea leaves in Alice's cup. "Qettah tells me that tonight is a most propitious night for having a baby," Amira added. Alice looked over at the astrologer, who sat at a table by the dovecote, studying charts and graphs, occasionally consulting the brilliant night sky. Alice laughed. She was nine months pregnant and a week overdue. "I shall try to comply!" she said.

Nefissa, who was sitting beneath an arbor of bright-blue wisteria, exchanged a knowing smile with her sister-in-law. Every birth in the Rasheed house was accompanied by fortune telling, star-gazing, superstition, and magic, heightening the mystery of an already exciting event. She could see that it baffled Alice, who had told Nefissa that births in her own family had always been somber, hush-hush affairs.

Others had also come up to the roof to enjoy the spring night and share in the drama of Qettah's mystical forecasts—aunts and female cousins who were unmarried Rasheeds, or had been married to Rasheeds, and who now, being husbandless, were under Ibrahim's protection. They ate and gossiped while Amira and Qettah read the omens.

Nefissa was watching two toddlers playing on a blanket—one-year-old Camelia, whose mother had died in childbirth nearly a year ago, and Nefissa's own little girl, Tahia, fourteen months old. Nefissa's four-year-old son, Omar, had chosen to go tonight to the cinema with his uncles. But Nefissa could concentrate on neither her sister-in-law's impending childbirth, nor the two little girls. She was thinking of the time and trying not to look anxious.

Tonight she was going to meet her English lieutenant at the princess's palace, and they were going to be alone.

The women gathered on the Rasheed roof awaiting the important event entertained themselves with sweetmeats and tea and chattered in Arabic and, for Alice's sake, in English. Alice loved the sound of Arabic; she had even started learning to speak it. When Qettah pointed to a star rising above the dome of a nearby mosque, sparkling like a beacon between two minarets, and said, "There is Rigel, a very strong sign," Alice replied uncertainly, *"Al hamdu lillah,"* and again shared a look with Nefissa, who winked.

As the other women encouraged Alice, saying that she was starting to speak Arabic like an Egyptian, Nefissa looked at her watch again. She was so excited she wanted to shout from the rooftop. But she was also cautious, afraid of being disappointed again. Since their meeting in her carriage four months ago, they had set up several rendezvous, all through the princess, in whom Nefissa had confided. But each attempt had come to nothing——twice the officer had not shown up; once Nefissa had had to stay home; and once the princess had let them down.

Would they be successful tonight? she wondered. Would his commanding officers let him go, would the princess keep her word? Nefissa thought that if she could not get a chance to be with him, to feel his touch, to know his kiss, she would die.

Finally, she rose and said, "It is time for me to go."

Amira looked at her. "Where are you going?"

"The princess is expecting me."

"With Alice so close to her time?"

"It's all right," Alice said, knowing about the romantic rendezvous, relishing being in on the secret.

Amira watched her daughter leave, and wondered where Nefissa had found such a strong will. Amira had taught her children obedience, but they seemed to have minds of their own. Fatima had been like that, Amira thought suddenly, wondering as she often did where her lost daughter Fatima was at that moment, where she had disappeared to after Ali had cast her out of the house. Amira had once even thought of trying to find her, enquiring through friends and acquaintances, but Ali had forbidden it, and although it had caused her pain, Amira had dutifully obeyed.

"Oh!" Alice cried, and everyone turned to her. When she put her hands on her abdomen and said, "I think it's time," they jumped up and rushed to her.

Amira murmured, "Praise God," and went to help her daughter-in-law into the house, while Qettah fixed her eyes on the stars.

—

As a close friend of the princess, and well known at the palace, Nefissa was escorted inside by a tall, silent Nubian in a white galabeya, red vest and red turban, one of an army of servants employed in the two-hundred-room palace in the heart of Cairo, their sole purpose being to attend to the needs and comforts of the princess and her new husband. Built during the Ottoman era in an exotic mixture of Persian and Moorish architectural styles, the palace was a maze of corridors, rooms, and gardens, and as Nefissa followed the Nubian through elaborate marble archways, she heard in the distance an orchestra playing a Viennese waltz—the princess and her husband, entertaining guests.

Finally she was brought to a part of the palace she had never visited until recently; the servant lifted a velvet drape, and Nefissa entered a vast room with an enormous fountain in the center. She recognized it as a beautiful old harem, no longer used. The floor was of a highly polished marble so richly dark blue that it looked like deep water; Nefissa was almost afraid to walk on it, and thought that, if she looked down, she would see fish glinting in its depths. There were low divans around the walls, covered with velvet and satin spreads; hundreds of brass lamps were suspended on chains, all of them lit, casting reflections on marble columns and arches and a high ceiling inlaid with intricate mosaic. Just below the ceiling there were screened balconies overlooking the room, where Nefissa imagined the long-ago sultan must have sat and watched his women in secret.

Nefissa saw curious murals on the walls, scenes of nude women bathing in the central fountain, some even entwined in erotic embraces. The women, of all ages and types, seemed afflicted with a kind of languorous melancholy, prisoners of their own beauty, caged like birds for one man's amusement. Were these the portraits of women who had really lived? Nefissa wondered, as she became captivated by their doelike eyes and voluptuous limbs. Was she gazing upon the faces of women who had once had names, and who had dreamed perhaps of freedom, and the real love of a man? As she studied the scenes, she saw that in each, in the background, was a man, darker skinned than the women, dressed in a long blue robe. He appeared to be strangely detached from the activities of the bathers, neither aroused by them nor disapproving of their sensuous play. But who was he? Certainly not the sultan, who would appear larger than life, in sumptuous clothes, and surrounded by nymphs. What had the artist meant by including so odd a figure?

Nefissa turned away from the strangely disquieting paintings, and felt her heart race. She had been waiting forever for this night. What was her English lieutenant going to be like? She wondered, as she began to pace, praying that he would show up. In her fantasies he was a gentle and considerate lover. But she had heard stories among the princess's circle of friends, liberated women who mingled freely with foreign men, and who complained that the English lacked passion. Would he be as detached from their lovemaking as the mysterious man in the murals? Would he walk in, sweep her off her feet, satisfy himself, and say good-bye?

When Nefissa heard the mournful cry of a peacock somewhere out in the garden, her anxiety mounted. It was getting late. She had waited in this strange harem, with its ghosts of sad, imprisoned women, twice before, and both times she had been disappointed. She felt her anxiety turn to panic. Time was running out, not just for tonight, but for her freedom. Nefissa tried not to think of the men her mother was attempting to match her with, wealthy, eligible, and not unattractive. How long was she going to be able to keep finding excuses for not marrying this one or that one? How long would Amira's patience hold out? When would she finally say, "Mr. So-and-So is perfect for you, Nefissa, and he is a respected man. You must marry again, your children need a father."

But I don't want to get married again, she wanted to say, not just yet, for then my freedom will end and I will never have an opportunity to know what it's like to experience an evening of wonderful, forbidden love.

Nefissa heard a door open somewhere behind her, then footsteps crossing the marble floor.

The velvet drapes stirred, as if by a breeze, and suddenly there he was, removing his military hat so that his blond hair gleamed in the light from the overhead brass lamps.

Nefissa caught her breath as he looked around the vast chamber, his polished boots echoing on the marble floor. "What is this place?"

"It's a harem. It was built three hundred years ago."

He laughed. "It's like something out of *A Thousand Arabian Nights*!"

"The *Thousand and One*," Nefissa corrected him, hardly believing he was there, that she was there with him, and that they were finally alone together. "Even numbers are unlucky," she added, wondering where she found the voice, the courage to speak. "And so Scheherazade told one more tale after the thousandth."

He looked at her. "My God, you're beautiful."

"I was afraid you would not come."

He walked up to her, close, but not touching. "Nothing could have kept me away," he said quietly.

When Nefissa saw how he turned his cap around and around in his hands, her heart flew out to him.

"I frankly never expected to meet you like this," he said. "You're so—protected. You're like one of these—" he gestured to the murals—"a woman bound in veils, a prisoner behind wooden screens."

"My mother is very protective. She thinks the old ways were better."

"What if she were to find out about us?"

"I can't even think of it. I had a sister, she did something, I don't know what. I was only fourteen at the time, I didn't really understand, but I heard my father shouting at her, calling her names. He sent her out of the house without even a suitcase, and we were forbidden ever to speak her name again. Even now, no one mentions Fatima."

"What became of her?"

"I don't know."

"Are you afraid now?"

"Yes."

"Don't be." He reached out to touch her; she felt fingertips brush her arm.

"I'm leaving Egypt tomorrow," he said. "We're being shipped back to England."

Nefissa was used to the dark, seductive glances of Arab men which, whether intentionally or not, burned with promise and male challenge. But the Englishman's eyes were open and blue like a summer sea, with an innocence and vulnerability that she thought more exciting than the other kind.

"Then this is all we have?" she said. "Just this hour?"

"We have the entire night. I'm not expected back until morning. Will you stay with me?"

She went to a window and looked out at the deep, indigo night, in which white roses bloomed and a nightingale sang a sweet, sad song.

"Do you know the story of the nightingale and the rose?" she said, unable to meet his eyes.

He stood behind her, so close that she could feel his breath on her neck. "Tell it to me."

"Long ago," she began, feeling as if she were on fire, that if he touched her, she would become a flame, "long ago, all roses were white because they were virgins. But one night a nightingale fell in love with a rose, and when he sang to her, something stirred in her heart. Then the nightingale came close and whispered, 'I love you, rose,' and the flower blushed and turned pink. But then the nightingale came even closer, and the rose opened her petals and the nightingale took her virginity. But because God had decreed that roses should remain chaste, the rose turned red with shame. That is how red and pink roses came into being, and to this day, when the nightingale sings, a rose's petals will tremble, but they will not open, because God had never meant for a bird and a flower to mate."

Putting his hands on her shoulders, he turned her to him. "And what of a man and a woman? What did God intend for them?"

He took her face between his hands and brought her lips to his. He smelled of cigarettes and whiskey, both forbidden to her, and she tasted them now, on his lips and tongue.

He pulled away and, removing his belt and holster, stood silently facing her. With fingers that trembled uncontrollably Nefissa undid the buttons of his military tunic. He wore no shirt under it, and the pale, taut skin, the supple chest and broad shoulders, touched her strangely. She ran her hands over the powerful muscles and the flat abdomen, fascinated. She could not help comparing this man's spare, lean body with that of her late husband, who had been soft, delicate, almost feminine.

With a sensuality she had never thought she'd experience, the lieutenant pushed her blouse from her shoulders and unfastened her skirt.

"My God, you're beautiful!" he repeated, staring at her.

And there was no need for any hurrying at all.

—

"Why does Britain want to take Palestine from the Arabs and give it to the Jews?" asked an indolent young man who was high on hashish. "The Arabs didn't take that land from the Jews, but from the Romans, fourteen centuries ago. Tell me what European country would be expected to give up territory it had held and occupied for fourteen hundred years? What if the Indians demanded Manhattan back? Would the Americans give it to them?"

On Hassan al-Sabir's houseboat, moored on the Nile, several friends reclined on low couches, sharing a water pipe and occasionally helping themselves to grapes and olives, cheese and bread, from a brass tray. Ibrahim was among them, thinking about Alice, wondering when the baby was going to come. He and Hassan were close friends; they had both been at university in Oxford, where anti-Eastern prejudice had formed a special bond between them that remained after their return to Egypt. Like Ibrahim, Hassan was twenty-nine, attractive and rich. But unlike his friend, Hassan was a lawyer, and very ambitious.

"I suppose it's all a matter of who was in Palestine first," Hassan said, bored. "But why bother yourself about it? It's none of our affair."

But the young man insisted, "We're not the ones who persecuted the Jews during the war. We recognize the Jews as our brothers, as we all are descended from the Prophet Ibrahim. And we have lived peacefully together for centuries. This new Israel would not be a homeland for a persecuted people, but just another excuse for further European occupation in the Middle East!"

Hassan sighed. "You are becoming dangerously political, my dear fellow. And tiresome."

"I know what will happen. They will not come to live as Semites among Semites, as our brothers, but as Europeans looking down upon the miserable Arab. Didn't it happen here? We aren't allowed to join the Turf Club or the Sporting Club, because they don't allow *gyppos*! We have to make Egypt for Egyptians, or else we'll go the way of Palestine."

An intense young man with sharply defined cheekbones said, "Britain will never leave Egypt. Not while they want our cotton and the Canal."

"By God," said Hassan with a laugh, glancing at Ibrahim, who clearly had no interest in the conversation, "why bother yourselves over such things?"

"Because Egypt has the highest death rate in the world. One child in two dies before the age of five. We have more blind people than anywhere else in the world, too, and what have our so-called protectors done about it? In the eighty years the British have occupied Egypt, they haven't attempted to bring pure water to our villages, or build schools, or establish a medical service for the poor. They might not have done anything specifically to brutalize us, but they've been indifferent to us, which is just as bad!"

Hassan rose from the divan and, gesturing to Ibrahim, went out on the deck. Although he had an apartment in the city, where his wife, mother, unmarried sister, and three children all lived, Hassan spent most of his time on his houseboat, where he entertained friends and women. Tonight he was wishing he had invited prostitutes instead of the junior partners from his law firm. "Sorry, old boy," he said to Ibrahim as he lit up a Dunhill. "I shan't invite them again. I had no idea they had all these thoughts and opinions. I say, you're looking rather happy."

Ibrahim's smiling face was set toward Garden City, and he was thinking that the Nile's movement was as slow as the passing of time. "I was just thinking about Alice, and what luck that I found her."

Hassan had entertained the same thought when he had first set eyes upon Ibrahim's blond bride, himself possessing a preference for fair women. "God has truly blessed you, my friend," he said. "By the way," he added, inspecting his reflection in the window and liking the handsome young man he saw, "a cousin of my sister's husband came around requesting a post in the Ministry of Health. Can you use your influence, as a favor to me?"

"I golf with the minister on Saturday. Tell your wife's in-law to telephone me day after tomorrow. I shall have a posting for him."

Hassan's valet, a staid Albanian, came out onto the deck. "Your house just telephoned, Dr. Rasheed. Your wife is in labor."

"Praise the Lord!" Ibrahim declared. "A son, I hope!" And he hurried out.

=

Ibrahim quietly closed the bedroom door behind him, leaving Alice to sleep peacefully after her labor; he joined his mother in the grand salon, where she and Qettah the astrologer were going over the star charts, and where the newborn child slept in a cradle under Amira's watchful eye. Kneeling to look at his child, Ibrahim was filled with tenderness and love. She was like a cherub in a European painting, he thought, one of God's little angels. Fine platinum filaments, like cornsilk, grew on her head. Yasmina, he thought. I will name you Yasmina.

He was suddenly overcome with remorse that he had not welcomed his first daughter, Camelia, into the world with this same love. But he had been so griefstricken over his young wife's death that he had barely looked at the baby. And even now, a year later, Ibrahim could not make himself feel the love for his first daughter that he felt for this new one. His joy was suddenly cut short by the vision of his father, and the sound of Ali's voice saying, "Once again you have failed me. Six years have I lain in my tomb, and still I have no grandsons to show that I was ever even alive."

Please don't make me not love this child, Ibrahim pleaded silently with his father. But in Ibrahim's mind he heard Ali reply "You are a father of daughters, that is all you are."

Amira laid a hand on her son's shoulder. "Your daughter was born under Mirach, the lovely yellow star in Andromeda, in the seventh lunar house. Qettah says that this foretells beauty and wealth for her." She paused, sensing her son's inner struggle, and said, "Do not despair, son of my heart. Next time, it will be a son, *inshallah*."

"Will it, Mother?" he said, bowing beneath the mantle of guilt his father had bequeathed to him.

"We can never be sure, Ibrahim. Only God in His wisdom bestows sons. The future was written in His book long ago. Take comfort in His compassion and infinite understanding."

Her words about God worried him; he had cursed God the night Camelia was born. "Perhaps I will never have a son, Mother. Perhaps I have brought misfortune upon myself."

"What do you mean?"

Ibrahim felt Qettah's dark, impassive eyes watching him. Although the old woman had been to the Rasheed house before, and had even been present at his own birth, Qettah's presence always unsettled him. "The night Camelia's mother died in childbirth. I didn't know what I was doing. In my grief, I cursed God." He couldn't look at his mother. "Am I now cursed because of it? Will I never have a son?"

"You cursed God?" Amira said. And suddenly she was recalling the dream she had had the night before Ibrahim came home from Monaco—a dream of evil jinns and afreets in a dark and dusty bedroom. Had it foreshadowed a terrible future? One in which no more sons blessed the Rasheeds?

There was one way to find out.

On Qettah's instructions, Amira brewed thick coffee, heavily sugared, and instructed her son to drink it. When he had done so, Qettah upended the cup on its saucer and waited for the coffee grounds to dribble down, forming a pattern. When she had read Ibrahim's fortune, she closed her eyes.

She had seen daughters. Only daughters.

But there was another message in the coffee grounds. "Sayyid," she said respectfully, in a voice that was surprisingly young, even though Ibrahim suspected the astrologer was nearly ninety. "In your grief you cursed God, but God is merciful and does not punish those in distress. Nonetheless there is a curse over this house, Sayyid. But where it comes from, I cannot say."

Ibrahim swallowed painfully. My father, he thought. My father has cursed me. "What does it mean?"

"The line of Ali Rasheed will vanish from the earth."

"Because of me? Is this certain to happen?"

"It is only a possible future, Sayyid. But God is merciful, and has shown us the way for you to bring blessings back to your family. You must go out into the streets and perform an act of great charity and sacrifice. God loves a charitable man, my son. Through generous acts He may lift the curse because He is merciful and compassionate. Go at once. Try."

Ibrahim looked at his mother, and then hurried out of the house, driven by fury at his father, by memories of a man who would address his own son as "dog" because he thought it would build character. Ibrahim climbed into his car with tears in his eyes, not knowing where he should go or what form the act of charity should take. All he could think of was the sweet angel, Yasmina, lying in her cradle, whom he wanted to love but could not because of fear of his father's ridicule. And Camelia, born the night he had cursed God. And all the baby girls to come, down through the years, until there was no son to carry on the Rasheed name, and the family disappeared.

He started to pull the car out of the drive, then braked abruptly and rested his head on the steering wheel. Dear God, what was he going to do?

When he looked up, he saw the fellaheen girl standing there. She was holding a baby. He had seen her before, staring at him as if perhaps she knew him. He had never spoken to her, never really looked at her, but now, as she stood in the moonlight, he was suddenly reminded of a similar night a year ago. Did the girl look familiar? No, she couldn't be the one who had given him water, had eased his terrible nausea and misery when he had awakened beside that canal. "What is your name?" he asked.

She stared at him with enormous eyes and when she spoke her voice was shy and small. "Sahra, master."

"Your baby doesn't look well," he said.

"He does not get enough to eat, master."

Ibrahim regarded the girl with the hollow eyes, the baby with barely enough flesh on its bones, and a strange feeling came over him: the feeling that God's hand was upon him. And an idea, stunning in its genius and simplicity, came to him. "If you give me your son," he said, gently, so as not to frighten her away, "I can save him. I can give him a life of riches and happiness."

Sahra gave him a puzzled look. She thought of Abdu. Had she the right to give away his son? But this man so strongly resembled Abdu . . . what could that mean? Sahra had been hungry for so long that she had difficulty thinking. She looked at the big house, where orange blossoms bloomed and golden light spilled from the many windows, and she thought of how Madame Najiba made her go out every day with her baby and beg for alms. And then she looked at the man whom she had once met beside the canal, and who again, in her confusion, she thought must somehow be connected with Abdu. "Yes, master," she said shyly, and held her baby out to him.

He told her to get in the car, and they drove off.

—

Hassan stared at him. "You want to *what?*"

"I want to marry this girl," Ibrahim said, pushing past his friend, bringing Sahra in with him. "You're a lawyer. Draw up the contract. You will represent her family."

Hassan followed him into the main salon of the houseboat, still littered with the remnants of their party. "Are you out of your mind? What do you mean you want to marry her! You have Alice!"

"Hassan, think, man! It's not her I want, it's the boy. Alice gave birth to a girl tonight. And the astrologer told me God asks for a charitable act. I will take this child, a boy, as my own."

Hassan was silent for a moment, studying the beggar girl, then, realizing what Ibrahim was thinking, said, "Do you seriously expect to get away with saying this child is your own? Have you gone mad? Ibrahim, you were in Monte Carlo for nearly seven months. No one would believe this baby is yours."

"The girl says the baby was born three months ago. That means he was conceived a year ago. I was in Cairo then. If I declare this child to be mine, in front of witnesses, then under the law that makes him so."

Hassan reluctantly agreed; suddenly remembering the woman who was due to arrive at the houseboat within the hour, he decided to draw up the marriage contract. After his valet had witnessed both their signatures, Hassan and Ibrahim shook hands. The marriage was legal. Then, because the law required four male witnesses for the next step, Hassan had the valet bring the cook and houseboy into the room, where they listened in silence as Ibrahim said to them, "I declare this child to be mine, of my body, to carry my name. I am the father; he is my son."

Hassan hastily filled out a birth certificate, and the witnesses made their marks.

Finally Ibrahim turned to Sahra and, according to custom and law, recited, "I divorce thee, I divorce thee, I divorce thee."

He took the baby from her and said, "This child is now mine, before God and according to the laws of Egypt. You must never make a claim on him, or tell him who you are. Do you understand this?"

Sahra said, "Yes, master," and fainted.

=

Amira stared at the baby in Ibrahim's arms and then looked at her son in disbelief. "This child is *yours?*"

"He is mine and I have named him Zachariah."

"Oh my son, you cannot claim another man's son as your own! It is written in the Koran that God forbids the taking of another man's son!"

"He is mine. I married his mother and I declared the boy to be mine. I have the legal papers."

"Legal papers!" she cried. "It is against *God's* law to adopt a child! Ibrahim, son of my heart, I beg of you! Do not go through with this." Amira felt her panic rise. To take a child from its mother . . .

"In all respect and honor to you, Mother, Qettah told me to go out and perform a charitable act. I have done so. I have saved this child from the streets."

"God will not be tricked, Ibrahim! Don't you see, this will bring bad luck upon our house! Please, son of my heart, don't do this. Restore this baby to his mother."

But when he said, "It is already done," and she saw the look of helplessness in his eyes, and the fear and confusion, she said, "So be it. *Inshallah.* As God wills. Now it is to be our secret. No one is to know where this child came from, Ibrahim. Tell none of your friends, no member of our family. The secret is to remain here, between us. For the sake of our family's honor." Her voice broke as she added, "Tomorrow we will introduce your new son to the world. You will present him at the mosque. And then he will be circumcised."

Amira struggled for self-control. "And now, what of the mother? Where is she?"

"I will see that she is taken care of."

But Amira was in the grip of her old fears. "No," she said, "the boy must be with his mother. We cannot separate them. Bring her in. I shall place her as a servant in our house. In this way she can nurse the child, and he will not be taken from her."

Amira then took the frail bundle into her arms. "I will raise you as my grandson," she said to the infant. "If Heaven created you, then earth can find a place for you."

As she looked into the infant's eyes, she thought again of her strange dreams of a desert camp and a night raid, which not even Qettah had been able to interpret, and she wondered if they had portended this night, or if they were omens of events still to come. Then she thought of the babies who had been born upon the return of those dreams— one-year-old Camelia, Yasmina, only hours old, and now the adopted Zachariah. She thought of her own child, Nefissa, who earlier had left the house with flushed cheeks, and who still had not returned, although the hour was late. And Amira imagined the mighty hand of God, writing in His book of destinies.

"Listen, my son," she said to Ibrahim. "In the morning you will go to the mosque and distribute alms to the poor. And you will pray and atone for what you have done. And I, too, will pray, for God is merciful."

Amira spoke calmly, but she was afraid.

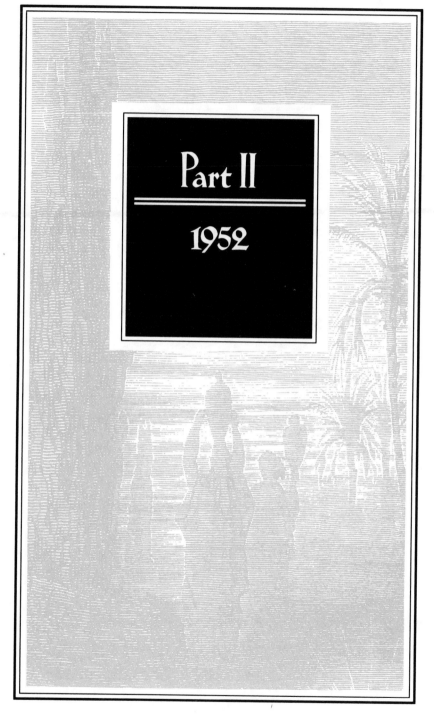

Part II

1952

CHAPTER 8

I say, what's going on? Is today a holiday or something? Why are the streets deserted?"

The taxi driver looked in the rearview mirror at the man he had just picked up at the main railway station; he wanted to tell the Englishman that today was a bad day for his kind to be in Cairo; he wanted to say, "Didn't you hear about the massacre at the Suez Canal yesterday, when your soldiers slaughtered fifty Egyptians? Haven't you heard the oaths now being sworn all over the city to avenge this atrocity? Didn't you hear the government warning British citizens to stay off the streets?" The driver also wanted to add, "Don't you know why it was so difficult for you to get a taxi? Only a madman would pick up an Englishman! And don't you know that I only agreed to take you to Virgins of Paradise Street because you offered so much money, and business is bad today? And am I not, therefore, just as crazy as you?"

But the driver only looked at his passenger and shrugged. The man was clearly ignorant about these things, and other things besides, such as basic common courtesies. Everyone knew that it was insulting for a male passenger to ride in the back of a taxi instead of up front with the driver. A passenger was more than just a fare, he was a temporary guest in the driver's car.

But Edward Westfall, the twenty-six-year-old son of the Earl of Pemberton, was oblivious. Whatever the cause for the strangely empty streets of Cairo on such a crisp Saturday morning, and whatever the reason for his driver's lack of verbosity, these were not his concerns. He was having such a high time of it, so enjoying this "schoolboy's lark," as his father had called it, that nothing could dampen his excellent mood.

"I'm here to visit my sister," he said, as they headed down a broad avenue in the exclusive Ezbekiya district. Neither Edward nor the driver were aware that, at that same moment, young men with clubs and axes were gathering to launch a holy war. "It's to be a surprise," Edward went on, sitting forward on the seat as if trying to make the taxi go faster. "She has no idea I'm coming. She's married to Farouk's personal physician. We might even be dining at the palace tonight."

The driver shot him another look. He wanted to say, "Don't brag about that, it's another count against you—English, and a friend of the king. Turn around and go home, while you're still alive." But instead he merely said, "Yes, Sayyid," and thought about the money.

"I can't wait to see her reaction!" Edward said, as he pictured the happy reunion. How long had it been since they had last seen each other? Alice had left home right after the war, in June of 1945, to visit friends on the French Riviera, returning to England only for a brief visit, accompanied by her new husband, Dr. Rasheed. That was six-and-a-half years ago.

"This is my first time in Egypt," Edward continued, wondering about the sounds he heard in the distance. Were they explosions? "I'm going to invite Alice on a sailing trip up the Nile to Lower Egypt, so we can visit the ancient monuments. I don't think she's done that yet."

The driver cast him another contemptuous look, and thought: You've got it backward, fool! You go *up* the Nile when you go south to Upper Egypt. Lower Egypt is north, where the Nile flows *to*. But he didn't say anything because he, too, had heard the explosions that could have either been near or far away. And was he smelling smoke? But the street still seemed peaceful, deserted.

"I say," Edward said, looking ahead through the windshield. "What's going on?" An angry mob had appeared, carrying sticks and torches.

"*Y'Allah!*" cried the driver, slamming on his brakes. He took one second to survey the angry faces and clenched fists, then quickly turned the car down a side street.

"Good heavens!" Edward exclaimed, as he was flung back onto his seat.

When they reached the end of the street they saw a building on fire, flames and smoke pouring out of the windows, a large crowd gathered on the sidewalk. Strangely, there wasn't a fire engine or hose in sight, and none of the onlookers was doing anything to help. Edward frowned when he saw a sign fall off the façade and tumble to the sidewalk. He could just make out SMYTHE & SON, ENGLISH HABERDASHERS, EST. 1917.

Throwing the car into reverse, the driver steered back down the street, screeched to another stop, then plunged headlong down an alley. Edward, thrown this way and that, shouted, "What's happening, man! Why weren't those people trying to put out the fire? Oh my God! Look there!"

At the end of the alley they came upon another fire, one that had just been started; angry young men in galabeyas were throwing flaming rags through the broken windows of an English furrier. "I say," Edward said, as the driver tried to maneuver the taxi past the mob. "I don't think I like the look of this."

===

As the taxi disappeared around a corner, the leader of the mob raised his fist and shouted, "Death to nonbelievers!" And his several hundred comrades shouted it back.

One young man in the front of the crowd, his eyes blazing with excitement, felt the power of God in his veins. This was what Abdu had worked for for nearly seven years, ever since he had left his village—to bring Egypt back to God's ways and the purity of Islam. His only wish was that Sahra could be here to see his triumph. Funny little round-faced Sahra, whom he still thought of and loved, even though he believed she was married to Sheikh Hamid, was now possibly even a widow, considering Sheikh Hamid's age. Abdu pictured her in the village shop, being respectfully addressed by Hamid's customers. How many children did she have?

The day he had left the village, after making love with Sahra on the canal bank, Abdu had been dogged by feelings of remorse. He had taken her virginity; no blood would have been spilled on her wedding night.

But when he had recalled how hungrily the old sheikh had looked at her, and what a large bride-price he had offered her family, Abdu had decided that Hamid was one of those men who, in order to get the woman he wanted, was not beyond resorting to subterfuge, a pinprick to his own finger before wrapping the handkerchief around it—a trick as old as the Nile. By the time Abdu had arrived in Cairo and found the address that had been given to him, he had been so overwhelmed by the city called the Mother of Cities, and the passion and determination of the Brotherhood, that all other thoughts had vanished. Sahra became a sweet memory.

His whole earlier existence was now like a distant dream. He sometimes thought about that youth who toiled in the fields, or played backgammon in Hadj Farid's café, or made up verses for Sahra, and wondered who that young man could have been. That wasn't the Abdu he was now, the Abdu who had been born the night he arrived in Cairo and began to listen to the word of God for what seemed like the first time. The frail old village imam, whose weekly preachings in the mosque put most people to sleep, had none of the fire and inspiration the Brotherhood leaders did. The village preacher taught the same Koran, the same holy message, but the Brethren spoke the verses in such a way that Abdu seemed to feel them, taste them; they seemed to feed his hungry soul as if they were bread and meat. How clear it all was to him now, how bright and narrow and straight the road of purpose stretched before him—to bring Egypt back from the brink, back to God and His grace.

The leader directed the mob to a halt, pulled himself up on a lamppost, and began a fiery speech. They were going to show the world that Egypt would no longer suffer an imperialist overlord, he said. The British were going to be driven out in their coffins!

The young men cheered and brandished their homemade weapons. *"La illaha illa Allah!"* they cried. Abdu shouted as loudly as the rest of them. "There is no god but God!" And when the leader cried, "To the Turf Club!" the mob surged like a tide down the next street, Abdu running at the head of them, his heart pounding, his green eyes ablaze with glory.

—

The commander-in-chief of the British Army stood up, raised his glass and said, "Gentlemen, to the new heir to the throne!"

As the six hundred men at the banquet tables drank a toast in honor of the prince, Hassan leaned over and murmured, "What we're really toasting is the royal poker, you understand," and Ibrahim smiled.

The banquet at Abdin Palace was to celebrate the birth of Farouk's son, and a congenial mix of foreign dignitaries, officers of both the Egyptian and British armies, and government officials was in attendance. They sat beneath blazing chandeliers and feasted on asparagus, cold cucumber soup, duck *à l'orange,* raspberry sherbet, roasted gazelle, and cherries flambé, all served on gold plates accompanied by imported wines and brandies and heavily sweetened Turkish coffee. But despite the amicable talk and gentlemanly laughter, Ibrahim sensed that an undercurrent of unease flowed among the tables. Some of the laughter sounded forced, some of the conversations too loud. Arab and Briton smiled at one another, but there seemed to be more diplomacy than genuine friendship in those smiles. Everyone knew that, given the unrest in the city brought on by the Ismailia massacre, His Majesty had been advised to postpone today's celebration. But Farouk wouldn't hear of it. If anyone had need to worry, he assured them, it was the British. *He* had nothing to fear.

The king had never looked so happy. When Queen Farida failed to produce a son, Farouk had divorced her, publicly reciting three times the formula, "I divorce thee," after which he had married a sixteen-year-old virgin whom he had wooed with an extravagance that had been faithfully chronicled in gossip magazines around the world. For every single day of their courtship and honeymoon, Narriman had received a gift—a ruby necklace one day, Swiss chocolates the next, her favorite orchids, a kitten. In return, she had given Farouk his first son. Neither massacres nor rumors of revolt were going to spoil today's celebration.

Ibrahim sat a few seats down the head table from Farouk, close at hand should the royal body suffer from a sudden attack of indigestion. Although slim and handsome a mere sixteen years ago, on this January afternoon Farouk weighed two hundred and fifty pounds, and ate with a voracity that still astonished his friends—three courses to another man's one, and ten orange fizzes by latest count.

As he watched the king signal for yet another helping of fish, Hassan leaned over to Ibrahim and said, "What baffles me is, how do he and Narriman manage it? In bed, I mean. The old boy's stomach must stick out farther than his—"

"What was that?" Ibrahim said, interrupting him. "Did you hear something just now?"

"What?"

"I don't know. It sounded like explosions."

Hassan looked around the vast banquet hall where the six hundred men enjoyed themselves amid an Eastern opulence that had lately been coming under attack. Tall windows framed by brocade draperies admitted a soft winter light that illuminated gigantic marble columns, velvet-covered walls, and gold-framed paintings. Noticing that none of the other guests seemed to have heard anything unusual, Hassan said, "Must be firecrackers, honoring the prince."

Hassan thought for a moment. "You don't really think there's going to be a muck about this Ismailia thing, do you?" He was also thinking about the string of alarming events that had occurred since Egypt's humiliating defeat in the Palestine war, four years ago. First a police commandant was assassinated, and then the governor of the Cairo province, and finally the prime minister had been shot while walking into the Ministry of the Interior. The streets were rife with demonstrations and strikes and riots to protest the continued British presence in Egypt. Only last year, people were killed during a demonstration in front of the British Embassy. And then, yesterday, there had been that ghastly massacre at Ismailia . . .

But Ibrahim reassured his friend with a smile. "Egyptians might be a passionate and sometimes irrational species, but we aren't mad enough to come right out and attack British citizens. Besides, all this talk about revolution is merely an exercise in futility. Egypt hasn't been ruled by Egyptians in over two thousand years. You certainly don't think things are going to change now? Look, His Majesty isn't the least bit troubled, and now there's an heir to the throne. This unrest will die down, it's just another passing fancy. Tomorrow the mob will be agitating for something else."

"You're right!" Hassan said, suddenly cheered. He drained his champagne glass and it was instantly refilled by the footman who stood behind his chair. There were footmen attending to the individual needs of each of the six hundred guests, silent servants who stood in long white galabeyas, red fezzes and turbans on their heads, white gloves on their hands. "I wonder if the test match results are in," Hassan said, helping himself to crusty French bread and soft, warm Brie. "Manchester was favored . . ."

But Ibrahim wasn't listening. He was thinking of the delicious surprise he had for Alice: a trip to England.

She missed her family very much, he knew, especially her brother, Edward, with whom she had once been very close. And since the loss of their second baby to summer fever, Alice had been so depressed that Ibrahim had tried to think of ways to cheer her up. He had even taken her along on Farouk's honeymoon, said to be the longest and most extravagant honeymoon in history, consisting of a party of sixty traveling on the royal yacht, all wearing matching blue blazers, white trousers and nautical caps. They had disembarked at various ports in a fleet of Rolls-Royces, and stayed at the best hotels. Farouk showered his new queen with priceless jewels, masterpieces of art, haute cuisine and haute couture, and indulged in his passion for gambling, losing $150,000 to Darryl F. Zanuck at a Cannes casino in the course of a single game. It had been a magic-carpet journey that had had the whole world buzzing, but the pregnancy Ibrahim had hoped would result from the trip had not materialized.

Hassan leaned over and said quietly, "Look lively, old boy, here comes the royal brat."

A nanny brought the baby out, wrapped in a chinchilla blanket, and when the six hundred officers and dignitaries rose from their seats to honor the heir to the throne of Egypt, Ibrahim thought of his own son, Zachariah.

No one had questioned the sudden appearance of the infant; men frequently had wives they told no one about. Even Hassan had broken down and married a blond, who would not have let him touch her if he hadn't, and whom he now kept on his houseboat, his Egyptian wife knowing nothing about her. Ibrahim had simply informed everyone that he had divorced the baby's mother, and then Amira had quietly installed Sahra as a servant in the house. Little Zakki was now six years old, a charming but frail boy who tended toward dreaminess. What astonished Ibrahim was that the child actually bore a vague resemblance to himself, an observation which reconfirmed for Ibrahim that God indeed had been guiding him the night he had adopted the boy, despite Amira's concerns. He chose to ignore her warnings—there was no curse on the Rasheed family, not with Egyptian cotton selling at record high prices, and Ibrahim's cotton farms producing such a high yield that he could hardly keep track of his rapidly multiplying bank balance, which was why everyone was referring to cotton as "white gold." The family was happy and healthy, and Ibrahim lived a life of comfort and ease that surpassed even the life his father had enjoyed.

And soon he and Alice would be on their way to England. Perhaps they would take Yasmina with them. After all, she had a grandfather there, and aunts and cousins. Yes, definitely, he thought, suddenly pleased with the idea, imagining the fun he and his five-year-old daughter were going to have on board ship.

A courier came into the banquet hall and engaged in a whispered conference with the king and his commander-in-chief. Ibrahim wondered if something was up, if perhaps trouble really was brewing in the city. If so, and with such anti-British feeling gripping Cairo, he thought about Alice at home, and wondered if private citizens might be targets of revenge.

=

As Edward's taxi made yet another turn, they saw more flames and more smoke, men breaking windows and throwing fire bombs, more buildings on fire. Having tried different routes to get to Garden City but finding the way always blocked, the driver finally said, "I take you to a safe place, Sayyid," and he steered the car down a narrow alley. A minute later they pulled up in front of the Turf Club. "All English in here," he said, reaching over the seat to open Edward's door. "You are safe here."

"But I asked you to take me to Virgins of Paradise Street. What the deuce is going on? Is it a riot?"

"Please go inside! Cairo is very dangerous place for you! Go inside, you are protected in there, *inshallah*!"

Edward got out with some reluctance, stunned by the stench of smoke in the air. He regarded the entrance to the Turf Club for a moment, then, deciding it was better to press on to his sister's house, turned to get back into the cab. But the taxi was already speeding away from the curb and around the corner. With all his luggage.

When a nearby explosion rocked the street, Edward ran up the steps of the club and found the place in turmoil. Members were pouring into the lobby, knocking over furniture and potted plants, men in white cricket flannels, ladies in swimsuits and sun hats. Even the native porters in long galabeyas and fezzes were pushing to get out.

As Edward forced his way through, trying to locate someone in charge, getting elbowed in the ribs and his toes stepped on, he saw a jeep pull up at the front; a group of men jumped down and ran up the steps with cans of gasoline and crowbars. Edward stared in horror as drapes and furniture were doused and then set aflame. As everything caught fire, including the overhead ceiling fans, another mob came swarming in, and when the panicked club members tried to get out, the rioters struck them down with iron bars. Screams filled the air, and blood began to flow.

Edward tried to find his way in the smoke, dodging flying glass as liquor bottles exploded behind the bar. He managed to stagger to the reception desk, which had been abandoned, and from there he could see, through the open doors, firemen out in the street with hoses. But as soon as the water began to hit the burning building, rioters attacked the hoses with knives, slashing them until no more water came.

As he tried desperately to find a way out through the smoke, he saw Britons in fashionable sporting clothes sprawled on the floor, their blood staining the tiles. Fighting down his own rising hysteria, he searched for an exit. The front was blocked by a mob, and curtains were ablaze. And then he thought: the swimming pool! But as he fought his way through the lobby toward the open terrace doors, his path was suddenly blocked by a young Egyptian in a long galabeya. Edward found himself gazing into a pair of green eyes that blazed with something more than a reflection from the fire. He thought for an instant that he might try reasoning with the fellow, after all, *he* wasn't one of these resident Englishmen, just a tourist, only arrived today. But a pair of brown hands grabbed for his neck, and Edward found himself struggling with the stranger, and thinking how absurd this all was.

Finally his attacker reached for a vase, and as it came crashing down on Edward's skull, the odd thought entered his mind that Alice was going to be disappointed.

=

The kitchen was a big sunny room with marble walls and floor, warm enough to keep out the January cold while the cook, a Lebanese with red cheeks and fly-away hair, oversaw the work of her four assistants at the two stoves and three big ovens. The population of the mansion on Virgins of Paradise Street varied from year to year, as girls got married and moved away, elderly members died, new wives were brought in, and babies were born. On this crisp Saturday in January, twenty-nine Rasheeds were in residence, from newborn to elderly, as well as twelve servants who lived on the roof; the kitchen was busy day and night. The women chatted as they worked, and the radio was turned to a musical program, the distinctive voice of Farid Latrache filling the air with love songs. In the midst of such industry, Amira prepared glasses of lemonade to take out to the garden, where several of the women and children were enjoying the fresh winter sunshine.

As she added a bowl of sugared apricot balls to her tray, Amira glanced at Sahra, who was peering through one of the windows as she pounded lumps of dough into flat rounds of bread. Amira knew what the girl was looking at. In the nearly six years since Ibrahim had brought Zachariah into the house, Sahra watched the boy whenever she could. And although the fellaha had promised that she would never tell anyone that she was really the boy's mother and that Ibrahim was not his father, the danger was still there. So Amira kept a close watch on her.

As Amira carried the tray down the steps into the garden, she looked up at the sky. Was that distant thunder she had just heard? But the sky was clear. Alice was quietly reading as she watched the children. Six-and-a-half-year-old Camelia was dancing with her eyes closed, to a song only she could hear. She had once said to Amira, "Wasn't it nice of God to give us dancing, Umma?" Amira often thought that inside the little girl with the dusky complexion and amber eyes was a spirit that soared, that was set free; Camelia could dance like a fluttering bird, or like a rose opening its petals. Amira had already decided that when the girl was older she would be given dancing lessons.

And there was Yasmina of the creamy white skin and dark blond hair, stretched on the grass, deeply engrossed in a picture book. At five and a half, she was already exhibiting a thirst for knowledge; she had once said that books were so wonderful because every time you turned a page, there was something new, something you didn't know before. Yasmina was ahead of the others in her *alif-ba*'s, even though she was the youngest.

Tahia, who was the same age as Camelia, was playing on the lawn with her dolls. She had already declared that, when she grew up, she wanted to have many babies. So unlike her mother, Amira thought, wondering how to get Nefissa to marry again.

Finally there was Zachariah, a pretty child, gazing dreamily at a butterfly. Amira frequently marveled about this boy who, by some strange workings of God, resembled his adopted father. But in physical appearance only; Zachariah hadn't Ibrahim's fondness for personal comforts and simple, direct thoughts; the boy liked to ask about angels. He would stare up at the sky and wonder aloud what God and heaven looked like. A strange, blessed child, Amira thought. Only six years old and already he could recite twenty suras of the Koran. You would say, "Zakki, recite sura four, verse thirty-four," and he would promptly say, " 'Men have superiority over women because God has made the one superior to the other.' "

Omar, Nefissa's first child, came into the garden, a chubby ten-year-old who looked as if he were constantly searching for mischief. Amira tried to be patient with the sullen boy; it wasn't his fault that his mother had never disciplined him properly. Amira sighed. Another reason why Nefissa should marry again.

"Mother Amira," Alice said, as she bit into a sugared apricot ball, "do you smell smoke?"

"Perhaps fellaheen are burning off fields on the other side of the Nile."

Omar suddenly shoved little Zachariah out of his way, causing him to fall on the gravel path, and Camelia and Yasmina immediately rushed to pick him up. If only there were more children! Amira thought. A house of this size should have many children playing in the garden. Amira longed for more grandchildren of her own. But Nefissa refused to remarry, no matter how many eligible men Amira tried to match her with, and, so far, Alice had produced only one living child for Ibrahim, Yasmina.

"Look at me!" cried Camelia as she trailed dried papyrus stalks behind her, "I'm a peacock!"

Amira froze. Suddenly, she *saw* a peacock—not her granddaughter pretending, but a real bird, as blue and shimmering and alive as if it were actually there, strutting before her.

It was a memory, she realized. She was remembering a peacock from somewhere long ago.

She sat down suddenly. She never knew when memories like this would come, whether in dreams, or when she was awake, as she was now, sitting in her garden with the past overwhelming her like the ocean swells she had once observed from the seaside villa in Alexandria. It was the same each time: an unexpected memory would suddenly wash over her, illuminating a long-ago moment in such stunning detail that for an instant it was totally real. And then it would pass, leaving her breathless.

Every time this happened, Amira pictured her mind as a deep well, with bubbles trapped at the bottom. Once in a while, for no apparent reason, a bubble would break free and rise to the surface of her mind, releasing the memory it contained. Sometimes they were familiar memories, ones she recognized, such as the day she had met Ali Rasheed in the harem on Tree of Pearls Street, but often they were forgotten fragments from her past—a face, a voice, a sudden rush of terror or joy. Or a peacock. As the years passed, the bits and pieces came back, forming a patchy mosaic of her early life, but so much still remained to be filled in: her life before the raid on the desert caravan—for she was certain now that she was the child in her dream—where and when the raid took place, what became of her mother afterward. And what of the peculiar square tower she sometimes saw in those dreams?

It amazed Amira that she should have forgotten such important facts in her life. Would they ever fully return? she wondered, as the vision of the peacock began to fade. And what had happened to block those memories of her earlier childhood?

"Children," she called. "Come and have some lemonade."

Yasmina's eyes grew big and round when she saw the apricot balls—they were her favorite, which was how she had earned the nickname "Mishmish," Arabic for apricot. But before she could reach the bowl, Omar elbowed her out of the way and took a big handful. Still, Amira had made sure there was enough for all of them. As she felt the warm sun on her shoulders, inhaled the fragrance of the garden, she was suddenly filled with a luminous joy. She saw the future: in ten or fifteen years these children would be married, and there would be new babies in the house. She thought: I shall be a great-grandmother, and not yet sixty! *Praise God, Lord of the Universe for His generosity and beneficence. Let it be like this always . . .*

She frowned suddenly. The smell of smoke was getting stronger. What could it be? She looked at her watch. Maryam and Suleiman would be back from the synagogue soon, she would ask them if they had seen anything out of the ordinary in the city.

Suddenly realizing that the smoke was from no ordinary fire, she stood up and said, "Come along, children. Time to come in and do your lessons."

"Oh Umma," they protested, "must we?"

"You have to learn to read," she said, as she inspected Zachariah's knee, which he had scraped when Omar pushed him. "Because then you will be able to read the Koran. God's word is power. When you have perfect knowledge of the Koran, then you are armed for anything in life. No one can take advantage of you, or hurt you, when you know the Law."

Alice laughed. "They're just babies, Mother Amira."

Amira smiled to hide her rising alarm—the smoke was getting stronger. And now she could hear shouts in the streets. "Come along, quickly. Do your lessons today, and tomorrow you will have a picnic at Grandfather's tomb."

This cheered them, and they ran into the house laughing, because the prospect of a day at a grave was always fun. Once a year Ibrahim took the children to the City of the Dead, where they put fresh flowers on the graves of Ali Rasheed, Camelia's mother, and Alice's baby. Afterward, they always enjoyed a picnic lunch. Then they would come home and Amira would explain to them how the spirit went to paradise when the flesh was put in the ground. Zachariah in particular liked hearing her descriptions of paradise, and he couldn't wait to get there. But the girls were sometimes confused. If the Koran promised so many rewards to men in the afterlife—gardens and virgins—Camelia had once asked, then what was a girl's reward? And Amira had laughed and hugged her and said, "A woman's reward is to serve her husband for eternity."

A servant came running into the garden. "Mistress! The city is on fire!"

They joined the others up on the roof, from where they could see flames and smoke.

"It's the end of the world!" cried the cook.

Amira could not believe what she saw—a city on fire, and the Nile itself, reflecting the flames, also appearing to burn. Explosions followed one after another; and then there was rapid gunfire, as if it were a war zone.

"Declare the unity of God!" cried the cook.

"The Lord is exalted!"

Auntie Zou Zou came out, supporting herself on a cane. Her old eyes widened, and she cried, "Compassion is God's alone! The city is burning."

The servants started wailing and praying. "Are we under attack? Is the whole country on fire?"

Alice had turned as white as her wool cardigan. "Why isn't the government doing something? Where are the police, the soldiers?" Amira surveyed the billowing black smoke, which seemed about a mile and a half away, and tried to determine what was burning. Ali Rasheed had brought her up to the roof years ago, and pointed out various landmarks, so that Amira could at least know something of the city she lived in but had never seen. And the smoke was where Ali had said the British had built their fine hotels and cinemas. She anxiously sought Abdin Palace, where Ibrahim was attending a banquet, and tried to determine if it, too, was burning.

=

The hour was late, and flames were still leaping against the night sky, as the family waited anxiously for word of Ibrahim. Maryam and Suleiman Misrahi had arrived a short while before, after rushing to the Misrahi Imports warehouse, fearful that it, too, had been set on fire. But although it appeared that Suleiman's highly profitable import business had been spared, they had seen sights that had made them disbelieve their eyes: hundreds of buildings had been set on fire, nearly all of them British. And now, in Amira's grand salon, as the family gathered beneath the flickering brass oil lamps, watching the clock creep toward midnight, a voice on the radio solemnly listed the destroyed establishments: "Barclay's Bank, Shepheard's Hotel, the Metro Cinema, the Place de l'Opéra, Groppi's . . ."

As the clock was just chiming twelve, a shadow appeared in the doorway. Cousin Doreya was the first to see him. "God is merciful! Ibrahim!" And she ran to him, the others following.

As they embraced and kissed and brought him inside, Ibrahim assuring them that he was all right, that he had not been attacked, he turned to Suleiman and said, "Can you help me with something?"

They left, and returned a moment later supporting a young man between them, his head wrapped in a bandage. When Alice saw him, she gave a startled cry.

"Eddie! My God, Eddie!" she said, as she threw her arms around him. "What are you doing here? When did you arrive? You're hurt! Are you all right? What happened?"

He smiled weakly. "I wanted to surprise you. I guess I've done that."

"Oh Eddie, Eddie," she sobbed, as Ibrahim told the others what had happened at the Turf Club. "He was taken to Kasr El Aini Hospital, and they telephoned me at the palace, once he convinced them he really was related to me." He sat down with a sigh. "Everybody, this is Edward, Alice's brother."

Amira kissed him on both cheeks, and welcomed him, eyeing the bandage. "I am sorry you arrived on such a sorrowful day. Come, sit down, did they treat your wound well in the hospital? I don't trust them, I will take a look at it."

A servant brought a bowl of water, soap, and a towel, and after Amira inspected Edward's wound, and determined it was not serious, she washed it, applied a camphor ointment she had made herself, and rewrapped it with clean gauze. Then she ordered a medicinal tea to be brought up from the kitchen, containing chamomile for his nerves, dandelion to promote healing.

Suleiman said to Ibrahim, "What is happening now? Are the fires under control?"

"The city is still burning," Ibrahim said weakly. "And there is a curfew. The mob came within a thousand yards of the palace."

"But who is responsible for this?" Amira asked.

When Ibrahim said, "The Muslim Brotherhood is rumored to be one of the forces behind the riots," everyone remembered the terrible day, five years ago when, to protest the British stealing land from Palestinian Arabs, the Brotherhood had blown up movie houses that were showing what they called "Jewish-controlled American films."

"But is it a takeover of the government?" Maryam asked. "Has there been a coup?"

Ibrahim shook his head with a baffled expression. There had been no attempted takeover of the government, no move whatsoever to unseat Farouk. Nonetheless, there was no doubt that it had been a preplanned, very organized riot. The only question was, Who was behind it, and why?

"What is the king going to do about it?" Suleiman said.

Ibrahim didn't respond. He knew Farouk's policy would be to do nothing. After all, as the monarch himself frequently declared, the riots weren't directed against him, but toward the British. Farouk knew he looked good compared to the hated English, and fully expected to come out a hero in the end.

A voice came over the radio, solemnly reading from the Koran, a ritual usually reserved for the death of a high official, and as they listened, each of those gathered in Amira's grand salon concentrated on their separate fears:

Edward decided he was going to get his sister out of here and back to England.

Ibrahim thought about the boat tickets to England with which he had planned to surprise Alice. But he knew Farouk would never give him permission to leave now. The trip would have to be postponed until the trouble subsided, as surely it would.

Suleiman reached for his wife's hand, thinking of the Jewish establishments that had also been torched in the riots.

And Amira wondered what would become of her son, and her family, if the tide should turn against the king.

CHAPTER 9

The sweltering July evening was filled with the perfume of Cairo's many gardens, and the fertile smell of the sluggish Nile. Cairenes strolled down the sidewalks as movies let out and restaurants began closing up, and one young family in particular, having just enjoyed a film and ice cream at the cinema, filled the summer air with their laughter. But when they arrived at their apartment house, the husband found an urgent message waiting for him. He read it quickly and destroyed it, then, putting on his military uniform, he kissed his wife and children good-bye, asking them to pray for him, because he did not know if he would ever see them again. He hurried off into the night toward a dangerous appointment that had been set long ago. His name was Anwar Sadat, and the revolution had begun.

—

Nefissa was trying to cool off in the sunken marble tub of her private bathroom, enveloping herself in a delicious cloud smelling of almonds and roses. For the first time in her life, she had to suffer the hot summer nights of Cairo. Ever since the riots back in January, on Black Saturday, as the day was being called, there had been increasing outbreaks of violence, and tension had risen in the city. Ibrahim had decided that it wasn't safe for the family to travel, and so had left them all at home when he joined Farouk at the summer palace in Alexandria. But Nefissa was going to Alexandria whether Ibrahim liked it or not. And she was not going alone.

She laid her head back, closed her eyes, inhaled the heady fragrances of her bath, and thought about Edward Westfall, who was going to be her motoring companion to the coast tomorrow.

As she pictured his wavy blond hair, opal-blue eyes, and cleft chin, she raised her knees and felt the silky water cascade over her skin. She reached for a crystal bottle of almond oil, poured some into her hand, and began gently to caress her thighs. In her bath, Nefissa was sometimes almost able to bring herself to a kind of delicious precipice, on the other side of which, she knew, there must be something sweet and sublime. But she could never quite achieve it. She had a vague memory of long ago, when she was a little girl, exploring herself and discovering a stunning pleasure. She seemed to remember rewarding herself with that dizzying sensation whenever she wanted, but then had come the night of cutting—her circumcision. Amira had explained that the impurity had been cut out of her, that she was now a "good" girl. And since then, Nefissa had not been able to recapture that rare sensation, not even when she was married.

As that same pleasure continued to elude her now, leaving her only with a hint of what might have been, she thought of her lieutenant and their one night together, and reached for a sea sponge to lather herself with creamy almond soap. Why did women mutilate one another, she wondered. When had the cutting first begun? Amira had said it was started by Mother Eve, but if that was so, who had performed the operation, since Eve was the first woman? Could it have been Adam?

Why were boys' circumcisions performed in daylight, accompanied by a big celebration, while a girl's was done in the secrecy of night and no one spoke of it afterward? Why was it a matter of pride for boys, but shame for girls?

Nefissa sighed restlessly. She wasn't in love with Edward Westfall; she didn't think she even particularly liked him. But he reminded her so much of her beautiful lieutenant that whenever she looked at him, or he spoke to her, she felt a strange reaction deep inside.

What pleasure it gave her to think about that night in the old harem at the princess's palace, when she and her English lieutenant had made love until dawn! It still seemed like yesterday; Nefissa could recall every tiny detail of every delicious moment—the small scar on his right thigh, the salty taste of his skin, and how wonderfully he had made love to her. While the sad-eyed women in the murals had looked on, and while the nightingale had sung to the rose in the garden, Nefissa had experienced an ecstasy, a passion, of a kind she was certain most women only dreamed about.

And when they had said good-bye, as her beautiful officer had kissed her for the last time in the light of dawn, promising that he would write to her, that he would come back, Nefissa suddenly, in one brief moment, understood they would never see each other again.

He had not told her his name, not once among all the kisses and caresses and sweet words; they had kept the night a complete fantasy, as if they, too, were as unreal as the sultan's concubines painted on the walls. And in the years since, she had received no word from him. All she had was the handkerchief he had given her, made of fine linen and embroidered with forget-me-nots. It had belonged to his mother, he had said.

Nefissa rose languidly from the bath and rubbed herself down with a thick towel made of luxuriant cotton from her brother's own fields. As she applied a creamy moisturizer of lanolin, beeswax, and frankincense, mixed with Amira's herbs, she wondered again about her lieutenant. Was he still in England, married perhaps? Did he ever think about her?

Nefissa felt her youth slipping away; she was twenty-seven, and time's passing was following her like a shadow. Although she knew Amira was anxious for her to remarry and have more children, and although she had received offers from many well-to-do Egyptian men, Nefissa was not interested. She wanted to recapture something she had once had. Which was why she had started noticing Edward. If she put her mind to it, she could picture him in the lieutenant's uniform, see him standing beneath a lamppost and lighting a match. She didn't love him, she would never love a man as she had loved her lieutenant. But if the best was unavailable, then second-best would have to do.

As she slipped between cool, lavender-scented sheets, Nefissa told herself that she was looking forward to going to Alexandria with Edward tomorrow. She might not feel any passion for him, but he was English, after all, and blond and fair-skinned, and perhaps in the darkness of a bedroom she might almost believe she was making love again to her lost soldier . . .

=

Beneath the hot July moon, shadowy figures moved silently through the deserted streets of the sleeping city as armored columns emerged from the Abbasseya barracks, quietly rolling their mounted guns, tanks, and jeeps. They blocked the Nile bridges and all roads leading from Cairo, and took over General Military Headquarters, interrupting a late-night meeting at which the general staff had been voting to arrest the revolutionary leaders who called themselves the Free Officers. The switchboard was swiftly taken over, and orders were immediately issued to all staff officers and troop commanders to report at once to headquarters, whereupon they were taken into custody and locked up. An armored brigade was dispatched down the Suez Road to intercept British troops possibly coming from the Canal. Everywhere the revolutionary soldiers took up occupation, they met with little or no resistance.

By 2:00 A.M., Cairo was under the control of the Free Officers. All that was left to do now was push on to Alexandria and the king.

=

Edward Westfall stared at the gun in his hand. He had used it before, during the war; he was not afraid to use it again.

Dawn was breaking, and the open shutters of his bedroom windows admitted a warm morning wind and the call to prayer from Cairo's many minarets. Edward hefted the .38 Smith & Wesson in his hand and offered his own silent prayer: God help me. Please don't let me succumb to my weaknesses again. I am being seduced, and I can't help myself. Please God, deliver me from this vice which plagues me, which is destroying me, and which I am helpless to fight.

Edward had told everyone, including himself, that the reason he was still in Egypt six months after his arrival was because he was worried for his sister's safety. It was also what he had told his father when he had written back in January, asking the earl to ship some things to him because an unscrupulous taxi driver had absconded with his clothes and sporting equipment. "I can't get Alice out of Egypt," he had written, "because of some antiquated law about a wife needing a husband's permission to leave the country. And Ibrahim just doesn't see the danger." So Edward had asked the old man to include his service revolver from the war, one of the .38 Smith & Wessons Britain had distributed to her troops when the supply of double-action Enfields had run out.

Edward really had planned on rescuing Alice and Yasmina from this dangerous place. But that had been months ago, and was no longer the reason why he was still here. The real reason was a secret, one he would not confess even to his sister, a reason that he loathed to admit even to himself.

Memories of disturbing dreams came back, visions of dark, liquid eyes, ripe, sensuous lips, and long slender fingers that caressed him in secret places—the impure, forbidden thoughts he would not allow himself to entertain when he was awake, but with which his treacherous brain mocked him at night.

What was he going to do? How could a man remain pure in this culture that seemed to be both obsessed with sex and yet repulsed by it? A person couldn't walk down a Cairo street without seeing advertisements for movies about love, or hearing coffee-shop radios blaring out songs of passionate embraces, or overhearing ribald conversations about virility and fertility. Sex, love, and passion, it seemed to the very proper Edward, were as intricately woven into Cairo's daily tapestry as coffee, dust, and the hot sun. And yet earthly lusts, even innocent flirtations or affectionate hand-holding, were forbidden to all except the virtuously married, and even then confined to the privacy of their bedrooms. It was worse, Edward thought, than the puritanism of his own Victorian-style upbringing. Certainly the rules of sexual conduct were as specific in England as in Egypt: virtue and chastity were applauded, fornication and adultery condemned. But at least British society did not constantly flaunt in your face what you could not have. England had not created women who veiled their faces and yet who undressed you with temptress eyes. England had not invented the provocative belly, or beledi, or whatever-it-was dance. And certainly no English family proudly displayed the bride's virgin blood the morning after the wedding night! Even the perfumes were different here. Yardley's English lavender was a demure lady's fragrance, but the women of the East assaulted the nostrils with aggressive, sex-filled perfumes reeking of musk and sandalwood. The food, too, was spicier, the music livelier, the laughter louder, tempers quicker. Dear God, was even lovemaking wilder and more passionate in Egypt? How was a man to maintain his equilibrium and keep his appetites under control?

Edward had hardly slept. His head had been filled with the cloying odors of honeysuckle and jasmine, and the heat of the night had forced him to toss off his sheets and sleep naked, the scented breeze kissing his body. And now, with dawn bringing another hot new day full of sensual seduction, Edward already detected the rich breakfast aromas of eggs, fried beans, hot cheese, and sweet coffee.

He laid down the gun and rang reluctantly for his valet. He had agreed to go to Alexandria today with Nefissa. And he was dreading it.

His heart began to pound, and he started to sweat. What madness had possessed him to agree to such a folly? This was not what he had come to Egypt for, to fall victim again to his vices! After all, one of the reasons he had come in the first place was to get away from a disastrous liaison before his father had found out, not just to see Alice and the ancient monuments. One hint of scandal, and the earl would have cut him off without a penny. And now here he was again, hurtling headlong toward another sexual abyss.

Hearing servants in the hall, and knowing that at any moment his valet would be bringing in tea and brandy, along with hot water for shaving, Edward put on his silk dressing gown and went into the bathroom. He examined his face in the mirror. The injury he had received at the Turf Club had healed without a scar. He was, in fact, looking particularly healthy, thanks to Amira's care, some bracing tonics, and vigorous exercise. Edward was thankful the January riots hadn't gotten as far as Gezira Island, an exclusive club where the British continued to carry on their privileged pursuits, albeit on a quieter level. Edward had obtained membership in the club, where he went every day to play tennis, swim, and keep himself in shape. He knew he was attractive, and he knew that when women looked at him they saw not only fine, regular features crowned by pale blond hair, but a perfect physique beneath the impeccable clothes of the conscientious English gentleman.

The dark, liquid eyes flashed in his mind again and he wondered what *they* saw when they looked at him?

He groaned. How could he have agreed to drive to Alexandria with Nefissa! In Alexandria the seduction would be complete, and he would once again descend into the abyss. He should stay here, on Virgins of Paradise Street. He was safe in this house, safe among Amira's strict rules of moral conduct.

When his valet came in, Edward quickly slipped the revolver into his suitcase. It was for protection on the long drive. As the valet prepared the shaving cream, Edward drank the brandy, refused the tea and ordered more brandy. He held the glass with a very shaky hand.

═

Amira had just finished leading the women, female servants, and children in the morning prayer. After closing the prayer by looking over each shoulder and saying to their guardian angels, "Peace be upon you and the mercy of God," they dispersed, the servants to their household duties, the women down to breakfast, Zachariah and Omar running off behind them. Amira remained in the bedrooms with Yasmina and Camelia and Tahia who, although only six and seven years old, were learning to make beds. It was part of their training for when they grew up and got married; first they made their own beds, and then their brothers', then they picked up Zachariah's and Omar's strewn clothes and toys, and tidied the room the two boys shared. The girls worked fast because they were hungry; the house was filled with delicious aromas and they wouldn't be allowed to eat breakfast until these early-morning chores had been attended to.

"But we have servants, Umma," said Tahia, who, at seven years and two months, was the eldest of the girls. "They can make the beds."

"But what if you don't have servants when you marry," Amira said as she straightened Omar's bedspread. "Then how will you take care of your husband?"

Camelia said, "Are Auntie Alice and Uncle Edward bad because they don't pray with us?"

"No, they are Christians—like us, people of the Book. They pray in their own way." Amira had heard Edward's valet go up the stairs toward the men's side of the house, carrying the usual tray of tea and brandy. For the first time since the house was built, alcohol was allowed. Amira had protested, just as she had when Alice had once wanted to bring wine into the house. Then, Amira had prevailed. But in this case, as it was her son's brother-in-law's desire to have it, she had had to accede.

Elderly Auntie Zou Zou came clumping into the room on her cane. There were dark shadows under her eyes. She had not been sleeping well, she declared, her dreams were haunted by premonitions and omens. "I dreamt of a blood-red moon, and I saw jinns playing in our garden. The flowers had all died." Amira shooed the girls from the room, in case the old woman frightened them, and said, "It is written that nothing shall befall us save that which God has decreed for us. He is our Protecting Friend. Don't worry, Auntie. The king and Ibrahim are in God's hands."

But Zou Zou, who had been young and wild in the days of the great khedives of Egypt, said, "And it is also written than God does not change people until they change themselves. There is bad business coming, Um Ibrahim, and it is not right that your son is not here. What's a man for, except to protect his family?" When Zou Zou had begged Ibrahim not to go to Alexandria with the king, he had cheerily assured her that everything was all right. How could he be so blind? In the six months since Black Saturday, King Farouk had changed his government three times, and the latest rumor was that he planned to place his brother-in-law—a man whom the army despised—in charge of his cabinet. And so once again tension gripped Cairo. "I am fearful, Amira," she said. "For your son's safety, and for the safety of the family. With him in Alexandria, what protection have we, after all?" She turned and followed the children in the direction of breakfast.

In the breakfast room on the first floor, where the family was noisily addressing plates of eggs and beans, Nefissa stood by the open window, watching for Edward's car. She was wearing a lightweight linen traveling suit and carrying a crocodile make-up case. Alice came up to her. "I've made something for you." She handed Nefissa a beautiful corsage from the garden, made of crimson flowers that matched the girl's crimson lips and brought out the sparkle in her dark eyes.

Nefissa glanced over at Amira, who was helping to feed two very small children, and whispered excitedly to Alice, "If she only knew! Mother would lock me up and throw the key into the Nile!" Nefissa was planning to commit a shocking indiscretion: she was going to dismiss the chauffeur and drive the car to Alexandria herself. Months of secret driving lessons had finally rewarded her with a freedom and power she had never known before. "It's bad enough I've given up my veil and refuse to wear black," she whispered as she pinned the corsage to her linen suit, "but if Umma knew I also drove a car! Does Edward know I'm going to be driving?"

"My poor brother hasn't a hint! He thinks you'll be chaperoned by a driver. Will you stop along the way?" Alice was as anxious for the seduction to take place as Nefissa was. She would do anything to get Edward to stay in Egypt.

Suddenly they heard the gate bell ringing frantically, and a moment later a servant admitted Maryam Misrahi into the room. "Do you have your radio on, Amira? Turn it up! There has been a revolution! During the night, while we slept!"

"What? But how?"

"I don't know! The streets downtown are filled with tanks and soldiers!"

They tuned to Radio Cairo and heard a voice they didn't recognize, belonging to a man they had never heard of, Anwar Sadat, who was talking about Egyptians governing themselves at last. Others came into the room, all the women and servants, gathered around the radio.

"He doesn't mention the king," a cousin said, listening carefully to Sadat's speech. "He doesn't say what they've done with him."

"The king will be killed," cried another, "and so will Ibrahim!"

As the others suddenly panicked, embracing one another and crying and wailing, and as little Tahia burst into tears, Amira hid her own alarm and said calmly, "We cannot let fear rule us. Remember that understanding comes from God, and that we place ourselves in His safekeeping." She turned to a servant and said, "Telephone everyone, tell them to come. We will follow the news together here, and pray. Round up all the children. Keep them occupied with games, and reassure them." Then she gave instructions to the cook to start boiling water for tea, and to prepare large amounts of food, as relatives would be arriving soon to await news of Ibrahim. Finally, she said to Nefissa, "You will not be going to Alexandria today."

—

"This is preposterous," King Farouk said, waving a hand of dismissal toward Sadat. "How can you claim a revolution when only a few guns were fired, a few drops of blood shed?"

But a nearly bloodless revolution had indeed taken place. Within three days of taking over Cairo, the Free Officers had stunned the world by seizing control of all communications, government offices, and transportation, bringing Egypt to a virtual standstill. Farouk had been cut off; the British were unable to send help because the revolutionary army controlled the trains, airports, harbors, and major roads, and although the American military attaché in Cairo said that Washington demanded an explanation of what was happening, no military assistance was offered from that quarter. Farouk was helpless. A few shots had been exchanged between his royal guard and the revolutionary forces that surrounded the palace, but Farouk had called them back, locked the gates and sealed himself inside. Finally, one of the Free Officers, Anwar Sadat, came and offered the king an ultimatum: leave the country by six o'clock that night, or suffer the consequences.

When the king started to protest, Sadat politely reminded him of the Black Saturday riots, in which every movie house, nightclub, casino, restaurant, and department store in Cairo's European section had burned to the ground—over four hundred establishments in all. It was being said that had Farouk taken action just two hours earlier, had he not been so concerned with his own pleasures, all this could have been prevented. But now, the soft-spoken Sadat added, the king was a very unpopular man.

Farouk was also aware of another uncomfortable fact: that the majority of the Free Officers wanted him executed, but that he had been spared by a single vote, that of General Abdel Nasser, who wanted no bloodshed. "History will sentence him," Nasser had said. Farouk decided that the longer he stayed in Egypt, the shorter his life would be.

He gave Sadat his decision on the spot.

It struck Ibrahim that this might be the last time he would be in this palace, or even in Farouk's company, which was hard to believe after so many years of existing in the royal shadow. Was it really possible that there would be no more midnight calls summoning him to Abdin Palace? Farouk had never read a book, never listened to music, never written a letter; movies were his entertainment, along with gossiping on the phone at all hours of the night. As his personal doctor, Ibrahim was one of the few who knew that Farouk had been raised in a harem until he was fifteen, pampered by an iron-willed mother, so that he had remained childlike, preferring toys to politics, and was completely un-equipped for survival. When he had been warned days ago about the Free Officers, he had shrugged them off as "pimps," and on the night of the coup itself, when he had been told of unusual troop movements in Cairo, he had dismissed the news as insignificant. Ibrahim realized that this was no man to rule a country as great as Egypt. The revolution-ary officers were right, the time had come for Egypt to have a real leader.

And now, stranger, more confusing thoughts tumbled about in Ibrahim's mind. Was this truly the end of the king's reign? Who was going to take his place? And where did the royal physician fit in? Ibrahim found himself gazing at the heavy black velvet drapery over an arched doorway and was startled to find himself thinking: that is what my future looks like.

Finally the document of abdication was brought, and in a vast, sunlit marble hall that, with its towering and breathtaking friezes, resembled an ancient Roman palace, Farouk stoically regarded the paper. It con-tained two sentences in Arabic: "We, Farouk the first, whereas we have always sought the happiness and welfare of our people . . ." Nearly weeping, the king took out his gold pen, and as Ibrahim watched Farouk sign the abdication, he saw that the monarch's hand shook so badly that his signature was illegible. And when he signed a second time, in Arabic, the king misspelled his name, because he had never learned to write the language of the country he ruled.

Ibrahim helped Farouk bathe one last time, and dress for the final voyage in his white Admiral of the Fleet uniform. Then the king sat for the last time on the jeweled throne of Ras-el-Tin Palace and said good-bye to his close friends and advisers. To Ibrahim he said in French, "I shall miss you, *mon ami.* If you or your family come to any harm because of your association with me, I pray to God for forgiveness. You have served me well, my friend." Ibrahim accompanied him down the great marble staircase and out into the palace courtyard where, beneath the hot afternoon sun, the royal band played the Egyptian national anthem, and the Nile-green, crescent-moon flag of Egypt was lowered, folded, and handed to the king as a farewell gift.

But Ibrahim stayed at the foot of the gangway as Farouk walked up to the deck of the *Mahroussa*. For the first time in years, he would not be in close proximity to the king, and it made him feel curiously naked and cut adrift. Farouk made a calm, dignified farewell as he stood with the three princesses, his sisters, his seventeen-year-old queen and six-month-old son. The moorings were cast off and, as the yacht began to sail, twenty-one guns boomed a salute from a nearby naval frigate.

As he watched the *Mahroussa* sail away, Ibrahim could recall only the good memories: when he had brought Camelia, Yasmina, Tahia, and Zachariah to the palace to meet the king, and Farouk had given them candies, and sung his favorite song to them, "The Eyes of Texas Are Upon You." He recalled Farouk's wedding day, when millions of peasants had poured into Cairo for the event, and there was such a warm feeling for the king that Cairo's pickpockets had taken out ads in the newspapers, announcing a one-day moratorium on stealing in honor of the royal pair. And farther back, a night in 1936 when the Rasheeds had been vacationing in Alexandria, and Ibrahim had seen the new monarch arrive to claim his throne, a trim, exotically handsome young man on a ship gliding among a flotilla of thousands of candlelit boats and feluccas. All of Egypt had gone wild that day for Farouk, whose name in Arabic meant "one who knows right from wrong."

Finally, as the *Mahroussa* moved slowly out of the harbor, Ibrahim recalled the day his father had introduced him to the young king, and how Farouk had taken an instant liking to Ibrahim, appointing him to the post of royal physician. He was overwhelmed with sadness. Tears stung his eyes as he realized that the *Mahroussa* was sailing away with more than Egypt's deposed monarch. It was taking Ibrahim's memories, his past, the reason for his existence. And the image of the heavy black velvet drapery returned.

CHAPTER 10

Alice couldn't believe her eyes.

She had just come into the garden with a basket, tools, and a wide-brimmed straw hat to keep the Egyptian sun off her fair skin; when she saw what had happened against the eastern wall, she exclaimed aloud, dropping to her knees and leaning forward for a closer inspection—just in case her eyes were deceiving her.

But this was no illusion. At the ends of the dark green stems, tiny buds were indeed starting to open up; three had already blossomed into large, crimson flowers. Finally! After four years of nurturing and watering and weeding, of building a shady shelter, of watching and waiting and digging up her failures and starting again—after so much work and so much hope and the fear that she might never bring English flowers to this hot Mediterranean garden, Alice had succeeded in bringing to bloom her favorite crimson cyclamen.

She couldn't wait to show them to Edward. They were just like the ones that grew at home. But as she started back toward the house, Alice remembered that her brother had left that morning with Ibrahim and Hassan to go to a soccer match, and they wouldn't be back till afternoon. Alice had not been invited, of course, because women did not attend such events. She told herself that she didn't mind. She had adjusted to so many customs when she came to live on Virgins of Paradise Street; although she still sometimes stood in the garden and contemplated the high wall surrounding the estate, wondering if it was there more to keep the occupants in rather than intruders out, and although there had been moments when she had resented having to stay with the women in one room while Ibrahim and Eddie joined the men in another, Alice decided that Egyptian society had not been as difficult to get used to as she had at first expected. "I am so fortunate," she had written to a friend back in England, "I am married to a wonderful man, and live in a beautiful big house with more servants than I think we had at home!"

As she returned her attention to the garden, she heard a little girl singing nearby, and paused to listen, recognizing Camelia's voice. That child was born with music in her brain, she thought, and she tried to make out the Arabic lyrics the child was singing. After seven years, Alice was proud of the progress she had made in Arabic, and although she had a little trouble with Camelia's song, she was able to get the gist of it. It was, as most Egyptian songs were, about love: *"Lay your head on my breast, warm my breast, pierce me with your love arrow."*

When she heard Yasmina's voice join in, Alice wasn't surprised. Although a year apart in age, the two half-sisters were as close as twins, always together, and even, Alice had discovered on nights when she had gone into the girls' room to check on her daughter, sometimes slept in the same bed.

To her surprise, the sound of her daughter's voice made her feel homesick for England. She was longing more and more to see the ancestral Tudor home of the Westfalls, and the misty green countryside; she missed riding to hounds with her friends, and shopping at Harrod's; she yearned for bacon and ale, shepherd's pie and bangers, weeks of rain, and a ride on top of a red double-decker bus. And she missed her friends, who had declared that they would come to Egypt and visit her, but whose promises over the years had begun to fade until their letters no longer contained any plans for a visit. Only one of her friends, Madeline, had come right out and written, "It's too dangerous to travel in Egypt now. Especially for a British subject."

But I am happy here, Alice reminded herself. I have a good life with Ibrahim, and a beautiful little girl.

But a nagging thought, triggered by the sound of Yasmina's voice, was now undermining that certainty. Alice searched the garden, as if she could discover this new doubt among the flowers and shrubs. She examined her life and concluded that she truly didn't mind that she and Ibrahim slept on opposite sides of the house; her own parents had had separate bedrooms for nearly all their married life. Nor did she really mind that Ibrahim often attended social events without her, such as today's soccer match. But, on this warm August morning, she realized for the first time that something was missing. She couldn't figure out what.

Leaving her garden tools, Alice peered through a cluster of hydrangeas and saw Camelia and Yasmina playing in a patch of sunlight. Her smile turned to shock when she saw what they were doing. Each draped in a single length of long black silk, the girls were practicing wrapping the melaya around their bodies, over their heads and across the lower halves of their faces, imitating women seen all over Cairo. To Alice's further surprise, the two girls, aged six and seven, were doing a remarkable job of mimicking the way those women walked, sashaying their hips and constantly readjusting the slippery fabric.

"Hello, children," she said, emerging into their private patch of sunlight.

"Hello, Auntie Alice!" said Camelia, twirling around in her melaya dramatically. "Aren't these lovely? Auntie Nefissa gave them to us!"

Nefissa's discarded veils, Alice thought, recalling the change that had come over her sister-in-law in recent years. Nefissa had said, "I no longer want to live the way my mother does. I want to be a free woman." And Nefissa had boldly announced to Amira that she wasn't going to wear a veil outside anymore, and Amira, to Alice's surprise, had not argued with her.

So now the little girls were playing "dress-up" in the melayas, just as Alice had once done with her mother's old gowns. But there was a difference: Lady Frances's outmoded evening dresses had not been a symbol of repression and slavery.

Alice was suddenly gripped with a strange new fear. Ever since the overthrow of Farouk and the establishment of the revolutionary government, there had been talk of making the English leave Egypt, so the country could return to the old ways. She had thought nothing of it until this moment. Return to the old ways! She pictured the many rooms in the Rasheed mansion, filled with portraits of long-dead ancestors: powerful-looking men in turbans and fezzes, accompanied by faceless women hidden beneath veils. Women with no identities, Alice thought, except through the men they stood with.

Women, she thought darkly, who had to sit by while their husbands took other wives.

It had been so difficult, when she had wakened the morning after Yasmina was born, to learn that Ibrahim had had another wife! A wife she hadn't known about. And to be told that the son of that union was going to be raised in this house! When Ibrahim had explained to her that the other wife had meant nothing to him, that they had divorced by mutual consent, that it was she, Alice, he loved, and no one else, Alice had tried to tell herself that it was not Ibrahim's fault, that it was just part of his culture. But she had said to him, No more wives, I must be the only wife. And he had agreed.

Even so, there were times when she would look at little Zachariah, or hear his laugh, and she would feel the old pain: Ibrahim already had a wife when he married me!

Other images began to flood Alice's mind: the English tea parties she had attended with other English wives, the dances and balls she went to with Ibrahim, where men and women mingled, the Punch-and-Judy shows to which she took Yasmina, and the playgrounds where she met English nannies watching over children who resembled her own daughter. And she thought now: What if the British did leave Egypt? Would all the Englishness be gone as well?

She imagined a frightening future, with women again veiled, restricted to their homes, their husbands taking other wives. Alice had learned to accept the curtailed freedoms—not being able to go anywhere she wanted unless she was escorted, not being able to leave the country without her husband's permission, finding herself left alone with the women when she and Ibrahim visited Egyptian friends. She had even, after a while, come to accept the fact that Ibrahim had already had a wife when they had married in Monte Carlo. But reverting to the old ways was unthinkable.

And now, looking at her six-year-old daughter innocently wrapped in the archaic black veil, hiding her body, her identity, beneath it, Alice experienced a fear she had never felt before. What would this little girl's future be like, how would she be treated, what chances would she have in this culture in whose language the word for chaos, *fitna,* also meant "beautiful woman"?

The little girls had been speaking Arabic, and Alice had responded in the same language, but now, as she sat down on a stone bench and drew Yasmina to her, she reverted to English. "I was working in my garden just now, and I remembered a funny story from when I was a girl. Would you like to hear it?"

"Oh yes," they both said, coming to sit on the grass beside her.

I will tell Yasmina about England, Alice thought as she searched her memory for a story. I will fill her with my memories, so that if that other future should come to pass, then my daughter will be armed. "When I was a little girl," Alice said, "we lived in a big house in England. It was a beautiful house, given to our family by King James, centuries ago, and because it was so old it was inhabited by a lot of mice. Now, one day your grandma noticed that a mouse had been in the kitchen during the night and—"

Yasmina said, "Do you mean Umma?" "Umma" was the children's name for Amira.

"No, darling. Your other grandmother, *my* mother, Grandma West-fall."

"Where is she now?"

"She died, darling. She went to live with Lord Jesus in heaven. Now then, Grandma Westfall was terrified of mice, and so she had Grandpa and Uncle Eddie search everywhere for that mouse. Where was he hiding? They searched and searched but they couldn't find that little mouse. And then one morning while Grandma was having her tea, she saw a long pink tail sticking out from under the tea cozy. Grandma let out a cry and fell in a dead faint to the floor!"

Yasmina and Camelia screamed and clapped their hands. "The mouse was living in the tea cozy!"

"And Grandma had picked up that tea cozy every morning for weeks without knowing that the mouse was inside it!"

As the girls laughed and Camelia started pretending she was a mouse, Alice heard a voice call, "Hello there! Good morning!" They saw Maryam Misrahi's red hair before they saw the woman herself.

"Auntie Maryam!" the two little girls called out, and Camelia imme-diately jumped up, hastily wrapping the melaya about herself.

"Always the little show-off," Maryam said with a laugh, first patting Camelia on the cheek, and then Yasmina.

She turned to Alice. "How are you this morning, my dear? You are looking so well."

As Alice replied, it struck her for the first time how different Maryam and Amira were. Alice knew that they had been friends for years, that they saw each other nearly every day, but it had not occurred to her until this moment that where Maryam was outgoing and perhaps a little flamboyant, Ibrahim's mother was quiet and more conservative. And Maryam had an active social life beyond her home, whereas Amira, to Alice's continued amazement, had yet to set foot in the street beyond her gate.

And now that she thought about it, Alice decided it was beyond her understanding how Amira could be happy in such a cloistered life. And yet, astonishingly, Amira had once confessed that she stayed inside of her own volition. The confession had come the day Amira had received a letter from Athens, from an old friend, Andreas Skouras, informing her of his marriage to a Greek woman. Amira had been uncharacteristically open that day, confessing to Alice that she sometimes regretted not marrying Mr. Skouras when she had had the opportunity, and Alice, hearing about the former minister of culture for the first time, had seen her mother-in-law in a new light. Amira, she had realized, was still a young woman! Which made her choice of such a sequestered life all the more baffling.

As Camelia and Yasmina went off to play, Maryam said, "I heard from my son Itzak today."

"The son who lives in California?"

"He sent me some photographs. Here is one of his daughter, Rachel. Isn't she a pretty little girl?"

Alice looked at the group of people standing happily on a beach with palm trees behind them.

"She's a year younger than your Yasmina. My," Maryam said with a sigh, "how time flies. I have never seen her, you know. One of these days, Suleiman and I must go there. Here is another picture I thought you would like to see. I asked Itzak to send it to me because it's the only one we have. It was taken years ago, at Itzak's Bar Mitzvah. There, do you see anyone you recognize?"

It was another group photo, taken beneath an ancient olive tree. Alice recognized Maryam and Suleiman Misrahi, looking much younger; the son Itzak; and Ali Rasheed, Amira's barrel-chested husband, whose portrait dominated nearly every room of the house. Now, strangely, he seemed to dominate this picture, too. Finally there was Ibrahim, a young man of about eighteen.

Alice was struck by how strongly Yasmina resembled her father, and the fact that Ibrahim was not looking at the camera, but at his father, Ali.

"Who is this young girl?" Alice asked.

"That's Fatima, Ibrahim's sister."

"Fatima! I have never seen a picture of her. Do you know what became of her? Ibrahim won't talk about it."

"Perhaps someday he will tell you," Maryam said. "I'm going to see if I can get copies made of this photo. Itzak wants to have it, but I want it too, and I'm sure Amira will want it, to put into her albums." Maryam laughed. "Those albums of hers. I should have the patience she does. I still keep pictures in boxes."

"Maryam," Alice said, as she and Maryam walked back to where the cyclamen were blooming, "there aren't any pictures of Amira's family in her albums—her own parents, brothers and sisters. Why is that?"

"Why don't you ask her?"

"I have, and each time she says that when she married Ali, his family became hers. But still, she should have *some* pictures of them, shouldn't she? In fact, she never speaks of her parents."

"Ah well, you know how it can be between parents and their children sometimes. Things don't always go smoothly."

Thinking of her own father, the Earl of Pemberton who, to this day, still refused to talk to his daughter, Alice nodded and said, "Yes, you're right." She had hoped that he would come around when Yasmina was born, but, except for a yearly Christmas present to the girl—a generous check desposited in a trust fund—the earl had never acknowledged that he had any children other than Edward.

Alice wondered: Is that what happened between Amira and her parents?

And then something else occurred to her, something which she had never brought up with any of the family but which, feeling surprisingly at ease with Maryam, she did. "There are also no pictures of Zachariah's mother in any of the albums. Did you know her?"

"No, I didn't. None of us knew about her. But that is not unusual with Muslim men."

"Do you know her name, or where she is now?"

Maryam shook her head.

"Maryam," Alice said quietly, sensing that this might be her only moment with the one person outside the family who knew them so well, and in whom she could confide. "Do you think I fit in well here?"

"Whatever do you mean, my dear? Aren't you happy?"

"Oh, I'm happy, it's not that. It's just that . . . it's hard to explain. Sometimes I feel like a clock running at a different speed from everyone else, or like a piano slightly out of tune, as if I weren't synchronized with those around me. Sometimes, in the evening after dinner, when we're all in the salon, I look around at my husband's family and they all seem slightly out of focus, the scene is somehow askew. It isn't them, of course, because they are where they belong. It's me. I'm like a square peg trying to fit into a round hole. I am happy here, Maryam, and I do so want to be. But there are times . . ."

Maryam smiled and said, "What is it you want, Alice? You say you're happy, and you do seem happy, but perhaps you want something more? This isn't England, I know, and I know you had quite an adjustment to make when you came here. But something must be troubling you, even if you can't say what it is."

Alice looked up at the house, which was blushing a deep pink as the sun rose, and she imagined that she could see through the thick stone walls, right into the many rooms. "At this moment," she said, so quietly that it was as if she were talking to herself, "Amira is going through the house and taking inventory of everything—the sheets, the china."

Maryam laughed. "Amira is the most fastidious woman I know when it comes to knowing exactly where everything is! I've told her she can come to my house any time and count my sheets. God knows I don't even know what's in some of my closets!"

"Yes, but Maryam, that's what *I* want to do," Alice said, as she envisioned her mother-in-law going from room to room with a servant and a clipboard, counting the linens, setting aside pillowcases that needed mending, making neat stacks of starched, monogrammed sheets. "I envy her," Alice added, and suddenly realized what it was that was missing from her life: She longed for a home of her own. She suddenly understood something else about herself, something about her new fears for Yasmina and Ibrahim. It would be easier for her, should the British leave Egypt, and the old ways return, if she was in her own house. She would be better able to fight the old traditions—and save her daughter and herself from becoming slaves to them. As she and Maryam walked, Alice thought excitedly: I shall bring it up with Ibrahim tonight. We must have a place of our own!

=

All Cairo was buzzing over the latest news about the deposed king. Ibrahim's family, gathering in the salon after dinner, was no exception.

"Who would have thought their majesties were so extravagant?" declared a spinster cousin over her knitting.

Because Farouk and his family had sailed away on short notice, taking with them only what they could carry from the Alexandria residence, the five hundred rooms at Abdin Palace, and the four hundred at Qubbah, had revealed the true extent of Farouk's outlandish life-style. Sunken malachite bathtubs, huge wardrobes containing thousands of tailored suits, collections of precious stones and gold coins, vaults filled with reels of erotica, American movies, and comic books. There was also a hidden collection of keys to fifty apartments in Cairo, each key labeled with a woman's name and a rating of her sexual skills.

A lot of the queen's belongings had also been left behind: Narriman's wedding gown, studded with twenty thousand diamonds, a hundred handmade lace nightgowns, five mink coats, high-heeled shoes fitted with solid gold heels.

Experts from Sotheby's in London were being brought in by the Revolutionary Council to evaluate everything, after which they would hold an auction, the proceeds going to the poor. It was estimated that the value of the royal family's confiscated property was going to exceed seventy million Egyptian pounds.

"I don't like all this talk," Nefissa murmured to Ibrahim, who was sitting next to her on the divan as, with the rest of the family, they drank their after-dinner coffee. "The princess was my friend."

Ibrahim didn't reply; he had too much on his mind.

"To be thrown out of one's own home," Nefissa said quietly, as she absently ran her fingers through her son's hair. Omar was now a chunky eleven-year-old. "And then to have one's private things publicly displayed. I wonder if Faiza is still in Egypt. I haven't been able to find out." Thoughts of the princess brought back memories, the "Night of the Nightingale and the Rose," as Nefissa had come to call it. And from that memory her thoughts strayed to Alice's brother, Edward, whose blond hair and blue eyes nearly matched those of her lieutenant.

Was he as disappointed as she, she wondered, that they hadn't gone to Alexandria two weeks ago? Was he anxious to try to get away again? Nefissa wasn't to be deterred. If they couldn't take a motoring trip north, they could always go south. She knew Edward was interested in the ancient monuments, and that he had yet to visit the pyramids at Saqqara, nineteen miles from Cairo. Tonight, when the opportunity arose, she was going to suggest a day trip with a picnic lunch, just the two of them.

Ibrahim did not respond to his sister's comments; he did not like all this gossip about the king, either. After all, who knew Farouk better than he? Of course, how could one not talk about the strange, quiet revolution that had taken place while Egypt slept, organized by men previously unknown but who now headed the new Revolutionary Command

Council? What amazed Ibrahim and everyone else was that Farouk had not been executed but, at the insistence of Gamal Abdel Nasser, had been allowed to leave the country. But now people were being arrested everywhere; anyone suspected of having the slightest connection with the former monarch was brought in for questioning. Rumors were starting to circulate, whispered stories of torture, secret executions, and sentences of life imprisonment. What therefore, Ibrahim asked himself, was to become of the king's personal physician? Who could have been closer to Farouk than his doctor?

Am I and my family now in danger because of the post I held in the palace, a post which I did not seek, but which my father got for me?

Suddenly a masculine voice called from the outer hallway, *"Y'Allah! Is anyone home?"* And Ibrahim was pleased to see his friend, Hassan al-Sabir, come in, wearing a black tuxedo, his fez cocked at an angle.

The children ran to him, crying, "Uncle Hassan!" He laughed and lifted Yasmina into the air, calling her "his little apricot."

Then he greeted the women, starting with Amira. "And who is this lady who is so beautiful she shames the moon?" he said, slipping into the Arabic he knew she preferred to have spoken in her home.

"Welcome to our house," she said politely. "God's blessing on you."

As Ibrahim watched Hassan charm his way around the room, the center of attention as he somehow always managed to be, he caught a quickly veiled look on Amira's face as she, too, marked Hassan's progress. Ibrahim had always sensed that his mother didn't like Hassan al-Sabir. But why was this, when he charmed everyone else?

Despite the ceiling fans and the open windows, the room was baking in the August heat. Ibrahim signaled to a servant to bring cigarettes and coffee, and led Hassan out onto the balcony to catch the Nile breeze.

"What is the news?" Ibrahim asked quietly, as the servant lit his cigarette for him, then discreetly left. "I hear talk that the new government is going to sequester land. My friends at the Cotton Exchange are saying that all wealthy landowners are going to have to give up their holdings, and the big farms are going to be broken up and given to the peasants. Do you think there is any truth in this?"

Hassan, who owed his wealth to an inheritance, shrugged. "Rumors, I imagine."

"Perhaps. Still, all this talk about arrests. I heard that they've sentenced Farouk's barber to fifteen years of hard labor."

"His barber was a scoundrel involved in court graft. You were Farouk's doctor. Hardly a political criminal. Listen," Hassan said, flicking cigarette ash over the side of the balcony, "these so called Free Officers, they don't frighten me. I know their type—peasants, all of them. The leader, Nasser—his father is a postman. And his second in command, Sadat, is a *fellah*, born and bred in a village so poor that even the flies avoid it. And he's as black as midnight, too," Hassan added with disdain. "They won't be able to pull it off. The king will be back. You'll see."

"I hope you're right," Ibrahim said. He'd been worried since the night the king sailed away.

Hassan shrugged again. Whichever the way the wind blew, he intended to go with it. Besides, as a lawyer he was profiting from the revolution. His caseload had never been so full, and no one complained about his escalated fees. For as long as this revolution lasted, Hassan al-Sabir intended to make a profit. "I tell you what, my friend. You need cheering up. What do you say we go to Mohammed Ali Street," he said, referring to the section in old Cairo that was a center of lower-class dancers, musicians, and accommodating women. "I know a certain young lady who is an acrobat in bed. She can be yours tonight, if you like."

Ibrahim shook his head. "I'm perfectly happy here," he said, looking through the open doors into the brightly lit salon and noticing how the overhead lights seemed to form a halo around Alice's hair. He didn't need Mohammed Ali Street; he decided he would invite Alice to his rooms tonight.

"But can Alice be enough for you? We are men of appetites, Ibrahim. Why not take a second wife, like I did? Even the Prophet, may God bless him with eternal peace, understood men's needs."

As Hassan paused to exhale a stream of smoke into the hot August night, the tranquility of the balcony was suddenly disrupted by a high-pitched voice calling, "Daddy!"

Ibrahim picked Yasmina up, swung her in the air, and then propped her on the wrought-iron railing that surrounded the balcony. "Auntie Nefissa just told us a riddle!" she said. "See if you can guess it!"

Hassan watched how Ibrahim instantly gave the child every inch of his attention, smiling like a schoolboy, and remembering how often Ibrahim would talk about his daughter, reporting on what she had said or done, boasting the way most men boasted about sons, he was surprised to find himself envying his friend. He himself didn't enjoy such a close relationship with his daughters, who were away at boarding school in Europe and to whom he sometimes felt connected just by cards and letters. Hassan could see that Yasmina, with her blond hair and blue eyes, was going to grow up to be a beauty someday. Just like her mother. He pictured the girl ten years from now, a stunning sixteen-year-old, ripe for marriage.

Alice's brother, Edward, entered the salon and paused in the doorway, his gaze going straight to Nefissa, with a look of hunger on his face so clear that Hassan nearly laughed out loud. Poor Edward, seduced by Egypt. When he heard the gate bell ring below, Hassan wondered if anyone interesting might be paying a visit to the Rasheeds. Then he saw one of the servants, appearing very upset, come into the salon and hurriedly murmur something to Amira. She turned pale, then nodded, and the servant returned a moment later with four men in uniforms, carrying rifles. They had come to arrest Ibrahim Rasheed, they said, for crimes against the Egyptian people.

"Good God," Hassan said, as he followed his friend inside.

"Surely there is some mistake," Ibrahim said to the officer in charge. "Don't you know who I am? Don't you know who my father was?"

They apologized, but insisted that he must go with them.

"Now see here," Hassan began, but Ibrahim interrupted him. "There's obviously been some mistake, and I suppose there's only one way to clear it up."

He kissed Amira, saying, "You're not to worry, Mother." Then he turned to Alice. "I shall be all right," he said, also kissing her.

"I'll wait up for you," Alice said, her face pale with fear, and as she watched the soldiers take her husband away, she remembered what she had seen in the garden that morning, and how it had frightened her: Yasmina and Camelia playing dress-up in black melayas.

CHAPTER 11

In his dream, Ibrahim was startled to see Sahra, the kitchen girl, enter the men's side of the house. She was leading Zachariah by the hand; she was barefoot, and wearing the simple dress of a villager. He noticed for the first time that she was pretty; he also realized that she was no longer a girl, but a woman.

"What are you doing here?" he asked.

She opened her mouth to speak, but the voice of God came out. "You tried to trick Me, Ibrahim Rasheed, and you cursed Me as well. This child is not yours, but another man's. You had no right to take this boy. You have broken My sacred law."

When Ibrahim cried, "I don't understand!" his own voice awoke him, and the first thing he was aware of as he returned to consciousness was a sharp pain at the back of his head. The second was the stench. As he tried to sit up, he was overcome with nausea. Dizzy, he attempted to make sense of the shapes around him, but his vision was blurred. He groaned. He couldn't think. He realized he was sitting on a bare stone floor, engulfed in intense heat; a strange droning filled his ears. When he drew in a deep breath, he gagged. The stench was overwhelming—a miasma of human sweat, urine, and feces.

But where was he?

And then it came back to him: the soldiers arresting him at his home, the drive to General Military Headquarters downtown, with him protesting his innocence until a man hit him with a rifle butt. He had expected to be taken to one of the Free Officers, but instead he had been pushed into a dingy office where a sweating, irritable sergeant had put two questions to him: "What subversive acts went on in the palace?" and, "Name those who took part in them." Ibrahim recalled trying to reason with the man, to explain that there had been a mistake, until finally he had lost his temper and demanded to see someone in authority. Then he had felt a sudden, sharp blow to his head, and afterward . . . nothing.

As he explored the sore place on the back of his head, his vision began to clear. He was in a large prison cell with high stone walls and a filthy stone floor, and he was not alone. The cell obviously contained more men than it was originally intended to hold, mostly dressed in ragged galabeyas, some pacing, muttering to themselves, others sitting in a stupor against the walls. There were no chairs or benches, no bedding except for moldy straw, and no toilet, just some overflowing buckets.

Was he still dreaming? If so, this was a nightmare, more real than any he'd experienced before. He looked down at himself and discovered that he was still in his tuxedo; his crocodile shoes were gone, as were his gold watch, two diamond rings, and pearl cuff links. His pockets were empty. He didn't even have a handkerchief.

When he saw the window in the opposite wall, he staggered to his feet and clumsily made his way toward it. But it was too high for him to reach, and although the blazing August sun streamed through, nothing gave him a clue as to his whereabouts. Had they brought him to the Citadel, at the edge of Cairo? Or was he far from the city, in the desert somewhere? He could be miles from Virgins of Paradise Street.

As soon as his head had finally cleared and he became more stable on his feet, he crossed the cell, avoiding contact with the other prisoners, who seemed to have no interest in him, and finally reached the barred door, through which he could see a dim, stone hallway. "Hello?" he called out in English. "Is anyone there?"

He heard the jangle of keys, and a young man appeared, wearing a sweat-stained khaki uniform, a military revolver stuck in its belt. He looked at Ibrahim blankly.

"Listen," Ibrahim said. "This is a mistake."

The man continued to stare at him.

"Didn't you hear what I said? Are you deaf?"

Someone tapped his shoulder, and Ibrahim recoiled. A heavyset, bearded man in a dirty blue galabeya grinned at him and said in Arabic, "They don't speak English here. Even if they do, they don't. No more English since the revolution. That's the first lesson you have to learn."

Ibrahim switched to Arabic. "This is a mistake, I'm telling you," he explained in Arabic to the soldier. "I am Dr. Ibrahim Rasheed and I demand to speak to the person in charge."

The guard gave him a sullen look.

"Look," Ibrahim said, trying to be patient. "You must inform your supervisor that I wish to speak to him."

The guard walked off.

As Ibrahim looked around the cell, he found to his dismay that he had to urinate. Then he realized the bearded prisoner was still standing beside him. "God's peace upon you, my friend," the man said. "I am Mahzouz."

Ibrahim took in the shabby galabeya, the missing teeth and scarred face, and gave him a dubious look. "Mahzouz" was Arabic for "lucky."

The man smiled. "The name was given to me in better days."

"Why are you in here?" Ibrahim asked.

Mahzouz shrugged. "Like you, I am innocent."

Ibrahim brushed off his jacket and discovered that his bow tie was gone. "Do you have any idea how we get communication past that guard?"

Mahzouz shrugged. "God will choose the moment of your release, my friend. Fate rests only with the Eternal One."

Now that his head was no longer foggy, just throbbing slightly, Ibrahim assessed the situation. He knew that the best place for him was near this door, in case the guard returned with someone in authority. Unfortunately, the door seemed to be everyone else's favorite place, too, and there wasn't an inch of space. As he started to make his way back across the cell, where he would have a perfect view of the door, he heard keys rattling in the corridor. To his horror, before he could take even one step forward, the prisoners suddenly came to life and made a wild rush for the door. The oldest and weakest were pushed out of the way, and one man screamed as he was pinned against the bars of the door. Ibrahim remained motionless as he watched the men grab for the rounds of bread that had been brought in, along with a giant pot filled with beans.

The stampede lasted only a few seconds; the guards left and the prisoners hunched over their food, fighting for whatever fell to the floor. Ibrahim watched Mahzouz come slowly across the cell, eating his own beans and bread with an almost exaggerated insouciance, and as he came close, Ibrahim saw maggots in the beans.

"You know, my friend," Mahzouz said, with his mouth full, "you should have taken some. It is hours until the next meal. And let me give you some advice," he added, eyeing Ibrahim's fine tuxedo. "Keep close watch on your clothes. You're dressed better than the commandant of this prison. And he won't like that."

Ibrahim turned away. The pain in his bladder brought him back to the moment. With great reluctance, and a mingling of shame and indignation, he made his way to the darkest corner, held his breath against the stench, and relieved himself. Then he settled down again on the filthy floor, his back to the wall, noticing bleakly that someone had carved the name of God in one of the stones. Keeping an eye on the barred door and listening for the return of the guards, Ibrahim reassured himself that, before the sunlight departed from the high window, he would be free.

=

A nudge against his shoulder brought Ibrahim sharply awake. He looked up at the high window, and saw the sunlight was now slanting, and turning an amber yellow. He was amazed that he had dozed off, and then he saw that Mahzouz had come over and was sitting next to him. "You don't seem very worried, my friend."

Ibrahim rolled his shoulders to ease the stiffness. "It's only a matter of time before my family will arrange for my release."

"If it is so written in God's Book," Mahzouz said, and Ibrahim wondered if the man was mocking him.

As he remained with his back firmly against the wall and his eyes on the door, it occurred to Ibrahim that he had not heard the Call to Prayer. So this prison was far from the city. Did the officials expect the men to forget their duty to pray? How was a man to gauge the hour? Ibrahim mentally withdrew from the nightmare he had been plunged into, telling himself that he had nothing to do with this filth, the rats in the straw, the man who had hitched up his galabeya and was picking lice off his naked body, or the one who was retching in the corner.

More bread and beans were delivered, and Ibrahim remained where he was. He discovered that the heat in the cell didn't die with the day, and he became aware of his own body odor. It was his custom to bathe two or three times a day, during the summer, and he also desperately wanted a toothbrush, a razor, hot water, and soap. As the last of the daylight vanished from the high window, Ibrahim went through the prostrations of the fourth Prayer, apologizing to God that he had not been able to perform the required ritual washing beforehand.

=

Finally the cell was plunged into darkness, and the men settled down for the night. As he shifted around on the hard stone floor, Ibrahim comforted himself with the thought that dawn would bring freedom. He removed his tuxedo jacket and folded it under his head for a pillow. But when he woke up the next morning, the jacket was gone and he noticed with some suspicion that two prisoners were enjoying coffee and cigarettes. He also realized that he was extremely hungry, and remembered that he had last eaten over twenty-four hours ago, at home. He wished now he had helped himself to more lamb and rice, and not passed up the sweet baklava.

He made his way to the door again and, pressing his face to the bars, tried to see up and down the corridor. "You out there!" he called in Arabic. "I know you can hear me. I have a message for your superior. Tell him that he is going to be very sorry he has kept me in here."

The insolent guard materialized suddenly, grinning.

"Listen here," Ibrahim said, not bothering to hide his irritation. "You clearly don't know who you're dealing with. I'm not one of these"—he gestured around the cell. "Tell your superior to contact Hassan al-Sabir. He's my attorney. He'll explain what a mistake this all is."

But the guard only grunted and walked away.

Ibrahim called after him, "Don't you know who I am?" He had been about to add: "When the king hears of this . . ." But there was no longer a king.

He leaned against the bars, at a loss. He tried to imagine Hassan in the same situation. His friend had a natural arrogance that commanded respect; he would get attention in no time. But Ibrahim didn't know how to be arrogant. He had never had to push his weight around; people were naturally subservient to him.

Well, he was certain to be out of here in a few hours. No doubt it had taken his family a while to find the right authorities, locate the prison where he was being held, and then sort through the bureaucratic paperwork that Alice's brother would call "red tape." As he picked his way back to his spot against the wall, Ibrahim wondered what Alice was doing at that moment. She must be terribly worried. And what of little Yasmina? Was she asking about him? Had the sight of soldiers taking her father away frightened her?

The guards brought in more food, sparking another inhuman stampede. To Ibrahim's annoyance, his stomach was urging him to join in, but he refused to eat the rotten beans and bread the others devoured so ravenously. If he knew his mother, she was preparing a feast for him right now, and tonight he would dine on his favorite meatballs stuffed with eggs. He might even avail himself of a little of Edward's brandy—a restorative.

As the prisoners noisily consumed their breakfast, Ibrahim went to the bars and tried to catch the guards before they left. But they ignored him and disappeared down the dark corridor.

"Depressing, isn't it?"

He turned to see Mahzouz, who was wiping the last of the bread around his lips before swallowing. "No matter what you say to them," the man said with a smile, "they always ignore you. Those dogs only know one language." And he rubbed his fingers together.

"What do you mean?" Ibrahim said.

"Baksheesh. Bribery."

"But I haven't any money. It was taken from me."

"This is a fine shirt, my friend. Finer, I would wager, than our new leader, Nasser, wears. How much did you pay for it?" Ibrahim had no idea. His accountant handled the tailor's bills. He walked away from Mahzouz without another word, and as he crossed the cell to his regular place, felt his irritation rise. When, a few minutes later, keys sounded in the corridor announcing an unscheduled visit from the guards, he jumped up along with the ablest of the prisoners, and tried to push his way through the excited mob. "Here I am!" he called to the guards. "Dr. Ibrahim Rasheed! I'm back here!"

But they hadn't come for Ibrahim. Instead they led another prisoner out, a man who, by his smile, was either being released or moved to a better cell. Mahzouz had explained to Ibrahim that such things happened: A man's family bribed the prison officials and got him better accommodations.

Ibrahim was puzzled. If that was so, then what was *his* family doing?

And then he thought in alarm: What if they have arrested all of us?

But that wasn't possible. There were too many Rasheeds, and only a few had had any dealings with the king. Besides, there were the women, his mother especially, who would surely not be arrested. And she would be working for his release.

Although he tried to reassure himself once again that he would be out by nightfall, Ibrahim felt his confidence slip.

=

When he awoke to his third dawn in prison, he decided he had had enough. In front of his barely interested audience—many of these men, like Mahzouz, had been incarcerated for so long that their minds had gone numb—Ibrahim went to the bars and began to shout for some attention. He felt weak. He still hadn't eaten. And he had cramps in his abdomen from trying to keep his bowels continent. He might urinate in the corner, because he had no choice, but he was not going to squat like an animal over those buckets.

"You have to let me out!" he shouted through the bars. "Good God, man! I'm a close friend of the prime minister! Talk to the minister of health!"

He began to panic. Where were his family, his friends? Where were the British? How could they allow this farce of a revolution to go on?

"There will be serious consequences if you don't do as I say! I'll see that you're all fired! You'll be sent to the copper mines! *Do you hear me?*"

He turned to find Mahzouz standing next to him, his eyes glinting with amusement and compassion. "It won't work, my friend. They don't care about your fancy friends. Remember what I said." He rubbed his fingers together again. "*Baksheesh.* And I recommend that you eat something. Everyone tries starvation at first. But you won't be any good dead, will you?"

The next time the guards brought food, Ibrahim hung back and waited until the last minute to take one of the rounds of bread. Straw had been baked right into it.

"You don't expect me to eat this, do you?"

"You can stick it up your arse for all I care," the guard said, and went away.

Ibrahim threw the bread down and it was immediately set upon by others. As he made his way to the back wall on unsteady feet, he thought, I must get a grip on myself. Everything will be all right. This can't go on much longer . . .

—

He was visited by nightmares, but when he awoke he saw that he was still in a nightmare. There was no relief, either in sleep or in reality. When the food came around again he grabbed some bread and plunged it into the beans, eating ravenously. And when the need arose, he squatted over one of the buckets.

=

On the seventh day, guards came for one of the prisoners, but this man did not smile. And when he was brought back a while later, he was unconscious. They dragged him into the cell and threw him down. Mahzouz came over to Ibrahim and said, "You told me you are a doctor. Can you help him?"

Ibrahim looked closely at the crumpled figure. The man had been tortured.

"Can you help him?" Mahzouz repeated.

"I . . . I . . . don't know." Ibrahim had never seen wounds like this. And it had been years since he had taken care of an injury or an illness.

Mahzouz gave him a contemptuous look and muttered, "Hah! Some doctor!"

That night, when the guards came to remove the body, Ibrahim ran to them and said, "Please, you must listen to me." When one of them eyed his tuxedo shirt, which was by now sweaty and grimy, Ibrahim immediately stripped it off and thrust it at the man. "Here. Take it. It would cost you a month's salary," he said, having no idea what the man's salary would be. "Get a message to Hassan al-Sabir. He's a lawyer. His office is in Ezbekiya. Tell him where I am. Tell him to come and get me."

The guard took the shirt without a word, and when Hassan did not appear over the next few days, Ibrahim realized his bribe had been useless.

He began to pray in earnest, asking God once again to forgive him for cursing Him the night Camelia was born. He said he was sorry about adopting Zachariah, breaking God's commandment that no man should claim another man's son. He was sorry, sorry, sorry. "Just please take me away from here!" His pleading moved from God to the guards. "Listen, I'm a very rich man. You can have anything you want, just let me go." But they were only interested in what he could give them right then. And all Ibrahim possessed was his undershirt and shorts, tuxedo trousers and cummerbund.

=

He dreamed he was holding Alice in his arms, and the children were playing at his feet. Strangely, he thought of them in terms of flavors: Alice was vanilla ice cream, Yasmina tasted of apricots, Camelia was filled with dark honey, and Zachariah was made of chocolate. Did a man dream this way about his family? And when he woke he was distressed to realize he had lost count of the sunrises. Was this the thirtieth, or had that been yesterday? It would be September now, maybe almost October. At least the killing August heat was dissipating.

Ibrahim scratched his beard and tried to pick out the lice. And then he realized Mahzouz wasn't there.

Had they taken him away during the night? Had he been released while Ibrahim was napping? Had he been tortured and died?

Many of the prisoners had been removed for interrogation. What Ibrahim couldn't understand was why the guards had not come for *him*. It would give him a chance to explain, and to speak to someone higher up in authority. He noticed that the prisoners weren't being questioned in any kind of order, because some of those who had been removed were newcomers. Some days no one was taken; some days, three or four were dragged off. When they were brought back, he had tried to see what he could do for their wounds, but he was helpless. It occurred to him that even if he had the supplies, he wasn't sure he remembered enough of his medical school training to be of any use.

He wondered if Farouk had returned to Egypt. Was the revolution still going on? Did his family think he was dead? Was Alice now wearing black? Had she gone back to England with Edward?

Ibrahim started to cry. None of the others paid any attention. They all broke down at one time or another.

How could he have known that he would miss the filthy Mahzouz?

=

And then he had another nightmare: his father, Ali Rasheed, scowling at him and shaking his head as if to say, You have disappointed me again.

=

The latest prisoners to arrive said that the Prophet's birthday had been celebrated a few days ago, which meant Ibrahim had been locked up for exactly four months. During which time no one had come to see him, no one had asked for him, no one had brought food or clothing or cigarettes, and he hadn't left the cell once, not even for questioning.

He was numb. His life had been reduced to the one patch of cell he had laid claim to where "Allah" had been carved into the stone; he was possessive of this patch, and of the lumpy straw he used as a mattress. It was his entire world, the territory of the forgotten man. He no longer fretted over the flesh melting away from his bones, or the beard growing down to his chest. And his dreams, although as bizarre as his reality, no longer alarmed him. He no longer missed his silk dressing gown or his water pipe, he no longer wished he could be on Hassan's houseboat, enjoying a lively game of cards with amusing companions. He no longer craved cigarettes and coffee. What he wanted most was to see the sky, to feel Nile grass beneath his feet, to make love to Alice, to take Yasmina to the park and point out the wonders of nature to her. His life had shrunk to a basic cycle of waking up each morning, wondering if today would bring freedom; the daily rush for bread and beans; visits to the buckets; listening for the guards' keys; and waiting, waiting, until, with nightfall, torpor stole over him and he delivered himself into sleep. He had long since ceased praying five times a day.

On the day that the young prisoner was brought in, Ibrahim was struggling with a thought. He wasn't sure what it was; he had awakened thinking that something of great importance was about to be revealed. But it eluded him. All through the day, he wrestled with it. He knew his thinking had been affected by his meager diet; malnutrition and dehydration had robbed him of the sharp wit he required to reach the profound revelation that hovered at the edge of his consciousness. And when the young man was brought in, his body wasted with disease and torture, Ibrahim did not know that his personal epiphany was at hand.

The young man who was tossed roughly into the cell was ignored by the other prisoners. Ibrahim went and knelt beside him, more out of hunger for word of the outside world than from concern for the man himself.

They talked briefly, the youth lying down because he was too weak to sit up. Ibrahim learned that he was not a new prisoner at all, but had been arrested nearly a year ago during the riots of Black Saturday. Since then, the young man explained weakly, he had been moved from cell to cell, and tortured in between. He was a member of the Muslim Brotherhood, he said, and he knew he was going to die soon. But he added, "Don't worry for my sake, my friend. I go to God."

Ibrahim wondered what it was like to die for something one believed in.

The young man's green eyes rested on Ibrahim. "Do you have a son?"

"Yes," Ibrahim whispered, thinking of little Zachariah. "A fine boy."

The young man closed his eyes. "That is good. It's good to have a son. My only regret, God forgive me, is that I depart this earth leaving no son to carry on for me." As the final breath left Abdu's body, he pictured the village of his boyhood, and the girl Sahra he had lain with, and he wondered if she would perhaps join him someday in paradise.

Ibrahim rested his hand on the man's shoulder and murmured, "I declare that there is no god but God, and Mohammed is his Messenger."

And then he remembered the dream about Sahra and Zachariah he had had weeks ago, when he had first woken up in this place. And suddenly the thought that had been eluding him all day became brilliantly clear. He understood everything now. This was God's punishment on him for calling Zachariah his own. His being here wasn't a mistake after all; he was *supposed* to be here. He belonged here. And with surrender came acceptance, and a curious kind of peace.

It was then that the guards came for him.

CHAPTER 12

The Call to Prayer began, first with the muezzin singing out from the minaret of Al Azhar Mosque, then another at the next mosque picked up the prayer, followed by another and another, their voices blending together over the domes and rooftops of the city, stringing the Call like pearls across the wintry morning sky.

Those gathered in the Rasheed house, especially the men, did not think it strange that a woman had just led them in prayer. She was no ordinary woman but Amira, Ali's widow and, in the four months since her son's mysterious arrest, the head of the Rasheed clan. It was Amira who had brought them together to the house on Virgins of Paradise Street, and who now kept them united in the family crisis. The grand salon had been turned into a command post, where every family member was put to work—answering the telephone, making phone calls, printing petitions to be circulated, preparing articles and statements for the newspapers, writing letters to anyone who might help the cause of Ibrahim Rasheed. Amira was at the center of it all, organizing and giving orders: "I have just learned that the father of the editor of *Al Ahram* was a close friend of Grandfather Ali. Khalil, go to the newspaper office, tell him of our misfortune. If his father is still alive, perhaps he will help." The male family members went out on her assignments and reported back to her, while the women cooked and served for the large population now in residence. All the bedrooms were occupied, as family members who lived as far away as Luxor and even Aswan had come to take up the cause of getting Ibrahim released from prison.

As the first rays of sunlight broke over the eastern hills, the telephone was already ringing, a typewriter was busy clacking away. Zou Zou's grandson, a handsome man who worked at the Commerce Exchange, came in, accepted a cup of tea, and sat down with Amira. "Times have changed, Um Ibrahim," he said wearily. "A man's name no longer means anything. His honor, his father's honor, carry no weight any more. All the officials are interested in is baksheesh. Lowly bureaucrats who once couldn't sit at the same table with us now have uniforms and strut around like peacocks, demanding huge fees for their help."

Amira listened patiently as she saw in his eyes what she saw in the eyes of the Rasheed uncles and nephews—confusion, frustration, loss. The social classes were collapsing; aristocratic men such as the Rasheeds no longer wore the fez, once the proud symbol of their status. No one knew his place any more; the title "pasha" had been stripped from the lordly class, and newspaper vendors and taxi drivers were rude to men to whom they once bowed. The vast farms that had been held by rich landholders for generations were being seized and divided up among the peasants; large institutions—even the banks—were being nationalized. The military ruled the country, and there was no one to stop them, not even the

British, who saw their own presence in Egypt coming to an end. Now there was talk of socialism in every Cairo coffeehouse, and a frenzied kind of egalitarianism was sweeping Egypt.

Amira did not understand, nor did she pretend to. But if such change was God's will, then so be it. But where was Ibrahim? Why had he become a victim in this upheaval? And why was she unable to find him? Worry and sleeplessness had taken their toll. Amira had lost weight, and her forehead showed new lines. She had been forced to sell some of her jewelry and use some of her personal savings in order to pay the high bribes the petty officials demanded. She was also praying more than she ever had before, and practicing the special magic Ali Rasheed's mother had taught her long ago, magic that was supposed to keep the bad luck that had come to Egypt away from the house on Virgins of Paradise Street.

She had summoned Qettah to cast Ibrahim's fortune, but the elderly woman had only shaken her head, saying, "His birth-star is Aldebaran, Sayyida, the star of courage and honor. But I cannot tell you if your son will live in courage or die in honor."

As more visitors arrived with reports, news, and hearsay, the nephew of Ali's older brother came rushing in. "Ibrahim is still alive! He is being held at the Citadel!"

"*Al hamdu lillah*," Amira said. "Praise the Lord."

Everyone clustered around Mohssein Rasheed, a student at the university who had suspended his studies in order to help search for his cousin. They all spoke at once, but it was Amira who commanded his attention. "Mohssein, why is he being held there? What was the reason for his arrest?"

"They say they have proof of *treason*, Auntie!"

"Treason!" She closed her eyes. A crime punishable by death.

"They say they have witnesses who have testified under oath to what he said."

"Liars!" cried the others. "Liars who have been bribed!"

But Amira held up a hand and said calmly, "Praise to the Eternal One that we have found Ibrahim. Mohssein, go to the Citadel and find out what you can. Salah, go with him. Tewfik, go at once to Hassan al-Sabir's office in Ezbekiya. He will want this new information."

As Nefissa was bringing in a note that had just been delivered by someone who knew a man who knew a man who, for a fee, could get word to Ibrahim, Suleiman Misrahi arrived. He was looking older, his hair thinning, his eyes sunken. Although his profitable import business had not yet been touched by the revolutionaries, the government take-over of large corporations and cotton farms worried him. He had also heard talk of the revolutionary government building new Egyptian facto-ries to manufacture products such as automobiles and farm machinery, items that were currently imported from other countries. Suleiman dealt mostly in luxuries like chocolate and lace; would they, also, become nationalized?

"Thank you for coming, Suleiman," Amira said, as she received him in a small parlor off the salon, reserved for private meetings with guests.

Her feelings for Suleiman, a good, kind, and gentle man, were strong and warm. She thought now about how devastated Maryam had been, years ago, to learn that it was not she who was responsible for their childlessness, but he, and how she could not bear to tell him the truth. Amira had often wondered if Suleiman really would be angry if he ever learned that his children were not really his but had been fathered by his brother Moussa.

"The situation is deplorable, Amira," he said. "I have attended some of the trials. Trials! They're circuses! Everyone is accusing everyone else. If you name someone who committed a crime worse than you, they let you go. The revolution has been reduced to a farce, and I am ashamed now to say that I am Egyptian." He shook his head in despair. These were mad times. The American film *Quo Vadis*, which had been banned because Nero reminded Farouk too much of himself, had now been released and was the number-one hit in Cairo. Thousands flocked to see it, and every time Peter Ustinov, playing Nero, appeared on the screen, people shouted, "To Capri! To Capri!"—Farouk's current place of exile.

Suleiman reached into his breast pocket and brought out a sheet of paper. "It has taken me some time and quite a bit of baksheesh, but I have finally been able to get what you asked for, Amira. Here is the address of one of the men on the Revolutionary Council."

Back in August, after Ibrahim had been arrested and attempts to locate him through normal legal channels had proven futile, Amira had asked for a list of the members of the Revolutionary Council, men who called themselves the Free Officers. She had learned that they were all young, under forty, and when Suleiman had read the names to her, she had asked him to locate the residence of one in particular.

"It wasn't easy finding this address," he said now, handing her the piece of paper. "The Officers know they are targets of counterrevolutionaries. But I finally went to a friend who owes me a favor, and who is a friend of this man's brother. What will you do with this information? Who is this man, Amira?"

"Perhaps he is God's sign of hope."

=

"Amira," Maryam said, "you *must* let me go with you. You haven't left this house in thirty-six years. You'll get lost!"

"I shall find my way," Amira said quietly, draping the black melaya over her head. "God will guide my footsteps."

"But why not take the car?"

"Because this is a mission for myself alone, I cannot risk the safety of another person."

"Where are you going? Will you at least tell me that? Is it to the address Suleiman gave you?"

Amira continued to arrange the melaya around herself until only her eyes showed. "It is better that you don't know."

"Do you even know how to get to wherever it is you're going?"

"Suleiman gave me directions."

"I'm fearful, Amira," Maryam said softly. "The times we are in frighten me. My friends are asking me when Suleiman and I are moving to Israel. Such a thought hadn't even entered our minds!" She shook her head sadly. When the news had come out, three years ago, that 45,000 Jews had left Yemen for Israel in an exodus called Operation Magic Carpet, Maryam's friends had started asking why *they* weren't going. But why should they? Egypt was their home. Even their name, *Al Misrahi*, meant "Egyptians." But other Jews were leaving Cairo, and now attendance at the synagogue was down.

"Maryam," Amira said, "I shall be fine. My strength is in God."

Before she left, Amira spent a moment with the picture of Ali that she kept at her bedside. "I am going into the city now," she said. "If there is one chance to save our son, this is it. God has illuminated me. He will guide my feet. But I am afraid. This house has been my haven. I have been safe here." Finally she was at the garden gate, the winter sunshine warming her shoulders. Through this gate she had been brought many years and many memories ago. She glanced toward the orange trees and saw Alice working in her flower garden, trying to coax English carnations out of Egyptian soil. The children were nearby, their play subdued. Because of Ibrahim's incarceration, the Prophet Mohammed's birthday, recently celebrated, had been a somber affair for the little ones, and now it looked as if there wouldn't be much of a joyous celebration for the prophet whom Alice revered, Jesus, whose birthday was just two weeks away. We are a house in mourning, Amira thought.

Making sure the black silk melaya was secure around her, that not even her hands or ankles showed, she took a deep breath, opened the gate and stepped out.

——

Please God, Alice prayed as she dug into the hard earth, restore Ibrahim to me, and I shall be a good wife to him. I will love him and serve him and give him many children. I will forget how he deceived me about Zakki's mother. Just bring him safely home.

Not even Edward was consolation to her these days; it seemed that the longer her brother stayed in Egypt, the more morose he became. He had grown so quiet; he seemed constantly embroiled in his own thoughts. Alice had once believed it must be love, that passion for Nefissa had consumed him, but now she didn't know what to think. She knew he carried a gun with him all the time, saying it was for their safety, because Britons had become targets of the radicals. But was that really the reason?

She looked up from her gardening to see Yasmina standing there, her eyes the color of the blue morning glories that cascaded over the stone wall. "Mama," she said, "when will Daddy be home? I miss him."

"I miss him too, sweetheart." Alice took the girl into her arms, and when she saw Camelia and Zachariah standing there, also looking lost— they were motherless and fatherless, after all—she opened her arms to them and they ran into her embrace.

She was just suggesting that they go into the kitchen and see if there was any mango ice cream left from last night's dinner, when she saw

Hassan al-Sabir come into the garden. Of them all, Ibrahim's friend seemed the least affected by recent events. Alice jumped up. "You have news of Ibrahim?"

His dark eyes flickered as he thought how, for the past four months, that was always the first thing she said to him. "I saw the Dragon leave. Where was she going?"

Alice pulled off her gardening gloves. "Dragon?"

Hassan suspected that Amira didn't like him, although he had no idea why. "Ibrahim's mother. I didn't know she ever left this house."

"Goodness, she doesn't. Where do you suppose Mother Amira has gone? Children, go into the house now, Uncle Hassan and I have to talk in private."

Hassan looked around. "Where are Nefissa and Edward?"

"Nefissa is trying to find out if Princess Faiza is in Egypt or if she left with the rest of the royal family. If Faiza is still here, she might be able to help us find Ibrahim. And Edward—" she sighed—"I suppose Edward is in his room." She was afraid her brother was drinking a lot; she was also afraid he was going to go back to England, and she couldn't bear the thought of losing both him and Ibrahim. "Do you have anything to report?"

He surprised her by reaching over and brushing a strand of blond hair from her cheek. "To be honest, my dear," he said, "I think you should prepare yourself for the worst. I don't think Ibrahim is ever coming home. These are very uncertain times. Men who were your friends yesterday are your enemies today. You know how hard I've worked for Ibrahim's release, tried to find out where he is, or when he will be brought to trial. But even I am helpless, and I am one of the few men left in this city who still has connections. Citizens who were loyal to the king will not be treated lightly, I'm afraid."

Tears came to Alice's eyes; he put his arms around her. "You need not be afraid while I am around."

"I want Ibrahim to come home!"

"We all do," he said. "But there is only so much anyone can do, the rest is in God's hands." He placed a finger under her chin and lifted her face. "You must be very lonely, Alice," he said. And then he tried to kiss her.

Alice drew back in shock. "Hassan!" she said.

"Beautiful Alice. You know I've wanted you ever since we met in

Monte Carlo. You and I were fated for each other. But you married Ibrahim."

"Hassan, stop it," she said, pulling back. "I love Ibrahim."

He took her arm. "Ibrahim is gone, my dear Alice. It's time you faced that fact. You are the equivalent of a widow, a young and beautiful widow. You need a man."

"Please don't!" she said; she pushed him away and stumbled back against the trunk of a pomegranate tree. He pinned her to the tree and again tried to kiss her; she struggled and cried out.

"You know you want me as much as I want you," he said as he tried to slide his hand beneath her blouse.

"But I don't want you," she sobbed. "Stop it!"

He laughed. "I've been waiting for over eight years for this chance."

She broke free, stumbled toward her basket of gardening tools, and as Hassan reached for her, she spun around and brandished a hand rake in his face. "I'll use this, Hassan, I swear I will. Leave me alone."

He looked at the sharp prongs, inches from his cheek, and his smile faded. "You aren't serious."

"I'm deadly serious," Alice said. "You are disgusting. You're a monster. If you touch me, I'll make sure you look like a monster for the rest of your life."

He looked from the rake to Alice, then back to the rake, then he suddenly smiled and stepped away from her, holding up his hands. "You prize yourself very highly, my dear. Too highly. It's not worth risking disfigurement for you. The sad thing is you have no idea what you've missed. I would have made love to you in such a way that you would not have wanted to go back to your husband again, even if he did come back. After an hour with me, you wouldn't want any other man ever again." He laughed, and it was not a pleasant laugh. "Poor Alice," he said. "What you don't know is that someday you will come to me, begging for me, but you'll never get another chance. You will remember this afternoon. And you will regret it."

—

Amira was lost. Her destination was an address on Shari el-Azhar, and Suleiman had given her simple directions as to how to get there: "Go north on Kasr El Aini until you come to the great traffic circle in front of the British barracks. This used to be Ismail Square, but now it is called

Liberation Square. You will see two shops, one selling pastries, the other with luggage in the window. These mark the entrance to the street that will take you to the General Post Office. Go east on this street until you come to another large traffic circle, where the post office is. Shari El Azhar branches off to the east from this circle—follow it until you come to the Great Mosque. This address is on a small street opposite the mosque. The doorway is blue, and there is a pot of red geraniums on the steps." Out of fear that someone might find Suleiman's note, Amira had memorized the directions and destroyed it.

But there were two things she had not counted on: that she might get turned around, and that the overcast day would make it impossible to determine the position of the sun. Now, two hours after stepping through her garden gate, Amira realized she had made a wrong turn, and that she was unable to determine east from west. She tried not to think of the big gray sky hanging over her. Although she had spent many afternoons and evenings on the spacious roof of their house, where she tended a grape arbor and raised pigeons for the family table, the sky above Virgins of Paradise Street was a different sky from this one— there, she had felt protected, here she was not.

Amira stood on the busy street corner and looked around her at the towering buildings. She had learned the city from her roof garden, and had memorized every dome, minaret and rooftop. But now she was below, in the middle of it, and it seemed an alien, terrifying place. Which way to turn? Where was Shari El Azhar? Where was Virgins of Paradise Street?

And Cairo was full of so many people! There were tanks in the streets, and soldiers were everywhere. As she hurried along, clutching her melaya protectively about her, she thought that everyone must be staring at her, thinking, There goes Amira Rasheed. Her husband, Ali, is frowning down at her from paradise! She had panicked several times when she had come to intersections and seen red and green lights, policemen directing the frantic traffic. She had stepped off a curb without looking and almost been run over. Sellers of vegetables, chickens, and spices had hawked their wares in her face. She had passed men on street corners arguing, or haggling over a price, or laughing at a joke. And she had seen women going arm in arm down a busy street, laughing and pointing things out in shop windows. She had been spellbound.

And her son was somewhere in prison, or possibly dead; she had to find him.

Feeling conspicuous on the street corner, Amira decided to plunge ahead, only to find herself in a street that she realized she had been down earlier. She felt her heart begin to pound. She was walking in circles! And then she glimpsed something between two buildings that gave her hope: the dull, metallic flash of the Nile.

Following the sidewalk so she wouldn't have to make another terrifying street crossing, Amira found herself approaching a bridge. By now she had joined other foot traffic: village men in galabeyas pulling carts heaped with vegetables, women in long black dresses carrying bundles on their heads, students in modern dress with books under their arms. It was none of these who captured Amira's attention—it was the river. She could not take her eyes off it.

She had never seen it except from the roof—a silky ribbon of changing colors. It had looked far away, artificial. But now, looking down at the water from the arch of the bridge, she was overwhelmed. She had seen the river before! Where? When? Long ago.

The river hypnotized her. Its fertile smells reminded her of childbirth. Its surface appeared to be slow, innocent, but Amira thought she could see deeper, down to the swifter, more dangerous current. And another memory came back: herself, at fourteen, her belly swollen with her first child, whom she named Ibrahim. And her husband, Ali, saying in his wise way, "The Nile is unique. She flows from the south to the north."

Amira had asked, "The river is a woman?"

"She is the Mother of Egypt, the Mother of Rivers. Without her there would be no life here."

"But God gives us life."

"God gives us the Nile, and she nurtures us."

Amira stared at the wide, powerful river that reflected the pewter sky and the white lateens of the feluccas that skimmed its surface, and she again heard Ali say, "She flows from the south to the north." She watched the current, following it until it disappeared around a curve. That way is north, she thought.

And then she realized that her left hand lay to the west, her right to the east. And she believed that this was a sign from God.

She was no longer afraid as she retraced her steps along the bridge, turning left on the first major street and following it, always keeping the Nile in sight. When she reached the traffic circle in front of the British barracks, she knew where she was. Keeping the Nile in her mind's eye as she turned eastward, she walked resolutely along the busy street until she came to another traffic circle from where she was able to recognize one of the minarets of Al-Azhar Mosque, which Ali had pointed out to her so many years ago.

Finally she saw the blue door with the pot of red geraniums on the steps.

She rang the bell and a servant answered. Amira introduced herself, saying that she was calling on Captain Rageb's wife. After admitting her to a small parlor, the servant left. While she waited, she prayed that this was the person she sought, that she had not made a mistake.

The servant returned, and Amira was taken upstairs to an elegant salon not unlike her own, but smaller. A woman greeted her, and as soon as Amira saw her, she said a mental prayer of thanks to God. She lowered her veil and, after the preliminary greetings, said, "Mrs. Safeya, do you remember me?"

"Indeed I do, Sayyida," the woman said. "Please sit down."

Tea and pastries were brought in, and Mrs. Rageb offered Amira a cigarette, which she gratefully accepted. "It is nice to see you again, Sayyida."

"And you. Is your family well?"

Safeya pointed to a collection of photographs of young girls on the wall. "My two daughters," she said with pride. "The eldest is twenty-one now, and married. My youngest is going to be seven shortly." She looked directly at her guest. "I named her Amira. She was born while my husband, the captain, was stationed in the Sudan. But you know this."

Amira was remembering the necklace Mrs. Rageb had worn the day she had come to Virgins of Paradise Street, seven years ago—a blue stone on a gold chain to ward off bad luck—and how Amira had known the woman was afraid. She noticed that Mrs. Rageb was no longer wearing the necklace.

"Tell me, please," Amira said, "do you recall our conversation in my garden seven years ago?"

"I shall never forget it. I promised you on that day that I should forever be in your debt. If you have come to make a request, Mrs. Amira, my house and everything I own are yours."

"Mrs. Safeya, is your husband the Captain Youssef Rageb who is on the Revolutionary Council?"

"He is."

"You once told me that your husband loves you, and that he considers you his equal and listens to your advice. Is this still true?"

"More than ever," Safeya said softly.

"Then I have indeed come to ask a favor of you," Amira said.

CHAPTER 13

Alice lay quietly in bed for a moment, wondering what had wakened her. It didn't take much these days—she was sleeping lightly, worrying constantly about Ibrahim. The bedside clock showed well past midnight. She listened to the silence of the house, and was startled to hear footsteps going past her door. When, a moment later, someone else went by, she realized that that was what had roused her—people hurrying down the hall. But she heard no talking, no cries of alarm. Getting out of bed, Alice opened her door in time to see Nefissa and a female cousin disappear around the end of the hall in the direction of the children's rooms.

Pulling on her dressing gown, Alice went after them.

—

Camelia didn't like being wakened before it was morning; she loved sleep and dreams, and the coziness of bed. When she felt a hand gently shaking her, she thought it was her sister Mishmish, who sometimes woke her during the night because she had had a bad dream, or she was afraid Daddy was never coming home. But when the seven-year-old opened her eyes, she was surprised to find Umma leaning over her.

"Come along, Lili," Amira said gently. "Come with me."

Camelia rubbed her eyes and followed sleepily as Umma led her to the bathroom. Camelia glanced back at her sister Yasmina, who was still asleep in her own bed. Then she went inside and Umma closed the door.

The bathroom's bright light hurt Camelia's eyes; she was surprised to see Auntie Nefissa there, and Cousin Doreya, and Raya, and even old Auntie Zou Zou. "I will hold her," Nefissa said, opening out her arms to Camelia, and giving her an encouraging smile. "I will be her mama tonight."

Because she was still sleepy, Camelia didn't question what the women were doing; she sat down on the floor, on a thick towel Auntie Nefissa had spread out, and then leaned back into her aunt's arms. But when Doreya and Raya drew her legs apart, Camelia began to resist. "What are you doing, Umma?" she said.

Amira moved swiftly.

—

In the dark bedroom, Yasmina was dreaming. As she lay curled up in bed, her arms around the English teddy bear her Uncle Edward had had sent to her from England, she was comforted in her sleep by a pleasant dream of Daddy coming back from his long holiday, and the house being happy again. There was a party, and Mummy was wearing her white satin evening gown and diamond earrings, and Umma was bringing big bowls of ice cream from the kitchen, and apricots and brown sugar.

And then she saw Camelia dancing and laughing and calling to her. "Mishmish! *Mishmish!*"

Yasmina opened her eyes. The bedroom was dark, thin ribbons of moonlight spilling through the shutters. She listened. Had she dreamed her sister was calling her? Or had it really—

A scream tore the air.

Yasmina jumped out of bed and ran to her sister's bed, but she found it empty, the covers rolled back. "Lili?" she called. "Where are you?"

Then she saw a light under the bathroom door.

She ran to it, and just as she got there, the door opened and Umma came out, carrying a sobbing Camelia. "What happened?" Yasmina asked.

"It's all right," Amira said as she laid the seven-year-old in her bed, tucking her in and wiping away her tears. "Camelia will be all right."

"But what—"

"Come along now, Yasmina," Nefissa said gently. "Back to bed."

The bedroom door suddenly opened and Alice stood there in her dressing gown, blond hair disarrayed, eyes still puffy with sleep. "What happened? I heard a scream. It sounded like Camelia."

"She will be all right," Amira said, stroking Camelia's hair.

"But what happened?" Alice noticed that the other women were fully dressed, even though it was the middle of the night.

"Everything is fine. Camelia will be healed in a few days."

Alice looked at the others, who smiled and assured her everything was going to be all right. "Healed? But what happened to her?"

"It was her circumcision," Nefissa said. "In a few days she will have forgotten all about it. Come and have tea with with us."

"Her *what?*" Alice said. And then she heard one of the women murmur to another, "The English don't do this."

Amira laid a hand on Alice's arm and said, "Come, my dear, and I'll explain. Nefissa, will you stay with Camelia, please?"

After the women had left the room, and Auntie Nefissa had gone into the bathroom, Yasmina crept out of bed and went to her sister, who was sobbing softly into her pillow. "What is it, Lili?" she asked. "What happened? Are you sick?"

Camelia wiped her eyes. "I hurt, Mishmish," she said.

Drawing the blanket back, Yasmina climbed in and put her arms around Camelia. "Don't cry. You heard Umma. You'll be all right."

"Please don't leave me," Camelia said, and Yasmina pulled the blanket up over them both.

=

A silver tea service was set up in Amira's bedroom, and as she poured two cups, she said, "Is it true that circumcision is not practiced among the English?"

Alice gave her a perplexed look. "Boys sometimes, I think. But Mother Amira, how can a girl be circumcised? What do you do?" As Amira explained, Alice stared at her in shock. "But that's not the same as a boy's circumcision. Isn't this harmful?"

"Not at all. When Camelia grows up, she will just have a small scar. I removed only the tiniest part. Otherwise, she is the same as before."

"But why do you do this?"

"It is done to preserve a girl's honor when she grows up. The impurity has been removed, she will be a chaste and obedient wife."

Alice frowned. "But doesn't that mean she won't be able to enjoy sex?"

"Of course she will," Amira said with a smile. "No man wants an unsatisfied woman in his bed."

Alice looked at the clock on Amira's nightstand; it was nearly two. The house, the garden, and Virgins of Paradise Street were dark and silent. "But why did you do the circumcision at this hour, and so secretly?" she asked. "When Zachariah was circumcised there was a big party, a celebration."

"A boy's circumcision has different meaning than a girl's. For a boy, it means he has been brought into the family of Islam. But a girl's involves her shame, and so it must be done quietly." Seeing Alice's baffled look, she added, "This is a ritual that every Muslim girl undergoes. Camelia is now assured of finding a good husband, because he will know she is not easily aroused and therefore can be trusted. It is for this reason that no decent man will marry an uncircumcised woman."

Alice's perplexity deepened. "But your son married me, didn't he?"

Amira sat down and took Alice's hand. "Yes, he did. And because you married the son of my heart, you are the daughter of my heart. I am truly sorry you are upset. I should have prepared you for it, explained, and then invited you to take part, so that next year, when it is Yasmina's turn—"

"Yasmina! But surely you're not planning on doing this to my daughter!"

"We shall see what Ibrahim says."

Alice looked at the tea in her cup and suddenly she could not drink. Rising unsteadily, she said, "I want to check on the girls."

═══

Nefissa was sitting beside the bed, embroidering. "They are both asleep," she said to Alice with a smile, gesturing to the two little girls curled together beneath one blanket.

Alice looked first at Camelia, whose black hair lay damp on her pillow, and then at her daughter, whose blond curls mingled with her sister's darker ones. And as she laid a hand on Yasmina's forehead, she recalled the girls dressing up in the melayas, and saw again a frightening future—

one in which Egypt had returned to the old ways, a world of veiled women and female circumcision.

I will not let that happen to you, sweetheart, she vowed silently to Yasmina. I promise you that you will always be free to be yourself.

Suddenly, she wanted to talk to her brother. Kissing each of the girls, she said good-night to her sister-in-law, then made her way through the large, silent house, across the main salon, and up the massive stairway into the men's wing. Eddie will understand, Alice told herself. He can help me find an apartment. I will take Yasmina—the three of us will live there until Ibrahim comes home.

She started to knock on her brother's door and then, remembering that he was a heavy sleeper, she walked in. His sitting room was blazing with light, and two men were there. It took Alice a moment to realize what they were doing: Edward was bent over, and Hassan al-Sabir was behind him; their trousers were around their ankles.

They looked up, startled. Then Alice gave a cry, turned, and ran.

She stumbled down the stairway; running across the polished floor of the entry hall, she slipped and fell. Through tears, she tried to find a handhold, but as she struggled to her feet, she felt a hand grasp her arm. It was Hassan. She tried to run, but he spun her around in the pool of moonlight that came through the window. "So you didn't know," he said with a smile. "By your look I would say you never even suspected."

"You're a monster," she gasped.

"Me? Come now, my dear. It is your brother who is the monster—he played the female role, he is the shamed one."

"You have corrupted him!"

"*I* have corrupted *him*?" Hassan laughed. "My dear Alice, whose idea do you think it was? Edward has wanted me since he first arrived here. You thought it was Nefissa he wanted, didn't you?"

She tried to pull away, but he drew her closer and said with a hard smile, "You seem jealous, Alice. But of which of us are you jealous, I wonder?"

"You disgust me!"

"Yes, you've already told me that. So I decided that since I couldn't have the sister, then the brother would do just as well. I imagine you're both rather much the same, from that angle."

She broke free and ran.

CHAPTER 14

Ibrahim was coming home! On this blustery day in January of 1953, there was so much activity in the kitchen that the cook and her assistants kept bumping into one another. Many guests and family members had arrived to welcome Ibrahim home, and the ovens had been going night and day, turning out casseroles, roasts, breads, and pies.

Sahra had been set the chore of grinding lamb into a paste for meatballs, a skill she had learned for village festivals and which she now performed cheerfully. Her master was coming home! The man who had saved her and her baby from a life of beggary and starvation, and who had called her son his own and had given Zachariah the life of a prince. Sahra herself had even been a doctor's wife for one minute, much finer than being the wife of a shopkeeper for a lifetime. And she had been allowed to breast-feed her son for three years, to hold him and rock him, even if she could never acknowledge him as her own. And now the two had celebrated another birthday under this roof: Sahra was twenty-one, Zakki, seven.

She knew it must all have been part of God's plan—conceiving Abdu's son beside the canal, leaving the village, and finally coming into this wonderful house that was like a palace. Hadn't her mother told her the night she fled the wrath of her father and uncles that she was in God's hands? Abdu, wherever he was, would be pleased if he knew. And now the master was back and the house was going to be a happy place again!

The guests were all crowded into the grand reception room—Rasheeds, other residents of Virgins of Paradise Street, Ibrahim's friends from the nightclubs and casinos—all in their finest clothes, all anxious to bring him back into their fold. He had been away for six months. When they heard a car backfiring, the children ran to a window and screamed when they looked down and saw Uncle Mohssein's car pull into the drive.

"Daddy's here!" they cried, jumping up and down. "Daddy's here!"

The noise in the reception room rose as they listened to the progress of the two men up the stairway. No one had seen Ibrahim since August; he had not been allowed any visitors, not even after a letter had arrived saying that he would be released within the next few weeks. And so the image that stood in everyone's mind, as Mohssein led his cousin into the room, did not match the apparition that now stood in the doorway. Everyone fell silent and stared in shock at the stranger with the gray hair and gray beard. Ibrahim Rasheed looked like a skeleton; there were enormous black hollows under his eyes, and his suit hung on his emaciated frame.

Amira came forward and put her arms around him. "Blessed be the Eternal One who has brought my son home."

The others came up, tears in their eyes, trying to smile, reaching out to touch him. Nefissa was openly weeping, while Alice slowly made her way to him, her face as pale as the silk dress she wore. When she embraced him, Ibrahim broke down and wept.

The children approached shyly, not certain who this man was. But when he held out his arms and called them by their nicknames— Mishmish, Lili, Zakki—they recognized his voice. Ibrahim embraced his two daughters, Camelia and Yasmina, sobbing into their sweet-smelling hair, but when it was Zachariah's turn, Ibrahim stepped away before the boy could touch him, and reached for Amira's arm. "I don't know how it is that I am home, Mother," he said in a faint voice. "Yesterday I thought I was going to be in prison forever. This morning I woke up and they told me I was to go home. I don't know why I was there, or why they released me."

"It is God's will that you are free," she said with tears in her eyes. Not even Ibrahim would ever know of her secret pact with the wife of the Free Officer. "You are home now, and that is all that matters."

"Mother," he said quietly. "King Farouk is never coming back. Egypt is a different place now."

"That, too, is in God's hands. Your fate is already written. Come now, sit down and eat." As she led him to the divan of honor, upholstered in gold brocade and red velvet, Amira hid her fright at feeling the thin arm beneath his sleeve, and at the haunted look she had seen in his eyes. She knew he had been tortured in that terrible place; it was the one piece of information Safeya Rageb had been able to give her. But Amira would never ask him about it, and she knew her son would never speak of it. Her task now was to restore him to health and happiness, and to help him find his place in this new Egypt.

When Alice looked around and said, "Where's Eddie?" the children jumped up and said, "We'll go get him, the sleepy head!" And they ran out of the room, a squealing mob.

They returned a moment later. "We can't wake up Uncle Eddie," Zachariah said. "We shook him and shook him, but he won't wake up!"

"He's hurt his forehead," Yasmina said. "Right here," and she pointed between her eyes.

Amira left the room, Alice and Nefissa following.

They found Edward in a chair, impeccably dressed in a blue blazer and white trousers, his face freshly shaven, his hair slicked down with pomade. When they saw the neat bullet hole between his eyes, and the .38 in his hand, they realized that the noise they had heard just as Ibrahim had arrived had not been a car backfiring. At the moment one life had returned to the house on Virgins of Paradise Street, another had departed.

Alice was the first to see the note. She read phrases that would haunt her for the rest of her life: "Not Hassan's fault. I loved him and I thought he loved me. Now I know I was the instrument of his revenge against you, dear sister. To hurt you, Alice, he destroyed me. But don't mourn for me. I was doomed the day I arrived here. I left England because of my vice. I knew that if Father found out it would ruin the family. I can no longer live with my shame." And he had added one line addressed to Nefissa: "Forgive me if I misled you."

Alice hadn't realized she was reading aloud until she heard the sudden silence in the room when she stopped. Amira took the note and, using Edward's lighter, set fire to it. When it was reduced to black ash in the waste basket, she told Nefissa to find the box of bullets, to spread them on the desk, along with whatever cleaning materials Edward might have used for his gun.

Then she turned to Alice and said, "No one is to know about this, do you understand? You must tell no one—not Ibrahim, not Hassan, no one. Alice? Nefissa? Do you understand?"

Alice looked at her brother. "But what about—"

"We will make it look like an accident," Amira said, as Nefissa placed a chamois and oil with the bullets. "He was cleaning his gun, it accidentally went off. This is what we will tell everyone. Now, both of you, promise me this is what you will say."

Nefissa nodded dumbly, and Alice whispered, "Yes, Mother Amira."

"Now we will call the police." But before they left the room, Amira paused and laid a gentle hand on Edward's neatly combed hair, closed her eyes and murmured, "I declare that there is no god but God, and Mohammed is His messenger."

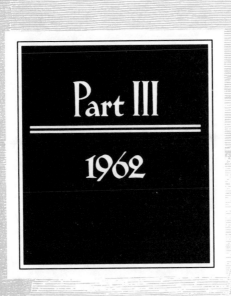

Part III
1962

There was only one thing on Omar Rasheed's mind as he watched the seductive dancer on the screen: getting into bed with his cousin.

The dancer's name was Dahiba, and the way she moved across the screen in those high heels and that Rita Hayworth evening gown, her hips and breasts and long legs turning his blood to liquid fire, made twenty-year-old Omar think he was going to burst. Dahiba herself wasn't the object of his youthful lust; it was seventeen-year-old Camelia who aroused him to such frenzy, sitting next to him in the dark movie theater, her arm brushing his, the pungency of her musk perfume filling his head. Omar had desired his cousin since the night the family had attended a recital at her ballet academy and Camelia had danced in a leotard, a frilly skirt, and white tights. She had been fifteen, and it was the first time Omar had noticed that she was no longer a little girl.

"Isn't Dahiba *beautiful?*" Camelia said, her eyes riveted on the screen.

Omar couldn't reply. He had no idea what it was like to make love to a woman, since sex outside marriage was forbidden in Islam. A boy had to wait until he had a wife before enjoying intimate relations, and usually, as in Omar's case, that sublime event didn't take place until the young man had finished school and gotten a job, so that he could take on the responsibilities of a family. Like many of his friends, Omar could not expect his wedding to take place before he was twenty-five. And since society forbade young unmarried people from even holding hands, Omar was occasionally driven to seek relief with the similarly sexually frustrated young men he met at the public baths; but this was only a temporary satisfaction. What he wanted was a female.

"Bismillah! Dahiba is a goddess," Camelia said with a sigh. The movie was typical Egyptian fare: a musical comedy involving mistaken identities, star-crossed love, and a peasant girl winding up with a millionaire husband. The theater was packed and noisy, the audience singing along with the music and clapping the beat to Dahiba's dance, while hawkers walked up and down the aisles selling sandwiches, fried meatballs, and soda pop. When the villain appeared on the screen—his thin mustache and fez marking him instantly as the recognizable bad guy—the audience shouted insults. And when Dahiba, in her role as the virginal Fatima, spurned his advances, the audience cheered so loudly it seemed the roof of Cairo's Roxy Cinema might cave in.

It was Thursday, the night for going out since there was no work or school the next day; as Egypt was the second-largest producer of films in the world, making it possible to go to a different movie every day of the year and not see the same movie twice, nearly everyone went to the cinema on Thursday evenings. Especially the Rasheed cousins: Omar and his sister Tahia, Camelia and her brother Zachariah. Yasmina was not with them tonight. They wore their best clothes, Omar and Zachariah in tailored shirts and slacks, and smelling of cologne, Tahia and Camelia, also perfumed, wearing long-sleeved blouses, their skirts below their knees. Although hemlines were rising in Europe, the Rasheed girls were dressed conservatively.

The film ended, and the two thousand people crammed into the seats and aisles of the movie house stood for the Egyptian national anthem, while the face of President Nasser smiled down at them from the screen. As the four young Rasheeds went out into the fragrant spring night, laughing and chatting about the movie, they each entertained secret thoughts: sixteen-year-old Zachariah was trying to recall the beautiful lyrics of the songs he had just heard; Tahia, seventeen, was thinking that romance was the loveliest thing in the world; Camelia was deciding that she was going to be a famous dancer like Dahiba someday; and Omar was wondering where he was going to find a girl who would let him have sex with her.

When he caught his passing reflection in a store window, he felt his confidence blossom. Omar knew he was good looking. He had lost his baby fat and had developed a lithe, angular physique; he possessed penetrating dark eyes and had finely arched eyebrows that met over his nose. At the moment he was an engineering student at Cairo University, but when he obtained his degree and a job with the government, and received the allowance entitled to him from his late father, he knew there wouldn't be a woman in all Egypt who could resist him.

But that was in the future; the reality was that he was still only a student, still living with his mother on Virgins of Paradise Street, and still relying on his Uncle Ibrahim for spending money. What woman would look at him? On the other hand, here was his cousin Camelia, warm and alive on his arm, wafting her perfume in his face, tossing her black hair and flashing her honey-brown eyes. Unlike every other female in Egypt, it was possible that Camelia might not be totally off bounds to him.

"I'm starving!" she said when they reached an intersection. "Let's get something to eat before we go home." The four young people linked arms, the girls in the middle, and ran laughing across the street to where vendors in galabeyas busily dispensed kebabs, ice cream, and fruit to the hungry movie goers. Omar and his sister and Camelia bought *shwarma*—hot strips of lamb and chunks of tomato stuffed into pita bread—while Zachariah had a hot sweet potato and a glass of tamarind juice. He hadn't eaten meat since a terrifying incident that had occurred when he was seven years old. On the feast day of *Aid el-Adha*, which commemorated the prophet Ibrahim's readiness to sacrifice his son Ismail, Zachariah had watched a butcher preparing a lamb for the feast. After the animal's throat had been slit and all the blood drained out, the butcher, crying, "In the name of God!" had pumped air into the carcass to separate the skin from the flesh. Zachariah had watched in horror as the animal got bigger and bigger while the butcher struck the carcass with a stick to distribute the air beneath the skin. The seven-year-old had screamed. And he had not eaten meat since.

As they ate, trying to keep from being buffeted by the sidewalk crowd, Zachariah was troubled by one aspect of the film they had just seen. The "bad woman" in it had been a divorcée of loose morals, a stereotype in most Egyptian movies. It made him wonder about his own mother, of whom he still knew nothing because his father refused to speak of her. Zachariah couldn't believe his mother was anything like the divorced women in the movies. After all, old Auntie Zou Zou, who had died the year before, had been divorced, and had remained a pious woman for most of her life.

Zachariah knew what his mother must have been like, even though there were no photos of her in the family albums. She would have been beautiful, he decided, and religious and chaste, resembling the saintly Zeinab, whose mosque the family visited once a year on her holy day. Zachariah loved to fantasize about going in search of his mother, and the tearful reunion they would have. Omar had once said, "If your mother is such a wonderful woman, why has she never come to see you?" Zachariah's only answer was that she must be dead. Martyred now, as well as sainted.

When they stepped off the curb, Zachariah took Tahia's elbow. As her cousin he was permitted this liberty, but the shock that shot through him at the feel of the warm skin beneath her sleeve was far from cousinly. Unlike Omar, who had only really noticed Camelia two years ago, Zachariah had been in love with Omar's sister for as long as he could remember, back to when they were children playing in the garden. Tahia reminded him of his fantasy mother; she was a model of Muslim virtue and chastity. The fact that, at seventeen, she was nearly a year older than he was didn't bother him; she was small and delicate and, despite eight years of education at a private girls' school, still innocent and ignorant of the greater world. And also unlike Omar, whose ambitions went no further than a quick, hot encounter, Zachariah's thoughts centered upon marriage and the noble, spiritual aspects of love. He and Tahia were cousins; they were fated to marry. As they hurried along the sidewalk, alive with youth and happiness, Zachariah composed a poem in his mind: "Tahia, if only you were mine! I would make rivers of happiness flow beneath your feet! I would command the moon to make bracelets of silver for you! I would command the sun to send down necklaces of gold! Green grass beneath your slippers would be emeralds; raindrops on your body would turn into pearls. I would work magic for you, my beloved. Magic, and much, much more."

Tahia didn't hear the poem, of course, and anyway she was laughing at something Omar had just said about the somber Russians in the streets, a familiar sight ever since the Soviets had come to help build the High Dam at Aswan. Cairo shops sold Russian goods and displayed signs written in Russian, but Egyptians couldn't warm to people whom they called "heavy blooded."

Zachariah began to sing a love song— *"Ya lili ya aini."* "You are my eyes"—and the others joined in. They were drunk on youthful power as they hurried down the street, dodging pedestrians. The streets were brightly lit; music poured from open doorways. Fellaheen women sat on the sidewalks in black melayas, shucking ears of corn and roasting them over open fires, a sign that summer had almost arrived. The warm air was filled with the aroma of meat and fish sizzling on grills, and the sudden, heady bursts of perfume from flowering trees. It was a great time to be young and alive and in Cairo.

As the foursome reached Liberation Square, on the other side of which, on the spot where the British barracks had once been, the new pharaonic Nile Hilton rose, Camelia was oblivious of the possessive way Omar's arm tightened around her elbow. She was thinking of the great Dahiba in the movie they had just seen. All of Egypt adored Dahiba; how wonderful it must be to be so talented and famous! Camelia believed she was born to dance. She could remember how naturally it had come to her when she was little and had imitated the women who danced the beledi at Umma's parties. When Umma had agreed with Ibrahim that his oldest daughter had talent, Camelia had been enrolled in a ballet school. She had been eight years old; now, ten years later, Camelia Rasheed was the academy's star pupil and there was talk of signing her on with the National Ballet. But Camelia didn't want to be a classical ballet dancer. She had other, wonderful, secret plans. She had decided she would tell her sister Yasmina about them when she got home.

Omar noticed the way young men in the street glanced at Camelia, furtively, and then looked quickly away when they realized she was with male relatives. A lingering look, perhaps a bold word of greeting, and Omar and Zachariah would be required to set upon the offender with insults and fists. Only the month before, when the five Rasheed teenagers had been out shopping, Yasmina had gone off to browse by herself, and a young man had brushed up against her, his hand grazing her breast. She'd given him a sharp rebuke, but it was Omar and Zachariah who had driven the boy into the street, hurling insults and abuse at him until other pedestrians joined in and the shamed boy had disappeared down an alley. Secretly, Omar hadn't blamed him. A public crowd, such as in the market or on a bus, was the only opportunity a young man was given to feel a girl. Omar himself was frequently guilty of such "accidental" grazes. In fact, he sometimes followed a girl, hoping to get lucky. So far, he had gotten away with it. So far, no brothers or male cousins had jumped on him for threatening a family's honor. And it occurred to him now, as they struck out across Liberation Square, dodging taxis and buses, that Camelia was a perfect target. After all, *he* was the male cousin in this case. Who would she report him to?

Surely not to her father, because Omar knew Uncle Ibrahim's secret. And he laughed now, to think about it.

===

"How did you get these scars?"

Ibrahim rolled away from the woman and reached for the cigarettes beside the bed. They always asked him about the scars after they had made love and taken a closer look at his body. It had bothered him at first, but now his response was automatic. "During the Revolution," he said, in a tone that usually shut them up.

But this one persisted. "I didn't say when, I said how."

"With a knife."

"Yes, but—"

He sat up and drew the sheet over his thighs and groin to hide the evidence of the torture he had suffered in prison. His torturers had thought it funny when they had cut him there, pretending they were going to castrate him and stopping just within inches when he screamed and begged them to stop. No one, not his mother, nor Alice, knew about Ibrahim's special interrogation at the prison.

The woman snaked an arm around his waist and kissed his shoulder. But he stood up, pulled the sheet around himself like a toga, and went to the window. Cairo's bright lights and traffic glared back at him. The window was closed, but he could hear the noise of the street, three storys down, the cacophony of car horns, café radios, street musicians, laughter, arguments.

It amazed Ibrahim how Egypt had changed in the ten years since the Revolution. He recalled how, after the Suez War, in which Egypt had been defeated by Israel, aided by France and Britain, an explosion of Egyptian national pride had taken place. The slogan "Egypt for Egyptians" had swept the country from the Sudan to the Delta like an enormous Nile tide, resulting in a mass exodus of foreigners from Egypt. The face of Cairo was changing. All restaurants and shops and businesses were owned by Egyptians; clerks, waiters, and office workers were Egyptian. There were other, more subtle signs of the caretaker having departed: sidewalks were neglected and crumbling, paint was peeling from façades, shops had lost their chic European look. But Egyptians didn't care. They loved their new unity and freedom; they were drunk on national pride. The hero of this curious multirevolution was Gamal Abdel Nasser, and Egyptians loved a hero. Nasser's picture was seen in store windows, at news kiosks, on billboards, even on the marquee of the Roxy Cinema across from Ibrahim's office. On one side of the film's title was Nasser's smiling face; on the other was the face of another hero, the American president, John Kennedy, whom Middle Easterners loved because he had brought to the world's attention the torture and imprisonment of Algerians by the French.

As Ibrahim watched the pedestrians in the street below, spilling off the sidewalk and impeding the flow of traffic, he recognized members of the "new" aristrocracy: military men and their wives. Pashas in fezzes had vanished, the new lords of Egypt wore army uniforms and escorted women who tried to dress like American movie stars. This new class, arrogant and self-important, spoke disparagingly of the old departed aristocracy while they flocked to public auctions where the estates of the exiled nobility were put on sale. The wives of the newly prosperous officers snapped up china and crystal, furniture and gowns once owned by important families; the more renowned and "old" the name, the more desirable the goods. Ibrahim sometimes wondered what would have happened to the Rasheed estate if he had stayed in prison, or had been executed, or if they had left Egypt, as friends had advised. Would his mother's jewelry, which had been in the family for two hundred years, adorn one of these high-heeled women? Would Nefissa's fur coats embrace the shoulders of a woman whose father was a cheese-maker?

For the sake of his mother and sister, Ibrahim thanked God he had insisted they stay, because, once the uncertainty and fear of the revolutionary years had passed, the Rasheeds had entered a new prosperity. Despite the government sequestration of large farm holdings, restricting each family to a mere two hundred acres, Ibrahim and others of his class had gotten around the law on a technicality: the two hundred acres were *per family member*. Because of the size of the Rasheed clan, Ibrahim's vast cotton holdings had barely been touched. And so Amira and the other women in his house still had their servants and jewelry and automobiles. And for this, at least, Ibrahim was thankful.

"Dr. Rasheed?"

He looked at the woman's reflection in the glass. She was still lying on the bed, smiling invitingly. But he was finished with her. He would pay her and never see her again. Next week, it would be a new prostitute.

"You have to go now," he said. "I have a patient coming."

He watched her in the window as she dressed, slipping her voluptuous body into a tight skirt and sweater, touching up her bouffant hairdo and heavy eyeliner in the dresser mirror. He hadn't lied. He did have a patient coming. He had scheduled the appointment for this hour on purpose, so he could get rid of the woman without lying. Besides, it was not unusual that he should be seeing a patient at this time of the evening; Dr. Rasheed's practice was now so busy that he scheduled patients at all hours.

In the two years following his release from prison, Ibrahim had lived quietly, almost reclusively. He hadn't gone out, had not contacted his old friends, but instead had pored over medical books until his old education came back to him, the profession he had allowed to atrophy while he had attended King Farouk. When he was ready, he had taken this small suite, which consisted of a tiny waiting room, an examining room, his office, and an adjoining private apartment where he could retire between appointments. For a time, he had enjoyed a slow, low-key practice. But then his life had taken an ironic and unexpected turn: he had become fashionable.

He stared at the flashing lights of the Roxy Cinema across the way, and saw the woman reflected in the glass, moving around the room behind him, picking up the money he had left on the dresser, counting it, slipping it into her sweater. With a final glance at Ibrahim, she was gone and he was alone again.

When he had come timidly out into the world and quietly opened his medical practice not far from Liberation Square, Ibrahim had kept his past a secret; no one was to know about his former alliance with royalty. But word had somehow leaked out, and soon it was known all over Cairo that King Farouk's personal physician was now in private practice. Rather than hurting his reputation, as he had thought it would, his past made him a celebrity. The same officers' wives who were buying up the estates of exiled aristocracy flocked to the king's former physician with their ailments. Dr. Ibrahim Rasheed was in great demand.

Not that he was a particularly skilled practitioner, or had developed any love for medicine. Ibrahim was just as indifferent to his profession as he had been back in medical school, when he had pursued the career because it had been his father's. He had returned to medicine because it gave direction to his life.

A crowd suddenly surged from the movie theater and when Ibrahim saw the four young Rasheeds, he remembered that it was Thursday night. As he watched them making their way through the crowd, laughing and talking, Ibrahim remembered being young once, long ago, before prison and King Farouk. He had been young and happy and optimistic. Just as these were: Nefissa's beautiful children, the conceited Omar and tender Tahia, and his own sweet daughter, Camelia. Even her way of walking was more fluid and artful than anyone else's. He searched the crowd for Yasmina, and then remembered that Thursday was when she did volunteer work at the Red Crescent.

Ibrahim saw Zachariah, but his eyes didn't linger for long upon the boy who now caused him such pain. Zachariah, the bastard son of a fellaha, whom Ibrahim had had the arrogance to call his own. Was Amira right, had he mocked God? Not a day went by in which Ibrahim did not wish he could turn back the clock and relive that fateful night.

He left the window and stubbed out his cigarette. It was time to get ready for Mrs. Sayeed and her gallstones.

=

Yasmina came breathlessly into the grand salon, where the family was gathering for Um Khalsoum's monthly concert on the radio. "Sorry I'm late!" she said, pulling off her scarf and shaking out her blond hair. She kissed Amira first, and then her mother, who asked, "Are you hungry, darling? You missed dinner."

"We stopped for kebab," Yasmina said, as she took a seat on the divan between Camelia and Tahia.

Thursday evening was the one occasion in the week when both sexes got together, the men and boys on one side of the salon, the women and girls on the other. The nineteen members of the Rasheed family were settling around the radio, with snacks and glasses of tea. While waiting for the concert to begin, Amira worked on the family photo albums, which no longer had blank spaces where the disgraced daughter, Fatima, had once been displayed. Amira had gradually filled these with pictures of other family members, and as she pasted a photograph in the last blank space that her daughter had once occupied, Amira thought: Fatima is thirty-eight now.

"Mishmish," Zachariah called from across the room. "We saw the new Dahiba film this afternoon!"

Omar gave Yasmina an insolent look. "Where have you been?"

"At the Red Crescent. You know that."

"Who walked home with you?"

Yasmina didn't mind when Omar interrogated her this way; it was his right as a male blood relative to do so, and she was obligated to answer. "Mona and Aziza. They walked me to the gate." Omar needn't have worried; Yasmina would never think of going down a street alone, because boys felt free to hurl insults and pebbles at girls who walked alone. She wondered if it was true what Umma had said about that sort of thing never happening in the days of the veil.

"Oh, Mishmish!" Camelia said. "You should have seen Dahiba dance!" And she stood up, placed her hands behind her head, and did a slow hip roll. Omar's eyes nearly popped out of his head.

"Why *are* you late, darling?" Alice said.

"We went to a hospital!" Yasmina was excited. She was graduating from high school in June and then in September she would start University—not Cairo University, where Omar went and where Zachariah was soon to attend. Yasmina was going to go where Camelia was currently enrolled, at the prestigious American University, which, although co-ed, was small and private and had a better guarantee of a girl's safety. And she knew exactly what she was going to study—science.

When Ibrahim came into the salon, the family greeted him respectfully. He kissed his mother first, then Alice. Camelia was disappointed to see that Hassan al-Sabir was not with him. Ibrahim occasionally invited his friend to listen to Um Khalsoum's monthly concert at the Rasheed house. But because Umma always seemed uncomfortable when Hassan came over, his visits were infrequent. Still, Camelia was hopeful. The crush she had had on her father's friend when she was little had blossomed into an adolescent love.

"We went to the hospital today," Yasmina said to her father as she moved closer to him.

"Did you?" he said, giving her a special smile.

"We visited the children's ward, and when they asked for a volunteer for the demonstration, I raised my hand!"

"There's my clever girl. Just like I've taught you. It doesn't do to be shy if you want an education. Maybe someday you'll come to work with me in my office. Would you like that?"

"Oh, more than anything! Where can I start?"

He laughed. "When you're done with school! I'll teach you how to be a good nurse. Ah, the concert is starting."

Um Khalsoum was such a popular singer that the Arab world came to a halt every fourth Thursday of the month, as television sets and radios from Morocco to Iran were tuned in to her concert, a phenomenon President Nasser took advantage of by frequently scheduling speeches in the minutes before her show. When he came on, Amira set aside the photo album. She liked Egypt's charismatic president. She had voted for him six years ago, not because she knew anything about him, but because it was the first time women had been granted the vote in Egypt, and Amira had gone proudly to the polls. She liked him not so much for his politics, which she had little interest in, but because he was an Egyptian and a modest man. The son of a postal clerk, Gamal Nasser ate beans for breakfast like everyone else, and he prayed every Friday at the mosque.

Tonight, however, the president startled the world with what would be a historical speech: Nasser addressed the controversial issue of family planning.

Due to the socialist government's improved health-care programs, he explained, infant mortality was down, fewer people were dying of cholera and smallpox, the death rate was down. However, the result was an alarming population explosion. The population had grown, Nasser reported gravely, from 21 million in 1956 to 26 million in 1962. If this kept up, he said, Egypt would sink under the weight of her own people. The time had come for conscientious birth control, a measure, he assured his audience, that would ultimately improve the condition of the family, the most important institution in the Middle East.

Amira looked around the room at her family, her pride. She said a mental prayer of thanks to God for her good fortune; Amira was fifty-eight, in excellent health, and could expect soon to become a great-grandmother.

As Ibrahim listened to the president's speech, he thought again about his "son" and was ashamed. Zachariah was a nice boy, very popular, but Ibrahim couldn't help being uncomfortable around him. The more Nasser spoke of contraception, the more Ibrahim felt his frustration rise. All this talk about preventing babies from being born. And when Nasser went on to explain that, in order to spare the mother—even if it was just anxiety over another pregnancy—birth control was permitted by Islam, even going so far as to quote from the Koran: "It is written, 'God desires ease for you. He does not desire hardship for you, and has not laid upon you any hardship in religion,' " Ibrahim thought, What about the rights of a man who has no son?

He glanced over at Alice. He watched her slender white hands, and marveled at how remarkably soft and unblemished they were, considering he couldn't recall a day in the past nine-and-a-half years when she had not worked in her garden. As he saw how gracefully she turned the pages of her seed catalog, he imagined them caressing him, and he was startled to feel a stab of desire. He had not been able to sleep with his wife since his release from prison.

And then it came to him: he was forty-five and in his prime, and Alice was only thirty-seven; they might yet have another child. He wondered why he hadn't thought of it before: he could still father a son! The more he considered this, the more his mood brightened, and he almost smiled at the irony of the moment, that Nasser's plea to curtail the birthrate had given Ibrahim the idea of increasing it.

As Tahia listened to the president's speech, she was thinking that Gamal Nasser was romantically handsome; she liked the idea that his wife's name was also Tahia. Yasmina was thinking that birth control should be free and available to all women. But they weren't all listening to the president. Zachariah was composing another poem for Tahia, and Camelia was deciding that she was going to have to find a way to meet the great Dahiba. And Omar's frustration mounted. So many babies being born and no one could accuse Omar Rasheed of being responsible! He looked hungrily at Camelia, who had kicked off her shoes and whose red-lacquered toenails showed through her stockings. There was no longer any doubt. One way or another, he was going to have her.

CHAPTER 16

Nefissa guessed that the handsome young waiter was around twenty, the same age as her son, so he *couldn't* be flirting with her, surely it was her imagination. And yet when he brought tea, serving it with a little more flourish than necessary, she saw the same flash in his dark eyes that she had noticed earlier, and now she was nonplussed.

Nefissa watched him walk away as she absently stirred sugar into the tea. It was a perfect June day, not yet summer-hot but laced with a kind of languid balminess, a day for sitting on the terrace of the Club Cage d'Or and marking the time as it passed as slowly as the river.

She had spent the day shopping in the few stylish dress salons left in Cairo. The new patriotic push to buy Egyptian-made goods meant that fewer good-quality items were available, and the excursion had taken hours; worse, she had had to travel by taxi because the Rasheeds had let their chauffeur go, such ostentation being frowned upon in this new socialist society.

Even the place where she was having tea had changed. The Cage d'Or used to be a very exclusive club, restricted to the aristocracy and, of course, the royal family. As she watched the wives of fishermen on the opposite bank stoking charcoal fires and gutting fish, Nefissa recalled the days when she had come here as part of Princess Faiza's entourage. Her husband had been alive then, Omar just a baby. They had been young and rich and beautiful, and they had gambled the nights away at the Cage d'Or's roulette tables. Now the club was a tearoom during the day and a dance spot at night, open to anyone who could afford it, mainly, from what Nefissa saw, military men and their wives. No one from her own class came here any more.

She sipped her tea and sighed. Those wonderful old days of class and privilege were long gone. Nasser had opened everything up to the public—the royal gardens had been turned into public parks and Farouk's palaces were museums. Ordinary people could now peer into the private chambers where Nefissa had once kept Princess Faiza company. The princess herself was gone, as were most of the old crowd, who had departed for Europe or America in hopes of better prospects. The number of Nefissa's friends had dwindled; she didn't even have Alice any more. The bond she had shared in the early years with her sister-in-law had been severed the night of Edward's suicide.

"Would Madam care for anything else?"

The waiter startled her. She hadn't seen him coming. She squinted up; the sun was behind him, creating a halo. He seemed to be standing too close to the table, his smile was too familiar. She had watched him wait on customers at the other tables, curt and businesslike. What interest could he possibly have in her?

"No, thank you," she said, realizing she had hesitated a little too long. She reached into her purse and brought out a gold cigarette case with her initials engraved in the corner, a tiny diamond at the foot of the "R." Before she could find her lighter, the waiter was holding out a lighted match, and as she lit her cigarette, she found herself wondering what it would be like to be made love to by such a beautiful young man.

And she was reminded again of her loneliness.

Now that Omar and Tahia were almost adults, they rarely had need of her, being busy with their own friends, interests, and chasing after the future. Nefissa filled her days with shopping, visits to the hairdresser, gossiping on the phone. She spent endless hours at her vanity table, trying new cosmetics, testing perfumes, manicuring her nails, and pampering her skin, pursuing beauty as if it were a holy cause. She told herself that all this—the careful makeup, the weight watching, the meticulous wardrobe—was because she took pride in her appearance. But she knew what truly drove her. She wanted to be in love again.

She had turned down the many marriage prospects her mother had arranged for her, some of whom had been rich and quite attractive, because she had wanted something she had once had long ago with her English lieutenant—true romance. But romance had not come, and the years had slipped away without her realizing it, until she finally woke up one morning and realized she was thirty-seven, the mother of two teenagers. What man would want her?

"Dahiba is going to be dancing here," the young waiter said with a knowing smile. "Starting tomorrow night."

Nefissa wished he would go away. His very presence, his smile full of innuendo, seemed to mock her. "Who is Dahiba?"

He rolled his eyes. *"Bismillah!* Our most beloved dancer! You can't go out much in the evenings, madam. I'm surprised," he said, adding quietly, "a rich lady like you."

So that was it—he wasn't interested in her, but in her money. She was both repulsed by him, and yet, to her secret shame, attracted to him. She was galled to find herself wondering if he thought she was beautiful—*hoping* he did.

"I work in the evenings as well," he continued, "tonight, as a matter of fact. I work until three in the morning, and then I walk home to my flat, which is not far from here."

She stared at him, wondering why she tolerated his insolence. To be so blatantly offering himself to her for money was insulting. When their eyes met and held for three heartbeats, Nefissa suddenly turned away and reached for her purse. She had to remember who she was, that she had once been close friends with royalty; Rasheed women did not pay for love.

=

Omar had been biding his time ever since the night of President Nasser's speech four weeks ago, when he had decided he was going to have Camelia one way or another. It wasn't easy; either she was always with someone or he was, and so many people lived in the house that it was impossible to arrange for a chance encounter alone. Omar didn't require much time; he knew he could be quick. If he could just catch her on the stairs, or behind the bushes in the garden . . . And he wasn't worried about the struggle she might put up. Although ten years of ballet had clearly made her strong—she possessed a dancer's lithe, muscular build—Omar knew he was stronger. And besides, once he got started she might just give in.

As he watched Grandmother Amira, wrapped in a black melaya, walk away down Virgins of Paradise Street, he knew this was an opportunity that could not be missed. Even though Umma went out a bit these days, ever since the time of Uncle Ibrahim's imprisonment, she did not go out with great frequency. She never went shopping or to restaurants or to the cinema, as his aunts and female cousins did; Umma visited the mosques of Saints Hussein and Zeinab on their holy days, and once a year she went to the cemetery to pray at the grave of Grandfather Ali. Today was the day for her annual visit to the bridge that connected Gezira Island to the city; no one knew why Umma made this small pilgrimage all alone, going to throw a flower in the river, but Omar could count on at least half an hour of freedom from her ever-watchful eye. Fifteen minutes was all he needed.

Now he had to pray that Camelia would come back from her ballet lesson at her usual time, and not stop somewhere with friends.

There she was, coming through the garden gate!

Omar had it all worked out: he would lure her behind the gazebo, pin her down and cover her mouth. If she later accused him, he would deny it. Everyone would believe him rather than her, because a woman's testimony carried one half the weight of a man's, it was so written in the Koran.

"Ya! Camelia!" he called as she came down the path. "Come here! I have something to show you!"

"What is it?"

"You have to come and see."

She gave him a dubious look and then, curious, put her books down and followed him around to the back of the gazebo, where the hibiscus was blooming. "What is it?" she asked again.

He grabbed her and pulled her to the ground, throwing himself on top of her. *"Y'Allah!"* she cried. "Get off me, you oaf!"

He tried to cover her mouth but she bit his hand. And when he reached down to undo his pants, she gave him a great shove that sent him sprawling.

As she started to get up, frowning at the grass stains on her blouse, Omar was on her again, trying to push her skirt up. She hit him on the breastbone and he howled in pain, falling on his buttocks. Camelia scowled down at him. "Are you crazy, Omar Rasheed? Has a jinni taken possession of you?"

"By the mercy of God, what is going on here?"

They turned to see Amira coming around the gazebo, the black melaya billowing around her shoulders, a furious look on her face. "Omar! What are you doing?"

He scrambled backward, out of her way. "Umma! I . . . uh . . ."

"Oh, get up, oaf," Camelia said as she brushed off her skirt. Then she reached down and slapped his head. *"Mahalabeya,"* she said. "Rice pudding!" She gathered up her books. "You and I are not betrothed, and we never will be. So don't try that again." And she marched off.

Omar got to his feet and stood sheepishly before his grandmother.

"In all respect and honor to you, Umma, I thought you went to the river," he said.

"I did, but as I got to the end of the street, I realized I had forgotten to take flowers with me."

She didn't say anything more and Omar continued to stand there, staring at the ground. He felt her eyes on him, the power of her disapproval.

Unable to bear the silence any longer, he raised his head. And when he saw her dark, intelligent eyes, a memory suddenly came back: He was eight years old, and Umma had caught him in the garden pulling the wings off a butterfly. He hadn't heard her coming. She had delivered a stunning whack to his head that had sent him reeling. In all his life, that was the only time anyone had ever laid a hand on him.

She continued to glare at him, the June breeze stirring strands of her black hair that had come loose from the bun at the nape of her neck. She was his grandmother, but all the same Omar could see her as others did: beautiful, her strong will evident in the square jaw and piercing eyes.

He swallowed with a dry throat and said, "Forgive me, Umma."

"Forgiveness is God's," she said. "Omar, what you did was wrong."

"But I burn, Umma," he said softly.

"All men burn, Omar. You must learn to control it. You must not touch Camelia again."

"I want to marry her!"

"No."

"Why not? We're cousins. Who else would she marry?"

"There is something you do not know. When your uncle's first wife died, your mother nursed Camelia. But you were also still nursing at her breast. It is written in the Koran that a union between two people who were suckled at the same breast is forbidden. It is incest, Omar."

He stared at her in dismay. "I didn't know that! Camelia is my sister, then!"

"And you cannot marry her."

Tears rose in his eyes. *"Bismillah!* Then what will I do?"

She laid a hand on his shoulder and said with a gentle smile, "It is not for you to decide, Omar. Your fate is already written in God's book. Say a prayer to the Eternal One. Trust in His time."

Omar recited the prayer, but as soon as Amira left the garden, he kicked furiously at a clump of lilies until he had uprooted and destroyed them. Then he rushed into the house, straight to his mother's apartment, and barged in without knocking.

"I want to get married," he said. "Right away."

Nefissa looked up from her dressing table, startled. "Who is the girl, darling?"

"No girl. Any girl. Find me a wife!"

"What about your studies? What about the university?"

"I want to get married. I didn't say anything about giving up school. I can be a student and a husband at the same time."

"Can't it wait until you receive your degree?"

"I have three years to go, Mother! I will perish before then!"

She sighed. The impatience of a twenty-year-old. Had she been like that? "All right, my darling," she said, coming up to him and running her fingers through his thick black hair. The image of the waiter at the Cage d'Or sprang into her mind. And suddenly she was alarmed to think that her own precious son might, out of desperation, as turn to an older, rich woman. "I will go and talk to Ibrahim."

=

As Hassan followed the servant up the stairs to the men's wing, he whistled, he felt so good. The visit he was paying on Ibrahim today had been a long time in the planning; there had been moments when he had thought he couldn't wait, and he had had to remind himself to proceed with caution. Ibrahim wasn't the same old friend he had once been; six months in prison had changed him. Hassan could no longer predict what Ibrahim's reaction would be to anything. In the old days, Ibrahim had been as simple to read as a child's picture book, but now, with his spells of depression, his periods of melancholy when he wouldn't see anyone, and his new, strangely quiet temperament, Ibrahim required delicate handling. And what Hassan was coming to see him about today was delicate in the extreme.

What on earth had happened to his friend in prison? Hassan wondered as he ascended the big staircase. Ibrahim refused to speak of it; in the nine-and-a-half years since his release, not one word had been offered. Hassan often wondered how Ibrahim had been able to get out of prison, when all the efforts of the Rasheeds and himself had met with complete failure. Every channel had been blocked, and then suddenly,

Ibrahim had been set free, and Ibrahim himself claimed not to know why.

The servant knocked and then opened the door, and Hassan was delivered into the familiar comfort of Ibrahim's apartment. They greeted each other warmly, and Hassan accepted his friend's offer of coffee. He would have preferred whiskey, but when Edward died, the whiskey had gone, too.

Poor old Eddie, Hassan thought, as he made himself comfortable on a divan. Had his death truly been accidental? How did a man shoot himself precisely between the eyes while cleaning his gun? But the police report had ruled his death as accidental, and Amira, who had found Edward, insisted that it was so. Still, Hassan didn't trust her. He suspected that that woman would cover up anything to protect the family honor.

"It's good to see you," Ibrahim said, and in such an almost cheerful way that Hassan decided luck was with him today. Surely Ibrahim was going to say yes to his proposal.

They lit cigarettes, an English brand, Hassan noted with appreciation. "It's good to see you, too, my brother. May God bless you with health and long life." Hassan the English gentleman was gone, no more "old fellow" and "I say." Now he spoke only Arabic, and used traditional phrases. They talked for a few minutes about cotton prices and the progress of the Aswan Dam, then Hassan said, "May I be permitted to state my purpose, dear friend? I have come on a special errand tonight. This is a day of days for us, Ibrahim. I have come to ask for your daughter's hand in marriage."

Ibrahim gave him a startled look, then said, "You've caught me by surprise. I had no idea you had this in mind."

"I've been divorced now for nearly three years. A man needs a wife, as you yourself have often told me. And as my high position in the government calls for me to attend many state functions, even to host a few myself, a wife is necessary. I waited, of course, until her birthday, which was just a few weeks ago. Otherwise, she would have been too young."

Ibrahim looked up. "Hm? Oh yes, too young. I don't know. You're forty-five, Hassan."

"As young as you, my friend!" Which was true only so far as chronological age. Although Hassan had maintained a youthful vigor and passed for a much younger man, Ibrahim had aged. His hair had turned gray in prison, and his once-vigorous frame had never recovered its earlier robustness. "I suppose we can at least discuss the matter," Ibrahim said. "We had talked of Camelia joining the ballet company, but I never—"

"Camelia! I am talking about Yasmina!"

Ibrahim stared at him. "Yasmina! But she's only just sixteen!"

"Of course we'll wait until she's eighteen for the wedding, but I see no reason why you and I can't agree to the betrothal now."

Ibrahim frowned. "Yasmina? No, I couldn't agree to it."

Hassan held himself back. He could not allow his impatience to ruin everything. He must have her! Yasmina—as beautiful as a moonbeam.

"She wants to go to university," Ibrahim said.

"All girls do now. These modern times make them forget what they were created for. But as soon as they're pregnant they give up ideas about education."

"But why Yasmina?"

Hassan paused. He couldn't very well say, "I've always wanted Alice, but I'll take her daughter instead." So he shrugged and said, "Why not Yasmina? She's young and beautiful. She's poised and graceful and well mannered. And obedient, all the virtues a man looks for in a wife." Silently he added: Besides, I'm not marrying to get sons, I have four already. This time around I'm getting married to have fun in bed. And the sexual education of pretty little Yasmina should be delightful indeed.

As Ibrahim began to think about it, he realized that he found Hassan's unexpected proposal almost welcome. Yasmina would eventually have to marry, and Ibrahim knew that there were few men he would approve of—what man could be better worthy of his favorite daughter but Hassan, with whom he had been friends since their college days?

"This is no hasty decision on my part," Hassan said carefully. "I have thought highly of her for some time, you know. And you and I are like brothers, my friend. How many years have we been together? I've always felt like a member of this family. Remember when you and Nefissa and I took that felucca on the river and capsized it?"

Ibrahim laughed, a rare sound.

Hassan pressed on. "Why not make my membership in this family official? It should comfort you to know that she will not be marrying a stranger, we know each other very well, I think. And I believe she bears some affection for me. And you know she will continue to live in the style she has known all her life. I am a rich man, after all."

Ibrahim remained silent.

"Besides, a man in my position must be careful in choosing a wife. She must be presentable and know now to carry herself on occasions involving the highest officials of state. She must be—I will utter the forbidden word—an aristocrat. And so my field of choice is limited, as you know."

"Yes," Ibrahim said thoughtfully. "It is agreed then. Let us have the document drawn up—"

"I just happen to have brought it with me." As he watched Ibrahim bring out a fountain pen, Hassan added, "I shall be your son-in-law, isn't that amusing?"

═

Nefissa had been about to knock on her brother's door when she had heard her name mentioned. She recognized Hassan's voice; he was talking about the time the three of them had capsized a felucca. Nefissa had only been married a year at the time, she hadn't thought Hassan would even remember the incident. And now, after hearing the rest of the conversation, she felt her heart begin to race. She couldn't believe it. Hassan was asking her brother's permission to marry her!

She had heard various phrases: "We know each other very well—she bears some affection for me—she must be aristocratic—know how to carry herself on occasions involving the highest officials of state." So the old days of class and privilege *weren't* gone, Nefissa realized with sudden happiness. The classes were still there, only the titles had changed. Everyone knew Hassan was moving up in the government; talk of a judgeship in the High Court was rumored. He would require a wife equal to such status—an aristocrat, a woman who had once been close friends with royalty.

Feeling like a young girl again, she hurried back to her apartment and quickly combed her hair, put on some lipstick and a quick spray of jasmine perfume. She hurried down to the garden, and when she saw Hassan emerge, she stepped in his path.

"I couldn't help overhearing," she said. "I hope you don't mind that I listened at the door?"

He gave her a baffled look.

"The marriage proposal!" she said, laughing. "You didn't have to go to Ibrahim. I make my own decisions these days." She put her arms around his neck. "Oh, Hassan, I have desired you for such a long time. I shall be a good wife to you, I promise."

"You?" he said. And then he laughed. "We weren't talking about you! We were talking about Yasmina!" He pulled her arms from his neck. "There was a time when I might have considered you, Nefissa, back when you were young and attractive. But why should I want a woman who's all used up when I can have the choicest young virgin in Cairo?"

She stared at him in horror. "Hassan! You can't mean that."

As she watched him leave, Nefissa thought back to the one beautiful night in her life when she had been truly loved. Her handsome lieutenant, who had disappeared; she wanted him back. Someone *had* to love her as she had once been loved.

CHAPTER 17

The dreams had begun again, in more detail and more powerful than ever, disturbing Amira's sleep with the familiar images—the desert encampment, the peculiar square tower—but now with a baffling new one: a tall, ebony-skinned man in a scarlet turban. Who was he, and why was he only now entering her dreams? Did he belong in the house on Tree of Pearls Street, or had he been part of the home she could not recall, back before she was kidnapped from the caravan?

Even more perplexing, Amira thought as she tried to solve the riddle of the dreams, was why she had started having them again. No babies were about to be born into the family just now. What were the dreams trying to tell her?

"What is impotence, Umma?" Yasmina asked.

They were in the kitchen, putting cups and saucers in the sink. Amira had just concluded her weekly afternoon tea, which she now held every Friday while the men were at the mosque. After she led the female members of her family in the noon prayer, she opened her garden gate and friends and visitors came, as they always had. She and her granddaughters were cleaning up, a task which the servants could have done, but which Amira thought beneficial to her granddaughters' domestic training.

Amira had not heard Yasmina's question. As she washed and polished the silver teapot, her mind was trying to work out a solution to an urgent problem: That morning, before leaving for the mosque, Ibrahim had informed Amira of the agreement he and Hassan had arrived at the night before; Hassan al-Sabir was now engaged to marry Yasmina. Amira had said nothing to her son, but had felt a terrible forboding steal over her.

"Umma?" the girl said. "Did you hear me?"

Amira looked at her granddaughter, so pretty and fair, her white-gold curls tamed by two barrettes. And she thought: If it is all I do between now and my dying breath, I shall save this child from the hands of Hassan al-Sabir. "What did you say, Mishmish?"

"I heard Um Hussein asking you for a cure for impotence. What is impotence?"

"It is a condition that renders a man incapable of carrying out his duty as a husband."

Yasmina frowned, uncertain what that duty entailed. She and her fellow classmates at the all-girl high school often whispered about boys and marriage, but as most of their information was conjecture, Yasmina had only a vague notion of what the marriage duty was. "How is it cured?" she asked.

Before Amira could reply, Badawiya, the elderly Lebanese cook, said from her place at the chopping block, "By a younger wife!" And the others in the kitchen laughed.

Amira put an arm around Yasmina and said, "If God wills it, Mishmish, that is something you will never have to worry about."

"Well, I'm not going to get married for years and years!" the sixteen-year-old said. "I'm going to university to study science. I know exactly what I want my future to be."

Amira glanced at Maryam Misrahi, who had helped bring in the left-over pastries. Maryam gave her friend a look that said, The girls these days! And Amira smiled to hide her distress. She had not told Maryam about the horrendous betrothal Ibrahim had agreed to.

Camelia, who was at the kitchen door anxiously watching for Zachariah, said impatiently, "I wish *I* could see into my future!"

Maryam came and stood next to her, looking at the colorful garden. "Do you know how we read the future when I was a girl?" she said. "You took an egg and warmed it between your hands for seven minutes. Then you cracked it open into a glass of water. If the egg floated, it would mean your future husband would be rich. If it sank, he would be poor. If the yolk broke, he would be—"

"I'm not talking about husbands, Auntie Maryam! I want to know if—" She stopped herself. Umma mustn't know what she was up to. Camelia returned to her nervous vigil for Zachariah, who had said he had something important for her.

"Umma," Yasmina said, as she took a raspberry tart from the tray Badawiya had just brought from the oven. She bit into it, finding it deliciously sweet and warm. "Why do women come to you when they're sick and not go to a real doctor like Papa?"

Amira carefully dried the cups and placed them in the cabinet. "They come to me out of modesty."

"But Papa has female patients, too."

"I do not know those women, Mishmish. But the ones who come to me do not wish to expose themselves to a strange man."

"Why aren't there more women doctors then? Shouldn't there be the same number of women doctors as men doctors? Doesn't that make sense?"

"So many questions!" Amira said, glancing again at Maryam.

Maryam envied Amira, with all these young people about, and the promise of more babies soon to come into the house. Maryam's own children had left home long ago and now lived in different parts of the world, even as far away as California. Maryam had seen her grandchildren in person only once, and now her first great-grandchild was on the way. Perhaps it was time to take a long vacation and visit the children. After all, she and Suleiman were in their sixties. How much longer could they put it off, just because Misrahi Imports was losing profits and Suleiman had to work night and day? Wasn't family more important than business? I'll bring it up tonight, she decided, when he comes home for Sabbath.

Sahra was in the kitchen as well, listening to all the talk as she lifted a tray of hot sesame buns out of the oven. She was thirty years old now, and growing plump. And she was no longer a kitchen girl. As Badawiya, who had been with the family since before Ibrahim was born, grew older and less able to do things, Sahra gradually took over, and it was understood that someday, when Badawiya retired, Sahra would be the main cook for the Rasheed family.

She smiled when she heard Camelia sigh, "Oh, where *is* he?" Sahra was devoted to the master's children, just as she was devoted to the master, and over the years she had been able to piece together a kind of story. Because the family's annual visit to the cemetery came fourteen days after her own birthday, Sahra had been able to calculate that the mother for whom Camelia went to pray had died the night Sahra had seen the master weeping beside the canal. That must have been the night, therefore, that Camelia was born. Sahra's heart went out to the poor motherless girl, and to her sister Yasmina as well, because it was the disappointment of her birth that had driven the master to adopt Sahra's son, Zachariah. In a way, Sahra felt like a kind of mother to all three.

"Auntie Maryam," Camelia said as she looked out the window, absently rubbing her shoulder, which was bruised from Omar's boorishness. "Have you been to see that film yet, the one starring Dahiba?"

"Your Uncle Suleiman is too busy to go to movies."

"Oh, but you should go! You have never seen anyone dance like Dahiba! Maybe you and grandmother could go together."

But Amira, who had overheard, laughed and said, "Where do I have time to go to the movies!" Then she said to Yasmina, "Mrs. Abdel Rahman telephoned this morning to ask if I would take my special hyssop tea to her sister on Fahmy Pasha Street. The children are down with summer fever. Will you come with me, Mishmish?"

"I'd love to, Umma. I'll get us a taxi."

Just then Zachariah came into the kitchen. When he kissed his grandmother, she asked, "Is your father home from the mosque?"

"His car is just pulling in," he said, retrieving a pickle from a jar and crunching it.

One of the kitchen girls was preparing the small birds known as *assafeer,* plucking them, cutting off their beaks and legs, and tucking their heads into their bodies. As she rubbed them with seasoning and threaded them onto skewers, Zachariah turned away, a look of revulsion on his face. Sahra thought how like his father Abdu he was, possessing a boundless compassion for all living creatures.

He was like Abdu in other ways as well, Sahra decided, in his love for making up poems, his love of God and the Koran, and physically, too. Zachariah had the same wide shoulders and green eyes, the same gentle smile, that it was almost like being with her beloved Abdu again. She wondered if he had any memories of the first three years of his life, when she had breast-fed him.

When Amira finally left the kitchen, Camelia rushed up to her brother. "Did you get it for me, Zakki? Did you get it?"

The day after they had gone to the movies, a month ago, Camelia had come to him and said, "Oh Zakki, I simply *must* find out where Dahiba lives! I *must* meet her. I want to study with her. Look, I've memorized her dance routine, the one she performs in the movie. I just know that when she sees me do it, she'll take me on as a protégée. But I have to find out where she lives! Please find out for me."

Now he grinned and produced a piece of paper. "This cost me fifty piastres," he said. "I had to bribe someone at the Cage d'Or, where she dances."

"It's her address!" Camelia cried.

"I walked by her place, Lili," he said excitedly. "She lives in a penthouse apartment, and she has body guards and a Chevrolet! I saw her come out of the building. By God, Egypt still has a queen!"

"I shall faint!" Camelia cried. Then she kissed him and said, "I shall adore you for the rest of my life, Zakki! Thank you, thank you!"

"What are you going to do?" he called after her. But she had already gone.

═

"Where are we, Grandmother?" Yasmina asked, looking out of the taxi. They were in a section of Cairo she had never visited before, on a street called Tree of Pearls.

Amira did not reply immediately. She and Yasmina had paid a visit to Mrs. Abdel Rahman's sister and her sick children, but when they left, instead of telling their driver to take them back to Virgins of Paradise Street, Amira had asked him to bring them here. And now they were in front of the very place where Amira had first met Ali Rasheed, forty-six years ago.

Amira believed that the house had been torn down, but this was only partly true. The main building still stood—a large stone residence not unlike her own house on Virgins of Paradise Street—but the grounds and gardens had been divided, and shops and apartments now abutted the nineteenth-century mansion. Girls in uniforms hurried up the front steps with book bags and lunch boxes. The house was now a school.

This house, Amira marveled, as she studied the ornate façade as if expecting powerful memories to spring from it, this house where I had once been imprisoned in a harem is now a place where girls become educated and are free. She closed her eyes and tried to travel back over the years, tried to make her thoughts go on a journey into the past, to travel and explore the marble corridors, to see if she could find herself there, remember anything more about a terrified seven-year-old among strangers. Could she envision her mother there also? Or where? In a desert?

Why can't I remember being brought here? Why do I only remember the day I left this place?

Try as she did, Amira could not bring back the memories. But although the past remained elusive, one thing did come to her—a sudden understanding. I was brought here, but not with my mother; that was when I was taken from my mother; there's something . . . She was trying to protect me, I was grabbed away and watched over by a tall black man wearing a scarlet turban.

Looking at Yasmina, Amira thought: This is what my dreams were saying, this is why I came here today. But why now? Am I being warned about something? Is Yasmina to be taken away from me to go and live with a man who is not of our family?

"What is it, Grandmother?" Yasmina said. "Why are we here?"

Amira wanted to say, Do not fear, granddaughter of my heart, I will not let any harm come to you, I will not lose you. Instead she said, trying to sound reassuring, "Someday, when I understand it all myself, I will tell you. But now let's go home. I must speak with your father."

=

Ibrahim stood at the window in his private sitting room, watching Alice in the garden. As he saw how lovingly those slender white hands divided bulbs and roots, scattered seeds, and patted down the moist earth, he experienced a yearning that was like a physical pain. The garden that had become the focus of her life had started out ten years ago as a small patch; now it took up nearly the entire east side of the house, a riot of bright-blue morning glories, pinkish-purple fuchsias, and flame-red roses, flowers that would not normally flourish in Egypt's harsh, dry heat. Alice's constant loving care and vigilance had created a miracle.

How he prayed that she would show him as much care and devotion.

What had happened to their marriage? They hadn't even really spoken to each other in a long time, beyond the daily amenities, the clichés of life. How could he put things right between them again, take them back to the way they were before the Revolution, before his life had started to disintegrate?

For a long time after his release from prison Ibrahim had had no interest in sex, with Alice or anyone else. But as the months had passed and his physical wounds had healed, Ibrahim had hoped that Alice would return to being a loving wife. But she had not come to his bed; if he insisted, there was no mutual lovemaking, just the pantomime of a desperate man trying to find his way back to sanity in the arms of an indifferent woman. It was then that he had turned to the embraces of prostitutes. Their artful pretend-love gave him momentary peace. But it was only momentary; he wanted his wife. And he wanted a son.

He heard a discreet knock on his door and was surprised to see his mother there; she rarely visited this side of the house. "May we speak, my son? There are urgent family matters that require your attention. Omar has become a problem. He cannot control his sexual urges. I caught him yesterday assaulting Camelia."

"Assaulting Camelia?"

"No harm was done, but he cannot be trusted. He needs to be married. I have an idea." She sat down on a luxurious divan, purposely placing herself beneath a stern portrait of Ibrahim's father, Ali. "Let us betroth Omar to Yasmina. And let the wedding take place soon, after she graduates from high school."

"But I told you this morning, Mother. Yasmina is betrothed to Hassan."

"The girl is too young for Hassan. Would he allow her to continue her schooling? But Omar still has three years of studying left. He and Yasmina can be students together. That is much better for Yasmina than marrying a man thirty years her senior."

"In all honor and respect to you, Mother, you married a man who was forty years older than you."

"Ibrahim, this wedding between Hassan and Yasmina must not take place."

"Hassan and I have already signed the agreement. I have given my word."

"You should have consulted with me first. And what about Alice? Has a mother no say in the choosing of her daughter's husband? It is up to *us* to find a man for Yasmina, *you* have only to sign the marriage contract."

"But what are your objections to Hassan? I've never understood why you don't like him."

"The marriage simply cannot take place."

"I will not break my word to my friend." He returned to the window, to looking out at Alice. Amira came and stood next to him. After a moment she said, "There are problems between you and your wife."

"It is nothing that a son should discuss with his mother."

"But perhaps I can help."

He turned haunted eyes to her, and she remembered what Zachariah had told her: "Father wakes up at night screaming. I can hear him, all the way down the hall." Ibrahim was silent for a moment, then looked at his hands. "I don't know what the problem is between Alice and me, Mother. But it is there, and I want a son."

"Then listen to me. I can give you a potion to put in a drink for Alice."

He gave her a dubious look. "A potion?"

I saw it used once, long ago, in the harem on Tree of Pearls Street. "Believe me when I say that this potion works. Alice will comply, and if God wills it, she will bear you a son."

He turned from the window. "No potions, Mother." "That is not the answer I am seeking. And now I am weary. I want to rest for a while."

"We need to settle the issue of Yasmina's betrothal."

"By the Prophet, may God increase His blessings upon him, it is already settled!"

But she said quietly, "It is not. What I am about to tell you, son of my heart, causes me great pain. I have kept it a secret for all these years, to spare you further suffering, but God guides my conscience now." She drew a deep breath. "Son of my heart, whom I love more than my own life, I tell you that you have no covenant with Hassan al-Sabir. He is not your friend or brother."

"What are you saying?"

Her heart raced. Once uttered, it could never be taken back. "It was Hassan who got you arrested and thrown into prison."

He stared at her. "I don't believe you."

"By God's mercy, it is true."

"It cannot be."

"I swear by the oneness of God, Ibrahim."

"How do you know this? Someone has lied to you!"

She thought of her promise to Safeya Rageb, to keep her intercession for Ibrahim a secret. "I know it, that is all. It is part of your official file: Hassan al-Sabir named you as a conspirator against the Egyptian people. You can look it up yourself if you wish."

"I'll do better than that. I will ask Hassan."

===

Yasmina and Tahia tried to keep from giggling as they huddled behind empty crates bearing labels that read CHIVAS REGAL and JOHNNIE WALKER. They were hiding outside the service entrance to the Club Cage d'Or, waiting for Zachariah to give them the signal. He had gone inside to arrange everything, and now Camelia, shivering beneath her coat despite the warm June night, thought he was taking too long. Something must have gone wrong.

She had tried to see the great Dahiba at her apartment, but had failed. When the doorman wouldn't let her into the building, Camelia had had to bribe him. And then the elevator boy wouldn't take her up to the penthouse; more baksheesh. The two bodyguards playing cards outside Dahiba's door had also demanded payment, so that by the time Camelia knocked on the door and was confronted by a butler, she didn't have any money left. It wouldn't have helped anyway; the butler fetched Dahiba's secretary, who came out and informed Camelia that Madam did not receive visitors, she did not audition amateurs, and she certainly did not take pupils. And so Zachariah had come up with a plan. He told Amira that he was going to take the girls to see a variety show, and when Umma and the others were in the salon listening to a program on the radio, the teenagers had left the house and headed for the nightclub where Dahiba was dancing.

"Poor Zakki," Tahia said, watching the open doorway that led to the club's kitchen. "He hates lying to Umma."

"He didn't lie," Yasmina reminded her. "Zakki just said he was bringing us to a show, and he did, didn't he? Here he comes!"

Zachariah came around behind the crates and whispered, "It's all set, Lili! There's a woman inside the door, she's the ladies' room attendant. She'll take you through the kitchen to a place at the back of the stage where you won't be seen. By God, did I have to pay her plenty!"

They kissed her and wished her luck, and Camelia hurried inside, trying not to let any of her costume show beneath her coat.

When the attendant deposited Camelia behind the curtain, warning her not to move because Zachariah had told her that his sister just wanted to watch, Camelia peeked out at the audience and felt her heart race. The nightclub was packed with women in expensive dresses and men in uniforms festooned with medals. She froze when she saw a short, chubby man at one of the front tables. He was Hakim Raouf, the famous movie director, and Dahiba's husband.

The band started setting up, and then the lights dimmed around the club and spotlights widened on the empty stage. The music played for a few minutes, allowing the audience to settle into the mood, and then, to a roar of cheering and applause, Dahiba came out. Camelia gasped. She was even more electrifying in person than in the movies. She opened her number dramatically, enveloped in a blue chiffon veil sparkling with rhinestones, executing bold moves around the stage that were a combination of ballet and modern dance. After a few minutes she dropped her veil to reveal a dazzling costume of turquoise satin and silver lamé, with a wide hip belt strung with long silver fringe. She stopped, held up a hand and began slowly to undulate her hips. The audience roared again—this was Dahiba's signature entrance.

From this proximity, and in person, Camelia realized that Dahiba wasn't really beautiful; she wasn't even very pretty. But she had presence, and as Camelia watched how the dance made the audience hers, how she manipulated them, made them clap, or laugh, or grow somber, she realized that Dahiba wasn't just entertaining the audience, she was making them *feel*.

Camelia held her breath as she watched for her own opportunity. Finally, Dahiba moved to the edge of the stage, as she always did, to engage in interaction with her audience. When the beat picked up for a segment in which Dahiba danced to the beledi rhythm, Camelia threw off her coat, quickly checked her costume of red and gold, and came out onto the stage. At first the audience was confused, and then, when Camelia began to dance, they began to clap. Dahiba turned, saw the girl dancing, and when she saw the questioning looks from her band, signaled them to keep playing.

Although the stage was large, Camelia restricted herself to a small space, choreographing her dance not out of bold, showy gestures, but utilizing intricate, intense torso and hip movements, her arms raised gracefully outward. She didn't look at Dahiba, but kept her eyes and her smile on the audience, who clapped louder and shouted *"Y'Allah!"*

Dahiba signaled to her band: the beat slowed and they stopped playing until only the flute remained, filling the smoky air like a snake charmer's music. Still Camelia didn't miss a step. She altered her movement with the shift of mood, pausing, then beginning a wave in her pelvis that rippled up to her chest and down again.

The audience went wild. When they realized that this was not planned, that the honey-eyed girl had staged a coup, men climbed up on their chairs and shouted, "O sweet angel from God!" They whistled and cheered and blew kisses to the outrageous girl. From her place at the edge of the stage, Dahiba studied the frenzied audience. Her husband, Hakim, also seemed to be delighted.

When the music ended, Camelia blew a kiss to the audience, then ran back behind the curtain, where the club manager immediately grabbed her, threatening to call the police. As he started to usher her away, Dahiba suddenly materialized. "What did you think you were doing out there?" she said.

Camelia could hardly speak. Up close, she saw Dahiba's heavy eye makeup, the fine lines around the eyes and mouth and, more startling, a hardness that was never evident in any of her movies. "Oh, ma'am, I just wanted to audition for you! I've been trying to meet you, but—"

Hakim Raouf appeared then, laughing and mopping his crimson

cheeks. "By the head of Sayyid Hussein, God bless him and upon him salvation. That was some show! Come, come, little girl. We'll have tea!" And he snapped his fingers at the bewildered manager.

They went to Dahiba's office and dressing room, and as she and her husband lit cigarettes, Dahiba asked, "What is your name?"

"Camelia Rasheed, ma'am."

Dahiba's eyes flickered. "Are you related to Dr. Ibrahim Rasheed?"

"He is my father."

"How old are you?"

"Nearly eighteen."

"You have had formal dance training?"

"Ballet."

"And you wish to study with me?"

"Oh yes, more than anything!"

She gave Camelia a long, thoughtful look. "I don't allow others on my stage with me. No dancer does. You should know that, and you could have been arrested for your recklessness. Still, the audience loved you."

"It's a good gimmick," Hakim said, as he loosened the collar around his chubby neck. "Perhaps we should add it, my pumpkin."

Dahiba punched his arm in a playful way. "And perhaps we could add a performing baboon as well. Do you want the part?"

To Camelia she said, "You are too muscular. You have the shoulders of a man, and you have slim hips. You would have to gain weight. A skinny dancer is not very appealing to the eye, she is not sensuous enough. Also, your style is outdated and amateurish. We don't just dance the beledi any more. Oriental dance borrows from all disciplines. But you hold promise. With the right training you might become great." She smiled. "Possibly even as great as myself."

"Oh, thank—"

Dahiba held up a hand. "But before I agree to take you on, I must warn you that your family will not approve. Oriental dancers are looked upon as women with no morals. We are despised because we draw men's attention to female sexuality. We draw them away from thoughts of God and the piety that Islam commands. Men desire us and so they despise us for making them desire us. Do you understand what I am saying? Many men will want you, Camelia, but few will respect you. Even fewer will want to marry you. Can you live with that?"

Camelia glanced at the flushed face of Hakim Raouf and said, "You haven't done so badly, ma'am."

Hakim grabbed her hand, kissed it, and declared, "Blessed be the tree from whose wood your cradle was made! By God, I am in love with this girl!"

As Dahiba laughed, Camelia added, "I want to dance, that's all I know."

"Then I will tell you why I will take you as a student, Camelia Rasheed. My first student, in fact. Performance is nothing if it consists only of skill. By God, but we Egyptians do love emotion and drama, which a good dancer can only offer through her personality. You have that charisma, Camelia. Your dancing was barely adequate, but the audience was won by your brazen audacity. You have the ability to manipulate your audience, and that is half the performance. Does your family know you are here?"

Camelia hesitated. Then she said, "No. They wouldn't approve. But I don't care! I won't tell them I'm taking lessons with you."

"You will have to come to my apartment at least three times a week. Where will you say you are going?"

"I'll tell Umma that I'm taking extra dance lessons. She'll think it's ballet. It won't be lying, really."

"And if she should find out?"

Camelia wasn't going to think about that yet. All she could think of was that Dahiba was going to be her teacher, and that someday, like Dahiba, she was going to be famous.

===

Ibrahim knocked on the door of Hassan's houseboat, and when the valet opened it, Ibrahim pushed him aside and marched straight to Hassan, who was reclining on a divan, smoking hashish.

"My friend! How wonderful of you to join me. Sit down and—"

"Is what I hear true, Hassan?" Ibrahim said, still standing. "Did you give my name to the Revolutionary Council? Did you cause me to be put in prison?"

Hassan kept on smiling. "By God, where did you get such a preposterous idea? Of course not."

"My mother told me."

Hassan's smile vanished. The Dragon again! "Then she told you a lie. Your mother has never liked me, you know."

"My mother does not lie."

"Then someone gave her misinformation."

"She says it is in the records. That I can find out."

Laying his pipe aside, Hassan sat up, ran his hands through his hair, and said, "Very well, I will tell you. Those were dangerous times, my friend. From one day to the next, none of us knew who would be alive to see the next sunset. I was arrested. To save myself I gave them names. Perhaps your name was among them, I don't remember. You would have done the same, Ibrahim, I swear by God that you would have done the same."

"They asked me to name names, Hassan, and I did not do it. I suffered hell and torture before I would betray a brother. You have no idea what you have put me through, Hassan al-Sabir," Ibrahim said quietly, tears rising in his eyes. "Those six months in prison ruined my life. You and I are brothers no longer. And you will not marry my daughter."

Hassan jumped up and caught his arm. "You cannot break our contract, by God!"

"As God is my witness, I can and I will."

"If you do this, Ibrahim, I promise you will live to regret it."

=

Ibrahim found Amira in the salon, listening to the evening reading of the Koran on the radio. "You were right, Mother," he said. "Hassan al-Sabir is no longer my brother. Arrange for Yasmina's betrothal to Omar. The wedding will take place immediately after she graduates from high school."

Then he said, "And give me the potion for Alice. I must have a son."

CHAPTER 18

W hy is it customary to remove all the hair, Mother Amira?"
Alice asked as she watched the female relatives apply the
sugar-and-lemon paste to Yasmina's skin.

"The tradition goes back to when the Queen of Sheba came to visit
King Suleiman. Before her arrival, Suleiman had heard that the queen,
for all her beauty, had hairy legs. In order to find out if this were true,
he ordered constructed in front of his palace a walkway of glass, with
water flowing underneath. It is said that when the Queen arrived, she
thought she was about to cross a pool of water, and so she lifted her
skirts. The story about her legs was true, and so Suleiman invented a hair
remover in order that he could marry her. It was this very sugar-and-
lemon formula that we use today, and it is customary for every bride to
use it on the eve of her wedding in order that she might please her
husband."

"But even her eyebrows?" Alice asked, marveling at the skill with
which Cousin Haneya had applied the paste above Yasmina's eyes, and
then removed it so that only the thinnest half-moon of brow was left.

"She will paint them in, as we do. A woman is more beautiful this
way."

The depilatory ritual was accompanied by a party for all the Rasheed
female relatives. They had come to the house on Virgins of Paradise
Street dressed in their finest clothes to shower praises, gifts, and advice
upon the new bride, and to feast and gossip and dance. Qettah the
astrologer was there also, the ageless woman who had been present at
Yasmina's birth. Much older now, she had to squint over her charts and
calculations as she forecast the horoscopes of Omar and Yasmina—a
match of the star Hamal in Aries, a cruel and brutal star, with the softly
yellow Mirach in Andromeda.

Yasmina was excited. Tomorrow she was going to be a wife, and in
a home of her very own! Breaking with the tradition that a son brought
his wife to live in his mother's house, Omar had taken an apartment near
the river. Now that he was going to receive a generous inheritance from
his father, he had declared, he could afford his own place, and independence.

When all the sugar paste was removed, Yasmina bathed, and her cousins massaged the oils of almond and roses into her tingling skin. Then she was helped into new clothes, her hair was dressed, and she was escorted into the salon to join the merrymaking.

Alice hugged her daughter. "I am so happy for you, darling." And then she said a surprising thing. "There is something you should know, now that you will be married. You will have an income of your own, my darling. You are going to receive an inheritance from your English grandfather, the Earl of Pemberton."

"But you told me he never approved of your marriage to Papa!"

"My father was a narrow-minded man, but he had a strong sense of duty. When he died two years ago, he left a portion of his estate to you. There's some money in your name, to be released to you when you get married, and one of the family houses." To Alice, the earl had left nothing.

It was finally time for Amira to explain to Yasmina what to expect on her wedding night, when she would be alone with Omar. They went into the bedroom and closed the door against the music and laughter, and when Amira described to her granddaughter what Omar was going to do, Yasmina said, "Did your mother tell you these things when you married Grandfather Ali?"

"One of your duties as a wife," Amira continued, avoiding Yasmina's question because the family did not know about the kidnapping, or that Amira did not know her real family, "is that when you go to bed at night, you must always be sweet smelling. Before falling asleep, you must ask your husband three times: 'Is there anything you desire?' If there is nothing, then you are free to go to sleep. But remember, it is not for you to tell him of *your* desire. A woman who initiates the act is a suspect wife."

As Amira talked about the mystery of a man and woman being together, Yasmina was reminded of a similar talk they had had, when Yasmina had been twelve and had discovered blood on her nightgown. "Each woman has a moon that lives in her," Amira had explained. "Its cycle is the same as that of the moon in the sky, it waxes and wanes the same way. It is there to remind us that we are part of God and His stars."

But now Amira was giving instructions: "It is wise to resist him at first. This shows to your new husband that you are not roused to passion and so he will respect you. Never act as though you are enjoying it, for then he will accuse you of loose morals. But while resistance is wise,"

Amira added, "refusal is forbidden. And when he enters you, invoke the name of God, or else a jinni might possess you first."

But Yasmina wasn't worried about the marriage act; she was going to be with her cousin Omar, so she knew she had nothing to fear.

=

A carriage decorated with flowers and drawn by four white horses pulled up in front of the Nile Hilton, and the bride and groom stepped down. The many guests were already there, ready to join the *zeffa*, the procession that would lead into the ballroom where the wedding reception was to take place. Amid cheers and applause and zaghareets, Omar in a tuxedo and Yasmina in a white wedding gown with a long train followed bagpipers in galabeyas, beledi dancers in glittering costumes, musicians playing lutes and flutes and drums. For luck, friends and relatives tossed coins at the bridal couple as the noisy procession wound slowly through the hotel and finally into the ballroom. Omar and Yasmina were placed on two flower-covered thrones and there they would stay for the entire evening, while their guests feasted from groaning buffet tables, entertained by singers, comedians, and dance troupes in endless succession.

As Alice took a place on the women's side of the ballroom, she thought about how strange it was that there should be no church ceremony, not even a ceremony in the mosque. There had been no ceremony at all; in fact, religion did not seem to enter into this wedding. Egyptian custom required only that two male relatives representing the bride and groom—in this case Ibrahim and Omar himself, since Omar's father was dead—signed the contract and shook hands. The bride, in another room, was then informed that she was married. No vows, no kiss at the altar.

As people congratulated her on the marriage of her beautiful daughter, with Alice shaking hands with more relatives than she had thought it possible for one family to contain, she pondered the strangeness of this Egyptian preference for cousins as marriage partners. And she had discovered there was even a precise formula: the first choice for a girl was the son of her father's brother; if one was not available, then the son of the father's sister came next. And it was not for the young people to do the choosing and deciding. The mother of a marriageable girl found an eligible boy and called upon his mother. Over the course of several visits they discussed the boy's future prospects as a provider, the girl's health and childbearing qualities, the status of each family, and above all, each family's honor. Finally, the bride-price that the boy's family was to pay was agreed upon, the bride's parents announced the gifts they would give the couple, and the male guardians met and drew up the papers. Only then was the couple informed.

It seemed to Alice a rather cold and calculating way to get married, but perhaps it was better than the love-match method, since so much more than just love was considered. Because, after all, how long did love last? She looked over at Ibrahim on the men's side of the room. Theirs had been a love match, and see how it had failed.

But just why had love left their marriage? Alice wasn't sure, nor did she know exactly when the happiness between her and Ibrahim had died. Perhaps it was the night of Camelia's circumcision, or possibly earlier, when Alice had caught the two girls playing with melayas and had been afraid of the future once the British left Egypt. And then they *had* left, and some of the old ways had returned, as predicted. But the failure of their marriage stemmed also from Ibrahim himself, from his coldness after he had returned from prison. Alice had waited and hoped for the old passion to come back, but a love that was already endangered, she realized, could not survive for long on such a slender thread of hope. Especially as, with each passing day in which Alice had waited for Ibrahim to send for her to come to his bed, she had dwelt more and more upon the fact that he had already had a wife when he married her in Monte Carlo, a fact that she had once been able to forgive, but which she now believed had contributed to the fact that the roots of their love had not been planted deep enough to grow.

Ibrahim looked her way and their eyes met briefly. He was thinking of the potion Amira had given him. He was going to mix it into Alice's drink tonight, after the party.

And then he looked at Yasmina, his beautiful golden angel, the baby who had captured his heart in her first hour of life. He prayed that she would be happy with Omar, that her life was always going to be perfect and fulfilled. He was glad she had married his sister's son and not a stranger. And especially he was glad she had not married Hassan. Hassan, the brother who had betrayed him and whom he would never forgive.

Amira sat in a place of honor nearest the bridal couple, for the first time in her life appearing without her protective melaya. She was among the most fashionably and expensively dressed, in a black beaded gown with long sleeves and a hem that brushed the floor. At Alice's suggestion, she had replaced her old-fashioned bun with a modest but modern bouffant hairstyle that curled just below her ears. Even so, around her neck and shoulders was a black chiffon scarf, to be drawn over her head and across her face when she left the hotel after the party.

Amira was so filled with joy at the sight of Omar and Yasmina on their thrones that she silently recited her favorite sura from the Koran: "God will reward them with the gardens of Eden, gardens watered by running streams, where they shall dwell forever." Then her thoughts shifted to marriage matches for her other children. It was going to be hard work, she knew, and require a lot of care. Well-to-do parents always had a more difficult time in this endeavor than the rest of the population, because their prospects were fewer. Anyone could marry "up," but no one married "down."

And so Amira was pleased to notice the way Jamal Rasheed kept his eyes on Camelia all evening. A recent widower in his forties, with six children, he was comfortably situated—he owned several apartment buildings in Cairo; he was a Rasheed, being the grandson of the brother of Ali Rasheed's father. Amira decided that she would send him a message in the next few days, alerting him of her intention to visit, and the reason why. Camelia had never voiced the desire to go to university as Yasmina had; Amira believed she would be pleased that her grandmother had arranged such a good match for her.

Then there was shy Tahia, who was also seventeen and who had just received her high school certificate. She, too, had voiced no intention of continuing with school and seemed to Amira to be obediently waiting for her mother and grandmother to arrange a match.

And there was Zachariah, not truly of her own blood, but she felt a duty to settle his future all the same. Amira loved him and was proud of him, and she recalled the day the family had celebrated his having learned all hundred and fourteen chapters of the Koran, at only eleven years old. Amira was uncertain about how to arrange a marriage for Zachariah; he wasn't like the others—the spiritual aspects of life seemed to come ahead of anything else for him. Perhaps he might study to become an imam first, and preach at the mosque on Fridays.

When Yasmina caught Amira's eye, she smiled and shifted in her chair. She was becoming weary from sitting for such a long time, she was anxious to move into the new apartment and start a new life. She was a wife now. And next month she was starting at university! She and Omar would take the tram to school together, and ride home together, and study in the evenings at the same table. Someday he would have a job with the government—President Nasser had promised all university graduates a civil service job after college—and she would have babies. She and Omar would be very smart, educated, modern parents who shared equally in all responsibilities, hampered by none of the old-fashioned inequities of the older generation. Life was so wonderful that when she saw her sister at the buffet table, she couldn't help but wave, thinking she was going to faint with happiness.

Camelia, helping herself to generous portions of kebab and rice in an effort to gain the weight Dahiba had demanded, returned her sister's wave. But her mind was on other matters, foremost being her disappointment that Uncle Hassan hadn't come to the wedding. She had hoped he would be here so they could talk, and maybe he would notice that she was no longer a child. She often wondered if he had ever thought of getting married again. She also wondered why he hadn't come to the wedding.

A beledi dancer came onto the stage, skilled, but not superior, and Camelia thought of the past eight exhausting but blissful weeks she had spent studying in secret with Dahiba, a demanding and exacting instructor. Dahiba would say "Give me this rhythm," or "Give me that rhythm," and Camelia would be expected to do it, without music. Dahiba was also teaching her about costuming and cosmetics, and how to flirt with the audience. The afternoons with Dahiba were so sublime that Camelia was starting to resent having to go to the ballet studio first. But she couldn't stop ballet, because then she would no longer have an excuse for going out in the afternoon three times a week. But she was learning fast, Dahiba had said. Possibly within a year, when she was eighteen, Camelia might have a small part in the show.

When Zachariah walked by with two plates, she winked at him. Thanks to him, and to the help of Tahia and Yasmina, Camelia was beginning to see her dream come true. When he did not return the wink, nor even smile, she remembered the unhappy news he had received that afternoon: a classmate of whom he had been very fond had killed himself that morning. "He was a bastard, Lili," Zachariah had said, with tears streaming down his cheeks. "His mother was never married, he never knew who his father was. The boys at school taunted him mercilessly about it, but he withstood it bravely. And then he fell in love with a girl in his neighborhood and hoped to marry her, but when his mother paid a call on the girl's mother, the girl's mother said that no family, no matter how lowly, would allow a daughter to marry him. What decent woman would want to marry a man who didn't know who his father was? He could not lead an honorable life, so he chose an honorable death."

Zachariah returned to his table, where he handed a plate of food to elderly Uncle Kareem, who could only walk with a cane. As he watched the acrobats on the stage, he glanced at Tahia, who was sitting with Umma, Auntie Alice, and Auntie Nefissa. Zachariah was worried that Umma might try to find someone to marry Tahia. He was only sixteen, how could he ask to be betrothed to her? He was going to have to work up the courage to approach Grandmother. When a famous comedian came out on stage, the audience laughed before he even opened his mouth, but Zachariah noticed that Uncle Suleiman, sitting next to him, didn't laugh, and he wondered why.

Suleiman Misrahi was worrying about his business. Every day the government imposed stricter rules on the import trade in an effort to boost consumerism in Egyptian-made goods. Profits were down so sharply that Suleiman had had to let a lot of old, loyal employees go. It was even looking as if he might have to sell the big house on Virgins of Paradise Street and move into an apartment. He was sorry he had had to tell Maryam they could not take a trip and visit the children. He was even sorrier that no wine was being served at this reception; he could use some now, in quantity.

The last and most important beledi dancer appeared. She performed, not for the audience, but for the bride, a dance symbolizing the bride's transition from virgin to sexual being. Wearing a revealing costume and moving seductively, she evoked independence, sexuality, and unharnessed feminine power, all directed toward the demure bride, who sat stiffly and primly in virginal white, demonstrating by her serious manner that she was not moved by the dance.

When it was over the party came to an end, the guests departed, and the immediate family members climbed into taxis to escort the bridal couple to their new apartment.

The men stayed in the parlor as the women escorted Yasmina into the bedroom, where they helped her out of her wedding gown and into a nightdress. They arranged her on the bed and lifted up her shift, then Amira held Yasmina from behind while Omar took his position on the bed. When he wrapped the handkerchief around his finger, the women turned their backs, and Amira looked away. Yasmina cried out, blood was drawn.

=

As Ibrahim and Alice entered the house, he undid his tie and said, "It was a good wedding, wasn't it, my dear."

"I don't like that barbaric virginity ritual."

He took her arm. "Will you come to my room for a few minutes?"

"I am tired, Ibrahim." It was what she always said.

"Let's drink a toast to our daughter's happiness. I have some brandy."

She looked at him. The wedding had made her sentimental; she remembered her own wedding, so long ago, to a handsome man whom she had vowed to love and obey until she died. She went with him. Ibrahim watched her carefully as she sipped the brandy, and realized with relief that she didn't detect the underlying flavor of Amira's potion. She was soon tipsy. "I'm not used to drinking!" she said, laughing.

But rather than make her romantic, as Ibrahim had expected it to, the drink only made her groggy. He kissed her, but she didn't return his kiss. But she didn't push him away either, so he slipped the strap of her evening gown off her shoulder. When she didn't resist, he continued to undress her, but she hung like a rag doll in his arms, a dreamy, faraway look on her face. She didn't seem to be aware of what he was doing; she even giggled.

This was not what he wanted, Ibrahim thought, as he carried Alice into the bedroom and laid her on his bed. He had wanted her to be a willing partner, to be warm and responsive. But he also wanted a son. As he slipped under the covers and took her into an embrace, Ibrahim felt more shameful than he ever had with any of his prostitutes.

=

Zachariah couldn't sleep. He kept thinking of his friend, who had drowned himself in the Nile. Had heaven embraced him? Zachariah wondered, as he went down to the garden to find relief from the hot

August night. Has Latif today gazed upon the face of the Eternal One?

He was startled to find Tahia sitting there in the moonlight. Sorrow for Latif vanished as he thought: she is a mirage shimmering in the wilderness of longing.

"May I sit with you?" he asked, and she smiled and moved over on the marble bench.

He began to sing softly a popular love song, "*Ya noori.* You are my light."

When she started to cry, he was startled. "What is it? What's wrong?"

"I shall miss Mishmish! Oh Zakki! We're all growing up! We shall all leave and never see each other again! Our happiness will be gone! We shall never play in this garden together again!"

He clumsily reached for her and was surprised when she put her arms around him and buried her face in his neck, wetting it with tears. He held her close and said soothing things, calling her *Qatr al-Nana,* beautiful dewdrop, and touching her hair, marveling at its softness. Tahia was so warm and giving in his arms that his feelings overwhelmed him. "I love you," he blurted. "The angels themselves must have rejoiced when you were born."

And then his lips were seeking hers, and he found them soft and willing. He wanted more, but he stopped at the one kiss. When he and Tahia eventually made love it would be as God decreed in the Koran—in marriage only.

"I will speak to Umma," he said, holding her face in his hands and thinking how the moonlight turned her tears into diamonds. "We shall be as happy as Omar and Yasmina."

===

Yasmina watched Omar as he slept, and thought how strange it seemed to be in bed with her cousin, with a boy she had grown up with. The lovemaking had been nice, they had actually laughed, it was fun, but she wondered when the passion was supposed to come, the romance she heard about in songs and movies.

Quietly leaving the bed, she went to the window and looked out. She had never felt so happy. The wedding had been beautiful, and now here she was in a home of her own. But what monopolized her thoughts on this balmy summer evening were the words her father had spoken a few weeks ago, when she had come home from the Red Crescent. "Perhaps someday you will work with me in my office," Ibrahim had said. "I'll teach you how to be a good nurse."

But as she hugged herself now, still warm from Omar's lovemaking, Yasmina thought: No, not a nurse. I shall be a doctor.

CHAPTER 19

Camelia's first thought when she saw the man was that he was very handsome. The second was to wonder if he was married.

He was the government censor, on hand at Saba Studios to make sure Hakim Raouf's latest film did not depict poverty, political discontent, or, in this particular case, Dahiba's belly button. Camelia tried not to stare at him as she stood out of the way of the cameras and crew while Hakim gave directions to his actors. This was the fourth time Dahiba had invited her to come and watch a movie being made, and each time the seventeen-year-old had thought she would faint with the glamor of it all. But on this blustery December day, Camelia was even more excited, because this was also the week of the *Mulid al-Nabi,* the nine-day festival celebrating the Prophet's birth, a time when people bought new clothes, exchanged presents, set off firecrackers, and ate mounds of sweets. As a special treat Dahiba's husband had ordered a dessert buffet set up in the studio, spread with cakes, pastries, fruit, and sweetmeats, the favorite being "palace bread," which was made of flat bread fried in butter, then soaked in honey and coated with thick cream.

Camelia watched the attractive government censor help himself to a handful of dates stuffed with candied orange peel and then stir several teaspoons of sugar into his coffee. She wondered if he had noticed her.

Of course she wouldn't dream of going up to him and starting a conversation, just as she would be shocked, insulted even, if he should similarly approach her. But she did want to catch his eye. If only she were allowed to dress with a little more allure! But Umma always made sure her girls left the house modestly dressed, which meant long sleeves, hems below the knees, and collars that buttoned up to the neck. Amira always made especially sure Camelia wore a scarf to hide her luxurious long black hair, which would, she declared, be a temptation to men; but Camelia always removed it as soon as she was out of sight of Virgins of Paradise Street. She didn't think it was fair that her brother and male cousins could wear anything they wanted, as if only women aroused temptation. And besides, Camelia wondered, were men so weak that they lost all control at the sight of a lock of hair? The girls at school joked about it, saying that men must be silly creatures indeed if they got excited at the sight of a split end. But at least Amira allowed makeup, as she herself spent time every morning at her vanity table before joining the family for breakfast. And so Camelia took care to apply kohl around her amber eyes, draw in perfectly arched black eyebrows, and apply a smoky red lipstick that complemented her olive skin. Did the government censor at least think she was pretty?

Hakim Raouf shouted, "Action!" and Dahiba began to dance, with the censor paying careful attention. The scene was set in a nightclub, and Dahiba was cast in the role of a dancer who pretended she didn't recognize her philandering husband, who was in the audience, disguised. Another comedy. Raouf had once complained to Camelia that a man as brilliant as Nasser—"The man, by the head of Sayyid Hussein, who shipped fifty thousand transistor radios, all tuned to Cairo Radio, to the rural areas of the Middle East!"—imposed controls on films that practically guaranteed box-office failure. Dahiba's husband often grumbled about "pulling up tent stakes and moving to Lebanon, where they have more freedom and appreciate artistic creativity."

He shouted, "Cut!" and called for someone from wardrobe to make an adjustment to Dahiba's costume. Then he went up to his wife, who was taller than he, even more so now that she was in high heels, and murmured something in her ear. She laughed.

Camelia loved watching Dahiba with her husband. They made such an unlikely couple—she, so tall and graceful and elegant, he, so short and chubby and untidy. But they had purposely chosen each other. Dahiba's parents had been killed in a boating accident when she was seventeen, leaving her without a family, and so she had been free to choose her own husband. She had picked Hakim Raouf and they had been together for the past twenty years.

That is what I want, Camelia decided, as she glanced again at the censor. I am going to choose my husband for myself, and we are going to be happy and a little crazy together.

And there would be children, too, Camelia promised herself, because Dahiba had assured her that it was possible to have babies and a career.

As she was watching the handsome censor, he suddenly looked her way, and kept his eyes on her for a moment longer than was proper before looking away. Camelia felt her heart do a somersault.

Finally, the scene was over; shooting was done for the day. As Camelia gathered up her coat and purse and library books, she saw Dahiba engage the censor in a conversation. He asked her something, and she laughed, shaking her head. Then he looked at his watch and nodded.

"What did you think of the scene?" Dahiba asked when she joined up with Camelia, putting an arm around her.

"You were wonderful! He couldn't take his eyes off you," Camelia said, nodding toward the censor.

"Of course he couldn't, my dear. It's his job! He was making sure I wasn't dancing too provocatively. Anyway, I invited him to join us for tea this afternoon."

"You did? Did he accept?"

"He asked me if you were my daughter. I told him you were my pupil."

"But is he coming to tea?"

"He asked if you were going to be there. When I said yes, he accepted."

"I shall faint with joy!"

"Four o'clock, my dear. Don't be late."

Camelia nearly ran all the way home, mentally sorting through her wardrobe to decide what to wear. She knew what the tea would be like—he would appear surprised to see her there, and then, as was customary, he would take care to spend the rest of the visit showing no interest in her. If he accepted an invitation to tea a second time, then it meant that he liked her, and it would be permissible for them to exchange a few words, under Dahiba's watchful eye. Perhaps the third invitation would be for dinner, and Camelia would be allowed to sit next to him, and they could talk a little about themselves. Or maybe they could go on a picnic, or to a concert, with Dahiba and Raouf chaperoning. Camelia's mind reeled with the possibilities!

When she arrived home, a light rain was falling and she found most of her female relatives in the big kitchen, talking and laughing as they cooked.

Amira was overseeing the making of sugar dolls, the traditional children's treat on the Prophet's birthday. Auntie Alice was there as well, her cheeks flushed, her blond hair swept back with combs, as she made an English plum pudding for Christmas. Because the birth of the Prophet Mohammed coincided with the birth of the Prophet Jesus only once every thirty-three years, when it did, the house was filled with double the excitement, twice the bustle. Auntie Alice would bring out Christmas decorations, and set up a little tree which she strung with tinsel, and as she placed a nativity scene under the tree, she would tell the children the story of Jesus' birth. They were all familiar with the story, because the Virgin Birth was in the Koran; there was also an ancient tree in Cairo beneath which Mary and Joseph had rested in their flight to Egypt. When Camelia saw Maryam Misrahi in the kitchen, she remembered that a *third* festival was being celebrated—Hanukkah. Auntie Maryam had brought over her special *harosset*, a date-and-raisin dessert she always prepared for the Jewish Feast of Lights, which commemorated the rededication of the Temple in Jerusalem, the very place from which Mohammed had been lifted to heaven to receive Islam's Five Pillars of Faith from God. Seeing all the bustle and activity in the kitchen made Camelia think that, given the three sacred festivals occurring at the same time, this must be the holiest week in the year.

As she pulled off the scarf she had tied on her head before entering Virgins of Paradise Street, she called out a breathless hello to everyone, and helped herself to an apricot tart.

"There you are, Lili," Amira said. "Did you get the books you needed?"

Camelia had told her grandmother she was going to the library to find some books for her Arabic literature class. She had not mentioned that she would be stopping at Saba Studios afterward. "I found two of them, thank God. I have plenty of homework tonight!"

"Did you take a taxi, as I asked?"

Camelia sighed. Umma had only recently started letting the girls go out alone unchaperoned by a male relative, a concession she had made with reluctance. But with Tahia and Camelia going to school, as well as

Hanida's two daughters, and Rayya's girl, and Zubaida's twins working as typists at *Al Ahram* newspaper, necessity had forced Amira to allow them more independence.

"It's so cold and invigorating out, Umma!" Camelia said. "I decided to walk. But nothing happened," she added quickly, when she saw her grandmother's questioning look. To Umma's old-fashioned thinking the streets of Cairo were still fraught with evils and temptations that threatened a girl's honor. But during Camelia's walk from the studios there had been only one incident—village boys in galabeyas throwing pebbles at her and calling her names. Camelia had ignored them, as she always did. Other than that, the walk home had been uneventful. After all, what could possibly happen to her on a crowded street in broad daylight?

"I have some wonderful news for you," Amira said, as she wiped her hands on the apron protecting her black silk skirt. "I want you to telephone your ballet teacher and cancel this afternoon's lesson. We are going to be honored by an important visitor."

Camelia stared at her. Amira didn't know about her secret dancing lessons with Dahiba, and the ballet lesson was her excuse to go. This afternoon, the ballet lesson was going to be her excuse to attend Dahiba's tea with the government censor! "But Madame won't like it," she said quickly, referring to the director of the ballet academy. "Madame gets angry when—"

"Nonsense," Amira said. "You haven't missed a lesson in years. This one time won't hurt. Shall I telephone her myself?"

"Who is the visitor, Umma?"

Amira smiled with pride. "It is our distant cousin, Jamal Rasheed. And he is coming to speak to *you*, granddaughter of my heart."

Maryam lifted her glass of tea and said, "*Mazel tov*, my dear."

Camelia stared at her grandmother and Auntie Maryam in disbelief. Then she recalled how Jamal Rasheed had been to the house several times, to visit Amira, Camelia had thought. But now she realized in horror that his purpose had been to look her over.

"Look how amazed she is," Maryam said, smiling. "You are a lucky girl, Lili. Jamal Rasheed is a rich man. He is known for his piety, and for his kindness."

"But, Auntie," Camelia cried, "I don't want to get married!"

Amira smiled. "Such a thing to say. Jamal Rasheed is a good man, and he is very comfortable financially. He even has a nanny for his children, so you won't be expected to take care of them."

"It's not Jamal Rasheed, Umma! It's any man! I just don't want to get married right now!"

"In God's name, why ever not?"

"I can't, that's all!" Camelia said. "Not right now!"

"What's gotten into you? Of course you will marry Mr. Rasheed. Your father and he have already signed the engagement contract."

"Oh, Umma! How *could* you!"

To everyone's surprise, Camelia ran out of the kitchen and out through the front door, slamming it.

She ran all the way to Dahiba's apartment house in the rain, burst through the lobby doors, and flew past the startled doorman. When she headed for the stairs, he said, "Wait—" But it was too late. Camelia didn't see the woman scrubbing the marble steps, and that they were still wet. Camelia's feet flew out from under her and she fell, her ankle catching in the iron railing, so that she landed in a twisted position, one leg up and one leg down.

Everyone came rushing to help, and someone telephoned the penthouse for Dahiba. A few moments later a stunned Camelia limped into her teacher's apartment, sniffing back her tears.

"Dear child," Dahiba said, helping her to the sofa. "What happened? Shall I call a doctor?"

"No, I'm all right."

"But what happened? The doorman said you ran through the lobby as if jinns were after you."

"I was so upset! Umma told me I am engaged to an old man who has six children! She says I have to marry him! But I want to be a dancer!"

Dahiba put an arm around Camelia's shoulders and said, "Come along. We'll have some tea and talk about this." But when the girl stood up and Dahiba saw a spot of blood on the couch, she said, "Is it your monthly time?"

Camelia frowned. "No."

"Go into the bathroom and check yourself."

Camelia came out a minute later and said, "It's nothing, just a spot."

"Tell me again how you fell." And when Camelia made a scissors motion with her fingers, Dahiba said, "Listen to me, child. You must go home at once and tell your grandmother about this. Tell her what happened. Tell her how you fell."

"I can't tell her I was here!"

"Then tell her you fell in the street. But you must tell her about this, at once. Go now, hurry."

"But why? I told you I'm not hurt. I don't have any pain anywhere. And the man from the government will be here soon for tea!"

"Never mind him. Just do as I say. Your grandmother will need to know."

Camelia walked home, worried and confused, and when she found Amira in the garden, anxiously watching for her under an umbrella, Camelia said, "I'm sorry, Umma. I shouldn't have run away from you like that. Please forgive me."

"Forgiveness is God's. Come inside, your clothes are wet. Where did you learn such disrespect?"

"I am sorry, Umma. But I can't marry Jamal Rasheed."

Amira sighed. "We will talk about it," she said, and turned toward the house.

"Umma," Camelia blurted. "I had an accident."

"An accident? What sort of accident?"

She described the crowded street, the slippery sidewalk. "My legs went like this," and Camelia gestured with her fingers. "And then there was a spot of blood." Amira asked her the same question Dahiba had, about her monthly time, and when Camelia said it was two weeks away, Amira's look also turned grave. "What is it, Umma?" Camelia said in alarm. "What happened to me?"

"Trust in God, my child. There is a way to take care of it. But we mustn't tell your father." Ibrahim had been in such a deep depression since his break-up with Hassan that Amira didn't want to burden him with another woe.

She knew what she had to do. There were surgeons in Cairo who specialized in these cases, men who kept a secret for a high price.

=

The address was on 26th of July Street. Amira had been told on the telephone to come after the evening prayer, and to bring cash, and now she and Camelia were climbing a stairway to the apartment on the fourth floor. Amira held Camelia's hand as she knocked, and when a middle-aged woman in a clean butcher's apron answered, Amira said softly, "Tell Dr. al-Malakim that we are here."

To Amira's surprise, the woman said that she was Dr. al-Malakim, and opened the door for them to enter.

They were led through a parlor that was illuminated by a single lamp; Amira saw modest furniture, flowered wallpaper, and family photos displayed on top of a television set. There was a strong aroma of onions and roasting lamb in the air, and an underlying odor of disinfectant. The woman led them through a curtain and into a bedroom; a fresh white sheet had been stretched tightly over the bed, and Amira glimpsed a rubber sheet underneath.

"Have her lie down there, Sayyida," Dr. al-Malakim said, as she went to a small table that had been laid out with cotton pads, a hypodermic syringe, and metal pans containing surgical instruments in a greenish solution. "She only needs to remove her panties, nothing else."

"This won't hurt?" Amira said. "You said on the phone that it wouldn't hurt."

The woman gave Amira a reassuring smile. "Please have faith, Sayyida. God has given me this skill. I will give her an anesthetic. Perhaps you will want to wait outside?"

But Amira took a seat on the edge of the bed and held Camelia's hands. "Everything will be all right," she said to the terrified girl. "We'll be going home in just a few minutes."

As the doctor pulled a stool to the foot of the bed and repositioned the lamp, she said in a kindly voice, "Tell me how this happened."

When Amira repeated what Camelia had told her, the woman reached for a syringe and said, "Now then, child, first the injection. Recite the *Fatiha,* very slowly . . ."

═══

"What did she do to me, Umma?" Camelia asked as they got out of the taxi. She was still groggy from the anesthesia, and she felt a dull throb between her legs. Amira helped her into the house and up to her bedroom, thankful that they encountered no one along the way.

"When you fell," she said, as she helped Camelia into her nightgown, "your maidenhead was broken. It happens sometimes. In some girls, the membrane is fragile. But there are doctors who know how to reconstruct it, so that on your wedding night you will still be intact, and therefore family honor is preserved, *inshallah*. That is what Dr. al-Malakim did for you."

Camelia was filled with shame, she didn't know why. "But I didn't do anything wrong, Umma. I had an accident, that's all. I am still a virgin."

"But we would have had no proof. On your wedding night there would have been no blood, Jamal Rasheed would have repudiated you, and our family would have been dishonored. But now you are restored, and no one need know about our visit to Dr. al-Malakim. Sleep now, my darling, and think of God's perfect peace. Tomorrow you will have forgotten all about this."

But Camelia stayed awake for a long time, waiting for the pain to go away. When it grew worse during the night, she didn't say anything, for fear of giving the secret away. And when she woke up with a fever the next day, she still kept her secret to herself. But when she fainted in the kitchen that evening, and Amir felt how alarmingly the girl's forehead burned, Ibrahim was called.

Now Amira had to tell him what they had done. "She has an infection that has spread to her abdomen," Ibrahim said gravely. "I will have her admitted to the hospital."

=

Camelia spent nearly two weeks in Kasr El Aini Hospital, and when she was out of danger, visitors came. The family did not know about the fall she had had, or the illicit operation to restore her virginity; they had simply been told that she had had a fever. The Rasheed aunts and uncles and cousins came with flowers and food and spent the day camped in Camelia's room, spilling into the corridor outside. Dahiba sent flowers and cards, and spoke to her on the phone. "I won't come, because it would embarrass your family to have a dancer there. Get well soon, my dear. Hakim is fretting about your health. And Mr. Sayeed, the government censor, has asked about you."

On the morning that Camelia was discharged from the hospital, Ibrahim told Amira, "Because of the scarring caused by the infection, she will never be able to bear children." He couldn't bring himself to look at Camelia. Now he thought: Am I to be robbed of grandsons, too?

When she was brought home from the hospital, the family greeted her with condolences, as if someone had died. They showered her with pity and sympathy because Jamal Rasheed had broken their engagement, a sign that no man would ever want her. The aunts and female cousins cried for their poor sister, who had no place in society because she could not be a wife and a mother, and was now condemned to a life of virginal spinsterhood.

When Amira was alone with her granddaughter, she said, "Fear not, I will take care of you, granddaughter of my heart. For as long as you live, you will have a home in this house." Camelia thought of the women who had lived there while she was growing up, the unwanted, discarded women, the ones who were past usefulness and those who were stigmatized, all banding together under Amira's roof like frightened birds.

"Why did it happen, Umma? I did nothing wrong."

"It is God's will, granddaughter of my heart. We must not question it. Every step we take, every breath we draw was preordained by the Eternal One. Take comfort in the knowledge that your fate is in His beneficent care."

Umma was right, Umma had always been right; Camelia would surrender to God's will. And she pictured the handsome government censor whom she would never know.

CHAPTER 20

It was the mystical night of *Lailat al-Miraj,* commemorating the hour when the Prophet Mohammed rode through the skies on a white winged horse from Arabia to Jerusalem, there to be lifted up to heaven to receive the five daily prayers from God. As the khamsin moaned through the dark streets of Cairo, obliterating street lamps and headlights with veils of sand, the ancient mashrabiya screens of the Rasheed house rattled and squeaked, and antique brass oil lamps, long since converted to electricity, swung and swayed on their elegant chains. The twenty-six family members and servants who currently resided in the house were gathered in the salon, where Ibrahim was leading them in prayers.

Amira sat with a black veil drawn over her head, listening to the cadenced chanting of the Koran, but having difficulty keeping her thoughts upon prayer. Where, she wondered, were Omar and Yasmina on this special night when families came together in spiritual fellowship?

=

Out in the city, where doors banged and shutters rattled as the fierce desert wind raced down the wide avenues and twisted alleys, Yasmina groped her way along walls. Traffic was scant, and few pedestrians were abroad; she felt as if she were all alone in a chaotic universe. But she persevered, her coat wrapped tightly around her swollen body, a scarf across her face to keep the stinging sand out of her nose and eyes. She could hardly walk, she was in so much pain.

Omar had hit her so hard she had thought he was going to hurt both her and the unborn child, and so she had fled. As she stumbled through the windy night, each step seeming a mile, each breath bringing more pain, she prayed that she would make it to Virgins of Paradise Street, where she knew she would find golden windows, safe and welcoming.

=

Inside the warm salon, Ibrahim continued to lead the prayers and as Camelia recited along with the others, her thoughts were settled upon the fact that her eighteenth birthday was less than a month away. But the prospect brought her no joy. In the four months since her accident, she had not danced with Dahiba. She had also quit school and the ballet academy, and hadn't seen any of her friends. She decided that she was going to become like one of the elderly maiden aunts, a woman existing on the periphery of other people's lives. But at least Zou Zou, for example, had had memories to sustain her, of her gypsy lover and adventures duping the slave traders. What memories did Camelia have, besides the brief fantasy of tea with a handsome government censor?

Even Ibrahim, reading from the Koran, was not listening to the holy words he pronounced. The recitation was mechanical; his mind was distracted by thoughts of progeny and heirs. His hopes for getting Alice pregnant had so far produced no results. But now there was new hope—Yasmina's baby was due in a month. Would Ibrahim be blessed with a grandson?

The prayers ended and it came time to tell the story of how Mohammed was lifted to heaven on his winged horse, and God decreed that Believers must pray fifty times a day, but the prophet Moussa interceded and talked Mohammed into asking the Lord to reduce the number to five. As Ibrahim told the tale, he glanced at Alice, who sat with a Bible in her lap. Memories of their random nights together over the past months, when he had given her potion-laced brandy, so consumed him with guilt and feelings of shame that he made a personal vow: no more subterfuge to try to get her pregnant. He would leave the matter of a son in God's hands.

Suddenly, there was a frantic knocking on the door downstairs, and a moment later a servant was helping Yasmina into the salon. She collapsed on a divan as the family rushed to help her.

Alice pushed through and took her daughter into her arms. "My baby, my baby," she said. "What happened?"

Yasmina said, "Omar," and wailed in pain.

Amira turned to Ibrahim and said, "Send for Omar," but Yasmina said, "No! Don't call Omar! Please—"

Ibrahim sat beside her. "Tell me what happened. Has he hurt you?"

When Yasmina saw the fury in her father's eyes, she was suddenly afraid for Omar, and, in her pain, she became confused. "No . . . it was nothing. It was my fault."

And now that she was here, and safe, Yasmina was beginning to think that perhaps it *was* her fault. She had talked back to Omar when she shouldn't have. She had announced her intention to continue her studies; he had denied her permission because of the baby. And Yasmina had said that she would not obey. And so he had struck her.

"It's all right, Daddy," she said now. "Just let me stay here for a while."

The police arrived then, saying that they had come to arrest Yasmina Rasheed for deserting her husband.

The family erupted in a noisy argument, half of them shouting insults at the policemen that they should do such a thing on a holy night like this, the other half thinking that Yasmina should not have run away, no matter how badly Omar treated her. But she had no choice anyway, she had to go back home. Under the *Beit el-Ta'a,* the House of Obedience Law, it was Omar's right to have his wife arrested for running away, and if necessary, the law permitted the policemen to literally drag the offending woman back to her husband.

When Yasmina refused to go with the officers voluntarily, her aunts and female cousins wrung their hands and wailed. If the neighbors were to learn of this, they would call Yasmina *nashiz*, "freak," the term applied to a wife who disobeyed her husband.

"Then we have no choice," the policemen said apologetically. And one of them reached for Yasmina.

She screamed and sank to her knees.

Haneya said, "Pray for us! The girl is in labor!"

"If it is in God's time," Amira said calmly, helping Yasmina to her feet, "then it is not too soon. Come, we must hurry. Send for Qettah."

Yasmina's labor was brief, and the baby was brought into the world beneath the canopy of Amira's enormous fourposter, where generations of Rasheeds had been born. It was a boy, born under Antares, Qettah announced, the double-star in Scorpio, in the sixteenth lunar mansion. The household celebrated, and Ibrahim smiled for the first time in weeks. As Yasmina gazed at her new baby with intense love, forgetting the beating she had recently received, she said, "I had hoped he would wait and be born on my birthday." When she was going to be seventeen.

Alice and Ibrahim were at her bedside, smiling with tears in their eyes. "I can't believe I'm a grandmother," Alice said, laughing. "I'm only thirty-eight years old, and I'm a grandmother! I have a secret to tell you, darling, to tell you both." She looked at her husband and said, "I am also going to be a mother. I'm pregnant."

"Oh, my love," Ibrahim said, taking her into his arms. "Never has a man been more blessed than I." Then he sat on the edge of the bed, took his daughter's hand in his and said, "Truly God smiled upon me the night you were born. And now you have given me a grandson. And, God, willing, I shall have a son as well," he added, reaching for Alice. "You have both made me very happy."

—

As Yasmina sat by the open window of her apartment, watching the Nile churn beneath the force of the khamsin, she cradled the baby in her arms, and the feel of his warmth through the blanket, the little knobs and soft places of his body, made her forget her sorrow. Although Omar had allowed her to remain on Virgins of Paradise Street to recover from childbirth, the day she came home with the baby he had punished her. But that was two weeks ago, and since then he hadn't laid a hand on her.

Yasmina prayed that it was because of the baby; perhaps having a child reminded Omar that he had responsibilities now, perhaps also he respected Yasmina a little, for having given him a son.

She looked at the time, thinking that Omar wouldn't be home for hours, and an idea came to her. She would bundle the baby up and find a taxi, and pay a visit to Virgins of Paradise Street. It would be her first official visit home as a mother. As she quickly got ready, suddenly excited, she pictured the welcome at the other end, the embraces and laughter. She would no longer be one of the little girls of the house, but a respected wife and mother.

When she went to the door she found it was stuck, which was puzzling, because this was a new building and the doors shouldn't be warping yet. She pulled on it harder and discovered that it wasn't stuck at all, but locked. Omar must have locked it behind him when he left for school that morning.

Going first through her purse for her key, she then searched the other likely places that she might have left it, but the key was nowhere to be found. Annoyed with herself for having misplaced it, she decided to telephone the landlord, who had a master key, but when she picked up the phone, she found that it was dead. She stared at the instrument in her hand. Suddenly she felt cold. Had Omar locked her in on purpose and disconnected the phone? No, it wasn't possible. For all his occasional cruelty, Omar wouldn't go that far. He had simply locked the door without thinking, and telephones in Cairo were unreliable at best. As Yasmina put Mohammed back in his crib and went into the kitchen to prepare dinner, she assured herself that when Omar came home he would apologize and they would laugh about the silliness of it. She decided to fix his favorite dish: stuffed breast of lamb.

But to her surprise, Omar didn't come home for dinner. She sat up all night waiting for him, and when he didn't come home the next day, Yasmina's alarm turned to terror. He *had* locked her in and gone away. So she tried to pick the lock, but was so frightened that her hands shook and she succeeded only in dismantling the knob, causing it to fall away into two halves, one inside the apartment, the other into the hall.

Frantically, she took a hammer and screwdriver to the door, hoping to lift it from its hinges, but the hardware was covered in many thicknesses of paint. She banged on the door and cried for help, with little hope; she and Omar lived on the top floor, and the occupants of the other two apartments were away much of the time. And even then, they wouldn't have helped. No one interfered when a husband disciplined his wife.

When Omar finally came home at the end of the third day, Yasmina was almost out of her mind with worry and fear. He kicked the door down, and threw the broken knob at her. "What have you done to this door!"

"You were gone, I was afraid—"

"You need to be taught a lesson, Yasmina. First you defy me by saying you are going to school when I forbid it. Then you dishonor me by running away. All of our neighbors know about it. They laugh at me behind my back. I'm going to turn you into an obedient wife."

When he went through the apartment, unscrewing light bulbs and breaking them, she followed him, praying that the baby wouldn't wake up. "What are you doing, Omar?"

"Teaching you a lesson you won't forget."

He pushed her away, dragged the TV set from the wall and yanked out the cord. He did the same to the radio, broke the rest of the bulbs so that the apartment was plunged into darkness, and then went to the door and put the knob back together.

"Wait," Yasmina said when he started to leave, "Don't go. Please don't leave me. We don't have much food. The baby needs—"

But he slammed the door behind him and she heard the key turn in the lock.

=

When she awoke to a pounding at her door, Yasmina didn't at first know where she was. It was dark; she was hungry and her head ached. And then she realized she had somehow fallen asleep on the living-room floor. Finally it came back: Omar had locked her in . . . how many days ago?

Why was he doing this to her? Why would he go for days being nice to her, and then suddenly turn, like this? What had she done to deserve such treatment?

She made her way in the darkness to the bedroom and when she lifted Mohammed out of his crib, his mouth immediately sought her breast. She wondered how much longer she would have milk for him; she hadn't eaten since the day before. When she heard the pounding again, she groped her way to the front door. "It's locked," she said. "Who's there?"

"Stand back," she heard Zachariah say, and in the next instant he kicked the door open.

Camelia and Tahia rushed in. *"Bismillah!"* they cried when they saw Yasmina. "What is going on here?"

"He locked me in!" Yasmina said, and Tahia put her arms around her.

"We've been trying to telephone you," Camelia said, looking around the dark apartment. "Omar came to the house, and when we asked about you he said you were too busy with the baby to come and visit. I *knew* there was something wrong."

"You're coming with us," Zachariah said. "Get the baby ready."

They moved quickly, grabbing a blanket and Yasmina's coat, but when they turned to leave, Omar was in the doorway, a thunderous look on his face. "What do you think you're doing?"

"We're taking our sister home," Camelia said. "Don't you dare stop us!"

"Get out of my house, all of you. My wife stays here!" When he grabbed Yasmina's arm, Camelia whipped off her shoe and pounded him over the head with it. Omar howled and tried to protect himself, and the others ran out, taking Yasmina and the baby with them.

Their arrival caused an uproar in the household of Virgins of Paradise Street. The family was shocked at Yasmina's appearance, and enraged when they heard what Omar had done. The women brought Yasmina and the baby into the salon, all talking at once, shouting that Omar should be thrashed, demanding to know where Nefissa, his mother, was.

"The fires of hell for that boy!" Hanida cried.

"Where is Uncle Ibrahim?" shouted a hot-tempered nephew. "It is his duty to deal with this!"

"There is no power save God's," wailed elderly Auntie Fahima.

It took Amira a few minutes to restore order, and when she did she said, "Judgment is the Lord's. All of you be quiet now. Rayya, send everyone away. See that the children are put to bed. You boys also get ready for bed. Tewfik, make sure that Uncle Kareem's cane is by his bed. All of you, go to your rooms now and allow God's peace to enter our house."

When everyone was gone and the house was quiet, Amira said gently, "You must return to your house and make amends with your husband,

Yasmina. You are a wife now, you have a responsibility to your husband."

"He does terrible things to me, Umma. Why? How can he be like this?"

Amira brushed Yasmina's hair from her face and said, "Omar has always been a naughty boy. He's like his father, who died before you were born. Perhaps it is passed on in the blood, I do not know. But always remember that a good wife acts as a veil around family secrets."

=

Omar arrived, demanding to see Yasmina. Ibrahim took him into the small reception room, closed the door, faced him squarely, and quietly ordered him not to lock his wife up again.

He laughed. "It is my right, Uncle. Under the law, a husband may lock up his wife if he chooses, to keep her from running away again. And you cannot interfere."

But Ibrahim said in a deadly tone, "The law may not be able to protect Yasmina, but *I* can. If you harm her again, if you lock her up, or threaten her, or cause her unhappiness, I will curse you, Omar. I will cast you out of the family and you will no longer be my nephew, you will no longer be a Rasheed."

Omar's blood ran cold. He knew Ibrahim had the power to do it, to render him nonexistent, just as Grandfather Ali had done to Auntie Fatima, whose name was forbidden, and whose pictures had been destroyed. Upon Ali's word, she had simply ceased to be. And so would he.

Omar trembled with fury and fear as he struggled to contain himself. "Yes, Uncle," he said in a tight voice.

"And because I do not trust you, I shall telephone Yasmina every day. I shall visit her once a week, and she will be free to come here with the baby whenever she wishes. You will not stop her, you will not intervene. Is that understood?"

He bowed his head. "Yes, Uncle."

=

As Camelia watched them go, her heart went out to Yasmina, because now she had been labeled, even in the eyes of the law—she was *nashiz,* freak. And suddenly Camelia saw that their situations were very much the same. I, too, have been labeled a freak, she thought, because of an unfortunate accident; I, too, am condemned to a prison because of ignorance and prejudice.

Camelia felt a strange new emotion stir within her. It was almost like an awakening, as if she had been asleep these past four months and was only now opening her eyes. She wanted to run after her sister and bring her back, but the law was on Omar's side. Camelia's feelings of utter helplessness drove her to search for her grandmother, whom she found at her vanity table, preparing for bed.

"I ask permission to speak with you, Umma," she said respectfully. "I am upset about Yasmina and Omar."

Amira sighed. The burdens of family! "They will work out their differences, God willing."

"But the laws are unfair to women, Umma," Camelia said, sitting down on the bed. "It's wrong to force a woman to stay in an unhappy marriage."

"The laws were created for a woman's protection."

"Protection! In all honor and respect to you, Umma, but every day the newspapers are full of accounts about the inequities suffered by women. Only today I read about a young woman here in Cairo whose husband took a second wife. He left the country with her, leaving the first all alone with a small child. The husband has no intention of returning to Egypt, but he refuses to give this woman a divorce. She even tried petitioning the court for a divorce, so that she might be free to marry again, but they will do nothing unless her husband agrees to it. She has written countless letters to him and he does not answer. So this young woman is condemned to a lonely life and all because of that selfish man."

"An isolated case," Amira said, brushing her hair.

"But it isn't, Umma. Look through the paper yourself. You only listen to the radio, but the papers are full of such stories. There was another one about a man who died recently. At his funeral it was discovered that he had three other wives besides his first one, each in a different quarter of town, none of them knowing about the others. Each widow had thought she was going to receive his full inheritance, but instead the four had to divide what little he had left them."

"He was not a good man."

"But that is my point, Umma. He was not a good man, but it was his legal right to have several wives without informing any of them that there were co-wives! The law is unfair to women. Just as it is unfair to Yasmina. What about all those poor women who don't have a family like ours to see to their interests and stop a sadistic husband from beating them?"

"By the mercy of God," Amira said, setting down her brush and facing Camelia, "I have never heard you talk like this. Who has put these ideas into your head?"

Camelia was startled to realize that she had been echoing Dahiba's words. During the months that she had been taking secret lessons from the great dancer, Camelia had picked up her mentor's politics and philosophy as well.

Amira said, "You don't understand, Lili. You're too young. Our laws are based upon God's laws, we are therefore guided by God's command-ments, and God can only do good, blessed be He, Lord of all crea-tures."

"Show me where it is written that we must endure torture."

Amira's tone turned hard. "I will not have you questioning the revealed Word of God."

"But the House of Obedience Law is not based on God's word, Umma! The Prophet tells us that no woman should be forced into a marriage she does not want."

"It is written that a wife be obedient to her husband."

"That's a law for women. There are laws for men, too, Umma. But the ones governing men are ignored."

"What are you talking about?"

Camelia searched for an example. "All right, you make us dress modestly and act modestly because it is so written in the Koran. And yet when we were growing up, you allowed Omar and Zakki to dress and act any way they desired."

"It is their right as men."

"Is it?" Camelia went to the Koran that stood beneath a portrait of Ali Rasheed, lifted the heavy book from its wooden stand, and thumbed the pages. "Look, Umma, read here. Chapter Twenty-four, verse thirty."

Amira gazed down at the page.

"Do you see what I mean?"

Amira said quietly, "I can't."

"But it's very plain." Camelia read the passage: " 'Tell the believing men to lower their gaze and be modest. That is purer for them, God is aware of what they do.' You see? It's the same law as for women, but it is only enforced when it comes to women." Camelia realized to her amazement that she was further quoting Dahiba as she said, "The laws of God are just, Umma, but the laws of men, which they have subverted from the Koran, are not just. Look, I'll show you another example."

But as Camelia went through the pages, Amira said again, "I can't."

"Shall I fetch your glasses for you?"

"I mean, Camelia, that I cannot read. I never learned how to read."

Camelia quickly sat down, a stunned expression on her face.

"It has been my shame," Amira admitted as she rose from the vanity table. "It has been my . . . deception. But your grandfather taught me the Word of God, even though I could not read, and therefore I know God's laws."

"There is no shame in not knowing how to read," Camelia finally said. "Even the Prophet, God's blessing upon him, could not read or write. But in all honor and respect to you, Umma, perhaps Grandfather Ali did not teach you all the laws."

"Quickly say a prayer, child. You dishonor your grandfather, who was a good man."

When Camelia saw the look on her grandmother's face, the pride shimmering in those dark, lively eyes, she was immediately repentant. But, as Umma had always said, words once uttered could not be called back. More quietly, Camelia said, "I respect and honor God's laws, but the laws made by men are wrong. I am only eighteen years old and I have been sentenced to a life that is more of a death than a life, because I cannot have children. I am being punished for something I had no control over. For something that has nothing to do with honor but with physical disability. You always taught us that the Eternal One is compassionate and wise. The Lord said, 'I wish ease for you.' Umma, Yasmina should be allowed to divorce Omar."

"When a woman divorces her husband, she brings dishonor upon her family."

"But Auntie Zou Zou was divorced, and so is Auntie Doreya and Auntie Ayesha."

"They are only related to Grandfather Ali, they are not his direct descendants. It falls to the grandsons and granddaughters of Ali Rasheed to preserve the family honor."

Camelia reached for her grandmother's hands and said passionately, "And so we must suffer in the name of honor? Yasmina must stay in a terrible marriage because of family honor? And because that woman on 26th of July Street infected me, I must live a useless life in the name of honor?"

"Honor is everything," Amira said softly, her chin trembling. "Without it we are nothing."

"Umma," Camelia said, "you were the mother who raised me, who taught me about God, who taught me right from wrong. I have never questioned or doubted you. But there must be more to life than just honor."

"I cannot believe that a granddaughter of Ali Rasheed speaks these words. Or that she thus addresses her grandmother. I fear for these corrupt times when a girl contradicts an elder, and twists the word of God to suit her own ends."

Camelia bit her lip. Then she said, "I ask your forgiveness and your blessing, Umma. I have to find my own life in my own way. I am leaving this house tonight, I must find where I belong. Pray for me."

Long after Camelia had left the room, Amira stood hidden behind the mashrabiya screen, and as she watched her granddaughter disappear down the street with a suitcase, she thought of the little baby she had brought into the world on a windy night such as this, eighteen years ago.

The night Ibrahim had cursed God.

CHAPTER 21

Zachariah saw angels.

At least he thought he did. But the graceful beings who seemed to float around him in soft golden light were only Amira, and Sahra, the kitchen woman. It was the final week of Ramadan, the month of fasting, and the last thing Zachariah remembered was the unbearable heat in the kitchen.

He felt a hand beneath his head, and something warm and sweet-scented touching his lips. "Drink this," he heard his grandmother say.

After a few sips, Zachariah's head cleared. And when his eyes focused and he saw Umma's worried look, he said, "What happened?"

"You fainted, Zakki."

When he saw the cup in Amira's hand and realized he had just drunk tea, he struggled to sit up. "What time is it?"

"It's all right," she said gently. "The tea is permitted. It is past sunset. The family is in the salon, eating. Come, you will join them."

He sat up and realized he was in his own bedroom. Then he saw Sahra, his old wet nurse, hovering behind Amira. "You fainted in the kitchen, little master," she said. "We brought you here."

Amira stroked his head and said, "Have you been fasting too much, Zakki?"

He sank back into the pillows. I am not fasting enough, he thought, and wished now he hadn't even ingested the tea, sunset or not. Realizing that the month of Ramadan would be over soon, and this period of fasting and atonement would end, Zakki was gripped with panic. So little time was left for him to save himself!

Every day of the fasting month, from sunrise to sunset, the seventeen-year-old had tried to fulfill this Fourth Pillar of the Faith by abstaining from food, water, tobacco, and even cologne, in order to defeat the passions that were Satan's weapons. Since everyone knew that eating and drinking strengthened the devil's arsenal, then abstinence kept God's enemy at bay. But there was more to the Ramadan fast than keeping food and drink out of the body, there was also the fast of the mind, which Zachariah had tried faithfully to practice. Earthly thoughts were part of abstinence, as all concentration must be upon God, and so, just as swallowing a piece of bread voided the physical fast, so did an impure thought invalidate the spiritual fast.

And on every single day of this holiest of Islam's months, Zachariah had annulled the fast of his mind.

Amira said, "You are too zealous, child. It is forbidden to fast continuously, and yet I believe that is what you have been doing. God requires only that we purify ourselves from dawn to sunset, after which we may eat to our heart's content. Remember that God is the Merciful and the Nourisher."

Zachariah turned away. Umma couldn't possibly understand. He *wanted* to be pious, he wanted the Lord to fill him with grace, but how worthy could he be if he couldn't keep lustful thoughts about Tahia out of his mind? Food and water were easy to avoid; but his mind betrayed him every time he looked at her and remembered their one kiss on the night of Yasmina's wedding.

"What is it, my dear?" Amira said. "I sense that something troubles you. Is there a problem at school?"

He leveled his green eyes at Amira and said, "I wish to get married."

Amira gave him a surprised look. "But you are not even eighteen, Zakki. You have no profession, you would have no way of supporting a wife and family."

"You let Omar get married, and he's still in school."

"Omar has his father's inheritance. And he is only one year away from graduating and obtaining a job as a government engineer. Your situations are different."

"Then Tahia and I can live here, with you, until I finish school."

She sat back. "Tahia? Is she the one you want to marry?"

"Oh, Umma," he said with passion, "I burn for her!"

Amira sighed. These boys, always burning! "You are too young," she said again. And then suddenly she remembered: Zachariah was not really a Rasheed. Could he possibly be allowed to marry Tahia?

=

After Amira left him, she went up to the roof and saw the winking stars. Up there, she thought, was Zachariah's birth-star, but no one knew which one it was. *Just as I do not know my own birth-star.*

How can we chart our courses, she wondered, as the sounds of celebration from all over the city reached her. How can we know our futures if we do not know our stars?

She thought of the dreams that still troubled her, their remarkable intensity and sharpness of detail—the camp in the desert, the mother losing her child, the tall Nubian in a scarlet turban—and she wondered yet again what they were trying to tell her. *It is a lonely feeling, not to know one's ancestry.*

Zachariah wanted to marry Tahia, but was it wise to permit such a union? Was it not possibly inviting calamity by marrying Tahia to a boy whose ancestry was unknown, whose fortune could not be read? Amira felt sorry for him and wanted to make him happy, but she also recognized a greater duty to her daughter's daughter. Tahia needed a secure, dependable man, who was already known, whose honor was beyond reproach.

And Amira knew exactly who that man should be; she had already read Jamal Rasheed's stars when she had chosen him to marry Camelia.

=

Canons and drums sounded all over the city, and when the official gunshot announcing the end of Ramadan was broadcast over Cairo Radio, people launched into the streets in new clothes to go calling on relatives, taking presents for the children. The joyous three-day celebration of *Eid al-Fitr* had begun.

Zachariah and Tahia sat in the garden on the same marble bench where they had experienced their first kiss, nearly a year ago. They did not share in the happiness of the festival—Tahia was engaged to marry Jamal Rasheed before a month was out; she would be moving into his house on Zamalek. She was not excited about the prospect, but, unlike Camelia and Yasmina, it would not occur to her to disobey Umma and refuse to marry Mr. Rasheed.

They sat in silence beneath the stars and the slender crescent of the new moon, holding hands and inhaling the fragrance of jasmine and honeysuckle. Finally Zachariah said, "I will always love you, Tahia. I will never love another woman. I will never marry, but instead will devote my life to God." He said this without knowing that he echoed the words his own father had spoken to Sahra beside the Nile, nearly eighteen years ago.

=

Ibrahim looked at the woman in his bed and decided that she was going to be the last prostitute he saw. After he had had his fortune read by three different fortune tellers, with all three promising that the child Alice was carrying was a son, Ibrahim decided that he had paid his debt in prison, God had forgiven him for his past signs and was granting him a new start in life.

==

The first thing Nefissa noticed about the man was his hair. It was slightly thinning but unmistakably blond. And each time their eyes met, Nefissa tried to gauge the color of his—were they gray or blue? The guests were attending a reception for a well-known journalist, and Nefissa, being a close friend of the hostess, a socialite she had known during the Farouk years, had been invited. She wanted to meet the intriguing gentleman, but she was still recovering from Hassan's humiliating rebuff, even though it had happened a year ago. As she was wondering what she should do, the hostess, a keen-eyed woman who dabbled in matchmaking and who had not failed to notice the game of eye-contact tag going on between two of her guests, came up to Nefissa and said in a quiet, conspiratorial tone, "He is a professor teaching at the American University. He is quite good looking, I think, but what makes him even more attractive is the fact that he is single. Shall I introduce you to him, darling?"

==

Inside the Cage d'Or, Camelia was backstage, making final adjustments to the white satin galabeya she was going to wear for her dance debut. It crossed her mind briefly that she wished her family could be here to see her first public performance. But the night she had left Virgins of Paradise Street, she had been taken in by Dahiba and Hakim; they were her family now. And when she finally made her entrance onstage, joining Dahiba for their new act together, Camelia felt her soul soar up to the glittering chandeliers. The audience applauded and shouted *"Y'Allah!"* She smiled and began to dance.

==

As Yasmina cuddled Mohammed against her breast, she pored over the biology book Zakki had given to her on her birthday. She barely looked up when Omar came from the bedroom, the fragrance of his cologne preceding him. And when he said he was going out again, she nodded and turned the page. She was no longer afraid of him. Whatever her father had said to him in private, it had brought him in line. He spent his nights out now, with friends, but she didn't care. She had Mohammed, the center of her universe, and she had her books. Someday, she was determined, she was going to return to school. She was going to find independence. Which was one reason why, on those few occasions when Omar came home drunk and called her to bed, Yasmina had secret insurance against further pregnancies: contraceptives obtained from one of President Nasser's new birth-control clinics.

===

Alice arranged flowers in vases in the salon, peonies and roses collected from her garden. As she studied the effects of pink with yellow, she contemplated the new life growing inside her, what she hoped would be a new little Eddie. He would be blond and blue-eyed like her brother, and she would take him to England and teach him about his English heritage.

===

Amira gave the large moving van a wistful look as the last of Maryam's furniture went into it. Suleiman had sold the big house on Virgins of Paradise Street and now the Misrahis were moving to a small apartment near Talaat Harb Square.

Amira looked at the woman who had been her best friend and neighbor for many years, ever since they were both young brides. They had raised babies, shared secrets, comforted each other, and danced the beledi together. Where had the years flown?

"You will come and visit us often?" Maryam said, as the doors of the van slammed shut. "You won't let distance separate us?"

"There was a time," Amira answered, "when I would have hesitated to leave my house. In fact, I was afraid to leave. But that time is long past. Of course I will come and visit you, you are my sister."

Amira linked her arm through Maryam's and, remembering the days when she had been terrified to go out into the world, when she had not even discarded her veil, even though Ali had given her permission to do so—thinking, too, of how that brutal separation from her mother long ago had left her with a legacy of insecurity—Amira realized that she was very much looking forward to visiting Maryam in her new apartment on Talaat Harb Square.

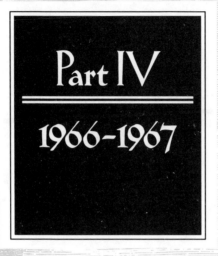

Part IV
1966-1967

W e must be careful now, Yasmina. A deep wound such as this can be tricky." Ibrahim was speaking in English so that the child's mother, a fellaha who had recently come to live in the city, would not understand and become alarmed.

"What happened?" Yasmina asked. She had just arrived at her father's office to fill in for his nurse, who had the evening off.

"A stairway broke—There, there," Ibrahim said, switching to Arabic. "Be a brave boy. Just another minute and we'll be all through."

As her father gently rinsed the wound, Yasmina gave the child a reassuring smile. He was like many of the children crowding into the nearby neighborhood. Peasants leaving their farms and pouring into the city in search of better prospects were being crammed into flats and apartments meant to hold one tenth the number; they filled rooftops and alleys with makeshift shelters, garden plots, chickens and goats; they slept in stairways and broken-down elevators. And so accidents frequently occurred, with archaic wooden balconies suddenly giving way, whole buildings collapsing without warning, or, as in the case of Dr. Rasheed's young patient, rotten stairs splintering. The boy had gotten a nail in the calf of his leg.

"All right now, Yasmina," he said, returning to English. "We have washed the wound thoroughly, syringed out the dirt, and soaked the wound in potassium permanganate. What do we do next?"

Yasmina had put a white lab coat on over her dress, and bound her hair up in a white scarf, as her father's nurse always did. She handed her father a basin of purple liquid she had just mixed. "Gentian violet," she said, "unless an antibiotic ointment is indicated."

"Good girl," Ibrahim said, gently applying the solution to the boy's skin while the mother, an ageless woman wrapped in a black melaya, watched silently. "As you know, a deep wound that does not bleed much, such as this one," he said, "is likely to become highly infected. This boy is lucky, his mother knew enough to bring him to me. Very often, when they see no bleeding, they assume the wound is minor and ignore it. Septicemia and tetanus develop, and the victim dies. There," he said, setting aside the basin and removing his gloves. "We never suture a wound of this type, so I'll leave you to bandage it while I draw up some penicillin."

As Yasmina wrapped the skinny leg with clean gauze, it occurred to her that the child was about the same age as her own son, and yet this fellaheen boy was smaller than three-year-old Mohammed, causing her to wonder if the fellaheen really improved their lot by coming into the city, or if they were better off staying on their farms by the Nile.

After administering the shot, which made the child, who had been quiet up until now, burst into tears, Ibrahim said to the mother in Arabic, "Bring your son back to me in three days. In the meantime, feel his forehead. If he gets warm, bring him back right away. If his leg becomes hard and rigid, or if he seems to move his head a lot, bring him back. Do you understand?"

She nodded, shy eyes peering over the black cotton melaya she had held across her face through the whole visit. When she reached beneath the cloak and came out with money—half-piastre coins—Ibrahim refused them, saying, "Prayers are more valuable than money, Umma. Pray for me at the next holy festival."

After the woman and child were gone, Ibrahim went to the sink and washed his hands. "We probably won't see them again, Yasmina. If the wound becomes infected and the boy gets sick, his mother will most likely take him to a magician to have the jinns exorcised." He looked at his daughter, who was cleaning up the instruments and supplies, and he felt his heart fill with pride. To give free medical treatment to the local peasants was his own idea; Ibrahim confessed that such work left him with a deep feeling of satisfaction at the end of each day. But he did not expect such service from Yasmina, who must certainly feel more comfortable with his wealthy patients. And yet here she was, helping him out during his "free clinic" hour when the fellaheen came.

"Are you sure this is what you want to spend the rest of your life doing, Mishmish?" he asked. "Being a wife and a mother is a noble occupation. Why do you want to be a doctor? As you can see, it can be a frustrating business."

She gave him a teasing smile. "Why did *you* become a doctor, Father?"

"I had no choice. Your grandfather, God give him peace, dictated to me how my life was going to go."

"What would you have preferred to do?"

"If I had it to do over again," Ibrahim said, as he dried his hands, "I would go and live on one of our cotton farms in the Delta. I had thought for a while that I would like to be a writer. Of course, I was young at the time. Don't all young people dream of being writers?"

Yasmina watched him as he carefully brushed his hair, using broad sweeps above each temple, where she noticed a distinguished silver was replacing the gray. Yasmina thought that her father, nearing fifty, was still very good looking, and even though his waistline had filled out a little, she decided that it made him look like a man of substance. She could see why her mother had fallen in love with him.

As she separated the clean instruments from the used, and carefully disposed of the gloves and soiled gauze, as Ibrahim had taught her to do, she watched him out of the corner of her eye while he jotted notes on an index card, his gold pen catching the light. And she realized that her father was entering the age that Yasmina thought was the most becoming to Arab men, the mid-life stage when they seemed to shake off youthful pretensions and self-involvement and take on the finer qualities of maturity and dignity. She had observed the same features in her university professors, in the older men who sat in the coffeehouses, even in elderly street beggars, and she wondered if it was perhaps a national or racial trait, this natural stateliness that seemed eventually to come to most Arab men. Even her husband, Omar, although only twenty-four, was already exhibiting early signs of it, most likely, Yasmina suspected, because of his frequent dealings with community leaders and prominent businessmen.

She imagined the day when Ibrahim would pose for a family portrait as Grandfather Ali had done, sitting on a chair as if it were a throne, surrounded by devoted subjects—his family. Yasmina saw herself in the group, at his right hand.

"We no longer own the farms in the Delta, Father," she said teasingly. "You would have been thrown out of your writer's paradise. And then what would you have done?"

Ibrahim went to the window and looked out at the neon lights that were starting to flicker on as day gave way to night. Now that the siesta hours were over, people were launching themselves into the streets for an evening of business or entertainment. Cairo! Ibrahim thought, as he watched a line form in front of the Roxy Cinema. City of restless souls. "Probably I would have gone into the streets and sold potatoes," he said, watching an elderly sweet-potato vendor wheeling his cart among the theater patrons.

Ibrahim turned and looked at Yasmina, who was replacing the supplies in the white metal cabinets. She had removed her scarf, and her blond hair tumbled down her back. From this angle she resembled Alice, he thought; she possessed the same grace, the same careful movements. But Yasmina's ambition had not been inherited from her mother. Perhaps, he thought, she had gotten it from himself, but it was a determination he had not been aware he possessed.

When Ibrahim took a moment to explore the prospect of Yasmina becoming a doctor, imagining how he could convert the room adjoining the office, where he had once brought prostitutes, turning it into a second office and examining room, he found that the idea very much appealed to him. If she were to become a doctor, he thought, then he could bring her into the practice with him; she would treat the women and children, while he saw to the men; they would work as a team, share opinions, consult with each other, the Doctors Rasheed. And she would be here every day, bringing her own special luminescence to his office.

"But you have a son, Yasmina," he said. "Shouldn't you be devoting all your time to him?"

"I do, mostly. Auntie Nefissa likes to have him, too. Right now, they're at a puppet show."

"Well, until Tahia does her duty and produces a child, Mohammed is Nefissa's only grandchild."

Yasmina turned around and faced him. "Father, I have managed to earn two years of university credits. In another two years Mohammed will be starting school. I would like to go into medical school then."

"Aren't you too young to be a doctor?"

"I shall be twenty-six when I finish!"

"An old woman," he said. "I don't know, Mishmish. Medical school is no place for a young lady of your class and breeding. It doesn't seem proper. I think I would rather see you give me more grandchildren. After all, Mohammed is nearly four. He needs brothers and sisters."

She laughed. "My son has more cousins than he can handle. A brother or a sister would only confuse him!"

Yasmina knew the family was wondering when her next child was going to come. They didn't know about her use of birth control, or that she had briefly considered obtaining a divorce from Omar, three years ago. But a discreet enquiry into the process had revealed that, while a man wishing to rid himself of a wife simply had to recite "I divorce thee" three times, a woman could obtain a divorce only on a few specific grounds: if her husband had been put in prison for a long term; if he had a terminal illness; if he was certified insane; if he had beaten her so severely that she was permanently injured.

An older woman with whom she did volunteer work at the Red Crescent had offered her some advice. "Lawyers! Courts! Petitions!" Zubaida had declared. "Any woman with a brain between her ears knows the quickest and easiest way to get a man to divorce her. Didn't it work for me, twice? Both husbands, egotistical donkeys, a big mistake marrying them. But there is an old remedy, my mother called it putting poison in the stew. Its ingredients are simple: keeping an untidy house, allowing noise while the husband entertains male friends, providing insufficient food for honored guests, letting the children be disrespectful in front of others—all little darts to wound his masculine pride and honor. If those fail, a good ridiculing laugh in bed while he attempts sex does the trick."

But Yasmina was not that desperate, and besides, since Omar had graduated from the university and gotten a good job with the government, he was away on overseas assignments, often for months at a time. His absence plus her secret use of a contraceptive, as well as the time she spent pursuing a university degree, were what made life with Omar tolerable. It even seemed, she was beginning to think, that their relationship might be improving; Omar was more respectful of her lately, and when he had returned from his last assignment overseas, he had brought her a gift. Supposing that this was how marriages grew, and that in time perhaps even love would come into their lives, Yasmina was beginning to see a fuller picture of her future.

"But I want more, Father," she said. "Yes, it's a wonderful thing to be a mother. But I feel confined in such a role. When I attend classes at the university, or when I come here to help you, I almost feel like a different person, as if I am waking up, or becoming my real self. How I envy Camelia her dancing career!"

"Your grandfather did not approve of women becoming doctors."

"But it is *you* I'm asking for help, Father, and you are not Grandfather Ali."

"No," he said slowly, surprised by her words. "I am not my father, God rest him. Very well, Mishmish. After your mother and I return from our trip to England, we will talk about it."

She gave him a hug and as Ibrahim returned it, he realized that he was secretly pleased with Yasmina's ambition and her courage to speak up to him. If only he had had such courage . . .

There was a knock at the outer door, and when Ibrahim went to open it, he was surprised to find his niece's husband, Jamal Rasheed, standing there.

"Forgive the intrusion, Ibrahim," he said, "but necessity has its own laws. May I come in?"

Alarmed my Jamal's abruptness, forgoing the customary polite exchange, Yasmina offered him a chair and said, "Is it Tahia? Is she all right?" Although her cousin had left the house on Virgins of Paradise Street when she had married Jamal Rasheed, Yasmina continued to see her often. She knew that Tahia was trying to get pregnant, but so far had been unsuccessful.

"My wife is fine, God be thanked. Ibrahim, the military police have been around, asking questions."

"What sort of questions?"

"About you. About your political leanings, about your bank account and investments."

"What? But why?"

"I do not know. But I have just now learned from a friend, I cannot tell you who, that the Rasheed name is on a certain list."

"What list?"

"The one belonging to the Visitors of Dawn."

Ibrahim went to the outer door, peered up and down the deserted corridor, then locked the door, came in and locked the inner door, also, before saying, "How can we possibly be on this list? My family has no argument with Nasser's government. We are peaceful people, Jamal."

"I swear upon the chastity of Sayyida Zeinab that it is true. You must be careful, my brother. The military police are powerful; Minister Amer is greatly feared. Now that the Army is in charge of everything, if a man so much as criticizes Cairo's unreliable telephones, he is arrested and his property seized in the name of the state."

Jamal looked around, as if one of Nasser's notorious spies might be hiding in Ibrahim's examination room. "Listen to me, Ibrahim. Your family is in danger. No one is exempt from these madmen. They come in the night, force their way in, and arrest the men of the family. Many are never heard from again. This time it is not like before, during the Revolution, when you were arrested. This is far, far worse, for they can take your house, your bank account, all that you own."

Suddenly, from the street below, came a clamor of honking horns and cheering voices. Yasmina got up and closed the window as Jamal continued in a low voice. "Ibrahim, you know my sister, Munirah, who is married to the rich manufacturer? They came to her home late last night. She and the children were forced out into the street while the soldiers impounded the house and everything in it. They stripped the rings from her fingers and the necklaces from her daughters' necks. Then they took her husband and eldest sons away. You don't hear about these things because the newspapers are afraid to print them. But it is the rich who are the targets of this scourge."

"In the name of God, is there no way we can protect ourselves?"

"I'll tell you what I have done. I signed over the deeds of my apartment houses to Tahia and my female cousins. Then I closed my bank account and hid the money. If the Visitors of the Dawn come to the house of Jamal Rasheed, they won't find much. Believe me, Ibrahim, there is nowhere to turn, no one you can trust. Even some of those who once had power have been stripped of that power."

"But why should my name be put on that list? By God, I have led a

peaceful life since the day Farouk sailed from Alexandria. My family and
I are blameless! What does Minister Amer have against me?"

"Ibrahim," Jamal said, "it is not Amer who is after you. It is his under
secretary, a man little known to the people, but one of immense power.
And once he places a name on that secret list, there is no escaping it."

"Who is this man?"

"Someone who was once your friend. Hassan al-Sabir."

=

"Poor Ibrahim," Alice said, as she accepted a cup of coffee from
Maryam Misrahi. "I'm afraid all he remembers of England is how my
father shunned us when we went there for our honeymoon. Eddie was
wonderful to Ibrahim, of course. Edward was like my mother, they both
adored the East. But my father believed I had married beneath myself."
She paused and heard faint strains of music coming from the next
apartment—Arabic music, which she had never quite gotten used to.
"I'm so glad we're taking this trip," she said. "I feel almost as if England
is being given a second chance!"

"Family is important," said Suleiman who, at seventy, had the appearance of a man who has settled comfortably into retirement. "Maryam
and I would like to travel and see the children, but they are spread all
over the world, and I fear we aren't up to such an odyssey any more."
He looked at Amira, who was also visiting, and said, "Your son is a good
man, to spare the time from his medical practice and take his wife back
to her homeland. It is something I wish I had done when I was younger,
traveled around the world and visited my children."

"I thank God for Ibrahim," Amira said, measuring sugar into her
coffee, hiding her anxiety in the small rituals of spooning and stirring.
She chided herself for her groundless fear—that she might never see her
son again once he left—and she fought to hide it from her friends. "May
God grant you safe journey," she said softly to Alice, "and a speedy
return."

A modest balcony jutted out from the Misrahis' apartment, not big
enough to accommodate people, but large enough for the pots of
geraniums and marigolds Maryam cultivated. Its best feature was a large
sliding-glass door that could be opened to admit the sultry September
evening air, along with cooking aromas and sounds of traffic. As the
diaphanous curtains stirred in the late summer breeze, Alice took her

coffee and went to look out over the small balcony, which also had a view of the Nile. "I heard somewhere," she said, "that lotuses are called brides of the Nile. Why is that?"

Amira joined her daughter-in-law at the open door and regarded the mighty water that flowed beneath the stone bridge; she sensed the river's power, inhaled its scents. Was there a more beautiful river than the Mother of Rivers? she wondered. Was there a more beautiful and blessed land than Egypt, Mother of the World?

"Ali told me that long ago, in the days of the pharaohs," Amira explained, "a young virgin was sacrificed every year just before the annual flooding of the river. She was thrown into the Nile, and if she drowned she became the bride of the river, endowing the flood with rich silt and the promise of plentiful crops and an abundant harvest. But now only the fragile lotus flower is the bride of the Nile."

Alice pressed a scented handkerchief to her throat. In twenty-one years, she had yet to become acclimated to Egypt's heat. "You yourself come to the river every year on the same day and toss a flower onto the water. Is it for the lotus ceremony?"

Thinking of the day she had gone to see Safeya Rageb, the first day she had set foot out of the house, Amira said, "No, that is not the reason. I was lost in the city once, and Ali spoke to me from the past, on that bridge, down there. He set me on the right path, and guided my way. It was in that moment that I recognized the power and mystery of the Nile." She looked at Alice. "Did you know that the river is haunted by the souls of those who have drowned in it? Not just the brides, but fishermen, swimmers, people who commit suicide. The Nile is the giver of life, and the taker of it."

"It gives us damn good fish, though," Suleiman said behind them, as he reached for his coffee.

Maryam laughed. "Since his retirement, food has become my husband's passion!"

Suleiman waved away his wife's comment and addressed Alice. "Soon, my dear, you will be enjoying England's delectable bounty— scones, strawberry jam, and cream. Devonshire tea, marvelous! I had it once, when I was there in 1936. I can taste that jam still."

Maryam laughed, and went back into the kitchen. Alice turned to her mother-in-law. "Mother Amira, why don't you come to England with us? You've never been out of Egypt."

But Amira smiled and said, "It is a trip for you and Ibrahim. Make it a second honeymoon." And, she added silently, make it an occasion to heal yourself.

Ibrahim had come up with the idea for the trip shortly after Alice's miscarriage, when she had lost the child she had hoped would be a son, and had slipped into a deep depression, and, like a wonderful medicine, the prospect of going home had cheered her up. No, Amira would not think of going with them. Besides, she had plans of her own. She had decided to go on a journey herself, to the holy city of Mecca, in Arabia.

"I don't have any close relatives in England anymore," Alice said. "Just an elderly aunt. But my friends are there." She paused and looked out at the brightly lit, noisy city that she thought of as a crazy quilt of East and West, and which, once in a while, sometimes seemed very alien to her. She would be in a shop she had visited many times, bargaining in Arabic over the price of fabric or a pair of shoes, as she had done for two decades, and all of a sudden everything would fall out of focus; the words would sound garbled and meaningless in her mouth, the smell of the shop and the street outside would overwhelm her. And she would wonder for an instant where she was and why she was there. Afterward, when she felt herself slip back into synchronization with Cairo, she would think of the heat and the sand that had gotten under her skin, and she would imagine that only the fog and mist of England could cleanse her.

But there was a more urgent, secret reason for her wanting to go to England. After the miscarriage she had discovered a hidden depression running steadily, deep inside her, like a cold subterranean stream that never surfaced. She had begun to think about her mother, and wonder if *she* had sensed a similar chill within herself. What had driven Lady Frances to commit suicide? Melancholia, it said on the death certificate.

Alice had decided to go to England and seek answers. The elderly aunt, Penelope, had been her mother's best friend. Perhaps Aunt Penny knew why Lady Frances had taken her own life. Alice needed to know if it had been due to some external cause, or if it were inborn, like a genetic tendency, and could not have been avoided. Alice needed to know because she was going to be forty-two next year, the same age her mother had been when she died.

"Friends are good," Suleiman said, getting up stiffly. Like Maryam's, his hair was completely white, and he wore his clothes like a man who feels he has earned the right to look comfortable. "So many of our friends have left Egypt. They prosper though, in Europe and America. Still, I believe President Nasser has good intentions for Egypt. Tell me about the place where you were born, Alice, perhaps I passed through it in 1936."

Amira went into the kitchen where Maryam was lifting freshly baked baklava out of the oven. "More and more these days," Maryam said, as she poured cold syrup over the hot pastry, "Suleiman lives in the past. Is that what happens to old people, Amira? When the future is smaller than the past, do they start to look backward?"

"Perhaps it is God's way of preparing us for eternity. Here, let me help you with that. I, too, have been thinking more and more about the past lately. It is strange, Maryam, but the older I get the more I remember of those long-ago days, as though I were drawing nearer to them rather than moving farther away."

"Perhaps someday, God willing, you will remember everything and you will be blessed with the childhood memories with which we are all blessed."

To be blessed with memories of the past! Amira thought. But, in order to seek the past, she knew she must travel the road back, find where she came from, who she really was. Was my mother killed that day and left in the desert? Amira wondered, or was she also abducted and placed in another harem? Is she possibly still alive even? I am sixty-two; she would be in her eighties, maybe even younger. If she gave birth to me when she was a girl of fourteen, as I was when I had Ibrahim, then she could still be a healthy woman today somewhere in this world, and perhaps, on hot musky nights such as this, she looks at the stars as I do, and wonders about the little girl who had been torn from her arms.

Amira considered the square minaret that appeared more frequently in her dreams than any other memory. Where on earth did it exist? The few square minarets found in Cairo were elaborate structures, covered with intricate decoration, but the one of her dreams was plain and unadorned. Each time it appeared to her, Amira sensed that it was trying to tell her something, as if it were whispering, *Find me, and you shall find all the answers—your mother's name, where you were born, your birth-star.*

I will make the pilgrimage to Mecca and, God willing, I will find the trail that brought me to Egypt, and follow it back to my beginnings. Possibly even to my mother.

When they came back into the parlor, Suleiman snipped off the end of his cigar, examined it a moment, then said, "So, Yasmina wants to be a doctor, does she? And why not? My Itzak in California, his daughter Rachel is planning to go to medical school. It's a good profession for a girl. Women understand pain and suffering. Men do not. When do we ever experience it? Maryam, let us go to California and visit Itzak. Amira, do you remember my Itzak? Of course you do, you helped bring him into the world. He writes to me in English, he tells me he isn't teaching his children Arabic because, he says, they are American. But I say they are Egyptian, by God, and if I have to go there and—"

They heard a loud knocking at the door. "Who could that be?" Maryam said, wiping her hands on her apron. But before she could go and see, they heard a loud crash and suddenly men in uniforms were swarming through the apartment.

Suleiman shot to his feet. "Who are you? What do you want?"

"Suleiman Misrahi?" said the officer in charge.

"I am he."

"You have been accused of speaking treasonous words against the government."

Amira's hand flew to her breast. It was the nightmare of Ibrahim's arrest and imprisonment all over again. Everyone had heard of these late-night raids by Nasser's military police, and the rumors of banishment to detention camps without a trial. But those arrested were members of the subversive Muslim Brotherhood, or other antigovernment groups. What could they want with an elderly Jewish couple?

"There is some mistake," Maryam began, but she was shoved out of the way. She fell against a china cabinet and felt a sudden sharp pain in her ribs.

Alice ran to her, and Amira stepped up to the officer in charge. "You have no right," she said. "This is a house of peace."

But she was ignored, and she and the others watched in horror as the soldiers went through the apartment, pulling clothes from closets, emptying drawers, stuffing jewelry and money into their pockets. One of the men swept an arm across the sideboard, sending a silver menorah to the floor, along with framed pictures of Misrahi children and grandchildren.

The menorah, the picture frames with the photos ripped out, and Maryam's antique silverware were all dumped into a gunnysack and hauled out into the corridor.

"Alice," Amira said quietly, so that the soldiers wouldn't hear. "Telephone Ibrahim, quickly."

Finally, the men seized Suleiman.

"No!" cried Maryam.

"You are under arrest," barked the officer, "for subversive acts against the government and people of Egypt."

Suleiman turned a bewildered look on his wife.

"Please," she begged. "There is some mistake. We have done nothing—"

But a soldier pushed Suleiman roughly through the doorway and out into the hall. The elderly man suddenly clutched his chest, gave a cry, and sank to the floor.

Maryam ran to him. "Suleiman? *Suleiman!*"

CHAPTER 23

Ibrahim stopped first to warn Amira and Alice. They were with Maryam, sitting shivah for Suleiman, while friends came with condolences and to sing kaddish, the Jewish prayer of mourning. Because Maryam's apartment had been confiscated and she had literally been put out on the street with only the clothes she was wearing, the seven-day observance was being held at the home of the rabbi of her synagogue. After that, she would have to find a place to live. Amira had begged Maryam to move into the Rasheed house, but Maryam had declined. With Suleiman gone, she had said that she could not stand the pain of returning to Virgins of Paradise Street, where they had lived happily for so many years.

No one knew why the Misrahis had been targeted by the Visitors of the Dawn. The soldiers were breaking down doors and making arrests all over the city, their victims primarily being rich people. No other Jews

had been hit, and certainly no one in the Misrahis' reduced circumstances. Suleiman had sold his import business; he and Maryam had been
living on a modest pension. With the help of family members, Amira was
trying to find out why the soldiers had come to arrest Suleiman, and
where their belongings had been taken. So far, she had learned nothing.

A servant came in and informed Amira that her son was asking for her.
"You have news?" she said, meeting Ibrahim at the door.

"I have spoken to everyone I know, Mother, every government man
who owes me a favor, but they can do nothing, they are all afraid for
their jobs. I doubt we shall ever know what became of the Misrahis'
possessions. There is no one else we can turn to."

Amira thought of Safeya Rageb, who had been responsible for
Ibrahim's release from prison nearly twenty-five years ago. Hoping that
Mrs. Rageb might help Maryam, Amira had gone to her, only to learn
that Captain Rageb, one of the original Free Officers, was no longer in
favor with the government. He had been quietly "retired," and Mrs.
Rageb's days of granting favors had ended.

"But I came for another reason," Ibrahim said. "Our family is in
danger, Mother. We have been targeted by the military police. I want
you and Alice to go home as soon as possible, hide our valuables, and
warn the women that if soldiers come to the house, they are to stay
calm."

He turned to Alice and said, "I am sorry, my dear, but we will have
to postpone our trip to England for just a little while. Do you want to
go ahead without me?"

Alice said, "No, I'll stay. We'll go when it is safe."

Maryam came to the door. "What is it, Amira? Ibrahim, what is
wrong?"

"*Allah ma'aki*, Auntie Maryam," he said. "Forgive this intrusion, but
my mother is needed at home."

"Yes, of course," Maryam said. "In these dangerous times you
should be with your family."

Amira said, "I will come back as soon as I can."

Maryam laid a hand on her friend's arm and said, "I know you have
been trying to find out where our belongings went, my dear sister.
Trouble yourself no further. What has happened is God's will. I have
made a decision: my son wishes me to go back to California with him,

and live there with him and his children. We will leave as soon as we've"—her voice broke—"finished saying good-bye to Suleiman."

Ibrahim said, "Mother, you and Alice take my car, I'll get a taxi. We must hurry."

"Is the danger so near, then?"

"I pray to God it isn't."

"But where are you going?"

"There is one person left in all Cairo who might yet save us. Pray for me, Mother, that he will grant me a hearing."

The house on Pyramids Way, set amid sugarcane fields and palm groves, could barely be seen from the road, its brilliant whitewashed walls glimpsed through ancient date palms, fig and olive trees, and flowering shrubs; massive sycamores guarded an emerald lawn and limestone walkways, while heavy wooden shutters stood closed against the sun and prying eyes. As Ibrahim got out of the taxi, he peered through the protective growth and thought, A very rich man lives here.

He knocked at a door so intricately carved that he felt as if he were visiting a mosque, and a servant in an immaculate white galabeya admitted him into an elegant living room. Rugs and animal skins covered a highly polished floor, and overhead ceiling fans kept the hot air moving.

The servant vanished, and a moment later Hassan appeared. Ibrahim thought his former friend had changed little in the four years since they had last spoken, except perhaps Hassan seemed a little more self-assured, a little less hungry than he had been the night Ibrahim had broken the marriage contract. And he advertised his wealth in the long, richly embroidered caftan he wore, the gold watch, the heavy gold rings.

"Welcome to my humble house," Hassan said. "I have been expecting you."

Ibrahim looked around and said dryly, "Humble? This is hardly the austerity I would expect from one of Nasser's henchmen."

"The spoils of war, my friend. Merely my rewards for serving the socialist cause. My servant is bringing coffee. Unless you prefer tea or whiskey?" Hassan went to a mahogany liquor cart with crystal decanters and glasses, and poured himself a drink.

Ibrahim decided to come right to the point. "I have been warned about the Visitors of the Dawn. Is that warning valid?"

"Such a way for old friends to greet each other. Where are your manners?"

"Why is my family on that list?"

"Because I put you there."

"Why?"

Hassan looked at his drink, took a sip, then said, "You are very direct, very straightforward. It's unlike you. Yes, I put your name on that list, and for just one reason. So that you would come to me with a bribe to remove it."

Ibrahim gestured around the magnificently furnished room. "I am hardly richer than you."

"It isn't money that I want."

"What then?"

"Can't you guess?"

Ibrahim considered the treasures surrounding him: the massive elephant tusks crisscrossed above the fireplace, the antelope-foot cigarette holder, the zebra skin covering the polished floor. An ancient Egyptian statue, which Ibrahim did not doubt was genuine, and which he did not doubt had been illegally obtained, stood on a pedestal beneath handsome Scottish bagpipes adorning a wall, framed by a tartan. Hassan's pillage, he thought, wondering if Maryam and Suleiman's priceless antique silver menorah was also somewhere in this house, already part of Hassan's collection.

"I desire another trophy," Hassan said, when Ibrahim did not answer him, and when he saw how he looked at the treasures.

"What do you mean?"

"Actually, I only want what is really mine, something which you took from me when you broke our agreement. Give it to me, and your family will be safe."

Ibrahim's look was deadly. "And what is that?"

"Yasmina, of course."

—

"Here we are, darling," Yasmina said to Mohammed as the taxi pulled up in front of the Rasheed house. She hugged him and gave him a big smile, trying to hide her fears. Omar had left the country yesterday, on an engineering assignment in Kuwait, and because of the arrests going on around the city, hitting randomly and unexpectedly, he had insisted she move herself and the boy into the house on Virgins of Paradise Street. We'll be safe here, little one, she thought as servants came to help with the luggage, looking at the stately, rose-colored mansion beckoning like a calm harbor.

As she stepped out of the taxi, carrying her heavy son because she didn't want to put him down until they were safely within the high walls, she thought of her school friend, Layla Azmi, who was married to a wealthy man. The military police had forced their way into Layla's house, made a list of everything in it down to the last candlestick, told her she had three days to get out, and that she was not to take a single thing with her. Then they had driven off with her husband, and she hadn't heard from him since.

Nefissa came hurrying down the path and took the three-year-old from Yasmina, saying, "Praise God, now all the family is here. And how is the grandson of my heart today?"

Servants collected Yasmina's luggage and carried it into the house with uncharacteristic urgency. Fear, she saw, had infected even the peaceful atmosphere on Virgins of Paradise Street.

As they stepped from the September heat into the cool interior of the house, Nefissa said, "Ibrahim has told us to hide everything. If you have brought jewelry with you, Yasmina, we will have to put it somewhere in case . . ." She stopped before saying, "the military police come." She didn't want to frighten Mohammed.

Yasmina found the house a hive of activity, paintings being taken down from walls, china and crystal removed from display tables, and Amira at the center of it all, supervising. In the salon, Yasmina was pleased to see Jamal Rasheed and, to her joy, Tahia. They embraced warmly, but Yasmina saw the worry in her cousin's eyes.

When Zachariah came into the room a moment later, removing his gold wire-rimmed glasses to rub his eyes, Yasmina embraced him, too, and murmured, "Praise God we are all together."

He turned to Amira and said, "I had no luck, Umma. I have wasted another morning at the office of the defense minister, trying to find out about the Misrahis. This time I was told the minister has gone out of town! It is impossible to see him. There are hundreds crowded into his waiting room and out into the hall, all with petitions like ours!"

Zachariah glanced at Tahia, but couldn't look at Jamal. Since Tahia's wedding, Zachariah had not allowed himself to even contemplate the physical side of her relationship with the older man. But this morning Jamal had proudly announced that Tahia was expecting their first child, and Zachariah couldn't bear the thought of what her pregnancy was proof of.

"Zakki," Amira said quietly, so as not to alarm the others, "don't worry about the Misrahis any more. Maryam told me today she is going to California with her son. We have other, more urgent matters to attend to."

He looked around, noticing for the first time that everyone was busily stripping the house. The job of collecting all the jewelry had fallen to Alice, who was going from bedroom to bedroom, making sure all drawers, jewelry boxes, and purses were emptied of anything of value. Basima saw that all designer fashions, satin and silk undergarments, crocodile shoes, and fur coats were brought into the salon and folded into empty flour or potato sacks. The boys then carted these off to the kitchen, where Sahra oversaw their placement around the big tiled room, in full view so that soldiers seeing them might not suspect their true contents. Rayya helped Doreya remove paintings from the wall and wrap them, while Haneya assisted Alice in the garden, digging holes to receive the pots of jewelry that had been collected. Everyone worked quickly and silently, without the joy and merriment that usually accompanied household projects. Night was coming, which meant the soldiers could arrive at any time, and the women had nowhere near rendered the house bare, with everything of value safely hidden or disguised.

"Will this work, Umma?" Zachariah said. "Everyone knows we're rich."

"They will think we have fallen on hard times," Amira replied. "Our cotton holdings have dwindled to nearly nothing, and your father practices medicine in a middle-class neighborhood that is rapidly turning fellaheen. When the soldiers come, they will see a once-wealthy family reduced to penury, living off a small income and their pride." Amira had also closed out her own personal bank account and hidden the cash in the pigeon coop.

When she turned to supervising the stripping of the divans, the luxurious satin and velvet throws being folded and carried up to the roof to be hidden in the fruit shed, with plain blankets laid down in their place, Yasmina went to Zachariah and said, "Where is Father?"

But the twenty-year-old shrugged. "He left the house this morning right after breakfast. Umma and Auntie Alice were at Auntie Maryam's, and he told them to come home and hide everything. I didn't go to classes today. Mishmish, do you know what's going on? Why are we in danger?"

Thinking of Jamal Rasheed's visit to her father's office the night before, she was tempted to tell her brother what she knew, that Hassan was behind it all. But Zachariah seemed so lost and confused. Although he had been born five months before Yasmina, she felt like the older sibling. So she smiled and said, "Don't worry. It will soon pass and everything will be all right." Then she took her son from Nefissa and hurried upstairs.

In the bedroom she had shared with Camelia when they were little, Yasmina found her suitcases already there, one open on the bed, ready to be unpacked.

As she put her son down, he said, "I'm thirsty, Mama." She took him into the bathroom, filled a glass with water, and then sat on the edge of the tub to watch him drink, marveling, as she always did, that this little boy was hers. She smiled at the concentration with which he drank—all ten tiny fingers grasping the glass, his eyes downcast, his eyebrows forming a furrow. Yasmina had observed the same intensity in other things Mohammed did, even if it was only playing with his building blocks, and she wondered if she was already seeing him as he was going to be as an adult. He would be handsome, she could tell, like most of the Rasheed men, and perhaps a little vain, but he had already learned to laugh at himself, the way Egyptians did. Even now, after he finished drinking, he looked down and saw that he'd spilled a lot of the water on his shirt. He shrieked and laughed and called himself a hopeless donkey, and then he surprised Yasmina with an adult remark that he had picked up from one of his uncles: "God must love clumsy people, he made so many of them!"

She laughed and drew him to her, and he giggled and said, "May we play 'Happy Families,' Mama?"

Her moment of joy died suddenly, as she remembered the danger the family was in, and the errand she must run.

"I tell you what," she said, stroking the hair that never seemed to stay combed, "we'll play in a little while. I have to go out, but when I come back we'll play any game you want." Then she hugged him again and thought: I will not let any harm come to you.

As they went back into the bedroom, Nefissa came in, saying, "Such turmoil! Cousin Ahmed and his wife and children are coming in from Assyut. The house will be full tonight!"

"Auntie, I have to go out for a while. Will you watch Mohammed? Everyone is so busy that I'm afraid he might get ignored."

Nefissa sat on the bed and pulled the boy onto her lap. "Nothing could give me more joy," she said, producing a piece of candy from her pocket and giving it to him.

When Yasmina suddenly dropped her purse and retrieved her belongings with trembling hands, Nefissa noticed what she had not seen upon her niece's arrival—that the young woman was highly agitated. "If the Visitors of the Dawn frighten you so," she said, "then wouldn't it be better to stay here?"

"This is an appointment that cannot wait, Auntie."

Nefissa's curiosity was piqued. "What—" she began. But Yasmina rushed out.

When Mohammed squirmed on her lap, Nefissa put the three-year-old down and decided to unpack for her niece. She started with the opened suitcase on the bed, lifting out the carefully folded nightgowns and lingerie. But as she drew out Yasmina's plastic toiletries bag, it fell open and the contents spilled out. As she replaced them, she came across something that at first baffled her. When she realized it was a diaphragm she was stunned.

Birth control? No wonder no children had come after Mohammed! But surely Omar didn't know about this.

As she finished putting everything back into the bag, she saw that a lipstick had fallen to the floor, and when she picked it up, she found a piece of paper that must have dropped from Yasmina's purse. An address was written on it, in Yasmina's handwriting.

=

"What did you say?" Ibrahim said, taking a step closer to Hassan.

"I said I want Yasmina. If you give her to me, I shall take your family's name off that list."

"You dare!"

"She is mine! You promised her to me and then you broke that promise, proving that you are not a man of honor. On that day, you and I ceased to be brothers. But we need not be enemies. Tell Yasmina to pay me a call and we can—"

"Go to hell."

"I hadn't thought you would be so resistant. After all, your entire family's welfare is at stake."

Ibrahim's hands curled into fists. "And we will fight you as a family. You accuse me of having no honor. Then you don't know me. I would rather see my family on the street than lose our honor."

"Remember, my friend, you already have a prison record—for crimes against the Egyptian people."

"If you touch my daughter—"

Hassan laughed. "I remember when we were young, Ibrahim, and you would go on and on to me about how you wanted to do this or that, and how you were going to stand up to your father about it. And then I would see you, nearly a grown man, standing before him with your head bowed, saying, 'Yes sir,' like a schoolboy. Don't make a fool of yourself, my friend. You will only regret it."

"Yes, I have done things in my life that I am now sorry for," Ibrahim said, startled to hear himself make such a confession, further surprised to realize that he meant it. "They were the actions of a weak man," he said. "I am not proud of them. You mention my father. He was a strong man, and next to him I did feel weak. But my father is with God, and I am on my own. If I have to fight you, I will."

He stepped up to Hassan. Their faces were so close he could smell his friend's familiar cologne. "Stay away from my family," Ibrahim said. "Stay away from Yasmina, or you will regret it."

Hassan's smiled. "Threats, Ibrahim? *I* have the power here, not you. Remember, I put you in prison once already."

"I know," Ibrahim said quietly.

"According to your record, they . . . interrogated you. Is that right?"

Ibrahim's jaw tightened. "You will not provoke me into fighting you, not here, not now."

"I don't want to fight you. I want Yasmina."

"You will never have her."

Hassan shrugged. "One way or another, she will be mine. And you will learn once and for all that I am not a man to be trifled with, a man with whom you can make contracts and then break them. You humiliated me, Ibrahim, and now I intend to do the same to you."

=

As Yasmina's taxi arrived in front of the house set far back from the road on Pyramids Way, she did not see another taxi just depart, nor the passenger inside. Her mind was on what she was going to say to Hassan. As she followed the path through the trees and shrubs, she felt confused. Why was Uncle Hassan doing this? When Jamal had spoken his name in her father's office the night before, she had thought it was a mistake. But, seeing the look on her father's face, she had thought, Can there be any truth in it?

At the front door, which was large and intimidating, she felt her resolve weaken. It couldn't be true. Not Uncle Hassan. And yet . . .

He hadn't been to their house in over four years. He hadn't attended her wedding, or Camelia's birthday party, or Zachariah's high school graduation. For a close friend of her father's, worthy of being called Uncle by his children, Hassan al-Sabir had been curiously absent from their lives in recent years. She took a deep breath and knocked, and a moment later was following a servant into a living room that looked like a museum. Hassan was there, and as he rose from the couch, Yasmina realized that this was the first time she had ever been alone with him.

"Yasmina! My dear," he said. "Well, well, this is a surprise. You've grown. You're a woman now." He clasped her hands and smiled. "Welcome, and God's peace upon you."

"God's peace and His blessings upon you, Uncle Hassan."

His smile deepened. "So I am still your uncle, am I? Please, sit down."

Yasmina regarded the leather sofa spread with leopard skins; her eyes grew wide as she took in the rest of the surroundings.

"As you can see, my dear," he said, "I am doing very well these days."

She was drawn to a framed photograph on the fireplace mantle—a picture of two young men in white polo flannels, leaning on each other and laughing.

"That is your father and I at Oxford, many years ago," Hassan said, joining her. "Our team won that day. It was one of the best days in my life."

"Uncle Hassan, I came to talk to you about my father."

Hassan went on staring at the photograph. "My experience at school would have been a very lonely one if it hadn't been for your father," he said quietly. "I was all alone in the world, my father had just died, my mother had died years before, and I had no brothers or sisters. If it weren't for Ibrahim Rasheed befriending me I would have been wretched." He looked at Yasmina. "I loved your father very much—more than he knew, I think."

She thought Hassan's look had softened, making him seem younger. "Uncle Hassan, do you know why I've come to see you?"

"First give me news of your family," he said, taking a seat on the sofa and beckoning to her to join him. "Are they well? Tell me," he said as he moved closer to her, "how is your grandmother taking the Misrahis' misfortune?"

"The Misrahis? Umma is very upset, of course. We are all upset. But why—?"

"I hear she's been rushing around like a chicken without a head, trying to make things right."

Yasmina frowned. "I beg your pardon?"

"Did you know that I've always privately called your grandmother the Dragon? She has never liked me. From the very first day Ibrahim brought me to your house, when we returned from Oxford. That was long before you were born, my beautiful Yasmina." He lifted a lock of her blond hair and sifted it through his fingers. "I saw it in her eyes, when he introduced me to her. She was smiling, and then she suddenly went cold. For no reason, little Mishmish. And did you know that I wanted to marry you? Your father and I even signed the engagement contract. But the Dragon made Ibrahim break it. She said I wasn't good enough for you."

She stood up quickly, nearly tripping on the zebra-skin rug. "Uncle Hassan, I heard something last night which I find impossible to believe. It is about the Visitors of the Dawn and a certain list of names."

"Yes, the list. What about it?"

"I was told that my family is on that list."

"What if it is?"

"Uncle Hassan, do you have anything to do with the Visitors of the Dawn?"

"But of course, sweet Mishmish. The *Zuwwar el-Fagr* are under the direct command of Defense Minister Hakim Amer, and I am his right-hand man. And so whatever they do is a result of my orders. As a matter of fact, I was responsible for the search and seizure of the Misrahis' apartment in the first place. *I* sent the soldiers there."

"You! But why? What had they done?"

"Nothing, they were quite innocent. I used them as bait, so to speak."

"What do you mean, bait?"

"I want something, and this is my way of getting it. I was the one who added the Rasheed name to that list. Upon my order, the soldiers will visit your house on Virgins of Paradise Street, and I assure you, they will be most thorough. They will strip it bare, and then confiscate the house itself. Your grandmother and the others will be out on the street. Unless, of course, I get what I want."

Yasmina began to tremble. "What is that?"

"You, of course." He stood up and walked toward her. "I can take the Rasheed name off that list. I can make your house safe from the Visitors of the Dawn. But it will require a certain, shall we say payment from you. Here, now."

She stared at him in shock.

"Blame your father, Yasmina, it was he who dishonored our friendship, by marrying you to Omar instead of to me. I have waited all this time to take my revenge. And now I shall have it, through you. Your father can't stop me this time, I shall have you after all."

She wrapped her arms around herself, shivering. "And if I refuse to cooperate?"

"Then I will send soldiers to Virgins of Paradise Street. And I assure you that no one will be spared."

"I won't give you what you want."

"Yes, you will." He reached for her and drew her to him. When she tried to push him away, he gripped both of her wrists with one hand and tore her blouse. "Now you won't tell anyone about this," he murmured, slipping his hand under her bra and cupping a firm young breast.

She broke away and ran across the room, stumbling over a table, sending a vase crashing to the floor. He caught up with her, swung her around, and pinned her against the wall.

"After all," he said, "in these cases it is the woman's honor that is ruined, not the man's. Remember, you came here of your own free will. You will do everything I say, and I shall enjoy it very much. And who knows? You might enjoy it yourself."

=

Out on the road, Nefissa pulled her car up to the spot where she had seen Yasmina get out of a taxi. Her grandson was with her; she had taken Mohammed for ice cream, and then curiosity had led her to the address that had fallen from Yasmina's purse. She gazed for a moment at the secluded villa behind the trees, and then, seeing a woman sweeping the path that led to the house, she rolled down her window and called, "God's peace upon you, Mother. Can you tell me who lives in this house?"

"Fear God, Sayyida, that is Hassan al-Sabir," the woman said in a low voice, "a very powerful man."

Hassan al-Sabir!

But what on earth was Yasmina doing with Hassan?

CHAPTER 2 4

The audience in the crowded Cage d'Or nightclub jumped to their feet and cheered: "*Y'Allah!* Camelia! Dahiba!"

It was time for Dahiba's drum solo, the climax of their show, and so Camelia blew kisses as she left the stage. Although it was autumn, the evening was warm; she was anxious to get out of her costume, which was a plain white cotton galabeya with a simple scarf around the hips. Because of the atmosphere of austerity prevailing over Nasser's new Egypt, Camelia and Dahiba, like all other entertainers in Cairo, had put away their flamboyant costumes, removed the glitter from their shows and modified their choreography to give the audiences more beledi, "folk," and less showy Oriental. But even with such curbs, their audiences were always packed and enthusiastic.

Backstage, Camelia was surprised to find Yasmina waiting for her. The sisters had seen little of each other in the past few months, and Camelia was shocked to see dark circles under Yasmina's blue eyes. Camelia was further alarmed when she realized Yasmina did not have her son with her; Mohammed always went everywhere with his mother. Despite her appearance, Yasmina smiled and hugged her sister, and declared that she was dancing better every day. "And have you seen this, Lili? Read it!"

Camelia read aloud the newspaper article Yasmina had circled: "The lovely Camelia, new to the Cairo club scene, is a dancer of unsurpassed excellence, possessing the suppleness of a serpent, the grace of a gazelle, and the beauty of a butterfly. This reviewer predicts that one day Camelia will surpass even the great Dahiba, her mentor." The piece was written by Yacob Mansour, whose reviews Camelia had never read before.

Yasmina laughed. "He is in love with you, Lili! You have a secret admirer!"

Camelia already had several admirers, men who made enquiries of Hakim Raouf about his wife's protégée, and who sometimes sent flowers and messages backstage. But twenty-one-year-old Camelia was not going to allow herself to fall in love. She was going to devote herself to becoming the greatest dancer Egypt had ever known, and a husband or a lover did not figure in her plans.

When Camelia saw the shadow behind her sister's smile, and how Yasmina's hands trembled, she led her into the dressing room, picked up the phone, and asked for tea to be brought, then turned to Yasmina and said, "What's wrong, Mishmish? You look so tired."

"It's nothing. I just have . . . something on my mind."

"You are trying to do too much," Camelia said as she pinned her long black hair on top of her head and proceeded to remove her stage makeup. "Being a mother to Mohammed, taking classes at the university, working in Father's office as his nurse." But when she saw her sister's stricken look in the mirror, Camelia turned around and said, "Mishmish, I know something is wrong. Please tell me."

"I don't know how to say it, Lili," Yasmina said quietly. "A terrible thing has happened."

"What are you talking about?"

"I did something, no, what I mean is, something happened to me, the day after Suleiman Misrahi died. I haven't told anyone, not even Mother. There's no one I can confide in, Lili, except you. And I don't even know how to tell you."

"Just tell it, like we used to when we were growing up. We never kept secrets then, did we?"

"Camelia, I'm pregnant."

Camelia experienced the quick stab of jealousy she always did when a friend or female relative announced a pregnancy—such joyful news was never going to be hers to announce—and then she quickly felt remorseful. "But that's wonderful!"

"No, Lili, it isn't wonderful. You know that I have been practicing birth control. Omar doesn't know about that, no one knows. Only you."

"Well, no contraceptive method is foolproof, Yasmina. Mistakes happen. I know you want to go to medical school, but you'll just have to put it off a while longer."

"You don't understand, Lili. The child is not Omar's."

The roar of applause came through the thin walls, and heavy footsteps thudded past the dressing-room door. Camelia got up, turned the key in the lock, then sat back down. "If the child is not Omar's, then whose is it?"

Yasmina told Camelia about Jamal Rasheed's visit to the office, his warnings of danger, and finally that he had found out the name of the man who had put the family on the list for the Visitors of Dawn. "I went to his house. I kept thinking—Uncle Hassan, it couldn't be! But he admitted everything to me, and he said it was because he wanted *me*, that he and I had been betrothed but that Father had broken the contract."

"By all the saints," Camelia murmured. "This is impossible, Yasmina. And then what happened?"

"When I realized what a foolish thing I had done in going there, I started to leave. He grabbed me, I tried to fight him. But he was too strong."

Camelia closed her eyes and murmured, "May he burn in hell. Oh Yasmina! And you have told no one about this?"

Yasmina shook her head.

"Uncle Hassan . . ." Camelia said in disbelief. "And to think how I worshiped him when I was little! I even had fantasies about marrying him! And now to discover that he is the son of Satan!"

"And I am carrying his child."

"Yasmina, listen to me. You must not tell anyone about this. They will judge you harshly. Remember Auntie Fatima, whose name we could never even speak. We don't know what it was she did, but Grandfather Ali would never forgive her. He threw her out, and even her own brother and sister won't talk about her."

"And they will do that to me."

"Allah, Yasmina! What do you think? You went to a man's house on your own, the worst thing a woman can do. Hassan did not force you into his house."

"I went there just to talk to him, Lili. And he overpowered me."

"You are the victim, Yasmina, but you will be punished all the same. That's the way it is. Now listen, Omar will believe the child is his. He's so conceited, his vanity will blind him to any lack of resemblance to himself. And everyone else will believe the child is his. What reason would they have for thinking otherwise? We must never tell anyone the truth, Mishmish. You would be ruined, and the family would be destroyed. For everyone's sake, but for yours most of all, you and I shall keep this a secret."

Yasmina sighed. "You're starting to sound like Umma."

"Perhaps this is what she would have said to you if you had gone to her. Now then, I am going to dinner after the show with some friends. I want you to come along. Don't shake your head. You don't get out enough, and these are very nice, respectable people. You are going to have a beautiful baby, and I am going to see to it that you forget all about Hassan al-Sabir."

Later that night, as Camelia lay in her bed, warm autumn moonlight spilling across her satin bedspread, she heard Yasmina's words again: "You're starting to sound like Umma." And it amazed her to realize that, in many ways, Umma had been right. Sometimes it *was* necessary to keep secrets in order to protect the family honor.

―

"California is such a strange place," Maryam had written, "I wonder if I shall ever fit in. But how strange and wonderful to attend a synagogue that is crowded! Suleiman would have been happy to see this. My heart is in Egypt with you, my sister, and with Suleiman."

Amira took the letter from Zubaida, who had just read it to her, and gazed at the writing. Although she couldn't read the words, she felt Maryam's spirit in the ink and paper, and it brought comfort in this troubled time.

The Visitors of the Dawn had not yet struck the Rasheed house, but the family was prepared: the salon had been stripped, the women wore no makeup or jewelry or expensive clothes, and the food that came from the kitchen consisted of Sahra's humble village recipes. But everyone was sleeping poorly, and each time someone knocked on the door, nerves snapped.

Amira carefully folded Maryam's letter into her pocket, and when she looked up, was startled to see Camelia standing in the salon.

"Umma?" the girl said.

"Granddaughter of my heart! Praise the Lord!"

"Oh, Umma! I was afraid you wouldn't see me! I'm so sorry for the things I said to you!"

Amira smiled through her tears. "You were eighteen and knew everything, like all eighteen-year-olds do! You've grown, you have filled out."

"I am a dancer now, Umma."

"Yes," Amira said. "Yasmina has told me."

"It is a very respectable act, Umma! I wear a beautiful galabeya. It has long sleeves and comes down to my ankles. And when I dance the beledi, oh, Umma, you should see how happy the people are!"

"Then I am glad, for God has found a place for you. Perhaps, in His infinite compassion, when He took away from you with one hand, He gave to you with the other. Make people happy, make their hearts sing, for that is God's precious gift to you."

"I want you to meet Dahiba, my teacher."

"The woman you have been living with?"

"Dahiba is very respectable, Umma. Have you seen her movies?"

"When I was young, your grandfather took me to a movie theater. There were special sections in those days, screened balconies where women could sit without being seen. Ali sat in the audience with the men, and I sat in a balcony with his mother and his first wife, who was sickly at the time, and his two sisters. The film was about adultery, I recall, and I was shocked. It was the first movie I had ever seen, and the last. No, I have not seen Dahiba's films."

"I want you to meet her, Umma. Come with me, let me show you where I live. You'll love her, I know you will!"

=

Like the rest of Cairo's rich, Dahiba and her husband Hakim Raouf had scaled down their life-style and stopped displaying their wealth. Although Raouf had friends in the government, and Dahiba was a favorite among members of the president's cabinet, they did not feel safe—no one did. So, along with her extravagant costumes, Dahiba had put away her furs and jewels, Raouf had dismissed their chauffeur. He drove the Chevrolet himself, and Dahiba arrived at the Club Cage d'Or like an ordinary citizen.

The were sitting in the living room, drinking coffee and eating oranges while they read movie scripts, when Camelia burst in. "I've brought someone to meet you!"

"*Al hamdu lillah!*" cried Raouf. "It is President Nasser himself!"

She laughed. "No, it's my grandmother. And she's waiting in the foyer."

Raouf's smile fell as he exchanged a glance with his wife.

"My dear," Dahiba said, rising from the sofa, "I don't think this was a good idea. Your grandmother will not approve of me, you have said so yourself."

"Yes, but we've had a long talk and she says she wants to meet you! You know how much I've wanted to be friends with Umma again. It was because of Yasmina's—It was something Yasmina said to me the other night at the club that made me decide to make amends with Umma. And she received me with so much joy! Perhaps deep down inside she doesn't approve of dancers, but please give her a chance. It means so much to me."

Dahiba looked at her husband, who quickly stood up and said, "I'm needed at the studio. I'll go out through the kitchen."

"I must warn you," Camelia said excitedly. "My grandmother is very old-fashioned. She doesn't go to movies or to nightclubs, so she's never heard of you. I hope you're not offended by that." She went out to the foyer, and came back, holding the door open for Amira. "Dahiba," she said, "I have the honor to introduce you to my grandmother. Umma, this is Dahiba, my teacher."

A moment of silence hung in the air, disturbed only by faint sounds of Cairo traffic in the street below. Then, with a sad smile, Dahiba said quietly, "Welcome to my house. Peace to you and the compassion of God."

Amira did not reply but stood there like a statue.

Dahiba sighed. "Won't you at least offer me a greeting, Mother?"

Amira turned, looked at Camelia and, without a word, walked out.

"Wait!" Camelia cried, running after her. "Umma, don't go!"

"Let her go, child," Dahiba said. "Let her go."

"I don't understand. Why did she leave? What happened?"

"Come here and sit down."

"Why did you call her Mother?"

"Because Amira *is* my mother. My real name is Fatima. I am Fatima Rasheed, and I am your aunt."

=

November light filtered through the gauze curtains into the living room as steam from the teapot filled the air with the scent of mint tea. Dahiba poured first for Camelia, then for herself, and settled back to talk.

"Are you angry with me?" Dahiba asked, "for not telling you?"

"I don't know. I'm confused. You told me your parents died in a boating accident."

"I made that up. I've never told anyone except Hakim who my real parents were. And I never told you, Camelia, because I had no idea what my mother might have said to you about her outcast daughter. I was afraid you wouldn't want to dance with me, if you knew who I really was."

"But how is it no one in the family ever found you out? Surely someone would have seen you, in a club or one of your movies!"

"I was young when my father banished me. By the time I became famous, certainly by the time I appeared on a movie screen, I had changed physically. I had matured, and cosmetics further altered my appearance. Besides, no one was looking for me on the stage or the screen. I did run into Maryam Misrahi once. I was coming out of the ballroom at the Hilton, and she was in the florist's shop in the lobby.

I don't know if she recognized me or not, or if she noticed that I was the dancer advertised on the poster outside. I thought she would come up and say something to me, but she didn't."

"What happened?" Camelia asked, putting her cup down and leaning forward. "Umma never told us anything about why you left the family."

Dahiba went to the window and looked out at the shadows collecting in the street below. A man in a dirty galabeya was pushing a cart piled high with plastic sandals. "I was just seventeen," she said quietly, "the same age you were when you sneaked onto the stage and danced for me that night."

She lit a cigarette and blew a plume of smoke into the dusky sunlight. "I was Mother's favorite, and she worked very hard to make the best marriage match for me—a wealthy pasha, distantly related. It was 1939, I was fifteen. On our wedding night there was no blood. Mother asked me if I had been with a boy, but when I told her about a fall I had had, and the stain on my skirt afterward, she realized what had happened. I was still a virgin but, like you, I was no longer marriageable."

Camelia gasped. "That was why you made me run home and tell Umma about my accident on the stairs!"

"I knew she would think of the operation to restore the hymen. They performed it even in those days, and she had wanted me to have one. But Father—your Grandfather Ali—said no, that it would be a lie and therefore dishonorable. He did not let a day go by in which he didn't express his disappointment in me. My very presence had cast a shadow over the house. And even though Mother was kind and tried to understand, I grew rebellious. It wasn't a fair society, I decided, that made victims of the innocent.

"I started going out unveiled. I made friends with a dancer, who took me to dangerous and exciting places—the coffee shops on Mohammed Ali Street. It was there"—Dahiba sighed—"among the dancers and musicians that I met Hosni, a devil of a man who was handsome and smooth and penniless. Hosni was a drummer who, like all musicians on Mohammed Ali Street, hung around the coffee shop waiting for jobs. When he saw me dancing one night, he thought we could be a team. He married me, told me he loved me. And so we got a small apartment and spent our days and nights in the coffee shops with other musicians and dancers, waiting for someone to hire us for weddings or parties.

Father was furious, of course. He equated dancers with prostitutes, and so he disowned me. I didn't mind. Hosni and I were at the very bottom of society's ladder and people looked down on us, but we were inexpressibly happy.

"And then . . . we had been married for nearly a year when I ran into a dancer friend in the Khan Khalili, where I was having a costume made. She asked me how I was feeling, was I unhappy, and so on. When I asked her why I should be unhappy, she said that she thought I would be upset about Hosni divorcing me. I was shocked. I hadn't known it, but he had recited the divorce formula three times in front of witnesses. He had legally divorced me, leaving me alone with no money, and he hadn't even sent me notice that I was no longer married to him! I never saw him again."

"But why did he divorce you if you were so happy together?"

"Camelia my dear, a man is only interested in a woman if he cannot have her. Once he possesses her, then he loses all interest, and so the only way a woman can hold on to her husband is to have a baby. Everyone knows that a man does not necessarily have to love his wife, but he will always love his children. Hosni divorced me because I didn't get pregnant. I was an affront to his virility."

"What did you do then?"

"I couldn't go back to Virgins of Paradise Street, so I tried to earn a living on my own as a dancer. I had a hard life for a while, Camelia. I won't go into it, but I did some things I was ashamed of. And then Hakim Raouf saw me in a wedding *zeffa* procession. He said he wanted to put me in a film. After a while, he fell in love with me, and despite the fact that I told him I didn't think I could have children, he married me."

"Uncle Hakim is a wonderful man."

"More wonderful than you think." Dahiba went to the sideboard where she kept silver and linen, unlocked a special drawer and brought out a battered notebook. "Besides dancing," she said, handing the book to Camelia, "I also write poetry. Most men would be furious to find their wives writing such words, but Hakim encourages me. He even hopes that someday I might publish."

Camelia opened the book and turned yellow pages. She came to a poem titled, "The Sentence of Woman," and she read:

"The day I was born
I was condemned.

I did not know my accusers.
I did not see the judge.

The verdict came down as
I drew in my first breath.

Woman."

Camelia read on, poems full of bitterness and disillusionment, about the grasping dominance of men, God's unfair laws, society's blind ignorance:

"God promises virgins in paradise for believers.
They are not meant for me when I die.
But for my father.
My brothers.
My uncles.
My nephews.
My sons.
No virgins wait for me in paradise."

Dahiba said, "When you came out on the stage that first night, I thought you looked familiar. And then when you told me your name, oh! What a strange feeling it gave me! There you were, my brother's daughter, and so like Amira around the eyes and mouth. I had a very hard time containing myself that night. I wanted to hug you and kiss you—my only family. But I was afraid you would run away, because of the terrible stories I was sure the family might have told you."

Camelia shook her head in wonder. "They never even spoke your name, and all your photos were taken out of the album."

Dahiba nodded. "That would be why none of the younger family members would recognize me. Even Ibrahim and Nefissa must have only vague memories of what I look like."

"It must have been awful for you."

"Until I met my dear Hakim, it was. To be cast out of your family, especially a large family like the Rasheeds, and to be treated as if you were dead . . . it is a terrible thing, Camelia. Many times, in those early days before I met Hakim, I truly did wish I were dead."

Dahiba returned to the sofa and extinguished her cigarette. "So, Umma leaves the house now. I never thought she would."

"I think the first time was when Papa was in prison. No one knows where she went—"

"Ibrahim was in prison? How much I have missed! Tell me, were you born in your grandmother's big fourposter bed? So was I, we were all born there, all the way back into the last century. *Bismillah,* there is history in that house! The stories I could tell you!" She laughed suddenly. "I can picture the Turkish fountain, where Uncle Salah went wading one night. He had smoked too much hashish, took off all his clothes and said he was a fish! Does the big stairway still have that great curving banister? Your father and Nefissa and I used to slide down it in the morning, and Umma would get so angry! And there was that downstairs closet that creaked for no reason. We kids said it was haunted."

"We said that, too, my brother Zakki and Yasmina and I."

"I remember the garden, with its papyrus and dusty old olive trees. Is it still the same?"

"Auntie Alice has changed it. The garden is very English now, with carnations and begonias. But it is very beautiful."

"Is there a stain on the kitchen wall beside the south window, a yellow stain shaped like a trumpet? That was put there many years ago, Camelia, even before I was born, and I am forty-two. There are so many stories in that big house—"

"Did you know my mother? She died giving birth to me."

"No, I'm sorry, I didn't know her."

"Auntie—" Camelia said, adjusting to their new relationship. "Why don't you make amends with Umma? Why don't you go to her and explain?"

"My dear child, there is nothing I would wish for more than to be reunited with my family. But when I married Hosni, my father said terrible things to me and Mother did not speak up in my defense. I was only a girl, she was a grown woman. It is for her to make the first step. Oh, Camelia, there is so much I want to tell you about the family, and so much I want to ask as well! But—" she frowned—"will you leave me now and go back to your grandmother? I doubt she will take you back unless you break completely with me. And if you stay with me, you might never see her again."

"If God wills it, then so be it," Camelia said. "I shall stay. You are my auntie, you are my family. And I will never stop dancing."

C H A P T E R   2 5

The traffic into the airport was chaotic. As Nefissa maneuvered her Fiat through the congestion, she wondered what had happened to cause such a commotion. There had been talk of war for weeks. Ever since Israel's April attack on Syria, Egypt had been on military alert. Just as in the days of the Revolution, Cairo had once again been gripped with tension, as people clustered around radios in coffee shops and snatched up newspapers filled with war propaganda. Had Israel finally declared war on Egypt? Nefissa wondered. She reached for the radio to get the news, then changed her mind. She didn't want to think of war right now; her son was coming home today and she was brimming with her own wonderful news.

When she finally got inside the terminal, she discovered that many flights had been canceled, leaving travelers stranded and infuriating those who, like herself, were there to meet incoming passengers. As she pushed her way through the crowd, she prayed that Omar's flight from Kuwait was one of those still scheduled to arrive before commercial flights were canceled altogether. Judging from the frenzied chatter all around her, Nefissa had guessed correctly: President Nasser had just declared a state of emergency; Egyptian troops were being called up. The country was going to war.

The ticket counters were mobbed, but when Nefissa tried to get the attention of an airport attendant, she was pushed around, and the shouting drowned her voice. When she saw the disembarking passengers filing through the customs exit, she elbowed her way against the tide to see if this was the Kuwait flight, the one on which her son was supposed to be, Omar having been called home for reserve military service. As she searched for him, she bumped against a tall handsome man carrying a diplomatic passport and an English raincoat. Their eyes met for an instant, both murmured, "Pardon me," and continued in their separate directions.

But Nefissa stopped and looked back to see him disappear into the crowd. For a moment he reminded her of . . . She shook her head and walked on.

Before the man with the raincoat reached the airport exit, he paused and looked over his shoulder. That woman . . . her eyes . . . They reminded him of eyes he had once fallen in love with, twenty-two years ago, when he had been a young lieutenant stationed in Cairo during the war. Eyes above a veil, hidden behind a mashrabiya screen. They had spent a night of fantastic lovemaking in an ancient harem . . .

But his car and driver were waiting, and he raced off.

Nefissa stopped again and looked back. Was it possible? Had it been *he*? Those blue eyes, that straight nose—she could never forget!

As she started to go back and follow him, she heard a voice over the public-address system announcing the arrival of passengers on the Kuwait flight. For an instant, Nefissa gazed in the direction the stranger had gone, then, shaking her head, turned and hurried toward the customs exit.

When Nefissa saw Omar coming through, she waved and called out to him. She could hardly contain her excitement.

She wanted to blurt her news as soon as they embraced, but this chaotic airport was not the right setting. She would wait until they were in the car and speeding along the highway, just the two of them. She would listen while Omar told her about his newest assignment in the Kuwait oil fields, then she would tell him in just the way she had rehearsed it: "I have decided to move in with you and Yasmina. A mother belongs with her son and grandchildren; it isn't right that I am still living at Virgins of Paradise Street, in my mother's house. I deserve to have a house of my own." Omar would agree, of course. It was he who had broken with tradition when he had taken an apartment for himself and his bride. But where did that leave his mother? It was her right to manage her son's household, as any mother in Cairo would attest.

It was Nefissa's dream, to take care of Omar and Mohammed. After a brief affair with a professor at the American University, and an unfulfilling flirtation with an English businessman, she had come to accept the fact that she was never going to recapture the romance she had found one glorious night when she was twenty. It was futile, she told herself, to try to find her English lieutenant in other men—she was even imagining seeing him in airports! And so she had gently let go of the dream. And replaced it with another.

"I am so glad to have you home, my son," she said, as she slid into the passenger seat of her car while Omar got behind the wheel. "You have an important job, but it takes you away for too long."

"Is everyone well, Mother? Yasmina, how is she? The baby is due soon, praise God."

They made it out of the airport congestion and were speeding along the desert highway, along which army tanks were rolling eastward, toward Sinai. Nefissa did not comment on Yasmina. Her niece was the one flaw in an otherwise perfect plan.

Ever since Nefissa had decided that she was too old to still be living in her mother's house, taking second place to Amira, and deciding that, at forty-two, she deserved to be dignified with her own home and a daughter-in-law to help her, she had started on her plan. After finding a larger apartment, in Cairo, she had chosen new china and silver patterns—she would get rid of those Omar and Yasmina were currently using—picked out new furniture, drapes and carpets, pictures for the walls. Although it had been a deliciously exciting project, the problem of Yasmina had loomed like a disagreeable shadow.

Nefissa had no proof, but she suspected that the baby Yasmina was carrying was not her son's but the child of Hassan al-Sabir. After all, there was the contraceptive she had found hidden among Yasmina's toiletries. If Omar had known of the birth control, he would have expressed surprised that Yasmina was pregnant; but he had not. And then there was Yasmina's mysterious visit to Hassan's house. She had not returned to Virgins of Paradise Street until two hours later, wearing a brand-new blouse, not the one she had left in.

Nefissa had kept her suspicions to herself. Revealing them, she had decided, would most likely ruin her plans for moving in with Omar. If he were to divorce Yasmina, he might move back into the house on Virgins of Paradise Street, which he would visit between his long absences. And Nefissa would continue to exist in Amira's shadow.

She wanted a household of her own, and a family to manage. What did it matter about the baby, if the truth were kept secret? There could even be an advantage, Nefissa had decided; she could let Yasmina know that she knew the truth about the baby, promising to keep the knowledge to herself as long as Yasmina recognized Nefissa as the head of their family.

When the first dun-colored buildings started to come into view along the highway, dusty new apartment blocks waiting for low-income families to move in, Nefissa decided to tell Omar of her plans. But he spoke first. "And do you know what, Mother?" he said. "I miss Yasmina. I have learned a lot while I've been working abroad, and one thing I've learned is the value of a good wife. I was impatient with Yasmina when we first got married. She didn't understand my needs and I had to teach her. But now," he stretched and smiled, "I see us having a good life together."

Nefissa had to smile. The way her son was talking, as if he weren't just a boy of twenty-five!

"And now Yasmina is pregnant," he said. "And I was beginning to wonder if there was something wrong. Mother, I have wonderful news. The oil company I have been assigned to has offered me a permanent job, as one of their senior engineers!"

"That's marvelous, Omar," she said, noticing how he tilted his chin with pride as he spoke. He had also cultivated a dignified mustache, she noticed, and wore an expensive, well-tailored shirt. In her mind and heart she had kept him a little boy, but it struck her now for the first time that her son was a man. "What about this war with Israel?"

"How long can it last? If there is even going to be a war, which I doubt. In any event, the company has promised to hold the job open for me until I return. And I have already found an apartment in Kuwait City, and put money down on it so that it won't be let to someone else while I'm away. It's small, but it will do for now for me and Yasmina and the children. The company has promised me promotions, so in time we will be able to afford a house and then you will be able to come and stay for long visits, Mother. How would you like that?"

When she didn't reply, he looked at her. "Mother? Are you all right?"

"You're going to *stay* in Kuwait? You're leaving your job with the government?"

"There is more money in private enterprise, Mother. And I would like to have a normal home life, with my wife and children."

"But . . . what about me?"

He laughed. "You will come and visit us! And every time you come, the children will climb all over you and make you so tired you will want to hurry back to Cairo!"

Her eyes widened in horror. He was *leaving*? She was going to be left behind on Virgins of Paradise Street, to become just one more of the aging spinsters and widows Ibrahim supported? The late afternoon, which had started out so bright and sunny, seemed to turn dark and cold. Nefissa watched her plans crumble as she pictured the lonely years that lay ahead, devoid of romance, with no son to take care of. She knew she could not let it happen.

=

Yasmina was helping her mother arrange flowers for Omar's homecoming party when she felt the baby kick. It was due to be born soon, and she wished Camelia could be here. But she was up in Port Said, with Dahiba and Raouf, filming a movie. Yasmina had several times in the past months come close to confessing the truth about Hassan and the baby to her father. But Camelia had helped her to keep her resolve, and she was glad now she had had the strength to remain silent. Working with her father in his office and seeing the pride in his eyes as he spoke of plans for helping her through medical school—Yasmina could not destroy that. Her secret about the day she had gone to see Hassan, whom she had not heard from since, was a small burden to bear if it kept her father happy.

Sahra came into the salon with a platter of steaming grape leaves stuffed with lamb and rice; behind her, two servants carried bowls of cabbage salad and deep-fried eggs sprinkled with oregano and onion. All the women of the family had come for the occasion, laughing and gossiping, complimenting one another's dress, jewelry; Tahia was there too, with her new baby, Asmahan, now two months old. They all worked to bring cheer into the large salon. Even though the threat of a surprise attack by the Visitors of Dawn had abated since Defense Minister Amer's attention had turned from the Liquidation of Feudalism to the threat of aggression from Israel, the Rasheed house was still plain and stripped of its richness. And so the family created a festive atmosphere with laughter, food, drink, and flowers.

Amira was at the window with little Mohammed, watching for the car that was bringing his daddy home from Kuwait. She pointed out the stars that were beginning to appear in the clear May sky. "You see? There is Aldebaran, the Follower, because he follows the Pleiades." She pointed to Rigel, Arabic for "foot." "Do you see Rigel in Orion's left foot? All the stars have Arabic names, great-grandson of my heart, because it was your ancestors who discovered them. Doesn't that make you proud?"

"What star were you born under, Umma?"

"A very lucky one!" she said, giving him a hug.

Ibrahim came into the salon. "Quickly, turn on the television, Mother. Nasser is speaking."

They gathered around the set and listened as President Nasser warned the Egyptian people to brace themselves for Israel's attack. "I do not want war," he said. "But I will fight for the honor of all Arabs. Europe and America speak of the rights of Israel, but where are the rights of the Arabs? Not one of them speaks of the rights of the Palestinian people in their own homeland. We alone will make the stand for our brothers."

"Declare the oneness of God!" cried Doreya.

"Praise His mercy!"

As everyone started talking at once, the face of Um Khalsoum appeared on the TV screen; she began to sing the Egyptian national anthem, "My country, my country, my love and heart are yours. Egypt, Mother of all lands, it is you I seek and desire." And several of the women in the Rasheed salon started to cry.

Amira's nephew, Tewfik, jumped up and said, "We should attack first, before the Israeli aggressors attack us!"

Uncle Kareem, who sat closest to the television set because of his advanced age, thumped his cane and said, "War is not a solution, you young dog! War only begets more war! God's way is peace."

"But Uncle, in all respect, didn't Israel attack Syria just last month? And is it not up to us to be prepared to defend the honor of all Arabs? The whole world is against us, Uncle. The United Nations' troops have been stationed on the Egyptian side of the border for eleven years, and when Nasser suggested that they should be moved to the Israeli side for a while, Israel refused to take them. Is this fair? Whose side is the world on, Uncle? We must drive Israel into the sea!"

"Stupid boy," said sharp-tongued Doreya. "How do we drive Israel into the sea? Her American backers make her more powerful than we are! They are making fools of us. Didn't Golda Meir call Arab women frivolous and superficial, saying we spend more money on makeup and clothes than on necessities!"

"Please, please," Amira said. "Let us not provoke a war in our own house!"

"Respectfully, Auntie," Tewfik said, "Israel is our enemy."

"Egypt, Israel! We are all the children of the Prophet Ibrahim. Why do we fight among ourselves?"

"The state of Israel has no right to exist."

"Declare God's mercy, you witless child! All people have a right to exist."

"In honor and respect to you, Auntie Amira, I don't believe you understand."

"What happens, happens," she said. "God's will, not ours."

When little Mohammed burst into tears, Amira turned off the TV set. "We are frightening the children." Then she thought: If war is indeed inevitable, we must be prepared. Tomorrow she would take the women and girls to the Red Crescent to donate blood, after which they would tear up bed sheets and roll bandages.

She suddenly thought of Camelia, up in Port Said making a film. She thought: At a time such as this, a family should be together.

Instructing Doreya and the other women to distract and entertain the children, Amira went into her bedroom and closed the door. Kneeling on the floor, she opened the bottom drawer of her dresser and lifted out the white pilgrim's robes, carefully folded for the day when she would make the journey to holy Mecca—a dream she had had to set aside until the danger from the Visitors of Dawn had passed. Beneath the robes was a wooden box inlaid with ivory, its lid inscribed with the words: *God, the Compassionate.* Although much of the jewelry that had been buried in the garden had been dug up over the past few months and donated to the Red Crescent and other organizations raising funds for the war effort, Amira had kept her most precious, most sentimental pieces in this ornate antique box filled with mementos. On top were three pieces of jewelry she would never part with: the first was a pearl necklace, given to her by Ali on the occasion of Ibrahim's birth. The second was an ancient Egyptian bracelet of lapis and gold, said to have belonged to Rameses II, pharaoh of the Exodus. It had been given as a gift to Farouk by a collector, and the king had in turn bestowed the priceless object upon Amira after she had given him a fertility potion made of herbs from her garden, a potion, Farouk swore, that had given him his only son. The third was the ring Andreas Skouras had given her before he left Egypt— the engraved carnelian set in gold, bearing the engraving of a mulberry leaf, to signify that Andreas drew his life from Amira as the silkworm did from the leaf. She had kept it to remind her of the man she had once loved, and whom she had almost married. At the bottom of the box was an envelope. She opened it and brought out the photographs that had been removed from the family album years ago.

When Ali had banished their daughter from the house, Amira had taken Fatima's photos out of the album, but they hadn't gone far. She had placed them tenderly beneath the pilgrim's robes. Looking at Fatima's young, smiling face brought back the shock of seeing her six months ago, when Camelia had taken Amira to visit her friend Dahiba. The memories that had rushed back, as she had stood speechless in Fatima's living room! And then the fury, that Fatima should befriend Camelia without telling the girl who she really was. And then the flood of love and compassion, and the desire to bring Fatima back into the family. Camelia had begged Amira to forgive Fatima, but Amira had said, "It is Fatima who must come back and ask for forgiveness." But Dahiba, being as stubborn as her mother, had not come, and Amira now regretted her own obstinacy.

There was a gentle knock at the door, she said, "Enter," and when Zachariah came in, Amira received a shock. He was dressed in an army uniform. "But how?" she said. "They rejected you before!"

"I tried again," he said simply, "and this time they took me." He wouldn't tell her the truth, that it had occurred to him that just as a man could bribe his way *out* of military service, so could he bribe his way into it.

"I did it for Father," he said. "So that he would be proud of me. If you had seen the look on his face when I told him the army had rejected me as physically unfit for service! Why do I always seem to disappoint him, Grandmother? I have memories of when I was little, and Father held me on his knee and told me stories the way he does now with Mohammed. But he stopped."

"Prison changes a man, Zakki."

"Does it make him stop loving his son?"

"In many ways, that is how your father was treated by his own father.

Ali believed in being stern and distant with children. I know at times it hurt Ibrahim. I was his mother, but I could not interfere. But now, God forgive me, I look back and believe my husband was wrong. For now I sometimes glimpse Ali in my son, especially when I hear him speak so coldly to you. Forgive him, Zakki. He knows no other way."

"Here is Omar!" they heard Zubaida cry in the salon. "*Al hamdu lillah!* Praise God, He has brought Omar home to us!"

"Your father will be proud of you, Zakki," she said quietly, as they left the bedroom. "If perhaps he does not show it, remember that he is proud of you all the same."

The family smothered Omar with hugs and kisses, and when they saw Zachariah come into the salon in his uniform, they cried out and declared what a blessed day this was, that God had chosen two Rasheed sons to be heroes of Egypt.

While everyone was fussing over the two cousins, Nefissa took her brother aside and said, "Ibrahim, we must talk. Now. It is important."

As Yasmina was embracing Omar, she saw her father and aunt leave the room. And when she caught a glimpse of Nefissa's rigid profile, she became alarmed. But she chided herself for being foolish. She had been jumpy lately, certain that everyone knew her secret. But it was only her imagination. Surely her father and Nefissa had any number of important things to discuss. How could they know about Hassan and the baby? But when her father returned a moment later, to stand in the doorway of the salon with a strange look on his face, her pulse began to race. He gestured to her, and then he called to Amira and Omar.

When they were in the small parlor off the grand stairway, a room designed for private audiences with visitors, Ibrahim quietly closed the door, turned to Yasmina, and said, "Is there something you wish to tell me?"

In this proximity, her father just steps away from her, Yasmina saw something in his eyes that frightened her. "What do you mean?" she said.

"By God, Yasmina," he said softly. "Tell me the truth."

Amira said, "Ibrahim, what is this about? Why have you brought us in here?"

But he kept his eyes on Yasmina, and she saw that he was struggling for control. "Tell me about the child," he said.

She looked at Nefissa and whispered, "How did you know?"

Ibrahim closed his eyes. "God deliver me from this hour."

Now Omar said, "What is going on? Mother? Uncle?"

Yasmina reached for her father. "I can explain. Please—"

He drew back. "How could you!" he boomed, startling everyone. "My God, daughter, do you know what you have done?"

"I went to Hassan," she said, "hoping to persuade him to take our name off the list—"

"You *went* to him?" Ibrahim boomed. "On your own? Good God, girl, couldn't you have left it to me to take care of? Have you no faith in me? And then—to let him—"

She held out her hands pleadingly. "No! He forced me! I tried to fight him, I tried to get away!"

"It doesn't matter, Yasmina! You *went* there. No one forced you to go to Hassan's house."

"Ibrahim!" cried Amira. "What is going on here?"

"My God," said Omar, suddenly understanding.

"Oh, child," Ibrahim said, with tears in his eyes. "What have you done to me? It would be better if you had plunged a knife into my heart. He's won, don't you see? You have given Hassan al-Sabir a victory. And you have caused me to lose face!"

"I was trying to save the family," Yasmina sobbed. She turned to Omar. "I didn't want to deceive you."

"The child is not mine?" he said.

"I am so sorry, Omar." Yasmina began to shake. She turned to Nefissa. "How did you know?" she whispered. And then she thought: Camelia was the only one who knew, Camelia who had promised not to tell.

Tears rose in Omar's eyes as he said, "That I should have come home to this. Oh God, Yasmina." He pressed a handkerchief to his eyes and sobbed, "I divorce you . . ."

Nefissa started to weep.

Ibrahim turned his back on them and said in a voice not his own, "Hassan said he was going to humiliate me, and he has succeeded. I have lost all honor. Our name has been degraded."

"But, Father," cried Yasmina, "how can that be? Hassan hasn't told you about my visit. He hasn't bragged to you, or to anyone about it."

"He didn't need to! My God, girl, that is his power, don't you see? By remaining silent, he is proving how powerful he is. Hassan knew my humiliation would be far worse if I were to learn this from someone other than him. All this time he has been sitting smugly back, waiting for the final victory."

Yasmina reached for Ibrahim. "No one need know, Father. It need not go beyond these walls."

But he drew away from her. "*I* know it, daughter. *I* know. It is enough." Ibrahim looked up at the ceiling, his face pale and drawn. "What do you think of me now, Father?" he murmured. Then he leveled his gaze at Yasmina and said, "A curse came upon this house the night you were born. A curse from God that I alone am to blame for. I regret the hour you were born."

"No, Father!"

"You are no longer my daughter."

Amira stared at him, seeing not her son but her husband, Ali. And then she saw another vision, her nightmare, in all its power and terror: the child being taken from its mother. As if tonight were a prophecy being fulfilled . . . "My son," she said, taking Ibrahim by the arm, "please do not do this."

But Ibrahim said to Yasmina, "From this moment on you are *haram*, forbidden. You are not of our family, your name will never be spoken in this house again. It will be as if you were dead."

CHAPTER 26

Yasmina and Alice were jostled by the airport crowd as people fought to get aboard the last scheduled flights out of Egypt. Fear was in the air; the noise was almost deafening as foreigners clutching hastily packed bags waved tickets and passports in a frantic push to get past harried attendants and through the boarding gates. Yasmina and her mother hurried toward the plane, the final BOAC flight to London.

No one from the family was there to see her off; Yasmina had had no contact with any of them in the three weeks since the night her father had declared her dead. The labor pains had started then, and Alice and

Zachariah had rushed her to the hospital where, eight hours later, she had awakened from the anesthetic to find her mother at her bedside, telling her that the baby had been stillborn. Which was God's blessing, Alice had said tearfully—it had been deformed.

The following days remained a blur in Yasmina's memory. Because Omar's unit had been called up, she had had the apartment to herself, where her body had healed while her mind had retreated into a state of numbness. But now, as she neared the boarding gate, elbowed and shoved by panicked people running from impending war, Yasmina felt the protective numbness fade away, and her pain emerge. Mohammed was going to stay with his father on Virgins of Paradise Street, so that both babies—her little boy and the new child—were lost to her. She thought she would die of grief.

It was Alice who had got the passport and tickets. "War is coming, my darling," she had said. "And then you will be trapped here. You have been cast out of the family, you have been made dead. You have no name, no identity, no place to go. You must leave, Yasmina. Find another life and save yourself. In England you have the house and the trust fund left to you by my father. And Aunt Penelope will help you."

"How can I leave my son?" Yasmina had asked, already knowing the answer. Omar would never let her see the boy again.

As they neared the ticket attendant, who was arguing with a passenger about inadequate papers, Yasmina turned to her mother and said, "It's best that you can't come with me. If we were both to go, then Mohammed would be lost to me forever. Now that you must stay, you can tell him about me, show him my picture every day, and never let him forget me."

Yes, Alice thought, Mohammed, her grandson. And the granddaughter Yasmina knew nothing about, the child just born, who was not dead, but sleeping in a crib on Virgins of Paradise Street.

"Mother," Yasmina said, "I don't know which pain is worse—the pain of losing the baby, the pain of Father casting me out, or the pain of knowing that Camelia betrayed me. But at least, with you here, the pain of losing my son will be eased a little, knowing that you are here to keep me in his heart."

"I wish I could go with you," Alice said. "But your father would not give me permission. He is a proud man, Yasmina, and to lose his wife would be another humiliation. I wish I had taken you away when I had my first fears, back when you were a little girl, and Egypt frightened me. I never really belonged here, and neither do you. I want you to save yourself, Yasmina."

Alice suddenly embraced her daughter, holding her tightly, herself a storm of pain and emotions. *It was for you, my darling, that I lied about the baby. I did it so that you could escape from this place as I never could. If you knew about her, if you had held her even once, you would have stayed, and been doomed. May God forgive me . . .*

As she felt Yasmina tremble in her arms, Alice was filled once again with a cold hatred for Hassan al-Sabir—the monster who had seduced and corrupted first her brother Edward, and then her daughter.

"I will write to you and tell you about Mohammed," she said, drawing away from Yasmina. "And I will tell him about you every day. I won't let them erase you from his memory."

Yasmina regarded her mother through tear-filled eyes as people pushed around them. "I don't know when we will see each other again, Mother. I will never come back to Egypt. I have been pronounced dead; I am a ghost. So I must create a new life for myself somewhere else. But I promise you this, Mother, that I will never again be a victim. I shall become strong, I shall be the one with power. And when you and I are together again, you will be proud of me. I love you."

Yasmina finally boarded the plane and sank wearily into her seat. Her breasts were still sore, waiting for the baby that would never nurse there; her arms ached to hold a poor little deformed thing that she believed hadn't survived its traumatic birth. Thinking she could sleep forever, Yasmina rested her head back and closed her eyes.

And so she did not see the newspaper sticking out of the coat pocket of the passenger getting settled across the aisle. Yasmina didn't see the headline on the front page, which read: UNITED ARAB REPUBLIC MOBIL- IZES 100,000 RESERVE TROOPS. Nor the smaller headline that ran beneath the photograph of a handsome, smiling face: HASSAN AL-SABIR, UNDER SECRETARY OF DEFENSE, FOUND MURDERED.

Part V
1973

CHAPTER 27

The house of Qettah the astrologer was tucked behind the shrine of the blessed Saint Sayyida Zeinab, in a shabby little alley called Pink Fountain Street. But there was no fountain there, and the color was not pink but the dun of the sandy bricks from which the Old City had been constructed centuries ago. There had once been sidewalks and cobblestones, but filth on the sidewalks had gradually piled up so that the level of the street was several feet higher, with only a narrow rut down the center. The inhabitants wore faded galabeyas and dusty melayas, their children played in the dirt, and the women gossiped from rickety balconies that leaned so far into the street that daylight was nearly blocked out.

It was in this ancient alley that Amira had urgent business, and as she hurried under a stone arch that was one of the gateways to the Old City, no one paid any attention to her. In this quarter, which had flourished before the Crusades, she was just another female form wrapped head to foot in black, only her eyes and hands showing. As she neared Sayyida Zeinab Mosque, she prayed that Qettah could help her.

Amira's past had spoken to her again in a strange, new dream. And she prayed that it was a good sign, in these uncertain times. Supernatural happenings were being reported all over Cairo—ghostly sightings and unexplainable phenomena: falling stars streaked the sky nearly every night, rain had fallen at the Sudan border where rain had never fallen before, and over the course of several weeks, a vision of the Virgin Mary had floated above the oldest and most venerated Coptic church in Cairo. Thousands had flocked to see Her, and church patriarchs had declared that the Holy Mother was telling Her followers that, since the Israelis had captured Jerusalem and Coptic Christians could no longer go there to see Her, *She* had come to Cairo to see *them*. All were ill omens and signs of the quiet hysteria that had infected Egypt because of Egypt's shameful defeat in the Six-Day War, in which fifteen thousand Egyptian soldiers had perished, and thousands more had been horribly wounded. The six years since had been an uneasy time of no declared war, no declared peace, with skirmishes continuing to break out in the Canal Zone. Even now, the Israelis were bombing targets in Upper Egypt, as far south as Aswan, threatening the High Dam, which, if hit, would send a twelve-foot wall of water rushing through the Nile Valley, flattening all villages and flooding Cairo itself. The people were afraid, they had lost their heart and their pride, morale had been reduced to dust. It was a sign, everyone said, that God had turned His back upon Egypt.

As Amira joined the press of humanity outside Sayyida Zeinab Mosque, she thought of her own prophetic sign—a new dream, which had been coming to her in her sleep over the past weeks, in which she saw a beautiful boy, about fourteen years old, beckoning to her. The dream always filled her with peace and joy; it never frightened her. Surely, she prayed, this is a good sign.

The crowd outside the mosque was so thick that donkey carts could not get through. Although the shrine had for centuries been a gathering place for crowds of beggars, the blind, orphans, and widows, hoping to receive the saint's grace, the numbers outside the ancient stone walls had swelled since the Six-Day War; in fact, mosque attendance all over Egypt had gone up six hundred per cent. Worse even than Egypt's defeat was the fact that Israelis now occupied one of Islam's most sacred places, the Dome of the Rock, from where Mohammed had ascended to heaven. To reverse this ignominy, imams in their pulpits were calling for the people to return to God. They pointed to the American TV sets and Japanese radios in shop windows in this modern and progressive Cairo, a hotbed of loose morals, where women now had careers and chose their own husbands or, even worse, were living alone. These were the signs of godlessness, the imams declared. The Israelis, they said, had won the war because they were a pious people. What then of Egyptians?

Amira, swallowed up in her black melaya, moved through the crowd as one of them, looking like just another *bint al-balad,* "daughter of the country," which was what the lower-class women called themselves. As she passed between a young woman in a black cotton melaya sitting behind a pyramid of onions, and a seller of jasmine garlands, squatting on the ground and picking his teeth, Amira thought of how the world had been turned upside down. In her younger days, the veil had been a status symbol of the rich, indicating that the wearer's husband was wealthy, his wife protected, waited on by servants, free from even the smallest task, while women of the poor class didn't wear a veil, as it hindered their work and daily toil. But now rich women went about unveiled, as a symbol of their modern status, while the lower class had taken up the melaya in imitation of their wealthy predecessors.

Holding the edge of the black silk over her mouth, she squinted up at the deep blue sky above Cairo, and as a hot, sandy wind pricked her cheeks, she remembered that tomorrow, the first day of spring, the khamsin was due to start. Odors filled her head—cookfires, sweat, animal dung, and jasmine—and she felt the invisible presence of God hovering over the city, watching and waiting.

She finally got through the crowd and after passing by small dark shops like brigands' caves, she found the alley and the doorway recessed beneath a crumbling arch. She knocked, and the familiar face of old Qettah peered out. She was not the same Qettah of nearly thirty years ago, who had been present at Camelia's birth, but the astrologer's daughter, herself now quite old, who had taken over when her mother had died. Their secret art, the elder Qettah had once explained to Amira, had been passed down through the generations, since the days before Islam. Each astrologer in her turn was called Qettah, and when she gave birth to a daughter, the woman would be taught the secrets of the stars in preparation for the day she would take her mother's place. Since the days of the pharaohs, all had been called Qettah.

As Amira slipped into the dim interior, she murmured, "God's peace and blessings upon this house." To which the astrologer replied, "And upon you, His blessings and mercy. You honor my house, Sayyida. Make it your home, and may you find solace within."

Amira had never before visited the astrologer, but the apartment of the elderly seeress was as she had imagined it would be, cluttered with star charts, astrological instruments, pens and inks, and ancient amulets. But Amira had expected to see cats, for "Qettah" means "cat" in Arabic. The astrologer even claimed that her line had descended from a cat, which Amira believed. Yet there were no signs that any animals lived here.

While tea brewed in a tarnished pot, they sat at a table and Qettah took Amira's hands in hers. The fortune teller studied the smooth palms, then said, "What star were you born under, mistress?"

Amira hesitated. The only other living person who knew this secret was Maryam Misrahi, living in far-away California. "I do not know, Venerable One," she said.

Keen eyes studied her. "What lunar mansion?"

Amira shook her head.

"Your mother's birth-star?"

"I do not know." She added quietly: "I do not know who my mother was."

Qettah sat back, and her bones creaked with the chair. "This is a sad thing, mistress. Without knowing the past we can never know the future. All is in God's hands. Your fate is written in His great book. But I cannot read it for you."

"But I did not come to have my future read, Venerable One. I came to have a dream interpreted, and perhaps to find answers to my past."

"Tell me the dream."

As Qettah listened with her eyes closed, Amira said, "I see a handsome young boy, not yet a man, tall and straight, with large beautiful eyes and a full mouth, smiling. He is dressed in elegant robes, and when he holds his hand out to me, it is a graceful gesture. In the dream, he doesn't speak, but I sense a message from him—I feel as if he is trying to reach me, trying to tell me something. The dream lasts only a few seconds, and then the boy vanishes."

"Do you know who he is?"

"No."

"Have you had this dream more than once?"

"Several times."

"Does this boy frighten you?"

"This is the wonder of it, Venerable One. I feel love for him. Who is he? Is he someone who is trapped in my lost memory? He beckons to me, as if he were telling me to search for him, to find him."

Qettah studied Amira with keen eyes. "And you think he is from your past?"

"I sense this most strongly. But I do not recall him in my memories. Could he have been someone who lived at the house on Tree of Pearls Street, where I lived as a girl? Is he perhaps the spirit of a son I never had? Is he my brother, and belonging to that most remote part of my memory which is lost to me?"

"Perhaps he is none of these, Sayyida. Perhaps he is a symbol of something in your life. We will see."

The tea was ready and Qettah poured some into a small chipped cup, inviting Amira to drink. When there was only a teaspoon left, Qettah took the cup in her left hand and swirled it three times, in large circles. Then she turned it over into the saucer and lifted it to read the leaves.

Silence crept into the room, broken only by the occasional rattling of the mashrabiya screen as wind whistled through it. Amira felt the edges of her melaya flutter against her ankles, she stared at Qettah's improbably wrinkled face and thought of each deep line as a chapter in the old woman's life. But Qettah's expression was unreadable.

Finally the astrologer looked up from the tea leaves and said, "He is a real boy, Sayyida. Someone in your past."

"Is he still alive? Where is he?"

"Have you ever dreamed of a city or a building, Sayyida? A landmark that might identify his whereabouts?"

"I have memories of a square minaret."

"Ah, the mosque of al-Nasir Mohammed perhaps, on Al Muizz Street?"

"That is not the one. The minaret I dream of is not in Cairo, but far away, I fear."

Qettah studied the leaves again, and then nodded, as if to confirm her reading. "You say you are a widow, Sayyida?"

"For many years now. Who is the boy? Is he my brother?"

"Sayyida," Qettah said with wonder in her voice, "he is not your brother, he is your betrothed."

Amira frowned. "I don't understand. I have no betrothed."

"This is the boy you were intended to marry, long ago. You were engaged to him."

"But . . . how is that possible? I have no memory of this!"

Setting aside the cup and saucer, Qettah brought out a small brass phial, which she gave to Amira to hold between her hands for seven counts. She then poured the contents onto the surface of a bowl of water, and the perfume of roses suddenly filled the air, along with another underlying fragrance Amira could not identify, but which reminded her of the sunrise.

Qettah fixed her eyes on the swirling oil, and after a moment, said, "You will be taking a journey, Sayyida."

"Where to?"

"To the East. Ah, the betrothed is here again."

Amira peered into the bowl, but saw only pearlescent ribbons of oil on water.

"Sayyida," Qettah finally said, placing her hands on the table, "the signs show that your path was somehow diverted from its original destiny. You went where you should not have gone; you did not go to where you should have gone."

"So my dreams of a raid on a caravan are not merely dreams, but actual memories. I had thought they were, but was never certain. Perhaps my mother and I were on our way to see this boy when the raiders attacked and kidnapped me."

"This was not supposed to happen, Sayyida. Another life was intended for you."

"In the name of the Eternal One," Amira said. "What shall I do?"

"The young man beckons. Go to him. Go to the East."

"But where in the East should I go?"

"Forgive me, but that I do not know. Make the pilgrimage to Mecca, Sayyida. Sometimes," Qettah said with a smile that broke her face into a thousand creases, "God illuminates us through prayer."

Amira left the Old City in great excitement, and followed winding alleys until the streets began to broaden and she was once again on a wide boulevard where tall modern buildings loomed and cars sped by. Here she saw further signs of war and defeat—sandbags piled up in front of doorways and windows covered with dark-blue paper. A city, she thought, braced for Armageddon.

She also saw signs of the changing times. The modest melaya and galabeya, so prevalent in the poor quarter, were nearly absent in this modern Cairo, as young men went by in blue jeans and Western jackets, and girls displayed their legs beneath short skirts. A billboard dominating Liberation Square showed a blond woman in a white bathing suit drinking a bottle of Coca-Cola. Next to it, another billboard advertised a movie, depicting a scene in which a man in a tuxedo held a gun, while the seductive shadow of a woman hovered behind him. When the signal light changed, Amira tugged her melaya tighter about her and hurried across the street; because she could not read, she was unaware that the billboard had been for a Hakim Raouf movie, and that the actresses in the credits were Dahiba and Camelia Rasheed.

Before heading for the spacious tree-lined avenues of Garden City, Amira crossed Liberation Square and joined the heavy pedestrian and motor traffic that poured between the massive stone lions guarding El Tahrir Bridge. She found herself searching the faces of the men she passed, to see if she recognized the beautiful youth of her dream in any of them. Is he here, she wondered, a breath away from me? Have our paths crossed a hundred times and we do not know it? Does he dream of me as a girl, and wonder who I am, why he should be having this dream?

She paused to look at the Nile. Tomorrow was the festival of *Shamm el-Nessin*, "Sniffing the Breeze," the one holiday shared by Muslims, Coptic Christians, and even atheists, in celebration of the first day of spring. Families would be gathering on the banks of the river for picnics and egg hunts. At least one drowning would be reported.

Amira gazed down into the water and felt, mingled with her excitement, a sense of pending disaster. Everyone was saying that President Sadat was leading Egypt toward another conflict with Israel. If so, how many were going to die this time? What other young men from the house of Rasheed would shed their blood in the desert?

And then she thought of the boy in her dream. She was certain that he held the key to her past, and to her identity. But where in all the world was she going to find him?

—

"Here, Sahra, let me help you with that," Zachariah said, as he lifted the heavy kettle of hard boiled eggs from the stove and placed it in the sink.

Secretly pleased by his attention, Sahra said, "God bless you for your help, young master. I'm a little under the weather this morning, but I shall be fine tomorrow, God willing."

The kitchen was crowded and noisy as children around the large table painted eggs and tied ribbons on chocolate bunnies. Tahia, one of the adults supervising, gave Sahra a curious look, and remembered that Auntie Doreya had complained of malaise at breakfast. Tahia hoped there wasn't something going around, a late winter flu perhaps, that might upset the children's fun tomorrow at the spring festival.

When six-year-old Asmahan suddenly screamed, two other little ones burst into tears, and Omar's youngest, the eight-month-old twins, howled. "Children, children," Tahia said, trying to restore order. "Mohammed, you shouldn't have done that. A great big boy like you, picking on your cousin." She put her hand to her lower back and straightened. She was eight months pregnant.

Nefissa, also sitting at the table with the children, said to her daughter, "Don't scold the boy, Tahia. It was Asmahan's fault," and she stroked ten-year-old Mohammed's hair as she fed him a piece of chocolate. Nefissa thought he was so like his father, when Omar had been that age, that she gave her frowning grandson another hug.

Tahia exchanged a look with Zachariah, who privately thought Mohammed needed stricter watching. The boy wasn't to blame; his father was away most of the time on government assignments, and although his stepmother Nala, Omar's second wife, was a good disciplinarian with their other four children, it was Nefissa who had authority over Mohammed, and she was spoiling him as badly as she had once spoiled Omar.

"When I was a girl," Sahra said, as she brought another batch of eggs to the table, "the wealthiest man in the village, Sheikh Hamid, distributed little ducklings and chicks made of sugar and almonds to the children. The more fortunate of us received new clothes, and nobody worked in the fields, we would picnic and listen to the firecrackers being set off by boys on either side of the canal. There were some Christian families in our village, and I remember that it was the only time our families all celebrated together." When she turned back to the sink, she put her hand on her abdomen and winced.

Zachariah nestled an egg in a napkin and showed little Abdul Wahab how to draw on it with a wax pencil. "Have you ever been back to see your family, Sahra?" he asked, watching Tahia out of the corner of his eye. Her lush, pregnant body flooded him with desire. He had once thought that purity was seductive, but now he found fecundity more so.

"No, young master," Sahra said, gulping down a large glass of water. She couldn't remember having ever been this thirsty. "I haven't been back since I left, when I was a girl."

"But don't you miss your family?"

She thought of her beloved Abdu, who had planted Zachariah in her, and whom Zakki now so strongly resembled. "My family is here," she said, silently blessing Abdu's memory.

"Mama!" cried one of the little ones. "Got to go pottie!"

"Again?"

"I'll take him," said Basima, and she scooped up the child and hurried out.

Haneya's daughter, Fadilla, frowned as she watched her aunt leave the kitchen. At twenty, Fadilla was still unmarried, which surprised everyone because she bore a strong resemblance to her great-grandmother, Zou Zou, who had been a beauty. "I was up all night with it myself," she said. "I wonder if the family has caught something."

"That makes the sixth case of diarrhea in the house," Tahia said. "I think Umma has a medicine for it."

As she opened a cupboard and surveyed the neat rows of jars and bottles and phials, all meticulously labeled with Amira's secret symbols, Zachariah watched her. On the day Tahia had been wed to the elderly Jamal Rasheed, Zachariah had vowed to her that he would not touch another woman. And he had kept that vow. But he was also keeping another, secret vow: that he was waiting for when she would be free again. Because he knew now for certain that they were destined to be together.

He had seen it in a vision, the day he had died in the Sinai Desert.

Feeling his gaze on her, Tahia looked over at Zachariah and smiled.

Poor Zakki, she thought. The terrible things the Six-Day War had done to him! His hair was receding, his shoulders were stooped, and he wore glasses with thick lenses. Zachariah was middle-aged at twenty-eight; one of her children had even erroneously addressed him as "Grandpa Zakki." If only he could have kept his job. Facing youngsters every day in a classroom might have helped him to stay young, but Zachariah had had one of his "spells" in front of his pupils, terrifying them, and so the headmaster had let him go. Now Zakki was looked after by the whole family, especially the women, who doted on him and watched for spells. He didn't have them often; the last one had occurred over a year ago. But when they struck, he was as vulnerable as a newborn baby.

Tahia didn't know exactly what he saw when the trouble came over him; only once, in the months after he came back from the Sinai, did he try to describe the "landscape of his lunacy," as he called it—a horrific image of barren desert, burned-out tanks, charred bodies, jets swooping down from the sky and strafing the sand so that it shot up in geysers. The medics said Zachariah had actually died on the battlefield, his heart had stopped beating, he had drawn no breath, and they had pronounced him dead. But then, a moment later, miraculously he had opened his eyes and was alive again. Where he had gone to in that long moment between heart beats, no one knew.

But Zachariah knew. He had gone to paradise.

And because of it, he had returned from the war a man filled with such beatific peace, such a calmness, that, in his presence, others grew calm and tranquil. Everything about him, it seemed to Tahia, was supernaturally gentle—his eyes, his voice, his hands, as if his man-soul had departed his body and an angel-soul had taken its place. He frightened her sometimes, he seemed so otherworldly, but he also made her heart swell with love for him. The war had changed him, as it had changed Egypt, and it had changed Tahia herself as well: at twenty-seven, she harbored her very first secret—that, although Jamal Rasheed was her husband, Zachariah was her love.

Amira came into the kitchen then, calling out, "*Sabah el-kheir.* Morning of goodness." The children stopped what they were doing, stood up respectfully, and said, "*Sabah el-nur, Umma.* Morning of light." Then they resumed their noisy industry.

Because she had gone straight to her rooms upon returning from her secret visit to Qettah, to shed her dusty melaya and freshen up before joining the family, Amira did not look as if she had just returned from the crowded Zeinab Quarter. Her outfit, a smart black wool skirt and black silk blouse, stockings and polished, high-heeled shoes, gold bracelets, diamond and antique emerald rings, and a simple pearl necklace had transformed her from *bint al-balad* to *bint al-zawat,* "daughter of the aristocracy." Just as she had always taught her girls that a woman's beauty was her second most cherished asset after her virtue, Amira had taken extra care with her makeup, the eyebrows perfectly drawn, lips skillfully outlined and shaded to hint youthful fullness, and blusher applied to a youthful complexion that had known only the finest creams and oils. Her hair, once black, was now a rich auburn, thanks to a weekly henna rinse, and was worn in a French twist pinned with diamond clips. Amira walked with grace and authority, and because she was fashionably plump, the sign of a woman who has borne children and lives well, she did not have the appearance of approaching seventy.

She paused to smile at the children, chattering like monkeys while they painted eggs as well as themselves. She thought of them as precious twigs sprouting from the various branches of the Rasheed tree; nine of them, her own great-grandchildren, possessed her distinctive, leaf-shaped eyes—not a Rasheed trait. What leaf-eyed ancestor had donated his or her looks to these babies? she wondered. Whose blood have I passed along? Perhaps I will find out when I learn who the boy is in my dreams, calling to me.

Peals of laughter brought her back to the kitchen. If only it was like this every day, she thought, feeling her good spirits restored. The house full of the happy noise of children! But with young couples setting up homes of their own these days, and unmarried women choosing to live alone, the resident population of the house on Virgins of Paradise Street had shrunk. Omar's five children—Yasmina's son Mohammed, nearly ten years old, and the four younger ones by Omar's second wife—and Tahia's children—six-year-old Asmahan and her three younger brothers and sisters—did not live here. Nor did the young women helping the children to paint eggs: Salma, the wife of one of Ayesha's sons who had been killed in the Six-Day War; Nasrah, wife of Amira's nephew, Tewfik; and Sakinna, a cousin on Jamal Rasheed's side of the family. Lovely girls, Amira thought, but with modern ideas. Only Narjis, named for the narcissus flower, seventeen-year-old daughter of Amira's niece Zubaida, appreciated traditional modesty. In fact, the girl's cousins teased Narjis about having taken a step backward, because she had adopted the new "Islamic dress" that some university women were starting to wear.

The futures of all these children and young women, whether they lived in this house or elsewhere, were Amira's responsibility. She had already paid a visit to Mrs. Abdel Rahman down the street to discuss a match between Sakinna and the Abdel Rahman son, who was graduating from the university this year. And for Salma, who had been widowed too long, Amira had her eye on Mr. Waleed, who held a well-paying post in the Ministry of Education. And Rayya's tempestuous sixteen-year-old daughter, who was arranging eggs in baskets, would be ready for engagement in a year or two. For her, Amira would look for a man who would be firm and take her in hand. But what to do about Fadilla, the twenty-year-old beauty who had announced her intention of choosing her own husband?

"There will be five more for dinner tonight, Sahra," Amira said as she went to the counter to examine the nine plump chickens being prepared for roasting. "Cousin Ahmed telephoned, he and Hosneya and the children will be joining us for the holiday." Which would bring the total of house guests to over fifty, a figure which gave Amira some degree of solace. In troubling times it was good to have the family together.

She looked through the kitchen window and saw that, overnight, the mishmish tree had bloomed, promising an abundant apricot harvest. It made her wonder about the other Mishmish, the banished granddaughter. Like Ali before him, who had proudly refused to speak Fatima's name, Ibrahim had not spoken of Yasmina since she went away.

My son said that we would not mourn for you, granddaughter of my heart. But I mourn for you, and I have done so every single day since that terrible night.

When Amira heard Zachariah say to Sahra, "Come, sit down. You don't look well," she marveled at how their secret had survived all these years. When Ibrahim had brought the beggar girl into the house twenty-eight years ago, Amira had feared she would tell the truth about the baby. But Sahra had never once betrayed that confidence; to this day, she was taken to be the family cook, and Zachariah the Rasheed heir.

The door to the garden swung open and Alice came into the kitchen, dressed to go out. Sweeping past Amira, she kissed her grandson, Mohammed. "Look what I have for you, darling," she said, handing him an envelope. "This just came. An Easter card from your Mama."

As the other children tried to look at the pretty card from America, Alice said to Mohammed, "You know, when I was a little girl back in England, we would rise very early on Easter Sunday and go outside to look into the pond and watch the sun dance."

He regarded her with big eyes. "How can the sun dance, Grandmother?"

"It dances for joy over the resurrection of Jesus." When she tried to wipe chocolate off his cheek, Nefissa took the card out of his hand and said, "Come here, baby. Grandma has a treat for you."

Alice looked at Ibrahim's sister, whose face was hard beneath her makeup, and she thought: Long ago we were friends; now we are rival grandmothers.

"I'm going out, Mother Amira," Alice said. "Shopping with Camelia."

"Alice, my dear, you look pale. Are you all right?"

"I have a touch of diarrhea," Alice said, pulling on her gloves.

"The whole family seems to have come down with something. I'll prepare a tea of savory leaves. Alice, may I have a word with you?"

They stepped out of the hearing of the others, and Amira said, "I have decided to make the pilgrimage to Mecca, and I would like you to go with me."

"Me? You want me to go with you to Saudi Arabia?"

"I have been wanting to make this journey for a long time, but I can never find the right opportunity. But I consulted with Qettah this morning, and I realize that now is the time for me to go. Would you like to accompany me?"

Alice thought for a moment, then she said, "Is it a long trip?"

"It can be long or short, however we wish it to be." She gave Alice a searching look. "I will go there to pray at the Ka'aba. Arabia is a very spiritual place, a good place to contemplate one's life. But anyway," Amira said, "think about it. I must go to see Ibrahim now. I want to leave as soon as possible."

===

The auditorium of the Cairo Women's Union was packed; over a thousand women had come to hear Muammar-al Qadaffi, president of Libya, speak on the future of Arab women. When Camelia entered the hall, she stood out from the crowd in such a way that others stared. Because of her willowy dancer's body and high heels, she gave the impression of being very tall. Heavy kohl outlined her amber eyes, and her thick black hair was caught up carelessly in a single clip, creating a stormy cloud around her head. Women usually stared at her with envy, men with lust. But in the years that she had been in the public eye, Camelia Rasheed's name had been linked to not a single scandal, not a hint of romance, despite her arresting beauty. And so her reputation increased the envy, the lust.

She took a seat in one of the front rows, between the director of the

Red Crescent and the wife of the minister of health. Now that Sadat was president, Egypt was once again the art center of the Arab world, and Camelia had become a well-known celebrity. Women came up to congratulate her on her latest film, saying, "Your family must be so proud." But as far as Camelia knew, none of her family ever went to her movies or attended her nightclub shows. Even though she was once again welcome at Virgins of Paradise Street, her relationship with Amira was still strained. "You are a Rasheed," her grandmother would say. "And Rasheed women do not dance in front of strange men." The reconciliation Camelia had hoped for between Umma and Dahiba had never materialized, each stubbornly insisting that the other must take the first step.

She wished Dahiba were here today. But, unable to get her poetry published in Egypt, Dahiba had been forced to go abroad, and had flown to Lebanon to meet with a publisher who had agreed to publish her work. Others had not been so lucky. Only last year, Dr. Nawal al Saadawi, Egypt's greatest feminist writer, had been placed on the government blacklist and her books and papers confiscated. Some women here today were feminists, Camelia knew, some were not, many were undecided, not knowing how to apply the recent influx of Western feminism to a society whose values and traditions differed so from those of the West. But Camelia had found her position: it was time, she believed, for the women of Egypt to step into the twentieth century and claim their rights as human beings equal to men. Starting with, she decided now, thinking of her friend Shemessa, who had recently undergone a messy illegal abortion, a woman's right to have control over her own body.

Finally the program began. The audience settled down, President Sadat introduced the guest speaker, and when Qadaffi came onstage, instead of beginning his talk, he surprised everyone by turning his back to the audience and writing something on the chalkboard behind the podium. The hall was silent at first, and then murmurs began, growing into loud talk. Camelia stared in shock at what the Libyan president had written: "Virginity. Menstruation. Childbirth."

Turning to the stunned gathering, Qadaffi went on to explain that equality for women was impossible because of their anatomy and physiology; he declared that, like cows, women had been put on earth to bear children and suckle their young, not to work beside men.

The audience exploded.

Women shot to their feet, enraged and insulted, and when he defended his position by saying that women had inferior constitutions and could not be expected to withstand the rigors that men did—the heat in factories, the heavy loads of construction workers—a celebrated journalist rose and spoke in such a commanding voice that the meeting grew hushed. "Mr. President," she said, "have you ever passed a kidney stone? Men assure me that it is very painful, unendurable in fact. Imagine therefore, Mr. President, passing a stone one hundred times the size of a normal one, the size, let's say, of a watermelon. Would *you* be able to bear it?"

The women clapped and cheered until Camelia thought the roof would fall in. She looked at her watch. The meeting had started late; she wondered if Alice was already outside waiting for her.

=

As Alice's taxi pulled up in front of the Cairo Women's Union, she thought: Saudi Arabia! And she was surprised to find that the prospect of going there with Amira was exciting. And perhaps, as Amira had said, it would be an opportunity to reflect upon her own life, too.

Alice's depression had deepened since Yasmina had left Egypt. What she had once imagined as a cold subterranean stream eroding away the rock and stone of her soul now seemed more like a raging river, boiling just below the surface of her skin. Sometimes she even heard it in her ears, like two massive waterfalls. "High blood pressure," Dr. Sanky, the English doctor on Ezbekiya Street, had said, giving her some pills she never took. It wasn't blood pressure, Alice knew, it was melancholia, the old-fashioned word that was written on her mother's death certificate under "cause of death."

And now, as she considered taking a journey to Mecca with Amira, she thought about something she had seen from the car a few minutes earlier. The taxi had stopped at an intersection, and Alice had looked out and seen a poster, advertising 7Up, plastered to a crumbling wall next to an ancient mosque. And it had struck her that there was an invisible war being waged in Cairo, a quiet, unseen, deadly war—between the past and the future, between East and West. American soft drinks were in demand, while at the same time religious leaders were preaching about a return to the old ways. As the car had driven on, the image had stayed in Alice's mind: the modern bright red-and-green poster juxtaposed against a medieval minaret. The more she thought of the image, the more she understood its significance in relation to herself. Perhaps a trip would be good therapy, she decided. *A few weeks away from Virgins of Paradise Street and away from Ibrahim, a chance to stand back and take a good look at my life.*

When a long black limousine pulled into the spot vacated by the taxi, people on the street stopped to stare. Since the death of Abdel Nasser three years ago, and Sadat's ousting of the Russians, ostentation had returned to Egypt. This was Dahiba's limousine, the one she had kept in storage during the Nasser years. She was a bigger star than ever now, her shows were standing room only, and her movies drew huge crowds; Dahiba was a goddess, and Egyptians liked to see their goddesses live well.

It was not Dahiba, however, who alighted from the flashy car, but a miniature goddess with two long braids and a missing front tooth, who sprang to the sidewalk crying, "Auntie Alice! Auntie Alice!" Alice knelt to take the six-year-old into a tight embrace, inhaling the fragrance of freshly washed hair.

"Are you ready to go shopping today, darling?" Alice asked, as she stood up and waved at Hakim Raouf, who was getting out of the car.

Zeinab hopped up and down, holding on to Alice's hand. "Mama said I can have a new dress! May I, Auntie Alice?" The "Mama" she referred to was Camelia, who she thought was her mother. But little Zeinab with the withered leg was in fact Yasmina's daughter, and Alice was not her auntie but her grandmother.

"God's peace be with you, my lovely lady," Dahiba's husband called as he approached. Years and prosperity had added to the movie director's girth, but he carried it well, in expensively tailored Italian suits. A wave of cologne preceded him, as well as the scent of Cuban cigars and, despite it not yet being noon, a hint of Scotch whiskey. His florid cheeks puffed out in a genuine smile as he greeted Alice, but he refrained from embracing her as he would in private, since it would scandalize the passersby.

"Good day to you, Mr. Raouf. I hope things go well for you."

He threw out his hands. "Prosperous, as you can see, my beautiful lady! But I grow increasingly frustrated. The government will not let me make the films I want to. Films about *real* issues. Perhaps I should follow my wife to Lebanon, where there is more freedom."

Raouf had tried to make a movie about a woman who murdered her husband and his lover. But the government had stopped production. His message in the film was to have been: a man can kill a woman and virtually get away with it, but the law severely punishes a woman for the same crime. But the censor had said, "When a man kills a woman, it is to protect his honor. But women have no honor."

"We got a telephone call from Auntie Dahiba!" Zeinab said excitedly, tugging on Alice's hand. "All the way from Beirut!"

Alice's heart ached to look at the little girl, so perfect, so beautiful, except for the leg that forced her to walk so awkwardly. Zeinab was the image of Yasmina at six, but a sepia version, since although she had Yasmina's blue eyes, she had the dark coloring of Hassan al-Sabir.

Alice was about to enquire about the call when the doors of the auditorium opened, briefly releasing the feminine uproar inside, and Camelia appeared. "Hello, Auntie," she said, kissing Alice. "The meeting started late, so I sneaked out early. Do you hear those women in there? They want to roast President Qadaffi on a spit!"

Camelia lifted Zeinab into her arms and planted a big kiss on her cheek. "And how is my baby?"

Zeinab giggled and squirmed. "You saw me only an hour ago, Mama! Auntie Alice says she's going to buy me a chocolate egg. May I have it, Mama, please?"

Camelia's eyes briefly met Alice's in a silent communication. Neither was thinking of chocolate eggs, but of the unspoken issue constantly between them.

When Camelia had returned home from Port Said six years ago and asked where Yasmina was, Amira had sat her down and told her what had happened to her sister—how Ibrahim had banished her from the family; how her child had been born slightly deformed. Camelia tried to defend her sister: "Hassan forced her. She did it to save the family." But when Camelia saw the poor deformed baby Yasmina had rejected, her sympathy for her sister had turned to anger. "Take the child," Amira had said. "You can never bear children, but God has given you a daughter."

And so Camelia had adopted her niece and named her after Sayyida Zeinab, the Mother of Cripples.

Zeinab was now her life, and it was for the little orphan that Camelia kept her reputation spotless. She didn't take lovers; she was never seen alone in the company of a man. And a respectable, tragic story had been invented to explain the child: Zeinab's father had died heroically in the Six-Day War.

The child was also the reason why Camelia had stopped dancing at the Cage d'Or. Since Oriental dance had grown in popularity, a hierarchy had evolved—the highest class of dancers performed only in five-star hotels such as the Hilton. Those of lesser skill and more dubious moral repute danced at clubs and cabarets. And finally, also for Zeinab's sake as well as her own, since a female performer without a male protector was taken advantage of by hotel managements and was a target for lustful admirers, Camelia had asked Dahiba's husband, Hakim Raouf, to act as her manager.

As they walked to the limousine, Hakim saying that he had just received a phone call from Dahiba in Beirut to announce that her book was going to be published in October, Alice sensed Camelia's confused emotions, as she often did when she and Camelia were together and Zeinab was the catalyst to the past. But Alice was never going to tell the truth. She had learned from Amira the art of keeping secrets. Just as Alice had lied to the others about Yasmina leaving the child behind, and had lied to Yasmina about the baby being born dead, so did she continue to lie each time she wrote to Yasmina, reporting the family news but never mentioning the daughter Yasmina did not know she had. Alice had done it for one reason only: to give Yasmina the chance to break free of the family, to escape from Egypt as she herself never had.

"Guess what," she said. "Mother Amira has asked me to go to Arabia with her."

"So she is finally going," Camelia said. "For as long as I can remember, Umma has been planning to make the pilgrimage. How exciting for you, Alice!"

When they reached the car, Alice suddenly fell against it. "Merciful Heaven," she murmured.

Hakim caught her elbow. "What is it, my dear?"

"I haven't felt well all morning, and now—" she clasped her stomach and grimaced—"I'm going to throw up!"

"We'll take you to the hospital. Get in, quickly."

"No! No hospital . . . Just over there, down that street, Ibrahim's office. Hurry."

=

Amira waited until Ibrahim's nurse left the room before she said, "I couldn't wait to tell you, my son. Preparations for the journey must begin at once."

Ibrahim removed his white lab coat and hung it up carefully. "I am pleased that you have decided at last to go, Mother, but you're not going on your own, are you?"

"Of course not. Ibrahim, I've asked Alice to go with me."

"Alice! What did she say?"

"She said she would think about it, but I sense that she likes the idea. It will do her good, Ibrahim. Ever since Yasmina went away, you and Alice have not been happy. Perhaps a pilgrimage to the most holy place on earth will revive her spirit. Perhaps," she added, "you would like to come with us?"

As he watched his nurse, Huda, roll the medicine cart back into the examining room, Ibrahim thought about his wife. In the six years since Yasmina's departure, Alice seemed to have changed little, except possibly to grow quieter. She still tended her English garden beneath the penetrating Egyptian sun, still went to Fifi's once a week to touch up her fading blond hair. And she had cultivated a small knot of friends—the wife of a professor at the American University, both from Michigan; an Englishwoman named Madeline, married in a lukewarm way to an Egyptian; and Mrs. Flornoy, a Canadian widow who had settled in Cairo after her American husband had died of malaria. The four expatriate women got together two nights a week for bridge and nostalgia, a respite from the overwhelming Egyptianness of their lives. But Ibrahim knew that these mundane rituals were something for Alice to hide behind, that they were the daily, commonplace acts of living that kept her from confronting the pain and anger he suspected she must be feeling. For he felt them himself, and so he, too, lived according to a basic, uncomplicated plan: rise with the sun, go through the motions of prayer, eat breakfast, go to the office, see his patients, sleep through the siesta, rise for more prayers, dinner, more patients, and the late-night hours made busy with books, correspondence, radio. He rarely saw

Alice; he had not asked her to come to his bedroom since the night Yasmina left.

They never spoke of that terrible time in June, on the eve of Egypt's humiliating defeat; Ibrahim would not even let himself think about it. There were moments, however, when he thought of his old friend Hassan, who had died under mysterious circumstances. The newspapers had reported simply that Hassan had been murdered; there had been no mention that his genitals had been cut off. And the police had never found out who did it.

"I cannot go to Saudi Arabia with you, Mother," he said, reaching for his jacket, "but if Alice wishes to, then she has my permission to do so."

"It would do you good to make the pilgrimage, my son. God's grace will heal you."

Ibrahim considered the vastness of Arabia's desert and sky, and thought that they gave a man too much room for thinking. Besides, he knew that going through the motions of a pilgrimage was as fruitless as the empty prayers he now recited five times a day. How can God grant grace to a man who has lost his faith? To a man who once cursed Him . . .

He paused to watch his nurse get ready to leave for the afternoon. Huda was a vaguely pretty, capable nurse of twenty-two, who had to hurry home every day and cook for her father and five younger brothers. She had once laughingly told Ibrahim, "When I was born, my father was so angry that his first child was a girl, that he threatened my mother with divorce if she didn't give him a son the next time. *Bismillah,* he must have put the fear of Satan in her, because she never had another girl after that!"

Ibrahim had asked her what her father did, and when she had said, "He sells sandwiches in Talaat Harb Square," Ibrahim had envied a sandwich seller.

As he watched her put the last of the supplies away, he heard through the open window the radio in the coffeehouse downstairs. The newscaster's somber voice was bringing the latest reports: the last of the Russian military advisers had been expelled from Egypt, police had quelled another student riot at Cairo University, and two White House aides were accused of having previous knowledge of the Watergate break-in. Ibrahim closed his window. There was never any good news.

The newspapers were no better, with their daily reminders that cotton exports continued to go down and therefore his income from his Delta farms. This was a bad time for Egypt; even Egypt's greatest living writer, Naguib Mahfouz, was writing stories about death and despair. Ibrahim found himself thinking more and more about the old days, when Farouk had been in power. Had it really been twenty-eight years since he and Hassan, virile young men in their twenties with not a care in the world, had raced from casino to casino with their king?

He returned his attention to his mother, who had surprised him by suddenly showing up at his office. This was the first time she had ever been here. "How do you intend to go to Arabia, Mother?" he asked. "By boat? By plane?"

"Pardon me, Dr. Ibrahim, but I'll be going now," Huda said brightly, as she came back in and reached for her sweater. Despite having to care for six demanding men, she considered herself to be quite modern and liberated. And it was apparent that she had a crush on her employer. "Will you be taking your family to the river tomorrow for the *Shamm el*—" She turned toward the door. "What was that sound?"

Ibrahim rose to his feet just as the door flew open and Alice came in, assisted by Hakim Raouf.

"What is it?" he said, going to her. "What's wrong?"

"I'm all right, Ibrahim . . . I just need a ladies' room. Quickly . . ."

"Huda," he said, and the young woman was instantly at Alice's side, helping her into the next room, with Amira following.

Ibrahim turned to Camelia. "What did she tell you? Does she have a fever?"

"No, no fever, Papa. She said she was up all night with diarrhea. And so were some of the other members of the family."

Huda came out. "Doctor, come quickly. Mrs. Rasheed is vomiting."

Camelia and Hakim paced Ibrahim's office while they heard sounds of distress on the other side of the wall. A few minutes later, Ibrahim appeared in the doorway. "I don't know what it is," he said. "She's lost a shocking amount of fluid, but she's resting for the moment. I took a specimen. Preliminary microscopic examination might tell us something." And he disappeared again.

In the small room, barely larger than a closet, which served as Ibrahim's laboratory, he prepared a slide and prayed for a tentative diagnosis. "What is it, Ibrahim?" Amira said, struck by the fact that, as he peered through the lens of the microscope, Ibrahim reminded her of Qettah examining tea leaves. "What is wrong with Alice?"

"I am praying it's only an attack of food poisoning," he said. But when he focused the microscope and saw the distinctive, comma-shaped bacilli, moving so rapidly they resembled shooting stars, he sat back and whispered, "Oh my God."

CHAPTER 28

What am I going to do? I am only three months away from getting my degree. Is it fair they should send me back *now*?"

Jasmine looked into the terrified eyes of her neighbor, a young exchange student from Syria, and saw her own worries mirrored there. The United States had broken off diplomatic relations with various countries in the Middle East, and now was revoking visas and sending students back to Syria, Jordan, and Egypt. Jasmine had not yet received her notice, but she lived in fear of it from day to day. She couldn't go back to Egypt. Her family considered her dead; in six years she had received no communication from any of them, except for regular letters from her mother.

"They're sending us all home!" the girl said, rubbing her arms as she stood outside Jasmine's front door, where a light rain fell. "Have you received your notice yet?"

Jasmine shook her head, but she knew it was only a matter of time. Like her neighbor, she too was only three months away from her bachelor's degree; and she had just been accepted into medical school.

"Do you know Hussein Sukry," the girl was saying, "who has the apartment next to mine? He left last week. He was hoping to support his family once he got his chemical engineering degree. But now he is back in Amman with no degree and no job. What are we to do? Let me know if you hear of a solution," the young woman said, adding, "*Ma salaama*. God keep you," and she went back across the courtyard of the apartment complex, where raindrops were creating ripples on the surface of the swimming pool.

Fighting down her panic, Jasmine looked at her watch and, seeing that she would be late for her appointment if she didn't hurry, grabbed her purse, sweater, and car keys, and rushed out, slamming the door behind her.

A metallic sky had hovered for days over Southern California and this college community perched on a cliff overlooking the Pacific Ocean. As Jasmine hurried to the elevator that went down to the subterranean parking garage, she glimpsed the dull sky and thought how aptly it reflected her mood. Ever since the notices from Immigration and Naturalization had started arriving, a cold, gray depression had settled over the small body of Muslim students who attended the nearby university. Why were they being punished for the politics of their countries? What did the conflict between Israel and Egypt have to do with anything or anyone beyond their own borders?

As she stepped out of the drizzle and into the elevator, she thought of how the khamsins would be starting in Egypt now, the sandstorms that always heralded her own and Camelia's birthdays. Jasmine was going to be twenty-seven, Camelia, twenty-eight.

When the elevator doors opened, she hurried blindly out, colliding with a young man.

"I'm sorry!" she said, helping him retrieve the books and papers he had dropped. "I didn't see you!"

He said, "No sweat," and handed her her purse. "Hey, it's Jasmine, right? In the front apartment?"

Pushing her blond hair back from her face, she found herself looking into a smile she recognized. It belonged to a young man with red-gold hair and beard, horn-rimmed glasses, patched jeans, and sandals. His name was Greg Van Kerk, and he lived four doors down from her.

"Yes, Jasmine Rasheed," she said. Five years ago, in England, when she had applied for a visa to the United States, she had changed the spelling of her first name. "I'm sorry I nearly knocked you over."

He laughed. "I can't think of a better way to begin my day. Except maybe to have my car start. It never fails, in the rain." He gestured to a battered VW behind him. "It never starts in a month with an R in it.

And wouldn't you know it, today is the one day I *have* to get to school."
He looked at the car keys in her hand. "I suppose you're on your way
to the campus?"

Jasmine hesitated. Although she and Greg Van Kerk had been neighbors for a year, exchanging words at the mailbox, saying "Hi" when
they passed in the courtyard, he was a stranger nonetheless. After six
years of living among Westerners, Jasmine still had not learned to relax
in the company of a man who wasn't a relative. Reminding herself that
this was a different country, with different rules, and that he was someone who needed assistance, she said shyly, "I will give you a ride, if you
wish."

Two minutes later they were on the Pacific Coast Highway, heading
for the green promontory where a university of twenty thousand students looked out over waves crashing picturesquely against rocks.

"Sure doesn't feel like spring," Greg said, after a spell of silence. "I
mean, when does Southern California ever have this much rain?"

Spring, she thought as she held tightly to the steering wheel. *Shamm
el-Nessim.* The family would be down by the Nile or at the Barrage
Gardens, picnicking and showing off their new clothes. And in three
days her son Mohammed was going to celebrate his tenth birthday—a
day she privately celebrated—and mourned—each year. She had sent
him a present, a long letter, and a photograph of herself.

"Nice car," Greg said, touching the dashboard of her new Chevrolet.

Jasmine recalled that Greg Van Kerk lived in one of the cheapest
apartments in the complex, and did part-time work as a handyman
around the place to help pay for his tuition. Thinking of the dented VW,
and noticing his patched jeans, Jasmine was reminded again of her good
fortune. The house and trust fund in England, which her grandfather
had left to her, brought in a small but steady income—the old earl's
guilt money, she suspected, after he had disinherited his daughter for
marrying an Arab.

Traffic slowed, and they saw red emergency lights ahead. "Never
fails," Greg said. "Southern Californians freak in rain."

"Bismillah!" Jasmine murmured, thinking of her urgent appointment.

"What?"

"I said, 'In the Name of God.' It's Arabic."

"That's right, someone told me you're from Egypt. You don't look Middle Eastern."

After spending a year in England, Jasmine had come to America at Maryam Misrahi's invitation, and had discovered how unpopular it was to be Egyptian in America. After the Six-Day War, the situation had become explosive, Jewish and Arab students actually getting into fights at the university, and anti-Egyptian slogans being scrawled on the walls. During her very first days in the Misrahi house in the San Fernando Valley, she had overheard an argument between Rachel, Maryam's granddaughter, and Rachel's brother, a Zionist who had voiced his opposition to having an Egyptian live with them. "Daddy was born in Cairo!" Rachel had countered. "We are Egyptian, Haroun!" "My name is Aaron," he had shot back, "and we are Jews first." That was when Jasmine had cut her visit short and found an apartment of her own. And now that things were heating up again, as the saber-rattling increased on both sides of the Suez Canal, Jasmine was glad she blended, chameleon-like, with the Western crowd.

"I heard that the State Department is making Middle Eastern students go home. Is that going to happen to you?" Greg said, as the Coast Highway traffic came nearly to a halt.

"I don't know," she said quietly. "I hope not."

When he saw how she grasped the steering wheel until her knuckles were white, he wondered if it was because of the slick highway, the accident up ahead, or the State Department. He said, "It must be strange for you here. I mean, Egypt isn't like America, is it?"

When Jasmine realized she liked the sound of Greg's voice, she tried to relax. She glanced at him; he was slouching in the seat rather than sitting in it, and the American phrase "easygoing" came to her mind. She didn't sense any threat from him, no danger to her virtue. She thought of Amira's favorite warning—"When a man and a woman are alone together, Satan makes their third companion"—and she wondered where was Satan in this car. *He's back in Egypt, with my father and his curse.*

A memory started to surface: "It will be as if you were dead . . ." her father had said. Jasmine pushed it down, buried it, as she always did. *Suppress the past, don't think about it.*

"No, America is not like Egypt," she said, as a highway patrol officer directed them around the traffic flares.

When she said nothing more, Greg regarded her for a long moment and noticed for the first time how blue her eyes were, and that her hair wasn't exactly blond but a dark honey. "I like your accent," he said. "Sort of British with spice thrown in."

"I lived for a while in England before coming to America. And my mother is English."

"What was that swearword you said a minute ago?"

"*Bismillah* is not a swearword. The Koran instructs us always to have God's name on our lips. But Americans don't like to speak the name of God. This is strange to a Muslim, because the Prophet taught us to invoke the name of God as frequently as possible, to keep Him always in front of our thoughts. And also, because evil spirits fear the name of God, we speak it a lot to keep them away."

He gave her a startled look. "You believe in evil spirits?"

"Most Egyptians do." When she saw how Greg smiled at her, her cheeks burned.

"So what kind of doctor are you going to be?" he asked.

"I want to take medicine to people who otherwise have no access to it. My father has a practice in Cairo . . . a lot of poor people come to him because they are afraid of the government doctors, and because people who work at the government hospitals usually require bribes. My father does a lot of work for free, but sometimes he gets paid in chickens or goats."

"And you're going to go back and work with him?"

"No, I will go somewhere else. There is need all over the world." She gave him a shy smile and said, "I am talking too much."

"Hardly! Besides, I'm interested. I'm an anthropologist—well, working on my master's."

"I am a little embarrassed," she said, her voice barely audible above the rain. "Where I come from, an unmarried woman does not talk freely with a man she is not related to, because the reputation of an unmarried woman in Egypt is a very fragile thing."

She looked out at the churning gray ocean. She sensed Greg at her side, waiting for her to continue.

"In America," she said, "if a woman wishes to live alone, not to marry, she has that choice. But Egyptian men believe that all women want to be married, they cannot conceive of a woman not wanting to be married." She thought of Camelia who, according to Alice's latest letter, was still unmarried. "Here in California I have actually seen young women pursue men they were interested in. In Egypt, it is only the man who may do the pursuing. It is a man's world, Egypt," Jasmine added quietly.

Greg gave her a long look before saying, "Do you miss your home a lot?"

Jasmine thought that it was more than merely missing Egypt; she felt as if she were constantly hungry, physically and spiritually. She was starved for her own culture, where the day was broken into five parts by prayer; she missed the street vendors on Cairo's noisy corners, the smoky smells and rowdy celebrations, the people, so quick to laugh or cry or shout. Living alone in an apartment had none of the comforting feel of a big house, with its spirits of the generations who had lived before her, and the laughter of many children and cousins, people everywhere, all of them Rasheeds, sharing beliefs, fears, and joys. Here, she felt isolated, an entity cut off from the greater body, almost as if she were truly just a spirit. As if her father's death sentence had indeed been carried out.

"So are you the only one here?" Greg asked. "I mean, is your family still in Egypt?"

How could she explain her father's punishment to Greg Van Kerk? In what terms could she tell him that, if she had lived in a village, her father and uncles would have been justified in killing her for sleeping with a man who was not her husband, even if he had forced her? How could she convey to him her terror of being sent back to Egypt, because she was now a ghost among the living and would be an outcast in her country, suffering a worse loneliness and isolation than any she had experienced in England or America?

As the buildings and tall pines of the school grounds came into view, Jasmine thought: Do the dead also mourn? Because, although six years now separated her from that terrible night, not a day went by in which she did not grieve for the loss of her stillborn child and her beloved son Mohammed.

Through Alice, Jasmine maintained a frail link with the boy. She sent him cards and presents, and Alice sent photographs back, of Mohammed at the zoo, in his school uniform, riding a horse at the Pyramids. But the letter she always hoped to find in her mailbox, scrawled in a childish hand and starting "Dearest Mama," never came.

Mohammed was never really mine, she thought, guiding her car into a parking space. He never belonged to me. He belonged to Omar and the Rasheeds. "Yes," she said, turning off the ignition. "My family is in Egypt."

Greg paused to look at her. When he had first moved into the apartment complex a year ago and had seen the young blond woman who occupied the expensive apartment at the front, without a room-mate, keeping to herself and not attending any of the barbecues around the pool, he had thought she was a snob. After a few murmured exchanges in the laundry room and the parking garage, he had decided she was just shy. Now he thought: not shy. Modest. And it struck him that he had never ascribed that quality to anyone before. She wasn't exactly nunlike, but her demeanor, her conservative way of dressing, even her hair, which looked as if it might be wild if set free from those barrettes, reminded him of the sisters who had taught at the Catholic schools he attended as a boy.

But there was something even more compelling about her than exotic looks, a British accent, a hint of mystery; it was her air of overwhelming sadness, as if she were enveloped in a deep, powerful mourning. And it made him, for the first time in his life, forget for a moment his overdue rent and stalled VW, and wonder what had made her so profoundly sad.

"Would you like to go out some night?" he said. "Movies, pizza?"

She gave him a startled look. "Thank you, but I don't think it will be possible. I study all the time, and I must prepare for medical school."

"Sure. I understand. Thanks for the ride," he said to her over the top of the car. "So what are you going to do?"

"I beg your pardon?"

"I mean, about the State Department. What if they order you to leave the U.S.? What will you do?"

"I have an appointment with the dean of the medical school," she said, her voice hopeful but her eyes betraying doubt. "Since they have accepted me for the fall class, maybe they will help, *inshallah*."

"*Inshallah*," he murmured, as he watched her cross the lawn toward the university's massive red-brick medical facility.

—

Because of the threat of rain, Jasmine decided to take a short cut through Lathrop Hall, and when the glass doors swung closed behind her, she found herself facing a long corridor filled with people in white lab coats, hurrying this way and that with clipboards and stethoscopes, alone or engaged in animated conversation. Doors stood open to laboratories, classrooms, and offices with signs reading: PARASITOLOGY, TROPICAL MEDICINE, PUBLIC HEALTH EDUCATION, VECTOR-BORNE DISEASES. The air seemed filled with urgency and purpose; it was the world, she knew, where she belonged.

As she made her way down the busy hall, she decided that, if the dean of the school was unable to help her, perhaps someone here might. She couldn't possibly talk to everyone, but she could get to those who would be her teachers; they would certainly want to help her stay in school.

Near the end of the corridor, a hand-lettered notice taped next to an open door caught her attention—specifically, the word "Arabic." She stepped closer to read it: "Needed. Assistant to work on book project: translation of Third World health manual for use in the field. Duties include typing, medical research, handling correspondence. Knowledge of Arabic helpful but not essential. Evenings and weekends." It was signed by Dr. Declan Connor, Department of Tropical Medicine.

She looked inside and saw a very small office with barely enough space for the desk, chair, and filing cabinets, all of which appeared to be covered with journals, books, papers. She glimpsed a typewriter among boxes of index cards. The only occupant in the office, a man whom she presumed to be Dr. Connor, was on the phone, trying to explain to someone about requiring computer time.

When he saw her standing there, he waved for her to come in, and said, "They've put me on hold again. I'll explain everything to you in a moment. I'm afraid we're in a bit of a rush—the publisher has moved the pub date up on me. And the World Health Organization informs me that nearly every agency in the Middle East is asking for the book."

Jasmine was struck by two things at once: that he spoke with a British accent, and that he was very attractive.

"While you're waiting," he said, cradling the earpiece between his chin and shoulder, "you'll want to take a look at this." He thrust a book into Jasmine's hands and, before she could speak, he was talking into the phone again.

He had given her a large book resembling a telephone directory, titled

When You *Have to Be the Doctor.* It bore a cover illustration of an African mother and child standing in front of grass huts, and as Jasmine flipped through the pages she saw illustrations of sick people, wounds, microbes, instructions on bandaging and how to measure and administer medication, and diagrams of the ideal village layout. Although medical and pharmaceutical terms were used, the text was in plain and simple language. Someone had inked a few notes in the margins—on a page dealing with measles, the word *mazla* had been written, with a question mark after it.

Jasmine looked around the office, at the certificates and letters framed and hung randomly on the walls. There was a baffling poster of a young African male in trousers and a shirt, and he was clearly pregnant. Underneath, in bold print, was the question: "How Would *You* Like It?" The question was repeated below in what Jasmine presumed to be Swahili, since small print at the very bottom of the poster identified it as having been produced by the Kenya Family Planning Commission.

Among the clutter on the desk was a sign that read: "Definition of a vaccine: a substance which, when injected into a white rat, results in a scientific paper." On another scrap of paper, taped to the edge of the desk, someone had scrawled: "Old professors never die, they just lose their faculties." Then she saw a photograph of a man and a woman and a child, standing in front of a gate with a sign that read GRACE TREVER-TON MISSION; in the background Jasmine saw concrete block buildings with tin roofs, and African women carrying baskets on their heads.

She looked at Dr. Connor, still on the phone. She judged him to be in his early thirties, but the tweed jacket and brown tie, the dark-brown hair conservatively cut, made him seem older; he looked as if he had stepped out of the past. Most men around campus these days were like Greg Van Kerk, opting for jeans and sandals and longer hair, but Jasmine thought that Dr. Connor, despite his young age, seemed to have been completely bypassed by the hippy movement.

She tried to get his attention, but he held up a hand, indicating he would be right with her. She looked at her watch; she was due at the dean's office. She briefly considered walking out, but felt curiously compelled to stay.

"No, wait," Connor said into the phone. "Don't transfer me, I just want—" He gave Jasmine an apologetic look and said, "I feel like a rat in a maze. Yes? Hello? Look, don't transfer me again. This is Dr. Connor in tropical medicine . . ."

Jasmine watched, fascinated. Declan Connor seemed to fill the room with barely harnessed energy—it showed in the stiff way he stood, his clipped speech, the abrupt gestures. She saw that his shirt collar was bunched up over the top of his jacket, as if he had gotten dressed on the run, and as he spoke on the phone, he rummaged through papers on the desk, making Jasmine wonder if he was a man who always did two things at once. Connor gave the impression of hurrying in place.

She liked his looks, finding that the large straight nose and clean-cut cheeks and jaw—aggressive features, she thought—seemed to heighten his illusion of intensity. When he made a sudden move, knocking some papers to the floor, he gave Jasmine an embarrassed smile and she felt her heart give a strange leap.

"Yes, all right," Connor finally said into the phone, and hung up with an exasperated sigh. "It's just like government bureaucracy around here!" He flashed her a smile. "But don't let it worry you. If we can't get computer time then we shall do it the way our ancestors did—with pen and paper. Well, what do you think of it?" he said, gesturing to the book in her hands. "That book was first written back in the forties by a very great lady, Dr. Grace Treverton, in Kenya. It's been updated many times since, of course, but so far it only exists in English and Swahili. The Treverton Foundation has asked me to come out with an Arabic version, for health-care workers in the Middle East. You'll see I've already started making notes in the margins."

"Yes," she said, flipping back to a section titled, "Nutritional Education," part of which involved teaching villagers the importance of proper food handling and cooking. "But you probably won't need this part here," Jasmine said, showing him the entry on trichinosis with its commandment in bold type never to eat undercooked pork. "You'll be working mainly with Muslims, who don't eat pork."

"I know, but we work in Christian villages as well."

"And then there is this"—she flipped back to the page on measles—"you have written the word *mazla* here. If you mean to say measles in Arabic, the word is *nazla*."

"Good heavens. You didn't tell me you speak Arabic. Oh, hang on."

He reached for a pair of glasses and put them on. "You're not the student I hired."

"I apologize, Dr. Connor," she said, handing the book back to him. "I didn't have a chance to explain."

"Do I detect the accent of a fellow countryman? What part of England are you from?"

"I'm not from England. But I am half English. I was born in Cairo."

"Cairo! Fascinating city! I taught for a year at the American University there—used to get my shirts ironed by a chap named Habib, on Youssef El Gendi Street. He would fill his mouth with water and spray it over the shirts, and then he would actually press the shirt holding the iron with his feet. Habib was always trying to get me to marry his daughter. I told him I was already married, but he insisted that two wives were better than one! I wonder if he's still there. Our son was nearly born in Cairo. But he chose the Athens airport, of all places, to make his entrance. That was five years ago. We haven't been back to the Middle East since. Well! Small world! What can I do for you?"

She explained about her problem with the Immigration Service. "Yes," Connor said, "unfortunate business. Doesn't make a damn bit of sense. I've already lost three students. Have you received your notice yet? Maybe you'll be one of the lucky ones. A few do slip through the net." He paused and seemed to study her. Then he looked at his watch and said, "The student I hired is forty-five minutes late. There's a chance she won't show. It's happened before—a better job comes along. If she doesn't show up, would you take the job? You'd be perfect, speaking Arabic as you do."

Jasmine realized that she would very much like to work for Dr. Connor. "If I'm not sent back," she said.

"I tell you what, if you get a notice from the INS I'll write a letter to them for you. I can't guarantee it would help, but it can't hurt. And I mean it about the job. The pay is wretched, I'm afraid. The Foundation doesn't sell the book, it's given out free wherever it's needed. But we could have fun doing it." When he smiled self-consciously and added, "Let's pray you don't get that notice. *Inshallah, ma salaama*," Jasmine had to suppress a laugh. His pronunciation was atrocious.

=

As Rachel Misrahi pushed her way through the demonstrators outside the Student Union, she gave herself a mental kick in the pants. If only she hadn't persuaded Jasmine to use the Misrahi residence as her official address—"Saves you reregistering with the feds every time you change apartments"—because then Rachel would not now be facing the god-awful task of delivering to Jasmine the certified letter that had come from the Immigration and Naturalization Service in Washington, D.C.

Rachel Misrahi, twenty-five years old and pushing her stocky frame through a crowd of women holding placards that said, STARVE A RAT, DON'T COOK DINNER TONIGHT, was prepared to be mad as hell if Jasmine had to go back to Egypt. Rachel had helped Jasmine get into this school, which Rachel herself had attended as an undergraduate.

She didn't have time to listen to what the feminist protesters were angry about, but she accepted their leaflets and said, "Keep the faith, sisters," and finally made her way inside. She looked around the busy cafeteria, where she knew Jasmine ate lunch every Monday and Wednesday, between Biochemistry and Economics. Purchasing tea and a wedge of cheesecake, reminding herself that tomorrow the diet starts, Rachel claimed a littered table from which she could watch the entrance to the cafeteria.

As she observed the mob outside dispense leaflets and shout slogans, despite the increasing rain, Rachel thought of the few attempts she had made to draw Jasmine into a feminist discussion. "After all," she had said, "you come from one of the most oppressed societies in the world, when it comes to women. I would think you would be at the forefront of the battle." But Jasmine had been curiously silent on the issue; Jasmine was, in fact, strangely silent on the subject of Egypt or her family in general. Rachel had thought she would be homesick, as a lot of foreign students were, and therefore talkative about home. But Jasmine never spoke of Cairo, or the Rasheeds.

Finally there she was, weaving her way through the lunch crowd. "They can't help me," she said sitting down. "The dean said that if the INS revokes my visa, then I can't attend the school. One of the professors offered to help—Dr. Connor—"

"In Tropical Medicine?"

"He said he would write a letter, but he didn't seem hopeful."

"I wish I could help, Jas, I really do. My dad even spoke to a lawyer friend of his. He couldn't give us much hope. If war breaks out again between Egypt and Israel, you can be sure you won't be welcome here. Let's pray that peace breaks out instead."

When Rachel saw the naked fear in Jasmine's eyes, she wondered why she was so afraid to go home. Although Rachel felt genuine kinship with her—after hearing her call Grandma Maryam "Auntie" so many times, Rachel regarded Jasmine as a cousin—Jasmine remained an enigma. Her innocence, for example, perplexed Rachel, who knew that Jasmine had been married and had left a son behind in Egypt. How could a divorced woman seem so virginal, so chaste? Rachel recalled the time she had introduced Jasmine to some friends, a couple living together in Malibu. Jasmine had been genuinely shocked to learn that they weren't married. If it really was because of her upbringing, as Grandma Maryam had explained, and that possibly Jasmine could never assimilate into American life, why then did she seem so fearful about going home?

Rachel was about to voice this when suddenly a man appeared at their table, a knapsack on his shoulder and a grin on his face. When he said to Jasmine, "So, how did it go?" Rachel looked at him in surprise. And when Jasmine responded, and then introduced Greg Van Kerk to Rachel, she stared in further amazement: since when had Jasmine cultivated friendship with a male?

"Mind if I sit down?" he asked. "So what are you going to do now?" he asked Jasmine, with a familiarity that baffled Rachel.

"I must think of something," Jasmine said. "And pray that I don't get one of those notices."

"Uh-oh," Rachel said. "Please don't kill the messenger." She pulled the certified letter out of her purse.

Jasmine looked at it. "So," she said quietly, "it has come."

"Hey," Greg said, "it might not be bad news. Maybe it's a letter telling you you're one of the lucky ones."

Rachel slit open the envelope, unfolded the letter and handed it to Jasmine. She didn't take it, but was able to read enough to know that it wasn't good news.

She looked out at the demonstrators in the rain. In Egypt, such a gathering would never take place—the fathers and brothers of these young women would break up the meeting and take them home. Through the plateglass window of the cafeteria she sensed their pain and outrage. They were women who felt they had been betrayed; the glue that held them together was anger, even hatred, against the men who had oppressed them. Jasmine knew what it felt like to be powerless—it was Hassan al-Sabir, forcing her to submit to him in order to save her family; it was her father, punishing her for being a victim. And now policies established by men she didn't even know were destroying her plans and her life.

This was why she had decided to become a doctor. Physicians possessed power—real power, over life and death. And someday she was going to be a woman with power, never again to be a victim of men or curses or death sentences.

"Listen, Jas," Rachel said. "You might as well accept it. As Grandma Maryam always says, *inshallah,* it's God's will. Go back to Egypt, and when the political climate is better, you can come back."

"I cannot go back," Jasmine said.

"Well," Greg said, stretching his long legs in front of him and crossing his ankles, "there is one way you might be able to stay. I mean, there is a loophole you might use."

Rachel and Jasmine both said, "What's that?"

"Marry an American."

Jasmine stared at him. "Can it be done?"

"Wait a minute," Rachel said. "The Immigration Service caught on to that a long time ago. She would never get away with it."

"I didn't say she should run off to Vegas and marry the first man she saw. It can be done, if it's done right. There's no doubt that the INS will investigate for a while. I mean, friends and neighbors will be questioned to see if the couple got married for legitimate reasons and not just to dodge visa regulations, and she would probably have to stay married for at least two years. If Jasmine got a divorce before that, the INS would most likely return her to her former status and ship her back to Egypt."

Jasmine turned to Rachel. "Do you think I should marry a stranger to stay in the United States?"

"Why not? You said girls marry strangers all the time in Egypt."

"But that is different, Rachel. And anyway, who would do this for me?"

Greg stretched, and his shirt came out from beneath his jeans. As he tucked it back in, he said, "I'm not doing anything this weekend."

Jasmine stared at him, and when she saw that he was serious, she said, "But how can it succeed? I receive this notice from the government, and the next day I am married to an American? They would suspect."

But Rachel said, "Not if you put on a good act and fool them. And anyway, they can't prove you got this letter before you got married."

"But I did. I won't lie."

"For God's sake, it's not lying. I never gave you the letter, did I? I opened it, I showed it to you, but I never *gave* it to you. Listen, Jas, of all the reasons I can think of for getting married, this is probably one of the best."

Greg said, "Hey, I can understand if it bothers you because you believe marriage is a sacred institution or something—"

"No," she said. "In Egypt, marriage is not a sacrament. We don't get married in a holy building as you do. It is simply a contract between two people."

"Then that's what I'm offering, a contract."

She frowned, her perplexity deepening. "But what about you? You would be giving up your freedom."

He laughed. "Such as it is! The women aren't exactly beating a path to my door, and anyway I have to concentrate on getting my master's and then start on my Ph.D. I don't intend to be a penniless student all my life. Okay, you want to know what's in it for me? I like your car. Let me have it every other weekend and you've got a deal."

"Seriously—"

"I *am* serious. You appear to be financially comfortable and I'm not. It seems to me this arrangement could benefit both of us. My rent gets paid, and the feds don't ship you back to Egypt."

Jasmine grew thoughtful. *Could* it work? she wondered. Could she somehow escape the nightmare of being sent back?

Greg said, "You can keep your maiden name if you want, but I would advise against it. We'd want this marriage to appear as legit as possible."

But Jasmine liked the idea of shedding the name Rasheed, as if she were shedding a veil, or a stigma. But she still hesitated and, seeing this, Greg said, "Okay, you don't know anything about me. All right, here it is: Born in St. Louis at an early age, was told by Sister Mary Theresa that I'd never amount to anything, escaped the draft and therefore Viet Nam because of diabetes, which I control with injections. I like cats and kids, and my dream is to go to New Guinea and discover a race of people no one ever knew existed. And I'm self-sufficient. I don't need a maid, I do my own cooking and cleaning. My parents are geologists who travel all over the world, so I didn't grow up in a traditional household where the wife was stuck in the kitchen. Believe me, my sympathies are with *them*," and he gestured toward the feminists who were now dispersing in the heavy downpour.

Jasmine wondered: Perhaps this is what marriage should be, rationally arrived at between two equal partners, with no dominance or subservience, no bride-price, no fear of divorce if a son isn't produced. She studied Greg for a moment, liking the way his red-gold hair curled over his frayed collar, and realized that this was the first time she had felt that a man was looking at her as a human being and not as a sex object or baby producer.

"Before we enter into this," she said finally, "I must tell you that I was married before. I had a baby that died, and I still have a son in Egypt."

Now it was Greg Van Kerk's turn to stare in amazement.

"But I will never go back," she said. "My son is no longer legally mine, I have no rightful claim upon him."

"I'm not worried about that."

"I did not leave Egypt on good terms with my family, and so I can never go back." *You are* haram, *forbidden*. She shook her head as if to clear it. Don't let the memories come back. "I went to England to claim an inheritance from my mother's side of the family. My relatives there, the Westfalls, were good to me, and tried to help me. But I was sick for a while. I was on medication . . . for depression." As she paused to give him a moment to absorb this, Jasmine thought about her own mother's clinical depression, and the fact that Alice's mother, Lady Westfall, had committed suicide.

"And then Auntie Maryam, Rachel's grandmother," she continued, "invited me to come and stay with her family here in California. I am determined to become a doctor, but it is only fair to tell you, if we are going to live together, that the depression is still there."

"I know," Greg said, suddenly feeling like a knight on a white horse, and deciding that he enjoyed it. "I sensed some kind of sadness about you. Maybe what you need is someone to help you work it out."

"There is just one more thing," she added cautiously. "We shall legally be husband and wife, but I can't—"

"Don't worry about that. We'll just be roommates, two very busy students. I'm happy on a sofa bed. And I don't think even the INS can get spies into a bedroom!"

"I've got an idea," Rachel said, suddenly excited. "Both of you come over to my house tonight. I've got a huge family, and I'll invite a bunch of friends. We'll make the wedding announcement there. That way, when the INS agents start snooping around they'll have to deal with my mother and Grandma Maryam! You can get married on Saturday, at the Little Chapel of the Something-or-Other."

As her two companions began making arrangements, happily excited about their small conspiracy against the authorities, Jasmine felt her fear vanish and her spirits lift. And in the next moment she found herself thinking of Dr. Declan Connor and his offer for a job. And she suddenly realized she was hoping very much that the student he had hired would not show up.

CHAPTER 29

Despite the blowing khamsin wind, a funeral tent had been erected at the end of Fahmy Pasha Street, and all day a large, illustrious crowd of people came and went, to hear the reading of the Koran and to pay respects to the deceased. Afterward, the procession to the cemetery rivaled that attending the funerals of statesmen and movie stars; even President Sadat had sent a representative to follow the coffin down El Bustan Street. As Zachariah shouldered one corner of the heavy casket, he asked himself, Who would have thought Jamal Rasheed was so well loved?

Zachariah was one of only two members attending from the widow's side of the family; Tahia herself hadn't even been able to come. When word had reached Virgins of Paradise Street of Jamal Rasheed's heart attack, his pregnant young wife had been down with cholera. And she was there still, along with nearly everyone else in the house.

For some mysterious reason, Zachariah had not contracted the disease, was in fact the only member of the family, except for Ibrahim, who was not confined behind closed doors bearing Ministry of Health quarantine notices. Zachariah had been examined, found not to be a carrier of the disease, and so had been granted permission to attend the funeral.

He had not wanted to leave Tahia's side, but a man could not shirk his duty to carry a family member to his grave. And as he walked wearily beneath his burden, exhausted from long hours spent at Tahia's bedside and helping the women with the enormous task of nursing so many sick family members, Zachariah marveled that he could so reverently carry the man who had stolen Tahia from him. But, in her nearly ten years with Jamal, Tahia had been genuinely happy with him, even loved him in a way, she had confessed to Zachariah. Therefore he paid respectful homage to the man. But Tahia had been left alone with four little ones and a fifth on the way; it was she he must think of now.

I will take care of her, Zachariah vowed, now that we are free to marry. The promise that God had made to him during his moments of death in the Sinai desert, when he had glimpsed the wondrous afterlife awaiting Believers—moments in which, fleetingly, Zachariah had not wanted to return to earth—God's promise that he and Tahia were fated to be together was coming to pass at last. They would marry before next Ramadan, he decided.

Walking behind Zachariah, also shouldering the casket that bore his distant relation, Ibrahim wrestled with the mystery of the cholera outbreak.

The Rasheed family was the only one in the entire city that had come down with the disease. Forty-two members were ill and being nursed by a handful of women, and in the three days since Alice's collapse in Ibrahim's office, investigators from the Ministry of Health had not been able to locate the cause.

The khamsin drove stinging sand over the coffin and its bearers, and the crowd following Jamal Rasheed to his tomb covered their faces with handkerchiefs and coughed the grit from their throats. As the crowd, consisting only of men, since women did not walk in funeral processions, made its way beneath a dun-colored veil through which the sun barely shone, Ibrahim thought: Why did the cholera strike only our family and no one else? Why are my sister and wife and mother and aunts and nieces and female cousins all prostrate with illness, while I and Zachariah walk free?

As the hot desert wind assaulted them and seemed intent upon toppling the casket, Ibrahim kept his eyes fixed on Zachariah's back; the boy was a constant reminder of things Ibrahim wished to forget. The young fool hadn't even gone to war properly, fighting valiantly and coming home wounded, as Omar had. No, Zachariah had returned with an audacious story about having died and gone to heaven, an embarrassment to the family.

Finally they arrived at the cemetery and the pall bearers placed Jamal in the tomb alongside his parents and brothers. As the large stone was rolled into place, sealing the tomb, and dust and water was sprinkled upon it as the imam from Jamal's mosque read from the Koran, Ibrahim reminded himself that a man's thoughts at a funeral should be pious.

So he directed his mind to the man he had just interred, and from Jamal his thoughts went to the widow, Tahia, who was lying sick in bed on Virgins of Paradise Street, unaware of the fact that her husband had died. It was Ibrahim's responsibility to break the news to her, which he planned to do as soon as she had recovered. Then, because she was his sister's daughter, it was his duty to take care of her and her children. But that meant five more mouths to feed, and a sixth on the way. Growing children needed new clothes, they ate voraciously, and school costs were skyrocketing. How was he going to afford it all? His cotton revenues, as well as his other investments, had started to dry up during the Nasser years.

As he squinted up at the sky and observed the queer phenomenon of a "blue" sun that sometimes appeared during the khamsin, Ibrahim arrived at a decision: He would wait a respectable amount of time, but not too long, before next Ramadan, and find a husband for Tahia.

A group of reporters was at Cairo airport awaiting the arrival of Dahiba, Egypt's beloved dancer. No one knew why she had gone to Lebanon, but rumors had raced through the city—a secret operation, an illicit love affair—but only one story was true: that she had found a publisher in Beirut brave enough to publish her controversial poetry, which everyone said was certain to be banned in Egypt.

She sailed past the newsmen, deflecting their questions with a smile and a flirtatious quip, and went straight to where Camelia was standing with Hakim and Zeinab. She first kissed and embraced her husband, and then little Zeinab. Finally Dahiba turned to Camelia. "Now what is this all about? You said on the phone that there was a family emergency."

Camelia explained briefly about the cholera, adding, "Father's nurse is at the house, as well as a nurse from the Ministry of Health. But Umma won't let anyone else in. Auntie Nazirah and her daughters came all the way from Assyut to help nurse the family, but Umma turned them away. Cousin Hosneya tried, too. Umma wouldn't even let *me* in. She says she doesn't want anyone else to get the disease."

"It's like my mother to try to do everything herself," Dahiba said, as they hurried to the waiting limousine.

"And she is sick, too," Camelia added. "I saw her briefly at the front door. But she forces herself to get out of bed. You know Umma."

"Only too well do I know my mother. Where is Ibrahim right now?"

"Papa went to Jamal Rasheed's funeral this morning. I told you over the phone about the sudden heart attack—"

"Yes, yes."

"Papa said he was going to visit Auntie Alice afterward. When she collapsed in his office three days ago, he admitted her into a private hospital. But when the rest of the family started getting sick, he just quarantined the house. But nearly everyone is there, Dahiba! The family was getting together for the *Shamm el-Nessim*. Every bed is occupied!"

Dahiba asked, "Which hospital?" and when Camelia told her, she said to her driver, "Suez Canal Street, please. And hurry."

=

Alice opened her eyes and thought she was still dreaming, because Ibrahim was there, smiling down at her, stroking her hair. She was very weak, she felt as if she had just taken a long, wearying journey of which she recalled only snatches—a nurse helping her with a bedpan, someone sponging down her body, a soft, rhythmic voice reciting what she recognized as verses from the Koran. She looked at her husband. He was wearing a white surgical gown over his suit, and rubber surgical gloves. Ibrahim appeared to be older all of a sudden; had she been asleep for years?

"What—" she began.

"The danger is past, my dear," he said gently.

"How long have I been here?"

"Three days. But you're getting better now. The course of the disease usually runs six days or less."

She looked at the IV bottle suspended over her bed, the tubing going into her arm. "What do I have? What's wrong with me?"

"You have cholera. But you're going to be all right. I have you on antibiotic therapy."

"Cholera!" she said, trying to sit up but not finding the strength. "What about the others? The family? Mohammed! Is my grandson all right?"

"Our grandson is fine, Alice. Everyone in the house has the disease in varying degrees, some have it worse than others. They all came down with it at different times. Except for Zachariah. He didn't get it at all."

"What caused it?"

"We don't know yet, the Ministry of Health is investigating. They've tested our water and samples of the food from the kitchen. That's the way the contagion is transmitted, by eating or drinking something contaminated with the cholera bacteria. But so far, everything has turned up negative. What is even more mysterious, ours is the only house affected." He took her hand and squeezed it. "*Al hamdu lillah.* Praise the Lord, we found it in time. When cholera is diagnosed early and treatment is begun immediately, it is not fatal."

"When can I go home?"

"As soon as you are strong enough." He stroked her hair again, wishing he could remove the surgical glove and feel that blond softness. When Alice had collapsed in his office, Ibrahim had been amazed at the sudden fear he had felt, the realization, which had hit him like a shock wave, that he might lose her. So he had placed her in this private, expensive hospital where she received excellent care, instead of in one of the major government hospitals where patients had to bribe the nurses to take care of them. When had he forgotten how much she still meant to him?

Alice held his hand for a long, quiet moment, comforted by his presence. When she realized that Ibrahim had been the only one to visit her, she saw that she was in an isolation ward, with three other empty beds. Visitors would not have been allowed. But there were flowers and cards. "From your friends," Ibrahim said. "Madeline and Mrs. Flornoy were camped out in the lobby. I finally told them to go home. The roses are from what's-her-name, the lady from Michigan. Mother wanted to send you flowers from her own garden, but she was afraid the cholera might travel with them. My God, Alice, you had me worried."

She smiled weakly, as more memories of the past three days returned: Ibrahim at her bedside, giving orders to the nurse, administering injections, positioning the pillows, a worried expression on his face. With Ibrahim being so solicitous, looking so concerned, she could imagine herself falling in love with him again. This was what he had been like, years ago, in Monte Carlo. She had forgotten. And now she fancied her love being reborn out of her illness, like a phoenix from the ashes. But, unlike the mythical bird, her love had nowhere to fly to. Did Ibrahim love her, or was he this kind to all his patients?

"I'm going to let you rest now." His kissed her forehead, murmured, "God watch over you and keep you," and left.

Out in the hall, he was stunned to see Dahiba and Camelia standing there.

He stared at his sister, his mouth open. The whole family knew that Camelia had taken up with the long-ago disgraced Fatima, but Ibrahim had not set eyes on his sister since the day Ali had banished her from the house, thirty-three years ago. He had known it was only a matter of time before he encountered her, but this was unexpected.

Dahiba rolled up her sleeve and said, "Don't just stand there like a donkey, Ibrahim. Give me a vaccination against the cholera."

—

The khamsin wrapped Cairo in a sandy haze, out of which minarets rose like mystical spires. And from these spires the muezzins sang out the ancient Call to Prayer, unchanged from the time of Mohammed, thirteen centuries ago:

> God is great.
> God is great.
>
> I proclaim that there is no god but God.
> I proclaim that there is no god but God.
>
> I witness that Mohammed is His messenger.
> I witness that Mohammed is His messenger.

Come to prayer—
Come to prayer—

Come to success—
Come to success—

God is great.
God is great.

There is no god but Him.

As Ibrahim's nurse, Huda, hurried down the hall with a bedpan, she glimpsed Amira through the open door of her bedroom, going through the prostrations of prayer, even though she looked as if she were about to collapse. The young nurse wasn't impressed. Anyone could put on such a charade, it didn't mean they were pious. Wasn't that what her father and brothers did? If Huda had anything to be thankful for, it was this respite from their interminable demands—six men who wasted their afternoons in a coffee shop while she was on her feet all day in Dr. Ibrahim's office, and then insisting she cook for them as soon as she got home. It made her smile now to think of the old man and his five lazy sons trying to make sense out of pots and pans. With luck, Dr. Ibrahim's family was going to require her services for at least a week, perhaps longer, during which time her father and brothers should develop a keen appreciation for everything she had done for them.

She found Mohammed sitting up in bed, arms crossed, an angry look on his face. The illness hadn't struck the ten-year-old as hard as it had the others, and his recovery was quick; now he was fretful because there hadn't been a celebration marking his birthday. When she saw that he still hadn't eaten his breakfast, Huda tried to coax him to take a little. But he wanted his Grandma Nefissa to feed him.

"Your grandmother is sick," Huda said in exasperation. She was tired and longed for a rest. It was a lot of work, supervising this "hospital" on Virgins of Paradise Street. While a few of the Rasheed women were well enough to nurse the others, they needed guidance: isolation technique had to be monitored so that reinfection did not occur, bedpans had to be emptied with great care and soiled sheets had to be either boiled or burned, to keep the contagion from spreading beyond this house. And she had taught them the danger signs that they must watch for: intense thirst, sunken eyes, rapid pulse, rapid breathing, and fever, all of which were to be reported to her at once. The most crucial care was in the rehydration therapy, which was something only a trained nurse could do, in that it involved alternating intravenous solutions of saline with sodium bicarbonate and intermittent supplements of potassium. It also meant staying on top of each patient's fluid intake and calculating it against urine output, because the greatest threat from cholera was dehydration, which led to acidosis, uremia, renal failure, and, eventually, death. Huda felt very important to be supervising it all, just like the nursing matrons at the hospital where she had trained. But the job had its unpleasant aspects.

Everyone had diarrhea and was vomiting; the bedding had to be changed constantly, and the rooms smelled terrible. But because of the khamsin, Mrs. Amira would not allow the windows to be opened in case desert jinns should bring in further bad luck. If only Dr. Ibrahim would let Huda administer Lomotil or one of Mrs. Amira's antidiarrhea remedies! But he had said that the disease must be allowed to be expelled from the body. To keep it inside would make everyone much sicker. Huda had also asked Dr. Ibrahim to bring in more trained help—the one government nurse was spectacularly lazy. But his mother would not permit others to come in; the stubborn woman was actually turning help away from the door. Which was foolish; as long as one was inoculated, there was no danger from the disease.

Still, Huda was glad she had come. When Ibrahim had asked her to take care of his family, she hadn't been able to refuse. She was in love with him, and it was an opportunity to see how he lived. The young nurse had suspected that her employer lived well, but she hadn't expected a mansion filled with such beautiful things. Dr. Ibrahim's house was like a palace. Now she was certain he would pay her well for this sacrifice, perhaps even give her a handsome gift.

As she tried to get the boy to eat a little of the beans and egg, she looked at the photograph over his bed, the portrait of a very pretty blond woman. Huda knew she was Dr. Ibrahim's daughter, the one who had gone to America. Even though Mohammed was dark, Huda saw the resemblance to his mother in the shape of his face, the dimples high on his cheeks even when he didn't smile. And his eyes were the same shade of blue, an attractive feature when combined with the black hair and dusky skin. At ten, Mohammed showed signs of the handsome man he was someday going to be.

"Very well then!" she said, standing up. "If you won't eat, I shan't force you."

As she reached for the tray on the bedside table, she felt a sudden cramp in her abdomen. Without warning her knees gave way, and as she fell to the floor, she vomited.

Mohammed yelled for help, and Amira came in. As she assisted the nurse to her feet, she said, "Did you have any nausea?"

Huda glumly shook her head. Vomiting without preceding nausea was one of the first signs of the disease. Now she, too, had cholera.

=

The black limousine, no longer shiny because of the khamsin dust, pulled up in front of the house, and Dahiba and Camelia got out before it had completely stopped. Hakim wasn't happy about them going past the government quarantine signs, but he said nothing other than that he would take care of Zeinab in the meantime. Dahiba didn't even knock. She marched up the path, and opened the front door as if she had left this house only yesterday. *"Bismillah!"* she said. "It stinks in here!"

As they quickly made their way up the stairs to the women's side of the house, they saw stacks of clean sheets, basins of soap and water, hospital gowns and surgical masks outside the bedrooms. The strong odor of disinfectant did not cover the underlying smell of sickness.

Amira was in the hall struggling with a large bundle of dirty sheets, a white surgical gown over her black dress, her hair wrapped in a white bandanna. Dahiba sighed and shook her head, "My mother, the Sayyida Zeinab of Virgins of Paradise Street."

Amira looked up, startled. She stared for a moment at her daughter, then said, "Fatima, praise God."

"My brother tells me you won't allow the windows to be opened, Mother."

"The disease is carried on the wind. Desert jinns have brought cholera to this house."

"Cholera is caused by bacteria, Mother, a tiny germ you can't see."

"Can one see jinns? Please, daughter, go away, before you get sick."

"Ibrahim inoculated us, Umma."

"He inoculated his nurse, too, and she is sick."

"It doesn't work with everyone. I place my trust in God. Now I want you to get into bed."

"You must leave," Amira said, but with less conviction.

"Since when is a family not allowed to take care of its members? It is times such as these that give meaning to a family, otherwise what are we, what do we have?" Removing her scarf and rolling up her sleeves, Dahiba helped her mother into bed. "I am going to take care of things now, Umma," she said, "starting with you. And I shall have no argument about it."

Amira did not argue further. Her head fell back onto the pillow, she closed her eyes and thought, Praise to the Eternal One, my baby has come home.

—

When Ibrahim arrived he first made the rounds of the bedrooms, checking each patient, administering tetracycline as needed. He was upset to find Huda confined to bed; he had warned her that the vaccination was only 80 percent effective. But she was holding up well and taking her situation stoically.

Finally he went downstairs to the kitchen, where water was being sterilized for drinking, and servants were ironing great piles of freshly laundered sheets. Sahra, looking gray and fatigued, was at the table preparing lunch trays for the sickrooms. Ibrahim rarely visited the kitchen, as it was the women's domain, but he came in now as a doctor, trying to root out the cause of this minor epidemic.

It was frustrating; he had just spoken again with the health inspector, and they still hadn't located the source of the disease. Dr. Kheir said six other families within the vicinity now had it. What Ibrahim couldn't fathom was why every adult in this house, with the exception of Zachariah and himself, had caught the cholera. The very youngest had also been spared. Why? What had everyone else ingested that the babies and the boy and he had not?

He surveyed the kitchen, as if he might find the culprit squatting there—a jinni, as his mother believed. Then he looked at Sahra, who had had only a mild case and had responded immediately to the tetracycline. "Sahra," he said, "have you been washing your hands with soap before preparing the meals, as I told you?"

"Yes, master. I've been washing them a hundred times a day." And she held out her right hand to show him how raw it was.

He looked at the bowl she was holding, whose contents she was about to spoon onto the sickroom trays. "What is that?" he asked.

"It is *kibbeh,* master. Very good for sick people. You yourself have a fondness for it."

He frowned. "Yes, but kibbeh is always cooked, isn't it?"

"This is a new recipe, master, which does not call for the meat to be cooked. The butcher himself told me about it. He said it is very popular in Syria. But the meat is fresh, as you can see. And the butcher cubed it himself, while I watched."

Ibrahim brought the bowl to his nose and sniffed the mixture of lamb, onion, pepper and cracked wheat.

"There is nothing wrong with it, master," she said anxiously. "Everyone enjoyed it. There was none left over."

"What are you talking about? Have you prepared this dish before?"

"Four nights ago, master. Since the family was gathering for the holiday I thought something special—"

"The night before my wife fell ill?"

When she nodded dumbly, Ibrahim thought back to that evening, and suddenly remembered that he had not eaten dinner with the family because of an emergency at the hospital. And Zachariah would not have eaten the kibbeh because of his aversion to meat.

He hurried from the kitchen and telephoned the Ministry of Health. "Dr. Rasheed, I was just about to call you," Dr. Kheir said at the other end. "We have traced the disease to a new butcher in your area, a Syrian. He arrived a week ago from Damascus and we have found that he is a carrier. The bacteria is in the meat. Has anyone in your household purchased meat from him recently?"

Ibrahim ran back into the kitchen, yanked the bowl from Sahra's hands and smashed it on the floor. "Haven't I told you a thousand times that meat must always be cooked? You could have killed us all!"

"I—I'm sorry, master," she said. "It was special, for the holiday. The new butcher—"

"Is a *carrier,* Sahra. He gave us the disease!"

She stared at him with wide eyes. "But Mr. Gamal wasn't ill!"

"A carrier isn't sick with it, he just passes it on to others. Don't you know you could have killed us all?"

She started to cry. "I am sorry, master. Before God, I didn't intend any harm."

He ran his hands through his hair, suddenly feeling very tired. "My God, look what your mistake has cost us. And now my nurse is sick, and my mother as well."

"The Sayyida is sick?"

"Pray that we have caught it in time. At her age, this disease can be deadly."

"Yes, master," Sahra whispered, her face wet with tears.

＝

Zachariah woke before dawn, unable to sleep. Today Tahia was going to be told about her husband. He knew his father was planning on telling her, but Zachariah wanted to break the news to her himself. Deciding that he would take her breakfast to her, he went down to the kitchen where he found the servants in a turmoil. The ovens had not been lit, they said, and the bread dough had not been set overnight to rise.

Knowing that Sahra, as head of the kitchen, preferred to see to these duties herself, and therefore was usually the first of the household staff up in the morning, Zachariah went to her room behind the kitchen, wondering if she had finally come down with the cholera.

But, to his surprise, Sahra's bed had not been slept in, and her clothes were gone, along with the family photographs she always kept on one wall. Sahra herself was nowhere to be found.

CHAPTER 30

It's positively howling out!" Declan Connor said, peering through his office window. "I've never seen the campus so deserted."

A warm evening wind blew through the pine trees and alders and jacarandas that dotted the medical school grounds, sending dried leaves rolling along illuminated walkways, and tiny whirlwinds of litter and dust. Although Halloween was still days away, a human skull, painted orange to look like a jack-o'-lantern, glowed in the window of the anatomy lab across the way—a student prank.

Jasmine looked up from the typewriter and felt her heart skip to see two of him, the real Connor, and his reflection in the glass—a man who looked too serious and conservative for this liberal school, and who seemed to generate, as he always did, a personal energy that Jasmine felt even from this distance. Or perhaps, she thought, it was only in her imagination that she was touched by his infectious vigor. After working with Connor for six months, she knew what a determined, ambitious man he was.

"Well!" he said, coming away from the window. "Where are we now? The last chapter, is it?"

The last chapter. Jasmine didn't like the sound of it. It meant their work together would soon come to an end.

"It's a brilliant idea, this," Connor said as he stood behind her to see what she had typed. "I'm going to have a similar chapter added to the African version."

The new chapter had been Jasmine's idea; it was titled, "Respecting Local Customs," and was written for the non-Arab, laying out a few simple but important rules to enable the foreign health worker to get along with the villagers. After a few rather obvious recommendations such as, "Be friendly and helpful," and "Do not argue with the local native healer," she had listed the rules specific to Arab culture: never ask a man about his wife; never eat with the left hand; never pay a compliment to a woman about her children.

"You have no idea," he said as he leaned over her, his hand on the back of her chair, so that she smelled his Old Spice, "the problems that have arisen when well-meaning volunteers have committed such simple errors as breaking a tribal custom. The Kikuyu, for instance, consider it a great compliment if you lay your hand on top of a child's head. By not doing so, you can insult someone. Now this last one you have here, Jasmine, about not complimenting a woman on her children . . ."

While she explained to him about the evil eye and the fellaheen's fear of envy, she felt herself become very warm. If his hand should slip, if he should accidentally touch her—

Greg, she thought. She must keep thinking of her husband, Greg.

Even though Greg Van Kerk, whom she had married to avoid deportation, wasn't really her husband.

As they had expected, the Immigration and Naturalization Service had indeed investigated them, questioning the landlady, their teachers, Greg's friends, Rachel's family. The agents came to the door every so often with badges and notepads and personal questions, and Jasmine and Greg, pleasant and cooperative, were always able to send them away satisfied, their secret still safe. Legally, they had been husband and wife for nearly seven months; Jasmine was officially Jasmine Van Kerk. But, despite the marriage certificate, they were just roommates. As Greg had said, not even the INS could plant a spy in the bedroom.

She thought about the past six and a half months of saying good night and closing the bedroom door, hearing the springs of the sofa bed in the living room creak beneath Greg's weight. Six months in a comfortable relationship with a man who was intelligent and considerate, who had rescued her from deportation and who deserved her respect. If only she would fall in love with Greg.

But the problem was, she had married one man and fallen in love with another.

Declan went back to his own desk, and as Jasmine watched him go through their manuscript one last time, she couldn't help comparing the two men—Declan with his energy and intensity, which she found infectious, and Greg, so laid back that he seemed to possess the Arab philosophy of *bokra*—tomorrow—an attitude she quite liked because it reminded her of home. Declan was a meticulous dresser, Greg was not; Declan had made a success of himself and had ambition, Greg was still halfheartedly struggling with his master's thesis. But both men were kind, both made her laugh, and she was fond of one and in love with the other—the wrong way around.

She had no idea how Declan felt about her, but it didn't matter, she told herself each time she began to think about him, to wonder what it would be like to be with him. Connor was married, his road was set. Just as Jasmine's was set.

Although she was uncertain about her future with Greg, and where they were going, she knew where *she* was going: to learn medicine, and to take her skills wherever they were needed. That much she owed to Declan Connor. Through working with him and experiencing his energy and seeing how clearly he understood his purpose, Jasmine had sharpened and defined her own—to practice the kind of medicine she had watched her father practice in Cairo. Ibrahim Rasheed had once been a king's personal physician; he still commanded large fees. But he also treated the growing peasant population within the city. And there, working with him in his office, dispensing medicine, learning from him, Jasmine's dream had been born. Working with Connor, Jasmine had seen her goal become focused.

And she knew it was that she must concentrate on, especially in moments when she began to feel sad, knowing that Connor was leaving when the semester was over. "Sybil and I can't seem to stay in one place for long," he had explained at the beginning of their project, back in March. "We even met on a hospital ship. I know it's good to teach new doctors, and I've enjoyed working at this school, but I miss the field. As soon as this translation is finished, Sybil and I are off to Morocco."

Jasmine had met his wife, a professor of immunology, when Sybil had brought their son to the office, five-year-old David, a knobby-kneed little boy in short pants and English accent who had made her think of her own son, Mohammed. In that moment, Jasmine had envied Connor's wife.

He turned over the last page of the manuscript, a glossary of basic Arabic terms, and said, "It looks as if we've done it! *Al hamdu lillah!*" And Jasmine laughed, as she always did when he spoke Arabic, because he spoke it with a British accent. He had once told her his favorite story about himself and his personal approach to languages. "It was in Kenya, at the mission, and I was invited to say grace at an important dinner for visiting church representatives. I was quietly reminded that the prayer must be in Latin, but as I don't know any prayers in Latin, I had to think quickly. So I bowed my head and recited, '*Levator labii superioris alaeque nasi*,' the name for the little muscle on the side of the nose. They all said, 'Amen,' and we got on with the business of eating."

Now they were done with the book. They had only to insert Jasmine's new chapter and they could send the manuscript off to the London publisher.

"I have an idea," he said suddenly. "Let me take you to dinner. I haven't paid you anywhere near what you're worth, it would make me feel better if you'd at least let me buy you dinner."

Jasmine stared at her fingers on the keyboard. Dinner! They had spent six months working closely together on a project that had been confined mainly to this office, and usually in the evenings, sometimes late into the night. But intimate though it had seemed, there had always been the fact of work between them, the business aspect of their relationship, and Jasmine had been able to maintain her distance. But dinner would put them on a different, dangerous level.

"You can't possibly refuse me," Connor said, coming around her desk and turning off the typewriter. "I know you haven't eaten since dawn because it's Ramadan." He smiled and added, "I don't know how you do it. The Jews are more reasonable about fasting, just one day, on Yom Kippur. To do it for thirty seems like madness."

She put her hands in her lap to hide her sudden nervousness. "Ramadan is even harder in the summer when the days are longer!" she said.

"Yes, I remember. Even cheerful old Habib got irritable over his ironing. That was when I reminded myself never to be in Egypt during Ramadan. Now then, you choose the restaurant," he said. "Make it as pricey as you like."

"Will your wife be joining us?"

"Sybil is teaching tonight."

Jasmine hesitated. In Egypt the rules were clear: A woman did not go out alone with a man who was not a relative. Especially a married woman. But was she really married? She and Greg had signed a paper, and she had taken his name. That was all. But even though she told herself that it would be just a friendly dinner with Connor, a meal in a public place, she was afraid—of her feelings, and of revealing them.

"Besides, I have a surprise for you," he said, his eyes twinkling with a mischief she had come to recognize. He had had the same look the day he had played a prank on Dr. Miller in Parasitology.

"A surprise?" she said.

He went behind the filing cabinet and brought out a large square envelope. "I've been saving it for a special moment. Now's as good a time as any. Go ahead, open it."

Jasmine saw the British stamps, and Declan's home address in the Marina. As she opened it, he said, "I had them send it to the house because I didn't want you to see it before I did."

She slid out the contents and saw that it was a photocopy of a book jacket, the title in bold black letters, *Dr. Grace Treverton's When* You *Have to Be the Doctor: A Rural Health Care Handbook for the Middle East.*

"I submitted several sketches," Connor explained, "because we couldn't very well use the same illustration that's on the original version. As you see, they've made the child and mother look Middle Eastern, and the grass hut in the background is now a mud-brick dwelling. This is the final cover."

Then Jasmine saw the surprise, at the bottom, under the illustration: *Revised and Translated by Declan Connor, M.D., and Jasmine Van Kerk.*

"I'm afraid there's no money in it for you," he said, "no royalties, but your name will be seen by a lot of people. The Peace Corps has just placed an order for copies, and so has the French group Doctors Without Borders."

She kept her eyes on the cover; she couldn't look at him. "I don't know what to say," she said softly.

"There's nothing *to* say. All *I* can say is, thank God that student I hired never showed up." He fell silent and she felt him studying her. Then, more quietly, he added, "And of course it was smart of you to get married."

Jasmine hadn't told him the details, that she and Greg had been strangers at the time. She knew he assumed that she and Greg had already been lovers, and she wanted to maintain that illusion; it helped her to keep distant from Connor, and from her own growing feelings toward him.

"Well? What do you say? Dinner in town?"

She finally looked up and when she saw his attractive smile, and the way the overhead lights sharpened the chiseled lines of his face, she said, "Yes, that would be very nice," and felt her heart gallop.

But as they were getting ready to leave, the telephone rang. Jasmine picked it up; it was Rachel, sounding urgent. "Sorry to bother you, Jas, I know you're working. Can you come over right away? Grandma Maryam is asking for you."

She glanced at Connor. "But it's Yom Kippur, Rachel. Do you want visitors?"

"She isn't well, Jas. She hasn't been out of bed for a week, and she says it's important that she talk to you right away. Can you come?"

Jasmine hesitated. "Just a minute." She put her hand over the mouth-piece. "Dr. Connor, a friend of mine is ill and asking me to come and see her right away."

"But of course you must go. We can make dinner another night."

"All right, Rachel, tell Auntie Maryam that I'll be there as soon as I can."

When Jasmine hung up, feeling both relieved and disappointed, for she knew that now they never would make that dinner date, Connor said, "Wait a minute, Jasmine. Before you go I want to say something. I had planned to tell you tonight at dinner, but I'll tell you now because I might not get another chance." He paused and thrust his hands in his pockets. Jasmine had the feeling he had rehearsed what he was about to say. "Working with you on this project has meant a lot to me," he said, "more than I can say. You'll make a splendid physician, Jasmine, and I know you'll take your skills to where they're needed. I hope . . . well, I just hope we have a chance to work together again someday."

"Thank you, Dr. Connor, I hope so, too."

But when she turned to go, he stopped her. "Jasmine," he said, coming close to her, his hand on her arm.

They looked at each other for a moment, hearing the October wind make the dry trees outside crackle. Connor bent his head, and Jasmine, with her heart racing, raised her face to his.

And then he suddenly stepped back, before they could kiss. "I'm sorry, Jasmine. If you only knew—"

"Please don't," she said. "Perhaps someday our paths will cross again, Dr. Connor. If it is God's will. *Ma salaama.*"

"*Ma salaama,*" he said.

===

Rachel was waiting for her in the driveway. "What is it?" Jasmine asked, squinting in the late afternoon sunlight.

"I'm not sure. It's rather mysterious. My grandmother says she has something for you. Apparently it came in the mail a few days ago."

Jasmine's heart leapt. Something from the family! A letter? Her father asking her to come home?

As they went inside, Jasmine's stomach suddenly growled. She laughed and said, "Sorry, I've been fasting."

"Today's a Jewish holiday. Why have *you* been fasting?"

"It is the tenth of Ramadan."

Rachel didn't respond; she always felt vaguely uncomfortable when she remembered that Jasmine was a Muslim. And now, something new: jealousy over Jasmine's special relationship with her grandmother. Although of Egyptian-Jewish descent, Rachel felt little affinity for the country Jasmine and Maryam shared; she had never been to Egypt, her father's birthplace, and knew little about it. But Grandma Maryam's heart was still there, Rachel knew, and so Jasmine claimed a special part of Rachel's grandmother that Rachel herself never could.

The house was quiet. "The others have gone to Temple," Rachel said. "I stayed home with Grandma Maryam. She's grown very frail in the last few months, Jas. She's only seventy-two, and I can't find anything wrong with her. We're all quite worried."

This was the first time Jasmine had been in Maryam Misrahi's bedroom; it was filled with possessions she had brought from Cairo, even a few things Jasmine remembered from visits to the Misrahi house long ago. But a large portrait on the wall stopped her. It was of Maryam and Amira, years ago, two young women with marceled hair, Maryam faintly flapperish, Amira young and smooth-faced, with heavy sultry eyes like a silent movie star's. And she was wearing not the mourning black Jasmine had always seen her in, but a white dress that looked like gossamer.

"You resemble her, you know," came a voice from the bed. "Cover your blond hair, and you are Amira."

Jasmine had never been aware of how much she favored her Egyptian side; the blond hair and blue eyes seemed to be all that she had inherited from Alice's family. And she marveled now to realize that the young woman in the portrait—Amira—could almost be her twin.

She went to the bedside and was startled to see how Maryam had aged in just a few months. Jasmine regarded the white hair and recalled the red-haired woman who had been such a familiar figure in her childhood. "What is it, Auntie?" she asked, sitting down. "What is wrong with you?"

Maryam spoke in Arabic. "I was there the night you were born," she said. "Your grandmother and I always helped each other at childbirth. I helped deliver your Auntie Nefissa, and Amira brought my Itzak into the world. It was all so long ago. Another world, then, on Virgins of Paradise Street."

"Yes, it was," Jasmine said quietly, thinking of the magnificent Turkish fountain in the garden, the gingerbread gazebo where Amira held her afternoon teas, like a queen holding court.

"Are you enjoying medical school?" Maryam asked.

"There is a lot to learn, Auntie. It takes up all my time." Jasmine wished she could tell her about Connor. But Jasmine hadn't even confessed her secret to Rachel.

"You'll make a fine doctor. You are the daughter of Ibrahim Rasheed and the granddaughter of Amira, how could you be otherwise? What news have you of the family? I haven't heard from your grandmother in a while."

Jasmine told her about the latest letter from Alice, news about the cholera scare. "There is some worry that Tahia's baby will have discolored teeth because of the tetracycline. And Sahra, our cook, disappeared, no one knows where to or why." Jasmine didn't add how the letter had terrified her, until Alice had assured her that Mohammed had come down with only a mild case of the illness. It frightened Jasmine to think that her son might get sick and die and she wasn't there to help.

"Why did you send for me, Auntie?"

"Don't lock the past out of your heart, Yasmina. I can see it in your eyes, you don't want to talk about your family. I asked for you to come because today is the Day of Atonement. I want you to make amends with your father. Family is everything, Yasmina. Amira writes to me— well, she has her grandson Zachariah write for her as she dictates—and she talks about everyone in the family, and she asks about you. I don't know what happened between you and your father, Yasmina, but you must make amends."

"Auntie Maryam, my father and I can never be friends. He doesn't love me—"

"Love! Oh, child, you don't know what love is." Maryam reached for her hand. "My dear, I know why you married the American. I know that you wanted to stay in the United States. But please, listen to me, you do not belong here, any more than I do. You and I belong where our hearts are, on Virgins of Paradise Street. You have a son there, a little boy who needs his mother."

"They would never let me see him," Jasmine said, looking down at the aged hand holding hers. "Omar took Mohammed from me, and the law says I can't see my son." *And as far as my family is concerned, I am dead.*

"What does the law know about a mother's heart? Go back, Yasmina, and God will help you find a way." Maryam gave Jasmine a long, searching look, then she reached for something on her nightstand. "This came to me the other day. It is from my sister in Beirut."

Jasmine saw that it was a book, *The Sentence of Woman,* and it was written in Arabic. The author's name was Dahiba Raouf.

"She is your Auntie Fatima, did you know that?"

"Yes," Jasmine murmured in amazement as she turned the pages and saw the poems. When she came to the back of the book, and read, "An Essay by Camelia Rasheed," a shock went through her.

Maryam sighed. "You Rasheed women always were very opinionated. I wonder if Amira knows about this book."

Jasmine was spellbound as she read her sister's words: "In matters of sex," Camelia had written,

the man comes to the battle fully armed. His armor is society's approval of whatever he does, his weapons are its laws. The woman has nothing; she is defenseless. She comes to the battle without so much as a shield. She is doomed to lose.

Men are the sole proprietors of the planet. They own the grass and the seas and the stars; they own history and the past; they own women and the air we breathe. They even own the drop of semen they leave inside us; they own the products of a woman's womb. Nothing is ours. We don't even own the sunshine we walk through.

Jasmine was stunned. When had Camelia developed these ideas? How, in Egypt's society, had she learned to think like this, to take her feelings and opinions and place them into words and sentences?

She continued to read:

A man has the option of either claiming a child as his own or not. He can say, That child is not mine. How arrogant that men have given themselves this power, for it is the woman who grows new life in her body, with her blood, oxygen, and cells; she carries it, feels it there, sings to it, nourishes the new spirit from her own. And yet the man, for whom the sex act was but a moment of pleasure, can claim ownership of that new life in another person's body. He has the power to acknowledge it and allow it to live, or he can deny it and let it die.

Jasmine stared at the page. Was Camelia speaking of Jasmine and her son? Or had she been thinking of Hassan al-Sabir when she wrote this, and the disgrace that had befallen Jasmine because the child had been his and not her husband's? She closed her eyes and pictured her black-haired, amber-eyed sister. How brave of Camelia to write this! But how could she be so bluntly honest in these words, and yet be so deceitful to a sister? Had she been so in love with Hassan that jealousy had driven her to expose Jasmine's secret to Nefissa?

A folded newspaper clipping fell out from between the pages of the book. It had been cut out of a Beirut newspaper, and someone had written in the margin, "Reprinted from *Paris Match*." It was an interview with Camelia, "Egypt's newest rising star."

"Will you read it to me, please?" Maryam said. "My eyesight is so poor, and," she added sadly, "no one in this family reads Arabic any more."

The article was about how a celebrity like Camelia, female and unmarried, had to work very hard to protect her reputation. "It is not easy being a single woman in Egypt," she had told the *Match* reporter. "In Egypt, if a strange man speaks to a woman on the street, and she responds, even by saying, 'No. Go away. Leave me alone,' he takes this as an indication that she is available and he will pursue. The proper reaction is to ignore him, pretend he is not there; he will get the message and leave, respecting her and knowing that she is a moral woman. It is difficult, to treat a human being as if he were invisible or did not exist. In France you would call this rude, but it is the Arab way."

"Yasmina," Maryam said. "Why aren't you and your sister friends? A sister is precious, Yasmina."

She felt the older woman's eyes searching her face, but Jasmine would not speak of things she refused even to think about. If she denied the past hard enough, she could send it away. It never happened.

"Camelia betrayed a secret," she finally said, "and because of it, I was thrown out of the family, and my son was taken away from me."

"Ah, secrets," the older woman said, thinking of her own son, Rachel's father who, at that moment, was with the family at the Temple for Yom Kippur service—her son who thought Suleiman Misrahi was his father, and who called Moussa Misrahi "Uncle." She laid her hand on the slender book and said, "I understand about secrets, Yasmina. But

listen to me, today is the Day of Atonement. And Ramadan is the month
of atonement. Go back to Egypt. Ibrahim will welcome you. He will
forgive you."

"It's late, I had better go, Auntie. I'll come back soon to see you."

But Maryam shook her head. "I've kept Suleiman waiting too long.
It is time I joined him. And this new world in which Arab hates Jew—I
cannot understand it. I do not want to be a part of it. Good-bye,
Yasmina. *Ramadan mubarak aleikum.* May you have a blessed Ramadan."

=

When she came in, Greg was at the dining-room table, typing his thesis,
the floor around his feet littered with books, wadded-up bits of paper,
and half-empty coffee containers. "Hi!" he said. "Is the book finished?"

She leaned against the wall, feeling momentarily lightheaded from
having fasted all day. "I stopped by Rachel's. Auntie Maryam wanted to
see me."

"Is she sick?"

"She just wanted to give me something."

"By the way, an INS agent dropped by a while ago. You'd think they
had better things to do than harass us. He asked the usual questions,
tried to get nosy—Hey"—he got up and went to her—"are you all
right?"

"I'm sorry. Seeing Auntie Maryam . . . it upset me."

"Have you eaten yet? I'll be glad to cook. I'm in the mood for chili.
How about if I open two cans tonight, instead of my usual one? I know
how you love my gourmet cooking."

She wanted to go back to the school and see if Declan was still there.
She wanted to go out to dinner with him, and stay with him, and cry
in his arms. But she said, "Thank you, Greg, I would like that."

"Come on, sit down. Dinner will be ready in a few minutes." And
he went into the kitchen.

As he started opening cans, he felt her watching him from the doorway. She was doing this more and more lately, pausing to look at him
when she thought he was unaware of it. He sensed her perplexity, her
restlessness, and he wondered if she was experiencing the same budding
desire he had for her. She was a woman both virginal and sexually

experienced, a combination he found to be a powerful aphrodisiac. And she was so sad, she seemed so vulnerable and lost that she generated profound feelings in him of wanting to take care of her. "I don't know where I belong," she had once confessed. "My mother and I were the only fair-haired ones in the family. We never did quite fit in; people would stare at us. I wondered if maybe I could find a place among my mother's race, but in England I felt no connection. On the outside I look as if I belong here in the West, but my heart is Arab. And yet I can never go back. Is there a place for me in the world?" Greg realized now that he wanted to help her find that place, perhaps even to *be* that place.

It was the first time in his life that he had felt this way toward anyone. The only child of rootless scientist parents, raised by indifferent nuns, Greg Van Kerk had never learned what it was like to be needed, to be cherished. Cold science and hard religion had nurtured him; "family" meant getting Christmas and birthday cards from exotic places where the local geology was clearly more fascinating than a son. Now, his sudden "tropism," as he thought of it, toward Jasmine had him completely derailed.

The TV was on and a bulletin suddenly interrupted the program, the voice-over saying, "Egyptian troops are overwhelming Israeli soldiers along the Bar Lev Line on the Suez Canal's eastern bank." Jasmine suddenly buried her face in her hands and started to cry.

"Hey," said Greg. "Hey, what is it?" He turned off the television set and sat down next to her, putting his hand on her shoulder. "I'm sorry. You're worried about your family, aren't you?"

He couldn't bear the way her shoulders shook as she cried, she looked so fragile and helpless. He was overwhelmed again with the desire to comfort and protect her. He put his arm around her shoulders and was surprised when she turned and buried her face against his chest. Then he took her into both arms, and drew her close. When their lips met, it was in a kiss salty from tears, but passionate. Medical and anthropology books tumbled from the sofa. Greg spoke in half sentences, between hungry kisses, "I just can't bear—" "I've been so badly wanting to—" Jasmine didn't speak, imagining that Greg was finishing the kiss that Declan had started.

They ended up on the floor, Jasmine oblivious of the wet spot beneath her bare back, where a Coke had spilled. They drove at each other so fiercely that the coffee table was shoved aside, one of its legs breaking.

Jasmine saw the ceiling spin; and realized she was thinking of Connor.

CHAPTER 31

People were dancing in the streets, canons and skyrockets were exploding, and everyone was shouting, "*Ya Sadat! Yahya batal el ubur!* Hail Sadat, Hail the Hero of the Crossing!" And already, with the war only just over and Egypt victorious, an enormous billboard dominated Liberation Square depicting Egyptian tanks rolling across the canal, Egyptian soldiers planting a flag on the opposite side, and Sadat, in huge profile, watching over it all. He had redeemed Egypt. He had given his people back their pride.

From the humblest alley to the most magnificent mansion, families were rejoicing over the return of God's grace to Egypt. Lanterns had been strung in the garden and along the high walls surrounding the house on Virgins of Paradise Street, and music and laughter poured from the open windows out into the balmy November night as the family celebrated the signing of the cease-fire between Egypt and Israel.

The men were in the salon, smoking, arguing politics, and telling jokes, while the women bustled in and out of the kitchen with food and glasses of tea. The entire family was gathered there; except for Ibrahim, who had been called away to see to a neighbor's boy, who had had a firecracker go off in his hand.

Zachariah was listening to his cousin Tewfik rage about the deplorable state of the cotton industry: "Nasser's plan didn't work. The government pays the cotton farmer so little for his cotton that he is turning to crops whose prices aren't regulated by the government, such as winter clover. What does the government do to compensate for the drop in cotton production? It raises the prices on the international market so that our cotton costs twice what Americans charge for their best pima variety. It is no wonder we are going bankrupt!" As Zachariah helped himself to some fried squash and decided the dish could be improved with the addition with some onions, he wondered what had happened to Sahra. No one seemed to know why she had left so suddenly, or where she had gone. He missed her special dishes and he missed her homely tales of village life. Had the cholera frightened her off?

Hakim Raouf, speaking in his loud and booming director's voice, told a joke. "My friend Farid was bragging the other day that his felucca is so tall, he could not sail it under Tahrir Bridge. And then my friend Salah bragged that his fishing boat is so big that it, too, could not sail under Tahrir Bridge. So I decided to put them both to shame: I told them I had tried to swim under Tahrir Bridge and could not. 'How is that, Raouf?' they asked. And I told them, 'Because I was swimming on my back!'"

As the men roared with laughter, the women in the kitchen rolled their eyes. "Did you hear that husband of mine?" Dahiba said. "He was bragging about the size of his nose!"

The women laughed and continued gossiping over the stacks of pita bread and sizzling plump chickens, their cheeks glowing in the heat from the ovens. Children sat on the floor with toys, or nursed at mothers' breasts, or, like little Zeinab, sat at one of the tables, entertaining themselves.

She had brought Camelia's scrapbook, which she never tired of going through, fascinated by the photographs and newspaper and magazine clippings about her mother which, at six, she was barely able to read. The very first clipping, growing yellow now, had been written back in 1966, and Zeinab could pick out a few words—"grace . . . gazelle . . . butterfly." And she could read part of the author's name: Yacob Something.

She tapped the page and said to her cousins who were also at the table, "I am going to be a dancer like Mama someday."

"No you won't," ten-year-old Mohammed said. "You've got a gimpy leg."

Tears rose in her eyes and it gave him a good feeling. Mohammed liked making his girl cousins cry, especially Zeinab. He decided that females were silly things, although certain aspects about them fascinated him, such as Auntie Basima's large breasts, and the glimpse of smooth thigh he sometimes caught when the women danced. Unfortunately, he was getting too old now to be with the aunts and female cousins in the kitchen; it would soon be time for him to join the men. No more touching the girls whenever he felt like it, or sitting on wide, voluptuous laps. Female proximity was going to be denied to him until he was grown up, and that seemed like a long time away.

Camelia came into the kitchen with a platter littered with chicken bones, and when she saw the tears rolling down Zeinab's cheeks, and the triumphant look on Mohammed's face, she knelt beside the little girl and dried her face with a handkerchief. "Really, Mohammed," she said to her nephew, "you're a naughty boy to be so mean to your cousin." She cast a glance at Nefissa, who was usually quick to defend the boy. But Nefissa was preoccupied with arranging candies on a platter.

Camelia thought the downward curve of her aunt's mouth had deepened; at forty-eight she had the look of a middle-aged woman who resents life's passing. Camelia could not help comparing Nefissa to her sister Dahiba who, although a year older, looked much younger and was dazzlingly glamorous.

Camelia wondered if the bitterness that had seemed to be part of Nefissa's make-up for so many years had increased when Dahiba was welcomed back into the family. Or had that eternally disapproving look begun long before? Camelia knew that it was Nefissa who had told the family, on the eve of the last war with Israel, about Yasmina and Hassan al-Sabir. She also knew that Amira had made Nefissa swear never to speak of the matter again, especially with regard to Zeinab. The family knew the truth of the girl's parentage, but outsiders, and above all the child herself, must never know. The secret had been let out, and now it was sealed up again; Zeinab and the other children did not know that Yasmina was her real mother. Zeinab believed that Mohammed was her cousin, not her half-brother.

Camelia gave Zeinab a piece of candy and listened to the happy talk and laughter filling the kitchen. Who would believe that these women harbored so many secrets? Even Dahiba herself: only a few in the family knew about her explosive book, outlawed in Egypt. The older, conservative women, and the younger ones, such as Narjis, who were adopting the new Islamic dress, had not been told. But the educated and more modern cousins had been shown a copy of *The Sentence of Woman*, and they had quietly applauded Dahiba and Camelia's courage to speak out. Above all, they wanted to be sure Amira was kept from knowing.

Alice, who had been helping Nefissa with the candy, retreated to her room to draw a quiet breath. Yasmina's latest letter was still by her bed. "How ironic, Mother," she had written, "to learn that it is the man's sperm that determines the sex of a baby. And to think that an Egyptian man can divorce a wife if she does not produce a boy, when it is the husband's fault all along!"

And Alice had thought: How would things have turned out if *you* had been a son . . .

Ibrahim suddenly came into her room, surprising her. "Alice, there you are. Have you seen the fireworks?" He took her hand. "Come, up onto the roof! Cairo looks as if it spins among the stars!"

"Ibrahim!" she said breathlessly. When was the last time he had come to her room?

He led her up the stairs, telling her about the Abdel Rahman boy who was "going to be careful with firecrackers from now on, by God," and when they reached the roof, their eyes met a spectacular sight as rockets exploded over Cairo, sending gold and silver showers over domes and minarets.

Nearly shouting, Ibrahim said, "What greater proof do we have that God has come back to us than this victory over our enemy? What greater evidence that He has forgiven his children?" He paused, then, a little more quietly, said, "I should have forgiven Yasmina. Alice, do you hate me for sending her away?"

She looked into his eyes and was surprised to find tenderness there. "No, Ibrahim, I don't hate you. She's doing fine where she is. And I think she's happy."

"I regret sending her away. I still love her and want her to come back." He watched an enormous ball of blue and silver stars burst overhead. "Perhaps I will write to her and ask her to come home."

Alice noticed how he kept his eyes on the fireworks, and the proud way he held his head as the fiery eruptions cast light on his features. She thought how handsome he was, how much he still looked like the young man she had fallen in love with in Monte Carlo.

But when he finally turned to her, she saw a sudden seriousness in his face that alarmed her. "Alice, I brought you up here so we could talk in private. There is something I have to tell you."

"What is it, Ibrahim?"

"There is no other way to break it to you than to just say it. Alice, I am going to take a second wife."

A military truck went by in the street below and the men crowded onto it chanted, "*Ya, Sadat! Ya, Sadat!* With our blood and souls we sacrifice ourselves for you!"

Alice realized that the smoke from the fireworks was starting to fill the night air, as if all Egypt were ablaze. "A second wife? Are you divorcing me?"

"I would never divorce you, Alice. I love you and respect you. And I want you always to live here and be my wife. But I want a son, and you are past the age to give me one."

"A son! But you have Zachariah!"

He reached for her hand and began in halting terms to tell her about the night Yasmina was born. When he was finished, he said, "I loved Yasmina, Alice, but I needed a son. On his deathbed, my father made me promise that I would give him grandsons. I was frightened. And so I adopted the bastard child of a beggar girl. Sahra, who used to be our cook."

Alice began to tremble. "Zachariah is not yours? But he looks like you, Ibrahim."

"Sahra told me that I bore some resemblance to the baby's father. Perhaps that was part of my madness. I knew that what I was doing was against God's law, but I had cursed God, and I thought He intended to punish me. And now I deeply regret that act. It is not for us to interfere with God's plan, Alice. Whatever He had destined for Sahra and her son, it was wrong of me to change that course. But I believe that today I am forgiven, as Egypt is forgiven, and tomorrow will be filled with new hope."

"Who—" she began, but barely found her voice. "Who are you going to marry?"

"My nurse, Huda. She comes from a family that produces sons, and that is what I want. She knows that I do not love her, I have explained my purpose for wanting to marry her. And she has agreed to it."

He put his hands on her shoulders and kissed her gently. "Please don't be upset, darling."

Suddenly Alice wasn't standing on the roof among fireworks, she was back in the garden, staring in amazement at the cyclamen buds that had appeared so miraculously. Ibrahim and Eddie were at a soccer match with Hassan; Alice hadn't been invited because she was a woman. Two little girls were in the garden with her—Camelia and Yasmina, playing dress-up with Nefissa's discarded melayas. They were trying to veil themselves, trying to hide their bodies and faces as Egyptian women hid theirs. They had thought it was a game, but Alice had seen the seriousness of it. The British were leaving Egypt, and there was talk of returning to the old ways.

The old ways of veils, she thought now, and female circumcision and second wives. And she realized that the future she had feared had arrived. "It's all right, darling," she said to Ibrahim. "I don't mind. You need a son, of course. And I can no longer give you one. You go on down and join the others, I'll be there in a minute."

Ibrahim disappeared in the darkness, and Alice followed soon after. When they were both gone, Zachariah came out of the shadows, from where he had been watching the fireworks.

=

Tahia looked at Zachariah in dismay. They were sitting on the same marble bench they had sat on when they had first declared their love, the night Yasmina was wed to Omar. "What do you mean, you're leaving?" she said. "Why? Where are you going?"

"Tahia, I found out tonight that my father is not really my father, that my whole life has been based upon a lie." He told her what he had overheard on the roof, and she said, "*Allah!* Can it be true? Surely you didn't hear correctly!"

Zachariah wasn't upset; in fact, he felt strangely at peace, as if a long and difficult struggle had suddenly come to an end. "I understand so much now," he said quietly. "Why my father never loved me. Why, at times, I even sensed his resentment toward me. And why I would catch Sahra watching me. I always thought she told those stories about her childhood in the village just to entertain us, but now I realize that in some way she was trying to tell me about my real family. Tahia, I love you with all my heart, but I cannot marry you until I know the truth about myself. I'm going to look for my mother. I'm going to find the village where I was conceived. Perhaps I have brothers and sisters there, a whole other family, waiting for me."

"But how will you find it? Zakki, there are hundreds of villages along the Nile! Sahra never said where she was from!" Tahia was frightened.

Only last month, during Ramadan, Zachariah had fasted so zealously that he had had one of his spells, falling down, becoming incoherent. What if a spell were to come over him while he was going from village to village?

"Please! Ask Tewfik or Ahmed to go with you—"

"This is a journey I must make on my own." He took her hand between his and said with a smile, "Don't be afraid for my sake, I go with God. Perhaps that was the meaning of my revelation in the desert. Perhaps it was the Almighty's sign to me that I am about to embark upon a quest. And no one can walk the road with me, Tahia. Not even you, whom I love more than the beating of my own heart. Please," he said, "be happy for me. I shall be able to embrace Sahra as my mother. And I shall find my father, and pay homage to him."

She sobbed, and drew a delicate hand across her cheek. "And then you will come back to me, my darling Zakki?"

"I will come back, precious Tahia. Before God and the Prophet and all the saints and angels, I swear to you that I will come back."

＝

In Amira's private suite, Qettah once again consulted tea leaves and oil on water. Finally the astrologer smiled and said, "You have recovered completely from the illness, Sayyida. Fortune favors you, as she favors Egypt. This is an auspicious time for travel. It is time now for you to make the pilgrimage to Mecca, and find the boy who beckons to you in your dreams."

Amira escorted the elderly woman to the front door, paying her for the visit, and then, too excited to wait until the morning, decided to tell Alice at once that they could start preparations for their journey to Saudi Arabia.

＝

Alice sat at her vanity table, enveloped in a cloud of essence of almonds and roses from her bath. She had put on one of her old gowns from the days of the Cage d'Or, an elegant dress, still white and seductive. How long had it been since she had worn it? She smiled. The depression that had shadowed her for so long was strangely gone, as if someone had turned on a bright light to chase it away. She had never felt so at peace.

Alice got up and left the room, and as she made her way down the hall, passing the door to the bedroom that had once been her brother's, she recalled with appalling clarity the last two times she had seen him in there: the first, with Hassan al-Sabir, committing an indecent act; the second, with a bullet through his brain. She was not surprised to see Edward there in the hallway now, in his white flannels, and carrying a cricket bat. He hadn't aged a day, even though she had last seen him over twenty years ago. Of course. She was seeing his ghost.

"It's a warm evening for November," he said to her. "Perfect for a walk."

"Yes, Eddie," Alice said.

She went down the stairs and when she paused at the bottom, she heard the river of melancholia roaring again in her ears.

She passed revelers in the streets, and men crowded around radios and television sets listening to President Sadat. The Corniche was jammed with traffic; pedestrians laughed and cavorted along the sidewalk, paying little attention to the woman in the white evening gown who made her way down to the river, where fishermen were singing over their braziers.

Alice saw lights across the way, reflected in the water, and realized they were coming from the Cage d'Or. She tried to imagine the dazzled girl she had once been, standing on the terrace, swept away by the excitement and romance of her Arabian Nights fantasy.

She found herself at a deserted spot, away from the feluccas and houseboats, far from the noisy Hilton and its dock, where the Nile cruise boats were moored. It surprised her that the water was cold, and the mud unpleasant beneath her bare feet. She had somehow always thought the Nile would be warm; hadn't Amira called the Nile the Mother of Rivers? Alice's gown billowed out at the knees, and then around her thighs, floating for a few minutes on the surface, a white jellyfish. When the water reached her breasts, the fabric sank down and swirled around her legs as the river's current caught it. The tide tickled her armpits and then her chin. She thought what a curious optical illusion it was, as she went under, that the Cage d'Or looked as if it were the one drowning, not she.

As the water closed over her head and she saw her blond hair stream out in tendrils, she heard Ibrahim say, "Do you hate me for declaring our daughter dead and sending her away?" And Alice, in pure honesty, replied: No, because you implemented her release from this prison that has held me captive. Thank you, Ibrahim, for setting my daughter free.

Alice opened her mouth and brackish water rushed in. She spread wide her arms, lifted her feet and felt the gentle current cradle her. She felt as if she were flying; her body rolled over and over gently, as the water continued to pour down her throat. And then her head struck something hard.

She felt a sharp pain and saw an explosion of stars, and she thought they were skyrockets, celebrating Egypt's victory.

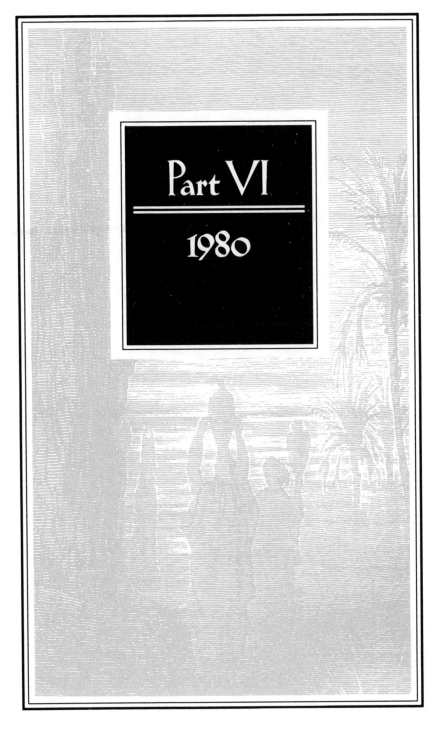

Part VI

1980

C H A P T E R   3 2

The country was rocked by the woman's blasphemy. In the streets and in the coffeehouses, it was all the people talked about: First she murders her brother, they said, and now she puts on a false beard and takes over the duties and privileges of a man. Should such a perversity of nature be allowed to live? Isn't the creature a walking obscenity?

"The woman is mad," grumbled a tax collector over his beer, "to deny her sex so, to thumb her nose at the role in life nature created her for."

"Who does she think she is?" said the owner of the coffeehouse. "Trying to be a man, demanding rights that were never intended for a mere female. Where would the world be if *all* women thought like that?"

A textile exporter raised his fist and cried, "Next thing you know, they'll be insisting that *we* have the babies!"

Dahiba couldn't help it. She laughed.

Hakim turned, giving her an exasperated look, and she said, "I'm sorry, my dear. But it's just so . . . so funny. Men having babies."

The actors in the outdoor coffeehouse that had been temporarily erected outside the Egyptian Museum relaxed and brought cigarettes out from under loincloths and long pleated robes. The onlookers crowded behind the ropes hooted to see people dressed as Egyptians from a long-gone past light up cigarettes.

"I am sorry, my darling," Dahiba said, going up to her husband and running her hand over his bald head. "Do the scene again. This time I promise I shall be quiet."

She knew how important this film was to him—and how dangerous. So far, the government censors were not interfering, but they were watching very closely. Would they be smart enough to see through Hakim's trick? "It is a film about our glorious past!" he had argued. "What can be shameful in a film about our pharaohs? There is nothing political in it, and I promise to keep the dancing scenes moral and decent."

But what the censors didn't know was the deeper message of the film, which, on the surface, was about a young woman in modern Cairo who falls asleep in the Egyptian Museum and dreams that she is Hatshepsut, Egypt's only woman pharaoh. But the dream is a parable. The young woman is married to a sadist who tortures her and, under the law, she has no recourse against him; in her dream, the roles are reversed, she becomes powerful and finally metes out punishment by castration. What the censors didn't know was that the actor who was playing the husband was also to play the castrated slave.

They were filming the dream sequence on an early November morning before Cairo became too noisy. And while ropes had been strung around to cordon off the bystanders, the crowd was growing so unexpectedly that uniformed guards carrying batons had been called in to provide further security.

Hakim and his crew were being very careful. Filmmakers in Cairo had been recent targets of Islamic fundamentalist groups who protested the production of "immoral films with messages that go against the teachings of Islam." Hakim himself had received threats for making films that depicted strong, opinionated women who preferred living alone to marrying. Ever since Egypt's victory in the Ramadan War in 1973, the growing tide of fundamentalism was calling for a return to the traditional and "natural" role of women, and the films of Hakim Raouf, Islamic conservatives declared, put ideas into the minds of young girls.

But it wasn't just among Muslims that Hakim and other directors had enemies; Coptic Christians were also voicing opposition to movies that they claimed constantly stereotyped members of their community in a negative light. Raouf had come under specific attack by both Copts and Muslims for having made a movie about a love affair between a Muslim woman and a Coptic man, which both sides declared offensive and so farfetched as to verge on parody.

"It is impossible to please everyone," Hakim said. "I am answerable to God and my conscience. I can no longer be at peace with myself if I make musical comedies or melodramas. As a filmmaker I have an obligation to speak with my heart."

Dahiba loved him for his courage, but today she had a bad feeling about the onlookers. Only the night before, a riot had broken out in the Coptic quarter of Cairo, where it was reported that a Christian had raped a five-year-old Muslim girl. Several people had been killed, buildings had burned, and it had taken over a hundred policemen to restore order.

"Hakim," she said quietly, shivering beneath the November sun, even though the morning was warm, "I think we should stop for the day. There are angry faces in the crowd. And you got that death threat the other day, signed with a Coptic cross."

They had also received threats because of Dahiba's book, *The Sentence of Woman,* which was still banned in Egypt and which, in the past seven years, had caused an uproar in the Arab world. Because she had retired from dancing six years ago, when she turned fifty, Dahiba had begun to concentrate on her feminist writings, none of which she had been able to get published, not even in Lebanon. "Shall we live like moles?" Hakim said. "God gave us minds and intellects and the choice of voicing our thoughts. If we give in, then others will follow, until Egypt is a silent place."

Dahiba had to agree. Still, she was afraid.

=

Inside her trailer, which was parked at the edge of the municipal bus compound in front of the Hilton Hotel, Camelia finished applying her Hatshepsut makeup. She was to play the renegade woman pharaoh; she was the star of the film. As she reached for the kingly beard that was to go on last, she glanced out the small window next to her mirror and saw truckloads of agitated-looking young men pulling up at the edge of the crowd. Several of them were carrying placards bearing the Coptic cross. She frowned, then turned to her fourteen-year-old daughter, who was doing homework at a small table.

When she saw the leg brace peeping out from under the hem of Zeinab's school uniform, Camelia felt a flood of love and, recalling the unwanted baby that had been placed in her arms fourteen years ago, marveled again that, through God's infinite compassion, she should be blessed with a daughter. It also made Camelia think of Yasmina. The years had not softened Camelia's anger toward her sister; her fury had in fact grown as her love for Zeinab had grown. How could Yasmina have given up the child? "She says she doesn't want it," Alice had said when Yasmina had left Egypt. "I tried to talk her into keeping the child, but she says it reminds her too much of Hassan." *Bismillah!* You don't punish a child for the sins of the father! But Camelia's anger was also mingled with fear—that someday Yasmina was going to show up to claim her daughter. *My sister had better be prepared to fight, because Zeinab is mine.*

"Zeinab dear," she said when she saw the young men jump down from the trucks, "please call Radwan in. Tell him I wish to see him. Quickly, darling."

Radwan was one of Camelia's personal bodyguards, a large Syrian who had been with her for seven years. When he stepped into the trailer, she said, "Radwan, will you please take Zeinab to my mother's house on Virgins of Paradise Street?"

"But Mama," the girl protested, "why can't I stay and watch you make the movie?"

Camelia gave her daughter a hug. Pretty little Zeinab, small for her age, with hair growing lighter each year so that now it was the color of antique brass. "It's going to be a long day, darling, and there are too many distractions here for you to do your homework. Go to your grandmother's and I'll come for you later." She turned to Radwan. "Take her out that way," she said, nodding in the direction of the Nile. "And hurry."

He nodded, his dark eyes flickering in understanding.

Drawing a robe over her pleated linen dress and elaborate jeweled collar, Camelia stepped out into Cairo's smoky morning and surveyed the unusually large throng collecting beyond the security ropes. Trouble was definitely in the air.

"In the name of God," she murmured. How could this be happening, when Egypt had finally started to make progress? Thanks to the diligence of Mrs. Sadat, the Status Laws had finally been passed by

Parliament, granting women more rights and increased representation in government. But now there was this disturbing revival of conservatism, with young women *voluntarily* taking up the veil.

Camelia looked to the left and saw Radwan climb into the back seat of her white limousine. As the car began to edge its way from the growing throng, she wondered if her handsome bodyguard was still in love with her, as he had once recklessly declared. Camelia frequently received declarations of love, now that she was a star, performing with twenty back-up dancers and a full orchestra. She always gently rebuffed such admirers, as she had Radwan. She didn't want lovers, or to be in love.

As she picked her way over cables to where the scene was being shot, Camelia felt hundreds of eyes watching her. She knew what was going through the minds of these onlookers, knew that they would be thinking of her in the exaggerated terms of which Egyptians were so fond: "There is Camelia Rasheed, our beloved goddess, the most beautiful woman in the world, the most desirable woman since Cleopatra, she who blinds even the angels." When she performed at the Hilton, men in the audience would call out, "You are honey! You are diamonds!" Once, when a drop of perspiration trickled from her cheek, down her neck and between her breasts, a passionate Saudi man had jumped on a table and cried, "Oh, sweet shower from God!"

Camelia had become used to such adulation. What she was not used to was love; she had never been in love, even though Cairo newspapers often referred to her as "Egypt's love goddess." It was a symbolic title only; the press knew that Camelia led a chaste and moral private life. There were things, however, that the press didn't know: that Zeinab wasn't really her daughter; that Camelia had never been married— certainly not to a hero who had died in the Six-Day War—and her biggest secret of all, that, at thirty-five, Camelia was still a virgin.

"Uncle Hakim," she said quietly as she joined him and Dahiba. "I don't like the feel of this crowd. Some angry-looking young men just arrived in trucks."

"We should leave," Dahiba said.

When Hakim saw the fear in their eyes, he said, "Very well, my angels. We shan't be reckless. After all, the braver the bird, the fatter the cat. I shall send the crew home. Maybe we can shoot this scene in the studio."

But just as he gave the signal to his cameraman, someone in the crowd shouted, "Death to the spawn of Satan!"

And suddenly the mob was surging forward, breaking the ropes. Mostly young men, shaking fists and wielding clubs, they pushed the security guards to the ground and swarmed over the cameras and equipment, smashing and destroying, before Hakim's crew could even react. The security guards tried to fight back, but the numbers were overwhelming. When a group of attackers fell upon the cameraman, beating him with sticks, Hakim rushed to his aid. One of the attackers grabbed a length of rope and threw it around Hakim's neck. Others joined in, dragging him along the ground. Then they threw the free end of the rope over a crane, and as they started to hoist him up, Hakim's face turned purple and his eyes bulged.

"Stop! Stop!" Camelia screamed, fighting her way through the mob. "Uncle Hakim! Oh my God—*Hakim!*"

=

Mohammed felt his skin burn with excitement, to see so many young men in white galabeyas going through the prostrations of prayer together. How many were there? Hundreds? A mere handful compared to the thousands they were keeping from crossing the university campus.

"It happens every day now," one of the bystanders said. "They fill the central courtyard and pray, so how can anyone disperse them? Still, we must get to class."

Mohammed also had to get to class, having just started his course of study at Cairo University. But the seventeen-year-old liked the students' prayer blockade. He wished he had the courage to join them. He also wished he could take up their uniform: a white galabeya, beard, and skullcap. How he envied these religious young men as they went around the campus, pounding on classroom doors, announcing the time for prayer, enraging professors and confounding students. They had a noble cause, a purpose. Didn't they burn, as he burned?

When the prayer was over and the young fundamentalists dispersed, Mohammed continued on through the campus, passing booths where religious books were sold at low prices. Zealous youths gave out free galabeyas or veils to any of the young people who stopped and listened to them. And not all of them were males; some were passionate girls who, wearing veils and long dresses, handed out flyers and pamphlets explaining the need to disavow the corrupt ways of Europe and America, and return to God and Islam. Students grabbed up tapes of sermons by fundamentalist imams; if they saw a man and woman walking together, they demanded to see their marriage license; bearded young men would hit girls with sticks if their skirts did not reach their ankles; they were demanding that all businesses and shops close during the Call to Prayer; they were calling for Jerusalem to be liberated from the Israelis; and they declared that any music, especially music from the West, was sacrilegious. Finally, the extremists were calling for a return of the segregation of the sexes, especially in school, among the virginal and unmarried; students insisted that males and females should not sit together in a classroom, and fundamentalist medical students refused to study the anatomy of the opposite sex. After all, they reasoned, hadn't the pious ways of Egyptians in 1973 given them a victory in the Ramadan War? Did that not therefore indicate that this was the way God wanted Egypt to go?

Yes, Mohammed Rasheed thought, believing that he burned for God.

And later that afternoon, when he returned home and joined his female relatives in the grand salon on Virgins of Paradise Street, he continued to mistake the heat that gripped him for religious fervor. But his thoughts were not of God but of a girl at school, with eyes like pools of ink. How was a boy to keep his thoughts pious when girls had such eyes, such thick cascading hair and inviting hips? The students were right, women had to be sequestered. They needed to be kept on a tighter reign, so that their rampant sexuality was not a threat to men.

Mohammed sank onto one of the divans and thought: Women are not to be trusted. Especially the beautiful ones. Wasn't his own mother beautiful? And hadn't she betrayed him by abandoning him? He never wrote to Yasmina, he didn't want anything to do with her. For the family to have declared her dead she must have committed a terrible sin, and therefore deserved to be ostracized. But whenever a letter arrived from California, he would secretly read it many times, and then weep over her photograph, in bed late at night, longing to touch that white skin and fair hair, and cursing her.

As he waited for one of the girls to bring him tea, he looked at his stepmother, Nala, quietly knitting on one of the divans. She was pregnant again. She had given Mohammed's father Omar seven children, suffered one miscarriage, and lost one baby to a heart defect. Nala had endured her many pregnancies without complaint. Mohammed thought this was right and natural.

When Zeinab brought him tea, he couldn't meet her eyes. Poor girl, whose mother danced lewdly in front of strange men. And how was it that Zeinab so strongly resembled his own mother, Yasmina? Because of this, Mohammed was uncomfortable around the girl he thought was his cousin.

As he drank the hot tea spiced with sugar and mint, filling his head with steam and fragrance, bringing back the memory of kohl-smudged black eyes and wide hips, Mohammed suddenly knew what he had to do. Tomorrow, at the university, he was going to trade in his jeans for the long white galabeya of the Brotherhood. It would be his shield against the dangers of women.

Out in the garden, Amira noted the position of the sun and decided that most of the young people should be home from school by now, starting to gather in the salon for the sunset prayer. So she collected the last of her harvested herbs and followed the path back to the house, passing what had once been Alice's garden.

Not a trace of the English Eden was left; the papyrus and poppies and wild lilies of Egypt had reclaimed the place where begonias and carnations had once miraculously grown. In seven years, Amira had not stopped grieving for the loss of Alice and Zachariah. But she consoled herself with the thought that what happened to them had been fated, that their destinies had been joined the moment Yasmina was born, and Amira had sent Ibrahim out into the city to commit an act of charity.

Amira entered a kitchen filled with golden afternoon sunlight, as well as the heavenly aroma of moussaka baking in the oven and fish sizzling in butter on the stove. As she put away the herbs and listened to the feminine chatter and laughter of girls and women engaged in various tasks, Amira thought how blessed she was: seventy-six, and in full possession of her health and wits, surrounded by eighteen great-grand-children, with two more on the way. Praise God's name! The house was full again, now that Tahia and her six children lived here, and Omar's eight, plus his wife, who always came to stay when Omar was overseas on a government job, as he was now. And all the children, grown and small, no matter what their relation to Amira, addressed her as Umma, because she was the mother of the family. As such, they were Amira's responsibility, because even though the duty of finding husbands for the girls fell to the mothers, it was ultimately Amira who chose them.

There was Tahia's fourteen-year-old daughter Asmahan, wearing the *hejab*, Islamic dress—her hair, neck, and shoulders covered by a veil—a self-righteous girl who strongly resembled her grandmother Nefissa, and whom Amira had once overheard telling Zeinab that her mother, Camelia, was going to burn in hell because she was a dancer. Other girls in the house wore the *hejab*, zealous university students who called themselves *mohajibaat*, "women of the veil," and who refused to sit next to men in the classroom. Their piety would make Amira's matchmaking plans easier. But some of their sisters and cousins were not so easy. Sakinna, whom the Abdel Rahman son had turned down, was still unmarried at twenty-three. Basima, still divorced, with two children, should be in a house of her own. And Samia, youngest daughter of Jamal Rasheed by his wife before Tahia, was too thin and therefore not a good bride candidate.

And there was Tahia herself, who had been widowed for over seven years. She was still lovely at thirty-five and would make someone happy. But whenever Amira brought up the subject, Tahia always said quietly but firmly that she was waiting for Zakki. In the seven years since his disappearance, no one had heard a word from Zachariah, but Tahia was unshaken in her belief that he was going to come back someday.

Amira herself was not so sure. Wherever the boy had gone, she had no doubt that he was on God's errand.

She went into the salon, where some of the family members were gathered around the television set for the late afternoon news. Today's story was about the escalating conflict between Coptic Christians and Muslims. In retaliation for the killing of a Muslim sheikh in a village in Upper Egypt, a Coptic church had been firebombed, killing ten people.

Amira looked at Mohammed, her scowling grandson, watching the imperious way he received a glass of tea from Zeinab. Brother and sister, but believing they were cousins, the two were similar in appearance, but in character as different as dill and honey. Amira was worried about Mohammed, about the way she caught him watching his girl cousins with falcon eyes. That boy had sex on his mind. Not that he was any different from his father at that age—Amira recalled when Omar had demanded they find him a wife—but there seemed to be a dangerous edge to Mohammed, as though a violent current ran in his veins. Amira wondered if it was the result of having been taken from his mother at a young age. She recalled how hysterical he had been after Yasmina had left, to the point where Ibrahim had had to medicate the boy just to get him to calm down. It might be wise, Amira thought now, to get Mohammed married young, before his hunger for sex drove him to an impulsive and calamitous act.

Finally, sadly, there was no question of marriage for Zeinab.

So much to take care of! And now, lately, Amira had been sensing more strongly than ever the call to Arabia. She had been having more dreams, more memories had returned. Strangely, the dreams of the beautiful youth who had been beckoning to her had ceased. Amira didn't know why. Had he perhaps been alive when she had dreamed about him, and was now dead? But although the intriguing boy was gone, more fragments had come to her. A voice from the past was haunting Amira: "We will be following the route the Prophet Moussa took when he led the Israelites out of Egypt. We shall stop at the well where he met his wife . . ." That must have been the road her mother's caravan had taken, when they were attacked by slavers. And the oasis in her dreams—was it Moussa's Well?

All of these fragments and dreams formed a mosaic of the past that was gradually being filled in. But what Amira still could not remember was arriving at the house on Tree of Pearls Street; she could not recall her first days in the harem. It was as though a door had been shut across that period, blocking out those days and her earlier years as well. Amira saw her past as a prisoner in a locked room. But where was the key?

She had not gone to Mecca when she had planned, seven years ago, because of Alice's death. And then the family had searched for Zachariah, and Amira had waited for news. Next, an epidemic of summer fever had swept through Cairo's children; and the following year had been pronounced by Qettah the astrologer as unfavorable for travel. But now the signs were good; Qettah had determined that this was an auspicious year for Amira.

As soon as the family was taken care of she was going to make the pilgrimage to Holy Mecca. And on the way back, follow the path the Israelites had taken. Perhaps she would find the square minaret and her mother's grave . . .

Down in the driveway, Ibrahim was getting wearily out of his car, telling himself that a man of sixty-three should not feel so ancient. Perhaps it was a sense of failure that made a man prematurely old. Because a man with no son was surely a failure. Guilt also drained a man, he decided. Since Alice's suicide, his conscience had not known a single moment's peace. He should have gone after her, especially considering her family's history—her mother and brother, both suicides. He might have saved her. And he had made a mistake with Huda, he realized now. Four little girls was what she had given him, making his sense of failure all the more acute.

He rested his head on the steering wheel.

The anniversary of Alice's death was in four days, and her image was haunting him—her pale face, the closed purple eyelids, the blond hair tangled with Nile mud. Some tourists in a felucca had pulled her out of the river. Because Ibrahim had gone alone to the morgue to identify her, he had been able to keep the true cause of her death a secret; only Amira knew the truth, the rest of the family believed Alice had been killed in a car accident.

Oh, Alice, my dearest, dearest Alice. It was my fault; I drove you away.

And Yasmina, the fruit of his union with Alice. She, too, he had failed. He had let her down when she thought she had had to succumb to Hassan's evil rather than go to her father for help. He had promised himself he would write to her in California, asking her to come home. But the right words never came. *Forgive me, Yasmina, wherever you are.*

But the person Ibrahim felt he had failed the most was his father. Looking down from heaven, Ali Rasheed would see only one grandson, Omar, the son of his daughter Nefissa. And great-grandsons, through Omar and Tahia. But there were no grandsons through his son; Ibrahim had failed.

Other problems weighed on him, too. The Rasheed fortune was no longer what it had been. Egypt's cotton, once called "white gold," had shrunk so far on the world market, due to bad government management and planning, that experts were predicting the eventual demise of the Egyptian cotton industry altogether. The fortune Ali Rasheed had amassed in cotton had shrunk, so that Ibrahim was left with a dwindling income and growing family responsibilities.

As he entered the large double doors, hand-carved and imported from India over a hundred years ago, Ibrahim looked at the foyer, with its marble floor and massive brass chandelier, as if for the first time. He had never before realized how large this house truly was. And as he contemplated the grand staircase, which split at the landing and continued up in two separate stairways, one to the men's side of the house, the other to the women's, an idea began to come to him.

"There you are, son of my heart," Amira said, coming into the foyer to greet him.

He marveled at his mother. A woman of her age, still beautiful, still managing this vast family as she always had. She smiled with carefully painted lips, and her hair, now white, was combed back into a French roll held with diamond clips. He felt the vigor of youth in the hands that clasped his. "Mother, I come to ask a favor."

She laughed. "There are no favors between mothers and sons! I shall do anything you ask, from my heart."

"I want you to find me a wife. I must have a son."

Amira's smile turned to a look of concern. "Have you forgotten the misfortune you brought upon our heads when you tried to make Zachariah your son?"

"A wife will give me a *legitimate* son," he said quietly, refusing to speak of the boy who had disappeared from their house seven years ago. Others in the family had searched for Zachariah, but they had never found him. "You have ways of knowing, Mother, you have powers. Find me a woman who will give me sons."

"God rewards the patient. Huda is pregnant. Let us wait and see before we do anything rash."

He took her hands in his and said, "Mother, in all respect and honor to you, I don't wish to follow your advice this time. Forgive me, but your judgment is not always the best."

"What do you mean?"

"I have been thinking about Camelia. Have you ever thought what her life would be like now if you hadn't taken her to that quack on 26th of July Street?"

"Yes, and I see now that had it not been for that unwise step, Camelia might today be happily married, the mother of many children. I am truly sorry for that."

"A woman needs a husband, Mother. And a girl should not be raised in nightclubs and movie studios. Zeinab needs a proper life. She needs a father. Camelia and Zeinab are my responsibility. I want you to help me look for a husband for Camelia."

"It is almost time for prayer," Amira said quietly. "Will you lead the family, my son? I wish to pray alone."

She went up on the roof, which was bathed in the glow of the last moments before sunset. As she gazed out over the orange-washed domes and minarets, she imagined that the blaze stretching across the Nile was not the rays of the setting sun, but a woman's gentle hennaed hand, closing the day.

When the Call to Prayer began, she unfolded her prayer rug and began the recitations.

Allahu akbar. God is great.

But her heart was not upon God.

As she knelt and touched her forehead to the rug, she thought of what Ibrahim had said about Camelia. He was right. Amira had failed in her duty to make certain of her granddaughter's happiness and future.

Ash hadu, la illaha illa Allah. I proclaim, there is no god but God.

She considered Ibrahim's continued urgency to produce a son, and felt vaguely displeased. All this talk about the line of Ali Rasheed, but there was another line, that of Amira Rasheed. Amira had produced a daughter, granddaughters, and great-granddaughters—but all these beautiful girls and women were not enough. A boy counted for more.

Ash hadu, Annah Mohammed rasulu Allah. I proclaim, Mohammed is the messenger of God.

Amira wondered for the first time in her life why family lines ran through the male, when only motherhood was certain. She pondered the deceptions over the years—the daughter of Ali Rasheed's third wife, having lain with a man and then been quickly married off to someone else who later thought the baby was his; Safeya Rageb, presenting to her husband a baby she declared was hers by him, but who was in fact her daughter's; Yasmina carrying a child that everyone thought was Omar's until Nefissa exposed the secret. How many more such lies and deceptions, Amira wondered, back through the centuries, through the millennia all the way to Mother Eve, simply because family lines did not pass through women? Did it make sense, when maternity was certain and paternity at best only a guess?

Hee Allah ahs Allah.

If the family line descended through women, then Yasmina's baby would have been received with celebration, no matter who the father, and Zeinab would now be with her true mother, the family would not be fractured.

Amazed by her thoughts, Amira forced her mind upon God and went through the prayer again, even though the muezzins had finished.

La illaha illa Allah.

But once again prayer eluded her as she thought: A wife for Ibrahim, a husband for Camelia . . .

——

They were in Camelia's apartment because Dahiba had refused to put her husband in a hospital, even one of the private ones. After the police quelled the riot and a doctor examined Hakim in Camelia's trailer, the two women had brought Hakim to the penthouse in the quiet and exclusive district of Zamalek, where they hoped he would be safe from the fanatics. Because Camelia was wealthy, her apartment was eighteen stories above Cairo, with panoramic views of the city, the Nile, and the Pyramids in the distance—a haven of twelve rooms, servants, and expensive furnishings for Zeinab and herself. And she now helped Hakim settle into a chair that faced a picture window looking out onto bright city lights and winking stars. "You gave me such a scare, dearest uncle. I thought they were going to hang you!" she said, wiping tears from her eyes.

He patted her hand, unable to speak. An angry rope burn circled his neck.

"Oh, Uncle, why would they want to hurt a sweet man like you? The Christians are a bloodthirsty people! They worship a man who is nailed to a cross! They must enjoy seeing people suffer! I hate them for what they did to you!"

A servant brought a tray of tea and biscuits, and, knowing that Hakim, like most Cairenes, had a passion for *Dallas,* Camelia turned on the television set. The screen came to life to the usual public-service announcements. *Dallas,* the most popular TV show in Egypt, made Cairo a deserted city on Thursday nights, and the government took advantage of the minutes before the show to air their important messages. Tonight's was part of a vigorous family-planning campaign that urged women to go to a government clinic for free birth-control devices, assuring them, with quotes from the Koran, that a smaller family was a happier one.

Dahiba sat down and went through the evening editions of all the newspapers she had been able to find, to see if the incident in front of the museum had been reported. "Here it is," she said. "The riot was started by Coptic Christian students. No one knows what set them off."

"Uncle has never hurt the Copts!" Camelia said.

"My God," Dahiba said suddenly.

"What is it?"

"This is one of those small, intellectual papers," she said as she handed it to Camelia, pointing to the article on the first page. "Look what they have printed!"

Camelia read: "Men dominate us because they fear us. They hate us because they desire us." She looked at Dahiba. "This is from my essay!" she said. "They've copied my essay from your book!"

Camelia continued to read the words she had written ten years ago: "Our sexuality threatens their masculinity and so they leave only three avenues open to us in which we may find respectability: as a girl-virgin, as a wife, as an elderly crone past childbearing. Nothing else is open to us. If an unmarried woman takes lovers she is branded a whore. If she rejects male lovers they call her a lesbian, because she threatens men's manhood. It is in the nature of a man to oppress that which threatens or frightens him."

Hakim groaned and said with a hoarse voice, "Why did God bless me with such intelligent women?"

"That is your essay, word for word," Dahiba said. "Do they mention your name?"

"No," Camelia said, and when she read the name in the byline, she thought it sounded familiar. "Yacob Mansour," she said.

"Ah, Mansour," Hakim whispered, his hand at his throat. "I know about him. He was arrested some time back for printing a story that was sympathetic to Israel."

"A Jew," Dahiba said. "Not a popular thing to be in Egypt these days."

"The Jews," Hakim sighed. "They are about the only group who aren't out for my blood!"

Camelia frowned, trying to recall where she had seen Mansour's name. And then it came to her. She left the room and returned with one of her scrapbooks, opening it to the first page, on which a yellowed news article had been pasted. It was a review dated November 1966, and the words "gazelle" and "butterfly" leapt off the page. The review was signed Yacob Mansour.

"It is the same man!" Camelia said. "Why has he printed my essay?"

"It took courage to do so," Dahiba said.

Camelia looked at her watch. "Where is this newspaper office located?"

Hakim sipped some tea and managed to croak out, "It's down a small alley off El Bustan Street, near the Chamber of Commerce."

Dahiba said, "You aren't going now, are you?"

"I'll take Radwan with me. I'll be all right, *inshallah*."

=

The office of the small newspaper was modest, consisting of two tiny, cluttered rooms where there was barely space to squeeze between desks. It looked out on an alley across from a rug maker's shop, and the front window, which had been smashed, was covered with cardboard.

Asking Radwan to wait inside the door, Camelia stepped through and saw two men hunched over typewriters, and a young woman standing at a filing cabinet. All three turned and stared at her.

"*Al hamdu lillah!*" declared the girl. She rushed forward and brushed off a chair, offering it to Camelia, and saying, "God's peace and happiness upon you, Sayyida! We are honored!" Then she shouted over her shoulder toward a curtained doorway, "Ya, Aziz! Run to Mr. Shafik's. Bring tea at once!"

Camelia replied, "And to you peace and the compassion of God and his blessings. I have come to see Mr. Mansour. Is he here?"

A man stood up from one of the desks and bowed. He was in his forties, slightly overweight, balding, with wire-rimmed spectacles and a shirt that cried out to be ironed. Camelia was reminded of Suleiman Misrahi and she realized how few Jews were left in Cairo.

"You pay our office a great honor, Miss Rasheed," he said with a smile.

Used to being recognized by strangers, Camelia said, "The honor is mine, Mr. Mansour."

"Did you know that I wrote a review of one of your performances fourteen years ago? I was thirty at the time and thought you were the most exquisite dancer that had ever graced the earth." He glanced toward Radwan in the doorway and added more quietly, "I still think you are."

Camelia also glanced at Radwan, hoping he had not overheard Mansour's words of bold familiarity. Lesser breaches of etiquette had brought the Syrian bodyguard to the immediate defense of his employer's honor.

The boy who had dashed out of the office a moment earlier materialized with a tray and two glasses of mint tea. Despite her anxiousness to learn why Mansour had printed her essay, Camelia went through the formalities of discussing the weather, soccer scores, the miracles that the new High Dam at Aswan had brought to Egypt. Finally she reached into her purse and brought out the paper, Mansour's article circled, and said, "Where did this essay come from?"

"I copied it from your aunt's book," he said, and when he saw her look of surprise, added, "I know you wrote these words. I thought your message was important, so I printed it. Perhaps this way we will open a few minds."

"But the book this was taken from is banned in Egypt! Did you know this?"

Mansour reached into his desk and brought out a copy of *The Sentence of Woman*.

Camelia drew in a breath. "You can get arrested for possessing this book!"

He smiled, and she noticed that when he did, his glasses got pushed up. "President Sadat professes to believe in democracy, allowing free speech. Every now and then, it is good to put him to the test."

Camelia thought that, considering how volatile his writing was, how forward he was with a woman he didn't know, Mansour was ironically soft-spoken. She had expected a man who shouted. "But doesn't this put you in jeopardy," she said, "printing my essay?"

"I once heard Indira Gandhi speak. She said that while it is true that sometimes a woman goes too far, it is only when she goes too far that others listen."

"You didn't mention my name in here."

"I didn't want to cause you trouble. The extremists"—he indicated the broken window—"especially the younger members of the Muslim Brotherhood, those fanatics in the white galabeyas, would not appreciate knowing this essay had been written by a woman. But since I am not Muslim, they would deal less harshly with me than they would with one of their own faith. This way, your words will be read and you will remain safe."

He looked at Camelia with smiling brown eyes and she found herself wondering something about him that she had not wondered about a man since she was seventeen and had had a crush on a government censor.

She wondered: Is he married?

CHAPTER 3 3

Jasmine stepped down from the bus and paused on the sidewalk before heading for her apartment building. Her heart was pounding. How on earth was she going to tell Greg the news? If it had hit her like a thunderbolt, then it was going to knock him completely off his feet. She was not looking forward to it.

As she let herself into the apartment she had shared with Greg for the past seven and a half years, feeling the first drops of November rain begin to fall, she saw that Greg had company in the living room, as usual. Jasmine was glad that tonight they were all men. Sometimes, wives or girlfriends came, and then Jasmine felt the compulsion to entice the women into the kitchen and leave the men in the living room, a habit from the old days. Sometimes the women would join her for coffee at the kitchen table, but mostly they wanted to stay with the men, and so Jasmine would comply, feeling uncomfortable among the mixed company.

She had once confessed this discomfort to Rachel Misrahi, who was now in medical practice in the Valley, and Rachel had replied, "You're an educated woman, Jas. A doctor, for God's sake. You have to get with the times and accept the fact that men and women are equal. Stop the role playing."

Tonight she was glad to see they were only Greg's male cronies from the anthropology department, a coterie of almost-Ph.D.s, who smiled and said "Hi" to Jasmine as she walked through, depositing her medical bag by the phone and heading for the kitchen where she shed her white lab coat and plugged in the coffee pot.

When she saw the dozen red and white carnations in a plain florist's vase, she smiled sadly. Dear Greg, every year at this time, without fail, he gave her carnations in remembrance of her mother's death. And each time, Jasmine would both wish he hadn't done it and be pleased that he had.

Dear Greg, for whom the spark of love had failed to ignite within her.

She went through the mail on the counter—bills, flyers for medical seminars, employment offers from two hospitals, another request for money from the University Alumni Fund, and a postcard from Rachel in Florida. Nothing from Egypt.

Seven years ago, a letter she had written to her mother had been returned with a letter from Amira: "Dear Alice is dead, God make paradise her abode. She died in an automobile accident." And Zachariah, Amira had added, had left to go in search of Sahra, the cook, who had also left the family.

And so both her mother, and her only frail link with the family, had been severed at once, as well as her only hope that her son Mohammed would ever be reminded of her. For Jasmine knew that, like Fatima before her, there would be no photographs, no mention of her. As far as Mohammed was concerned, now that his grandmother Alice was dead, his mother was also dead.

Only one more communication had come after that, six and a half years later when, last spring, Amira had sent a photograph of Mohammed at his high school graduation. It was the picture of an astonishingly handsome young man with the large liquid eyes found on early Christian coffin portraits. But Mohammed was unsmiling, as if determined not to expose his vulnerability to the camera.

The last item in the stack of mail, Jasmine was pleased to see, was a package from Declan Connor. He had sent her the latest edition of *When You Have to Be the Doctor,* and had enclosed a black-and-white snapshot of himself, Sybil, and their son, and a letter describing their work in Malaysia trying to fight rampant malaria. The letter was friendly and brief, with no hint of the romance that had almost blossomed between them seven years ago. Jasmine had not seen Connor since then, but they had kept in touch.

The kitchen door swung open and Jasmine glimpsed the television in the living room, and on the screen a news film of the recently released American hostages getting off a plane from Iran. "Hi," Greg said, kissing her. "How was work?"

She was exhausted. As the junior member of a pediatric clinic in a poor neighborhood, Jasmine worked the longest hours, but she didn't mind. Taking care of other women's babies helped to fill her need for her own child. Mohammed, her son, so far away, denied to her, and the deformed baby, stillborn . . . *No. Push the memories away.* She slipped her arms around Greg's waist and said, "Thank you for the flowers. They're beautiful."

He held her for a moment, then said, "I hope you don't mind the guys being over. We're making plans."

She nodded against his shoulder. Greg was always making plans, yet few ever came to fruition. Although he'd managed to get his master's degree, she had long since stopped offering advice on how he could get his Ph.D. dissertation finished.

"It's all right," she said. "I have to get over to the hospital for evening rounds. I just came home to shower and change, and pick up the car."

Greg went to the refrigerator, took out a beer, and said, "I'm glad you're here. I have news."

She gave him a look. "What a coincidence. So do I."

As he tossed his head back and swallowed some beer, Jasmine thought again about the irony of having married one man while falling in love with another. Seven years later, she was still married to one man, and still in love with the other. But she was fond of Greg, a comfortable affection had grown between them so that occasionally they even had sex. Jasmine suspected that they made love out of a basic need for human touch; they ignited no great passion in each other, and certainly none of the excitement she had once experienced with just a glance from Connor. When she had confessed to Rachel that her marriage with Greg was based on mutual respect rather than on love, Rachel had hailed theirs as a truly liberated marriage with none of the antiquated expectations or game playing that still encumbered relationships. But Jasmine yearned for an old-fashioned marriage, and found herself once again envying Sybil Connor.

"I'm pregnant," she said.

Greg nearly spit out his beer. "Jesus!" he said. "You don't give a guy a little warning."

"I'm sorry. How else can I tell you?" She searched his face. "Are you pleased?"

"Pleased! Wait a minute, my head is spinning. How did this happen?"

"I had to go off the pill, as you know, it was giving me headaches."

"I know, but there are other ways. I mean, when did it—"

"At the Labor Day barbecue." The last time they had had sex, Greg had been drinking beer out by the pool, where a group of them had been grilling steaks and burgers. He had talked Jasmine into "stepping inside for a few minutes."

"Well, it's great, I guess." He put his arms around her again. "Of course it's great. I know how much you love kids. We just never talked about it." He drew back. "But won't you have to quit work? How will we pay the rent?"

Medical school expenses had finally required her to sell the house in England, and seven years of living with a man who didn't hold a job had drained the trust fund. They now lived on what she made at the clinic, and this pregnancy threatened that security. Jasmine suddenly felt less free in this "equal" relationship than she had at any other moment in her life. She tried to keep her tone light as she said, "I guess it's your turn to get a job now. You'll have a family to support."

He turned away and took a long drink of beer. "God, Jasmine, that's not me. I mean, I have to get my own act together before I can think of having kids. I don't even know who I am or what I want yet."

"You're thirty-seven years old."

He laughed. "Yeah, that's how old my dad was when he got my mother pregnant. Quite a coincidence, huh?" He faced her squarely and said, "Jasmine, I'll be honest. I don't want to have any kid of mine suffer the kind of upbringing I did, all those private schools, never seeing my parents."

Jasmine closed her eyes, suddenly feeling very tired. "Then what do you suggest?" she said.

He plucked a magnet off the refrigerator door and turned it over in his fingers. It was a small plastic tomato with a smiling face.

When Greg didn't say anything, Jasmine went numb. "So what is *your* news?"

He put the magnet back, but it fell to the floor. "The guys and I are getting up an expedition to go to Kenya. Roger is doing a study on the Maasai—"

"I see," Jasmine said. Last year it had been New Guinea, and the year before Tierra del Fuego. He hadn't gone, but maybe this time he really would go. Jasmine realized that she did not particularly care.

"I have to get back to the clinic," she said. "Where are the car keys?"

"I took the car in for servicing this morning, remember? I told you I was going to." He reached for her. "Listen, Jas—"

"Yes, I know. But you said it would be ready by five. Didn't you pick it up?"

"I thought you were going to pick it up. That's how we've always done it—I take it in, you go and get it."

Yes, she thought. Total equality. Fair's fair. "All right, I'll take the bus."

"Jasmine," he said, taking her by the arm. "Please. I don't know what to say to you."

She pulled away. "We'll talk about it later. I have to catch the bus and get to the garage before they close."

=

As she drove the car along the Pacific Coast Highway, she watched the rain wash down the windshield and thought about Greg and their relationship. And she saw little change from when they had first met. They had lived together, but Jasmine's life had been so consumed with medical school, and then internship, and finally the clinic, that there had been little time left to devote to her marriage. Even so, she had made an effort to try to understand the man she had married, but with little success. She had sought Greg's depths but had found to her surprise that he had none. The pleasant, laid-back surface which she had initially liked turned out to be as deep as he got. She had attempted to get close to him, but even when they had sex, she sensed him drawing away. The one time she had met Greg's mother, during a stopover when Dr. Mary Van Kerk was flying from the caves of India to the caves of Western Australia, Jasmine had found a woman as hard as the rock she studied, and a stilted mother-son relationship in which both participants seemed to have forgotten their lines.

After that, Jasmine had started to compare Greg to Arab men. She thought about their lust for living, their spontaneity and ferocious humor, their universal reputation for being skilled and considerate lovers. Above all, she missed their mercurial passions. Arab men cried openly, they kissed one another, and to them there was no such thing as inappropriate laughter. And if a man impregnated a woman, he felt duty and honor bound to claim the child and provide for it.

Jasmine put her hand on her abdomen and was suddenly full of wonder. The shock had worn off, now she was surprised to discover that she was actually happy. In fact, she hadn't felt this good in a long time, not since she had been pregnant with Mohammed, and later, with the poor little deformed one who hadn't survived. Perhaps this baby will be a girl, Jasmine thought, finally allowing herself to become excited. I shall name her Ayesha, she thought, for the Prophet's favorite wife. And if Greg goes to Kenya, I shall find a way to raise my daughter on my own.

As she reached over to turn on the radio, she heard a muffled sound outside the car, and suddenly the steering wheel started to shimmy. Slowing down, Jasmine managed to pull the car over to the side of the rain-slicked highway. When she got out, holding a magazine over her head because she had forgotten to bring an umbrella, she saw that the right front tire had blown.

She kicked the wheel, then looked up and down the highway. There were few cars, and she realized that, if she was going to get to the hospital on time, she was going to have to change the tire herself.

As she maneuvered the jack under the slippery bumper, she grew furious with Greg, who should have taken care of the car himself. The jack wasn't cooperating. She pushed and strained, her anger growing, encompassing now Hassan, who had abused her, and her father, for banishing her. As she struggled, her fury mounted to rage, and she started to cry, the rain mingling with her tears of frustration.

Suddenly the jack slipped, and she fell back onto the hard blacktop. "*Allah!*" she cried, and a sharp pain cut through her abdomen.

===

Jasmine had been staring for a long time at the window of her hospital room. Because it was night, the glass reflected the single light above her bed and the dimmed lights in the hall beyond her open door. She had made it to the hospital on time, but as a patient in an ambulance. A passing motorist had stopped to help her, and had called the police from a highway call box. She had been rushed into surgery, diagnosed with an incomplete abortion. The surgeons had completed it, and since coming out of the anesthetic, Jasmine had been doing a lot of thinking.

And by the time Rachel arrived, coming quietly into the room and saying, "Oh Jas, I'm so sorry," Jasmine had arrived at some answers.

"Can I get you anything?" Rachel said, sitting down. "Are they taking good care of you? I may be a doctor, but I sure hate visiting friends in the hospital."

"Where is Greg?"

"He's down at the gift shop, buying you some flowers. He feels awful, Jas."

"So do I. You know, my mother lost two children—one died in infancy, and she miscarried the second. Isn't it weird how daughters seem to repeat their mother's lives?" Jasmine sniffed back her tears. She had difficulty speaking, she was so tired. "I've been lying here thinking about my father, reliving the special times he and I had together. I wish he was here right now, because there's so much I want to tell him, explain to him. And I want to ask him questions, too."

She winced and put her hand on her abdomen. "I look back," she said, "and see that, during those times with my father, helping the homeless fellaheen women and their children, I had gotten started on a road—my life's road. But I got sidetracked. I forgot the reasons why I married Greg in the first place, and so I stayed in the relationship. But I have to move on, Rachel, I have work to do."

"First you have to rest, and let your body heal. Time enough to be superwoman."

Jasmine smiled wearily. "You're the superwoman, Rachel. With your husband and baby and medical practice."

"You'd think I could lose a few pounds, running around like that. I'm going to let you rest now. If you need me, I'll be in the lounge down the hall."

By the time Greg came in with flowers and a stricken look, Jasmine was no longer angry with him, or even disappointed. He was simply a stranger who had shared her life for a while, and who would leave as a stranger.

He sat for a long time at the bedside, unable to speak. Finally he said, "I'm sorry you lost the baby."

"It was not meant to be. This is God's will." And finding comfort in this knowledge that everything was preordained, Jasmine observed another truth: the word *Islam* in Arabic means "surrender," and to surrender now to God's plan brought peace.

"I mean," he said, twisting his fingers, "it's not as though you had known about the baby for long. We didn't buy any baby furniture, or anything. We hadn't made any plans."

He looked at her with tears in his eyes. She saw bewilderment in his look, the need to be forgiven, although he didn't seem to know for what. And then she realized that he was carrying a burden that he was silently begging her to lift. Recognizing what it was, Jasmine said, "You and I got married for a specific reason, do you remember? We didn't marry for love or with the intention of bringing children into the world, but to avoid a legal situation. That situation has passed, and this is a sign from God that the hour has come for us to part."

When he started to protest, and she saw how feebly he did it, she said, "I believe now that I am not fated for marriage and children, for God has taken these away from me. He has another purpose in store for me."

"I am sorry, Jasmine," Greg said. "As soon as you get your strength back I'll move out. The apartment is yours."

It had always been hers; Greg had been but a guest in it. "We'll talk in the morning, when I'm discharged. I'm very tired now."

He hesitated, bound to the bed by his perplexity, his inability to grasp exactly what had happened. A baby—his baby—had been lost. Shouldn't he be feeling something? Weren't there certain words he should be speaking? He tried to tap some hidden program inside himself, a wellspring of compassion to fall back on that his mother might have implanted in him years ago when he wasn't looking. But there was nothing there.

And now he reflected on his relationship with Jasmine and realized that nothing had been there either. They had a few memories—celebrating their first wedding anniversary on Santa Monica Pier, both still waiting for love to blossom in their lives; popping the champagne cork when she graduated from medical school; Jasmine consoling him when his Ph.D. dissertation was rejected yet again. But what did these moments add up to?

And in that instant he recognized the stranger she had always been to him, the stranger she would always be.

He bent and kissed her cool forehead. "Here are the things you asked me to bring," he said, and after he closed the door, Jasmine opened the overnight case he had brought.

She lifted out the book he had placed on top of her toiletries—the newest edition of *When You Have to Be the Doctor,* which Connor had sent to her from Malaysia. She opened it and read the inscription he had written on the title page, next to their names: "Jasmine, if ever you're in quick need of a prayer, just remember that little muscle on the side of your nose." He had signed it, "Love, Declan." And she smiled.

Then she reached again into the overnight case and took out the leather-bound Koran that had made the journey from Egypt with her. It was in Arabic, and it had been a long time since she had opened it.

She opened it now.

CHAPTER 34

Yacob frightened her.

Rather, the thought of falling in love with him, of him loving her in return, was frightening. Camelia had worked hard to fight it, spending hours rehearsing for her show, immersing herself in choreography and costuming, filling her life so that she dropped into bed every night exhausted, entering a deep, dreamless sleep that not even Yacob Mansour could invade. But when she awoke each morning, he was first in her thoughts, the image of an unassuming man, slightly overweight, with wire-rimmed glasses and thinning hair. And then later, at the Hilton, as she danced and smiled and embraced the applause, she would find herself searching for him in the audience until, somewhere at the back of the room, beyond the lights and the frenzied crowd, she would see him standing there, quietly watching.

Did he feel the same toward her? she wondered. Surely he felt something, otherwise why was he in her audience so frequently? And yet not once had he come backstage, or presented her with flowers, or showered her with pound notes as other men did. In fact, in the four months since she had first met him at his newspaper office, Camelia had exchanged not another word with Mansour.

She didn't know anything about him, but guessed, by the suit he wore every time he came to a performance, that he was not well off, and she knew that his struggling newspaper was supported solely by donations. She still didn't even know if he was married, having purposely avoided trying to find out anything about him in the hope that her infatuation would pass. But it hadn't. It was growing.

Over the years Camelia had constructed a defense against falling in love, so that the few times she had found herself attracted to someone, the crush had died before it had had a chance to blossom. But for some reason, Yacob Mansour had found a way around that defense. And now she didn't know what to do.

She suspected that it wasn't wise to fall in love with a Jew these days. Years ago, before the wars with Israel, Egyptian Jews had coexisted peacefully with Muslims. Hadn't the Misrahi and Rasheed families been close? But three humiliating defeats by Israel had soured Egyptians toward their Semitic brothers; intimate relationships between members of the two camps were frowned upon, and especially intolerable was a situation in which the man was Jewish, the woman Muslim.

But Camelia couldn't get Yacob out of her mind.

She bought his paper every day and read his column. He wrote brilliantly, she thought, on volatile issues, calling boldly for the government to bring about needed reform; he was courageous, even reckless, naming names and detailing specific cases of injustice. Mansour also frequently wrote glowing reviews of her performances; he never made reference to her body, which would have been highly offensive, but his adjectives in praise of her skill and talent were endless. Did she read love between those laudatory lines? Or was she just imagining it? And was she herself truly falling in love with a man with whom she had exchanged only a brief dialogue, glimpsed at the back of an audience? How was she to know, if she had never experienced love? She had wanted to ask Umma for advice, but Amira's rule was: Marriage first, love follows.

As her limousine threaded its way through the congested streets of

Cairo, her bodyguard sitting up front with the chauffeur, Camelia looked through the darkly tinted window and marveled at how schoolgirlish this afternoon errand was making her feel. When was the last time she had felt so excited, so giddy? She was actually on her way to Yacob's newspaper office off Al Bustan Street; she was going there on legitimate business, and it had taken her three hours to get ready.

She shook her head and thought: I am thirty-five years old and have never been intimate with a man. I am as nervous as I used to be as a girl, when Hassan came to the house and I thought I would die of love. Hassan al-Sabir, whose murder was still on the police books, unsolved, and who, in Camelia's opinion, deserved what he got for what he had done to Yasmina.

She pushed the dark memory away as the limousine pulled up in front of a large gray edifice from which scores of girls in blue uniforms were emerging. Ever since Camelia had read a news story about a Muslim girl being kidnapped by Coptic Christians, she had personally come to collect her daughter every day after school.

Zeinab was outside the gate, saying good-bye to a red-haired girl. Except for the leg brace, she looked like any other energetic adolescent, a bit gawky, with two long braids down her back. Only the walk, as she limped toward the limousine, set her apart from the others. "Hello, Mama!" she said, kissing Camelia as she got into the car.

"Who was that you were talking to, darling?"

"She's my best friend, Angelina! She wants me to go to her house tomorrow. May I?"

"Angelina? Is she a foreigner?"

Zeinab laughed. "She's Egyptian, Mama! And she's the only girl in school who's nice to me and doesn't make fun of me."

Camelia's heart went out to her daughter, and she was sharply reminded that, in two months, Zeinab would be fifteen, and two years after that would be graduating from secondary school. What then? What was Zeinab's future? How was a crippled girl supposed to go through life? Zeinab would surely never marry, and she would need a protector. Hakim Raouf, though a wonderful uncle to Zeinab, was getting on in years.

She needs a father, Camelia thought.

"Mama?" Zeinab said as the limousine joined the heavy traffic on Al

Bustan Street, the chauffeur pounding on the horn instead of his brakes, Egyptian fashion. "May I go to Angelina's house?"

"Where does she live?"

"In Shubra."

Camelia frowned. "That is a heavily Christian neighborhood. It might not be safe."

"Oh, I'll be safe! Angelina's a Christian!"

Camelia looked out the window. What should she say now? She had tried to protect her daughter from the hatred that was dividing Cairo, that Camelia herself was starting to feel toward the people who had hurt Uncle Hakim. Within the secure walls of her eighteenth-story penthouse, Camelia had watched terrifying news films of burning mosques and slain Copts in a feud that was kept alive and escalating by the laws of revenge. When President Sadat had asked the Coptic pope, Shenouda, to take part in a peace conference, and Shenouda had refused, the Copts had emerged as the villains, and Camelia had thought: They want to continue the killing. And her distrust and fear of them grew.

"I don't want you to go to Angelina's, darling," she said, sweeping a few strands of hair from Zeinab's face. "It isn't safe these days."

Zeinab had been afraid her mother would say that. Ever since poor Uncle Hakim had been hurt, everyone was saying bad things about the Christians. But Angelina wasn't bad, she was kind and she was funny, and she had a marvelously handsome brother who sometimes came to the school to walk Angelina home.

"You don't like the Christians, do you, Mama?" she asked.

Camelia carefully chose her words, trying not to infect her daughter with her own prejudice. "It's not a question of like or dislike, darling, it's a fact of life. Until the authorities settle this dispute between the Copts and the Muslims, no one is safe. You are not to have anything to do with Angelina or any other Christians until it is safe. Do you understand?"

When Camelia saw Zeinab's crestfallen look, she put an arm around her daughter's thin shoulders and gave her a squeeze. Poor Zeinab, so self-conscious that she had a hard time making friends at school. Camelia understood the hunger in the girl's eyes, her quiet yearning for acceptance and friendship. We are alike, Camelia thought, my daughter and I. Zeinab wants to be friends with a Christian, and I am in love with a Jew.

"I tell you what. I have a quick stop to make, and then we'll go to Groppi's for dessert. Would you like that? We'll indulge ourselves, just the two of us!"

Zeinab said, "That would be wonderful," and fell silent. It wasn't fair that a few bad people were ruining things for everyone else. She so desperately wanted to visit Angelina's house that, even though she had promised she wouldn't, she was already trying to think of a way to go. Surely, Zeinab reasoned, it wouldn't hurt her mother if she didn't know.

Arriving at the alley, the chauffeur skillfully squeezed the big car into a space between a falafel vendor and a donkey cart loaded with oranges. Camelia hesitated before getting out.

She told herself that she was doing this for Dahiba, whose latest essay was in her purse. She was doing it for social justice and reform, to help her oppressed sisters. But as she checked her makeup one more time and felt her heart race, Camelia knew the real reason why she had offered to bring Dahiba's article in person to Mansour.

Radwan opened the door and pedestrians stared at her when she got out. When she asked the bodyguard to stay at the car, because of Zeinab, he frowned; Camelia knew Radwan was not comfortable with the idea of letting her walk down the narrow lane unescorted. Folding his massive arms, he planted himself against the car and watched her head down the alley, a tall, expensively dressed modern woman in high heels, with red lips and a cloud of black hair that drew stares from men and women alike.

The front window of the newspaper office was still patched with cardboard, but Camelia noticed with alarm that the door had been torn off its hinges. And when she stepped inside, she saw that the desks had been attacked with an ax; there were papers strewn everywhere, paint poured over them.

She found Yacob in the back room, sifting through some sodden pages. "Are you all right?" she said.

He looked up. "Miss Rasheed!"

"Who did this? Was it the Copts?"

He shrugged. "It could have been. Both sides would like to put me out of business. And it looks as if they have succeeded, for a while anyway. They stole our files and our typewriters."

Camelia felt her anger flare. First Hakim, and now Yacob. She most certainly would not permit Zeinab to visit Angelina and her Christian family. "Perhaps you should stop publishing your newspaper for a while," she said. "Your life is in danger. You must think about your family—your wife and children."

"No children," he said. He looked at her for a moment, and readjusted his glasses, as if trying to believe that she really stood there, that he really was seeing her. "I am not married."

Camelia suddenly found herself inspecting the photograph of President Sadat on the wall. She thought, how unpredictable are God's mysterious ways. Hadn't she just moments ago been thinking that Zeinab needed a father? And was there not something happening right now between herself and this man? She looked again at Mansour and noticed that the top button of his shirt was missing. He was hardly one of the rich businessmen and Saudi princes she was used to.

Could I marry such a man?

Yes. *Yes.*

"I won't give up, Miss Rasheed," he was saying. "I love this country. Egypt was great once, she can be great again. If you had an unruly child, you would correct it, wouldn't you? You wouldn't abandon it, even if that child might turn on you." He picked up a chair, tried to right it, but saw that a leg was broken. "I have a degree in journalism, Miss Rasheed," he said, as he looked to find a place for her to sit. "And I worked for a while on the big papers in Cairo. But I was told what to write, and I wouldn't do that. There are things that must be voiced." He regarded her in the dim light that filtered in from the outer room. "You understand this. You were forced to publish your essay in Lebanon. But as an Egyptian, I will publish my writing in Egypt."

She felt the intimacy of the small cluttered room, was aware of how close Yacob stood to her. "Even at risk to your life?" she asked.

"What good is my life if I do not follow my beliefs? As long as I can write and there is a printer who will print my words, I shall keep trying."

She nodded. "Then I'll help," she said. "You said you survive on donations. I shall make a donation. Tomorrow, you will have new typewriters and new desks, and you will be in business again."

Their eyes met, and for just a moment the noisy, ancient city around them vanished.

"But I am forgetting my manners," he said quietly. "Come, I'll send for tea," and he offered his arm to lead her into the outer office.

His sleeve rode up and Camelia said, "There's a bruise on your wrist—" But when she looked again, she received a shock. It was not a bruise, but a tattoo.

Of a Coptic cross.

=

Amira did not want to do what she was about to do, but she had no choice. She reached under the folded white garments, still waiting for the pilgrimage to Mecca she was soon going to make, and brought out the wooden box inlaid with ivory, its lid inscribed: *God, the Compassionate.*

God's anger with Ibrahim was evident in the daughter Huda had just given birth to, her fifth; in Fadilla's miscarriage; in Amira's failure to find a suitable second wife for Ibrahim; in her lack of success in finding a husband for Camelia; and finally, in Ibrahim's insane plan to divide the house, converting one half into rental units, leaving the other half for the family.

Amira was not going to allow that to happen.

Which was why a stranger was due to arrive at any moment, and for whom she must be prepared. With a sigh she closed the drawer that contained her pilgrim's robes and carried the box into the small, private parlor off the grand salon, a tastefully decorated room set aside for entertaining special guests without interference from the family. Amira had tidied the room and prepared the refreshments herself—this was a meeting the family must not know about. As she inspected the brass coffee urn, the platter of pastries and fresh fruit, she heard the doorbell ring. A moment later, a servant brought Amira's visitor into the small parlor, and left, closing the door.

Amira assessed Nabil el-Fahed in an instant: a man in his fifties, elegant, she thought, with not much gray in the dark hair, of a fine build that carried his tailored suit well, a good-looking man who reminded her of the late President Nasser, with a large nose and determined jaw. Wealthy, she thought, very wealthy. And unburdened, therefore, by financial troubles. "Peace to you and the compassion of God, Mr. Fahed," she said, enjoining him to take a seat as she poured the coffee. "You honor my house."

"And to you peace and the compassion of God and his blessings," he said, sitting down. "The honor is mine, Sayyida."

Amira had first heard of Nabil el-Fahed through Mrs. Abdel Rahman, who had spoken his praises after she purchased an antique sofa and chair from him. He was one of the best antiques experts in Cairo, everyone said, also an appraiser of rare and fine jewelry. And on top of that, honest. And so, in her desperation to save the house from being carved up and rented to strangers, Amira had decided that it was time to part with the jewelry she had once sworn would never leave the family— among it, the antique carnelian ring Andreas Skouras had given her as a token of his love.

"The khamsins will be starting soon," Amira said, as she handed Fahed coffee and a plate.

"Indeed they will, Sayyida," he said, helping himself to a square of baklava, an orange.

She sighed. "Then we will have dust and sand all over the house."

He shook his head in pity. "The khamsins are truly the housewife's scourge."

Being a professional appraiser, Nabil el-Fahed did a rapid assessment of his own. In Amira Rasheed, sitting on her gilt brocaded chair like a queen, he saw a woman of strength and will, her beauty coming from an inner power. Her clothes were costly and well cut; jewelry not excessive, just enough to speak of taste and class; a member of that older generation of noble, aristocratic women who had known the harem and the veil—a vanishing breed whose passing Nabil el-Fahed, lover of antiques and the older, better days, mourned.

When he had first walked in, Fahed had been quick to catch, on the opposite wall, a photograph of King Farouk in the company of a handsome young man. The woman's son, Fahed deduced, judging by the family resemblance. The antiques dealer mentally rubbed his hands together in delicious anticipation of viewing the items Mrs. Amira had no doubt invited him to appraise, most likely with the intention of selling. Judging by the size, age, and magnificence of the house, the age of the woman herself, the photo of the king, Fahed knew he could look forward to seeing something rare and priceless. Relics from the royal family perhaps? Such trophies were becoming scarce, their value skyrocketing as every collector was avid to own a remnant from Egypt's scandalous, glorious past. As he bit into the sticky-sweet baklava and followed it with sweet coffee, Nabil el-Fahed wondered what treasure Mrs. Amira was going to be dazzling him with.

While they continued to follow proper etiquette and discuss everything but the purpose of this meeting, Fahed discreetly scanned the rest of the photographs on the wall. And when he came to a picture of Camelia, he blurted, "*Al hamdu lillah!*" Which he quickly followed with, "A thousand apologies, Sayyida, but is this woman your relation?"

"She is my granddaughter," Amira said with pride.

He shook his head in admiration. "She is the light that illuminates your family, Sayyida."

Amira's eyebrows rose. "You have seen my granddaughter dance, Mr. Fahed?"

"God has blessed me with such good fortune. And forgive my forwardness, as you and I have only just met, but have you ever seen sunlight dance on the Nile, or birds dance among the clouds? They are nothing compared to the dancing of the Camelia."

Amira stared at him. The Camelia, he called her.

"I understand her husband died a hero in the Six-Day War, may God make heaven his abode. And left the lovely Camelia alone with a daughter."

"Praise God, Zeinab is a good child," Amira said slowly, a little taken aback by his rather improper introduction of Camelia into the conversation. There were set rules and etiquette for every dialogue, and Mr. Fahed was veering from propriety.

"It has long been my wish to meet the lady, but I would not offend her by approaching her without a proper introduction."

Amira blinked. Was the man saying what she thought he was? Amira smoothly recovered herself and, following his unexpected lead, said, "What an understanding wife you must have, Mr. Fahed, not to be jealous."

"My wife is a wonderful woman, Sayyida, but I am no longer married to her. We mutually agreed to a divorce five years ago, when the eldest of my sons got married and set his bride up in a place of their own. God blessed me with eight beautiful children, but they are on their own. And now that that part of my life is complete, and I am enjoying excellent health, praise God, I devote my time to collecting beautiful objects." He put down his empty coffee cup and shook his head. "It is astounding to me that your beautiful granddaughter has not remarried, Sayyida."

So, Amira thought, she was right. Mr. Fahed had just opened up a dialogue for marriage negotiation. As she replaced her cup in its saucer, she counted off the essential points Mr. Fahed had just proffered: he was not married, not looking for a childbearer, had his health, was financially established, wanted Camelia. Still, she said, "Men might appreciate watching a dancer, Mr. Fahed, but few wish to marry one."

"A weakness of the jealous, my dear lady! By the Prophet, God's blessings upon him, I am not such a man! When I possess an object of rare beauty, I show it off to the world!"

With a gracious smile Amira reached for the coffee urn, mentally adding two more favorable points to Mr. Fahed's list: not a jealous man, would permit Camelia to continue her career.

His eyes strayed again to Camelia's picture, and when he added, "Of course, a woman of Camelia's beauty and impeccable reputation, the widow of a war hero, would command a high bride-price. Anything less would be an insult," Amira poured coffee into the delicate china cups and thought: the final point, he will pay handsomely.

And then, wondering what star Mr. Fahed had been born under, she gently tucked the jewelry box behind a satin pillow and said, "My dear Mr. Fahed, if you wish, it would be my great pleasure to arrange an introduction between my granddaughter and yourself—"

═══

Yacob saw the shocked look on Camelia's face. "You didn't know I was Christian?" he said.

They were still standing in the small back room, Camelia frozen to the spot. "I . . . thought you were Jewish."

"Does it make a difference?"

She hesitated a moment too long before saying, "No. Of course not. Such things should never get in the way of business."

"Business?"

Camelia reached into her purse with a trembling hand. How could she have been so wrong! "This isn't a social call, Mr. Mansour. My aunt asked me to show you an essay she had written, to see if you would print it in your paper."

Because she wouldn't look at him, she missed the disappointment in his eyes. "I shall be glad to read it," he said softly, taking it from her.

Camelia kept her eyes averted as she tried to adjust to this new, terrible fact: that Yacob Mansour was a member of the hatemongers who had tried to kill Uncle Hakim.

He read out loud from Dahiba's typed page: "Women do not seek to subvert Holy Law, for that is written in the Koran, but to repair injustices that are outside the law. That which is written in the Koran we hold sacred, but those things which are not, we demand be corrected. The women of Egypt call for a law requiring a man to inform his wife promptly if he has divorced her; for a man to inform a wife if he has taken a second or third wife; the right of a first wife to a divorce in the event of her husband taking a second wife; the right of a woman to seek divorce if her husband causes her bodily harm; and lastly we call for an end to the brutal practice of female circumcision."

He regarded Camelia with an enigmatic expression. "What your aunt asks for is reasonable," he said, "but it will not be regarded as such by men. There are those who claim that feminism is a weapon of the imperialistic West to destabilize Arab society and destroy our cultural identity."

"Do you believe that?"

"If I did, I wouldn't have published your essay. Did you know that the edition we ran, with your essay in it, back in November, was so well received that we ran it again, and received even more requests for copies of it? Mostly from women, but from some men also."

He paused, and when she didn't speak, he said, "Why do we fight? Muslim or Copt, we are all Arabs."

"I'm sorry," Camelia said, unable to meet his gaze. "My uncle was hurt by Christians. They tried to hang him—it was horrible."

"There are bad people in every group. Did you think we were all murderers? Miss Rasheed, Christianity is a gentle religion, a religion of peace—"

"I have to go," she said, walking past him into the front office. "Please forgive me, but—"

Suddenly, two youths in white galabeyas came running down the alley, shouting, "No Christians!" Camelia turned, startled, just as they hurled rocks, shattering what remained of the window, sending shards flying. She cried out and Yacob quickly pulled her to safety. As they heard the running footsteps fade away down the alley, they held on to each other; and when there was silence again, they were still holding each other.

"Are you all right?" Yacob murmured, his arms tight around Camelia.

She whispered, "Yes," and felt the beat of his heart against hers.

And then his mouth was on hers, kissing her, and Camelia kissed him back.

She suddenly drew away: "Zeinab! My daughter is out there!"

She met Radwan in the alley, running toward her, his hand inside his jacket, reaching for the gun she knew was always there. "Wait!" she said breathlessly. "I'm all right! It was just—a prank."

When she saw how suspiciously the big Syrian glowered at Yacob, her heart thumped. She had been alone with a man who was not a relative, and she had let him kiss her. If Radwan knew, he would kill Mansour. "Everything is all right, Radwan," she said. "Mr. Mansour is an old friend. I'm all right, truly. Please go back to the car and tell Zeinab that I shall be there in a moment."

When the bodyguard was gone, Camelia turned to Yacob and said, "I won't come back here. And please don't come to my performances. You and I can never be. There is too much danger and—" Her voice broke. "I must think of my daughter. God keep you, Yacob Mansour. And may your Lord protect you. *Allah ma'aki.*"

CHAPTER 3 5

As dawn broke over the Nevada desert, Rachel turned to Jasmine, who was driving, and said, "I can't stand the suspense any longer. Will you *please* tell me where we are going?"

Jasmine smiled and stepped on the gas. "You'll see. We're almost there."

Almost where? Rachel thought as she looked out at the bleak landscape. When they had approached the lights of Las Vegas, two hours earlier, she had thought: Jasmine's brought me gambling! But it had turned out only to be a breakfast stop. An hour later they were on the highway again, heading north into a barren wasteland. And now sunlight began to steal over the hills to their right, illuminating red desert, eerie cacti, and stark mountains with dark shadows carved into their western faces. It was beautiful, but in a scary way, because Rachel had no idea where they were, or why.

"You've been acting crazy lately, Jas," she said to her friend. "And I'm crazy to have agreed to come along. Where *are* we going?"

Jasmine laughed. "Come now, you've been telling me for weeks how badly you needed to get away, even for only a day. Admit it, you're enjoying yourself."

Rachel did agree that the long drive had been strangely therapeutic, as they had followed the Thunderbird's headlights along the super highway that had been built solely to connect Las Vegas with Los Angeles. They had passed other cars, California Highway Patrol cruisers, a few RVs hauling boats to the Colorado River, and a large number of "turn-around" buses loaded with partygoers and gamblers. They had driven through small, bleached towns, closed up for the night, and passed the occasional garishly lit coffee shop. But mostly they had sped through silent darkness, racing toward a horizon littered with stars. As they had made their way through the maze of Los Angeles freeways, Rachel and Jasmine had talked about patients and medicine; and when buildings and signs of life had grown scarcer, Rachel had decided she was glad she had accepted Jasmine's invitation to take a night drive into the desert. After all, she didn't have office hours today, and Mort had offered to watch the baby. "I promise you we will be back for the late evening news," Jasmine had said.

And now, at last, after flying through the Mojave, between blacktop and night, they saw the sun lift off the red hills like a big yellow balloon. In a wink, the world was washed in daylight, and Rachel could make out a chain-link fence some yards off the road, bearing signs that read, GOVERNMENT PROPERTY: NO TRESPASSING. A moment later, she saw other vehicles up ahead, and Jasmine slowed the Thunderbird.

"Where *are* we?" Rachel said, rolling down her window and feeling the cold bite of desert air against her face.

Jasmine eased her car among others parked in the sand and pointed to a sign to her left. When Rachel read it, she said, "Nevada Test Site! Jas, what on earth are we doing here? And who are all these people?"

"We're at a rally, Rachel!" Jasmine said. "An antinuclear rally. I saw a notice about it in the paper. The government is doing an underground nuclear test today, and everybody's here to stop it. Come on!"

Rachel saw a break in the fence where a pickup truck had plowed through; other cars had followed it, and a large crowd was gathering in the chilly dawn. As she and Jasmine walked over the crunchy ground, zipping up their windbreakers and turning up their collars against the cold, Rachel estimated that several hundred people had come, with more still arriving, and most of them poured through the broken chain link and barbed wire. A few carried BAN THE BOMB and NO NUKES signs, but it was a curiously quiet and organized gathering, made up, Rachel noticed, of intellectuals and professionals, with a few suspicious-looking CIA types moving among the crowd with cameras. There were also media trucks from various television stations, as well as news vans, and reporters snapping pictures. Men in uniform were there in large numbers—Nevada state troopers and Air Force police. Military helicopters buzzed overhead.

As they were about to step through the breach in the chain link, Jasmine said, "We'd better not go in there. That's the secured zone, federal property. No one's allowed to cross over. If we do, we could get arrested."

"But all those people went in."

"Some of those people *want* to get arrested, for the publicity. The feds can't test their nuclear bomb if there are people anywhere on the site. We're not near the actual test site, but those few yards on that side of the fence are enough to bring the test to a halt."

"Then why are you and I here?"

Jasmine gave her a mysterious smile. "You'll see." As they drew closer to the fence, she searched the crowd.

"Wow, there are some celebrities here," Rachel said, astonished to recognize famous faces—the astronomer Carl Sagan, as well as Dr. Spock, and Nobel Prize–winner Linus Pauling. "Who are you looking for?" she asked. And before Jasmine could reply, she saw him, standing beside a news truck with a paper cup in his hand.

"Hey," Rachel said, "isn't that Dr. Connor, from medical school?"

"Yes," Jasmine said, watching him. "I haven't seen him for seven years."

Rachel stared at her. "Is *he* the reason we came?"

"And there's his wife, Sybil."

Jasmine watched Connor until she saw him look in her direction, and then turn away. And then he looked back again, nearly doing a double take. And when she saw the look of joy on his face, her heart skipped a beat.

"Hello there," he called, walking up to them. "Jasmine! I was wondering if you might be here today."

"Hello, Dr. Connor. I don't believe you've ever met my friend,

Rachel?" As she said it, Jasmine realized that it was Rachel who had interrupted their last evening together, when they had almost kissed. And as she wondered what might have happened if she and Declan had ended up going out to dinner, she wondered if he was also remembering that evening, and thinking about what might have been.

He had changed very little in appearance, she thought, except that he was more attractive than ever—rugged and sunburnt, with creases around his eyes. But there was no gray in his hair yet, and his stride bespoke the intensity and vigor she remembered, the energy that drove him. In seven years, she had received nine letters from him, from nine different countries.

"Where is your son, Dr. Connor?" she asked, stepping aside as more people, just arriving, pushed their way through the broken fence.

"Oh, we didn't bring David. Sybil and I came here hoping to get arrested." His smiled widened. "It's the only way to get any decent publicity for the cause." He looked past her and Rachel, then said, "Did your husband come with you?"

"I'm no longer married. Greg and I were divorced earlier this year."

Declan seemed to look at her for a long moment, looking into her eyes as if directly into her soul, and she wondered if whatever had once been between them was there still.

"I knew you were going to be here, Dr. Connor," Jasmine said a little breathlessly. "Your name was among those mentioned in the paper. I came because I wanted to tell you my news." She turned to Rachel. "And to tell you, too."

"The big surprise you promised me?" Rachel said.

"I've joined the Treverton Foundation."

"What?" Connor said. "Why, that's absolutely marvelous!" And for an instant Jasmine was afraid he was going to hug her. But instead he said, "Sybil and I are only passing through the United States on our way to Iraq, and I've been out of touch with the Foundation for a few weeks, so I hadn't been told. Then it's off to Egypt, is it? We have quite an active vaccination program along the Upper Nile."

"Oh no," she said quickly. "I'm not going to Egypt. I've volunteered for Lebanon—the camps. Their need seems to be great."

"Yes, the need is great everywhere," he said, pausing again to look at her. She saw something flicker in his eyes—a brief look of concern, or worry—and then it was gone. "I'm glad you've decided to join us," he said quietly. "I was afraid one of our competitors might snatch you up. One of those hospital ships that offer so much adventure. We need you." His eyes held hers for another moment, then Rachel said, "The program's starting." As they turned to face the pickup truck, Connor laughed and said, "We drew straws for the order in which we speak, since it's certain that only the first ones will get heard!"

A murmur suddenly went through the crowd, and everyone grew silent. Jasmine saw that a woman had climbed onto the bed of the truck and was speaking into a microphone.

"That's Dr. Helen Caldicott," Connor said, "the founder of Physicians for Social Responsibility. She's been called the mother of the nuclear freeze movement. Her theory is that missiles are phallic symbols, and that military leaders are in a competition she calls 'missile envy.' A clever play on Freud, don't you think?"

Jasmine stepped closer to the fence and listened to the Australian pediatrician speak stridently against nuclear arms. "You have to look at the planet as if it were a child!" Caldicott said, her voice ringing out over the heads of the spectators. "And that child has been diagnosed as having leukemia! Now imagine that it is your child. Wouldn't you overturn every stone to make sure that child lived?"

As she listened, Jasmine felt Connor standing so close to her that they almost touched. He had one hand on the fence, his fingers curled around the chainlink, the knuckles white. Jasmine had to keep herself from laying her hand over his.

"Well, it's my turn now," he said, when Caldicott had finished to applause. "Keep your fingers crossed that I get two words out," and he gave Jasmine a wink.

Connor joined Dr. Caldicott on the back of the truck, and accepted the microphone from her. He began to speak in his clipped British accent and in a voice so commanding that even the state troopers and CIA men paid attention. "The current proliferation of nuclear armament is not only irresponsible, it is an act of astonishing madness. It is this nation's shame," he said, "that expenditures for public health don't amount to even seventeen percent of that spent for military purposes." Jasmine kept her eyes on him as he spoke, watching how the desert breeze stirred his dark brown hair and snapped the collar of his tweed jacket. "What does this bode for the future of the planet?" he asked. "What legacy is this for our children? A legacy of bombs, radiation, and fear?"

When he looked right at Jasmine over the heads of the crowd, she felt her pulse quicken. A lone hawk circled overhead, inspected the silent assemblage, then swooped away from the path of a helicopter.

"The children of the world are the responsibility of us all!" Connor nearly shouted. "It is not just the duty of parents to see that sons and daughters inherit a healthy, peaceful planet, but the task of every single living individual."

Jasmine held her breath. She hadn't thought it was possible to be more in love with him than she already was.

A state trooper suddenly interrupted, speaking through a bullhorn. "You are trespassing on government property," he said to the crowd. "This is an illegal assembly. If you do not vacate the premises at once, you will be arrested."

Connor ignored the man and kept speaking.

The trooper repeated his warning, and when Connor refused to step down, the arrests began. Jasmine was amazed at how orderly and peacefully the demonstration was broken up, with no rioting, no fighting, little resistance. Connor got out of the truck, and a member of the Air Force police took him by the arm and began to escort him away; Jasmine saw that he walked calmly and with dignity toward the waiting military car. Sybil Connor followed.

"Well," Rachel said, "he got his arrest!"

A television reporter intercepted and thrust a microphone in Connor's face. "Any comments for our viewing audience?"

Connor gave him an angry look. "It is unconscionable that in this age children around the world are still dying of polio. You encounter a poor crippled child in Kenya and you have to tell him that that is how he will be for the rest of his life. There is no excuse for it. And while these blasted nuclear warheads are being produced at great expense and risk to the planet, forty thousand innocent children in the Third World die every day, from ordinary diseases that are easily prevented by immunization."

As he was led away, the reporter shouted after him, "Surely it is an impossible goal, Dr. Connor, to immunize every child in the world!"

"With resources and manpower—" he began, but he was pushed into the police vehicle, the door was slammed and locked behind him.

=

"You were right, I am glad I came," Rachel said as the crowd dispersed and she and Jasmine walked back to their car. "And Mort will be glad that I had the sense not to get arrested!" She waited on the passenger side of the car while Jasmine unlocked the doors. "But Dr. Connor is right, Jas, why *aren't* you going back to Egypt?"

"I made a promise to myself, Rachel," Jasmine said as she got in and unlocked the other door, "that I would never go back."

"But why?"

Jasmine shifted in her seat to face her friend. "Rachel, I'm going to tell you something I've never told a single other soul, not even Greg. I left Egypt in disgrace. In fact, my father threw me out because I went to bed with a man who wasn't my husband, and got pregnant by him. We weren't lovers, we were enemies. He forced me. He threatened to ruin my family if I didn't have sex with him. I resisted, but he was stronger. And that was how I left Egypt."

"Doesn't your family know that it wasn't your fault?"

"In their eyes it *is* my fault. In Egypt, honor is everything. A woman should even choose to die before dishonoring herself and her family. They took my son away from me and told me that I was as good as dead. I won't go back to them."

"But how do you know they aren't sorry for what they did?" Rachel said. "How do you know they don't want you back? Jasmine, you have to at least find that out. You can't go through life being mad at them."

Jasmine watched the military police cars drive past; she wondered where they were taking the Connors. She thought of the look of joy on his face when she had told him she was joining the Foundation. And maybe he *had* wanted to hug her, but had held back.

"Don't you miss your family, Jas?" Rachel asked.

She looked at her friend, at the concern in her eyes. "I do miss my son. And my sister," she said. "Camelia and I were very close when we were little." She started the car and slowly backed it onto the road, joining the rest of the departing vehicles. "How about lunch in Las Vegas?" she said.

"Yeah," Rachel said with a laugh. "And you can tell me all about the thrilling refugee camps you've volunteered to go to."

As Jasmine guided her Thunderbird into the line of traffic, she peered through the windshield at the military cars far up ahead and felt herself become electrified. She would not actually be working with Connor; perhaps she never would. But they would be working for the same causes, for the same Foundation. She wanted to drive up onto the nearby hill and shout her happiness to the world. Instead, she gripped the steering wheel and realized she very much needed to write a letter to Camelia.

C H A P T E R   3 6

The house was turned nearly upside down with excitement over Camelia's pending return from Europe. The servants had spent all morning cleaning, polishing, and sweeping, while Amira supervised flower arrangements, planned lunch and dinner menus, and assigned rooms to relatives arriving from out of town.

Only Nefissa, who was in the vestibule off the foyer going through the mail that had just been delivered, was not in a fever over her niece's return. Ignoring the sounds of industry throughout the house, girls calling to one another, and two radios tuned to different stations, she went methodically through the envelopes and cards, making mental notes of who received what and from whom, a daily ritual she considered her privilege due to her status in the household, being, after all, Amira's daughter, and the mother of Amira's only grandson. And she was pleased to find among the envelopes on this hot August afternoon a postcard from that very grandson, Omar, in Baghdad, saying that he would be home within the week. *Al hamdu lillah!* she thought. Praise the Lord. *And please grant my son safe passage.*

Omar's return meant that she, and Nala his wife, and the children would return to the garden flat in Bulaq. While Nefissa enjoyed these stays at Virgins of Paradise Street when Omar was away on an assignment, she was not the mistress of the house. In Bulaq, however, Nefissa ran the household like a queen, taking charge of the eight children, supervising the servants, planning the meals, and giving orders to the acquiescent Nala. Most especially she liked the fact that she was able to mother Omar again, as well as her grandson Mohammed who, of course, would go to Bulaq with them. Nefissa was worried about the way her mother had been watching Mohammed lately; Amira had her "marriage match" face on. But the boy was only eighteen, and a university student; besides, Nefissa felt that the privilege of finding a wife for her grandson was hers, not Amira's.

She continued to sort through the mail: there were letters for Basima and Sakinna—postmarked Assyut—for Tewfik a bill from the expensive tailor on Kasr El Nil Street, and for Ibrahim another sloppy note from Huda's father, the sandwich seller, undoubtedly requesting money again. Nefissa was of the opinion that her brother had demeaned the family by marrying so far beneath himself—his nurse, of all people! And what had the lazy girl produced in return? *Allah!* Five daughters!

When Nefissa heard the front bell ring, she looked out and saw Amira's rich friend Mr. Nabil el-Fahed, at the door. As a servant escorted him through the foyer and into the grand salon, Nefissa again wondered what business her mother had with this man. He appeared to be fine marriage material, extremely attractive, she thought, established, and doing profitably, she had heard, in his antiques business. But marriage material for whom? she wondered. Which of the many Rasheed girls did Amira have in mind for this man in his fifties?

When Nefissa came to the end of the mail, she froze. The last letter in the pile, addressed to Camelia, bore United States stamps and a California postmark. Another letter from Yasmina. Nefissa gripped it so tightly that she nearly crumpled it.

She knew what Yasmina's letter to Camelia was about, the same as the one that had come with the birthday card back in May, which Nefissa had opened and read before she destroyed it. Yasmina hadn't come out and said it, but it was clear that she was planning to return to Egypt. Nefissa didn't want her niece to return. She was working hard to erase Mohammed's mother from his heart, to make him forget Yasmina, to make him completely hers. He was her favorite grandson, because he was Omar's son. If life had passed her by, and love had eluded her, leaving her, at fifty-six, frustrated and unfilled, at least she had her grandson. And she wasn't about to share him with a mother who sent a birthday card every year and who decided to appear out of the blue after fourteen years. Ibrahim had pronounced Yasmina dead; let her stay dead.

She restored the mail to the basket for others to sort through, and left the vestibule with Yasmina's letter in her pocket. As she entered the salon, where Amira was serving tea to Mr. Fahed, commenting on the August heat and telling him about how the family used to summer in Alexandria, "back in the days of Farouk," Nefissa saw her fifteen-year-old niece, Zeinab, sitting at a window, her eyes fixed on the street below. And it sent a quick pang of envy and regret through Nefissa who, in a flash, saw herself sitting at the same place, staring anxiously through the same mashrabiya screen, more years ago than she cared to count. As she hurried on toward the kitchen, where the two cooks were arguing loudly about how many leeks should go into the spinach soup, Nefissa wondered again what turn her life might have taken if she had been able to marry her English lieutenant.

Zeinab wasn't watching for a man on this sultry afternoon, but for Camelia. Her mother had been gone for nearly five months, touring Europe with her orchestra, and she was due to come back today. As the girl inspected every car that turned down Virgins of Paradise Street, she toyed with the necklace Mr. Fahed had given her for her birthday, a teardrop pearl on an antique silver chain. Zeinab was confused about the new feelings that were stirring in her body. She had started noticing how muscular some of her male cousins were, she would admire their square jaws when they talked, and every time Cousin Moustafa left a room, she found herself staring at his rear end, so perfectly cupped in the tight pants he always wore.

She was shocked and ashamed by her thoughts. Why was she thinking such things? Was it because she had not undergone the secret operation the girls at school sometimes whispered about—the purifying excision they had had when they were little? Zeinab remembered being awakened by a scream one night when she was five years old; she had peeked into the bathroom and seen her cousin Asmahan on the floor, with Auntie Tahia restraining her and Umma holding a razor blade. What had they done to five-year-old Asmahan? Why hadn't they done it to her?

She had always felt different from the rest of the family, not just because of her leg brace, but in other ways. The Rasheeds were all dark, including her mother Camelia, but Zeinab's skin was pale, and her hair was growing lighter every year until it was now the color of Auntie Yasmina's, whom she had never met but whose photograph she saw every time she made her cousin Mohammed's bed. And sometimes Zeinab would catch Umma or Grandpa Ibrahim looking at her in a thoughtful way, as if she were a puzzle they were trying to solve. Zeinab was full of questions. Why didn't the family albums contain any pictures of her father, who had been killed in a war? Or pictures of his family? Where were her other grandparents and cousins? To enquire about such things, Umma had once gently told her, was disrespectful of the dead, and so Zeinab had kept her questions to herself.

But now there were new ones, "a flea market of questions," Uncle Hakim would say. And these latest were questions about boys and love and sex.

Her attention was suddenly drawn to a figure down on the street—her cousin Asmahan. Zeinab felt a pang of envy. Also fifteen, Asmahan was strikingly beautiful; everyone said she looked just like her grandmother, Nefissa, when she had been a girl. But, oddly, Asmahan chose to hide her beauty. Even in this steamy dusk, when pedestrians strolled along Virgins of Paradise Street in summer dresses, slacks, and shirts with collars open at the neck, Zeinab's cousin was draped in a long dress that went down to her ankles, a *hejab* around her head, gloves on her hands, socks on her feet, and—

Zeinab couldn't believe what she saw.

Asmahan's face was now completely covered by a veil! Not even her eyes peeped through! How could she see where she was going?

As Zeinab watched Asmahan disappear into the house, she wondered if her cousin was ever troubled by disturbing thoughts of boys. And not just boys, Zeinab realized in dismay as she heard masculine laughter fill the salon. Mr. Nabil el-Fahed, the wealthy antiques dealer, was sharing a joke with Umma. Zeinab had a massive crush on him. Ever since he had given her the teardrop necklace and told her how pretty she was. And so every time she dreamed about someday getting married, it was always to someone like Mr. Fahed.

Finally a taxi appeared at the end of the street, and when it came to a stop at the curb in front of the house, and Zeinab saw Camelia step out, she turned from the window and cried, "*Y'Allah!* They're here! They're back from Europe!"

Amira rose and murmured, "Praise God," smiling at Mr. Fahed. She had invited him to Camelia's homecoming for a secret purpose: so that he could observe for himself what a good mother she was.

They came in with suitcases and weary smiles, Camelia, Dahiba, and Hakim, while family members, mostly elderly women and young girls, clustered around them, praising God for their safe return. Tonight, after the men had returned from work and the boys from school, there was going to be a big party, after which Camelia was going to put on a special show at the Hilton Hotel.

As Zeinab flew into her mother's arms, embracing her tightly and drinking in Camelia's familiar sweet fragrance, she bit her tongue to keep other questions from spilling out. Why had her mother suddenly decided to tour Europe? She had made the announcement after they had returned from visiting that small newspaper office off Al Bustan Street. Zeinab didn't know what had happened—there had been the sound of glass breaking, and then Radwan running, and finally her mother coming back to the car, pale and shaken. Three hours later she had announced her intention to take her show to Europe.

But the reason for the trip no longer mattered, Zeinab thought, as she held on to her mother. Mama was back, now they could go home.

As Camelia embraced her daughter, she thought: How Zeinab has grown in just four months! She is almost a woman! And so pretty, with so much love to give. And then her thoughts darkened. What man wanted a handicapped wife? What man would look at her leg and not fear that the same deformity would show up in his children? From the hour of Zeinab's birth, everyone had known her fate, which was why she had not been subject to circumcision as a child. The purpose of female circumcision was to reduce sexual desire, thus keeping a wife faithful to her husband—in Zeinab's case, an unnecessary precaution.

But if Camelia didn't have to think of finding a husband for her adopted daughter, Zeinab still needed a male protector, especially now that she was entering womanhood, and doubly vulnerable. Camelia knew only too well what dangers lurked in the world, dangers to which even the most protected of women could be susceptible. Hadn't her own sister been married, a respected wife and mother, when she had become a victim of Hassan al-Sabir?

The sudden memory of Yasmina reminded Camelia of another of her fears, one which had been growing lately, as Zeinab approached adulthood: the fear that Yasmina would show up unexpectedly and demand to have her daughter back.

She is mine, Camelia thought now as she took the seat of honor in the salon. Yasmina abandoned her. Zeinab is my daughter, I shall never give her back, and she must never, ever be told the truth about her real father, that murdered monster Hassan al-Sabir.

The family took turns kissing Camelia in welcome, even Nefissa, who kept Yasmina's letter secure in her pocket; later, she would destroy it as she had the other. And when everyone had settled down and tea and pastries were brought out, Amira introduced Mr. Fahed to Camelia, Dahiba, and Hakim as "an old friend," although they had never heard his name before.

Camelia said, "Welcome to our house, Mr. Fahed. May God grant you peace." But she threw her grandmother a curious look. Why had Amira invited this stranger to the house at this time? There surely was a reason behind it; Camelia had never known her grandmother to act without a purpose.

Amira said, with unmistakable pride, "Mr. Fahed is an appraiser of fine things."

"Indeed?" Camelia said, wondering if some of the family's antiques were about to be sold. "It must be an interesting endeavor, Mr. Fahed."

He smiled and said, "It is an endeavor that, thanks to God, brings me into the company of such fine and gracious people as Sayyida Amira. I enjoy appraising beautiful things, so delightful to the eye. I am also," he added significantly, "a collector. I devote my life to surrounding myself by beauty, Miss Camelia. Which is why I have had the joy of watching your show many times."

There was a brief silence, in which the adults in the salon, including Nefissa whose face now registered shock, began to understand the true purpose of Mr. Fahed's visit. And when Amira added, "Mr. Fahed was just saying to me how extraordinary he finds it that you're not married, my dear," Hakim Raouf, also taken by surprise, skillfully stepped in. The duty of safeguarding a woman's honor in marriage negotiations normally fell to her father but, as Ibrahim was not present, her uncle assumed the role. "Alas, Mr. Fahed," Raouf said, barely disguising his delight for Camelia, "men like to watch beautiful women dance, but they don't wish to marry a dancer."

Fahed's eyes swept over Dahiba, who had retired from performing but who was still beautiful at fifty-seven. "You appear to be an exception, Mr. Raouf," he said, taking care not to make direct reference to Hakim's wife, nor to look at her for too long, as both would have been highly offensive. "As I would be, if I were married to a dancer whom all Egypt adored. I would not be so selfish as to hide her away from those who worship her."

Camelia, remaining silent now that Hakim was speaking for her, was amazed to realize that, after years of being passed over as marriage material, and having listened to marriage negotiations for her female cousins, this conversation, wonder of wonders, should be concerning herself! She listened in awe as Hakim and Fahed artfully discussed a subject without ever actually it bringing up—any direct reference on the part of either of them would be a gross impropriety—and she pondered the remarkable coincidence of it. Because hadn't she herself been thinking of marriage lately, for Zeinab's sake? But that was as far as Camelia's thinking had gone, because who could she marry, who would marry a dancer? And now here was Mr. Fahed actually proposing to her, through her family, and she began to wonder what it would be like to be married to such a man. He was certainly attractive, clearly well-to-do, and, judging by the way Zeinab smiled at him, had already won her daughter's approval.

As Hakim diplomatically extracted the vital details from Mr. Fahed— an address in the expensive Heliopolis district, a family background that included two pashas and a bey, and a solid financial base that impressed even the rich Raouf—Camelia watched the attractive antiques dealer out of the corner of her eye.

Mr. Fahed was not looking for a wife to give him babies. "I am a collector," he had said. "Of beautiful things."

But did she want such a husband?

She had gone to Europe to get Yacob Mansour out of her system. For four months, as she had danced before enthusiastic audiences at hotels and clubs in Paris, Munich, and Rome, she had not been able to forget the feel of Yacob's body against hers, the way he had held her so tightly and protectively when the vandals had broken the window at his newspaper office. Yacob had smelled of soap and tobacco, and a provocative spice she could not identify. And even now, as she pictured him, slightly pudgy, with thinning hair and old-fashioned, wire-rimmed glasses, she still felt his kiss burned into her lips, his body permanently imprinted into hers. In the end, she had failed to free herself of him. But she had made a decision. She would never see him again.

Especially now, with religious violence tearing Cairo apart. While she and Dahiba were away, the situation between the Muslims and Coptic Christians had worsened. Police were now stationed in front of every Coptic church in Cairo, Muslims were displaying the Koran on the dashboards of their cars, Christians had pictures of Pope Shenouda on their bumpers, and Muslims had stickers that read, THERE IS NO GOD BUT GOD. During the taxi ride from the airport, the driver had told her about the arrests that were going on around Cairo—"Anyone who is even suspected of having a tie to these acts of religious violence is being brought in."

For everyone's sake, Yacob Mansour was best forgotten.

When she realized that the conversation was drawing to a conclusion, with both Hakim and Fahed looking satisfied, Camelia turned to her grandmother's guest and said, "Will you be coming to my special performance tonight at the Hilton Hotel, Mr. Fahed?"

"By the Prophet's beard, God's blessing upon him! I would not miss it! And will you and your friends do me the honor of dining with me afterward?"

She hesitated for a fraction of a second, in which she saw Yacob Mansour's face, his glasses lifting on his cheeks when he smiled. Then she said, "We would be honored to dine with you, Mr. Fahed."

=

As soon as she came out onstage, she possessed it; and when the audience, having waited two hours for the performance to begin, saw their beloved Camelia, awash in gold and silver and pearls, they erupted into frenzied delight. She was their goddess, they were her worshipers. As she seemed to glide around the stage in her signature introduction, sweeping her veil through the air as if trying to gather the glittering light, men stood up and shouted, "*Allah!* Oh, sweet honey!" Camelia laughed and held out her arms as if to embrace them all, paying particular attention to those closest to the stage because she had promised herself that she would not search the audience for Yacob; she would find Nabil el-Fahed and single him out for a special smile. But she would not look for Yacob.

She released the veil and began a sensual dance, every muscle under tight control, abdomen rippling, hips shimmying in rapid, tight circles while her arms floated effortlessly up and out. She flirted with her audience; she played with them, and then drew back, becoming the Arab ideal of femininity: desirable yet inaccessible. Seeing Mr. Fahed at one of the coveted front tables, in a dark-blue, tailored suit accessorized with a gold Rolex and gold rings, rich, polished, and elegant, she gave him the special smile. She moved around the stage, her eyes sweeping the adoring faces until, finally unable to help herself, she looked all the way to the back of the room.

Yacob wasn't there.

When the music suddenly dropped away until only a flute was playing, the ancient wooden *nai* of Upper Egypt, which produced a haunting, mournful sound like that of a snake-charmer, the arcs dimmed, leaving Camelia in a single column of light. And as she began slow, hypnotic movements that made people think of cobras and smoke, her sad, melancholy moves seemed to come directly from her heart.

The number ended, and she retreated amid deafening applause. As her twenty back-up dancers took over, filling the stage with a lively folk dance performed in galabeyas and accompanied by shouts and zaghareets, Camelia hurried into her dressing room, where her assistants and a hairdresser helped her with a costume change.

Hakim startled them by bursting in and crying, "Mansour's newspaper office was bombed an hour ago!"

"What! Was anyone in there? Is he hurt?"

"I don't know. God pray for us, this is terrible! He printed Dahiba's article and now—"

"I must go," Camelia said, reaching for the black melaya she wore in her folk number. "Take care of Zeinab for me, take her to your place, and tell Radwan to stay with her, she is not to be left alone."

"Camelia, wait! I will come with you!"

But she was gone.

=

The alley was in chaos, with people jamming the way, making it impossible for the police cars to get by. Camelia parked at the end and elbowed her way through, and when she saw the gutted building, the glass and papers strewn everywhere, she broke into a run.

Yacob was inside, slightly dazed, picking through smoldering debris. "Praise God!" she cried, running into his arms.

The spectators gasped, recognizing her. Camelia's name was carried through the crowd along with cries of "*Allah!*" as everyone wondered what the beloved Camelia had to do with a subversive newsman.

She searched his face. Yacob's glasses were broken, and blood was streaming from a head wound. "Who did this?"

"I don't know," he said, still shaken.

"Oh, why can't we all live in peace!"

"You can't shake hands with a clenched fist." He stared at her, as if suddenly realizing she was there. "You're back from Europe!" And then he caught a glimpse of pearls and pink chiffon beneath the black cloak. "Your show! It was tonight! What are you doing here?"

"When I heard—" She touched his forehead. "You're hurt. Let me take you to a doctor."

But he took her hands and said in an urgent tone, "Camelia, listen to me. You must go away from here. Now, quickly. Arrests have been taking place ever since you left. Sadat is sweeping Cairo for intellectuals and liberals, who they say are fomenting sectarian strife. They are being arrested under the Law for the Protection of Values from Shame. And under this new law, anyone can be held for indefinite periods of detention. Last week, my brother was arrested. And then, yesterday, they came for Youssef Haddad, the writer. I do not know who bombed my office, Camelia. Perhaps it was the Muslim Brotherhood. Perhaps it was the government. All I know is you are in danger if you are seen with me."

"By God, I won't leave you! And you can't go home, it isn't safe. Come with me," she said, turning back to the alley. "My car is parked on Al Bustan Street. Hurry. The secret police might be here any minute."

=

Yacob stood on the balcony of Camelia's penthouse and felt the refreshing breath of the Nile against his face. She had washed and bandaged his wound, and now she was inside, tuning the radio for news. He gripped the iron railing and looked down at the black Nile where feluccas filled with tourists crisscrossed the current. He wished he hadn't come. The crowd in the alley had seen them leave together. Now she, too, was in danger.

"Nothing on the news about it," Camelia said, as she came out and stood next to him. She had changed from her cabaret costume into a white linen galabeya with gold embroidery on the sleeves and collar. Her hair was down, and she had removed her stage makeup. She had hoped the cold water on her face would cool her, but she was feverish, as if the August heat had permeated her skin and settled in her bones. After she had cleaned and bandaged Yacob's wound, they had sat on the sofa, their knees lightly touching. And when her fingertips had brushed his skin, she had felt a shock go through her.

She thought of the refined and rich Nabil el-Fahed, and decided that he had moved her to as much passion as one of his antique chairs. But Yacob Mansour, who still hadn't managed to replace a missing button on his shirt . . . What now? she wondered, watching his profile and realizing that, by bringing him here, they had both taken a dangerous and irreversible step.

He was looking up at the stars, studying their arcane messages, and finally he said softly, "Tomorrow Sirius will make its annual rising. You can see where it will appear on the horizon by following the three stars in Orion's belt. They point the way, there, do you see?"

He stood very close to her, his arm raised. Camelia nodded, unable to speak.

"In ancient times," he said, his gentle voice riding the Nile breeze, "before the birth of Jesus, Sirius was the star of Hermes, a young savior god, and every year Egyptians regarded the first sighting of the star on the horizon as a sign that the rebirth of Hermes was at hand. And those three stars in Orion's belt, which point directly to the place on the horizon where the star will appear, were called the Three Wise Men. And if you follow them"—he traced a path in the sky from Orion to the horizon—"you will find the star of Hermes." He looked at her. "I love you, Camelia. I want to touch you."

"Please don't," she said. "There are things about me that you don't know—"

"I know all that I need to know. I want to marry you, Camelia."

"Listen, Yacob," she said, speaking quickly before her courage fled. "Zeinab is not my daughter, she is my niece. But no one knows this. I am not a widow, I have never been married." She looked away. "I have never even . . . been with a man."

"And is this something to be ashamed of?"

"A woman of my age, whom Egyptians call the Goddess of Love?"

"How can you be ashamed, when all the holy women in history were virgins?"

"I am no holy woman."

"When you were away in Europe, every day was torture for me. I love you, Camelia, and I want to marry you. That is all I care about."

She left the balcony and went into the living room: a song was playing on the radio, and the seductive voice of Farid al-Attrach spun words of romance and love on the warm night air. "There is more," she said, turning to face him. "The reason I never married is that I cannot have children. I was ill when I was young, a fever—"

"I don't want children," he said, taking her by the shoulders. "I want you."

"But we are of different faiths!" she cried, pulling away.

"Even the Prophet had a Christian wife."

"Yacob, it is impossible for us to marry. Your family would never accept your having a dancer for a wife, and my family would not approve of my choosing a non-Muslim to be Zeinab's father. And what would my fans think, and your devoted readers? Both sides would accuse us of being traitors!"

"Is it traitorous to follow your heart?" he said softly, drawing her to him again. "I swear that I have loved you, Camelia, since the day I wrote that first review of your performance, years ago. I have wanted you since that day, and now that I have you, my cherished one, I am not going to let you go."

When he kissed her there was no more resistance. She returned his kiss and held him tightly. They made love first on the floor, right where they stood, sinking to the carpet that had once graced a magnificent salon in King Farouk's palace. They made love quickly, with the hunger and urgency of those who see their days rushing by. And then Camelia led him into the bedroom, where satin sheets the color of a sunrise spilled from an enormous bed, and this time the lovemaking was done slowly, each touch and sensation savored with the knowledge that their days from this moment on were going to be spent together.

And later, after they had bathed and dressed and caught their breath, they examined reality and agreed that, somehow, they would face the future, with all its complexities and difficulties, together. But it was as Yacob was reaching for her a third time that the hot night was shattered by a sudden pounding at the door.

Before either could react, the door came crashing down, and men with guns and badges and handcuffs rushed in and arrested them under the Law of the Protection of Values from Shame.

CHAPTER 37

When Jasmine heard the Call to Prayer, she was flooded with such feelings of warmth and security and home, that she laughed out loud. And her laughter woke her up.

She lay in bed for a moment, trying to remember her dream: Cairo's smoky morning, birds on rooftops noisily congratulating themselves on the dawn, the streets quickly becoming congested with Fiats and donkey carts. And over it all, the pervasive, earthy fragrance of the Nile.

Even though no muezzin called out over the Pacific Ocean to lead her in prayer, Jasmine performed the ritual ablutions in the bathroom and then knelt in the pale dawn and went through the prostrations. When she was finished, she remained kneeling, listening to the symphony of seagulls and crashing waves that came in on the September breeze. She knew that it was going to be a long time before she heard the Call to Prayer over Cairo again.

She had never heard from Camelia.

To the family she was still dead; not even her sister would forgive her. So be it. But if she couldn't return to Egypt, Jasmine was still leaving the United States. And now she had to finish the packing she had begun the night before, because Rachel was due at any minute to take her to the airport.

Jasmine packed with care, following the guidelines provided by the

Treverton Foundation. Since the Middle East was her destination, she packed lightweight cotton clothes, sun protection, insect protection, and reliable shoes. On top of these she placed her son's photograph—Mohammed at seventeen—as well as a photograph of Greg and herself on Santa Monica Pier, two hopeful people wondering when the magic was going to happen. She also packed *The Sentence of Woman*, which Maryam Misrahi had given her, and *When You Have to Be the Doctor*, in which she had folded an article from the *Los Angeles Times* that had appeared the day after the demonstration at the Nevada Test Site. The item was accompanied by a photograph of Dr. Declan Connor being arrested.

She closed and locked her suitcase just as Rachel appeared at the door, knocking as she walked in. "Ready?" she said, car keys still in her hand.

"Let me get my hat and my purse."

Rachel followed her into the bedroom which, stripped bare, looked as if it had never been occupied. "What are you going to do with your things?" Rachel asked, noting the pillowcase crammed with bedding and towels. In the living room she had seen boxes containing pots and pans, dishes, a record player.

Jasmine fixed the wide-brimmed straw bonnet to her head with a long, old-fashioned hat pin and said, "The landlady is going to donate it to the Salvation Army. I certainly don't need any of it where I'm going."

Rachel contemplated the one suitcase, the canvas carry-on, and Jasmine's purse, and marveled that a thirty-five-year-old woman, a doctor, could condense her life into such a small space. Already, the house Rachel shared with her husband Mort was so filled with furniture and possessions that they were talking about moving to a bigger place.

"Lebanon!" she murmured, shaking her head. "Why on earth did you choose to go to Lebanon? And refugee camps, at that."

"Because the Palestinian refugees are victims, and I know what it's like to be a victim." Jasmine looked at her friend in the mirror. "In Egypt, when someone is cast out of the family, as I was, it's as good as a death sentence. And a woman without a family has the hardest life of all. The Palestinians are outcasts, and the women and children are being hit the hardest. When the Foundation told me that they were putting this joint project together with the United Nations Welfare and Relief

Agency, I had to volunteer. But don't worry, I'll be all right." She reached for the canvas tote bag that served as her purse, and a few items spilled out onto the bed; among them was a photograph.

Rachel picked it up and looked at it. She had seen it before, a photo of five children in a garden, grinning enthusiastically. "Who are they again? I know one of them is you."

Jasmine took the picture, regarded it for a moment, and then pointed to the oldest of the children. "This is Omar, my cousin, he was my first husband. This is Tahia, his sister. She and my brother Zakki were supposed to get married, but my grandmother for some reason married Tahia off to an older relative named Jamal. And this is Camelia . . ." Jasmine regarded the dark-haired beauty in the photograph who stood with her arm around Jasmine.

"And this is your brother?"

"That's Zachariah. Zakki. We were very close. He used to call me Mishmish because I was mad for apricots."

"Didn't you tell me once that he disappeared?"

"He went looking for a cook who used to work for our family. No one knows what happened to him." Jasmine replaced everything in her purse, and when Rachel saw the Koran go in last, she said, "Are you sure about this?"

Jasmine looked at her friend, and said, "I don't recall being surer about anything else."

"Then why do I have the feeling you're trying to prove something? Jasmine, you need to reconcile with your past. I think you're walking around with a lot of anger inside you that you need to work out. Come to terms with your family, Jas, before you go running off to battlefields."

"You're a gynecologist, Rachel, not a psychiatrist. Believe me, I am reconciled with the past. Camelia never answered my letters."

"Maybe she just feels too bad about giving away your secret and causing your disgrace. Maybe you should try again."

"Whatever the reason for her silence, and for the silence from my whole family these past fourteen years, I have to make my own way in the world. I know what I'm doing and I know where I'm going."

"But—to Lebanon? You could get shot!"

Jasmine smiled and said, "You know, Rachel, it's strange to think, but the baby would have been born around my birthday, and if it had lived, right now I would have a four-month-old child, and you and I would be talking diapers instead of guns."

"Do you really think Greg would have left you to raise the child alone? I mean, he's a decent guy."

"Decent, yes. But you didn't see the terror in his eyes when I told him I was pregnant."

"Well," Rachel said, as she picked up the suitcase, finding it surprisingly light, "you'll find someone eventually."

I've already found someone, Jasmine thought, picturing Declan, who was currently in Iraq, trying to get medicine to the Kurds. Declan, whom she could never have.

Finally she paused to regard the woman who had been her friend during her loneliest hours, who had consoled her in the dark days following the miscarriage, and who, further back, had helped her enter a strange new world at the university, cushioning the trauma of culture shock. "Thanks for worrying about me, Rachel," she said.

"You know?" Rachel said. "I'm going to miss you something awful." Tears gathered in her eyes. "Don't forget me, Jas. And always remember that you have a friend, if you're ever in trouble and need help. Lebanon! Good God!"

They embraced, then Jasmine said, "We'd better get moving. I have a plane to catch!"

CHAPTER 38

Ibrahim came rushing into the salon. "I have found them!" he cried. "I have found my sister and daughter!"

"Praise God in His mercy!" Amira said, and the Rasheed relatives occupying the divans and floor space in the salon echoed her prayer.

Ibrahim had to sit down quickly in the September heat, and mop his forehead. These past three weeks of searching for the whereabouts of Dahiba and Camelia had been nightmarish, bringing back memories of his own months in prison nearly thirty years ago. The rest of the family, too, had been frantic. Upon hearing of the arrests, relatives from as far away as Aswan and Port Said had rallied to the house on Virgins of Paradise Street where, once again, as in times past, they filled all the bedrooms and kept the kitchen going night and day. The uncles and male cousins who had connections in Cairo immediately began to try to find out where the police had taken Camelia and Dahiba; some of the women helped, too—Sakinna, whose best friend was married to a high government official; Fadilla, whose father-in-law was a judge; and Amira, who numbered influential women among her friends.

But, after three weeks of inquiries, paying baksheesh, wasting hours in waiting rooms only to be told, "*Bokra.* Tomorrow," no information about Camelia and Dahiba had turned up. Until now.

As Basima brought Ibrahim a glass of cold lemonade, he said, "One of my patients, Mr. Ahmed Kamal, who has a high post in the Ministry of Justice, introduced me to his brother-in-law, whose wife has a brother in the Office of Prisons." Ibrahim quickly drank down the lemonade and again mopped his forehead. He was feeling the heat, and every day of his sixty-four years. "Dahiba and Camelia were taken to El Kanatir, the women's prison."

Everyone gasped. They were all familiar with the formidable yellow building on the outskirts of Cairo, a grim edifice set almost mockingly amid flower gardens and green fields. They were familiar also with the horror stories told about the place.

Amira, too, had heard the stories, and rumors that some women had been inside El Kanatir for years, without a trial, without any formal sentencing—"political detainees." Which was what Camelia and Dahiba were. She began immediately to organize the family. The women had already sold their jewelry for bribes; now food baskets would be prepared, suitcases packed with clothes and bed linens, money collected for baksheesh within the prison. Amira moved with furious energy—her daughter and granddaughter in that monstrous place!

As she was giving orders to the nephews and male cousins to begin drafting letters of protest to President Sadat, Ibrahim took her aside and said, "Mother, there is something else, something the others must not know. Camelia—" he stopped and looked around to make sure no one heard. "Mother, my daughter was arrested with a man."

Amira's finely painted eyebrows rose. "A man? What man?"

"A newspaper editor. Well, he owns the paper, writes for it, prints it.

A small radical press. He has published some of Camelia and Dahiba's writings."

"Writings? What are you talking about?"

"They have been writing essays, poetry. And these are the reason for the arrests. Camelia and Dahiba were writing some controversial articles."

"Was she at the newspaper office when they were arrested?"

"No." He bit his lip. "They were in Camelia's apartment. They were alone, and it was past midnight."

Before Amira could respond, they heard Omar in the salon, his booming voice saying, "Where is Uncle? I heard the news from my supervisor who is a friend of Ahmed Kamal! Are we off to El Kanatir then, by God?"

Amira said quietly to her son, "We will speak of this later. Don't tell the others."

When Omar saw his grandmother, he said, "God's praises and blessings upon you! Do not fear, Umma, we'll get our cousin and auntie out of that filthy jail!" At nearly forty, Omar had grown heavy from knowing too well the nightlife of Damascus, Kuwait, and Baghdad. And because he had spent eighteen years shouting orders at men in oil fields, he was loud even in the privacy of his home. "Where is that son of mine? It's time he was of some use around here. I want him to go to the office of Mr. Samir Shoukri, the finest lawyer in Cairo—"

The eighteen-year-old came in, dressed in the long white galabeya and skullcap of the Muslim Brotherhood, an organization which President Sadat had recently banned. "What is this costume?" Omar said, cuffing his son on the arm. "Are you trying to get us all arrested? By God, your mother must have been sleeping when you were conceived! Get into some decent clothes!"

Nobody was alarmed by the abuse, least of all Mohammed himself, who went off to change, for how else was a man to gain respect from his son if he didn't show him who was boss? Ibrahim could remember many times when his own father, Ali, had boxed him and called him names.

As they started to get into cars, some to pay calls on government officials to start working on their relatives' release, Ibrahim and Omar to confer with Mr. Shoukri, the lawyer, and the rest to go directly to the prison, Amira drew her son into the vestibule off the foyer and said,

"Bring me these writings for which my daughter and granddaughter were arrested. And find out what you can about the man who was arrested with Camelia—his name, his family. We have to see that this information does not get out, especially the fact that they were alone in her apartment when they were arrested. Camelia's honor is at stake."

=

Camelia and Dahiba had been placed, with six other women, in a cell designed to hold four. Only one of the others had been arrested, like them, for political reasons; the rest, although charged with different crimes, shared a similar history: abandoned by a husband, left without means of support, reduced to survival by begging, theft, or selling their bodies. One was in for murder, a prostitute who had slain her pimp and who would have been executed had it not been for the prison psychiatrist who, appealing to the president, had gotten her sentence commuted to life. Her name was Ruhiya and she was eighteen.

On the night of the sweeping political arrests, Dahiba and Hakim had been taken first, at their apartment. Although the police had burst in and ransacked the place, confiscating papers and books, they had granted them permission to send Zeinab with Radwan to Virgins of Paradise Street. Dahiba last saw her husband at the police station, where they were booked and fingerprinted without formal charges. She was taken away in a car, leaving Hakim shouting his protestations into the indifferent night. At dawn she had arrived at the prison where, once again, she had been processed without explanation, stripped of her clothing and jewelry, handed a rough gray tunic and a single blanket, and then rudely pushed into the cell she now occupied with seven others. In the twenty days since, she had received no word from the outside, had not even spoken with an attorney, or a prison official.

Camelia had been brought in later that same morning, having been separated from Yacob at her apartment, and then the two of them had been taken away in separate cars. She had been relieved of her beautiful gold-embroidered galabeya and given the rough tunic and blanket. Her one consolation during the past agonizing weeks was that her daughter was safely with the family. But what of Yacob? she had wondered every wakeful moment in the stone cell that contained only four cots and nothing else. Was he in a similar situation, in a prison cell with other men? Or had he perhaps already been tried and sentenced? Was he now serving a term of life imprisonment for treason? Was he still alive?

And what had become of Uncle Hakim?

In the first confused, terrifying hours, Camelia and Dahiba had drawn strength and comfort from each other, reassuring themselves that they would be released at any moment. The family would not leave them here, they said, Ibrahim and Amira had many important friends.

But then the hours had turned into days, and as the two had continued to assure themselves that their release was only a matter of time—despite the fact that one of their cellmates was also a political detainee who had been in for over a year without communication from the outside—they nonetheless realized that they must place their trust in God and the family, make the best of a terrible situation.

The other prisoners, recognizing the two newcomers, thought they should receive deferential treatment because they were celebrities. "They're real ladies," Ruhiya told the others, her voice filled with awe. "Better than us." And everyone agreed. But the fellaheen guard on their cell block, who believed that the evil eye had cursed her the hour of her birth, saw no reason to treat the new arrivals any differently. Let them come up with money, she decided, like everyone else. But Dahiba and Camelia had been stripped of everything of value and so had to live like the other prisoners.

At night, when lights were extinguished and fear or anger kept sleep away, the women filled the hot September darkness with quiet, desperate talk, and Camelia and Dahiba gradually came to know their cellmates, outcasts denied legal justice simply because they were female. From their stories, the Rasheed women had learned that the law executes the woman who kills a man, even in self-defense, but rarely even arrests the man who kills a woman, because he is considered to be defending his honor.

The law goes after the prostitute, but never after the man who solicits her service.

The law is blind to the man who abandons his wife and family, but punishes the abandoned woman for stealing food to feed her children.

The law is severe with a wife who leaves her husband, but grants a husband the right to leave his wife at his pleasure, with no warning, no provision for her care.

The law dictates that when a girl reaches the age of nine and a boy reaches the age of seven, they are the legal property of the father, even if he is no longer married to the mother, and he may take them away from her and not permit her to see them again.

The law permits a man to beat his wife or to use any means to keep her submissive.

Of the six sharing the cell with the Rasheed women, five were illiterate; they had never heard of feminism, and could not imagine why the two film stars were there.

=

"What arrogance men possess," Ibrahim read out loud, "to assume lordship over us. An arrogance which, compounded by their ignorance, makes bullies of them. A child, when feeling helpless, will lash out at the nearest innocent victim. Men do this, too. An example is the husband who beats his wife for giving him only daughters. But the sex of a child is determined in the husband's sperm, not in the wife's egg; it is therefore the husband's fault if no sons are produced. Yet does he berate himself for this? No, he turns his feelings of rage and impotence to the innocent." Ibrahim put the newspaper down.

Amira got up and went to the steps leading down from the gazebo, paused there and looked out over her garden, where trees still grew that had already been old when she had arrived here, sixty-five years ago.

She closed her eyes and inhaled the exotic fragrances that filled the air, and she thought: My granddaughter is a brave woman.

"Why was I never told of this?" she asked, turning to Ibrahim. They were alone in the gazebo; the rest of the family was either at the prison, trying to get food and money to Camelia and Dahiba, or muddling through Cairo's bureaucratic mazes, trying to secure their relatives' release. "How could this have gone on without my knowing?"

"Mother," Ibrahim said, joining her beneath the rose arbor that formed the entrance to the gazebo, "my daughter belongs to a new generation of women. I don't understand them, but they are finding their voice."

"And you were afraid to tell me of these writings? Ibrahim, when I was young, I had no say in anything, I was treated like an object with no mind, no soul. But my daughter and granddaughter possess a courage that fills me with pride. And now, this man who was arrested with Camelia. Where is he?"

"I don't know, Mother."

"Find him. We must know what has become of him."

Dahiba and Camelia were awakened from their afternoon siesta by the sound of keys jingling in the corridor, and then the warder's face appeared at the small opening in the solid iron door. Because it was neither mealtime nor the exercise hour, the women were suddenly alert—sometimes a prisoner was taken away without warning, never to return, her fate unknown. The door creaked open and the warder, a squat woman with fellaheen features and a stained uniform, said to Dahiba and Camelia, "You two. Come with me."

Dahiba took Camelia's hand as they left the cell, and the women called after them, "Good luck! God go with you!"

To their great surprise, they were taken to a cell at the end of the corridor, large enough for four occupants, but empty, with two neatly made beds, a table and chairs, and a window that looked out on palm trees and green fields. When the warder said, "This is your new home," Dahiba said, "Thank God, the family has found us!" A few minutes later, baskets of food were brought in, as well as clothes, linen, toiletries, writing materials, and a Koran. Inside the Koran was an envelope filled with ten- and fifty-piastre notes, and a letter from Ibrahim.

As there was far too much food for the two of them, Dahiba selected a loaf of bread, cheese, cold chicken, and some fruit, then turned to the warder and, handing her a fifty-piastre note, said, "Please distribute the rest of this among the women in the other cell. And send word to my family that we are well." When they were alone, they read the letter from Ibrahim. Hakim Raouf, he said, had also been arrested, but he was all right and Mr. Shoukri, the lawyer, was already working on his release.

What had become of Yacob Mansour, who had been arrested with Camelia, no one knew.

The family kept a vigil at the prison, arriving every day just after sunset, parking outside the gates in the hope of getting to see Camelia and

Dahiba. Occasionally one of the prison administrators would admit Amira or Ibrahim, there would be a polite dialogue with apologies—"Political detainees are not permitted visitors"—and assurances that tomorrow the news would be better, *inshallah*. And so notes were transferred back and forth between the family and Camelia and Dahiba, at great expense, and freshly cooked food was conveyed inside each day.

Ibrahim and Omar worked relentlessly for the women's release, making the rounds of government offices, calling in favors, meeting with well-connected men in coffee shops or in their homes. As Camelia and Dahiba had not been arrested on criminal counts—for which there existed certain procedures and protocol—but on undefined political grounds, their defense rested on shakier territory. To petition on their behalf placed the petitioner himself in a dangerous position; everyone knew of lawyers who had pleaded on behalf of state prisoners and then themselves ended up in jail. Those men who were most afraid to speak to Ibrahim passed him off with, "*Bokra*. Come back tomorrow." Others, sympathetic with his plight, but afraid, said, "*Ma'alesh*. I'm sorry. Never mind." And those who saw no profit in helping the Rasheeds shrugged and said, "*Inshallah*. Accept it. It is God's will."

Even Mr. Nabil el-Fahed, wealthy antiques dealer and friend of high officials, had become suspiciously unavailable after Camelia's arrest.

=

Amira led the women in prayer. They spread small rugs on the broken pavement of the prison parking lot and knelt facing Mecca. Despite the October heat, they went through the prostrations in perfect unison, twenty-six Rasheed women, ranging in age from twelve to eighty; two wore Islamic dress, Amira was in the traditional black melaya, the rest in skirts, blouses, or dresses. Omar's oldest daughter by Nala knelt in blue jeans and a Nike T-shirt.

After the prayer, they returned to their cars and chairs and umbrellas, taking up knitting or homework or gossip while Amira returned to the chair that had been set beneath a cottonwood tree, and fixed her eyes on the ugly yellow walls of the prison. Today marked the forty-sixth day of her daughter and granddaughter's incarceration.

She recognized her son's car pulling into the lot. "I have found Mansour," Ibrahim said quietly, so the others couldn't hear. "He is in prison, on the road leading out of the city. It is the same place where I was held, back in 1952."

She rose and held out her hand. "Take me there," she said. "I wish to speak to him."

=

Camelia was ill. As she lay on her bed, fighting down the nausea, memories of the cholera outbreak came back in chilling clarity. Although she had taken care to avoid prison food, the hands of the fellaheen warder who delivered the meals sent in from outside were never clean.

Dahiba sat by the bed and felt her niece's forehead. "You're warm," she said, her eyes filled with worry; she, too, was recalling the cholera.

"Whatever it is," Camelia said weakly, "why don't you also have it?"

"It's clearly something you ate that I didn't. Something spicy that is giving you a temporary upset. It is nothing, I'm sure—"

Camelia suddenly rolled over and vomited.

Dahiba ran to the door and shouted for the warder. "We need a doctor! Quickly!"

Expecting baksheesh, the woman came promptly. She looked at Camelia and said sourly, "He doesn't come to the cells. He is an important man. I'll have to take her to the infirmary."

As she helped Camelia through the door, the warder shoved Dahiba back. "You stay here," she said.

=

The superintendent of the men's prison on the Ismailia Road was more receptive to allowing prisoners visitors, under certain circumstances. In Yacob Mansour's case, generous recompense from Ibrahim Rasheed.

Amira asked her son to remain in the superintendent's office; she was escorted by a guard to a grim room with tables and chairs, and signs in Arabic on the walls which she could not read.

When a pale, ragged man was brought in, limping on bare feet, his hands and ankles manacled, she looked around to see who his visitor was. And when he was thrust into the chair opposite her, Amira was stunned.

His face was bruised and cut, the wounds left to fester; when he opened his mouth to speak, she saw that two teeth had been knocked out. Immediately, tears came to her eyes.

"Sayyida Amira," he said in a hoarse voice, as if he were parched, or had shouted too much. "I am honored. God's peace upon you."

"Do you know me?" she said.

"Yes, I know you, Sayyida," he said quietly. "Camelia told me about you. And I can see the resemblance, the same power in your eyes that is in Camelia's." When he realized he was squinting, he added, "Forgive me, they took away my glasses."

"They have mistreated you," she said.

"Please, what of Camelia? Is she all right? Have they released her?"

His soft-spokenness startled her, his gentle manner, the kindness in his eyes despite his suffering. She looked at his hands and saw a cigarette burn on one wrist; at its outer edges there appeared to be remnants of a tattoo.

"My granddaughter is in El Kanatir prison," she said. "We are working to get her released."

"But have they treated her well?"

"Yes. She writes us notes and tells us she is well. She has . . . asked about you."

His shoulders slumped. "You granddaughter is a brave and intelligent woman, Sayyida. She wishes to correct injustices in this world. She knew she was doing a dangerous thing, and yet she was determined to speak out. I love Camelia, Sayyida, and she loves me. We are planning on getting married. Just as soon as—"

"How can you speak of marriage when what you offer my granddaughter is a life of danger, of fear of arrest, fear of the police? And furthermore, you are a Christian, Mr. Mansour, my daughter is Muslim."

"I am told that your own son married a Christian."

"That is true."

He tilted his head. "Are we not all People of the Book, Sayyida? Aren't we first Arab, and then Egyptian? Your Prophet, peace upon him, spoke of my Lord in the Koran. He tells how the angel came to Mary and told her that she, who had never been touched by a man, would soon bear a child who would be called Jesus, the Messiah. If you believe what is written in the Koran, Sayyida, then do we not believe in the same things?"

She paused, in which she heard distant prison sounds—a gate clanging shut, men laughing, an angry shout. "Yes, Mr. Mansour," Amira said. "Indeed we do."

=

Dahiba paced the small floor of the cell, stopping to listen for Camelia's return.

When a warder finally came, she was surprised to see that it was not the usual fellaheen, but a woman she had never seen before. "Is my niece all right?" she said in alarm.

"Get your things together," the warder said crisply, looking at her watch.

"Where are you taking me? Is there to be a trial?"

"No trial. You are free to go."

Dahiba stared at her. "Free to go!"

"On the president's orders. You have been pardoned."

"But it was Sadat who had us arrested in the first place! Why has he now pardoned us!"

The woman gave her a surprised look. "Did no one tell you? Sadat was assassinated five days ago! There is a new president now, Mubarak, and he is granting pardons to all political detainees."

Quickly gathering their possessions together, dropping things in her haste to get out before the warder or Mubarak changed their minds, Dahiba collided with Camelia, coming back from the infirmary.

"Are you all right?" Dahiba said, thrusting a bundle of clothes into her niece's arms. "What did the doctor say? Why are you ill?"

"Auntie, what is going on?"

"They're letting us out! Hurry, before they decide it's a mistake!"

Outside the gates, the whole family was waiting. The bewildered aunt and niece were received with cheers and embraces.

"Hakim!" Dahiba cried, going to him. "My God, are you all right?"

Amira embraced Camelia, murmuring through her tears, "Praise God in his mercy."

But when Zeinab reached for her mother, Dahiba said, "Camelia is ill. We must get her to a doctor at once."

"No, I'm all right," Camelia said in amazement. "I'm pregnant! Umma, those doctors years ago were wrong! I *can* have children!"

The women stared at her in shock, and then a silence settled over the crowd as all eyes turned to Amira. She reached for Camelia's hands and said, "To everyone the fate God gives him, granddaughter of my heart. This is His will, *inshallah*."

"Umma, there is a man, Yacob Mansour—"

And just then Ibrahim's car appeared in the lot, and when Camelia saw Yacob in it, with a full beard, looking thinner, his face scarred, she ran to him, laughing and crying at the same time.

"But how is it you're here!" she said.

"It is thanks to your father. If it weren't for him, I might have perished in prison."

"We are going to get married, Umma," Camelia said.

And as everyone gathered round to congratulate them, Amira silently thanked God, sparing also a thought for the other granddaughter, Yasmina, praying that she, too, wherever she was, had found happiness and love.

Part VII

1988

The Toyota Land Cruiser raced along the dirt road that abutted the canal, scattering goats and chickens and kicking up a cloud of red dust. Fellaheen women at the river, hoisting tall jugs onto their heads, turned to see the familiar vehicle race by, the sun-bleached logo of the Treverton Foundation barely visible on its doors. When they saw how wildly Nasr the Nubian was driving, the women thought: An emergency for the doctor.

On the veranda of his small residence that looked out over green fields and the blue Nile, Dr. Declan Connor heard the car coming as he finished suturing and bandaging a man's foot, which had been sliced by a hoe. Both men turned as the Toyota roared up the track toward them, and when the fellah saw the dust the four-wheel-drive kicked up, he said, "My three gods, Your Presence! That man is in a hurry to get to paradise!"

The Toyota came to a squealing halt and Nasr's perspiring black face appeared through the settling dust. "The plane is arriving, Sayyid!" he shouted with a grin. "*Al hamdu lillah,* the supplies are here at last!"

"Thank God! Get over to the airstrip right away! Don't let anyone get his hands on the cargo!"

Nasr gunned the engine and the Toyota raced off down the dirt road.

"All right, Mohammed," Connor said. "We're done here. Just try to keep that foot clean."

Going inside for his hat, which hung on a hook next to a calendar with all the days marked off, Connor noted that the X through today's date marked exactly eleven weeks to go until he said good-bye to Egypt, and to the practice of medicine, forever.

As he made his way around the house to where another Land Cruiser was parked, the fellah limped after him and said with a grin, "The new assistant arrives today? Maybe this one will be a pretty nurse, Your Presence. With a big bottom."

Connor laughed and shook his head. "No more nurses, Mohammed," he said, as he climbed into the Toyota. "I've learned my lesson on that score. They've promised me a doctor this time. My replacement. The man who will take over after I leave."

=

Jasmine wondered if she was sick from the turbulent airplane ride, or if the malaria was upon her again.

The doctor in London had warned her that it might be too soon to travel, but she was finally going to be working with Dr. Connor again, and she had wanted to waste no time in coming. She had once vowed that she would never come back to Egypt, but when she was recuperating in a London hospital after falling ill in Gaza, a Foundation representative had visited her, explaining the need for a physician with a knowledge of Arabic to assist Dr. Connor in Upper Egypt. Jasmine had volunteered to go.

It was strange to be in this twin-engine airplane flying low over fertile fields and canals where buffalo turned their eternal wheels, blindfolded so that they wouldn't get dizzy; strange to be flying in a modern machine over a land that was both ancient and timeless, as if she rode a magic carpet over the little villages with their tiny domes and minarets—above it all without being part of it. When her flight from London had landed at Cairo International Airport, she had expected to feel some sort of psychological jolt, perhaps a mental relapse into anger and depression. And when she had stepped down to the tarmac and drawn in her first breath of Egyptian air in twenty-one years, she had braced herself for a stunning spiritual blow.

But nothing had happened. She had hurried with the rest of the passengers toward Customs and baggage claim, as if she were in any airport in the world, rushing to make any connecting flight. Still, she had felt slightly surreal, as though she were in a bed somewhere, having a strange dream. She had had the odd notion that if she looked at herself in a mirror, she would find that she was transparent. It was the medication, she told herself, plus the effects of the illness, wearing off but still influencing her mind. For why else would she have imagined, two hours later and taking off from the same airport in this small plane, that she was a ghost floating above Cairo? She had looked down and seen desert, and then green, and then, in the distance, the city where she had been born, cursed, and died. And it had struck her that she had taken the long way around coming here, to be at last up in the clouds with the birds and the angels and ghosts of the dead.

Am I back? she wondered as she felt the twin-engine De Havilland suddenly vibrate. Am I truly back? Or is this just another hallucination brought on by the illness? In London, when she had burned with fever, she had imagined she was back in medical school, in the cadaver lab where, for some reason, she was dissecting Greg.

Although it was a cool February day, Jasmine felt hot. Picking up the paper she had bought at the airport, with a headline that read, NEW BUSH ADMINISTRATION'S AMBASSADOR TO EGYPT ARRIVES, she fanned herself. She had scanned its pages earlier, reading the editorials, the movie reviews and, something new, "singles" ads placed by women seeking marriage partners. The ads listed the usual facts—age, education, family—but each also included a subtle color discrimination, as women described themselves in descending order of desirability from white, and "wheaten" color, to olive, and finally to black. On the front page was the story of a young man who had been overseas on a study program, and when he had come home had found a bottle of medicine in his unmarried sister's bedroom. Being told by a pharmacist that it was an abortifacient, he had killed the girl. But when the autopsy revealed that not only had the girl not been pregnant but that she was in fact still a virgin, it was further discovered that the victim had been having menstrual problems, for which the local chemist had sold her this "cure." When the defense attorney declared at the murder trial that his client was innocent on the grounds that his motive had been to defend family honor, the man was acquitted.

Jasmine set the paper aside and contemplated the panorama beyond her window—a great yellow ocean, the Sahara, bisected by a bright green strip, the Nile Valley. The demarcation between desert and vegetation was so sharp that it looked from the air as if a person could stand with one foot on thick grass, the other on sand. Jasmine saw herself like that, divided in two, one side wanting to be back in Egypt, the other fearing it. She had worked hard to distance herself from the cruel past and its unbearable memories. Was being here again going to tear open old wounds?

But she would not let herself think about the family in Cairo, or Hassan al-Sabir, who had been the instrument of her exile. She thought only of Declan Connor. Nearly fifteen years had passed since they finished the translation of the health manual; now they were going to be working together again.

The pilot said something over the drone of the engines, and when the plane began to lose altitude, Jasmine looked down and saw creamy sand dunes, rocky outcroppings, a jumble of ruins that might have been a cemetery, a primitive road scratched into the desert, and finally a shed, a wind sock, and a landing strip.

She saw two vehicles arriving in a cloud of sand, bumping over the rough road and braking to a halt at the end of the strip, where there was little more than a radio shack and a peeling sign that read AL TAFLA in Arabic and English. And then she saw the drivers of the Toyotas jump out and come running toward the plane, holding on to their hats as it taxied toward them, two men in khaki, wearing bush hats, a black Nubian and a sunburned white man. Connor! Her heart began to race.

=

When the plane came to a halt, the two men ran toward it, and a fellah in a galabeya came running from the radio shed, attracting the attention of a group of black-clad Bedouins squatting with their camels in the shade of an enormous rock.

"*Al hamdu lillah!*" Connor shouted to the pilot who waved from the open cockpit window. "*Salaamat!*"

"*Salaamat!*" the man called back. Like Nasr, the pilot worked for the Treverton Foundation, taking his plane into remote desert areas, or to the far reaches of the Upper Nile, wherever medical supplies and personnel were needed. While the Nubian went to open the rear cargo hatch, Connor helped the fellah chock the wheels and secure the aircraft. Then he went to the passenger door, praying that his replacement was on board. But when he saw a woman emerge, wearing blue jeans and a T-shirt, her long blond ponytail shining in the sunlight, he frowned. And then his eyes widened in amazement. "Jasmine?"

"Hello, Dr. Connor," she said, jumping down. "I can't tell you how good it is to see you again."

"My God," he said, taking her hand. "Jasmine Van Kerk! What on earth are you doing here?"

"Didn't the London office tell you I was coming?"

"I'm afraid communications this far up the Nile are aren't very dependable. I imagine I'll receive notice of your arrival in a week or two! This is marvelous! How long has it been?"

"Six and a half years. We last met in Nevada, at the test site, remember?"

"How could I forget?" he said. He held on to her hand for a moment longer, then said, "Well! Better get the cargo transferred. I hope they sent the jet-guns I asked for."

As Connor strode away to help Nasr load aluminum boxes labeled WORLD HEALTH ORGANIZATION into one of the Toyotas, Jasmine turned toward the east, the direction of the Nile, closed her eyes and took the cool wind in her face. They are five hundred miles away, she told herself. They are far away in Cairo; they cannot hurt me.

Connor finally came back and said, "Is this all your luggage?"

"Yes, just the one case."

He threw it into the back of the second Toyota and said, "All right, we'd better get going. We've got to get these vaccines into the refrigerator."

Jasmine had to grab on to the dashboard as Connor stepped on the gas and the four-wheel-drive swerved in the sand and raced away from the airstrip. When they turned onto a dubiously paved road that cleaved sand dunes, he said, "So you finally came back to Egypt. As I recall, you were resistant to the idea. Your family must have been glad to see you."

"They don't know I'm here. I didn't stop in Cairo."

"Oh? The last time I saw you, you were headed off for Lebanon. How was it?"

"Frustrating. And then I was assigned to the refugee camps in Gaza, which were worse. The world seems to have forgotten the Palestinians."

"The world doesn't give a damn about a lot of things."

Jasmine gave Connor a startled look. Although he still spoke in the British accent and with the compelling voice she remembered, she detected an edge that hadn't been there before. He had changed physically as well, she realized, as she regarded his profile against a backdrop of yellow, treeless desert. It occurred to her that he looked as if more than seven years had passed since she had last seen him, as if, in the meantime, life had dealt severely with him. Connor had always been tall and thin, but now the gauntness was more pronounced, the cheekbones and jaw more sharply etched. The intensity was still there, the vitality and energy she had once found so infectious. But now she thought she sensed an undercurrent of anger.

"I can't tell you how good it is to see you again, Jasmine. And how glad I am that you decided to come here. I've had a hell of a time with staff. London keeps sending me unmarried women, and I always end up having to send them home. They don't cause trouble, you understand, but, well, you know what the fellaheen are like. Unattached females are always trouble."

"What about men?" she asked, wondering if he truly was angry, or if she was imagining it; but noticing also how vigorously he handled the steering wheel, as if he were trying to tame it.

"I've had two male assistants," he said, squinting through the windshield's glare, his face almost angry. "The first was an Egyptian medical student putting in his stint required by the government. He spent a month being contemptuous of the fellaheen and left abruptly with a trumped-up health complaint. The second was an enthusiastic American volunteer who came hoping to convert the fellaheen to Christianity and had to be sent home after a week."

He shook his head. "Can't say I blame them, though. It's not easy dealing with the fellaheen. They're like children, they need watching. Sometimes they think that taking a medicine all at once is better than spreading it out. And that if one inoculation is good, then five ought to be five times as effective."

Steering the Toyota onto a dirt track that bordered the edge of vegetation, he said, "Last year, a fellah returned from Mecca with holy water, which he dumped into the village well, hoping it would bless everyone. The water turned out to be infected with cholera and we were threatened with a regional epidemic, so we had to get around fast and inoculate everyone in the area. But these people are terrified of injections and will do anything to avoid them. One unfortunate bastard, who didn't fear the needle, saw it as a way of making money. For a fee he took a man's place in line at the mobile clinic truck. He had received twenty cholera shots before we found out, and by then he was dead."

Jasmine rolled down her window and felt cool, dry desert air on her face. She drew in a deep breath to clear her head. It was suddenly too much—being back in Egypt, and with Connor again. "Then I'm glad to be of help to you," she said.

"You aren't here just to be my assistant, Jasmine. You're my replacement."

"Replacement!"

"Didn't they tell you that? You're going to be taking over after I leave."

"No, they didn't tell me. When are you leaving?"

"I'm sorry, I thought you knew. I'm leaving in eleven weeks. Knight Pharmaceuticals in Scotland has offered me a job as director of their tropical medicine division."

"Scotland! Is it for research and development?"

"Administration. A desk job, strictly nine to five, with no more patients, no more bush hospitals where we have two people to a bed. To be frank with you, Jasmine, I'm sick of trying to help people who refuse to help themselves. I'm also tired of sunshine and palm trees. Most men dream of retiring to the tropics, but I'm going where there's plenty of rain and fog."

She stared at him. "What about your wife? What will she be doing?"

He gripped the wheel as the four-wheel-drive raced along the desert track. "Sybil is dead. She died three years ago, in Tanzania."

"Oh. I'm sorry." Jasmine returned to the window and closed her eyes, inhaling the bracing air that was starting to deliver the moister scents of loam, grass, and river. Declan *was* angry; she saw it in his knuckles, and heard it in his voice. But angry at what, at whom?

They left the desert and were soon driving past fields of winter wheat and alfalfa watched over by ragged scarecrows and fellaheen bent over hoes, their galabeyas hiked up, waving cheerily at the passing car. Jasmine said, "How is your son, David?"

"He's nineteen now, in college in England. A bright boy. I'm amazed he turned out so well, considering the upbringing he had. But I intend to make all that up to him. As soon as I'm settled in at the new job, I'll have him stay with me. We'll go trout fishing."

"You make it sound as if you are leaving the Foundation altogether."

"I am. I'm going to put away my shingle, Jasmine. No more house calls."

As they bounced down the dirt track between fields of tall sugarcane, they came upon an old man riding a donkey sidesaddle, tapping it with a stick. He raised a hand in salute and said in Arabic, "Is this your new bride, Your Honor? When is your wedding night?"

To which Connor replied, "*Bokra fil mishmish*, Abu Aziz!" And the elder laughed.

"*Bokra fil mishmish*," Jasmine murmured, thinking of Zachariah, who had first called her Mishmish, and wondering what had become of him. In Amira's only letter to Jasmine she had said that Zachariah had gone off in search of Sahra, the cook.

Declan said, almost to himself, " 'Tomorrow when the apricots bloom.' A nice way of saying, 'Don't hold your breath.' "

Jasmine saw the tension in his neck and jaw. She wanted to ask how Sybil had died. "Your Arabic seems to have improved, Dr. Connor."

"I've been working on it. I remember how you used to laugh at my accent, when we were translating the manual."

"I hope I didn't offend you."

"Not at all! I liked the way you laughed." He looked at her, and then away. "And my accent *was* terrible. Even so, I always could speak Arabic better than I could read it or write it. Being born in Kenya and growing up speaking Swahili, which is heavily influenced by Arabic, always gave me an advantage. It's a beautiful language. Didn't you once say that Arabic sounded like water flowing over stones?"

"Yes, I did. But I was only quoting someone else. Do you still recite the names of muscles when you say grace?"

He laughed, and Jasmine thought he relaxed a little, she saw a glimpse of his former self. "You remember that, do you?" he said. She wanted to say, I remember a lot about the months we spent on the translation. I especially remember our last night together, when we almost kissed.

They arrived at the edge of the village, where squat mud-brick buildings faced railroad tracks. Many of the dwellings had blue doors, or hand prints applied with blue paint, the good-luck symbol of Fatima, the

Prophet's daughter. Some façades were painted with pictures of boats and airplanes and cars, indicating that the lucky occupant had made the pilgrimage to Mecca, and nearly all the houses were decorated with the name "Allah" in elaborate script, in order to keep out jinns and the evil eye. As they drove past women in doorways and old men on benches watching time pass, as Jasmine began to smell familiar aromas—beans cooking in oil, bread baking in ovens, dung drying on rooftops—she felt her twenty-one years of exile start to peel gently away, like petals dropping from a flower. Inch by inch, Egypt was insinuating its way back into her bones, blood, and muscle. What was going to happen, she wondered, when it reached her heart?

After waving to Nasr, who headed off in another direction, Connor turned the Land Cruiser toward the southern edge of the village, where a wider dirt road was accommodating donkey carts and camels loaded with sugarcane. "I'll show you the Foundation residence first," he said.

They passed a billboard that read A CHILD IS BORN EVERY TWENTY SECONDS. It had been put there by the Cairo Family Planning Association.

"There," he said. "That's our biggest problem. Overpopulation. As long as people keep turning out so many children, we will never defeat poverty and disease. And it's a worldwide problem, Doctor, not just a phenomenon of the Third World, people irresponsibly reproducing themselves. Balanced population growth means a small family, one man and one woman replacing themselves, and two children fill that bill. What is the point to producing more? Where is the thought for the future, consideration for the planet, when families consist of more than two children?"

He gestured back to the billboard they had just passed. "That doesn't do any good, of course, and the television and radio stations run birth-control ads every hour and a half, but the government propaganda isn't having much of an effect, especially here in Upper Egypt, where babies are being produced faster than we can inoculate them. Last year, family-planning clinics all over Egypt distributed four million condoms for birth-control purposes, but people ended up selling them as children's balloons, since a condom costs only five piastres and a balloon is thirty!"

Connor maneuvered the vehicle down a lane wide enough for a donkey and its panniers, and then they emerged into open space where

Jasmine saw the Nile stretch before her in the blazing orange glory of sunset. As he brought the Land Cruiser to a halt in front of a small stone house surrounded by sycamore trees, Connor said, "Back that way is the clinic, where you'll be staying. After I leave, you'll move into this house, the Foundation owns it. There are three rooms, electricity, and a servant." He paused to regard her for a moment. "It is good to see you again, Jasmine," he said more quietly. "I'm only sorry that we won't have much time together before I leave. Anyway," he reached into the back for her suitcase, "I'll take you over to the clinic. We have to leave the car here."

As they walked through the village, the westering sun seemed to drench the day with colors, and Jasmine delighted in the brightly painted façades—turquoise, lemon yellow, peach—a relief to the eye after the endless beige of the plain, mud-brick houses. By the time they reached the clinic, which was tucked between a tiny whitewashed mosque and a barber shop, the sun had dipped behind the red hills on the other side of the Nile, and a crowd was gathering in the lane, consisting, Jasmine saw, of men, children, and women past childbearing age. The girls and young wives, she knew, would be sequestered at home. Benches had been set out and colored lights had been strung overhead; banners fluttered in the breeze, bearing greetings written in both Arabic and English: WELCOME TO THE NEW DOCTOR, *AHLAN WAH SAHLAN,* (BENCHES PROVIDED BY WALEED'S COFFEEHOUSE). There were huge pots of steaming beans, platters of fresh vegetables and fruit, pyramids of flat bread, and enormous brass urns which, Jasmine knew, would contain licorice and tamarind juice.

"They've prepared a reception in your honor," Connor said, as they moved through a crowd that politely ogled the newcomer. Seeing the women in black melayas with children clustered around their legs, and men in galabeyas and skullcaps, Jasmine finally felt the jolt she had expected to feel at Cairo Airport. Suddenly she was back in Cairo, walking through the old streets with Tahia and Zakki and Camelia, laughing and eating shwarma sandwiches and thinking that the future was something that only happened to other people. She was dizzy for a moment, and she pressed her hand to the back of her neck.

The villagers stepped shyly away as she made her way through, and although they smiled, she saw puzzlement on their faces. An ox-bodied fellah in a clean blue galabeya stepped forward and shouted at everyone to be silent. When he turned to the new doctor, and said in English, "Welcome in Egypt, Sayyida. Welcome in our humble village, which you make shine with your honor. God's peace and blessings upon you," Jasmine saw confusion in his eyes. And she heard the villages murmuring among themselves: What is this? The Sayyid's replacement is a woman? Look how young she is! Where is her husband?

Jasmine said, "Thank you, I am honored to be here." They waited and watched, silence descending over the crowd, broken only by the sound of the banners snapping overhead. Jasmine looked at the faces surrounding her, knew the questions the villagers wanted to ask but were too polite. Searching for a way to open communication, she turned to a woman standing beside the clinic door, holding a baby. She was clearly not its mother, being elderly and with gray hair peeping from beneath her black veil. When she saw how Jasmine eyed the child, she drew it closer to her and covered it with her melaya, so that Jasmine smiled and said in Arabic, "Is that your grandchild, Umma? You do well to hide her, poor homely little thing."

The woman drew in a sharp breath and the onlookers gasped. But there was a spark of respect in the old woman's eyes as she said, "I am afflicted with ugly grandchildren, Sayyida. It is God's will."

"You have my sympathies, Umma." Then Jasmine turned to Khalid, the ox-bodied spokesman, and said, "In all honor and respect to you, Mr. Khalid, I heard you say that I am young. How old do you think I am?"

"My three gods, Sayyida! You are young, very young! Younger than my youngest daughter!"

"Mr. Khalid, I will turn forty-two when the next khamsins blow."

A murmur rippled through the crowd, and then Declan said, "I'll take Dr. Van Kerk inside, Khalid. She has had a long journey."

Jasmine followed him into a small reception room with freshly painted white walls, and sparsely furnished with an Ideal refrigerator, left over from the Nasser years when his slogan had been "Buy Egyptian," a map of the Middle East, dated 1986, with the area of Israel labeled "Occupied Palestinian Territory," and a few medical texts, including *When You Have to Be the Doctor*. The tall Nubian was just putting the last of the vaccines into the refrigerator, and when he stood up he seemed to fill the small room. "Welcome, Doctora," he said in a quick voice. *"Ahlan wah sahlan."*

"This is Nasr," Connor said. "He's our driver and mechanic. Khalid, the loud-voiced fellah outside in the blue galabeya, is also a member of the team. Khalid has gone through the sixth grade and speaks English, so he is our go-between when we make the rounds of the villages. He's our ambassador and smooths the way, so to speak."

Nasr bowed shyly and left.

"Your living quarters are through there," Declan said. "Not very fancy, I'm afraid."

"This is a palace compared to—" Jasmine suddenly slumped.

"What is it?" he said, taking her arm. "Are you ill?"

"I'll be all right. I came down with malaria in Gaza. I was treated in a hospital in London."

"You left too soon."

"I was in a hurry to come here, Dr. Connor."

He smiled. "Don't you think it's time you called me Declan?"

She felt his hand on her arm; he stood so close that she saw a small scar above one eyebrow, and she wondered how he had gotten it. "I'll be all right," she said, adding, "Declan," and liking the feel of his name on her tongue.

His eyes held hers for a heartbeat, then he went to the door and said, "The villagers are waiting to welcome you."

"Please tell them I will be out in a minute."

After he closed the door behind him, Jasmine stood in the gloom and thought: He has changed. But how? Why? The last letter she had received from him, four years ago, had been written by the old Connor—funny, ambitious, a crusader. But something had happened since then. She sensed a bitterness in the way he spoke; his words were laced with a pessimism she would never have ascribed to Declan Connor. Did it have something to do with his wife's death? she wondered.

She looked around the tiny clinic, already making plans to find more chairs, a folding screen, perhaps some plants. And then suddenly she was thinking of her father, and this surprised her. In the years that she had been working for the Treverton Foundation, being assigned to a variety of clinics, hospitals, and medical stations in remote areas, most of them understaffed and understocked, this was the first one that made her think of her father. And she wondered now if he was still practicing medicine, if he still had his office across from the Roxy Cinema. She was further surprised to find herself suddenly wishing he was there, in that small room with her, so she could ask his advice on how to make the best with what she had.

Why do I think of him now? she wondered. And then she knew: It is because I am back in Egypt. I am home.

Jasmine went into the bedroom and opened her suitcase. On top of her clothes were two letters which she intended to answer as soon as she was settled. The first was from Greg, who had gone to live with his mother in Western Australia, now that she was a widow; he had written to Jasmine to say that he still thought about her. The second was from Rachel, and it included a photograph of her two little girls.

Through the open window, Jasmine heard the villagers outside addressing Declan Connor. "We respect the new doctora, Your Presence, but a woman in her forties, with no husband, no children, what good is she? There must be something wrong with her."

Then she recognized the voice of Khalid, the team spokesman. "That woman in blue jeans, my three gods, Sayyid! She will keep our young men from wanting to go to work in the fields, she will make every wife jealous. This is very bad, Sayyid."

Jasmine closed the bedroom door.

Declan tried to reassure them by saying that Dr. Van Kerk was a qualified physician, and would take care of them. But they were worried about her morals, and how she was going to affect the orderly life of the village. Those few, like Khalid, who owned television sets and VCRs, knew all about American women—except for those in *Little House on the Prairie*, they were wanton and not to be trusted.

But when Jasmine came out a moment later, everyone fell silent and stared.

She had traded her blue jeans for a caftan, her blond hair was hidden beneath a scarf, and she was holding a Koran and a photograph. She addressed the group in Arabic: "I am honored to have been chosen to come and live among you. I pray to the One God," she said, laying a hand on the Koran as the villagers' eyes grew bigger, "that He grants us health and prosperity. My name is Yasmina Rasheed, my father was a pasha. But I am called Um Mohammed." She held up the photograph. "This is my son."

Exclamations of "*Bismillah!*" and "My three gods!" filled the evening air as admiration suddenly shone in their eyes. Such a fine grown son, the women said to one another, and herself the daughter of a pasha!

An elderly woman in the white robes of one who has visited Mecca said, "Respectfully, Um Mohammed, is your husband then in Cairo?"

"I have had two husbands, the last one divorced me when I lost a child. I am the mother of this son and two babies who did not survive."

"*Allah!*" the women said, murmuring condolences and clicking their tongues; the new doctora had experienced every woman's tragedy and grief. They took her by the arm and led her to the chair of honor, which had a tasseled pillow; food was brought, musical instruments produced. The men, on their side of the lane, lit water pipes and relaxed into telling jokes while the women clustered around the new doctora, urging her to taste this, drink that, exclaiming over her misfortune and agreeing that all men are dogs, especially those husbands who abandon their wives because their babies do not survive.

Declan looked at the photograph that was being passed around, and although he saw the face of a handsome Arab youth, the boy was clearly troubled. There was a trace of defiance around the mouth, the eyes betrayed unhappiness, and the forehead was creased, as if the boy had been confused at the moment the shutter snapped. He also saw a strong resemblance to Jasmine.

Khalid sat next to Connor with a grunt and said, "My three gods, Sayyid, but the new doctora is a big surprise."

"She is indeed," Declan said, watching Jasmine with the fellaheen women, smiling with the dimples he remembered from fifteen years ago. She had never mentioned a son before; the young Arab in the photograph had come as a surprise to him. He wondered what other surprises lay in store.

CHAPTER 40

There was poison in Mohammed Rasheed's blood—a poison that possessed blond hair, blue eyes, and a figure like poured cream. Her name was Mimi, she danced at the Club Cage d'Or, and she didn't even know Mohammed was alive. But he knew that *she* was alive, and as the young man wrestled with this new obsession, he gazed morosely around the small, bare office he shared with filing cabinets, stacks of papers from floor to ceiling, and a fan that didn't work. He was wondering how the dazzling Mimi would ever notice such an insignificant person as himself.

This was hardly what he had had in mind when he had been attending university. But none of this was his fault; everyone was saying that Nasser's scheme to grant government jobs to all college graduates, although initially a good idea, was backfiring. It had been a viable policy in Mohammed's father's day—Omar had received a prestigious, well-paying position. But that had been over twenty years ago. Now, the universities were pouring out graduates at a faster rate than the government could accommodate them, resulting in their being squeezed into an already top-heavy bureaucracy in which men were given titles but little work to do. Mohammed's duties consisted of taking tea to his boss, rubber-stamping mountains of useless forms, and funnelling citizens and their complaints through the bureaucratic maze with "*Bokra*. Come back tomorrow." Small accomplishment for a man who would be twenty-five in two months. He suddenly saw himself at thirty, and even forty, still stuck in this dingy office, still unmarried, still a virgin, and still burning for Mimi.

He was obsessed with her, with having her. If only he could get married, then he might flush the poison from his system. But marriage was almost as unattainable as Mimi herself, because, like every other young man in Cairo, Mohammed first had to save his money, to show that he could support a family, after which came the interminable wait for an apartment to open up in this city that grew more crowded each day. On his paltry salary, how was he to accomplish such a prodigious feat? He couldn't ask his father for help; Omar still had a mob of children to support. And Uncle Ibrahim had enough responsibilities with the crowd living at Virgins of Paradise Street.

Mohammed thought he would sacrifice anything if he could just hold Mimi in his arms . . .

When the telephone rang, startling him out of his daydream, he pushed aside papers that were supposed to have been processed weeks ago—but why bother?—and answered, "Sayyid Youssef's office," prepared to fob the caller off with the usual, "Sayyid Youssef is a very busy man," and then hint that a special fee might speed things up. Baksheesh was about the only way an underpaid government clerk like himself could get ahead.

But, to his surprise, it was his Uncle Ibrahim, sounding tense and agitated. "Mohammed, I've been trying to reach your Aunt Dahiba, but the telephones are out of order in her building again. Stop by on your way home and tell her to come to my office right away. It's very important."

"Yes, Uncle," Mohammed said, and hung up, wondering what it was about. Since he didn't want to go to his aunt's studio, he picked up the phone and dialed her number, Cairo fashion, pressing a number and then listening to see if it connected, pressing the next one, listening, and so on. But at the end of the last number, he was rewarded with the familiar silence of a dead telephone line.

He looked at his watch. Only one o'clock. Mohammed's hours were from nine to two, with a one-hour lunch break. But he knew he wouldn't be missed, so he decided to close up and go to the one place in the city where he could lose himself in a daydream about Mimi.

=

Ibrahim hung up the phone and looked out the window of his office, from where he had a view of congested Cairo. The streets were jammed with Fiats, taxis, limousines, pushcarts, donkey carts, and buses jogging along at a precarious tilt, and the sidewalks teemed with men in business suits and galabeyas, and women in Paris dresses or black melayas. Ibrahim had heard that the city's population had reached fifteen million, and that in ten years it would double—thirty million souls occupying a city that had been built to accommodate one tenth that number. And he recalled sadly the gracious days of Farouk's reign, when the traffic had been lighter, the sidewalks roomier, the city having an air of spaciousness and elegance. Where had all these people come from? He turned away from the depressing sight, knowing that his bleak mood was a result not of looking at the city he still so much loved but because he had just gotten the test results back from the lab.

They were positive.

The question now was how to break the news to the family.

He looked at the two photographs on his desk: Alice—young, vibrant, in love—and Yasmina, whose birth seemed like only yesterday.

He felt his heart move. Of all his children, including Camelia and the five girls by Huda, Ibrahim still loved Yasmina the best. Her banishment from the family had indeed been like a death; Ibrahim had mourned as surely as if he had buried her. There had been some consolation for a while, when Alice had maintained a link with their daughter in California. But Alice's suicide had severed the last fragile link, and Ibrahim would occasionally look up at the sky and wonder what sky was sheltering Yasmina at that same moment, at what place in the world she was.

Still, life was good. And he reminded himself that it profited a man nothing to dwell upon the unhappy past, that it was necessary at times to pause and take stock of his blessings. And Ibrahim Rasheed decided that he was more blessed than most. After all, he was a man of prestige and substance, and a vital component of society. In a country where poverty and a burgeoning population strained its medical-care system, good doctors, the caring and skillful ones, were hard to come by, and so Ibrahim was very much in demand. He thanked God every day for continued health and vigor: despite having turned seventy, he could boast possessing the constitution of a man much younger. What better proof than the fact that his new wife was finally pregnant.

But his brief moment of cheer came to an end. Remembering the lab results, Ibrahim dialed Dahiba's number once more, but again heard only silence at the other end.

=

"Hip sways on eight counts," Dahiba said, "ending with a sharply defined lock." Dressed in a leotard and skirt, she demonstrated while her student watched, holding her arms out, and swinging her hips while her shoulders and rib cage remained still. "Now listen for the *taqsim*. Let the music pour into you like sunlight, feel it shimmer along your veins and bones until you become that sunlight. This is a very difficult section, you have to feel it to be able to dance to it."

Dahiba and her student watched the tape player as they listened, as if expecting to see musical notes float out of it. They were the only ones in the studio; Dahiba no longer gave classes, and taught choreography only to individual, carefully selected dancers. Everyone wanted to learn from Dahiba, but not everyone was chosen. Mimi felt particularly fortunate.

"There," Dahiba said, as she stopped the tape and rewound it. "Did you feel that? Can you dance to that?"

"Oh yes, madam!" At twenty-eight, Mimi had a background of eight years in Oriental dance and ten years of ballet before that. She was good, and she was ambitious. Although she still only performed at clubs and not yet at the five-star hotels, she was rapidly making her way up in the competitive dance world, and her ambition shone in her blue eyes as she tightened the scarf around her hips and prepared to imitate her mentor. Mimi's real name was Afaf Fawwaz, but she was following the latest vogue for dancers to take French names.

As Dahiba pressed the "play" button and turned to watch Mimi, she saw her nephew Mohammed in the doorway, ogling Mimi as if his eyes were going to fall out of his head.

"Get away from there, boy!" she shouted, starting to close the door in his face. "Have you no shame?"

He fell back, stunned.

Mimi.

In a red leotard and black tights.

"Well, what is it?" Dahiba demanded.

"Uh—Uncle Ibrahim telephoned—you're to go to his office at once. He said it's important—" He turned and fled, Mimi's amused expression pursuing him like a jinni.

=

Feyrouz's coffeehouse faced the small square at the end of Fahmy Pasha Street, not far from the block of government buildings where Mohammed worked. It was a small, ancient establishment with a tiled façade decorated with elegant Arabic calligraphy. The interior was dim, the walls lined with benches where men passed the time of day drinking sweet coffee and playing dice or cards, making fun of their government leaders, their own bosses, and even themselves. Feyrouz's was the special hangout of young clerks; other coffeehouses around the city were the haunts of performers, intellectuals, displaced fellaheen, wealthy business-men, or homosexuals. There was a coffeehouse for everyone, and they were nearly all the exclusive domains of men.

As Mohammed turned off the main boulevard and entered the narrow lane, he saw, not the graffiti-covered walls or the red motor scooter chuffing by with four men on it, but Mimi's dimpled smile when he had stammered like a schoolboy in front of her. He had only seen her in person twice before: when she was stepping out of a taxi in front of the Cage d'Or, stunningly long legs preceding a voluptuous body, and in the Khan Khalili, as she was hurrying through the crowd with a costume over her arm. Other than that, he had only seen her on television, playing a small part in a popular soap opera. But it had been enough; he had fallen in love with her.

And now he had seen her close-up. In a leotard and tights. Practically naked.

As he entered the square, an Egyptian woman in Western dress emerged from a dry-goods shop and walked ahead of him, high heels click-clacking on the broken pavement. Mohammed's attention was suddenly diverted from Mimi to the abundant rear end captured in a snug skirt in front of him, and as he neared the coffeehouse, where his friends were already seated at a table inside, Mohammed suddenly reached out and grabbed a handful of firm, feminine buttock.

"Aiiee!" the woman shrieked, whipping around and whacking him with her purse. As Mohammed covered his head to protect himself, while pedestrians shook angry fists and hurled abuse at him, his friends sitting near the door of the coffeehouse laughed and howled.

"Ya Mohammed!" called out a handsome young man after the woman had marched off and the crowd dispersed. He sang, " 'In paradise, they say virgins dwell/Where fountains run with wine./If 'tis right to love them in the life to come/Surely 'tis lawful in this life as well!' "

With a red face, Mohammed made his way inside and took the jibes of the customers and proprietor like a good sport.

Feyrouz, a one-armed veteran of the Six-Day War who spent most of his time playing backgammon with old soldier friends, brought tea to the shamefaced young man, while his wife, a massive woman in a black dress and black melaya who sat all day by the cash register, sharing lewd jokes with the young men who came in, cried out, "By God, Mohammed Pasha! It is your hand that needs a zipper!"

They all laughed, Mohammed included, as he sat with his friends and accepted Feyrouz's glass of tea. As he tried to listen to the latest gossip and jokes his friends had to offer, his thoughts strayed again to Mimi. *Bismillah!* Taking lessons from Auntie Dahiba! Then might it not also be possible to meet her? It made a man's head spin!

Salah, a handsome young man who worked as a junior clerk at the Ministry of Antiquities, and who told wonderful jokes, a new one every day, which increased his popularity, said, "An Alexandrian, a Cairene, and a fellah were lost in the desert, dying of thirst. A jinni appeared before them and offered them each one wish. The Alexandrian said, 'Send me to the French Riviera, in the company of beautiful women.' And poof, he was gone. The Cairene said, 'Put me on a splendid boat on the Nile, with plenty of food and women.' Poof, the Cairene was gone. Finally it was the fellah's turn. He said, 'O jinn, I am so lonely, please bring my friends back!' "

The young men laughed and drank their tea, which was so thickly sugared that it was cloudy.

"Ya, Mohammed Pasha!" said mustached Habib, using the antiquated title with affection, as had Feyrouz's bawdy wife. "I have a prize for you." And he pulled a popular film magazine out of his pocket, thrusting it at Mohammed.

The four young men leaned in close as Mohammed flipped through the pages, wondering what the prize was, and when he came to a color photograph, they all cried out.

Mohammed's eyes nearly popped from his head. It was a picture of Mimi in a seductive gown.

"She is a rocket!" Salah declared.

"How would you like to be married to her?" said one of the others, jabbing Mohammed with an elbow.

"Any wife at all!" cried Salah, who, like Mohammed and the others, was hoping to save enough money to get married. "But you are lucky, Mohammed Pasha. Your uncle is a wealthy doctor who lives in a big house in Garden City. You can take your bride there."

Mohammed laughed with them, but felt the old gloom settle over him again. Salah might as well speak of fairy tales and fantasies. The house on Virgins of Paradise Street was run by Great-grandmother Amira, and Mohammed had no great yearning to be under her eyes. His father's house was no better, with Omar gone so much of the time and Grandma Nefissa giving orders to Nala and his half-brothers and sisters. By God, a man needed privacy with his bride! "*Bokra*. Tomorrow," he said miserably. "*Inshallah.*"

Salah clapped his friend on the back and said, "They say that Egypt

today is run by IBM!" And he enumerated on three fingers: "*Inshallah.
Bokra. Ma'alesh!*"

They all laughed, but Mohammed's laughter was forced. He couldn't
stop thinking of Mimi. The photograph in the magazine was from a
movie scene in which she played an evil woman who seduces a pious
man. Mohammed couldn't take his eyes off her blond hair, so long and
silky and pale, guaranteed to drive a man mad. By God, he thought, the
laws of the old days made sense, when a woman had been required to
cover her hair. How else was a man to lead a chaste and pious life?

Mimi's platinum curls made him think of his mother, who, for some
reason, the family pretended was dead. He never heard from her, except
on his birthday, when a card always faithfully arrived. He had saved them
all so that he now had a collection of twenty. Mohammed would not
allow himself to ponder the deeper, troubling questions: Why had she
left, why didn't she come back, and why would no one in the family talk
about her?

"By God!" cried Salah. "Let's go to the cinema and see this Mimi
film!"

"It's playing at the Roxy," said Habib, who downed the rest of his
tea and left a five-piastre note on the table.

As the young men jumped to their feet, causing the older patrons to
comment on the impatience of youth and what was the use of hurrying
when life was so short? Mohammed noticed a man just outside the
coffeehouse, watching him. Mohammed frowned. The man was familiar.
But from where? And then he remembered him from the days of the
Muslim Brotherhood, to which Mohammed had briefly belonged before
his father had made him quit. What was the man's name?

"*Y'Allah!*" said Salah, tugging his sleeve. "Let's go!"

As the lively young men left the square, laughing, arms linked, Mohammed felt the man's eyes on him. And as they joined the crowds on
the boulevard, Mohammed suddenly remembered his name. It was
Hussein, and Mohammed recalled now that he had been afraid of him.

=

As Dahiba gave baksheesh to the little boy who had watched her car
while she was in Ibrahim's office, she saw a crowd entering the Roxy
Cinema across the street. When she saw her nephew Mohammed among

them, she almost called out to him. And then she stopped herself. She got behind the wheel of her Mercedes, honked her horn and pulled out into the single lane of traffic; when, a few minutes later, traffic became tied up and she was stopped beneath a Rolex billboard, she put her head on the steering wheel and started to cry.

=

The women were gathered at the gazebo, Rasheed aunts and cousins and nieces, enjoying the cool weather and the bounty of Umma's kitchen, while Amira herself oversaw the harvesting of freshly blooming rosemary, the delicate blue flowers and gray-green leaves going into separate baskets held by two of her great-granddaughters—Nala's middle girl, a thirteen-year-old who didn't have a gift for herbs or healing, and Basima's ten-year-old daughter, who did.

Just as the mother of Ali Rasheed had passed on to Amira the ancient healing knowledge she had learned from her own mother, so had Amira through the years carefully seen to it that the secrets were handed down to the Rasheed women. Some of the recipes that made up her medicines were so old they were said to have been invented by Mother Eve, at the beginning of time. "Did you know," Amira said to the girls, "that the rosemary plant will not grow higher than six feet in thirty-three years so that it will not stand taller than the Prophet Jesus?"

"What do we use it for, Umma?" the ten-year-old asked.

And Amira thought wistfully: Yasmina possessed such a thirst to know, always asking which herb was used for what ailment. Yasmina, whom I mourn every time I mourn our beloved dead. "The flowers give us liniment, and from the leaves we will make an infusion to cure indigestion."

She looked up at the gray February sky and wondered if it was going to rain. Surely it hadn't rained so much in the old days? Someone on television had said that unexpected effects from the High Aswan Dam, completed in 1971, were only now being felt, and one of them was higher precipitation in the Nile Valley, due to evaporation from the immense Lake Nasser behind the dam. Rain now fell where it had never fallen before; ancient tomb paintings were being eaten away by moisture and fungus; stagnant pools of water along the Nile, flushed away during flood season in the past, now remained standing, producing disease. Not only were the times changing, she thought, but the physical world was changing as well.

The days seemed to be racing by now. Wasn't it only yesterday that Zeinab had been born, and last week, Tahia and Omar? Arthritis had settled in Amira's hands, and occasional spells of tightness invaded her chest. But she had entered her eighties with grace. Because for years she had taken great care of her complexion, using ancient beauty secrets, she had the face and carriage of a younger woman. But her soul, she sensed, was growing old. How many pages were left to her in God's book?

More memories had returned lately, more dreams. She felt as if she were swimming in some great cosmic circle, as if, the closer she neared the end of her life, the closer she came to its beginning. Now she saw the details of that long-ago caravan: the colorful tassels on the camel's fittings; stout tents pitched against the stars; men around a campfire singing: "Ya Moonbeam, spill across my pillow, warm my loins . . ."

The vision of the square minaret was now joined by the memory of a fragrance—something sweet and heavenly. Had she stood in an arbor when she had gazed upon that humble little tower? Or had she been inhaling someone's perfume? When would she find it? For years she had been saying, "This year I will go to Arabia." But the years had slipped through her fingers like sand. She had always said, "Tomorrow I shall go," until the tomorrows now numbered fewer than the yesterdays.

"Rosemary is good for relieving cramps," Camelia said, as she retrieved a delicate blue blossom from one of the baskets. She was sitting in the gazebo with her son, six-year-old Najib, a good-looking boy who had inherited his mother's amber eyes and his father's tendency toward chubbiness. Although the boy bore the tattoo of a Coptic cross on his wrist, Camelia and Yacob were raising him in both the Christian and Muslim faiths. Because of her dancing career, Camelia had had no more children after Najib; but Yacob was content with his son and with Zeinab, his adopted daughter. And their fears of a troubled future had not come to pass. Although violence continued to break out between Muslims and Copts, Camelia and her husband enjoyed a new prosperity, as his paper grew in circulation and his reputation as a writer gained stature, and Camelia became the number one dancer in Egypt. Her fans had not abandoned her for marrying a Christian, Yacob's readers had not deserted him for marrying a dancer. *"Ma'alesh,"* everyone said. "Never mind. It is God's will that you be together."

Camelia eyed the delicacies the servants had brought out, but she did not take any. Lent had just begun—between now and Easter, Coptic Christians were forbidden to eat anything that had a soul. They were, in fact, restricted to beans, vegetables, and salad, because cheese came from a cow, and eggs from a chicken. But Camelia didn't mind. Her life had been made richer by her union with Yacob, who had drawn her into the mystical and beautiful world of a people who had been in Egypt since before the time of Mohammed. The Copts, followers of St. Mark, enjoyed a history rich in stories and legends and miracles; Yacob had in fact been named for the first man whom the infant Jesus had healed during the Holy Family's flight into Egypt.

Camelia looked over at Zeinab sitting beneath cascading wisteria with a cousin's baby in her arms. At twenty, Zeinab was a lovely young woman. Only the leg brace detracted from her pretty face and winsome smile. And consider, Camelia thought, how wonderful she was with her little brother, Najib. From the hour Najib had been born, Zeinab had been like a mother to him. Surely there was a man in all of Egypt who would marry Zeinab, a good man who could look past her physical flaw and see the loving heart underneath?

Once in a while, when Zeinab laughed, or tossed her light brown curls, Camelia caught a flash of Hassan al-Sabir, and she would be reminded of the girl's origins. And then she would feel a stab of the old fear, that Yasmina might suddenly show up one day, and tell Zeinab the truth, that she was the product of an adulterous union, her father murdered, her mother banished. There had been little fear, over the years, that the secret might slip out among the family: the younger Rasheeds thought that Camelia was indeed the girl's mother, and the older ones guarded the truth. But Yasmina's appearance would shatter the carefully constructed illusion, and the truth, she feared, might destroy Zeinab.

Always ready to counter other people's opinions, Nefissa spoke up and said, "Rosemary! Everyone knows that the best remedy for cramps is chamomile tea," and she smiled down at the baby in her lap, her new great-granddaughter, Asmahan's child. At sixty-two, the downswept curve of Nefissa's mouth had become so permanent that even when she smiled, her lips curved down instead of up. Arrogance had also joined her features, in the arching of her carefully painted eyebrows, because now she was a great-grandmother, a most venerated rank.

Still, Nefissa didn't like to think of Tahia as a grandmother; how ancient it made her feel! Where had her youth flown? Hadn't it only been yesterday that she had shamelessly enticed an English lieutenant into her carriage? Nefissa tried not to dwell on the old days, but on her present bounty. Her only regret was that her daughter never remarried after Jamal Rasheed died. Tahia still held stubbornly to her belief that Zachariah was going to come back someday. How could she cling to such a mad dream, after nearly fifteen years had passed with no word from him? Perhaps he had drowned in the Nile, Nefissa thought, as she rocked little Fahima in her arms. Perhaps he joined Alice in damnation.

When Nefissa heard Zeinab laugh, she regarded the girl whose hair caught the sunlight and whose eyes closely resembled Yasmina's. There was something of Alice in her, too, in those long smooth arms, and the way she crooked her wrist. And when Nefissa saw the dimples in Zeinab's cheeks, she saw Hassan al-Sabir.

How long ago it seemed, her own infatuation with Hassan, her moment of humiliation when he had laughed and said, "Why should I marry you?" His murderer had never been found. A man such as he, the detectives had said, must have had many enemies. The list of people who might have wanted him dead had been too long to explore; the suspects, the police said, were as numerous as Cairo's population. And so, in the end, the culprit had gotten away. But Nefissa sometimes wondered if one day a clue was going to emerge and the identity of his killer revealed at last.

When the baby started to cry, she got up to take it over to Asmahan, who was gossiping with Fadilla, and as she went down the gazebo steps, she glimpsed through the open gate a car parked at the curb—her sister's Mercedes. Nefissa's curiosity was piqued. Why were Dahiba and her husband just sitting there and not getting out?

=

"We will go to America," Hakim Raouf said softly, tears streaming down his face. "We will go to France, to Switzerland. We will find specialists, a cure. By the Prophet, my love, if you die, I shall die. You are my life, Dahiba."

When he broke down sobbing, she took him into her arms and said,

"You are the most wonderful man ever to live. I couldn't have children and you didn't care. I wanted to dance and you let me. I wrote dangerous articles and you supported me. Has God ever created a more perfect man?"

"I am not perfect, Dahiba! I have not been the best husband to you!"

She took his face into her hands and said, "Alifa Rifaat's husband forbade her to write, so she wrote her stories in secret, locked in the bathroom, and it was only after his death that she was able to publish them. You are a good man, Hakim Raouf. You rescued me from Mohammed Ali Street."

"Shall I go in with you?"

"I wish to see my mother alone. I will be home later."

Dahiba came into the garden and signaled to her mother from the path. Amira looked at her in surprise. It was unlike her daughter to be rude.

Inside the house, Dahiba broke the news calmly and gravely: "I went to Ibrahim with a problem, Umma. He ran some tests. The tests say that I have cancer."

"In the name of God the Merciful!"

"Ibrahim thinks it might be too late to catch it. I shall require surgery, but he can't give me much hope."

Amira put her arms around her, murmuring, "Fatima, daughter of my heart," and while Dahiba spoke of surgery, chemotherapy, and radiation, Amira's thoughts considered another form of treatment.

God's treatment.

==

Mohammed hurried into the house, hoping to get upstairs unseen. When he heard a commotion in the grand salon, where the women were all talking loudly at once—something had happened, but he didn't care—he rushed to his room on the men's side of the house. After two hours of sitting in a dark movie house with an audience of cheering men, he was on fire. Mimi up there on the screen, so beautiful, so in need of being possessed! Inside his room, he sat on the bed, taped her picture next to his mother's and received a shock. Because his mother's photograph was an old one, the two women appeared to be about the same age, and there was a haunting resemblance that he hadn't noticed before. As he gazed at the two beautiful faces, he thought: How could beauty be so destructive? How could such loveliness cause such misery? Hadn't his mother made him unhappy for nearly all his life? And now, wasn't this second blond beauty making him equally as wretched?

Tears blinded him until the two photographs merged together, and Mohammed couldn't tell one from the other.

CHAPTER 41

By the Prophet's beard, a man needs a woman," Hadj Tayeb declared as Declan Connor examined him. An elderly fellah with a white beaded skullcap on his head and a white caftan over his bony frame, Tayeb had earned the title *Hadj*—pilgrim—when he had gone to Mecca. "It isn't good to keep your essence inside," he continued in an ancient croaking voice. "A man must have release every night."

"Every night!" cried Khalid who, as a member of the mobile health team, sat in the privileged chair next to the doctor. The rest of the men occupied chairs and benches in front of the coffeehouse that opened onto the village square. "My three gods," said the ox-bodied fellah from Al Tafla. "How can a man do it *every* night!"

Hadj Tayeb said piously, "I did."

"That's why you wore out four wives!" shouted Abu Hosni from inside the coffeehouse, and the men laughed.

"Truly, Sayyid," Hadj Tayeb said. "You should marry the doctora."

As the other men agreed, making racy comments about what a wedding night it would be, Declan Connor looked over at Jasmine across the village square where young fellaheen mothers were handing their babies to her like offerings. And he thought of how he had been thinking that very thing lately—of making love to the doctora.

It was a blue and gold noon, full of flies and dust and heat; the fellaheen were getting the square ready for tonight's celebration of the Prophet's birthday, when there would be storytelling, beledi dancing, stick dancing, puppet shows, and more food than the villagers had eaten in a month. The festivities would start after the sunset prayer, the young women retiring to the surrounding rooftops to observe unseen as the men, children, and women past childbearing age crowded into the square to share a sumptuous feast with the guests of honor, the Treverton Foundation mobile health team.

The square itself was the heart of this small, nameless village on the Upper Nile, with narrow, twisting lanes branching from it like the spokes of a square wheel. Here at the center of the peasants' lives were found the mainstays of every Egyptian village: the well, which was the realm of women; the coffeehouse, belonging to the men; the small, whitewashed mosque; the butcher shop, where even now the throats of sheep were being slit in accordance with the Koran; and the bakery, to which the villagers brought their lumps of dough every morning, imprinted with their identifying marks, to be baked in the ovens and picked up at the end of the day. Farmers with produce to sell squatted along the walls, watching over their oranges and tomatoes, cucumbers and lettuce, while itinerant peddlers offered plastic sandals, comic books, beaded skullcaps, and neat piles of spices—saffron, coriander, basil, and pepper, which could be bought for a penny and scooped into paper cones. The square was lively and noisy with goats, donkeys, and dogs clogging the air with their smells, children running excitedly about, and villagers clustering in curiosity around the two foreign doctors, as Jasmine and Declan Connor held their separate open-air clinics.

"You have trachoma, Hadj Tayeb," Declan said to the elderly pilgrim who sat on a wobbly chair in front of a Pepsi sign and elaborate calligraphic renderings of the name of Allah on the mud-brick wall. "It can be treated, but you must use the medicine exactly as I say."

Abu Hosni, who owned the coffeehouse—a cubbyhole between the village bakery and the cobbler—called out merrily, "By the Prophet, Your Honor, Hadj Tayeb is right. Why don't you marry the doctora?"

"I have no time for a wife," Declan said as he reached into his medical bag. "I'm here to do a job, and so is Dr. Van Kerk."

Hadj Tayeb said, "In all honor and respect, Sayyid, how many sons do you have?"

Declan applied tetracycline drops to each of the old man's eyes, and then, handing him the bottle with instructions to apply drops daily for three weeks, he said, "I have one son, in college."

"Only one? My three gods, Sayyid! A man must have many sons!"

Declan gestured for the next patient, a young fellah who hoisted up his galabeya to reveal a spectacularly infected wound, and as Declan proceeded to examine it, Abu Hosni shouted again from inside the coffeehouse, "Tell me, Sayyid, why is there all this talk of birth control? I do not understand it."

"The world is getting crowded, Abu Hosni," Declan said to the coffeehouse owner, who appeared in the doorway with a filthy apron over his galabeya. "People must start limiting the size of their families." When Declan received a puzzled look from the man, he said, "You and your wife have five children, is that so?"

"It is, praise God."

"And five grandchildren?"

"We are blessed."

"That is twelve people where once there were only two. Suppose every two people produced ten new people, can you see how crowded the world would be?"

The owner of the coffeehouse waved an arm in the direction of the desert. "There is plenty of space, Sayyid!"

"But your country cannot even feed the people who are here now. What will happen to your grandchildren? How will they live in a crowded world?"

"*Ma'alesh*, Sayyid. Not to worry. God will provide."

But Hadj Tayeb, puffing on his water pipe, said with a scowl, "The district nurse comes and holds classes for our girls. This is a dangerous thing, to give girls an education."

Declan said, "Educate a man, Hadja Tayeb, and you educate one person. Educate a woman and you educate a family." He returned to examining the fellah's wound, trying to keep down his impatience by reminding himself that he was leaving in five weeks, and trying at the same time to ignore the feminine laughter that suddenly erupted at the well, where the women were gathered.

He couldn't get Jasmine out of his mind.

They had spent the past six weeks traveling from village to village, trying to inoculate the children. It was not an easy task: the team, consisting of Connor and Jasmine, Nasr and Khalid, would arrive at a village, set up stations in the square, and, with the help of a district nurse or doctor, administer BCG-tuberculosis vaccines and jet-gun shots of DPT-polio to babies between three and eight months, and then DPT-polio boosters and combined yellow fever and measles vaccines to children between nine and fourteen months old. Pregnant women received tetanus injections because of the high risk of infection after the umbilical cord was cut.

It was long and hard work, because husbands had to be persuaded to allow their wives out of the house; the records were difficult to keep straight; and mothers needed to be convinced that girl babies also deserved to be inoculated. When they were finished, the Nubian Nasr and the district nurse would dismantle the jet-guns, pack away the syringes, and load the Toyotas while Jasmine and Declan set up separate consultation areas in the square, one for the women at the well, one for the men in the coffeehouse.

"This wound is serious," Declan said to the man he was examining, trying to concentrate on the job at hand and not on Jasmine. "You must go to the district hospital and have this wound cleaned out. Unless you do this, you could die."

"Death comes to us all," Hadj Tayeb declared. "It is written, 'Wherever you may be, death shall overtake you, even though you be in fortified castles. Nothing you do will prolong your life by one minute.'"

Declan said, "This is true, Hadj Tayeb. But even so, a man who was questioning the Prophet one day about fate asked if he should tie up his camel when he went into the mosque to pray, or simply trust God to guard it for him. And the Prophet replied, 'Tie up your camel and trust in God.'"

The others laughed and Hadj Tayeb grunted and returned to his water pipe.

"I am serious about this, Mohssein," Declan said sternly to the young fellah. "You must go to the hospital."

But the fellah assured Declan that he had paid ten piastres to the village sheikh to write a magic spell on a piece of paper, which was plastered to his chest.

"You were duped, Mohssein," Declan said. "This bit of paper isn't going to cure your wound. This is backward thinking, do you understand? We are in the twentieth century now, and you must go to the hospital and have this wound properly cleaned out, or the poison will spread to your entire body."

As Declan applied an antibiotic and then bandaged the wound, Khalid launched into a story about three fellaheen who paid a visit to a prostitute. But Declan had heard the joke countless times in the past six weeks and so he concentrated on examining the next man, at the same time surreptitiously watching Jasmine at the well with the women. They were showing her how to tie her scarf into one of the fashionable new turbans.

But Declan knew that, although the young wives and elderly mothers-in-law laughed and teased and flattered the doctora, there was more going on than a mere exercise in fashion.

Connor's experience in the Upper Nile had taught him that the women were the worriers of the race. While the men passed their hours at the coffeehouse, enjoying God's two most precious gifts to Egypt—abundant leisure time and endless sunshine—declaring that all a man needed to have paradise right here on earth was a wife with a big bottom and plenty of sons to work the fields, the women were going about the business of the future.

Which was what they were up to now, Declan thought, as he watched how they surrounded Jasmine, women in ruffled granny dresses—the fashion of the fellaha—enacting a ritual as old as time. Wearing a pastel caftan and standing taller than the fellaheen women, Jasmine was almost like a priestess in their midst, whom they approached shyly, or out of curiosity, exceedingly polite and deferential, murmuring and conspiring like handmaidens and keepers of mysteries. What were the secret requests they whispered to her? he wondered. Questions about fertility, perhaps, or conception, contraception, a means of abortion, potions of death or life. Whatever it was, there, by the humble village well, the future of the race was being determined, while the men warmed the chairs in the coffeehouse, telling jokes and saying, "Why worry? Your crops fails, *ma'alesh*, never mind. There is always *bokra*, tomorrow, God willing, *inshallah*."

Declan watched as Jasmine tried again, with the help of her giggling companions, to tie the turban around her blond hair, spreading a triangle of apricot silk on her head, then rolling the ends, winding them up and around and tucking them under at the back of her neck. When she lifted her arms, he could see the outline of her body beneath the caftan, the slim hips and firm breasts. A jolt of sexual desire shot through him like an arrow. It reminded him of the many evenings they had spent in his office, working on the translation. They had been fifteen years younger then, Jasmine like a girl, still innocent despite her education and having traveled halfway around the world, and himself still idealistic, still thinking the world could be saved.

He recalled now the first time he had seen her, when she had come into his office that rainy March day. He had been struck then by her looks, finding her exotic even before she had told him she was Egyptian. There had been something timid about her, and yet assertive too. Beneath the shy façade which, Connor noticed, most Arabic women cultivated in early life, he had sensed an unusual determination. And in the days following, as they had taken the health manual apart and put it back together in Arabic, as they had worked in the close confines of his office, making each other laugh, or sharing moments of seriousness, even then he had sensed in Jasmine a division, as if two souls were struggling to inhabit one body. She would talk freely about Egypt and sometimes even her own past, but when he tried to draw her out on the subject of her family, she grew silent. He saw a love for Egypt and its culture shine in her eyes, especially when she wrote her special chapter on respecting local traditions, and yet she also seemed to want to deny her own connections with this land and its people. It was almost as if she didn't know where she belonged, and it made Declan think of the book some of the students on campus were reading at the time, *Stranger in a Strange Land,* and he thought: She is like that.

And so when the project had come to an end and the manuscript was sent to London, he realized he had not learned a great deal about the young woman with whom, to his surprise, he had become infatuated. In their sporadic correspondence during the following years, he had learned little more—Jasmine had filled her letters with news of medical school, and then her internship, and finally her job in a clinic—so that by the time she arrived at Al Tafla, she was still a mystery to him.

But then, in the six weeks since she'd come, a curious thing had happened.

The team had taken the mobile clinic to the villages between Luxor and Aswan, and because fellaheen women were the same everywhere, they had immediately asked Jasmine, as they did any new female in the village—Are you married, do you have children, do you have sons?—because these facts established hierarchy and protocol; once you knew your place, you relaxed. At the start Jasmine had not been forthcoming with information, almost reluctantly bringing out her son's photographs, and talking about the two husbands—the one who had beaten her, the one who had left her after a miscarriage. She had spoken a little of a big house in Cairo where she had grown up, the schools she had attended, the famous people her father had known.

But that had been in the beginning. After the first two weeks, Connor had noticed a curious and subtle opening up, like a house with someone inside going around flinging up the windows, one by one, until the air and sunlight poured in. Now she mentioned names; she spoke freely of Great-grandmother Amira, Auntie Dahiba, Cousin Doreya. Her laughter, also, was coming more freely, more spontaneously with each passing day. She was even starting to flirt, Declan noticed—with old Khalid, with the dour women, with the children.

She is becoming Egyptian again, he thought, drawing up a syringe and trying to alleviate his patient's dismay. She is like a woman who has come home.

And yet, he thought as he watched her across the square, she had *not* gone home. As far as he knew, Jasmine had neither telephoned nor written to her family in Cairo; she was making no plans for a visit. Considering now the determination he had seen in her fifteen years ago, the near-desperation she had displayed because she might have to be sent back to Egypt, and observing how she came to life here in the villages, he wondered what drove her, what could make her so dedicated to helping these people while turning her back on the ones to whom she was related.

=

As Jasmine tucked the ends of the peach silk scarf under the turban she'd made of it, she glanced at Dr. Connor sitting outside the coffeehouse with the men. She saw him quickly look away.

He puzzled her. Although he still resembled the man who had taken the microphone on the back of a truck and fairly shouted for the establishment of a social conscience, and smiled the same smile that had made her heart soar fifteen years ago, inside, she knew he was different. She almost didn't know him. Jasmine wanted to ask: What happened to change you so? Why do you insist that you no longer care? Why do you say our efforts here in Egypt are futile? When she sometimes watched him sit alone in the evening, smoking one cigarette after another, squinting into the smoke as if searching for answers, she wanted to say to him, "Please don't go. Stay here." In five weeks she would lose him.

It wasn't just her love for him that made her want to help—the love that she knew had been born one rainy afternoon when she had taken a fateful shortcut through Lathrop Hall on her way to the dean's office. There was now another reason for wanting to help him. Declan Connor was the reason she had come back to Egypt. And for that, she would always be grateful.

Because a miracle seemed to have happened.

"Tell me, Sayyida Doctora," Um Tewfik said, as she nursed a baby at her breast. "Does your modern medicine really work?"

As Jasmine held a stethoscope to the chest of an elderly woman who complained of fever and weakness, she said, "Modern medicine can work, Um Tewfik, but it depends on the patient. For instance, a fellah named Ahmed came to me one day with a bad cough. I gave him a bottle of medicine and told him to take a large spoonful of it each day. He said to me, 'Yes, Sayyida,' and went away. But when he came back a week later, the cough was worse. 'Did you take the medicine, Ahmed?' I asked. 'No, Sayyida,' he replied. 'Why not?' I asked. 'Because I could not get the spoon into the bottle.' "

The women laughed and agreed that all men were helpless, and Jasmine laughed with them, at her own joke. She could not recall when she had felt so happy, or so alive. And this was the miracle.

As she examined a curious rash on her elderly patient's arm, Jasmine found herself thinking back to her first early days in England, over twenty years ago, when she had gone to claim her inheritance and had met her only Westfall relative, the old earl's sister, Lady Penelope. Jasmine had been received warmly in the woman's cottage, and, over tea, the elderly Penelope Westfall had said, "Your mother inherited her fondness for the Middle East from her mother, your grandmother, Lady Frances. Frances and I were best friends, I imagine she must have dragged me to see *The Sheik* a hundred times. Poor dear, married to my stuffy, unimaginative and decidedly unromantic brother! Frances committed suicide, you know."

But Jasmine hadn't known, and the news had come as a stunning blow. Her mother had never mentioned how Grandma Westfall died, that she had, as Aunt Penelope had put it, "Laid her head one day in the oven and turned on the gas." But this new knowledge had started Jasmine thinking about things she had not considered before: that Uncle Edward had supposedly accidentally shot himself while cleaning his gun, and that Alice had died in an automobile accident. But were these stories true, or had the truth been covered up? Was there in fact a history of depression and suicide in the family?

While Jasmine had never contemplated taking her own life, in those first months after she left Egypt she had known a deep and dark depression that had frightened her. And then, when she had made the decision to return to Egypt to work with Dr. Connor, and she had braced herself for the anger, the grief, all the emotions she had kept bottled up since Ibrahim's pronouncement of death, to her surprise, nothing of the sort occurred. She had experienced instead a miraculous rebirth, and with it had come the old happiness and joy that she had known long ago, as if they, too, had lain hidden away with the bad memories, repressed, not to be faced. Just to speak Egyptian Arabic again, which felt so good on her tongue, and to taste once more the food of her childhood, to hear the distinct, self-mocking laugh of the Egyptians, who took neither themselves nor life too seriously, to sit by the Nile and contemplate its changing from sunrise to moonrise, to feel the rich soil beneath her hands and the hot sun on her shoulders, to be connected again with the ancient rhythm of the Nile Valley—all these things had awakened and revived her both physically and spiritually.

But, in a strange twist of irony, with her rebirth had come the discovery that something seemed to have died in Declan Connor.

"Do you have blood in your urine, Umma?" she respectfully asked the elderly woman veiled entirely in black. "Do you have pain in your abdomen?"

When the fellaha nodded to both questions, Jasmine said, "You have the blood disease that comes from stagnant water." She would have administered an injection right then, but the health team had encountered such a staggering number of schistosomiasis cases in the last few days that their supply of the drug Praziquantel had run out. "You will need to visit the district doctor, Umma," she said, writing out instructions on a piece of paper. "This medicine will remove the sickness from your blood, but you must avoid walking through stagnant water from now on, because you will be infected again."

The elderly woman took the paper, looked at it for a moment, then silently moved away. Jasmine suspected that the doctor would not be visited, and that the paper would be boiled in tea to produce a magic potion.

"By the heart of the blessed Ayesha, Sayyida!" Um Tewfik said, as she removed the baby from her breast and covered herself. "Can you give me a potion to make babies? My sister has been married for three months and so far there are no babies. She is afraid her husband will get tired of her and look for another wife."

The others shook their heads in sympathy. Lucky women got pregnant in the first month.

"Your sister will have to go to a doctor for an examination," Jasmine said, "to find the cause of her trouble."

But Um Tewfik shook her head and said, "My sister knows the cause. She told me she was walking across a field three days after her wedding, and two ravens flew ahead of her. They sat down in an acacia tree and looked right at her, and she said she felt a jinni enter her at that moment. Clearly, Sayyida, that is the cause of her barrenness."

Seeing the firm set of the woman's jaw, Jasmine said to Um Tewfik, "Your sister could be right. Tell her to take two black feathers and wear them under her dress, down here," and she pointed to her own abdomen. "She is to wear these feathers for seven days, and recite the opening sura of the Koran seven times each day. Then she must put away the feathers for seven days, and after that wear them again. If she does this over a period of several weeks, the jinni will be cast out."

This was not Jasmine's first instance in prescribing magic. With each golden sunrise and each scarlet sunset, she felt Egypt reclaim her—the old, mystical Egypt Amira had taught her about long ago. So that now, when Jasmine listened to the wind, she heard the howls of jinns upon it; and when she delivered a baby, she recited ancient spells to ward off the evil eye. Jasmine understood the power of the centuries-old mysteries, she had seen magic cure what antibiotics could not, she had seen the power of superstition succeed where medicine had failed.

"Look at the way the Sayyid watches you, doctora!" Um Jamal said, and the women cast quick, shy glances at Declan across the square. "May I divorce, by God, if that man is not in love with you!"

The women's laughter floated up out of the square like the flapping of birds' wings, the young wives enjoying this rare occasion to mingle and socialize, because all too soon they would have to go back to their mud-brick homes and strict sequestration.

"Tonight at the feast of the Prophet," Um Jamal said, "I will cast a love-spell on the Sayyid for you, doctora."

"It won't do any good," Jasmine said. "Dr. Connor is going away soon."

"Then you must make him stay, Sayyida. It is your duty to do so. Men think they come and go as they please, but it is at our pleasure that they do so, although they do not know this."

And the younger women, only just beginning to realize their real hidden power, giggled.

"The doctora should marry the Sayyid and have babies," said Um Tewfik, and the older women agreed, nodding heads draped in black veils.

"I am too old to have children, Umma," Jasmine said, removing her stethoscope and folding it into her medical bag. "I will soon be forty-two."

But Um Jamal, a woman of impressive stature, past childbearing years and possessing an enviable twenty-two grandchildren, gave Jasmine a playful look and said, "You can still have babies, Sayyida. When I had my last, I was nearly fifty. May I divorce!" she added with a satisfied sigh, "if I did not give that man nineteen living children! He never looked at another woman!"

Although Jasmine laughed, she thought how sometimes, when an infant was placed in her arms, or when she saw mothers and daughters together, she would feel the ache of losing her own two babies. Even though she accepted her losses as God's will, she still sometimes wondered what it would be like to have a little girl of her own. She thought of the poor angel born on the eve of the Six-Day War. The child would have been twenty-one now, if she had lived. And it wouldn't have mattered to Jasmine that the baby was part of Hassan al-Sabir; she would have loved her with the same devotion these fellaha mothers showed to their own daughters.

And she thought every day about her son: Did Mohammed wonder about her, did he ever mention her or ask about her? Did he think of her as being alive, or was she like Auntie Fatima of long ago, a woman whose photographs had been removed from the family album, a woman as good as dead? Jasmine thought that just once she would like to observe Mohammed from a safe place. Not to approach him, not to upset his life or inflict pain or shame upon him, but only to watch him with a mother's loving eyes, to see how he laughed, how he walked, to hear his voice and imprint it upon her memory. Mohammed was a man now; Jasmine had carried the boy in her heart all these years, but she couldn't conjure up the man he must now be. Was he like Omar? Was he spoiled and selfish? No, she decided. Mohammed was part of her, he was part of Alice; there would be kindness in him as well.

Um Jamal said, suddenly grave, "In all honor and respect, Sayyida, you should marry the Sayyid. You are together all the time. It is not good, an unmarried woman with a man."

"There is nothing to worry about," Jasmine said, because the fact was that she and Declan were rarely alone together, or even together at all, because each time they came to a village and were given fellaheen hospitality, Jasmine and Declan were always separated, she to sit with the women, he with the men. And the sleeping accommodations usually meant that Jasmine was taken in at one house, Declan at another. The only times they were really together, so closely that they touched, were when they were in the Land Cruisers, bumping over rough roads, following dirt tracks between fields of cotton and sugarcane.

Finally she wished the women "*Mulid mubarak aleikum*,"—a happy Prophet's birthday—and the young wives vanished as efficiently as they had assembled earlier, disappearing down narrow alleys with babies in their arms or in slings on their backs, children clutching their mothers' brightly colored granny dresses. The older women, wrapped in black veils and shawls, dispersed to the few shady spots in the square, to eat nuts, gossip, and watch the afternoon pass until the evening celebrations began. Jasmine was left alone to pack up her medical equipment, and her memories.

She looked across the square, and Declan's eyes met hers.

=

When he realized he had been watching her, he quickly looked away. Snapping his medical bag closed, he said to the men collected in front of Abu Hosni's coffeehouse, "I'll see you at the festivities tonight, *inshallah*."

As he started to leave, a fellah in a ragged galabeya suddenly materialized from the crowd of onlookers and proffered a large Egyptian scarab carved out of limestone. "I sell it to you, Sayyid," he said cheerfully to Declan. "Very ancient. Four thousand years old. I personally know the tomb this came from. For you, fifty pounds."

"Sorry, my friend. I am not interested in old things."

"Brand new!" the fellah said, thrusting the scarab at him. "I personally know the man who made this! Best craftsman in all of Egypt. Thirty pounds, Sayyid."

Declan laughed and headed across the square, meeting Jasmine halfway. "I promised Hadj Tayeb I'd give him a lift to the cemetery," he said. "He wants to take offerings to his father's tomb. Shall I drop you at the convent?"

The convent, where Jasmine enjoyed the hospitality of Catholic nuns, while Declan had been given accommodations at the imam's house, was on the other side of the village. The festivities would be starting soon, and she and Declan would join the men's and women's groups, once again to be separated. "I would like to come with you," she said. "If it's all right. I am told there are some interesting ruins near the cemetery."

—

The Land Cruiser bounced over dirt tracks until cultivated fields and mud-brick houses were left behind and stark wilderness stretched ahead. Hadj Tayeb sat between Jasmine and Declan, holding on to the dashboard, pointing the way. The setting sun was in their eyes, a fiery ball in a pale, flawless sky, tinting the desert with rich hues of yellow and orange, streaked with the long black shadows of rocks and boulders. Finally, they saw what looked like a small village up ahead, but as they drew near, they heard no signs of life, just the desert silence and the lonely whistling of the wind.

The three stepped down from the vehicle, and the elderly fellah led Jasmine and Connor down narrow lanes that might have belonged to any village, past doorways and windows, and under crumbling stone arches. The "houses" were all domed, and they looked to Jasmine like row upon row of great beehives, constructed of mud brick, layered with dust and sand.

When they reached the tomb of the Tayeb family, the old Hadj pointed with a shaky finger and said, "The ruins lie over there, Sayyid, on the ancient caravan route."

As they left him to pray, striking across the plain with the last of the sunset in their eyes, Jasmine said, "The village women told me that the ruins have magic healing properties. The villagers go there sometimes to chip away stone from the columns, and make medicines of it."

There was little left of the goddess shrine that had served desert travelers thousands of years ago—only two of the original columns still stood; the rest lay broken among boulders and debris. A few ancient paving stones were visible where the sand had been blown away, indicating a causeway leading to what looked like a small sanctuary. Behind that rose a rugged escarpment thrust up millennia ago from the desert floor, a great, barren scar that separated the Nile Valley from the Sahara Desert.

"This was once a very busy caravan route," Declan said, as they picked their way among the rubble. The silence was profound, and the setting sun had turned the columns a stunning rust-red against the sky. "I imagine travelers stopped here to pray for a safe journey. They would have camped in those caves over there."

"It looks as if someone has been camping here," Jasmine said, poking the toe of her shoe into a circle of blackened rocks.

"Desert holy men are drawn to these lonely places. Mystics, mostly. Sufis. Christian hermits."

Jasmine came upon the statue of a ram. The head was missing, and the flat place where his neck had been made a perfect seat. As she sat down, she said, "Why isn't there any excavating going on here? Why haven't the archaeologists fenced this place off?"

Connor looked out at the barren plain stretching away to the horizon. In the distance, he saw the squat black tents of Bedouins. "Probably lack of funds," he said. "This looks like a small, insignificant shrine. Not worth the bother, I should imagine. Maybe Egyptologists were here once, in the last century, when European archaeologists plundered Egypt. Hadj Tayeb said that he and Abu Hosni had once convinced some of the captains of the Nile cruise boats to stop here and bring the tourists in. But after the long trek from the river, the tourists had been disappointed. And so the boats don't stop here any more."

Jasmine looked up at him, as he stood silhouetted against the lavender sky, the wind stirring his hair; it was longer now, with the first signs of silver at the temples. "Declan," she said, "why must you leave?"

He walked past her, his boots crunching over broken pavement that had been laid long ago. "I have to leave. For my own survival."

"But you are needed so badly here. Please, listen to me. When I arrived at the refugee camps in Gaza, I was so appalled by the conditions, the way the Palestinians are being treated, that I almost couldn't stay.

And then I went to the Treverton Foundation Clinic, and I saw what good they were doing—"

"Jasmine," he said, facing her as he stood in the shadow of a looming column, "I know all about the camps. I know all about the conditions people are living in, all over the world. But you and I aren't going to change it, not one bit. Look," he said, turning to the column. It was decorated with carvings so worn down by wind and sand that they could barely be made out, but as the sun shot its last rays over the escarpment and momentarily deepened the shadows, the engravings stood out in relief. "Do you see this?" he said, pointing to scenes of men working the fields, buffalo turning water wheels, women grinding corn. "These pictures were probably carved three thousand years ago, and yet they could have been done today, because the fellaheen live today exactly as their ancestors did. Nothing has changed. This is the lesson I've learned after twenty-five years of practicing medicine in the Third World. No matter what you and I do, people will remain the same. Nothing changes."

"Except you," she said. "You've changed."

"Let's just say I woke up."

"To what?"

"To the fact that what we're doing here—in Egypt, in the refugee camps—is nothing but an exercise in futility."

"You didn't use to think so. You once thought you could save the children of the world."

"That was during my arrogant phase, when I thought I could make a difference."

"You still can make a difference," she said, and he saw a challenging look in her eyes.

The sound of footsteps over the gravel suddenly disturbed the desert silence, and Hadj Tayeb came puffing toward them. "My three gods," he said. "God had better call me to Him soon, or else I'll be useless in paradise! Ah, these ruins. My village could make money if the tourists would come. But after they see Karnak and Kom Ombo, they look at this and say, 'Only two columns? Why should we pay money to see only two columns?' Abu Hosni and I are thinking of building new columns here, and making them look old. By God, but I am tired."

Connor said, "I'll go get the car. You two can wait here."

While they waited, Jasmine offered the elderly pilgrim her seat on the ram statue, which Tayeb accepted graciously, spreading his white gala-beya about himself. He squinted up at the sky, which was rapidly growing dark. "I do not like being in this place after the sun is gone," he said. Then he placed his hand on his chest.

"Are you all right?" Jasmine asked.

"I am an old man, God keep me."

When Declan returned and found Tayeb complaining of weakness, he brought the medical kit from the car and was about to open it when the old man lifted his head and said, "What's that sound?"

"It is the wind, Hadj Tayeb," Connor replied.

"Sounds like a jinni to me. By God, we had better leave this place, Sayyid. The ghosts come out at night, and look, the sun is gone."

"Wait a minute," Jasmine said. "I heard something, too."

The three stood motionless and listened to the wind whistle mournfully through the ruins. And then another sound joined the wind—a long, low moan.

"Someone is here!" said Jasmine.

They turned in the direction the sound had come from and listened again. This time it was more distinct.

"You're right," said Declan. "There *is* someone here. The sound is coming from that small structure."

The sanctuary, where the goddess of the shrine had once been housed, was the height of a man, and about ten feet square. They had to climb over rocks and debris to reach it, sometimes slipping in the gravel and loose shale; Declan took Jasmine's hand. The doorway was open to the east, where the sky was darkest, and so it was impossible to see inside. They bent down to listen.

There was another moan. "Allah!" said Hadj Tayeb, making a sign to ward off the evil eye.

Connor stepped inside and found a man reclining against an ancient altar, his eyes shut, breathing with difficulty. He wore the robe and turban of a Sufi mystic, and had a long gray beard down to his chest. There were bloodstains on his robe.

Declan knelt beside him and, saying quietly, "It's all right, old man, we've come to help," opened the medical kit to bring out a stethoscope and blood-pressure cuff.

While Connor monitored the man's vital signs, Jasmine lifted the hem of the coarse wool robe, and found a lower leg bone protruding through gangrenous flesh.

"He must have fallen and crawled in here for shelter," she said, reaching into the medical bag. In the dim light of the sanctuary, she quickly filled a syringe from an ampule of morphine. "This will ease your pain," she said to the man, although she wasn't sure he was even aware of their presence.

Declan listened through the stethoscope, then sat back and said, "Pulse is weak and thready. He's severely dehydrated and probably in a lot of pain. I'll start an IV and then we'll transport him to the district hospital."

But they were startled when the man suddenly said in a hoarse whisper, "No! Do not take me from here."

"We are going to take care of you, Abu," Jasmine said, using the respectful term meaning "father." "We are doctors."

He looked at her and she was surprised to see clear green eyes. When he grimaced with pain, and she saw strong teeth, she said to Declan, "This man is not old."

"No, but he's in a bad way," he said, signaling to Hadja Tayeb who hovered by the entrance. "Can you fetch the metal box from the back of the car, Hadj?" and the old man hurried off. Declan gently wrapped the blood pressure cuff around a shockingly emaciated upper arm. "His pressure's low," he said, "we have to rehydrate him right away."

While they waited for Tayeb to return with the IV setup, Jasmine laid her hand on the hermit's forehead. His skin was dry and crackly, as if he were a hundred years old, and yet she guessed that he was not much older than herself. Then she and Declan examined the wound and arrived at the same unspoken conclusion: amputation above the knee.

When Hadj Tayeb returned, struggling with the aluminum medical kit, Declan worked quickly to find a vein and get a drip started, wedging the bottle of dextrose solution on the altar stone above the man. Then he said, "Listen to me, Abu. We are going to splint your leg and carry you back—"

But the hermit said, "No," again, with a little more strength this time. "You must not take me away."

"What happened to you?"

"I was outside, on the escarpment, praying. I lost my balance in the wind. I managed to crawl down here."

"How long have you been like this?" Jasmine asked him.

"Hours, days . . ."

Because of the dirt he had crawled through, the blood had been able to coagulate so that he hadn't bled to death. But flies had had time to feast on the torn flesh. She wondered when his food and water had run out while he had lain in agony, waiting for help.

They had brought a canteen with them; she unscrewed it and, sliding an arm beneath bony shoulders, brought the water to his lips. He was able to take a few sips.

Finally the morphine started to work, and as he was able to drink more water, he slowly became coherent.

"There were some kind people here . . . Bedouins, on their way to Cairo. They fed me and gave me water. Praise God in His mercy."

"You're going to be all right," Declan said. "Just as soon as we have you in the hospital."

But the hermit seemed not to have heard, because he was suddenly staring at Jasmine.

He looked at her for a long time, his eyebrows coming together in a frown. And then he reached up a skeletal hand and pushed her turban back, revealing blond hair. A look of astonishment swept across his fleshless face. "Mishmish?" he whispered.

"What?" she said. "What did you say?"

"Is that you, Mishmish?"

She gasped. "What? What are you saying?"

"I thought I was dreaming. It is you, Mishmish."

"Zachariah? Oh, God, Zakki!" She looked at Declan. "He's my brother! This man is my brother!"

"What?"

"My brother. Oh, God——"

"I searched for her, you know," Zachariah said. "I searched for Sahra but I never found her."

"What's he talking about?" asked Declan.

"I went from village to village, Mishmish," he said in a failing voice. "I asked for her . . . but she vanished. It was not my destiny to find her."

"Don't talk, Zakki," Jasmine said, tears rising in her eyes. "We are going to make you well."

But he smiled and shook his head. "Mishmish . . ." he said, with a sigh that rattled in his chest. "After all these years, here you are. Praise His name, the Almighty granted me my final prayer that I might see you before I joined Him."

"Yes," she said, "praise His name. But, Zakki, I can't believe this! What are you doing here? How did you come so far from home?"

He gazed at her with unfocused eyes. "Do you remember, Mishmish . . . the fountain in the garden?"

"I remember it. Please save your strength."

"I need no strength for where I am going. Mishmish, have you seen the family since . . ." He suddenly grimaced. "Since Father sent you away? I was in such despair, Mishmish, after you left."

Her tears fell onto his hands. "Don't talk, Zakki. We're going to take care of you."

"God is with you, Yasmina. I can see His hand upon your shoulder. It rests there very lightly, but it is there."

"Oh, Zakki," she sobbed. "I can't believe I've found you. How awful it must have been for you, being alone like this."

"God was with me . . ." He heaved another sigh.

Declan said, "We have to move him now or it will be too late."

"Mishmish . . . the pain is going away."

"I gave you something for it."

"Bless you for that, sister of my heart," he said. Then he looked at Declan and said, "But you are in pain, my friend. I can see it in the aura surrounding you."

"Don't talk now, Abu, save your strength."

But Zachariah reached for Declan's hand and taking it, said, "Yes, you are in pain." He searched Declan's face, and seemed to read something there. He slowly shook his head. "You are not to blame. It wasn't your fault."

"What?"

"She says she is at peace, and she wants you to be at peace also."

Declan stared at him for a moment, then shot to his feet.

Zachariah turned to Jasmine. "Let me go to God now. It is my hour." He raised a hand and touched the golden hair that, freed from its turban, spilled over her shoulder. "God has brought you home, Mishmish. Your days of wandering in strange lands are over." Then he smiled and said, "Tell Tahia that I love her and will await her in paradise."

He closed his eyes and died.

Jasmine held him in her arms and, rocking his lifeless body, murmured, "In the name of God the Compassionate, the Merciful. There is no god but God, and Mohammed is His Messenger."

She held him for a long time, sitting in the desert silence as night shadows crept into the sanctuary, and a lone jackal howled in the surrounding hills. Hadj Tayeb wept openly. Finally Declan said, "We have to bury him, Jasmine."

But she said, "My mother wrote to me a long time ago and told me that Zachariah had had a mystical experience in the Sinai, during the Six-Day War. He died, she said, he actually died on the battlefield, and then he came back to life. She said he was different after that. He claimed to have seen paradise. He became very religious and Umma said he was chosen by God. And then he went in search of Sahra, our cook, although I don't know why."

"Jasmine," Declan said, "it's getting dark out. We have to bury him. Go and sit in the Land Cruiser with Tayeb. I will dig the grave."

"No. It's my duty to bury my brother. I want to be the one to lay him in the ground."

Night had fallen by the time they heaped stones on the grave so that scavengers wouldn't steal the body, and Jasmine had scratched the name of Allah into the rock that covered Zachariah's head. Hadj Tayeb ran his sleeve under his nose and said, "Praise God, Sayyida, your brother will rest in two heavens, for this place is also sacred to the ancient gods."

Jasmine started to cry, and Declan took her into his arms, holding her for a very long time.

CHAPTER 42

When Amira emerged from the car, everyone fell into a shocked silence.

The noisy Rasheed clan had just arrived in a convoy of automobiles and were milling happily about the dock with the rest of the holiday crowd, drinking in the bracing air of the sea and letting the hot sun soak into their bones. Back in Cairo, the khamsins held the city in a pall of hot sand and grit, but here at Port Suez, where the family had come to see Amira off—finally—on her pilgrimage to Mecca, the sun shed its golden blessings from a clear blue sky, and the water of the Gulf of Suez was such a brilliant turquoise that it hurt the eyes.

But it was Amira who now captured their attention, emerging from the Cadillac into the brilliant sunshine dressed in her pilgrim's robes. And she was such a vision of blinding whiteness that everyone gasped.

No one could recall having ever seen her in anything but black, and the white flowing robes and gossamer veil, which had lain in her drawer for countless, hope-filled years, had produced a curious transformation. Amira looked strangely young and virginal, as if the white had purified her years and bleached out all age and infirmity. She seemed to walk with a lighter step, her joints free from pain and stiffness, as if the robes were magic and could somehow bring back youth.

But it wasn't the traditional garments that had transformed Amira, it was the knowledge that she was going to holy Mecca at last, to the birthplace of the Prophet, where, today and for the past fourteen hundred years, only believers were permitted to enter. She had spent the past weeks in prayer and fasting in order to enter *Ihram*, the state of purity, removing all makeup and jewelry, all symbols of her earthly and secular life, clearing all mortal thoughts from her mind in order to concentrate solely upon God.

As Ibrahim assisted his mother toward Hadj Terminal, where ferries waited to take pilgrims down the Red Sea to the western coast of Saudi Arabia, the Rasheeds joined the throng of other embarking passengers and their families and merrily escorted Umma to the boat. They were all present except Nefissa, who had twisted her ankle and had had to remain in Cairo, and her grandson Mohammed, who had stayed to take care of her and keep her company. But Nefissa's daughter Tahia was there, holding the sticky hands of two little nieces.

Tahia, who had just turned forty-three, looked with pride at her daughter, Asmahan, whose birthday was tomorrow: she was going to be twenty-one and already she was pregnant with her second child. Tahia then looked over at Zeinab, who was also going to be twenty-one soon, but there were no prospects of marriage or babies for Camelia's daughter. Still, God worked His wondrous miracles. Hadn't the family once been told that Camelia herself would never be able to bear children because of the infection she had had as a teenager? And yet look at her son, Najib, a fine dark-haired, amber-eyed little boy of six. So who was to say what fate was written for Zeinab in God's book? Belief in God's compassion and mercy was what made life bearable, otherwise how could one survive? How many times had Tahia herself been tempted to leave her family and go off in search of Zachariah? But trust in God sustained her. When Zakki had fulfilled God's purpose, he would return. And they would be free at last to love and to marry.

Ibrahim's wife Huda walked behind Tahia with their five children—pretty girls with the distinctive Rasheed leaf-eyes, ranging from fourteen years to seven, and the center of Huda's universe. Ever since Ibrahim had rescued her from a life of drudgery, employing her as a nurse in his office and then taking care of her sandwich-seller father and lazy brothers, she had devoted herself to the producing and nurturing of these angels. She hadn't minded when Ibrahim had brought home a second wife, quiet little Atiya, because it had released Huda from the tedious bedroom duty. If anyone had asked, Huda would have said that she enjoyed lovemaking with Ibrahim, but in her heart she detested the act, and had suffered it only to produce children. Although she had hinted at times to Ibrahim that a rest from sex might be healthy, he had kept at it with prodigious determination. Especially as he had neared his seventieth birthday and still had no son as proof of his virility. Well, that was Atiya's burden now, and she was welcome to it.

As Ibrahim helped his mother into the noisy terminal, he looked over at Atiya, whose summer coat was pressed against her body by the wind, revealing the generous swell of her abdomen. She just *had* to give him a son. Seven daughters—nine, counting the little one that died in the summer of 1952, and the one Alice miscarried in 1963. But he drew comfort from the knowledge that God is merciful. Having no son was more punishment than any man deserved. Was his father, Ali, still watching from paradise, still waiting for the grandson from his son? What did years mean to a soul in heaven? Perhaps a lifetime seemed but a wink, and so Ali's impatience and disapproval of Ibrahim had not diminished. But now there was that promising mound beneath Atiya's coat.

As they followed the family into the terminal, Dahiba leaned on Hakim for support. Although Ibrahim had reported that they had been able to get all of the cancer during surgery, she had nonetheless been put on chemotherapy and radiation, which weakened her. But if Dahiba's physical strength was sapped, her spirit remained strong. These past four weeks had injected new meaning, new determination into her life, and into her husband's as well. For Hakim and Dahiba, life was going to go on even though the future lay behind a veil. They had accepted God's will, and would submit to His higher judgment; in the meantime, however, having tasted their own mortality and knowing that every person's hours were numbered, they had decided to dedicate their remaining days to leaving behind a significant legacy. For Hakim, it was to make the most important film of his career, a movie which, although not yet finished, was already creating a stir in Cairo, in that it dealt frankly and realistically with the true story of a woman who had been so profoundly brutalized by her husband, and then by a legal system that condoned his monstrous behavior, that she had been driven to murder. Hakim had no doubt that the film would be banned in Egypt, but he envisioned female audiences in the rest of the world cheering his heroine when she first fired the gun at the husband's groin, and then at his heart. Dahiba's project had been to submit once again the manuscript of a novel she had written ten years ago but which had been rejected. *Bahithat Al-Badiyya* (*Seeker in the Desert*) had been dismissed by publishers as autobiographical, a tool commonly used to belittle a woman's literary accomplishment in that it meant she had only one story, her own, to tell. But the manuscript had finally been bought, and, in President Mubarak's more liberal climate, was to be published in Egypt, and therefore throughout the Arab world. And so, despite her pain and weakness, Dahiba had come to Umma's seeing-off in high spirits.

But the family kept an eye on Dahiba. Although Camelia pretended to be enjoying the fresh sea air, the fabulous expanse of brilliant water, the tankers and cruise ships gliding past a backdrop of mauve coastline that was Sinai, she was worried about her aunt. Camelia knew the strain the chemotherapy was putting on her, and that the yellow scarf on Dahiba's head was meant to hide hair that had been lost through radiation. It was for these reasons that Camelia had come up with her wonderful surprise, a conspiracy the whole family was aware of, except for Dahiba and Hakim; and she trusted everyone to keep quiet. If there was one thing she could count on, it was her family's skill at keeping a secret.

The time came to say good-bye. As other pilgrims made their way onto the ferryboat, with families and friends seeing them off, Zeinab and two female cousins in their twenties took their places next to Amira. They, too, were dressed all in white, because they were also going to Arabia on the pilgrimage.

Amira embraced Dahiba and then Hakim, saying, "I go to Mecca to pray for my daughter's recovery. God is compassionate." And when she hugged Camelia, Amira murmured, "Do not worry, we will be back in time, *inshallah*," and gave her a conspiratorial wink.

Ibrahim embraced his mother for a long moment. He had wanted to send one of the boys with her, perhaps Mohammed, for protection, and Omar had seconded the suggestion, declaring that he didn't want his grandmother roaming Saudi Arabia on her own. But Amira had subverted their plan by choosing three girls to accompany her, rendering Mohammed's company unnecessary.

It wasn't just the pilgrimage to Mecca that made Ibrahim uneasy— after all, his mother would be among a large throng headed for the holy city. It was what she planned afterward, on the return trip. "I am going to try and trace the route my mother and I followed when I was a child and we went on a journey," she had said. He didn't understand what was so important about a trip she had taken long ago, and he was troubled by a premonition that he would not see her again.

"Be happy for me, son of my heart. I go on a journey of joy." And she turned toward the ferryboat, wondering if the sparkling blue sea it was to sail upon was the azure sea of her most recent dreams.

=

Mimi wore the latest style of Oriental dance costume: a slinky evening gown reminiscent of the 1950s, made of scarlet satin and crimson sequins; she wore high-heeled shoes with ankle straps, and one long evening glove on one arm, leaving the other bare. The clever lighting in the picture showed her blond hair to its best advantage, giving her a wild look. As if she could devour a man—eat him alive and make him beg for more.

As Mohammed stood outside the Cage d'Or, hands thrust into his pockets, he was oblivious of the people going into the nightclub, the

busload of tourists that streamed around him, the loud Arab businessmen arriving in search of a good time. He burned for Mimi. But he
didn't dare go in.

If only Auntie Dahiba hadn't gotten sick. On the night following the
afternoon he had come upon Mimi in his aunt's studio, Mohammed had
fallen asleep with Mimi's photograph in his mind, contemplating a plan
to meet her, a scheme nearly adolescent in its construction, but fueled
by an adult's lust. And then Auntie had gone into the hospital; she had
closed her studio and Mohammed's dream of meeting Mimi there had
been dashed. In the four weeks since, he had come nearly every night
to this club perched out over the Nile, to gaze at the place that had, years
ago, been one of Farouk's favorite gambling houses. And he had stood
here, staring at Mimi's picture on the marquee, wishing he had the
courage to go inside.

Why shouldn't he? He had money, and he was certainly old enough,
having celebrated his twenty-fifth birthday two days ago. The family had
thrown a big party for him, and he had received plenty of gifts. But little
money. And money was what he needed. Mimi would not be interested
in a penniless government clerk. As he was held entranced by that
cascading blondness, thinking that the annual birthday card had yet to
arrive from his mother from whatever part of the world she was in, he
was unaware that a man had come to stand next to him. And when he
heard a low voice say, "Western imperialist decadence," Mohammed
looked around to see whom the man addressed.

He was startled to see Hussein, who had watched him at Feyrouz's
coffeehouse, the man from his Muslim Brotherhood days, and whom
Mohammed had once been afraid of. When he realized that this was the
second time in four weeks that he had encountered Hussein—they had
nearly collided on the sidewalk a week ago when Mohammed had
emerged from the government building where he worked—he wondered now if those occasions had been just a coincidence.

"I beg your pardon?" he said, aware of two sensations: the hot, gritty
breath of the khamsin, and the dark, dangerous eyes of Hussein.

"You were with us once, brother," the man said. "I remember you
at our meetings. But then you vanished."

"My father—" Mohammed began, suddenly afraid, and wondering
why.

Hussein smiled, not a warm gesture. "Do you still believe, my friend?"

"Believe?"

Hussein gestured toward Mimi's picture. "This is the filth that is undermining Egyptian values and destroying our fundamental Islamic faith."

Mohammed looked at the poster, and then at Hussein. From inside the club, they heard strains of an orchestra tuning up. She would be on the stage soon, his beloved Mimi, dancing in front of all those strange men. He desired her, he detested her. Mohammed began to sweat.

Hussein stepped closer and said in a low voice that was almost a growl, "How can a man keep his thoughts upon God, how can a man remain faithful to his wife and family, when Satan throws such temptation in his path? These nightclubs are funded by Western dollars, they are part of a plot to strip away Egyptian pride and honor and decency."

Mohammed stared at Mimi's picture, at the swell of her breasts and hips, and suddenly realized that her smile was a mocking one. The khamsin seemed to blast his skin with thousands of needles. Sweat ran down his face, under his collar, and between his shoulder blades. He felt as if he were on fire.

"We must cleanse Egypt of this pestilence," Hussein murmured, "and return to the ways of God and righteousness. And we must use any means we can."

Mohammed regarded him in fear, and then turned and fled.

=

Nefissa was glad she had sprained her ankle and had therefore been unable to accompany the family to Suez, because her accident had necessitated Mohammed staying with her, and therefore he was unable to go to Mecca with Amira. Nefissa had been furious with her brother and son that they should have even made such a suggestion. It would only have given Amira one more opportunity to tighten her control over Mohammed, the way she controlled everyone else. But Nefissa was determined: the boy was hers.

And she had plans for him which no one, not even Omar or Ibrahim—not even Amira—was going to meddle with. Happiness might have eluded Nefissa all these years, but it could be hers yet, when her grandson was married to a girl she had already chosen, and the three of them took up residence in the new flat Nefissa had secretly paid for.

She was just looking at the clock, wondering where Mohammed was, where he went to every night, when she heard the door to the flat open and close. He came into the living room, where she was reclining on a sofa, her injured foot on a pillow. He quickly kissed her and turned away, but not before she saw that he looked pale and troubled.

"How are you tonight, grandson of my heart?" she asked, suddenly concerned.

He kept his back to her as he went through the mail he had picked up in the foyer downstairs. "I am well, Grandmother—" He stopped, and she saw his shoulders stiffen.

"What is it?" she asked.

"My birthday card," he replied in a tight voice. "It came."

Nefissa watched her grandson take a seat on the divan and stare at the envelope for a long moment before opening it. She had once been able to keep Yasmina's correspondence from Camelia, but she had not even attempted to keep these cards from her grandson. Mohammed looked forward to them every year; she even knew which drawer he saved them in. She knew that if she forbade him to have them, then he would have made a martyr of his mother and placed her on a pedestal. The available fruit, Nefissa counseled herself, was far less tempting than the forbidden.

When she saw him suddenly frown at the envelope, she said, "What is it, my darling?"

He brought it over. "I don't understand, Grandmother. Look, the envelope bears Egyptian stamps."

"Then it is not from her."

"But it is her handwriting!" Mohammed tore open the envelope and read the familiar, "*In my heart always, Your Mother.*" Then he examined the envelope more closely, and when he saw the postmark, he cried out. "*Bismillah!* She is in Egypt!"

"What!" Nefissa took it from him and brought the envelope into the light. When she read the postmark—Al Tafla, A.R.E.—she suddenly went cold. "In the name of God," she murmured. "Yasmina? In Egypt? Where is Al Tafla?"

He ran for the small atlas that was wedged in the bookcase between a dictionary and a collection of the poetry of Ibn Hamdis, and he frantically tore through the pages, his hands shaking because it was very important to find the exact spot, he had to know where Al Tafla was, precisely. He dropped the book, scrambled for it, then came to the page showing the green Nile Valley bisecting two yellow deserts. He quickly ran his finger down the river, then up again, up and back until: "*Y'Al-lah!* Here it is! It is south of Luxor and before—" He threw the book across the room, where it hit the TV set and tumbled to the floor, loose pages fluttering down.

Nefissa struggled to sit up, reached for the back of a chair, and pulled herself to her feet, wincing with pain. "Grandson of my heart," she said. "Please—"

"How can she be here," he cried, "and not come to see me? What kind of mother is that? Oh God, Grandmother! I am so confused!"

When she saw how he cried, how convulsively the sobs racked his slender body, she suddenly became alarmed, filled with a new fear. Yasmina in Egypt! What if she came back to claim her son? Legally, Yasmina could not touch him. But Mohammed was a man now, and one soft word from his mother could steal him away from Nefissa forever.

"Listen to me, my darling," she said, reaching for his arm. "Help me to sit down. There's a good boy. Now I must tell you something. The time has come for you to hear the truth about your mother."

He ran a hand under his nose as he helped her into the expensive brocade chair that was especially hers. It was from this fine seat that Nefissa gave orders to Nala and the servants, and coddled Omar, Mohammed, and the children. She drew in a steadying breath and said, "This will not be easy for me, grandson of my heart. The family has not spoken of your mother in many years, not since she went away. Please sit down."

But Mohammed couldn't sit. The khamsin rattled the windows like evil jinns playing pranks, and the apartment seemed too hot, too confining. He stood in the center of the living room, on the carpet his grandmother declared had once belonged to her friend Princess Faiza, and which she had purchased long ago at an auction.

"Tell me, Grandmother," he said in a tight voice. "What happened to my mother?"

She stiffened her back and said, "My poor boy, your mother was caught committing adultery with your Uncle Ibrahim's best friend." As she spoke the words, Nefissa was ashamed at the pleasure it gave her. "She was married to your father at the time."

"I . . . I don't believe you," he said, tears filling his eyes.

"Ask your uncle, when he returns from Suez. Ibrahim will tell you the truth. Even though she was his daughter. She had no honor."

"No!" he cried. "You cannot say that about my mother!"

"It pains me to tell you this, for she dishonored our family. This is why no one speaks of her. Ibrahim banished your mother on the eve of the Six-Day War, a dark day for Egypt, for all of us." Nefissa pressed her lips tightly together. She wouldn't tell him the rest, how Yasmina had begged for mercy, how she had pleaded to be allowed to keep her son, and how Omar had taken Mohammed away that night, never to see his mother again.

The young man remained rooted to Princess Faiza's carpet, shaking violently, sweat shining on his face. He suddenly ran from the room and Nefissa heard him vomiting in the bathroom.

When he came out, white-faced and stumbling, she reached for him, but he ran out of the flat and plunged blindly out into the streets, knocking people out of his way. He made his way to Feyrouz's coffee-house, where he prayed his friends were—Salah and Habib, to make him laugh, to make it all a bad dream waiting to be dispelled by jokes and laughter. But his friends weren't there. But Hussein was, with his dangerous eyes and dangerous ideas, and Mohammed sat numbly with him, cradling his head in his hands as Hussein talked of ridding Egypt of the godless. And as he listened, young Mohammed saw a black cloud roll toward him, like an evil fog, like the maw of an evil jinni about to devour him, and he said, "Yes," to whatever it was Hussein was proposing, while he silently vowed: I shall go to Al Tafla and punish her the way she should have been punished twenty-one years ago.

CHAPTER 43

Jasmine searched the night sky for her birth-star, Mirach in Andromeda, that she might draw strength from it for what she was about to do. But the stars had the sparkling brilliance of fireworks, making it impossible to pick out one from so many. So she looked at the moon shining over the Nile, large and round and silver, like a beneficent light, and she reached up to embrace its power.

After a silent prayer, she turned away from the river and made her way back into the sleeping village of Al Tafla, going through the dark alleys until she came to the house of the sheikha, the wisewoman who was also a fortune-teller and clairvoyant. Jasmine had to act quickly. In three days, Declan Connor would be gone.

=

Declan paced the creaking boards of his veranda, unable to sleep. He paused every so often to scan the midnight sky for clouds. All day the villagers had heard the distant rumblings of thunder; the air had felt electrified, and birds had been sighted in unusually large flocks. Was a storm coming? But how could there be, with no clouds? Declan pulled a pack of cigarettes out of his pocket and, lighting one, considered his own personal storm.

He was leaving Egypt in three days, and he couldn't get Jasmine out of his mind—the way she had felt in his arms when he had comforted her four weeks ago, after they had buried her brother. He was consumed with the memory of her body against his, her warmth, her breasts pressing against his chest, her tears dampening his shirt, and the way she had clung so tightly to him. He had never wanted a woman as he had wanted Jasmine in that moment, and he cursed himself for it. He had no right to feel such desire, not with Sybil lying in her grave.

He went to the edge of the porch and looked out over the dark river, where the moon traced a silver ribbon on its inky surface.

When he heard the rumble again, Declan realized that this time it wasn't the thunder they been hearing all day, but something else— distant drums. He threw down his cigarette and stamped it out. Definitely drums. But where, at this hour?

He slowly walked away from his small house on the Nile and headed toward the village, and as he drew nearer, the drums became more distinct, and he realized they were playing a definite rhythm. Who would be having a party in the middle of the night?

Al Tafla was closed up tight, no light shone from even Waleed's coffeehouse. No fellah or fallaha went abroad at night because of the jinns and evil spirits that populated the darkness. And despite the heat, doors were barred, windows were shuttered to keep out demons—or curses sent by envious neighbors.

Declan found the clinic dark and locked; there was no light in Jasmine's window. But, to his surprise, he saw torchlight flickering over the walls of the courtyard behind the clinic, where the oven, laundry tubs, and chicken coop were. Making his way down the alley that was so narrow his shoulders brushed the mud-brick walls, he saw, in the courtyard, men with musical instruments—wooden flutes, two-string fiddles, and wide, flat drums, which they were thumping rhythmically over hot coals. There were women present as well; Declan recognized Khalid's wife, Waleed's sister, the elderly and respected Bint Omar, all stepping back and forth over pans of burning incense and murmuring incantations. He couldn't make out the words; they weren't speaking Arabic.

And then he suddenly realized what they were preparing for—a *zaar*, a ritual trance dance for exorcising demons, in which the participants became frenzied and lost control of themselves. Although foreigners were not normally permitted to take part in zaars, or even to watch, Declan had secretly witnessed a trance dance in Tunisia—a *stambali*—and the dancer, a man, had dropped dead from a cardiac arrest.

Declan grew alarmed. Where was Jasmine?

He started to go in, but a woman barred his way. *"Haram!"* she said. "Taboo!"

But another woman, the village sheikha, intervened, approaching Declan with a dark, inquisitive eye. The sheikha was a powerful woman in Al Tafla, with tattoos on her chin to advertise her proud Bedouin origins, and with whom he had clashed over the issue of the brutal and barbaric custom of circumcising little girls. He was about to demand what was going on, and where the Doctora was, when, to his further surprise, she stepped aside and said, "You may enter, Sayyid."

A few of those sitting on benches around the courtyard acknowledged him with a smile or a nod, the rest moved around the small space as if limbering themselves up for an exercise. The women walked in slow circles, raising and lowering their arms, stomping their feet, moving their heads stiffly, while the drummers heated their drums over the coals and the fiddle player tuned his strings. The sheikha, in her flowing black robes, was going around lighting candles and incense until the sultry night air was filled with exotic smoke and perfumes.

Declan looked around for Jasmine. He knew better than to interfere with a trance dance, to try to stop it, but he wanted to know why it was being held here, at the clinic, and what Jasmine's part was in it. The man he had watched die in Tunisia had been young, and he had thrown himself into such a frenzy that he had hurt himself. Everyone knew that zaar dances could be dangerous, because they involved the expulsion of evil spirits, who were generally reluctant to leave. For Declan, it was the lack of conscious control that was dangerous.

Was someone ill? he wondered, as he took a seat next to Mrs. Rajat, who sat against the wall smoking a pipe with her eyes closed. Was this to be a healing zaar? Or was someone feeling unlucky perhaps in some way, and wanting to free himself of negative energies? Or had the thunder all day simply made the villagers nervous, anxious to fend off the jinns the storm was surely bringing? Declan sat warily against the mud-brick wall, which still retained the day's heat, and felt his uneasiness mount.

When all the candles were lit, the sheikha give a signal and the drummers, with the exception of one, silenced their instruments. The lone drummer, in a long white galabeya and white turban, moved around the courtyard, thumping a repetitive beat. The women closed their eyes and stood where they were, swaying slowly from side to side. After he made a few circles, the drummer changed his beat; he continued around the courtyard, thumb and fingers tapping out a hypnotic rhythm. After a moment, he changed the rhythm again, and another drummer joined him, adding a beat that altered the rhythm slightly.

Declan knew what they were doing. The fellaheen believed that each spirit had its own cadence, to which it responded when he or she heard it, and so the drummers were casting out lines, so to speak, to snare the spirits in their midst. Finally, one of the women began to dance. She jumped to life as if she had indeed suddenly been snared, and she moved in precision with the timing of the drummer. Declan was amazed to watch Khalid's wife, so generous of figure, move with such grace and agility. But she wasn't in a trance. Yet.

Other drummers joined in, creating at first a cacophony, but ultimately coming together in an orchestration of beats that meshed miraculously. More women began to dance, each with her own timing, with different movements, as each of their spirits responded to personal, inner rhythms. When Declan saw the sheikha vanish into the rear of the clinic, where Jasmine's quarters were, he was suddenly alert.

And when Jasmine came out, he shot to his feet.

But Jasmine didn't come out on her own, she was supported on either side by two women; her eyes were closed, her head leaned to one side. Had she been drugged, he wondered, or had she worked herself into this relaxed state? Her caftan was a dazzling blue, which he knew was a symbolic color intended to calm and soothe the spirits present.

Declan watched in fascination as the drummers walked in a circle around her, the hems of their white galabeyas sweeping the ground, while the women continued to support her. And when the sheikha began to speak in a loud and shrill voice, Declan stared at her in amazement. He had no idea what she was saying, what language she spoke—she seemed to be calling out names, as if summoning someone, perhaps the spirits themselves. She raised her arms, and her silhouette grew large on the opposite wall; although she herself remained still, her shadow appeared to dance, an illusion created by the flickering torches.

When Jasmine suddenly sank to the ground, Declan stepped forward, but a strong hand, Mrs. Rajat's, shot out and held him. The women moved away, leaving Jasmine kneeling with her eyes closed in the center of the circle. And when she started slowly to sway from side to side, the other musicians finally took up their instruments and joined the drummers.

Now the music was haunting, melodic, and mesmerizing. Declan remained rooted to the spot as he watched Jasmine sway from side to side on her knees, her arms held straight out, her head flung back. When her turban slipped, the sheikha darted in and grabbed it, shaking Jasmine's golden hair free. The women continued to dance around her, but Declan noticed that sharp eyes watched Jasmine; the circle took on a protective air, and he heard Mrs. Rajat and the others occasionally murmur words of reassurance, to let Jasmine know that she was safe and among friends.

Her swaying began to grow more pronounced, and she leaned so far back that her long hair brushed the ground behind her. Declan saw the moon rise over the surrounding rooftops, casting a supernatural light over her shimmering blue caftan.

The music intensified. Someone began to chant. Jasmine threw herself forward, swaying from side to side, brushing the ground with her hair.

Declan felt his pulse race with the increased rhythm of the drums. The torchlight flickered erratically, as though a tremendous wind were blowing through the courtyard, even though the night was still. The sheikha continued to call out her strange words, sounding as if she were commanding someone to appear.

And then Jasmine began to do a strange thing. With her arms held straight out from her shoulders, as if she were suspended by her wrists on invisible strings, she began to move her head in circles. Her long golden hair flew gracefully around, catching the torchlight and making Declan think of a Roman candle. Around and around it went, slowly at first, and then faster and faster, as the music picked up pace, and the sheikha rattled off her words so fast that they ran together.

As the music pulsated in his head, Declan felt sweat trickle between his shoulder blades; he couldn't take his eyes off that spinning hair—up, over, down and around, as Jasmine snapped her neck in an unnatural way. When he glimpsed her face, he saw pale, perspiring skin, her mouth slightly open, and her eyes—

Her eyes were open, but he saw only the whites. Her eyes had turned back into her head; she had reached the point of transcendence. She was unconscious.

"That's enough!" Declan said, stepping into the circle. "Stop!" When he reached for Jasmine, the sheikha blocked his way. *"Haram, Sayyid,"* she said. But he pushed past her, quickly gathered Jasmine into his arms and carried her out of the courtyard, away from the suffocating smoke and incense.

She lay limp in his arms as he hurried down the dark lane, but by the time he reached the Nile and was laying her gently on the grassy bank, she had started to come around.

"Declan . . ." she said.

"What the hell were you trying to do back there?" he said, kneeling over her and brushing her damp hair away from her face. "Don't you know trance dancing is dangerous? Damn it, you scared me."

"I was doing it for you, Declan."

"For me! Are you out of your mind? Do you know how worried I was?"

"But I wanted to—"

He suddenly took her into his arms and put his mouth over hers. "Jasmine," he murmured, kissing her face, her hair, her neck. "I was so frightened. I thought you might get hurt."

She kissed him back, hungrily, with her arms around his neck, holding tight to him.

"I shouldn't have sat through it," he said. "I should have stopped it before it got started."

"Declan, my love—"

"Dear God, I can't lose you, Jasmine." He pressed his face into her hair; his strong arms held her so tightly that she could hardly breathe. And then he was covering her with his hard body; she saw the tall green reeds around them reaching up to the stars. She inhaled the musky fragrance of the Nile as Declan said, "I love you, Jasmine," and then no more words were spoken.

=

They walked along the bank of the river, hand in hand, as the moon began its descent toward the horizon. Jasmine thought the Nile had never looked so beautiful. She delighted in the feel of Declan's hand in hers; it felt as if she were completely encompassed by him. That was what his lovemaking had been like—not so much a joining as an enveloping. Even though he had physically entered her, she had felt as if he were taking her into himself. Declan was the fourth man she had had intimate contact with in her life, but he was the first with whom the union had felt perfect and absolutely right. "Declan," she said, "you were permitted to watch the zaar tonight because I was performing it for you. I wasn't in danger. They know what to do if it goes too far."

He looked up at the sky and wondered if the stars had always been so brilliant, so numerous. "I was so worried," he said quietly, afraid to disturb the peace of the river. "Why on earth would you do something like that for me?"

"I wanted to give you a gift in return for what you did for me."

"And what did I do for you?"

"If it hadn't been for you, I might never have returned to Egypt, and I would not have been with Zakki in his final hour. But because I was there, my brother did not die alone and in pain. I have you to thank for that."

"But I didn't bring you to Egypt, Jasmine. I had nothing to do with it."

She stopped and looked at him, and saw how his handsome face was thrown into sharp chiaroscuro by the moon's glow. She had never felt so completely in love. "Ever since we buried Zachariah I have been trying to think of what I could do for you. My mind kept coming back to what he said to you, that you are in pain. And I thought that if I could take away your pain, this would be my gift to you."

"And you were trying to rid me of evil spirits?"

She smiled. "In a way. The people who were at the zaar tonight all honor and respect you, and so they joined together to generate positive energies and send them into you."

He sighed. "I'm afraid it didn't work. I don't feel very positive right now." He turned away and went to the water's edge, where the stars seemed to dance on the river's tide, and when he heard again the rumble of distant thunder, he realized that the desert storm was drawing closer. "You once asked me what changed me. It had to do with my wife's death. Sybil didn't just die, Jasmine. She was murdered."

She came to stand next to him. "And you blame yourself? Is that what my brother meant when he said it wasn't your fault?"

"No." Declan pulled a pack of cigarettes from his pocket. "That wasn't it."

"What then?"

He looked at the cigarette and match in his hand, then threw them both down. "I killed someone," he said. "Actually, I executed him."

Jasmine heard the night shift around them, the ancient, knowing night, and she smelled the fragrance of orange blossoms. She waited for Declan to speak.

"Sybil and I were working near Arusha, in Tanzania," he said after a moment. "I knew who killed her. It was the headman's son. Sybil had a small camera that he wanted. He had, in fact, stolen it from us a month earlier. I put the word out that I had gotten the medicine man to put a curse on whoever had taken the camera and that if they put it back, there would be no punishment, no questions asked. The next day, there it was, back in our Land Rover. But then, a month later, Sybil was found murdered on the track to our mission. Her throat had been slit by a native panga. The only thing missing from the car was that little camera."

Declan noticed a strand of blond hair plastered to Jasmine's damp throat. He carefully lifted it away. "Since the thief was the headman's son," he said, "I didn't think he would be brought to justice, so I immediately got the local elders together, and they held a quick meeting. Swift local justice would do the trick, they decided, especially when I told them what I had in mind. It was fair, they said, what I wanted to do.

"Four strong men held the thief down while I administered an injection. I told him it was a special serum that could determine innocence or guilt. If he was innocent of my wife's death, no harm would come to him, but if he was guilty it would kill him before the sun went down." He paused, then said, "At exactly sunset, he died."

"What did you inject?"

"Sterile water. Perfectly harmless. I didn't think he would die. I thought it would frighten him into confessing." Declan looked out at the dark river. "He was sixteen years old."

Jasmine put her hand on his arm and said, "It was written long ago when Sybil would die, just as my hour is written, and yours. The Prophet said, 'Until my hour comes, nothing can hurt me; when my hour comes, nothing can save me.' Zakki was right, it wasn't your fault. I want to help you, Declan. You carry a heavy burden. So do I. You have asked me why I don't go back to my family in Cairo. I will tell you why." She looked up at the springtime stars. "My father banished me from the family. He took my son away from me and cast me out. He did it because I had sexual relations with a man who was not my husband, and I became pregnant by him."

She turned to Declan, to see if she could read his reaction in his eyes. But all she saw there was reflected moonlight. She went on: "I did not love him, I was his victim. Hassan al-Sabir threatened to ruin my family, and I went to plead with him, but ended up by bringing dishonor upon my family. I know that I should have gone to my father—perhaps that is what angered him the most, that I made him think I didn't believe he could fight Hassan, that he was powerless. I don't know. The night my father banished me, he told me I had brought a curse upon our family when I was born. This is why I can never go back."

"Jasmine," Connor said, stepping closer to her, "I remember when you came into my office that first day, asking me if I could help you if you got a notice from the Immigration Service. I'll never forget the fear in your eyes. Three of my students had already been deported; they had come to me for help, too, but they weren't frightened. For them, being sent home had been an inconvenience, something to be angry and annoyed about. But you were afraid, Jasmine. And I've always wondered about it, because I think you are still afraid. What frightens you about going back? Is it because of that man, Hassan?"

"No. Hassan al-Sabir can no longer hurt me. I don't even know where he is, if he is still in Cairo, or if he is still alive even. I just don't want to have anything to do with *them*. My family disowned me, I am no longer a Rasheed."

She turned away from him, but he took her by the shoulders and brought her around to face him. "Jasmine, you said you wanted to help me. Forget about me. Help yourself. Exorcise your own demons."

For a moment she was lost in his intense gaze. Then she said, "You don't understand."

"I understand one thing—you say you're grateful to me for bringing you back to Egypt. I didn't bring you back, you brought yourself here. I was merely the excuse you needed."

"That's not true—"

"But you're not really back, are you? You work in Lebanon and Gaza and the Upper Nile. It's as if you're circling a sleeping giant that you're afraid to waken."

"Oh yes, Declan, I *am* afraid. I do want to see my family. I miss them so—my sister Camelia, and my grandmother, Amira. But I don't know how to go back!"

He smiled. "By taking one step at a time and not giving up."

"And yet you have given up," she said softly.

"Yes, I've given up. I've learned that science is useless in places like this. I've learned that no matter how hard I try to inoculate the children of these people, they still think a blue bead on a string is more effective. I've tried to teach them about the parasites in the river that cause illness and death, and the simple measures of prevention, but they prefer to trust in a magic amulet and walk in the infected water. They come to me during the day with their disease and malnutrition, but at night they sneak to the sorcerer's house for snake powder and talismans. And those ruins, where we found your brother, possess more healing power than my hypodermic syringe. Even you, Jasmine, believed that the zaar dance could help me. Don't you see how futile my efforts have been? Yes, I've given up. And that's why I have to leave, before the utter uselessness of it all destroys me, the way it destroyed Sybil."

"But superstition and magic didn't kill your wife."

"No, but it killed the boy who murdered her for a cheap camera. Jasmine, Sybil and I were in that village trying to convince the elders to urge their people to inoculate the children. We had just about gotten them convinced, thanks to Sybil's relentless efforts to wear down the resistance of the local sorcerer. And then I turned around and used the very witchcraft we had condemned! I set that village back a hundred years, after everything Sybil worked for. I let her down, Jasmine. I made a mockery of her death."

"No, you didn't," she said, touching his cheek. "Oh Declan, I so want to take away your pain. Tell me what I must do. Shall I go away with you?"

"No," he said, drawing her to him again. "You have to stay here, Jasmine. This is where you belong."

"I don't know where I belong," she said, putting her head on his shoulder and leaning into his strong body. "All I know is that I love you, Declan. That's all I know."

"For now," he said, bending his head to kiss her again, "it's all we need to know."

CHAPTER 44

D o not worry, my friend," Hussein said, as he set the timer on the bomb. "No one is going to be hurt. It's Monday, the club isn't open tonight." He paused to look at Mohammed, who was sitting in the back seat of the car, ashen-faced and trembling. Hussein added, "The bomb is merely symbolic, to show them we are determined to rid Egypt of godless decadence. I have set the timer to go off at nine o'clock this evening."

Mohammed looked out at the endless traffic streaming across the bridge, beneath which the Nile was an ominous dark green in the afternoon sun. Hussein's car was parked down the road from the Club Cage d'Or, and Mohammed could just distinguish the poster of Mimi out front. Then he looked again at the bomb Hussein had assembled. His throat was dry.

What was he doing here, with these dangerous men? What had he, Mohammed Rasheed, an insignificant government clerk, to do with them? He was confused. The past few weeks had been a blur, ever since the day he had discovered that his mother was in Egypt. As each morning had brought the hope that today she might come to see him, and each evening had seen those hopes dashed, Mohammed's anguish and spiritual turmoil had deepened. In his despair, he had gone every night to Hussein's apartment and sat and listened to young men talk passionately of God and revolution. Mohammed did not like Hussein and his friends, they frightened him, but they were an outlet for his misery and pent-up passions. They said that immodest and immoral women should be driven out of Egypt, and he agreed. And when they had suggested that, as a demonstration of their intent, they destroy the place where Mimi danced, he had thought, *That will show her,* although in his confusion he didn't know which of the two women he was punishing.

Now he sat in the car that was parked a distance away from the club, watching Hussein wire the clock to the bomb's battery terminals. He was terrified, he wanted to run.

He wrung his hands. How could his mother be in Egypt and not want to see her son? Was she even still at Al Tafla, or had she left Egypt without even coming to visit him?

It was time to plant the bomb.

"We give this honor to you, my friend," Hussein said, handing the box to Mohammed. "This is a way for you to prove your loyalty to the cause and to God. Here is the key to the rear entrance of the club. If you encounter anyone, a janitor or a watchman, give him baksheesh and say that you have a gift for Mimi from an important official, and that you have been instructed to deliver it personally to her dressing room. You will plant it by the stage, as I showed you on the diagram. God go with you, my friend."

On the other side of the club, at the main entrance, Camelia was just coming out and shaking hands with the owner. Everything for tonight's surprise party for Dahiba was going as planned; all the family would be there, as well as Dahiba's friends, members of her old orchestra, movie people and celebrities, and even a representative from the Ministry of Arts and Culture, to present Dahiba with an award. There were going to be reporters and cameras to record the event, which was to take place after a sumptuous dinner, and then Dahiba was going to be persuaded to dance again—her first public performance in fourteen years.

Camelia thanked the owner and hurried off to her waiting limousine, unaware that her nephew had just sneaked into the back of the club with a box under his arm.

=

Dahiba was watching Cairo's rooftops and domes and minarets turn golden in the late afternoon sunlight, and thinking what a wonderful place the world was, because she had been granted a second chance at life. The latest lab results had come back negative. The cancer was in remission.

Hakim came into the apartment carrying a large package, and looking suspiciously pleased with himself. "What is it?" Dahiba said when he handed it to her with a grin.

"A present for you, my darling. Open it and see."

Dahiba gently undid the ribbon and lifted the lid, and when she parted the tissue paper, she cried out in delight.

"Are you surprised?" Hakim said, his chubby face beaming.

"I don't know what to say!" Dahiba very delicately lifted the dress from the box and held it up see how the silver and gold threads woven into the gossamer black fabric shimmered in the sunlight. "It's beautiful, Hakim!"

"And it's genuine, too. My God, but it cost me!"

It was an "Assyut dress," a folk costume made of a beautiful and rare fabric that was nearly impossible to find any more.

"It's over a hundred years old," Hakim said, lifting the hem and feeling the rich material between his fingers. "It's like the one you wore for your debut performance at the Cage d'Or in 1944, do you remember?"

"But that was an imitation, Hakim! This one is real!"

"Let's go out and celebrate. Wear the dress and dazzle all of Cairo."

She hugged and kissed him and said, "What shall we celebrate?"

"That God has cured you of the cancer, praise His name."

"Where shall we go?"

His small eyes twinkled. "Let me surprise you."

===

As Amira looked out at the azure sea to the left of the road they were traveling, she thought of the family in Cairo. They would be getting ready for Dahiba's surprise party. She was sorry that she and Zeinab were going to miss it. She had promised Camelia that they would be home in time, but they had been delayed in returning from the pilgrimage to Mecca when she had been stricken with chest pains outside the city of Medina. The doctor there had recommended that she fly straight home to Cairo, but Amira was determined to find the caravan route of her childhood; she would not get another chance.

Looking out at the sparkling cobalt blue water of the Gulf of Akaba, Amira was elated. She felt purified, closer to God, for having been to Mecca, the most sacred spot on earth. She and Zeinab and the two cousins had prayed at the Ka'aba, the large black stone in Mecca where the prophet Ibrahim had been prepared to sacrifice his son Ismail; they had visited Hagar's well and drunk the sacred water; they had thrown pebbles at the stone columns that symbolized Satan, to drive the Devil out of themselves. And then they had taken a ferryboat up the coast to Akaba, and from there had hired a car and driver to take them across the Sinai Peninsula.

And now she was following the traditional route the Hebrews were said to have taken out of Egypt. But because the actual path had never been determined, and other routes had been suggested, Amira began to grow anxious. Her mother had said long ago that they were following the way of the Exodus. But was this the right one, or should she have taken the northern route, as others had suggested?

As if reading her mind, the driver, a Jordanian wearing a red-and-white checkered kaffiyeh on his head, said, "This is the Ninth Brigade Road, Sayyida." The large, dusty Buick sped along a highway with stark granite cliffs rising sharply on the right, and palm trees, golden beaches, and the deep-blue Gulf stretching on the left. The lavender coast of Arabia could be glimpsed across the water.

"But are we following the same route as the Prophet Moussa, when he led the Jews out of Egypt?"

"This is a popular route, Sayyida," he said. "But the monks at the monastery of St. Catherine's can tell you about it. God willing, we will stay the night there."

Finally the car turned off the coast highway and headed down a dirt road that cut through stony fields of daisies inhabited by brown desert larks, thrushes and partridges, desert hares, and small green lizards. It was a rough and hazardous road, and the driver was careful not to jostle his passengers too much. They encountered Bedouins along the way, standing outside their sprawling black tents and raising hands in salute to the passing car. As they rode through barren terrain where only sparse vegetation grew, and occasional clumps of palm trees struggled up from the harsh ground, Amira kept a sharp lookout. Should she find all of this familiar?

They eventually arrived at the monastery. "Gebel Moussa," the driver said, pointing to a lofty, jagged peak. "The Mountain of Moses." When Amira saw the craggy brown, gray, and red granite mountains, her heart raced. Should I remember these barren hills? she thought. Was it near here that our caravan was attacked? Was it here that I was taken from my mother's arms? Is she in fact buried nearby, and will I find her grave at last? So far, Amira had seen the azure sea of her dreams, had heard the bells of a camel caravan, and had been overwhelmed by a sense of familiarity in the alien terrain. What other memories was this place going to bring?

As they took the road toward St. Catherine's Monastery, nestled at the base of Mount Sinai, Amira and her companions encountered bus-loads of tourists, convoys of mini-vans, and back-packing students on bicycles, all going in the opposite direction.

"*Bismillah,*" said the driver. "This is not a good sign. I think we are too late. The monks have locked the gates for the night."

The road deteriorated to a dirt track and, as they passed a miniature white chapel, the driver said, "There is where the Prophet Moussa first spoke with God."

Finally they came to what looked like a fortress crouched among cypress trees. "I will take care of this," the driver said, as he parked the car and ran up a stone stairway. But he was back a moment later. "I am sorry, Sayyida. The monks have had enough tourists for today. They say come back tomorrow."

But Amira was gripped with a sense of urgency. If the chest pains at Medina had indeed been a warning sign, perhaps she did not have a tomorrow. "Zeinab," she said, "help me up those steps, please. I shall speak to the holy fathers myself." She fixed the driver with a look that startled him. "We are not tourists, Mr. Moustafa. We are pilgrims on a quest."

When they reached a gate set in the ancient wall, Amira had to pause and catch her breath. *Please God, do not let me die before I have found the answers I came to seek.*

Zeinab rang the bell and a bearded monk, wearing the dark-brown habit of his Greek Orthodox order, appeared. "Please, holy father," Zeinab said in Arabic, "will you please let my grandmother come in and rest? We have come a long way." When he appeared not to understand, she repeated it in English, and his face showed comprehension. He nodded, saying that he recognized the robes of the religious pilgrim, and welcomed the party inside.

They entered the whitewashed courtyard of the Christian monastery, and as Amira followed the monk over ancient paving stones, she thought: I have been here before.

=

As afternoon shadows crept through Al Tafla in Upper Egypt, Jasmine made the last of her house calls before returning to the clinic for evening consultations. "The Sayyid is leaving today, doctora?" Um Jamal asked, as Jasmine took her blood pressure in the small courtyard of the fellaha's house.

"Yes. Dr. Connor has somewhere he must go."

"Doctora, this is a mistake. You have to keep him here."

"Or go with him," Mrs. Rajat chimed in. "A young woman like you. Time enough to be old and alone, like me!"

Jasmine turned away from the women and carefully replaced her blood pressure cuff in the medical kit. She couldn't concentrate on her work. When she and Declan had made love two nights ago, after the zaar dance, it had been exquisite. And then they had talked afterward, long into the night, until dawn had found them making love again and Jasmine had felt her loyalties start to divide. As Um Jamal said, how could she let him go? But Declan wouldn't stay. "I love you, Jasmine," he had said. "But if I stay I shall perish. I have given and given to these people until there is nothing left of me to give. It's as if they've eaten away my soul, and I can only save myself by getting away. I must leave, Jasmine, and you must stay."

As she left Um Jamal's house and walked through the late afternoon sunlight, Jasmine tried to tell herself that it was her fate to live alone, that God had other plans for Declan and that the farewell they had spoken that morning was how it must be, that she would never see him again. But she discovered that even though she had been heading back to the clinic, her footsteps had brought her to the Foundation house by the river, where Declan was loading his things into the Toyota, in preparation for leaving for Cairo that night.

And then she saw him.

"Wait!" she cried.

He turned, and she flew into his arms. "I love you, Declan. I love you so much and I don't want to lose you."

He kissed her hard, driving his fingers through her hair.

She held tightly to him. "I have lost everyone I have ever loved," she said, "even my son. But I will not lose you. I want to go with you, Declan. I want to be your wife."

=

Mohammed was terrified. Everything had gone frighteningly well, just as Hussein had promised: no one had questioned him when he had walked into the club with the gift-wrapped box; no one saw him plant it at the edge of the stage near the dressing room. And before leaving, he had checked the timer one last time: it was set to go off at nine o'clock—just thirty minutes from now, he realized in cold fear as he approached the house on Virgins of Paradise Street.

It had been a nightmare trying to keep quiet about everything as he had passed the afternoon at Feyrouz's coffeehouse with his friends from the government offices. Salah had told jokes as usual, and Habib had teased Mohammed about his infatuation with Mimi. He had prayed that they wouldn't see how he sweated, or how he checked his watch too often, or that he had not been able to choke down Feyrouz's sweet tea. And now, with zero hour almost at hand, he realized he was going to throw up.

Dear God, what have I done? he thought as he entered a strangely silent and empty house. How will I live with myself after this? What if someone is hurt, or killed even? An innocent bystander! By God, I wish I could undo what I have done!

The silence of the house brought him out of his thoughts; he paused in the foyer to listen for the usual sounds of music, voices, laughter. But, for the first time that he could remember, his uncle's house was quiet and still. What had happened? Where was everyone?

"Mohammed!" cried his cousin Asmahan, who descended the stairs in a glittering evening dress and a cloud of perfume. "Why aren't you dressed?"

"Dressed for what?"

"Auntie Dahiba's surprise party! You were told about it weeks ago. The others have already gone. If you hurry, you can ride with me."

Party? he thought. And then he remembered: a surprise for Auntie Dahiba. Was it tonight?

"I had forgotten, Asmahan. Yes, I'll hurry and go with you. Where is the party to take place?"

"At the Club Cage d'Or."

=

Amira awoke with a tightness in her chest, and for a frightening moment did not know where she was. Then, remembering that she and her party were lodging overnight at St. Catherine's, she looked at Zeinab and the others, asleep on their cots. Without waking them, Amira got out of bed, wrapped her white robes around herself and stepped out into the cold desert night.

She prayed that her discomfort was due to the heavy evening meal they had taken with the monks, and not to heart problems. She needed to live just a little longer. No memories had returned. She and the girls had been given a tour of the monastery that was almost like a small village, visiting the beautiful church, the gardens, the ossuary where the bones of monks long dead were piled up. But her memory had not been jogged; if she had visited this place as a child, she didn't remember.

She went out into the deserted courtyard bathed in dazzling moonlight, and looked at the humble buildings hugging its perimeter. She thought again how curious it was to find an ancient mosque inside this Christian monastery; it had been built long ago to ward off Arab invaders, the monks said, and now the local Bedouins used it during

Ramadan and other religious occasions. Shivering with cold, she decided to go back to the dormitory. But something stopped her.

She looked up at the black sky, the splash of stars. Feeling suddenly as if she were being impelled by a will other than her own, Amira slowly climbed the stone steps to the parapet wall.

=

The limousine was caught in the heavy Cairo traffic. Dahiba looked out at the bright lights, the pedestrians rushing off to their evening engagements, and tingled with excitement. "I wish you would tell me where we are going, Hakim!" she said, laughing.

But he only squeezed her hand and said, "You will see, my darling. It's a surprise."

=

Mohammed looked at his watch. The bomb was set to go off in fifteen minutes. He broke out in a cold sweat as he blasted the car horn and tried to make his way through the heavy evening traffic.

When Asmahan had told him that the party was to be held at the Cage d'Or, Mohammed had tried telephoning the club, but the line was busy. Then he had considered calling the police. But there was no time. Deciding that he had to get to the club himself and try to disarm the bomb or throw it into the Nile, he had rushed out of the house and taken Asmahan's car. And now he was leaning out of the window and looking at the hopelessly snarled traffic up ahead.

My God, my God. Help me!

Finally, in blind panic, he abandoned the car, with the motor still running, and made his way on foot toward the river.

=

As Declan left Nasr and Khalid, having spent the evening giving them instructions on what to do until the new Foundation team leader arrived, he decided to see how Jasmine was doing. After they had made love earlier, she had gone to the clinic to start packing. She was leaving with him tomorrow.

When he reached the clinic, inhaling the rich cooking odors from the evening fires, he heard the muezzin call out over the speaker from the mosque next door. He tried the clinic door; it was unlocked, and he went in. Her bedroom door was open, but she wasn't there, and so he went through to the courtyard at the rear, where she had held the zaar dance two nights ago. He found Jasmine there, kneeling on a prayer rug in a pool of moonlight.

He had never seen her pray before, and he was held spellbound by the vision she created, in her white caftan and white turban, as she went through the prostrations as fluidly as if she were performing a choreographed dance. And when he realized that he could hear her, that the whispered Arabic prayer was coming from her lips, and when he glimpsed the look of utter devotion on her face—and something else, sadness perhaps, or apology—he suddenly threw down his cigarette, ground it out beneath his boot, and left.

=

Hakim came through the front entrance of the club with a very startled Dahiba on his arm. Everyone shouted, "Surprise!" And Dahiba's old band, up on the stage, began to play the song that had once opened her performances.

Mohammed burst through the back entrance, knocking waiters and cooks out of his way, and when he ran into the dining room, saw the whole family there—Uncle Ibrahim, Grandmother Nefissa, his stepmother Nala, all the aunts and uncles and cousins, from the eldest to the babies, even Ibrahim's pregnant wife, Atiya. And then Camelia was leading Dahiba onto the stage as everyone cheered and clapped, and flashbulbs went off.

"My God," Mohammed whispered. And then: "Get out of here! Everyone, get out!"

=

Amira walked along the parapet wall of the monastery, feeling the starlight wash over her shoulders, the cold desert wind cut through her white robes. She looked out over the desolate landscape, and tried to imagine the encampment of her dreams. Turning in a slow circle, she contemplated the dark jagged mountains against the stars, the walls and roofline of the monastery, until she came upon a curious silhouette against the sky. She realized after a moment that she was looking at the minaret of the little mosque that had been built inside the monastery.

The minaret was square—the minaret of her visions.

This is where we stayed.

And suddenly she smelled the sweet fragrance of her dreams—the scent of gardenias—and heard her mother's voice, clear and pure, saying, "Look up there, daughter of my heart. Do you see that beautiful blue star in Orion? That is Rigel, your birth-star."

Like a staggering blow, it all came clear in an instant, as if the Sinai had suddenly been illuminated by a new sun: the colorful tents and banners, the singing and dancing around the campfire, the visiting Bedouin sheikhs with their handsome black robes and their rumbling laughter. Amira had to grab the wall, as the memories flooded her like a deluge: *We have a house in Medina, and we have just been to Cairo to visit Auntie Saana, who is about to have another baby. Umma says Papa will be so glad to see us again, because he can't bear for the family to be separated. My father, who is an aristocrat, a prince of Arabia's largest tribe. And I was betrothed at birth to Prince Abdullah, who will someday be the leader of our tribe.*

"Allah!" she cried to the stars.

=

As Mohammed ran toward the stage, his father grabbed his arm.

Omar's eyes met his.

And suddenly there was a deafening noise and a ball of flame engulfed them.

=

As Amira gazed in wonder at the square minaret in the moonlight, and embraced all the new memories—the courtyard and fountain in Medina, the names of her brothers and sisters—she felt a sudden sharp pain behind her breastbone, and she saw a blinding light—

=

Jasmine awoke suddenly. She listened to the silence around her, and then, sensing that something was wrong, got out of bed, pulled on her robe, and went out into the night.

When she reached Declan's house she found the door standing open. He wasn't there, his things were gone, and where the Land Cruiser had been parked was just empty space and, beyond, the dark, silent Nile.

Epilogue
The Present

Jasmine parted the drapes of her hotel room and found an opalescent dawn breaking over the Nile. The city was just waking up to the call of the muezzin; fishermen were unfurling the triangular sails of their feluccas; and on the Corniche below, black-and-white taxis were starting to line up in front of the hotel. Tired and hungry, and overwhelmed with emotions—she and Amira had relived a lifetime in the course of one night—Jasmine turned and regarded the woman sitting across the room. Amira's white veil had slipped down, revealing wispy white hair on a small, frail skull.

"Oh Umma," Jasmine said, going to her.

She dropped to her knees and Amira drew her into a tight embrace. "I am so sorry, Umma," Jasmine said. "I have felt so alone. I wanted to come back, but I didn't know how."

As she held her, Amira said, "Years ago I used to have dreams of a child being taken from its mother. For a long time the dreams troubled me, for I thought they were portents of an event to come. But I eventually came to realize that I was reliving an event that had already taken place, when I was kidnapped from my mother. But, Yasmina, my granddaughter, the night your father banished you, I thought: This is the hour the dreams foretold. And then you were taken from me."

Amira lifted Jasmine's tearstained face and said, "But why did you go back to America after you had returned to Egypt before?"

Jasmine went back to her own chair, next to the room-service cart bearing the remains of a meal she had had sent up during the night. "Right after Declan left, I fell ill. I had malaria, a very bad attack. I was sent back to London, where I underwent a rocky recovery, after which the Foundation put me on leave until my health improved. So I went to California to stay with Rachel for a while."

"And then afterward you still did not come back?"

"I went with a group of doctors down to South America. There was a cholera epidemic there that was out of control. I only got back to America a few months ago."

"And you are well now, Yasmina?"

"Yes, Umma. I had contracted a new resistant strain of malaria, but there are new drugs, and I am better now."

Amira searched her face. "And Dr. Connor? Where is he?"

"I don't know. After I got well again in London, I wrote to him at Knight Pharmaceuticals in Scotland, but they said he never took the job. The Treverton Foundation didn't know his whereabouts either. And he's never tried to contact me."

"Do you still love this man?"

"Yes, I do."

"Then you must find him."

But Jasmine already knew that. When she had been unable to find Declan after she left Egypt, she had decided that he did not want to be found, that he wished to be left alone. But, as she and her grandmother had talked through the night, telling stories and disclosing secrets, speaking of love and loyalties and the values that matter, Jasmine had felt her love for Declan overwhelm her, as if it had been sleeping, waiting to be wakened. This time, she told herself, she would search for him until she found him.

She reached for the front page of a newspaper, dated nearly five years ago, which Amira had produced from her box of mementos. The headline read: TERRORIST BOMB DESTROYS NIGHTCLUB. "Because I was ill," Jasmine said, "I didn't read any newspapers or listen to any radios, and so I didn't know about this."

"That was the beginning of your father's decline," Amira said, rising stiffly from the chair she had occupied through the night. The contents of her antique box were now laid out on a table: photographs, newspaper clippings, keepsakes, jewelry—and the last birthday card Jasmine had sent to Mohammed, with the Al Tafla postmark that had ultimately led to tragedy. "Your father lost all interest in life, Yasmina. The doctors say there is nothing wrong with him, but he is wasting away and will die soon, because he does not want to live."

Jasmine watched her grandmother walk to the window and look out. Bathed in the glow of early morning, she seemed to Jasmine almost like an angel. "No one in the family knows I am here, Yasmina, except for Zeinab. It was she who sent you the telegram telling you that I was coming. She wanted to come with me, but there are some roads a woman must travel alone."

"Zeinab," Jasmine said. "My baby wasn't born dead. I had a daughter, and I didn't know it."

"We thought you had abandoned her, Yasmina. Alice said you didn't want the child."

"I think my mother wanted me to leave Egypt, and perhaps she knew I wouldn't have, if I had known the baby was alive."

Jasmine looked at the photograph of Zeinab. "I lost my son," she said softly, "but God has given me a daughter."

"Mohammed died a martyr's death, Yasmina. Those who saw it happen said that he tried to save the others. He must have seen the bomb, or saw it being planted, for he ran right toward it, shouting at everyone to get out. Your son died trying to save others, Yasmina, when he could have saved himself. He was given a true hero's funeral."

"May God keep him in paradise always. And it was not Camelia who gave away my secret," Jasmine said, her tone full of wonder. "My sister did not betray me after all."

"She did not. When I later asked Nefissa how she had learned about you and Hassan, she confessed to me that she had followed you to Hassan's house. Camelia kept your secret, Yasmina."

Thinking of Zeinab's father, Jasmine set the photograph down and said, "Who killed Hassan?"

"I do not know."

When she saw Jasmine's gaze settle again upon the terrible nightclub headline, Amira said, "It was through God's mercy that Zeinab and I were spared from the bomb. We were to have attended Dehiba's surprise party, but we were delayed when I fell ill outside Medina. Had it not been for that, your daughter and I might have been among these," and she laid her hand on the news photos of those killed by the bomb.

Amira regarded her granddaughter for a pensive moment, then she resumed her seat and, gathering her white robes about her, said, "And now, Yasmina, the final secret remains to be told. I have revealed to you that I did not know my family, that I was kidnapped from my mother's caravan. But what you do not know, what no one, not even your father knows—indeed, what not even I knew until it was revealed to me at St. Catherine's monastery—is what happened afterward. And this is difficult to tell."

Jasmine watched her grandmother, and waited.

"After the raid on my mother's caravan near St. Catherine's," Amira said at last, "I was taken to the house of a wealthy merchant in Cairo, a man with an appetite for little girls. The women of his harem fed me and bathed me, and put perfume in my hair, and then I was brought naked into a fabulous bedroom, where I saw a large man sitting on a chair that was like a throne. I was terrified as he stroked me and touched me and told me that I would not be harmed. Then the women lifted me up and lowered me onto his lap. There was pain. I screamed. I was six years old."

Amira looked down at her hands. "The wealthy merchant had me brought to him every night after that. Sometimes he loaned me to his friends or distinguished visitors, and watched while I 'entertained' them. I was thirteen when Ali Rasheed, a friend of the wealthy merchant, came one day and was permitted to visit the harem. He was taken with me and asked to buy me. The wealthy merchant agreed, as I was growing hips and breasts and no longer appealed to him. But he warned Ali Rasheed that I was not a virgin, and Ali said that it didn't matter. So he bought me, and I was taken to his house on Virgins of Paradise Street."

Amira cleared her throat. "Slavery was illegal by that time, and both Ali and the merchant could have been arrested had they been found out, because money had changed hands and I was Ali's slave. So when he brought me home, he freed me, and then he married me, and a year later I gave birth to Ibrahim."

Sounds of traffic on the Corniche rose to their open window and filtered into the room on the morning breeze.

"Oh, Umma," Jasmine said. "I am so sorry. It must have been terrible for you."

"So terrible, Yasmina, that I blocked it out of my mind. And as I buried that unbearable memory, I also buried everything of my life that came before it. But I had dreams . . . and strange feelings. Yasmina, do you remember the day we took a taxi to Tree of Pearls Street? Your father had betrothed you to Hassan, but as we sat in front of that school on Tree of Pearls Street, I decided I could not let it happen."

"Why not?"

"Because that wealthy merchant who abused me—his name was al-Sabir. Hassan was his son."

In the corridor outside, a service cart rattled by, a female voice called softly, *"Y'Allah!"*

Amira continued: "Although I did not remember the things that had been done to me in that harem, I had a feeling that there was no honor in Hassan's family. And so I could not let him marry you when he asked for you. That is why I made Ibrahim break the marriage contract, and why I married you to Omar."

The two women regarded each other across the room, recalling an afternoon they had shared in a taxi, long ago.

Amira said, "I understand now that what happened to me as a child—the kidnapping, the harem on Tree of Pearls Street—made me what I am. I was afraid to leave the house on Virgins of Paradise Street, I was afraid to remove my veil. I was even afraid for my children and grandchildren to walk the streets. Perhaps that was why I could not marry Andreas Skouras, even though I was in love with him, because I sensed that something shameful lay in my past."

"And now all your memories have been restored to you?"

"Through God's miracles, they have. I can tell you now what my mother looked like, I can describe the beautiful boy I had been betrothed to—Prince Abdullah—who had even, for a while, visited me in dreams, years ago. And I can even hear my mother's voice, saying to me, 'Remember always, daughter of my heart, that you are Sharif, a descendant of the Prophet.' "

"Will you look for your real family now, Umma? Your brothers and sisters?"

But Amira shook her head. "I already have my real family."

Jasmine smiled. "I want to go to Father now."

—

When they arrived at Virgins of Paradise Street, Jasmine had to wait a moment to collect herself. Her father was ill, which meant the whole family would be here; she would see familiar faces from long ago, and a host of new ones. But they would not be strangers to her. They would all be Rasheeds, and she would be bound to them, as they were bound to her.

When she entered the house, stepping over the threshold and feeling as if she were stepping through a time portal into the past, because nothing had changed, the garden, the gazebo, the massive carved doors were still the same, she found Nefissa in the foyer casting a disapproving frown over a dish one of the servants was about to take upstairs. She glanced up at Yasmina, smiled, then returned to the stew. And then her head snapped up again and she said, "*Al hamdu lillah!* Am I seeing a ghost?"

"Greetings, Auntie," Jasmine said, her heart racing—this was the woman who had caused her banishment, who was responsible for Mohammed being taken away from her, responsible ultimately for the tragedy that had occurred at the Club Cage d'Or.

"Yasmina!" Nefissa cried again, tears in her eyes, and she swept her niece into such a fierce embrace that Jasmine felt the breath knocked out of her. "Praise the Eternal One!" the older woman cried. "He has brought you back to us!" When the two regarded each other, Jasmine saw a plea in her aunt's eyes that reminded her of the pleading look she had seen in Greg's eyes, the night of the miscarriage. Nefissa was saying: Forgive me.

So Jasmine said, "God's peace and blessings upon you, Auntie."

And Nefissa cried, "*Al hamdu lillah,*" again, threading her arm through Jasmine's and leading her up the stairs, calling out breathlessly, "*Y'Allah! Y'Allah!*"

People came to the top of the staircase to see what the commotion was about, and after a moment of confused expressions, Jasmine saw smiles erupt here and there, and then more smiles, and finally shouts of "Praise the Lord!" In the next instant she was engulfed in a sea of faces both familiar and strange, smiles and tears, arms reaching out for her, to touch her, as if to reassure themselves that it was truly she.

When she saw Tahia, she held out her arms and the two embraced. "Praise God," Tahia said. "He has brought you back to us."

"Actually, it was Umma who brought me back," Jasmine said, and as everyone laughed, she thought of what she must later tell Tahia about Zachariah, and that his dying thoughts had been of her. "How is my father?"

Tahia shook her head. "He will not eat, he will not drink. He won't even speak to anyone. This happens on the anniversary of the bomb—do you know about that?"

Jasmine nodded. The bomb, which had killed her son, a waiter, and two musicians. Omar, too, had died. The only other casualty had been the unborn child of Ibrahim's wife, Atiya.

"But this time it is worse," Tahia said, as she led Jasmine to Ibrahim's suite. "He usually goes into a depression for a few days, and then comes out of it. But this one has lasted two weeks. I think he wants to die, God forbid."

Jasmine entered the bedroom, and was startled by its familiarity—like the rest, the garden, the foyer, her father's rooms hadn't changed since she came here to visit as a little girl. But they were smaller than she remembered, and no longer intimidating. The men who were holding vigil in the room stood up in shock when they saw her, and Jasmine was embraced again, one at a time, by uncles and cousins known and not known to her. They left the room and closed the door on the crowd in the hallway. Jasmine was left alone with the old man in the bed.

She was shocked to see how much Ibrahim had aged. There was almost no trace of the handsome, virile man she remembered as her father. He looked, in fact, older than Amira, his mother.

She sat on the edge of the bed and took his hand. At the instant of contact, she felt all trepidation, all doubt, and all anger melt away. What happened in the past between herself and this old man was over and done with; it had been written, and so it had happened. But now the future was written, and it was that which they must face together.

"Papa," she said softly.

Papery eyelids fluttered open. He stared at the ceiling for a moment, then looked at Jasmine. His eyes widened. "*Bismillah!* Am I dreaming? Or am I dead? Alice, is it you?"

"No, Papa. It's not Alice, it's Jasmine. Yasmina," she corrected herself.

"Yasmina? Oh—" He coughed. "Yasmina? Daughter of my heart? Is it truly you? Have you come back to me?"

"Yes, Papa. I am back. And the family tells me that you will not eat, that you are making yourself sick."

"I am a cursed man, Yasmina. God has abandoned me."

"In all honor and respect, Papa, that is nonsense. Look around you, at this magnificent house, and the furnishings, and the people all gathered outside your door. Would you count such riches as those of a cursed man?"

"I drove Alice to suicide and I have not been able to forgive myself!"

"My mother had an illness called clinical depression. I don't know if any of us could have helped her."

"I am beyond usefulness, Yasmina."

"Lying here and feeling sorry for yourself is not going to help, Papa. It is written than God changes those who change themselves. Why would God bother with a man who lies in bed and won't eat?"

"You are blasphemous and disrespectful," he said, but he smiled as he said it, and tears shimmered in his eyes. "You are back, Yasmina," he said, caressing her face with a trembling hand. "Are you a doctor now?"

"Yes, Papa, and a very good one."

He seemed to rest more easily among the pillows. "That is good. Yasmina," he said, and his hand sought hers. "You know, I have been looking back over my life. Did you know that Sahra found me by my car among the sugarcane, the morning after Camelia was born? I was throwing up, I had had too much champagne. By God"—he shook his head—"for a Rasheed! She gave me water and I gave her a white scarf. A year later, on the night you were born, she gave me her son." He looked at Jasmine. "That was Zachariah."

"Yes, Umma told me."

"Yasmina, do you remember King Farouk?"

"I recall a large man who gave us sweets."

"It was an innocent age then, Yasmina. Or—maybe it wasn't. I was not a very good doctor then, you know. But later on, I became a good doctor. Do you know when that was, when I changed? It was when you started helping me in my office. I wanted you to be proud of me. I wanted to teach you the right things."

"You taught me well, too."

"You know, I lived my whole life trying to please my father, even after he died. And now I shall be meeting him soon. I wonder how he will receive me."

"As a father always receives a son," she said. "Papa, you must make your peace with God."

"I am afraid, Yasmina. Does it upset you to hear your father admit that? I am afraid that God will not forgive me."

She smiled and stroked his white hair. "Everything we do was written long ago. Whatever happened was fated before we were even born. Take comfort in that thought, and in the knowledge that God is merciful and compassionate. Ask Him in humility and He will grant you peace."

"Will He forgive me, Yasmina? Do *you* forgive me?"

"Forgiveness is God's," she said. Then she added gently, "Yes, Papa, I forgive you."

She reached down and embraced him, burying her face in his neck. They cried together, then she sat back and, drying his cheeks, said, "I am going to see to it that you eat."

He started to weep again, but he smiled also, and then he started to fret. "I have wasted my years! I have treated time as if it were a cheap commodity. Look at me, foolish old man! Where is Nefissa with my soup? Where is that woman?"

As Jasmine rose from the bed, the bedroom door opened and three people walked in. Dahiba came first, smiling and saying, "Mother told us you had come back. Praise God."

Behind her came Camelia, her face a register of mixed emotions. Jasmine read cautious joy there, but wariness also. But she was amazed to see how little her sister had changed; Camelia was still tall and striking, still the glamorous film star.

And then a young woman came in, limping because of the leg brace she wore.

Jasmine had to suddenly reach for one of the bedposts. Zeinab, her daughter.

"Hello, Zeinab," she said. Jasmine looked at Camelia, and met her sister's eyes. Then she smiled at the girl and said, "I'm your Auntie Yasmina."

"Praise God!" Dahiba said, tears rolling down her cheeks. "We are a family again! We shall celebrate, we shall have a party!"

But there was one thing Jasmine had to do first.

=

She gave the taxi driver an address, and a few minutes later she was walking down a corridor in one of the older buildings in Cairo, scanning the names on the doors until she came to a modest sign that read TREVERTON FOUNDATION. The small reception area inside consisted of a desk, chairs, and posters on the walls from WHO, UNICEF, and Save the Children Fund. A young, well-dressed Egyptian woman looked up and smiled. "May I help you?" she said in English.

"I would like to locate one of your former members," Jasmine said. "We worked together in Upper Egypt and I was wondering if you could help me."

"May I have the name, please?"

"Dr. Declan Connor."

"Oh, yes," the young woman said. "He is in Upper Egypt."

"Upper Egypt! Do you mean Dr. Connor is here?"

"He is in Al Tafla, madam."

Jasmine could hardly contain her excitement. "Would you happen to be sending a plane down there tomorrow, with supplies?"

"I am sorry, madam."

Jasmine tried to think. She could take a flight to Luxor, but then she would have to drive down to Al Tafla. Sometimes flights were unreliable, as were the roads. She had to get to Declan as quickly as possible.

That left the overnight train.

=

Jasmine walked down familiar narrow lanes, past the village well where women were gossiping, and when she passed Waleed's coffeehouse, she was suddenly sent back five years, and it was as if she were arriving here for the first time.

She paused when she came to the clinic, where fellaheen waited patiently on benches outside, women on one side, men on the other. The door was open; Jasmine looked in.

Connor was inside, holding a stethoscope to the chest of a child who was sitting on the desk under the watchful eyes of his mother. Jasmine watched how gently Declan handled the child, reassuring him, telling him that he must be careful with what he ate from now on. Then he explained to the mother that the boy was all right, a mild attack of food poisoning, and that she must take care what he put into his mouth. As

Jasmine watched, she marveled at how little Declan had changed. She also wanted to laugh; his Arabic pronunciation was still appalling.

"There now. Off you go," he said, and when he looked toward the door, he froze.

"Jasmine!"

"Hello, Declan. I was—"

He swept her into his arms and kissed her hard on the mouth.

"My God, Jasmine! I was wondering when you were going to come back. I've been trying to find you."

"I wrote to you at Knight Pharmaceuticals—"

"I didn't go to Scotland," he said, holding her at arm's length, filling his eyes with the sight of her. "I signed on a hospital ship for a year, in Malaysia. When I came back to Egypt, I was told you had returned to England because of malaria. I went to London, and was told there that you had been put on hiatus by the Foundation, and you'd gone to California. I couldn't remember your friend's last name—Rachel. So I tried to find you through the California Medical Association, and then the AMA. I even tried the medical school. Finally I went to the house on Virgins of Paradise Street where you said your family lived. They gave me the address of Itzak Misrahi in California, I wrote to him, and he wrote back, saying you had joined the Lathrop Organization."

"Oh, no!" she said. "I went to Peru with an independent group of physicians to help the cholera victims. It was funded by Lathrop, but I wasn't a member. Declan, I tried to find you, too, I even wrote—"

"Never mind that," he said, kissing her again, while the fellaheen watched from the doorway, Um Tewfik and Khalid and old Waleed, grinning and agreeing among themselves that it was about time.

=

The wedding took place at the house on Virgins of Paradise Street. All the Rasheeds were there to take part in the traditional celebration, which included an elaborate zeffa procession, followed by a feast of cheese and salads, roasted lamb, grilled kebab, steaming rice and beans, sweet desserts, and coffee, while comedians, acrobats, and dancers entertained Jasmine and Declan, who sat on thrones, he in a tuxedo, she in an apricot lace wedding gown. Declan's son was also there, a twenty-five-year-old replica of his father and a recent Oxford graduate, who had been drawn into a lively discussion with Ibrahim, who had attended the same school fifty years ago.

Rachel Misrahi had come all the way from California to attend the wedding, and her father, Itzak, had accompanied her. After showing her the house next door, where he had been born but which was now the embassy of an African nation, he had spent hours reminiscing with Ibrahim about the days when they had been boys together, and Rachel had been fascinated to hear, for the first time, her father speaking Arabic.

Camelia and Dahiba danced a duet that had been part of their act years ago, as Yacob watched proudly with their son Najib, now a pudgy, handsome eleven-year-old. But his stepdaughter, Zeinab, was having a hard time concentrating on her mother's performance because of a cousin named Samir, an attractive young man who had been causing her to lose sleep lately, and who was now smiling at her from the other side of the salon.

Qettah was also there, to read the couple's fortune. She was not the Qettah who had been with the family during the Farouk years, nor the one whom Amira had visited in the Zeinab Quarter. She was the granddaughter, or possibly the great-granddaughter, of the old astrologer, and there was a younger woman with her, also named Qettah.

Two men observed the celebration from gilt-framed portraits: Ali Rasheed Pasha, in a fez and robes, surrounded by women and children, gazing sternly over a magnificent mustache; and King Farouk, young, handsome, and alone.

Sitting beneath these portraits, Ibrahim clapped along and shouted *"Y'Allah!"* as his daughter and sister performed a lively beledi dance. His wife, Atiya, was pregnant again, restoring his hope once more that God would give him a son. As he was thinking that there could not be a luckier or more blessed man than he, Ibrahim saw Zeinab laugh, and the way her cheeks dimpled made him think of Hassan al-Sabir, the man who had fathered her, the man who had once been his friend and brother.

Ibrahim allowed himself to think finally of that night, when he had banished Yasmina, when the world had been turned upside down and, grief-stricken, he had made his way to Hassan's house. The murder had not been accidental. Ibrahim had gone with the intention of destroying the man who had betrayed a friendship and threatened the honor of the Rasheed name. Ibrahim recalled now how, even at the very end, as he lay dying, Hassan had laughed at him. That was when Ibrahim had taken a knife to him and, using his physician's skill, had removed the weapon of assault Hassan had used on Yasmina.

Amira also clapped in time to the vivacious beledi dance, feeling younger and happier than she remembered being for a long time. The family restored and all together again, and seeing Itzak Misrahi, whom she had helped bring into the world, was almost like having Maryam back.

Remembering a dream she had had recently, in which an angel had said she would die soon, she asked herself, What was "soon" to an angel? Because there was still so much to be done. Nala's daughter, for instance, was ready for marriage, and the Abdel Rahman grandson, an important man with twelve people working under him, would be perfect. Hosneya's daughter, widowed with two children, needed a man to take care of her, and Amira thought that Mr. Gamal, a widower who had a fine job at the embassy next door, would be an excellent candidate. And wasn't young Samir smiling at Zeinab in a rather significant way? Amira recalled now that he had been at the house rather frequently lately, with feeble excuses, and blushing a deep crimson every time Zeinab appeared. Amira thought: I will speak to his mother tomorrow. And then I will help them with an apartment, if the boy cannot yet afford one.

Finally Amira thought of the childhood memories that had been restored to her, her birth-star, her true family line. And she promised herself that when her work was done, she would join her mother in paradise. But she could not make that journey yet, not while the family still needed her. Next year, or perhaps the year after, she would go.

ABOUT THE TYPE

This book was set in Galliard, a typeface designed by
Matthew Carter for the Mergenthaler Linotype Company in 1978. Galliard is based on the sixteenth-
century typefaces of Robert Granjon, which give it
classic lines yet interject a contemporary look.